The Cornish Girl

Joanna Hines

CORONET BOOKS
Hodder and Stoughton

Copyright © Joanna Hines 1994

First published in Great Britain in 1994
by Hodder and Stoughton,
a division of Hodder Headline PLC
Simultaneous Hodder and Stoughton hardcover edition 1994

A Coronet Paperback

The right of Joanna Hines to be identified as the author of
this work has been asserted by her in accordance with the
Copyright, Designs and Patents Act 1988.

10 9 8 7 6 5 4 3 2 1

All characters in this publication are fictitious and any
resemblance to real persons, living or dead, is purely
coincidental.

British Library CIP
A CIP catalogue record for this title is available from the British
Library

ISBN 0-340-60960-5

Printed and bound in Great Britain by
Cox and Wyman Ltd, Reading, Berks.
Photoset by Rowland Phototypesetting Ltd,
Bury St Edmunds, Suffolk.

Hodder and Stoughton Ltd
A Division of Hodder Headline PLC
47 Bedford Square
London WC1B 3DP

Cui dono lepidum novum libellum?

To Derrek,
of course.

The Falling Years

London, October 1660

Among the myriad minor sensations that absorbed the gossips that first autumn of Charles II's restoration was the scandal of Perdita Treveryan. The eldest child of Sir Richard Treveryan, her claim even to her father's name was dubious. In the next twenty years, the King's growing brood of royal bastards was to make illegitimacy almost fashionable but when Perdita first came to London the chill morality of the Protectorate still clung to the alleys and spires of the capital.

A bastard child was far from unusual: the novelty lay in Perdita's favoured position within her father's household. If she had been discreetly reared by a kindly yeoman and his wife far from the public eye, or if she had lived with the servants and been taught to minister to the needs of her two younger half-brothers, there would have been less cause for scandal. But no. Lady Treveryan's own firstborn child was not treated with more indulgence than the dark-eyed skinny girl who was a daily reminder of her husband's infidelity.

She was not Lady Treveryan's child, that much at least was common knowledge. Beyond that, all certainty ceased. Several theories were current concerning the possible identity of her mother. Favourite, at least among the superstitious, was the belief that she was the child of those elfin folk who had still lived in the wild hills of Cornwall where Perdita was born in the days before the Lord Protector Cromwell banished pleasure and magic from the country. For those requiring proof, the evidence was plain: look how Lady Treveryan, barren as an addled egg through fifteen years of marriage, had suddenly borne two sons in the space of as many years. To the credulous, and there were many still who believed such things, it was clear that a bargain had been struck: Perdita's welfare in return for the two fine baby boys.

The cynical preferred to emphasise Sir Richard's part in the matter. They were torn between scandal that he had foisted his bastard child on his poor wife and admiration for her cheerful acceptance of the outrage.

Kitty Treveryan was unaffected by either their scorn or their pity. She was armour-clad with that insensitivity which resulted from a lifetime's absorption in her own self. She did not gossip, for to gossip it is necessary to have at least a malicious interest in other people and Lady Treveryan had no interest in anyone except herself – in herself and in her immediate family, whom she saw as an extension of herself.

As for her husband, he never heard the rumours. Only a reckless man, or a fool, would have passed on such parlour tittle-tattle to Sir Richard. In all the bustle and excitement of the London of the newly restored monarchy, Sir Richard Treveryan remained aloof, a man apart.

A cold wind was blowing off the river and Perdita pulled her cloak more closely about her shoulders. She sat very upright in the overfull boat, her head slightly turned as though to examine the Palace of Whitehall which was now coming into view on the right-hand bank. She had, in fact, not the slightest interest in the Palace; her intention was to secure the admiration of the sturdy young waterman who was seated opposite her.

His eyes were grey-green like the tidal waters and his shoulders were bull-powerful from constant pulling at the oars. Perdita smiled, as though inwardly amused, and allowed the tips of her fingers to trail in the icy water: the gesture, she knew, showed to advantage the ivory skin of her wrist as it emerged from her velvet cuff.

At the other end of the boat Belinda, the old servant, fussed. 'Can't you row any faster?' and she tapped the shoulder of the less formidable of the two watermen who were seated with their backs to her. 'I'm sure you have slowed down. We hardly move at all.'

'Tide's on the turn,' he said, amiably enough. 'We'll try to get you home before dark.'

At the prospect of being still on the river once the sun had set, Belinda let out a wail of panic. 'Row faster, you scoundrel, you'll have my master to answer to if we are late!'

The older waterman spat, perhaps coincidentally, into the river, but the younger of the two, the one with the grey-green eyes, said, 'No call to blame us if you've stayed too long at the fair,' and as he spoke he smiled at Perdita and she absorbed his smile without turning her head to look at him.

Behind her, her two half-brothers squabbled at the back of the boat.

'We're hungry, Belinda,' said Nicolas, 'why didn't you bring any food?'

'This boat has water in it,' Ralph shrilled. 'We're sinking, I'm sure!'

A low moan from Belinda. 'This is all your doing, Perdita,' she scolded, 'I can't think where you disappeared to for so long. We'd have been home an hour ago but for you.'

At this the younger waterman examined Perdita closely. He made a note of her thoughtful dark eyes in a thin and clever face, and of something restless, a nervousness, yet kept under close control, in the set of her wide mouth. In particular he observed that there was something pinched and hungry in the young girl's face, for all her velvets and her lace and the jewel at her throat. He recognised those outward signs of a hungry and ill-cared-for heart: they were the same from the airy spaces of Hampton Court to the stinking hovels of Fish Lane, and, for all he knew, in the snowy wastes of Muscovy as well.

Perdita merely darted him a quick smile before replying coolly to Belinda's complaint. 'But there was so much to see. I had no idea it was getting late.'

Billy, the serving-boy, seated on a coil of rope at her feet, stared straight ahead and gave no sign that he had heard.

'Yes, Perdita, it's all your fault,' said Nicolas. 'Where were you?'

She smiled serenely. 'Only looking at the booths.'

But, in fact, she had seen almost nothing of the fair; nor had that been her purpose in arranging this expedition. She had seen it as a perfect opportunity to extract from Billy the serving-boy some information of desperate importance.

She had soon learned that though the boy looked timid enough he knew the value of what he had to give. The first sugared apple had merely revealed the information that yes, he did know something. It took half a dozen sweet buns to yield up the knowledge that yes, her father was indeed engaged in negotiations for her marriage. (Perdita had guessed as much.)

And the identity of her intended suitor? Billy was reluctant. Taking nothing for granted he knew the value of everything. Besides, his shrivelled stomach could barely cope with the sweet buns and sugared apple. Perdita grew angry and threatened him with dire punishments. He was unmoved.

A fortune-teller's booth came to their rescue. Perdita had paid the old man his money but did not allow Billy to hear what he said until she was certain that he had shared with her all he knew: Oliver Nashe, a well-to-do armourer from Coventry, was a widower with three children, the oldest only a couple of years younger than Perdita herself. She remembered now the man who had visited their lodgings about a week before. He had appeared kindly enough, although old in her young eyes. A bit uncouth perhaps, but she could hardly expect to marry into the gentry. And marriage would bring the respectability her illegitimate birth had denied her. She was not at all displeased with the information – it could have been worse, much worse. (And she thought with a shudder of the lumbering Devon farmer who had come courting her in the spring.)

She allowed herself a faint smile of contentment. And in the meantime there was the young boatman with the grey-green eyes and the rippling shoulders. The steady strokes of the oars kept time with Belinda's fussing.

A barge making its way upstream was nearly struck by a tilt boat racing down with the tide. There was much shouting and commotion and their own boat rocked dangerously.

'Lord preserve us, we are drowning!' And Belinda hugged herself with fear.

The watermen cursed each other amicably.

'Watch out, you oafs, you stupid clods!' the brothers yelped. 'Now I'm soaking wet!'

Billy, defeated by the sugared apple and the six sweet buns and the bucketing of the wherry, was sick over the side. Nicolas and Ralph watched him in silent fascination.

'Whatever has the boy been eating?' asked Belinda.

'Look!' Perdita suddenly wished to change the subject. 'There is Father waiting for us. He *must* be angry.'

Among the porters and the idle watermen on the Westminster Stairs, Sir Richard Treveryan stood a little apart, a tall gaunt figure, his dark cloak flapping in the wind.

A brief moment of hope flickered in Perdita's heart. He was waiting for them, he had been worrying about them. About her in particular.

It was nearly ten years since her father had ceased to visit their home, even in secret, ten years of his long exile in France. During his absence she had created an imaginary father for herself, a father powerful, wise and kind. A father above all loving. But it had been a stranger who met them on their arrival from Devon three weeks before, and a stranger he had remained, cold and remote – at least to her.

At the sight of her master Belinda grew frantic and forgot her fear of the watermen. 'Faster, you rogues, faster!' she squealed, striking their backs with her fists.

'He is waiting for us.' Ralph spoke with awe.

Perdita peered through the dusk. Sir Richard Treveryan was standing with his head tilted slightly back: keen falconer that he was, his eyes were most often fixed on far horizons. Not bothering with the fretful company now approaching in the boat.

She realised he must have come to the stairs to evade his wife's complaints, her habitual litany (at least since their arrival in London) that they should have a coach. 'If we only had a coach then I would not worry so when they were out.' But Treveryan, who loathed any kind of confinement, considered coach travel to be a form of torture by suffocation.

He lowered his gaze and saw them. Perdita began to lift her hand in greeting but already it was too late. He turned and began to walk briskly away from the river.

'Your precious brats are safe,' he would say to his wife in that mocking way he had.

Perdita's dreams of a father who waited for her by the

13

water's edge shrivelled and crumbled to nothing. She fought back her disappointment. He *would* not hurt her so. She must learn to be as hard and cold as he was. Green-cheeked Billy, who thought he was dying outwards from his heaving stomach, struggled past her to escape from the boat and she kicked his ankles to repay his bad manners.

And then she lifted up her chin and took comfort from the lingering pressure of the waterman's hand as he guided her from the boat and on to what Belinda, with loud thanks to the Lord above in all His mercy, described, though with dubious accuracy as the stairs were slippery with wet, as God's own blessed dry land.

Like all cynics Sir Richard Treveryan delighted in examples of human weakness and hypocrisy and on his return to London in the late summer of 1660 he had found no shortage of either for his amusement.

When he had visited the capital two years earlier to conduct some secret business for Charles Stuart, he had been heavily disguised. If any of the people whom he had met on that occasion had guessed his true identity they would not have scrupled to denounce him to Cromwell's men as a traitor and a spy. But now, with the return of the King and the regicides in their turn under sentence of death, every Londoner was declaring himself a monarchist born and bred. Sir Richard, like other returning exiles, was no longer a traitor and a rebel, but an acclaimed hero.

The threat of death had not much troubled him, so it was hardly surprising that he was alike indifferent to the exaggerated praise he now found heaped about his shoulders. Oliver Nashe, for instance, still gawped slack-jawed and foolish at the honour of marrying the daughter (illegitimate, it was true – but never mind that) of the man, not to say the hero, who had been wounded at Worcester. One rumour, which Sir Richard did not trouble to deny, would have it that his wounds had been received when he rushed in to defend the young King from Cromwell's men, thus enabling him to make his dramatic escape. What would they say, these month-old Royalists, had they known that it was boredom, not loyalty to the House of Stuart, that had driven him to Worcester nine years before? When each day tastes as dry and dull as the one before and the one following and every day to come until the end of time, amen, then soldiering, organising men to butcher their fellows in the name of half-understood ideals, will provide a way as acceptable as any other of passing the time.

And the exile that was so wretched for other Royalists had been for him a tolerable interlude. He had always preferred the rough clothes of a countryman to a courtier's lace and velvets. Following the inscrutable logic of diplomacy he had fought, in the King's name, first with the French against Spain and then, with equal dedication and resolve, with the Spanish against France. He derived some satisfaction from the symmetry of the European campaigns.

In fact, now that he was returned to his own lands once again he found that he somewhat missed the freedom of his exile. He had slept in his clothes under the southern constellations and shared the meagre food of his soldiers. There had been excellent hunting in the Pyrenees. And he had not seen his wife or his children for nearly ten years – in itself a blessing not to be underestimated.

Treveryan stood by the water's edge and watched the wherry as it slowly approached. When he had overheard his wife commanding a servant to seek them out he had surprised her by saying he would go himself. He had always preferred to be out in the open air and he liked the salt wind and the dirt of the river. It was one of the few places in this confounded city where he did not feel himself to be choking on gentility in small spaces. Happily his release was not far off. In two days there was to be a formal audience with the King and when that was done he intended to leave at once for the country. His wife could follow with the servants and the children when she would. Or not at all.

In the thickening darkness he could now make out the identity of the passengers in the little boat. He sent a servant to inform his wife of their arrival and began to walk away. He had no wish to be present when the noisy troop returned.

The illness which had detained him in Spain through the summer had left him prone to occasional bouts of lassitude; also with an increased liking for good wines and certain Venetian elixirs with pain-killing properties.

Oblivion, that gentle mist which erases the jagged blade

of memory and understanding, sweet nothingness was the only pleasure he now desired.

Kitty, Lady Treveryan, was surprised.

'Lord, child, I know even less of this than you,' she said, and her small features rumpled with bewilderment. 'However did you manage to discover so much?'

'Billy,' Perdita answered simply. 'I paid for him to visit a soothsayer yesterday at the fair.'

Kitty glanced sharply at the skinny boy, loaded with packages, who walked behind them and she lowered her voice. 'When you are mistress of your own house, Perdita, you must break this habit of bribing the servants or you will forfeit all respect.'

'I hope I'll not need bribery, then!' Perdita flushed angrily. 'I intend to know what's what in my own house without having to stoop so low!'

'Hmm. Well. That may be a fine thing, no doubt.' And Kitty lapsed into an unaccustomed silence, not wishing to be reminded of the times without number when she had been compelled to depend upon servants for whatever scant information she might glean.

They walked some little way without speaking before Kitty said lightly, 'Then you must take care and marry a man less secretive than your father. Mr Nashe seems a reasonable man.'

At the mention of her father Perdita made a curious and explosive noise, one most undignified but clearly expressing her disgust. 'Thank the Lord there *are* no other men like him!' she burst out. 'Surely he must be unique, I should think!'

And she spoke with such vehemence that Kitty stopped, looked searchingly at her and then called to Billy, 'Take those parcels back to the lodgings. We shall go on a little alone. Here, Perdita,' as the lad shuffled sorrowfully away, 'our rooms are so cramped that I'm sure the servants hear every word we say. And stop frowning so. If Mr Nashe should catch sight of you scowling like a baby with the wind he'll no doubt change his mind and you'll be left to die an old maid.'

'I don't care.'

'He's not to your taste?'

'How can I know? I've only seen the man once.'

'Hmm. He has money, you can tell by his clothes though they are quite out of the fashion. But a good wife could use his money to improve his appearance. I would judge him easy enough to manage, with care.'

Perdita frowned sulkily. 'I had hoped to love the man I marry.'

'Tch!' Kitty dismissed the romantic proposition. 'Love before marriage is nothing but fairy gold, all show and no substance, and anyone who tells you different is a rogue.'

Look at me, she could have added, look at me and believe what I tell you. She might have remembered another Kitty, the eager girl she had once been, so hot with love for the stranger who had burst into her narrow life that she had defied common sense and good advice to marry him that starry Christmas Eve when the bells rang out over Saltash and the Lord of Misrule was king. Look at me, she might have said, and be warned.

But she said nothing, did not even think of it. To dwell on the past, happy or sad, had never been Lady Treveryan's way.

Perdita exclaimed suddenly, 'I hate him! I do!'

'Mr Nashe? Why, what has he done to –?'

'No, not him. He's –' And she dismissed her little-known suitor with an airy sweep of her hand. 'It's Sir Richard I speak of.' She could not even bring herself to call him her father.

'Hate is strong –'

But Perdita swept on. 'He is deceitful and cruel and heartless and thinks of no one but himself.'

Kitty nodded her head thoughtfully at this unflattering portrait of her husband. 'Didn't I tell you the kind of man he was?'

'Yes. But I thought . . . He cares more for one of his mangy dogs than he does for me. Cares more for the servants than for his own child!' Her voice wobbled with self-pity.

'Nonsense, girl, he cares for no one but himself. Forget this fretting, Perdita, it does you no good.'

'I cannot be free of it.'

'Then you will have to act.'

17

'What can I do?'

'If you wish him to pay you some attention then you must seek him out, compel him to talk with you.'

Perdita seemed to shrink for a moment at the prospect. 'Could you not speak to him first, suggest to him that he should see me? Arrange it somehow?'

'Are you so very afraid of him?'

'Certainly not!'

'There there, no need to be all hot and bothered about it; plenty braver than yourself have found their courage failing when they had to tackle Richard Treveryan. *Sir* Richard Treveryan.'

'I'm *not* afraid of him. I'll talk with him today.'

'Then I wish you joy.' Kitty was already heartily bored by such an unpleasant subject and she caught the young girl by her arm. 'Look, Perdita, there's a place not far from here has very fine brocade. If you are to marry we'd do well to start purchasing the fabrics for your clothes at once.'

'Not now, Mother. You go without me, if you must. I need some time to think.'

Kitty pursed her lips and walked on alone. In her opinion there was nothing in this world that took precedence over a fine length of new brocade. But at the end of the street she paused and turned. Lady Treveryan, a small woman who had never been beautiful, or even pretty, and who had aged rapidly during the years of her husband's exile, watched her daughter for a few moments before the girl's tall figure was hidden in the crowds.

That dejected droop of the shoulders, footsteps wandering without direction . . . a small shrivelled memory of pain caused Lady Treveryan a brief moment of discomfort. She walked on.

The range of emotions at Kitty's command had always been limited, and any kind of sympathy was foreign to her. But today, listening to Perdita, she had known something close to genuine compassion. The gossips were right in one thing at least. In so far as she cared for anyone, Kitty cared for Perdita, her first child if not her firstborn. The daughter she had never thought to see.

The problem was that she understood the girl's con-
emotions only too clearly – memory served her

18

where imagination would have failed. People knew Kitty Treveryan as a shrewish and irritating woman. But years ago there had been a weak place, a soft underbelly which she had been careful no one should see, not even her husband. Especially not her husband – he who had been the only person in all the world to cause her real pain. She knew well enough what it was to batter her heart against the granite walls of Richard Treveryan's indifference.

But pain, even the memory of pain, was something she had always been zealous to avoid. Perhaps there was no need to spend much on further clothes for Perdita – after all, the gowns she had had newly made for this London visit would serve well enough for Warwickshire, and Oliver Nashe was barely a gentleman. A length of new brocade might better serve to make a new gown for herself . . . the bodice long and pointed at the front. Yes, she knew how it must be done . . . she would visit the dressmaker that very afternoon.

A cold drizzle was gusting from the Thames, bringing with it the salt smells of refuse and fish, but Perdita, so lost in her own unhappy thoughts, did not notice it at all.

Sir Richard Treveryan was arranging a marriage for her which was a better one than she had expected and she knew she should be thankful – but all she could think of was that, once settled in far-off Warwickshire, she would never see him or her family again. Her mother and brothers would miss her, she knew that, and even the servants would be sorry she was gone; but her father? He'd notice the loss of a favourite hunting dog sooner than he missed his firstborn child. In a life that had so far been devoted to the art of winning a place in the hearts of those around her, Perdita was contemplating her first defeat.

It was not a pleasant experience. Almost from infancy she had been one of those easy babies whose only apparent aim is to please. It was as though she had been aware, long before she could have understood the reason, that her position in the household was a precarious one; a favour granted that could as easily be withdrawn.

Her memory of those first years was vague. After the Royalists' defeat at Worcester Richard Treveryan had forfeited his remaining lands and his wealth. While he pursued a soldier's life in France and Spain, his wife returned to her father's house, and Perdita, at the age of seven, found herself facing the toughest challenge of her short life. Kitty busied herself in persuading the parliamentary committees that she should be allowed to keep at least those properties that she herself had brought to the marriage. Perdita, with equal determination, was intent on winning over the old gentleman who had let it be known that he would never call this cuckoo child his grand-daughter. Kitty was only partly successful; Perdita completely so. Ralph Jordan, Kitty's father, was no match for the small girl with the thin face and dark eyes and a smile that could wriggle right through to the heart of you. She teased him when he was merry, flattered him when he felt old, listened when he wished to talk. On the days when the household walked on tiptoe for fear of his ill-temper it was Perdita who was sent to humour him. And when he fell ill and was often in pain it was Perdita, then fourteen, whose quick hands alone could nurse him, Perdita whose soft voice soothed him, reading the psalms he loved so well to hear.

She held his hand when he was dying. As well as the expected sorrow (for she had grown genuinely to care for him) Perdita had known a fierce glow of triumph. The hardest battle of her life had been fought and most triumphantly won. She was a match for anyone. Or so, in her innocence, she had thought then.

She was excited when she heard the first talk of the King's return. Now her father was sure to come home too, the father she could barely remember. And if Ralph Jordan had learned to love her, the bastard child who had brought humiliation to his only daughter, then surely it was only a question of time before Sir Richard Treveryan learned to love her too.

From that moment when he stepped ashore at Blackfriars in the wind and rain of a bleak September afternoon, she knew that this would be a battle of a different kind. For the first time in sixteen years her courage failed her. His dark eyes looked at his family but appeared hardly to see them. She was to learn to dread those eyes: eyes that veiled secrets but betrayed no emotion; eyes that moved restlessly from the noisy trivia of the household and seemed always to be seeking out the open spaces where his beloved hawks could fly. Eyes in which Perdita could not see herself reflected at all.

In time, however, the little household, cramped in its temporary London lodgings, did achieve a semblance of kinship. Kitty chattered to him of plans for their future, which house they should settle in, what changes should be made. Sometimes he listened to her. He heard the boys' lessons and spoke sternly to them when they misbehaved. Even the servants had the benefit of an occasional word, a smile or a rebuke. Only Perdita was ignored. No matter how charmingly she smiled, how often she offered to fetch his glass, mend his clothes, make herself useful, no matter how witty or pertinent her comments, all her efforts were ignored. She began to feel herself not so much a bastard as a ghost child, not there at all.

But why?

As she struggled to seek some kind of explanation for his coldness the only answers she could find were stray fragments of rumour, half-remembered talk of sorcery and betrayal, the idle gossip of servants as they sat around the kitchen fire on winter evenings and told the old stories of ghostly lovers and demons that walked the moors at night, and then, in lower voices still, when they thought Perdita was asleep and could not hear their words, they murmured of her mother.

Her mother. The woman who, when she knew that she must lose the child, had named her Perdita, the lost one. She could hear their voices now as they spoke of a woman who had loved and lost and who, it was rumoured, had forfeited her life in the turmoil that had followed the civil war. A woman spoken of with awe and more than a touch of fear. Over the past few weeks Perdita had come to believe that this unknown woman who had died so many years before was the shadow still that blocked her father's love. Witchcraft? She remembered the whispered accusations, but she remembered Dorcas too.

How could she ever forget the servant who had loved her as much as any mother and on whose copious bosom her head had always found rest? Dorcas had said her mother

21

was an angel, that she had saved poor Dorcas from Hell and yet died herself of a broken heart. And when she spoke of her Dorcas rocked back and forth and cried and then laughed in her tears and grew hot and muddled and had to be soothed with a mug of warm ale.

But then as everyone knew, Dorcas's wits were addled long before and Perdita soon learned to mock her as the others did. Yet missed her now.

The memory of Dorcas was a kind of comfort. Even now, on those London nights when sleep evaded her, she had only to conjure up an image of that vast lap where a small child might lose her troubles, to breathe that rank smell, for the anxieties of her present life to be transformed into the empty sleep of infancy. She wished passionately that Dorcas was still alive so that she could ask her about her mother.

Perdita sighed. Questions, always questions, but no answers.

And why should she now be bothering with the old lives, lives that were part of a past that meant nothing to her, when her own life was even now opening up an intriguing prospect? In truth, she was mostly pleased at the idea of marriage to Mr Nashe. She was apprehensive too, of course, but from what little she had seen of him so far she guessed him to be a kindly man whom she could wrap around her little finger within six months. And Warwickshire would be a fresh start, no rumours of witchcraft or angels there, no shadows from another's past darkening her present life. Yes, a clean beginning in a new town, no longer a bastard daughter but a lawful wife – her heartbeat quickened at the bright new prospect of respectability.

But first, but first . . .

She paused, and looked around her. She had been so blinded by her thoughts that at first she could not make out where she was, but, recognising St Clement Dane's church, she realised that she must have walked nearly the whole length of the Strand. Around her church bells were chiming the twelve o'clock peal.

She turned and began hurrying back towards their rented rooms off King Street; she was walking as quickly as she could, as if the very fervour of her pace might fan a fire of resolution within her. Before she could launch herself on a new life then the mysteries of the old must be resolved. She had urgent and unfinished business – with Sir Richard Treveryan.

Perdita shook out her skirts and smoothed her hair. She pinned her brightest smile to her face and took a deep breath to calm herself before knocking gently on the door and then, in response to the gruff command from within, pushing it open.

'Father, may I speak with you?'

'Is it necessary?'

'Yes.'

'I'm very busy.' Sir Richard Treveryan barely looked up from the pile of papers he was working on.

'I will try to be brief, Father.' Now that she was actually standing in front of him, Perdita was more nervous even than she had expected. She almost hoped he would dismiss her at once, so that she might escape and rejoin her brothers at their game of cards, but instead Treveryan tossed aside the document he had been studying and, leaning back in his chair, said brusquely, 'Very well, then, but be quick.'

She shifted uneasily. Her throat was suddenly very dry. She glanced across at Viney, the elderly manservant who had shared exile with Treveryan and went with him everywhere. He was a thin, dark-haired man who was as little interested in the other members of the household as his master seemed to be. 'I'd like to speak to you alone. Please –'

'But we are –' and then, following her gaze, 'Oh, Viney. No need to worry about him, child. Graves will talk before Viney stoops to gossip. Isn't that right?'

'But Father, I'd rather –'

Treveryan frowned his impatience but, to her surprise and relief, it was Viney himself who came to her rescue. 'I had a mind to go out now, sir, to take these boots to be mended and to collect your new shoes for tomorrow.'

'Well, if you must. But do not delay. Whatever Perdita and I have to say to each other, it will not occupy me long.'

'Very good, sir.' And, with a brief glance in her direction that amazed her by being a smile almost of encouragement,

Viney picked up a pair of long leather riding boots and went out, closing the door quietly behind him.

'So? What is your business?'

For a moment the sudden realisation that she was, for the first time in her life, quite alone with her father, was almost more than she could bear; there was so much she wanted to say to him and such a woeful dearth of practice, that her carefully rehearsed phrases flew quite out of her brain. Her smile, which was intended to be charming but was in fact too defiant for charm, faded from her face and she stared helplessly at this tall stranger who sat before her. His dark hair was grizzled now with white and his gaunt features were shadowed by the fading light of an October afternoon. There was menace in his eyes. She swallowed once, opened her mouth to speak – but no words came.

Sir Richard Treveryan grunted impatiently. 'If your only purpose is to stand there gaping like an idiot then you may leave at once.'

'But I wanted to ask –'

'Hmm?' He was drumming his fingers on the oak surface of his desk. 'Let me guess. The servants have been babbling on about things that don't concern them and you like a fool have been listening. Is that so?'

'About my marriage, yes.'

'Your intended marriage, nothing is yet fixed. You wish to know about Mr Oliver Nashe?'

'Yes, sir, but only –'

He interrupted her. 'Well then, if I must: negotiations are progressing in a satisfactory manner,' and tipping his head back against the carved arch of his chair, Treveryan stared at the ceiling and spoke in a bored tone, as if reciting a catechism dredged from some far corner of his memory. 'In fact I have invited him to dinner tomorrow evening – he is eager to make your acquaintance. As you know, I have a formal audience with His Majesty in the morning. I daresay he will grant me some honour which will be intended to gratify my vanity at a cost less dear to him than the restoration of Trecarne. For myself, I'd as soon he bestowed his trinkets on his horse – but there, it does not do for returning heroes to be squeamish about his gracious royal gratitude. I have no doubt that Mr Oliver Nashe will be duly impressed by my close ties with royalty and I expect thereby to raise the value of your portion. He is wealthy enough, God knows, and can afford to be generous.'

His recitation ended, he turned his attention with some reluctance from the low beamed ceiling to the girl standing mute before him. 'Does that answer your question? I have work to do.'

'And do you think highly of him?'

A dismissive gesture. 'Of course not. But the man's no more a fool than the rest of them. Quite shrewd in his way, I daresay. If you take care no doubt you'll rub along together well enough. He has no outstanding vices that I know of, if that's what you're afraid of.'

'No. But –'

'What now?'

'I wanted to know –'

No longer able to restrain his impatience. 'I've told you all that need concern you now. More than you deserve.'

'. . . about my mother.'

It was the oddest feeling, now the words were out: as if the walls were folding down upon her.

Treveryan shifted irritably. 'Your mother? Why, she's downstairs trimming a new hat for tomorrow, or some such vital task. What of her?'

'No. My real mother. The one who –'

Her words diminished on a trembling breath. There was a silence, a huge engulfing silence. Darkness was spreading now in this room which was lit by only one small window and Perdita could no longer make out the expression on her father's face.

At length he stood up slowly and walked towards the fireplace. Two logs, still green, wheezed on the hearth; one of the hunting spaniels lying in a heap by the fire looked up expectantly at his approach, then slept again.

At last he spoke. 'Why in the name of all that's holy do you wish to know about her?'

'I wondered . . . she was my mother . . .'

'She gave you birth, that's all. The mangiest dog can do as much, and care more for her pups. The only mother you've ever had was my wife. Are you ungrateful now for what she's done?'

'Oh no, no! I owe her everything, I know that.' Perdita had early learned the delicate art of being grateful with dignity, but she could see from her father's gesture of impatience that to continue in this mode was a waste of time. 'But I need to understand . . . I've heard stories, strange rumours . . .'

'Ignore them, girl. If you listen to the servants' gibberish, small wonder your skull is so brimful of foolishness.'

She was careful to smile at his insult. 'It was not only the servants, Father. There were others, too, when they thought I was not listening.'

'Eavesdropping too?'

'I never intended . . . but once, when I was very small, I heard Lady Sutton say that my mother was – a witch.'

'Alice said that?'

'I heard also that my mother, my natural mother, made you care for her by sorcery and that in the same way she made your wife take me into her home. And that was how the boys came to be born, as part of the bargain.'

Sir Richard glanced up from his contemplation of the fire and looked at her with disbelief. His features, never handsome, were made strange by the dancing orange shadows of the firelight and the lines of boredom and contempt were exaggerated, etched deep into his face.

'My God,' he drawled, 'I never cease to be amazed by the eternal nonsense you women indulge yourselves with.'

'Then there is no truth in the stories?'

'Do you expect me to treat your question seriously?'

Perdita's cheeks flamed at the contempt in his voice. Her craving for understanding was met with nothing but scorn. She smothered her agitation, forced herself to speak calmly. 'And Dorcas said –'

'Dorcas now, as well?'

'Dorcas told me she was an angel.'

'How much more of this must I endure? If I remember rightly, Dorcas believed that goblins turned the milk sour and that the mountains of America are populated entirely by men with two heads. I only hope that when you are married Mr Nashe has more sense than to allow you time for such idiocy.'

If he had been angry with her, Perdita would not have

minded so much. It was the eternity of indifference in his voice that she found impossible to bear. A lifetime's training in caution and diplomacy was thrust aside by a mounting tide of anger and frustration.

'Father, you are not fair! You refuse to tell me what I need to know – and there is no one else that I can ask. What kind of a woman was she? Am I like her at all? Why did she give me up? And now, and now you mean to marry me off. And so far away, you'll never tell me. I won't ever . . . you shouldn't . . . it's not fair!'

'You grow hysterical. Go to your room at once.'

'No!' Perdita caught hold of his hands as though to wrest sympathy from him by force. 'No, no! You won't dismiss me, send me away. You won't. I won't go. I shall refuse . . . not marry Mr Nashe . . . I will not . . . be sent away . . . you must speak . . .'

He thrust her away. 'What's this? You're lucky I don't thrash you for your boldness. You go too far –'

Frightened by the force of her anger and of a feeling, unusual for Perdita, that she was no longer in command of herself, she fell to weeping. Sir Richard remained unmoved.

'A fine spectacle indeed. Perhaps I have misjudged you and your future lies in the theatre. Women are already appearing on the stage in France and they say the fashion will spread here. Still, if you insist on playing the heart-broken maiden then I suppose I must act the part of the stern father.' He sighed and walked over to the window and his profile was black against the dusky sky. 'Silence, girl, you achieve nothing by this wretched display. If I agree the details with Mr Nashe then you will marry him, as well you know. You do not have the stomach for rebellion.'

'I'll not be sent away.' Perdita spoke dully, swallowing her useless tears.

'No? Some other man has perhaps caught your eye?'

'No.'

'I'm glad to hear it. A lot of nonsense is talked these days about love and marriage. Love is a temporary weakness and a marriage needs firm foundations to survive the years.'

'Then did you never love?'

'Enough.'

There was a warning growl in his voice; his hand clenched

27

by his side. 'I've been patient with you far too long, God knows. Many a father would have punished you already for such disobedience.'

'But . . . all I asked . . . I sometimes think you hate me, and all because of her.'

'This witch again?' he laughed, a dry, cruel laugh. 'Or maybe Dorcas's angel? Well, you can set your mind at rest on that score. She was an ordinary girl enough. You might even say she was – a nobody.'

'You did not care for her?'

'How can one care for a nobody? She was an amusement, merely, and one that quickly became a nuisance. As you are doing now.'

The words were spoken with a fierce scorn and yet, suddenly, Perdita's deep despair was pierced by a ray of hope. Such scorn, verging almost on hatred and after such a long interval of time, could only be caused by feelings that had once been strong, passionate even.

'You did,' she breathed, 'you loved her!'

'Go!' His command crashed across the room. 'You are a witless fool and you deserve to be flogged!' And now there was nothing studied about his anger: all pretence at indifference had been swept away. He strode over to the door and for a moment Perdita believed he would strike her but instead he flung the door open. 'Go, and never dare to speak of this again!'

Perdita shivered. She was afraid. And she was triumphant. Some cold hard thing that had encased him, hidden him from her as surely as a suit of armour, had cracked. Not much, to be sure, but just enough to show her that the man who stood before her now, his face ugly with rage, had once been a man capable of pain and love.

She feared his violence, was glad to scurry past him. But even as she escaped she caught a glimpse of his face and saw his eyes, black as midnight, looking through her and beyond with an intensity of pain and something that was deeper than mere rage that quite took her breath away.

She knew now why Kitty feared him. More important, she knew now with an unmovable certainty, as she made her way through the gathering shadows of evening to the warmth and firelight below, that it was her natural mother, this woman long dead, neither witch nor angel but, as her father had said, an ordinary girl, a nobody, who cast a shadow down the years that blocked her father from her still.

Sir Richard Treveryan was still standing at the window when Viney returned and began to move quietly around the room, lighting the candles, attending to the fire. Viney said nothing, for he knew better than to intrude on his master's brooding silences.

'The foolish girl is under the impression that I ignore her deliberately,' Treveryan murmured, almost to himself. He laughed softly. 'If she only knew how I have to force myself to think of her at all, to be reminded of my duty to her to spend tedious hours with that oaf Nashe.'

Viney grunted, his usual non-committal comment.

'She even wanted to know about her mother. Her . . . natural mother.'

For the briefest moment Viney paused in his task and a shadow crossed his face. 'I knew that was who you meant,' he said, continuing as before.

'The sins of omission . . .' Sir Richard sighed, knowing that he had failed in his duty just now, had been too lenient. The young minx had stood before him and defied him and he should have punished her. Yet he had not. And his anger had quickly passed. Envy, that was it. When he saw his daughter, red-faced and afraid in her stupid defiance, he had actually envied her. She was wrong, she was muddle-headed and hysterical, but my God, she still cared.

It made him aware suddenly of the degree to which he had lost the taste for life. He felt old, not in his body, which was an irrelevance, but in his spirit. Never again would he be moved to tears or laughter as she still was. She derived more sweetness from a cup of clear water than he had from the finest wines of France. A glance from the eyes of a strutting youth would fire her more surely than a whole night he might spend with the most dextrous whore. He had no doubt she now believed herself to be in the utmost depths of despair; he even envied her capacity for grief.

Yes, her tantrum had stirred the ashes of a fire long dead. A few false sparks, but no real flame. Strange, he thought, how puny her rebellion seemed. For though he had never made a study of his daughter's character, he was sure she would prove easy to control. All outward fire, yet despite her brave words she did not have the necessary courage for rebellion.

Unlike her mother. Her mother so apparently dutiful, who had yet scandalised the narrow world she lived in not once, but twice, three times, during her stormy life. Oh, the bitter irony of it.

At moments like this it struck Sir Richard as strange that he could barely remember what Perdita's mother looked like. There had been no portrait painted; and the mother, with characteristic but surely unintended selflessness, had given him a daughter as near as possible in looks to himself. So much easier to overlook her bastard state.

Perdita, the lost one. Yet not so much lost, he thought, with the merest touch of bitterness, not so much lost as thrown away.

Angel or witch? He frowned. The ashes of the old fire glimmered for a moment, then were dead and grey again. The old riddle no longer even interested him. It had all been so long ago, after all.

The last sunlight of the autumn day gleamed behind the banked-up grey clouds over the King's palace at Whitehall. A sudden burst of light.

Old wounds ache sometimes with the turn of the seasons, and so it was with him. As summer gave place to the narrowing days of autumn he sometimes felt a sadness, an echo of a grief long gone. He considered it strange that it was at this falling time of year that his thoughts most often drifted back to Cornwall. Autumn, a season of no grace or beauty there. Westerly gales ripped the leaves from the oak woods before they had a chance to colour and the sea mist crept like a white curse up the creeks and hollows of the coast bringing salt aches to young and old alike.

He would never go there again. The fine house that he had built at Trecarne had gone to a Parliament man, and though he pretended regret in his dealings with the King, the truth was he was glad to be free of the burden of it.

Yet sometimes, just sometimes, in his dreams he heard the wind sighing through the Cornish woods again and heard the music of the tides, and then sometimes, in that moment between dreaming and waking, he heard a woman's voice speak his name with the soft warm voice of the Cornish, and he caught a glimpse of wide grey eyes that gazed on him and seemed to teach the eternity of love . . . and when the image broke and the present claimed him, he knew such a gaping wound of desolation that he felt his heart torn from him once again. And on those days he stepped from sleep to waking with a roar of pain like a man who has glimpsed into the fiery heart of hell itself.

It did not last, of course. In this life nothing lasted, and as for the next, well, he hardly cared. Old men do not grieve for the pretty faces of their youth. The illusions, the whole trickery of passion. He had been wrong to envy Perdita just now, still living in her dream.

Angel or witch? He laughed again. An ordinary girl, a nobody. And yet for a few brief months she had been his whole world. His whole world and – an illusion. The final irony of it was, of course, that she had not cared for him at all.

Margaret . . .

Mistress Hollar . . .

His own sweet Meg . . .

Part 1

Cornwall, 1630

1

The September hedgerows were drenched with dew as the three children trudged down the narrow track that led from their home to Porthew. The sun was not yet risen and the early air was chill. Little Tom, tumbled too soon from his bed, fretted to be allowed to ride the horse.

'There's room for me,' he whined, 'I could fit beside the baskets.'

'On the way home, Tom, when she's not so laden. Juno will be tired if she has too much to carry.'

'*I'm* tired now,' he said, 'I'm very tired.' He directed his appeal to Margaret, the elder of his two sisters, whom he rightly considered the more pliable.

'No you're not,' said Lizzie crossly, for she too found the walk to Porthew tiring and did not like to be up early, 'you're just lazy.'

Juno, a place on whose scrawny back was so ardently desired by Tom, followed at a little distance, picking her way daintily between the jagged stones of the lane. She was an unlikely animal to share the name of the queen of the gods. Thin and ungainly, with a large head and narrow shoulders, she had a coat of a sickly yellowish colour, rough and patchy. But she was patient and hard-working and Margaret loved her as she loved all their animals. Their farm was probably the only one in Cornwall to be populated almost entirely by the gods and heroes of ancient Greece and Rome. She had not, however, named the five roosters, anguished prisoners in their bouncing willow basket which was attached to the saddle with a stout cord. Their brief destiny was to be slaughtered. Hard enough to part with them as it was – if they had been named, the task might have proved impossible.

Tom was persistent. 'She's looking at me, Mattie,' he

wheedled, 'she's lonely. She *wants* me to ride her, I can tell. Please let me ride her. I'm so very small.'

Margaret laughed. 'Small, is it? A great stout boy like you with half a loaf inside you already today? Here, I'll carry you to the top of the hill and from there it's all the way down to Porthew. Oof, what a great lump you are.'

'He can walk, Mattie, you shouldn't spoil him so.'

'Oh, you're just as bad, you know you are.'

And Tom, who had long been convinced that the kind Lord God and Jesus Ahsaver had granted him two wonderful big sisters so that his every slightest whim should be instantly gratified, crowed and bounced on his lofty perch astride Margaret's shoulders: she was tall and strong and did not mind at all.

'Look, look! Over there! I can see a hare!' And pulling back an imaginary bow he blew the sound of a whistling arrow. 'Tew! I killed it.'

'Poor hare, leave it in peace.'

'I killed it!'

And then the sun came up: and a thousand cobwebs sparkled with dew on either side of the track and a lark rose up singing into the pale blue air above them.

Margaret beamed with the day. 'Did you ever see such a morning, Lizzie?'

'You say that every time,' said Lizzie, touching a hand to the new ribbons in her hair: more absorbed by her own prettiness than the beauty of the morning.

They reached the top of the hill.

'Down you get now, Tom. Look, there's Porthew.'

The bay was shimmering in the morning sunlight and from the town came the sound of church bells ringing. They could see the church, and boats in the harbour and little groups of people, some on foot and some on horseback and a few in jolting two-wheeled carts, converging on the town. The high day of all the year: St Ewan's Feast Day.

Tom, briefly, was silenced. Lizzie squealed with delight. Margaret thought with satisfaction of the carefully packed panniers – the brown eggs in their bed of hay, the butter wrapped in fresh green leaves, the round ripe apples and the jars of pickled samphire. No day in all the year to compare with this one.

36

Tom found his voice with renewed vigour. 'Will there be a dancing bear? Can I eat whatever I like? Will I go in a boat? Can I – ?'

'For mercy's sake, what a nuisance the boy is,' said Lizzie, 'he'll be hanging on our skirts all day. We should have left him at home.'

'Never mind,' said Margaret, 'when we've given the roosters away we can put him in their basket and shut the lid down and leave him 'til we're ready.'

'You won't, you won't.' Tom was skipping on ahead. Suddenly he sat down in the middle of the path and began tugging at his shoe.

'Whatever are you doing?'

'It hurts my foot. I don't like shoes.'

'You're never thinking of going barefoot?'

'I like bare feet best.'

'At home maybe, but not today.'

'Whatever will people think?'

'They'll take you for a beggar boy.'

The two girls whirled about his head in a flurry of out-raged propriety: a stone was removed from the troublesome shoe, soft hay from the egg basket was squeezed in to prevent blisters, he was stood up, dusted down and set on his way once more.

They could hear the sounds of cock crows and dogs barking across the valley, gulls calling in the harbour.

In her excitement Lizzie forgot that she had woken too early and that her legs were tired already. 'Lord, I'm so excited! Mattie, you've forgot your collar.'

'And so I had.' Margaret pulled from her sleeve a care-fully folded collar of white linen which she had put there for safety while she saw to the first before-dawn chores. She spread it across her shoulders while Lizzie smoothed and fussed and tucked.

'Pull your hair over it – so. Now no one can see the burn mark, it's good as new. There now, don't you look grand!'

Margaret's old dress of grey wool was transformed by the wide white collar. She laughed with delight at her own grandeur.

'I feel like gentry,' she said.

Lizzie patted the new blue ribbons that fluttered in her

chestnut curls. 'And *I* feel like a queen!' she declared.

Tom, catching their excitement, danced around them, his long curls whirling. 'And I'm a king!' he babbled. 'King of Kings, God save King Charles! Kingy, kingy –'

'Lord save the child, will he never stop his babbling?'

'Come on, let's run. I see Ambrose watching for us.'

'Giddy up, Juno, we'll miss the fair.'

'The fair, the fair!' And, wild with excitement, Tom careered off down the hill faster than his fat legs could scamper and he would have fallen headlong had not his two sisters caught him by the arms and whirled him along between them as they laughed and panted and raced to join the other country folk converging on Porthew for St Ewan's Feast Day.

Ambrose Treloar looked up from the axle he was mending and caught sight of the three figures tumbling towards him down the bracken-green hillside. He grinned. He had been watching for them since first light and now he raised a hand in greeting.

There was Tom, small and fat and squealing with pleasure, for his feet scarcely touched the ground in his giddy descent; and Lizzie, so neat and dainty with her pretty face and her tumbling chestnut curls. But it was on Margaret that his gaze lingered: Margaret so tall and strong and capable, with her wide smile and her grey eyes and that hair the colour of ripe corn, fair hair that was so uncommon in these Celtic parts. She had it from her mother, he knew, her mother from God knows where.

Ambrose watched Margaret as she ran down the hillside and he forgot the axle he was mending, forgot the farmer waiting by the roadside.

Some folk around here were suspicious of Margaret Pearce for her foreign mother, he knew that. Not that he was the sort to be bothered by a spot of gossip, not Ambrose. For after all, her father was a cousin to his mother so she was family on her father's side at least. His mother, he knew, favoured Lizzie as a possible wife for him. Lizzie had the good fortune to be Cornish on both sides.

For the two girls, so little alike in looks, were only recently sisters, not proper sisters at all. A few years back

Lizzie's mother (recently widowed) had married Margaret's father (whose wife had just died). And then Tom was born, a brother to them both. And they were fonder of each other than any real sisters that he knew.

Ambrose pondered slowly the problems and complications of kinship and love – and the axle cooled on the anvil and he had to thrust it back in the fire to heat again. He worked slowly enough even when not distracted by the sight of two pretty girls running down the hillside towards him on a fair-day morning, and the farmer waiting outside in the early sunshine was impatient to be on his way. A year ago he would no doubt have scolded Ambrose and chivvied him to work faster; but it would be a reckless man who chose to scold Ambrose Treloar these days.

Although he was not yet grown to his full strength, the youth was already a good head taller than any other man in the district – and he was reputed to have the strength of three.

The old folk, those who could remember back to Elizabeth's reign, were already declaring that the lad was likely to be a match to his grandfather, that mighty Walter Treloar whose feats of strength had passed into the annals of local folklore, a man who could flex a bow no other man could bend. And each year people still talked of the time when a crazed ox had broken loose on St Ewan's Day and roared through the crowd, scattering terrified people and animals like skittles. Only Walter stood his ground and laughed (so it was said), strode over to the maddened beast, lifted it high into the air and carried it through the empty street and back to the shambles yard. There he dropped it and, for good measure, struck it a powerful blow between the eyes to teach it some sense. One old lady and an infant were killed by the animal's charge but the ox, so they said, was meek as a maid from that day forward.

Ambrose knew the story well. In recent months he had been inclined to resent his grandfather's fame. It was time for the present young Treloar to make his mark. He nursed a secret hope that today a crazed beast might once again break loose and cause havoc among the fair-day crowds. He did not doubt that he could master a charging ox or bull. And Margaret would surely be impressed.

39

In all his dreams of strength and daring it was Margaret who stood witness to his triumph. And in his favourite imaginings, the ones which brought a broad smile of satisfaction to his face as he beat the white-hot iron to shape on his anvil, it was Margaret herself whom he rescued, and her wide grey eyes looked up at him, subdued at last by gratitude and love.

'Mother sent you this butter, Mistress Treloar,' said Margaret, unpacking the panniers carefully, 'and here's cheese . . . and you're to have two of the roosters too: they're young birds and will make good eating.'

Mistress Treloar watched eagerly and tried to peer into the baskets to see if there were any special treats that she was being denied. When she was certain that no more gifts were being offered she said, 'My thanks to your mother, Margaret, she's always good to remember her friends. And I trust she is keeping well.'

'Well enough, though as you know she suffers from rheumatics and cannot get about much.'

'We all have our trials, I'm sure. Now just you tether your horse here while you go into town and I'll see she comes to no harm. Come on into the kitchen and I'll give you all something to eat. Ambrose, you see to those roosters.'

Margaret hesitated for a moment before sliding her hand under the lid of the willow basket and removing first one outraged rooster, then a second, and handing them both to Ambrose. As he took them from her they appeared to grow smaller, for his huge hands enclosed them so easily they might have been no more than sparrows. He swung them both in the air and tilted back his head to watch them and his ginger hair was flecked gold in the early rays of the sun. For the briefest moment he released them, one after the other, and then, just as the birds tasted freedom, with a twist of his massive hands he broke their necks and their heads hung limp while their wings still beat a forgotten rhythm of escape.

It was quickly done, and cleanly, so Margaret could not explain why her stomach should heave at the sight of the killing. Afterwards she thought that her revulsion had been caused not so much by the death, which she knew to be necessary, but more by the smile of pleasure on Ambrose's broad face as the job was done.

Fortified by the bread and small beer that Mistress Treloar had given them, Tom and his sisters went back to the forge beside the house to talk with Ambrose before walking the last quarter mile into Porthew. The forge was open to the road at the front and it was pleasant to sit there with the sun warming their faces and to watch the little groups of people who made their way along the road to the fair. Almost all were friends, relatives or acquaintances and they exchanged greetings with the easy friendliness of a high day and holiday.

Ambrose was shaping a bar of metal into a meat hook and Tom watched fascinated, silenced for a moment as the hammer struck the metal and the sparks flew up into the black roof of the smithy. Ambrose worked with a slow rhythm and wished that it was Margaret, not Lizzie, who turned her head so often to look with admiration on his work.

'Don't you miss the wrestling, this afternoon,' his deep voice rang out over the sound of the hammer blows.

'Will you take part?'

'Indeed I shall. They say Robert Trelyn of Helston will come; no one has beaten him in more than six years. Not until today.'

'And can you beat him now, Ambrose?' Lizzie dimpled him her prettiest smile.

'Easily. I can beat anyone now.' And he picked up the cooling bar and bent it to shape with his leather-gloved hands. Tom plugged his thumb into his mouth: such visible excess of strength was almost too thrilling.

'And you must see the play, then, Ambrose,' said Lizzie. 'Did you know that Mattie has a special part?'

'What's that, then?'

'Quiet, Lizzie, I'm sure he isn't interested in my speechifying.'

'Of course he is. You know, Ambrose, don't you, that Sir John Sutton has recently wed for the second time?'

'Everybody knows that.'

41

'Well then, Parson Weaver thought it would be a fine thing to add a piece into the play in praise of love and marriage and all that sort of foolishness. And as a compliment to Sir John, seeing as he's such an educated man, Parson thought to put the speech into Latin. So of course it had to be Mattie to say it since she's such a fine clever girl and speaks Latin as if she was born a Roman.'

'Latin, eh?' Ambrose scowled. 'No need for that, is there?'

'It was meant as a compliment, Ambrose, to Sir John and his new wife.' Margaret explained the reasons to him carefully, as she always did. And as always Ambrose only grew the angrier.

'I don't hold with Latin, not at all. Damned papist language. I've got no time for it. Leave that for the monkey-gibbering Catholics, that's what I say.'

'But Ambrose, it isn't just Catholics. The Romans were speaking in Latin long before Catholics were even thought of.'

'Heathen then. Damned heathen language.' Ambrose's anger was not soothed by Margaret's defence of Latin. She was mocking him, he was sure of it, just as she had mocked him in Dame Erisey's little school when he was a hulking great lad and she was a tiny girl and he could make no sense at all of the scribbles on paper that she deciphered so easily. And still she made him feel like a foolish child, for all that he was taller than her by far and he could have picked her up and lifted her from the ground just by reaching out one strong hand. As always his anger found a physical expression and he lifted the meat hook he had been shaping, now cooled nearly to full strength, and bent it back to straight again. The bar snapped and he threw it into a corner in disgust.

Tom, hearing distant noise, jumped down from his stool and ran out into the road.

'Horses!' he shouted. 'Lots of horses coming! I can see them! And fine riders too!'

Margaret, whose eyes were better able to make out the printed page by candlelight than anything at a distance, could see nothing but a blur of dust, but Lizzie distinguished the riders quite easily.

At the front of the party was a laughing, good-looking

youth wearing a large cocked hat and fine clothes. About six or seven gentlemen and ladies followed him, all equally resplendent in their fair-day finery and riding horses as different from the proudly named Juno as a sleek greyhound is from a farmyard cur. Following them at a respectful distance came half a dozen serving-men, some on ponies and some running to keep up as best they could.

'It's the Suttons!'

The girls jumped to their feet and prepared to curtsy as they had been taught, for after all, the Suttons owned most of the land around Porthew, their own small farm included.

Lizzie curtsied her deepest for the good-looking Nicolas Sutton who rode at the head of the party, but he ignored them, kicking his horse into a canter with a jingle of spurs and harness which flashed and shivered in the bright sunshine.

'Good day, Treloar,' Sir John Sutton shouted as he passed and Mistress Treloar ran round from their house and dropped a curtsy so deep and unaccustomed that it was only with the greatest difficulty that she managed to stand again when they had passed.

'Oh fiddle it,' she wheezed, brushing the dust from her skirts, 'and I never properly saw the new Lady Sutton. That must be her on the bay mare.'

'You'll see her later on at the fair.'

'But then everyone will have seen her and I wanted to be the first.'

They watched as the little group of riders clattered down the road to Porthew, horseshoes winking sunlight as they kicked up the dust. And the scent of oiled leather, horses and fine velvets lingered even when the sound of the jingling harnesses had faded completely.

'And hasn't Nicolas Sutton grown handsome,' gasped Lizzie. 'Did you ever see such a hat as the one he was wearing? Oh, wouldn't I give my eyes to wear such fine clothes as they have,' and she touched her new blue hair ribbons, a little wistfully, now that their splendour had been eclipsed by so much greater finery.

'He's just back from the university,' said Mistress Treloar, 'and none too pleased with his father's marriage either, so I'm told.'

'He'll be looking to his own marriage soon enough,' said Ambrose gruffly. He resented the attention squandered on those gaudy weaklings. In his view size and strength were the only standards by which men should be judged. 'And a nice *rich* wife is being found for him at this very moment,' and he poked Lizzie playfully in the ribs.

'I can't see why he should want a rich wife,' said Lizzie, still petulant although her spirits were somewhat restored by his teasing, 'he has plenty of money already. There should be a law passed that people *with* the money should have to marry those who haven't any. It would be better spread.'

'What nonsense you do talk,' said Margaret; 'money isn't butter to be spread about the place. Come along, we should be on our way. We've calls to make yet and I must see Parson about the verses.'

'Are you coming to the play, Mistress Treloar? Mattie is speaking, you know.' For Lizzie was proud of her educated sister.

'Yes, Latin,' said Tom. 'She's speaking lots of Latin.' Though for him, 'Latin' covered any language he could not understand, including the Cornish that was still spoken among some of the more isolated families in that western part of the county.

'Well, maybe. We shall see.' Mistress Treloar was profoundly suspicious of Margaret's unnatural learning. It would bring the girl to a bad end, she was sure: no one ever heard of a learned woman but there was trouble there soon enough.

'I'll be along later,' said Ambrose. 'Just as soon as Father comes back to mind the forge. You can wish me luck for the fight.'

'Luck?' Lizzie was scornful. 'You don't need luck, Ambrose Treloar, it's those other poor fellows who'll need the luck if they are to stay on their feet for as long as it takes to say a quick prayer. But we'll be there to cheer you in your victory.'

'A fine girl Lizzie's grown to be,' said Mistress Treloar as she stood behind her son at the entrance to the smithy and watched the three children set off down the road to Porthew. 'A fine girl indeed. Lively and cheerful, but sensible too. She'll make a good wife for the right man some

44

day.' And she looked hopefully up at her son. But his thoughts were all of Margaret, and the wrestling match that afternoon, and his mother's words did not register with him at all.

Porthew greeted them with the rich smells of fish and tar, salt and decay; the raucous cries of the gulls and the soft rhythm of a September sea; voices raised in laughter, argument or song; the jostling of people and animals. There were traders and pedlars and men looking for work, wandering Irish and sailors from foreign ports, Bretons, Picards and Walloons. There were animals being bought and sold and a few being killed slowly for entertainment. But above all there was gossip. Gossip rich and heady as a hot spiced wine, each teller adding fresh seasoning to the story as they passed it on, moral or caution, scandal or commiseration, as seemed fit.

Margaret and Lizzie took a rooster and three cheeses to Joan Dawkins the fishwife and received in return a quantity of smoked pilchards and the news that Sir John Sutton's new wife was old and poor and must have married him by trickery. From Dame Treworgie (a jar of pickled samphire and two dozen eggs) they learned that the new Lady Sutton had achieved her married state by devious witchcraft and that she was now intent on murdering the poor man by the same fiendish means. Already – and Dame Treworgie had this for a fact, might God strike her blind if she told them a lie – Sir John was in the early stages of a wasting disease which the doctors could not understand at all and which was sure to kill him by Christmas. But from Mistress Calwodely, Aunt Jane to Lizzie since she was sister to her mother's father, to whom they gave soft cheeses for her toothless mouth, eggs and apples for baking, and who gave them in return three pairs of fine knitted stockings to keep out the winter cold, they heard that far from being tricked, or bewitched, Sir John had chosen his second wife most cleverly. For by marrying the mother he hoped to control the son, rival in love to his own handsome Nicolas. And the disputed prize was Miss Alice Laniver, long known to have favoured Lady Sutton's son, but now certain to marry young Nicolas as his father had planned.

And along the way they learned that young Jane Penhallick's baby had fallen down a well and drowned and she was out of her wits with grief ('Poor girl and she was such a good mother too') or from others that the same Jane Penhallick had long believed the child to be a changeling, not hers at all, and the tortured belief festered and grew until in a moment of loathing she had thrown the unfortunate infant to his death ('And now she raves all day because the little people have put a curse upon her for harming one of their own'). And they learned too that Robert Pascoe, who was famous throughout the district for his cruel treatment of his mother, had been visited on the anniversary of his father's death by an apparition ('His father for sure') and though no one was exactly sure what passed between them, from that moment to this he had treated his mother like a queen. But the truly amazing thing was that his hair, that thick mane of chestnut hair, had turned white as seafoam in the night.

And so, amid scandal and gifts and laughter, the freshness of the bright September morning mellowed into the warmth of a fine noonday.

Their duty visits accomplished, the three children made their way to the top of the town and the back door of the draper's shop where they were warmly greeted by a girl a little older than Margaret.

'Wherever have you been, Mattie? I've been watching for you all morning. Hello, Tom – my heavens, what a big fellow you are growing. Good day, Lizzie – come in all of you, come in.'

Meredith Hocken was a sturdily built girl with thin mousy curls and a pale moon of a face that would have been plain but for the expression, both mischievous and lazily sensual, that animated it. She had been Margaret's closest friend since their early meeting at Dame Erisey's little school.

'It's not like you to be indoors on a fair day.' Margaret set her basket down on the kitchen table. 'Is anything wrong?'

'Yes. No. Come in and sit down. I've been bursting to tell you all morning.'

'If it's about the new Lady Sutton then I've heard it already. And poor Jane Penhallick's baby too.'

46

'And about Robert Pascoe,' Lizzie chipped in. 'Do you really believe his father came to scold him from the dead? Or was it perhaps a dream?'

Meredith was scornful. 'Whoever heard of a dream make a man's hair change colour in a night? White it is, pure white. You should see it. And the look in his eyes makes you want to run away home and bolt the door behind you.'

'Then what is it? You almost look as if you had seen a ghost yourself.'

'I'm hungry,' said Tom, his head whizzing with the gossip which had galloped far beyond his comprehension. 'You must fetch me something to eat.'

His sisters were scandalised.

'Where are your manners?'

'What kind of way is that to speak?'

Tom was unmoved. 'You *said* Merry would feed me. You *promised* me she would.'

'Don't scold the boy,' said Merry. 'I'll forget to breathe next. I've pie and everything all ready for you.'

The table was laid with a fine crusty pie, fresh green salad and cheeses and a pitcher of milk. Since Merry was well known for her lackadaisical housekeeping, Margaret was surprised to see her fussing to do all properly. And there was a troubled expression in her normally languid eyes.

'Well, Merry,' asked Margaret, when at last all the dishes were set to her satisfaction and Tom's mouth was crammed so full of food he was unable to speak, even if he had wanted to, 'what is your news? Is your mother worse?'

'She's well enough, though she still takes Father's death hard. I hear her sometimes in the night . . . but now . . .' and she glanced towards the door that led from the kitchen to the shop at the front of the house, 'now *he's* come.'

'Who?'

'My cousin William. He arrived from Fowey late last night. I told you we had word that he was coming and we've been expecting him all week. And now he's here –'

'Oh, Merry –'

Margaret and Lizzie both leant forward to hear more of this newcomer and, like Merry, they glanced anxiously at the heavy oak door.

'What is he like?'

'You'll see for yourselves soon enough.' Merry spoke in a whisper. 'He's the most handsome man you ever did see,' and her eyes sparkled.

'Really?' Lizzie patted her hair. 'More handsome than Nicolas Sutton? We saw him this morning, you know.'

'Tch!' From Merry's look of contempt one would have thought Nicolas Sutton a mere serving-boy. 'Far more handsome. And what's more, Mother is determined that he should stay and care for the shop. She's in there with him now, explaining it all – or as much as she understands herself, poor thing. They've been closeted in the shop since dawn.'

'But when did he arrive?'

'Towards midnight. I thought he'd be tired after all his travelling but he hardly slept at all. And he eats no more than a sparrow and looks at the food as if he wouldn't give it to a dog.'

'And do you think he will stay?'

Merry smiled, the slow lazy smile that caused so many of the young men in the neighbourhood to overlook her plainness and her lack of housekeeping skills and come courting by her garden gate on the long summer evenings. 'I don't know,' she said. 'I certainly hope so, for I know Mother and I are hopeless managers and must find someone. But I can tell you this much for certain, if he does come to live here then all the girls for miles around will want to be my friend for he is the handsomest man you ever did see.'

Tom's eyes were glazed with over-eating and the three girls were chattering and laughing like finches in a wicker cage when the heavy oak door which led from the kitchen to the shop finally opened and yielded up its secret.

Mistress Hocken came in first. A short, stout woman, suffering now from shortness of breath and vague pains in her legs and head, the recent loss of her husband had left her more perplexed than grieving. Clearly her morning had been taxing for the poor woman; she had the blind look of someone who has been attempting to explain matters quite beyond their comprehension.

But no one was watching Mistress Hocken. Lizzie, forgetting manners, craned her head to see the figure standing in the shadows behind her. Margaret quickly brushed a few stray crumbs of pastry from Tom's fat cheeks. Merry adjusted the position of her plate.

'Margaret, Lizzie,' Mistress Hocken wheezed a greeting, 'and little Tom too. Merry has taken care of you, I'm glad to see. And now, this is my nephew, Mr William Hollar, my poor dead husband's sister's boy.'

Ducking his head to avoid the granite lintel, the young man stepped from the shadows into the brightness of the kitchen. He was, without doubt, the handsomest man Lizzie or Margaret had ever seen. Slightly above medium height and slimly built, he had hair the colour of dark honey and his eyes were violet blue as a summer twilight. His features were classically formed: straight nose, well-set mouth and chin. Seeing William Hollar for the first time, framed in the low doorway of Master Hocken's shop, Margaret understood at once how the Trojan hero Aeneas looked when he stepped ashore at Carthage, and why he won the heart of Dido.

Merry jumped to her feet. 'Cousin William, these are our good friends, Margaret and Lizzie Pearce from Conwinnion. And Tom too, of course. They are here for the fair.'

The violet-blue eyes rested briefly on their faces. 'I am delighted to make your acquaintance,' he said and his voice rippled soft as a breeze, and he inclined his head, and then, as though it was something he had forgotten to do earlier, he smiled.

There was an awkward silence. Somehow his presence had damped the laughter and the easy talk, but the girls were inclined to be forgiving. Gazing at those miraculous eyes, Lizzie wondered if he was married already (Merry had been strangely uncertain on this crucial point) and if not, whether brown curls (with new blue ribbons) and a cheerful disposition were perhaps what he looked for in a wife. Margaret noticed the fine linen at his throat and wrists and the elegant cut of his clothes. Tom alone was unmoved by the stranger's appearance: he was considering whether perhaps the last piece of pie might have been a mistake.

Merry, normally so outspoken, was temporarily numbed to silence by her handsome cousin. Margaret, who liked people too much ever to be ill at ease, said, 'I understand you came from Fowey last night. Did you have a good journey?'

'It was tolerable. I have been obliged to travel a good deal and it is always a tiresome business.'

As none of his companions had ever ventured further than Helston, the subject of travel was not one on which they felt inspired to contribute.

'It must be tedious, I'm sure,' said Lizzie, smiling prettily as she spoke, 'all that dreadful bumping around on horseback and those rough roads. Quite dreadful.'

Silence. Then, 'I came by sea.'

Another silence.

Mistress Hocken stared at the pie in a puzzled way, as though she had not altogether expected to see it placed on her table. 'Can I fetch you girls more to eat?' she asked. 'William, perhaps you are hungry now?'

'No, ma'am. My needs are very frugal.'

'And we've had more than enough,' said Lizzie. 'Tom's fit to burst his buttons as it is.' And she poked his taut stomach causing him to grunt as though in sudden pain.

'Merry has the things that Mother sent,' said Margaret, 'and now we'd best be on our way. I must see Parson – and Tom here wants to see everything.'

Lizzie stood up. 'You must come to the play this afternoon, Mr Hollar,' she said. 'Our Mattie is taking a special part. A Latin one.' There was a trace of hurt pride in her voice: already the handsome stranger had made her feel defensive, somehow ashamed of their little world, although she would have found it hard to say exactly why.

This time his courteous smile held a trace of a sneer. 'I fear I shall probably have to forgo that pleasure.'

'No matter,' said Margaret easily, and then to her friend, 'Will you come with us now, Merry?'

'Later. I shall catch you up at the play.'

'And don't forget the wrestling,' said Lizzie, 'Ambrose is to take on all comers and prove himself the strongest.'

Merry promised she would be with them as soon as she had cleared away – an unheard-of preliminary, normally – and Margaret, Lizzie and Tom were free to escape down the passage beside the house and into the warm sunshine of the street. For some reason they felt light-hearted, as if just released from school, and with a common instinct they skipped and ran down to the harbour, pausing only when the draper's house was out of sight. Panting and laughing they pronounced their complex verdict on the newly arrived Mr Hollar.

'Did you ever see such a proud man?' queried Lizzie.

'Can he really be Merry's cousin?'

'With such grand clothes I'm sure he thinks he's a gentleman.'

'And handsome – oh!'

'He didn't eat the pie,' said Tom.

'Perhaps,' said Margaret, after careful consideration, 'perhaps upcountry people are always like that when you meet them first. I daresay we'll find him friendly enough when we know him better.'

Mr William Hollar, newly arrived from Leyden by way of Plymouth and Fowey, retired to his bedroom, the very best in the house, and contemplated the events of the past twelve hours. As so often, his disdain just now had been part genuine, part mask to hide his deep unease. These simple country people brought back all too vivid memories of his own family, the parents he had been so eager to leave when hardly more than a boy. He despised his aunt with her idiot complaining, and his cousin Merry's slovenly ways nauseated him. He had noticed Margaret's old dress of coarse grey wool, and the brown marks on her collar where the iron had burnt it. And that other girl, thinking herself so fine with a few cheap ribbons in her hair.

Yes, his contempt was genuine enough. But yet . . . but yet . . . there was envy too. There was a freedom in their ways, for all that they were ignorant and ridiculous. That fair-haired girl had looked at him with such candour in her eyes . . . and William, whose whole life had been a secret, a hiding-away of truth, could only recognise, and envy, what he might never hope to attain.

He paced his bedroom restlessly. (Laughable to call this a best bedroom when he could scarce stand straight anywhere but plumb in the middle of it and there was dust and odour everywhere.) He sat down on the bed, his aunt's

51

marriage bed: it was hard and bulging and smelled of things not fresh. The sheets were so worn and discoloured with age he would not have expected a serving-boy to suffer them.

His fastidiousness, the superiority it implied, pleased him. But then he frowned. He had been too formal in his manner with those girls just now, he knew that. It was essential to make a good impression. If he decided to stay he must endeavour to win the respect of these West Cornwall rustics. Perhaps even their liking. If he decided to stay . . .

Sighing, he stood up and went to the casement window and, with difficulty, opened it. The noise and bustle of the fair rose up from the street below.

A party of gypsies clattered down the street on their pie-bald ponies. Pedlars and higglers with their weather-wrinkled faces, shouted and joked and argued with the passersby. From the open ground behind the shambles he could hear the roar of the bull-baiting. It was a thriving, complex world – and he alone knew none of it.

But if he stayed . . . All his adult life – and he was nearing thirty though strangers often took him for ten years younger – he had been a wanderer, with no place to call his own; an outsider. This past winter he had spent in Paris had been hard, so hard that he shrank from the memory of it, and since then, for the first time, he knew the lure of the settled life. He hungered for respectability. He yearned to walk down a familiar street and be greeted with deference by the passersby. 'Good day, Mr Hollar, how goes it with you this fine morning?' 'Well, thank you, and is your wife's tooth-ache better today?' These tokens of common respect that other people took for granted were a prize worth the seeking indeed. He wanted, in effect, just such a life as his aunt was offering.

When her letter had reached him in Leyden he thought at first that a forgiving God had heard his anguished prayers. But now that the prospect was fleshed out, real people in an all too real community and nothing at all like the idyllic Porthew of his imaginings, now his doubts were vivid enough.

Such a narrow, squalid little world. To think that this

house was considered one of the finest in Porthew, though to him it was little better than a hovel. He could well imagine the gossip that was the life-blood of this town, and the endless dull stories; who has said this and done that, babies and death and copulation, the animal sequence of life in this forgotten backwater . . . he must be insane even to consider staying. There was a physical revulsion that rose in his throat like a sickness: he was a proud free creature who fears the trap's cruel teeth – but who is yet too famished to resist the bait.

Enough, he told himself, enough. No decision need be made at once. And in the meantime he would do well to smooth the way should he decide to make his home here. He had been awkward and proud this morning, but he could put that to rights soon enough. This afternoon the people of Porthew would discover that the stranger who had arrived in their midst last night was a man they could respect. And maybe even like.

And he knew that he was lucky (that forgiving God again?) to fetch up in a place so remote that he was, as yet, unknown.

Towards noon there was a new rumour to spice the gossip of that Porthew Feast Day. Margaret and Lizzie first heard it when they were sitting on the harbour wall eating hazelnuts while Tom aimed the shells at the strutting gulls on the shingle below. Soon he grew restive.

'I want to see some more.' He tugged at Margaret's skirt. 'Let's go and see some more.'

'Later, Tom, there's plenty of time.'

'I want to go now.'

'You stay right here with us,' said Lizzie.

Made mutinous by the excitement of the day, Tom began to wander off.

'Come back here at once,' shouted Margaret. 'If you don't stay close by Lizzie and me then the gypsies will get you. I've seen them in town already and they are looking for little boys like you to eat for their dinners.'

Tom bounced back to his sisters' sides while they, oblivious to the danger he was in, continued to crack nuts and exchange greetings with the passersby. He watched wide eyed as a group of tinners from the north of the county walked past arguing drunkenly. They were a fearsome lot with their rough clothes and their underground, moldewarp faces. Were they, he wondered, the children-eating gypsies? He wrapped a cautious arm about Lizzie's knee. And watched.

A stout fishwife sauntered by.

'Good day, Lizzie, Margaret. Hello, young Tom. Did you hear that Mistress Hocken's nephew has arrived from Fowey?'

'Indeed we have. And what's more, we met him just now.' (It was largely to spread their information that the girls had chosen the strategic point on that harbour wall.) 'A fine-looking man he is, but very proud.'

'Do you think he will stay to look after the shop?'

'He's not yet made up his mind. But I know they are hoping he will stay.'

The fishwife shook her head. 'Poor Mistress Hocken, she has never been the same since her poor husband died. She took it very hard. Can't seem to manage at all.' And the fishwife, who had buried three husbands and grown richer and jollier with each passing funeral, shook her head pityingly. Tom watched her wobbling chins with fascination.

'It will be a relief to them to have a man about the place again, I'm sure,' said Margaret.

'And there's another newcomer in town today by all accounts,' said the fishwife in a low voice.

'And who might that be?'

She laid her fishbasket on the wall. 'The son to the new Mistress Sutton. The lady as married Sir John in such a hurry last month. A strange business, that was.'

Lizzie was full of interest. 'What do they say about him?'

'Nothing good that I've heard. His family had land up Bodmin way but it's all gone now. They've still one or two farms near here but they will probably have to be sold too. A most unlucky family by the sound of it.'

'And the son is here today?'

'Perhaps we saw him, Lizzie, with the Suttons when they came past Ambrose's forge.'

Lizzie frowned, trying to remember, but, 'I'm sure I would have noticed him,' she said at length.

Their next informant was more helpful. Joan Treworgie, daughter of Dame Treworgie to whom they had given the eggs and pickled samphire earlier that morning, had worked at the Suttons' home at Rossmere since she was hardly more than a child and she knew the family as only a servant can, that is, in intimate though often erratic detail.

'He arrived last week from the university,' she said, her voice heavy with disapproval, 'and there's been nothing but trouble ever since. He is in a fit of rage about his mother's marriage and she's at her wits' end to know what to do with him. Sir John would turn him out of doors if he could. The only time there is peace in the house is when he's out riding or hawking, which mercifully is often enough.'

'How dreadful.' But even as she spoke Lizzie craned her neck for a glimpse of this scoundrel in the crowd.

'And of course he has no money at all. His father was a madman who threw all his money away. Or drank it all. Not that the son cares a fig for that. Spends all his time in the stables or the mews and acts more like a hireling than a gentleman who has been to university – a scandal for a respectable family, that's what it is.'

It was not long before they met the young gentleman who was causing such upset at Rossmere. A little before noon Nicolas Sutton stepped out of the ale-house with a dark-haired youth about his own age and, noticing one of his father's serving-women talking with two pretty girls, he strolled over to be introduced.

Medium height, with brown curling hair and amiable features, Nicolas Sutton had the easy charm of a young gentleman who knows himself to be handsome – and a good deal wealthier than any of his neighbours.

'Good day to you, Joan. Are you going to introduce me to your friends?' Since his years at the university, little remained of his Cornish inflexions and Margaret and Lizzie wondered at the flat drawl of his voice.

Joan introduced them with the minimum of ceremony and Lizzie, whose dealings with good-looking young gentlemen had been meagre enough until now, flushed and giggled and leaned against her sister for reassurance.

'Delighted, ladies, to make your acquaintance,' and he

bowed, with an exaggerated flourish of his plumed hat. 'And this is my old friend and brother of a month, Richard Treveryan, an ill-humoured and disagreeable fellow, but we hope to teach him better manners by and by.'

His companion grinned broadly at this unflattering description, but Lizzie was unable to hide her surprise.

'Why, I thought –' she began, and then broke off, flushing deeper than ever before. She had been on the point of saying that she had taken him to be Sutton's serving-man, or groom, rather than his friend, for he was dressed in the leather jerkin and coarse linen of a countryman. He was taller than Nicolas, thin and muscular, with gaunt uneven features and rough dark hair – a raven to his friend's well-groomed peacock. He sketched the trace of a bow and Lizzie recovered herself.

'Why, I did not think you would be so tall,' she said stoutly, 'for your mother, I believe, is quite a little lady.'

He shrugged. 'You have been misinformed. She is generally considered to be uncommon tall.' And with that he appeared to lose all interest in the conversation.

Tom, his head still abuzz with half-remembered gossip, chipped in suddenly, 'Is she –?'

But Margaret interrupted him. 'You said, Mr Sutton, that you and Mr Treveryan are old friends?'

'Indeed we are. At Oxford we were often in trouble and did our best to help each other escape punishment.'

'It must be a fine thing to attend a university,' said Margaret wistfully.

'Enjoyable, at least,' said Nicolas. 'Treveryan here is the scholar, not me. If he had spent half the time on his books that he did on hawking . . . but who cares for the finer points of Lucretius when the skies are wide for birds to fly in?' and he beamed at them, delighted with the eloquence of his rhetorical question.

The puzzle which Tom was bursting with would be restrained no longer. He tugged at Treveryan's sleeve and demanded in a shrill voice, 'Is your mother truly a witch?'

There was a silence. Even Nicolas Sutton looked startled. Joan Treworgie's mouth fell into a scandalised O. Lizzie flushed scarlet and held her breath. Richard Treveryan himself had been gazing out to sea, deaf to Nicolas's bland phrases, and it was only with difficulty that he focused on the question framed by the small boy who was gazing up at him so intensely. He frowned, as though trying to recollect what had been said.

Margaret recovered herself first. 'Lord save the boy, what a dreadful . . . pay no heed to him, sir, for he –'

'A witch, eh?' Richard Treveryan stared down at Tom, his face hard and questioning. Suddenly the set of his mouth had a cruel twist, his eyes narrowed and his mouth twitched, and Margaret, afraid that he might box Tom's ears, prepared to whisk the child from danger at the first sign of movement. And then, unexpected as a shaft of sunlight in a storm, Treveryan was laughing, a burst of sheer delight at the young boy's mischief. Margaret and Lizzie glanced at each other anxiously, but when they saw that Nicolas was laughing as well, they considered it safe to join in; theirs was laughter of relief, however, rather than genuine amusement.

Tom flushed. Something told him he had narrowly escaped serious trouble, but none the less, his question yet remained to be answered.

'Is she? Is it true?'

'I do believe you have guessed her secret,' Treveryan said solemnly, 'but you must not tell anyone else or the poor woman is sure to burn.'

Tom gasped. 'Then it *is* true!'

'Why don't you ask her yourself?'

'Don't feed the boy such nonsense!' exclaimed Margaret.

Treveryan looked at her as if for the first time. 'I thought *you* were perhaps encouraging the young witch-finder.'

'It's wrong to joke about such serious matters.'

'Then I shall continue to do so.'

In spite of her annoyance, Margaret found she was smiling. 'Are you always so perverse, Mr Treveryan?'

He considered for a moment, then, 'Not always. I would hate to be accused of consistency.'

Seeing Margaret laugh out loud, Tom grew more and more confused. 'But she must be a witch!' he burst out.

'No, I'm afraid it's all lies,' Treveryan assured him, 'unless, that is, an evil temper and a vicious tongue are evidence of witchcraft –'

'Really!'

'In which case I'm sure the Devil could learn a good deal from her, if she only had the patience to teach him. But I know she's learned nothing from him.'

The two young men both seemed highly amused by the whole business, but Margaret and Lizzie were scandalised.

'Tom, you are very rude to ask such questions,' scolded Margaret, deflecting her anger from the gentlemen to the tousled head of her brother.

The church rang the noonday hour.

'Lord, I must fly.' Margaret jumped down from her seat on the harbour wall. 'I promised Parson I'd be ready by noon. Lizzie, keep a close eye on Tom and don't let him wander off. I shall see you after the play.'

'Is your sister one of the players?' asked Nicolas, watching Margaret as she hastened towards the church.

'Yes.' Lizzie's pride was obvious. 'She is to speak in Latin. I hope you will be sure and watch it, for her words are bound to be clever and it is all in honour of your father's marriage.'

Nicolas turned to his friend. 'Shall we go, Richard?'

Treveryan too had been watching Margaret depart, but now he merely shrugged and said, 'To hear the union between your father and my mother celebrated with public verses? I can think of nothing more grotesque.'

And Lizzie considered it most fortunate that Margaret had not been able to overhear this last and most cynical slander.

The Life of St Ewan was a long play which had been performed every feast day without fail since the death of St Ewan himself, or such was the general opinion among the inhabitants of Porthew. Although the basic plot never altered, many small flourishes were added each year of a topical nature, and so it was quite in keeping with tradition that, at the very moment when St Ewan, a notorious killjoy, had just delivered a speech in praise of the celibate life, an unidentified girl (Margaret) should step forward and proclaim the blessings of the married state in honour of Sir John Sutton's recent wedding.

The play was performed on a mound of earth near the

church. Sir John, his wife and several of their party, were seated on benches at the front while the rest of the audience milled around behind them, gossiping and drinking and occasionally paying attention.

At Margaret's first appearance there was a general hush. Most of the audience knew the play almost word for word and silence was only observed for the choicest moments, such as the scene when St Ewan defeated the last giant to survive in Cornwall who was, as usual, played by Robert Treloar, Ambrose's father, and for obvious departures from the script. The appearance of Margaret signalled just such a departure.

She spoke in a low, clear voice and as she had remembered her words she had no need of paper or book to read from. But she had no idea how to project the words and it was only by watching the movement of her lips that those at any distance from the stage knew her speech was even begun. The members of the audience strained their ears to hear her words – and those that were able to hear the words strained still more to make sense of them. Gradually the word 'Latin' whispered through the crowd like a subterranean breeze: 'Oh, Latin, is it?' 'I thought it was strange,' 'Of course, Latin for sure,' and, since the audience could neither hear nor, hearing, understand, the talk and laughter began again, somewhat louder than before.

Margaret noticed neither the silence nor the chatter. She stood in the centre of the stage, her hands hanging by her side, looking over the crowd with a faint smile on her face and said the lines as she had been taught. But when she had finished her verses she remained where she stood, irresolute, for Parson Weaver had forgotten to tell her how an exit should be made. Then, with a slight curtsy to Lady Sutton and a shy smile towards the audience in general, she retreated awkwardly. And though Lizzie, sitting to one side of the audience, was pink with sisterly pride, no one, however partial, could ever have described Margaret's first and last venture into the theatre as a resounding success.

Richard Treveryan stood on the fringes of the crowd, a little way behind Lizzie. Dressed as he was in the workaday clothes of a yeoman, he was not recognised as a member of the Suttons' party and so was not ushered to the seats at the front. He preferred it thus. His black eyes looked out from under a thatch of unruly hair and their expression was restless, searching. In spite of himself he was intrigued by the unusual figure of the girl who stood on the platform that served for a stage.

Her appearance bordered on the comical. He noticed the heavy working boots that looked as though they had been borrowed from some male relative. And her dress, which presumably was the very best she could muster for the occasion, was so drab and shapeless, a woman of quality would expect a better fit from a shroud than this poor girl had managed. She stood very still, stared straight ahead and spoke in the wooden monotone of one who has a job to do but who would be perfectly happy never to speak in public again. It should have been a comical sight altogether.

And yet . . . and yet . . . Richard did not find he was moved to laughter. For all her dreadful clothes and her clumping shoes there was still something about the girl that set her apart. She was self-possessed, quite unmoved by the inattention of her audience; he guessed that their approval would not much have interested her either. They could have hurled rotten apples or cheered with wild delight but the tall girl with the fair hair would have continued to talk in that low, soft voice which had just the trace of a catch in it. At first Richard had been startled to hear the Latin words spoken with the warm Cornish burr accenting each syllable. Now, as he listened, it began to seem the most natural way in all the world that the words should be spoken; the dead language sprang to life, was granted freshness by that voice which rounded each vowel like a caress. He became entranced, imagined briefly that the words were directed at him alone.

And then he forgot her uncouth clothes and saw only her tallness, her capable hands, the clear grey eyes gazing over the crowd and the wide mouth which hovered now on the verge of a smile.

And when she was finished and hesitated suddenly, uncertain how to proceed, a warm flush of colour spread across her throat and across her cheeks. She turned awkwardly, paused, and then turned back to smile towards her audience.

It seemed to Treveryan then, as Margaret's smile reached out across the heads of the milling rabble between them, that her shining eyes rested briefly on his face and that the wide curve of her lips was a gift for him alone. An unexpected warmth was kindled deep within him and he smiled back, a sudden boyish smile that took him by surprise and made him feel foolish and eager all at once.

If I were not otherwise absorbed, he thought, there might be pleasure to be had with a girl such as her.

Much later, when he came to know her better, he learned that she had long been afflicted with short-sightedness and so realised that she could not have seen him there at all.

'Are you glad it's over, Mattie? I was so proud of you – now everyone knows how clever you are.'

Lizzie had been quick to find her sister once Margaret's part was over. Margaret was flushed and a little bemused by the excitement of appearing in public.

'Was it truly all right?'

'Yes, yes, of course. And what's more, Merry's cousin William did come to watch after all. He was standing just across from me and he understood every word. At any rate, I saw him smile as if he was taking it all in.'

'Well, I'm sure no one else did. I might just as well have spoken gibberish.'

'Oh, look, here he comes now. Mattie, he's coming to congratulate you. Won't everyone be green with envy!'

It was true. Mr William Hollar was standing with Merry and, as she had predicted, he was the centre of a flurry of female attention. His honey-coloured head was circled by a bobbing ring of dark ones – and even an occasional grey: obviously the attractions of Mr Hollar knew no barriers of age – all vying eagerly for his attention. Catching sight of Margaret and Lizzie, however, he excused himself courteously and, with the proud Merry at his side, strolled over to greet them.

'Your speech was most impressive,' he said, smiling. 'My cousin forgot to tell me you were such a scholar and I had not expected Porthew to be a centre of learning.'

'Parson has been good enough to teach me and I like to learn,' said Margaret, and William noticed that she did not seek to deny the compliment – no false modesty here.

'And are you as talented as your sister?' He turned to Lizzie.

Lizzie giggled her disclaimer, then added, 'But I love to hear the stories she tells us.'

'Ah.' William smiled again, but seemed at a loss as to how to continue the conversation and appeared suddenly ill at ease.

It was Tom's shrill voice that broke the silence. 'What about the wrestling? You promised we'd see Ambrose once the play was done.'

'Do you like to see the wrestling, young man?' William looked down at Tom and smiled, as though relieved by the diversion.

Tom pummelled the air with his fists. 'I love it! I love to see them fight – and Ambrose is the strongest man in the world.'

'Is he now? Then I mustn't miss the sport. Your Ambrose sounds a fearsome fellow.'

Tom squinted up at the stranger warily. 'He's bigger than you are,' he said, 'and stronger too. You're just a weakling next to Ambrose.'

'Tom! Don't be so rude!' Margaret was beginning to think that the rooster's wicker basket might have been the best place for her outspoken brother after all.

'No, don't scold the boy,' said William. 'What he says is only the truth and no one should be punished for saying what is true.'

'Some true things are better left unsaid.'

William looked at her sharply. 'The child will learn to bide his words soon enough,' he said, and, reaching into his pocket, he pulled out a small coin. 'Here, Tom, you can buy yourself a treat.'

Tom beamed with pleasure and began at once to look around him, eyeing the booths with a new interest, though Margaret knew he would not spend it; her brother was a miser born.

'The wrestling has begun already, I think,' said Lizzie, watching the little groups of people drifting towards the open ground behind the ale-house. 'We'd best go now too if we want to be able to see anything.'

Margaret, who loathed any kind of fighting, had been hoping to linger so that they would be too far back in the crowd to see. It was one of the few occasions when she considered her short-sightedness a blessing.

But when they drew close to the fighting ground, there was a horror still closer for Margaret to endure.

A group of boys had captured a badger which they had tied by a cord to a stake near the path. Half a dozen small dogs were baiting it. The badger had put up a fierce fight and a couple of the dogs were bleeding heavily, but she was tiring now, as if she knew the struggle was hopeless. One of the dogs, a smooth-haired terrier more persistent than the rest, had caught hold of her right hind leg repeatedly and it was hanging, the broken bone sticking through the mess of blood and sinew. A group of bystanders was watching with interest and urging the dogs on to greater bravery.

Margaret turned pale, and Lizzie, scenting danger, tried to drag her past before it was too late.

'The poor creature!' Margaret exlaimed in anguish. 'How can they be so cruel? Tom, don't you dare to laugh to see it suffer so!'

'Don't make a fuss, Mattie,' Lizzie pleaded, 'you can't stop them, it's only a badger. It doesn't matter.'

'But it *does* matter.' Margaret turned in desperation to the oldest of the lads, a gangling boy with a heavily freckled face. 'Bob Dawkins, that's your dog, isn't it? Oh, for mercy's sake, can't you call it off? The poor beast can hardly stand and the dogs are suffering too. Oh, please make them stop!'

The boy barely troubled to glance in her direction. ''Tis none of your business,' he said. 'Besides, the dogs enjoy the sport.'

Margaret looked around wildly, searching for some way to end the savagery. Sensing their victim's growing weakness, the boldest of the dogs, the smooth-haired terrier, caught the badger by the tender tip of her nose and she screamed with pain.

'Come *on*, Mattie.' Lizzie and Merry were both tugging

at her arms. 'There's nothing you can do. 'Tis as good as dead anyway.'

'But at least it should die cleanly. Not like that.'

William Hollar stepped forward and spoke to Bob Dawkins. 'Here's a sixpence for you and your friends if you finish the animal off cleanly now.'

The boy looked at him sullenly, reluctant to end the sport, reluctant to pass up the chance of a sixpence. He was on the verge of accepting the offer when one of the bystanders called out, 'And here's a shilling from me to let it go on to the death.'

There was a murmur of approval from the onlookers and Richard Treveryan stepped forward and, with a quick glance towards Margaret, tossed a coin in the dust. Bob Dawkins retrieved it and grinned his thanks at the young gentleman. William inclined his head, acknowledging defeat.

Lizzie and Merry hustled Margaret away to the far side of the open stretch of ground – and then Lizzie had to go back again for Tom who had stayed to see the fun.

'You should not be so tender-hearted,' soothed William. 'Badgers are mere vermin after all.'

'I know,' said Margaret, though she was still shaking with anger and frustration. 'But there's enough suffering in this world surely, without inventing more and calling it sport.'

'Maybe so, but the common rabble enjoy to see slow murder done.'

Margaret shuddered. 'And you, Mr Hollar?'

'I despise all senseless cruelty.'

'Thank you. If only that villain had not intervened . . .'

But before William could acknowledge her thanks Margaret had turned pale: a crescendo of snarling and yapping and a shout of triumph from the crowd signalled that the badger's torment had reached its messy and inevitable conclusion.

By mid-afternoon Ambrose Treloar was well on the way to becoming a local hero. He had already vanquished John Ruan from the Lizard, and then William Makepouder, the hope and pride of the St Keverne men, had staggered from the ring in ignominy. A few pot-valiant farm labourers were swiftly dealt with, as was Sir John Sutton's groom, a brawny lad from Devon.

The Helston men were growing restive, eager for their own Robert Trelyn to beat this phenomenon: the greater Ambrose's feats of strength now, the greater would be their own man's glory when he finally put paid to the young giant. Ambrose, bare feet planted squarely in the dusty ground and wearing nothing but a pair of russet breeches, drank another pot of ale and felt himself ready for anything.

'I'm surprised you stay to watch this sport,' William said to Margaret, 'I would have thought it too warlike for your taste.'

'Ambrose is an old friend and would be mighty disappointed if we weren't here to see him win,' Margaret explained. 'But it's true that I do cheat: my eyes are not good for distances and if I stand well back I cannot see so much of what goes on.'

'An admirable compromise,' William acknowledged with a smile.

Lizzie and Tom had wriggled their way to the front of the crowd. At the edge of the improvised ring small boys, excited by the tension and drama of the wrestling, fought and tumbled together like puppies in the dirt.

'Who will take on Ambrose now?' a voice called out.

Then another: 'Where's this Robert Trelyn, then?'

'Gone back to Helston with his tail between his legs!'

A roar of laughter from the local men, mutterings from the huddle around the Helston champion.

'Go on, Robert boy, time to push him off his perch!'

Robert Trelyn, squatting on his haunches, watched Ambrose with shrewd black eyes, as he had watched since the fighting began. Cunning fighter that he was, he had hoped to let Ambrose fritter away his strength a while longer in copious draughts of ale and the defeat of weaklings. But now he saw that to wait longer would only indicate reluctance. So he stood up, kicked his shoes to one side, stripped off his shirt – and acknowledged the crowd with a grudging smile.

They roared their approval. This contest had been eagerly awaited and talked about for months; at last Ambrose's raw young strength was to be pitched against the experience and hard muscle of Robert Trelyn.

After the shouts had died down, a waiting silence descended on the crowd. Even the small boys forgot their fighting and sat cross-legged to watch. The two men circled each other slowly. The Helston man was generally accounted tall, but the top of his head was level with Ambrose's mouth. Yet he was tough. Ambrose, not yet twenty, still carried weight that was only puppy fat: every ounce of Trelyn's flesh was hard-packed muscle. And Ambrose was too confident.

He lunged forward suddenly, thinking to put his arms around Trelyn's waist and throw him to the ground as easily as he had his other victims, but his opponent twisted his body slightly, caught Ambrose off balance and sent him tumbling to the ground.

Even the Porthew men laughed: Ambrose was indeed a comical sight, the huge pink mass of his body sprawled in the dust as if pole-axed. Ambrose himself blinked with surprise and then grinned: it must have been a lucky accident, he thought, for defeat never entered his mind. But when it happened a second, then a third time, the Porthew men were no longer laughing and a purple flush of rage spread across Ambrose's broad face.

The third time, Ambrose rose slowly to his feet and, ignoring his opponent, he reached for the tankard that his friends kept filled for him. Trelyn waited patiently; he was enjoying the fight now and certain of victory. Then Ambrose turned and went for him again, eyes blazing, head down like a bull charging and with a roar of rage for this man who had thought to make a fool of him. As before, Trelyn twisted, half backwards this time and shifted his weight to wrong-foot Ambrose again, but his anger had made Ambrose canny and he was ready for him and his huge arms encircled Trelyn's torso. Swift as a snake Trelyn answered with a grip as strong. For a long time the two men remained locked together in an embrace, Ambrose's tawny chest crushed against Trelyn's dark one, both swaying slightly, each seeking to off-balance the other while keeping his own feet squarely on the ground.

The silence of the crowd was complete. The only sounds

were the grunts of the two men, the desperate shuffle of their feet. Both fighters were holding their breath, lungs filled to expand their rib-cage to the full, each man's arms crushing the other's ribs. Slowly, Trelyn's face was turning as purple as Ambrose's had been in his rage. His black eyes bulged; blue veins snaked across his neck and forehead.

Ambrose, in his anger, would have hung on to the death: his own or the other man's or both – it did not matter. Inexorable as granite, his mighty smith's arms crushed his opponent until the Helston man could take no more. Trelyn's feet slipped in the dust, his arms lost their grip, his mouth flung open to breathe and to cry out with pain and Ambrose roared in triumph and released his hold, only to dash him to the ground like a kitten, and then, his victory assured, he caught him round the waist once more and, while the crowd bellowed its delight, lifted him high into the air.

Robert Trelyn, champion wrestler of Helston and the surrounding area for over six years, was carried round the ring in ignominy while the Porthew men whooped and laughed and the noise of the crowd drowned his groans as his flailing arms tried in vain to protect his agonisingly cracked ribs.

Ambrose had never known such strength as the force that rushed through his veins. The man whom he held high above his head weighed no more than a small child. If he had tried to throw him now he truly believed he could have pitched him high in the air, over the church roof and into the harbour beyond. All things were possible to Ambrose in the white heat of his triumph.

'Let him down, Ambrose boy. The man is suffering now. Let him down.'

The man's voice – must have been his father's – seemed to come from somewhere among the little people far below him. Reluctantly Ambrose began to lower the writhing body, but first he looked over the heads of the spectators to where he had seen Margaret standing with the fair-haired stranger. He wanted to lay his victim at her feet; for fighting was what he did best and it was the finest tribute to her that he knew.

67

But he saw her face in profile, not looking at him at all. At the moment when the fight had gone out of Robert Trelyn and the local crowd had roared with the closeness of its victory, Margaret had turned from the blur of semi-naked bodies. She slapped her hands over her ears to block out the Helston man's scream of agony and defeat and, to distract herself, she was busy asking William Hollar rapid questions about his journey from the Low Countries.

Ambrose dropped his victim and strode off in disgust.

It was that time of late afternoon when the Feast Day celebrations unravelled rapidly into drunkenness and debauch. Long shadows were slanting across the harbour and the rough ground by Jack Pym's ale-house resembled the aftermath of a battle, so many bodies lying where they fell and only an occasional groan to show they were living still. Of those who did manage to set off in the general direction of home, a good many soon staggered into a ditch or hay-rick, there to pass a chilly and sore-headed night.

The men and women who remained more or less on their feet did so only to indulge in pleasures of a different kind. It was commonly accepted in Porthew that babies born towards midsummer, nine months after the Feast Day, did not necessarily resemble their legal fathers: red-haired children were born to the most exclusively dark-haired parents and embarrassed mothers were obliged to invent missing ancestors to explain a blue-eyed child among the brown.

Margaret, with growing anxiety, was searching for Lizzie and Tom.

When the wrestling ended she had been accosted by Dame Erisey, an elderly cousin by marriage of her father's, who insisted that Margaret come with her to her cottage which lay on the edge of Porthew, just above the harbour. Margaret was reluctant to go, but Lizzie and Tom promised to meet her by the harbour later. Dame Erisey made her a gift of three fine linen kerchiefs for the family so that Margaret was ashamed of her impatience and sat down to a glass or two of the old lady's cordial and listened to an account of her various illnesses and how her present aches varied from those she had been afflicted by in the past.

The town was in shadow and only the highest cliff-tops beyond still flamed yellow in the dying sunlight when Margaret eventually returned to the harbour . . . and to no sign at all of Lizzie and Tom.

The group of men singing catches by the harbour wall had not seen them, nor had the old women, sitting in their doorways with their spinning or their sewing and a little measure of something with which to toast St Ewan. She went back to Mistress Hocken's, but neither she nor Merry had seen them anywhere and William was in the shop once more, examining the ledger books, and was not to be disturbed.

Margaret returned to Jack Pym's ale-house where Ambrose was celebrating his victory with those of his friends still capable of raising a flagon to their lips. Neither Ambrose nor his companions were properly able by this time to focus on the urgency of her question – but they begged her to stay and keep them company since most of the young girls in the area had already been hauled home by their parents and those that remained were long since spoken for.

Margaret searched and asked everywhere but no one had seen a pretty girl with blue ribbons in her hair and a small boy. She asked the watch, but he too was celebrating the local saint and had no wish to go searching for lost children.

She found Tom first. He was curled up fast asleep on a coil of rope underneath the harbour wall. His face was grubby, streaked with tears and grime. Margaret shook him awake.

'What are you doing here, Tom? Where's Lizzie?'

At the sound of her voice Tom flung his arms around his sister and sobbed. 'The gypsies,' he choked, 'I was hiding from the gypsies. I didn't want them to eat me up.'

Margaret cradled him and scolded. 'But where is Lizzie? You're a bad boy to wander off like that and go hiding yourself away.'

'The man gave me a penny and told me to wait for you. Lizzie said it was all right,' said Tom, aggrieved that Margaret was cross when he had only done as he was told.

'Man? What man?'

'The man who took Lizzie away.'

69

'Oh Lord. What did he look like?'

Tom stared at her, not understanding the urgency of her question. 'I dunno,' he said.

'Think, Tom, for goodness' sake. You must be able to remember something about him.'

Tom frowned, trying his hardest. 'He had a big hat with a sort of feathery thing in it.'

Margaret's heart sank. She picked Tom up and carried him up the short hill to Mistress Hocken's house, there to be cleaned up by Merry and watched until the missing Lizzie was found.

She returned to the harbour. Little fires were being lit along the beach and the delicious smell of grilling fish mingled with the tar and the salt. Gulls flapped their wings and strutted and called greedily to each other. Their calls sounded to Margaret like mocking laughter. If Lizzie had gone with a gentleman (for only a gentleman wore a hat with a feather in it) then Margaret did not know where to look for her. She was worried for herself as well as for Lizzie: if anything happened then it was Margaret who was sure to get the blame. Although they were separated by barely more than six months, Margaret was taller, stronger and seemed much the older and was therefore generally held to be responsible for the others, foolish Lizzie as much as little Tom.

'Are you looking for your sister?'

Margaret looked up in surprise . . . and then, disgust. It was Bob Dawkins, the lad who had trapped the badger to be baited earlier in the day. His grin indicated that he knew only too well where Lizzie had gone.

'Where is she, then, Bob Dawkins?' Margaret asked sharply.

'She might not want me to tell you, I reckon.'

Margaret's anxiety burst out in a fury. 'You'd better tell me where she is right now, Bob Dawkins, or I'll –'

'All right, all right.' He backed away, still grinning. 'Just try looking in Robert Payne's stable, that's all, just try and see what you find,' and he scampered off, laughing.

Robert Payne was a well-to-do fish merchant with a fine house some distance beyond the ale-house. Margaret set off at once but as she passed the ale-house door Ambrose and half a dozen other youths tumbled out into the fresh air.

'Where are you off to, Mattie?' he shouted. 'Stay here and keep me company!'

'Go home,' said Margaret crossly, 'and sleep it off,' and she stumped on up the hill.

She climbed over a low wall into Mr Payne's back garden. The first outbuilding she came to contained nothing but a few sheep and a couple of heifers; the second two squealing pigs and several chickens, while in a third, behind a shaggy pony guzzling oats, she saw the white legs of her sister stretched across the hay and a finely dressed young gentleman half on top of her; the hat with the feather in it had been tossed aside by the door.

'Lizzie!' Margaret exclaimed. 'Get up here and come home at once!'

'Go away,' a man's voice, somewhat muffled, replied, 'leave us be. Can't you see we're busy?'

'Lizzie!'

The white legs scrabbled in the hay and Lizzie freed herself awkwardly.

The young gentleman swore and turned on the intruder. 'Get out of here, you interfering witch!' said Nicolas Sutton, his normally amiable face pink and furious.

Margaret flushed. 'I'll not leave without Lizzie.'

Lizzie pulled her skirts down over her ankles and glared at Margaret with an expression that managed to be excited, defiant and frightened all at once.

'By Christ, this is nothing to do with you,' said Nicolas. 'She came with me freely enough. Now leave us alone.'

'I'll do no such thing. She's no more than a child and you've no right to lead her on like that – it's not fair on the girl.'

Nicolas Sutton scrambled to his feet and advanced on Margaret in a fury. 'The devil take you for a meddlesome baggage. I tell you for the last time, get out of here at once!'

And he raised his hand and would surely have struck her, but the next moment, just as Lizzie screamed, there was a deep bellow of rage and what little daylight there had been in the stable was blocked by the huge body filling the doorway as Ambrose burst in and set on the young gentleman.

71

He fetched Nicolas a blow to the stomach that sent him flying across the little stable and then, before Nicolas could recover either his breath or his sword, Ambrose pounced on him once more and picked him up by the scruff of his elegant collar as if he were no more than a plucked pheasant.

'Say you're sorry to these girls,' roared Ambrose. 'Go on, now, you say you're sorry!'

'Put me down, you oaf!' squeaked Nicolas. 'My father is a Justice, you'll be sorry. Put me down!' And his feet ran helplessly through the air.

'Ambrose, are you mad?' Margaret was appalled by his rashness and quick visions of his body hanging from a gibbet flashed before her. 'You can't go assaulting the Suttons. Put the man down at once.'

'Put me down!' Young Sutton was purple with rage.

'Not until he says he's sorry!' Ambrose was so brimful of fight and strong ale that he would have happily taken on the whole tribe of Suttons if he could. 'I don't care who he is – mustn't go insulting you,' and he lifted Nicolas still higher so that his brown curls brushed against the cobwebs of the ceiling.

'Stop it! I'll see you suffer for this!'

'Ambrose, have some sense. There's no harm done yet.'

'He thinks he can do what he likes but I'll show him!'

Low laughter in the doorway caused Margaret to spin round suddenly. Richard Treveryan was standing in the entrance and his dark eyes were bright with amusement as he absorbed the scene before him.

'A fine state your whoring's got you into this time, Nick,' he commented.

'Richard, thank God – by all that's holy, man, don't stand there laughing at me. Make this bumpkin put me down or by heavens I'll –'

'Nick, you're in no position to make threats . . . but all right. Come along now, Treloar, put the young gentleman down, there's a good fellow.'

'Keep out of this,' Ambrose was sweating heavily, confused now, but still angry, 'he needs to be taught a lesson.'

'Maybe so, but you're hardly the schoolmaster, and besides,' Treveryan was mocking, 'I'm sure the girl was willing enough.'

Ambrose growled with rage and stepped forward. In his all-conquering mood that day he truly thought he could take them both on at once. At his first movement Treveryan drew his rapier and faced Ambrose, his face no longer laughing but cruel and cold.

'Set him down,' said Richard, 'or you're an even bigger fool than I thought.'

'Don't you go calling me a fool!'

'Then fight me if you wish. God knows, there's been little enough sport until now. Come on then, giant, let's see what you can do.'

Ambrose swayed towards him.

Margaret was appalled. 'Ambrose, what are you thinking of? Can't you see he's only baiting you?'

Treveryan pushed her aside. 'Keep out of this. And take your hoyden sister with you.'

At the deliberate insult Ambrose trumpeted his fury but, still holding the wriggling Nicolas in the air, he was uncertain how to proceed with the fight.

Treveryan's face was ugly, sneering. 'Staying safe behind your womenfolk?'

A gurgle of rage bubbled through Ambrose's lips and, trailing Nicolas Sutton behind him like a banner, he lunged at Treveryan.

Lizzie screamed and ran to Margaret's side.

Margaret shouted, 'Ambrose, no!' picked up a pail of water and dashed it in his face. There was a brief moment of pandemonium. Nicolas was dropped in the hay and Ambrose, spluttering and bewildered, clutched at his hand: a thin line of blood ran across it where Treveryan's rapier had slashed him.

Margaret seized Ambrose's injured hand and, as she did so, was careful to put herself between him and Treveryan's gleaming rapier. She faced him squarely.

'That's enough, Mr Treveryan,' she said, still shaking with anger. 'If this is your idea of sport then God knows you've had enough for sure.'

He laughed at her. 'Nonsense, girl, the fun was just beginning. You're a worse killjoy than your local misery St Ewan.'

Nicolas stood up, brushing straw and cobwebs from his

hair and shoulders. He reached out a hand to Lizzie and attempted a smile, though his face was still a choleric shade of pink. 'Here, Lizzie,' he offered, 'I can show you a quieter place . . .'

Lizzie stared at him wide-eyed and Margaret, with a sigh of exasperation, pulled her sister to her side. 'Leave her alone. It's not right of you to make up to her like this. She's hardly more than a child.'

'She's old enough to know what she wants.'

Margaret was furious. 'You *know* that's not true! You just wanted to be able to lead her on and not have to think of *her* at all. But she's the one would have to pay the price for your few moments of pleasure. Did you pause to consider that at all, Mr Sutton? No, you thought only of yourself, the way men always do!'

Lizzie slipped her hand into Margaret's arm. 'We were only talking, Mattie,' she whispered, 'and kissing a little bit.'

Treveryan had sheathed his rapier. 'Is your low opinion of men based on a wide experience?' he queried. 'Or have you simply been unlucky?'

Nicolas laughed, but it was against Richard Treveryan that Margaret's anger was now directed. 'It seems to me, sir, that the cruellest things are amusing to you. I might feel sorry for you if I did not despise you so much.'

At this Nicolas whooped his approval of her scolding, then smiled encouragingly at Lizzie. Margaret kept a firm hold of her hand.

'Mr Sutton, you will have to find your amusements elsewhere. Or do without. Come, Lizzie, Tom will be wondering where we are. Ambrose, you must come with us.'

'Cluck cluck cluck,' said Nicolas, 'listen to the mother hen gathering in her chickens.'

Margaret could feel Ambrose's anger, a mountain of fury behind her.

'I dunno,' he muttered, 'they should be taught a lesson.'

'But not by you, Ambrose.' Margaret was beginning to feel desperate. 'You can't win against the gentry, you know that.'

'Listen to the sensible hen.' It was Treveryan who spoke.

He had been watching Margaret closely and his expression suddenly made her uncomfortable and more than ever eager to be gone. She was confused now that he seemed to be taking her side.

He spoke soberly to Ambrose. 'Go on home, then, like a dutiful giant. Then no more will be said about this fight. But I should warn you that if you stay here, the watch has been alerted, and the constable will be here at any moment. You surely don't want to end up before the magistrate for assaulting his son, now do you?'

'He's talking sense, Ambrose,' Margaret conceded. 'Come, we'll walk back together.'

Ambrose shook the water from his hair. 'I don't like it –' he muttered.

'No more trouble, Ambrose. Not now.'

Still holding Lizzie by the hand, Margaret took Ambrose's arm and began to guide him from the stable. Treveryan remained standing by the doorway. Margaret wondered with sudden dread whether he meant to make Ambrose fight him after all. But his rapier was still sheathed and it was not Ambrose who had his attention.

'Mr Treveryan, stand aside and let us pass.'

The merest hesitation, then he stepped back with an exaggerated flourish. 'Madam, with sincere reluctance.'

And they could hear his laughter fading behind them as they hurried through the slanting evening shadows to the road.

Lizzie maintained a sullen silence until they were nearing home. She and Tom were riding Juno while Margaret trudged beside them. Tom was nodding in the saddle and more than once it was only swift action on Lizzie's part that saved him from falling off altogether. Margaret too was bone tired, but she hardly noticed it. She was deep in thought.

At last Lizzie burst out, 'You won't say anything to Mother, will you?'

'Of course I won't,' said Margaret swiftly, glad only that Lizzie's sulks were over. 'But whatever possessed you to go with him like that?'

Lizzie pouted. 'He spoke so nicely, Mattie, not a bit like

Ambrose and the other boys. You should have heard him. And he only said wouldn't it be nice to take a walk. He never said . . . I only meant to let him kiss me. There's no harm in that, is there?'

Margaret was frowning.

'Is there, Mattie?'

'Oh, don't ask me!' Margaret burst out with sudden intensity. 'Words are cheap enough!' And she strode on so quickly that Lizzie had to kick Juno into a bumpy trot to catch up with her again.

It was dark by the time they reached home and the moon was rising over the copse beyond their second field. Tom slithered from the horse and Margaret steered him into the kitchen where his parents were dozing by the embers of the day's fire.

'Well, Tom, and have you enjoyed your day?'

Tom stared at his mother with the unseeing eyes of a sleepwalker and then his mouth opened and his face disappeared behind an enormous yawn.

She laughed. 'Bedtime for you, young fellow, and you can tell me all about it in the morning.'

Margaret went out to tend Juno while Lizzie fetched in the salted pilchards and the knitted stockings and the rest of the day's booty.

Later still, when she and Lizzie lay together in the bed they shared under the sloping roof and the night was so quiet and still they could hear the waves breaking on the shingle a mile away and Tom was sleeping soundly in the truckle bed beside their own, Lizzie murmured sleepily, 'What a day it's been, Mattie, hasn't it? So many excitements.'

Margaret's head was still crowded with spinning images: there was Ambrose, his ginger hair haloed by sunshine as he lifted Robert Trelyn high in the air; that first glimpse of William Hollar as he stood in the doorway with his face shining with the beauty of Apollo; the noisy crowd half-listening as she made her Latin speech; Richard Treveryan's cruel smile and his rough hair and his mocking eyes and Nicolas Sutton's pink-faced helpless rage. She murmured in her turn, 'We won't forget today for a long long time,' and fell asleep.

In after years that Porthew Feast Day stood out in her memory as the last day of a childhood which came in time to seem blessedly happy and uncomplicated.

She was just three weeks short of her sixteenth birthday.

2

Less than a week after St Ewan's Day, on a morning veiled with mist, Lizzie scampered up the stairs with all the haste of a bearer of bad news.

'Mother, Mother! Mattie's been sick in the cow byre! She says it's nothing but she looks awful pale.'

Mistress Pearce struggled to raise herself in the bed. Her joints were a web of pain, pain which had kept her awake through half the night and which she now tried to escape in sleep. It was with difficulty that she focused on a world beyond her body and its multiple discomforts – but seeing Lizzie's flushed and anxious face, she did so now.

'Bid her come and see me, then,' she said, her twisted fingers pulling back the bed curtains, and Lizzie ran off obediently. Mistress Pearce propped herself awkwardly against the bolster and pulled a shawl around her shoulders. She had a sharp and pointed little face above a large and often useless body; her lips were pressed tight shut as though to prevent herself from moaning or complaint. There was a grey light seeping through the bedroom window: the sun was not yet risen but she could tell already that it was to be a damp day; she felt the dampness in the room, in her bedding, in her aching bones.

No sooner did Margaret appear in the doorway than Mistress Pearce's suspicions sharpened: her woman's instinct probed the secret the girl had so far managed to keep even from herself.

'Lizzie tells me you are sick again this morning.'

Margaret, grey-faced, leaned against the doorpost for support. 'It's nothing, no need to worry. I think perhaps that fish we ate was not quite fresh. I'm feeling better again already.'

'You've been with a man, haven't you?'

Margaret put a hand to her eyes as though to shield them

from the light. 'It's not that, I'm sure. Just a passing upset.'

'How long overdue are you?'

'Maybe, I lose track . . . perhaps a week . . . but I'm often late . . . I'm sure I shall be –'

Mistress Pearce waved aside her protests with an impatient gesture. 'Margaret, listen to me. You've been with a man and now you're carrying his child. I knew there was something days ago but could not be sure.'

Her accusation was without reproach, a mere statement of fact. She did not much like her step-daughter, who was a constant reminder of the foreigner she had herself replaced, but she respected her as a hard worker and a reasonable person to deal with. Her narrow world of pain was restricted to practical considerations and she had little patience for morality.

Margaret was silent a long while, and then she groaned, 'I suppose it must be true. I feel so wretchedly ill now that I hardly know what to do with myself.'

'The sickness will pass,' said Mistress Pearce, 'but the problem will not go away so easily. You must tell me this fellow's name and then we can decide what's best.'

Margaret shook her head. 'There's no point,' she said, 'I cannot tell you who it is.'

'Why not?'

'He'll not marry me, if that is what you hope. It's impossible.'

'Is he married already?'

Margaret did not answer.

'Either married then or too high born to marry you. Or maybe it's someone you're ashamed to admit to. Perhaps the lad who helped with the harvest?' She paused, her pointed features twitching like a ferret's as she tried to scent out the truth. But Margaret remained impassive, so she went on. 'Though I doubt that. This fellow has done little enough to help you, don't waste your time protecting *him*.'

'I gave him my promise.'

'Tch! Promises mean nothing. You're in trouble enough without making more for yourself by hanging on to some useless promise. Don't you realise how serious this is?'

Margaret nodded miserably and her eyes filled with tears but she said nothing.

'I always thought you had more sense, Margaret,' she grumbled, 'I always thought my Lizzie was the one who needed watching, not you. Even though you do waste your time with books and old stories, but still . . .' A thought occurred to her, but then she dismissed it as irrelevant. 'Your father must know about this.'

'Do you have to tell him?' Margaret was appalled.

'And how do you expect to keep him in the dark? All the world and his dog will know before long, my girl. Some secrets are not made for keeping.'

'Don't tell him yet, please don't. Perhaps . . . perhaps we are wrong. It may be just an upset or –'

'Or? Unwanted babies are hard to dislodge, I know that much, just as the wanted ones slip away all too easily.' She spoke with the heavy certainty of a woman with only two children to show for her eleven pregnancies.

'Listen to me, Margaret. This is a serious business, for us all. I'll not be responsible for keeping your father in the dark. There's only one solution. You must be married before you lose your name and bring disgrace upon the whole family. You'll have to tell your father the fellow's name even if you won't tell me. Now, go downstairs and light the fire. I'll come down presently and we shall tell him when he comes in for his meal. Has the sickness passed?'

Margaret nodded. 'I'm better now.'

It was only partly true. She went down the stairs to the grey-dark kitchen and began to sweep the ashes from the open hearth. A thin cat, a grey tabby, stalked over to her and, back arched and tail held high, he brushed against her arm as she worked. She pushed him away wearily and then, on a contradictory impulse, stroked his fur with rapid, anxious movements. Yes, the sickness had passed, thank heavens, but she was left feeling strangely light-headed and dreamlike. There was an eerie unreality about everything she did. For some days now, she had lost track of how many but it was certainly more than the week she had admitted to her step-mother, she had blinded herself to the certainty that was growing within her, a certainty too fearful to confront.

She went out to the fuel store behind the house and gathered furze and logs for the fire and then she paused, as she often did, to watch the sun rise above the five elms at the end of the orchard. A score of rooks flapped noisily in the branches, just as they did every day at morning and evening; the long grass sparkled with dew just as it had done a month ago and all the days of her life as long as she could remember.

Her sense of unreality increased. Impossible to believe that a passing sickness, a period missed, could signal the momentous changes her step-mother had described: disgrace to the family, a hasty marriage, unwanted babies . . . for here she was, gathering logs and furze and taking them in for the fire as she had done every morning and would surely continue to do for evermore while the rooks fussed in the branches of the elms and the dew sparkled on the grass.

And there was Lizzie, grumbling at the two slow cows as she drove them out to the meadow. The hog was in his sty, squealing to be fed, and the chickens scratched the ground and clucked and the pigeons flew down from the wood and stole their precious corn. The sounds and smells of the farmyard morning swathed her round in a soft cocoon of familiarity and her fears were lulled. An undertow of anxiety remained, a nagging pulse, but she endeavoured to ignore it. She sang softly to herself as she returned to the house.

Surely her life would never change. Not yet.

John Pearce was a straightforward man. He took pleasure in his work. He liked to watch his animals grow fat and to see his stores filled with corn and hay – and he relished the thought that he would be passing on to young Tom a far more prosperous heritage than his own had been.

Sturdy and thickset, he walked now with a stoop, as resilient as the blackthorn trees whose roots clung to the headland at the sea-end of the farm, tough enough to withstand any weather but curved like a wave by the endless gales that howled in from the Atlantic. Like the stunted Cornish trees he might bend but had never yet been beaten.

His first reaction to the news that Margaret was almost certainly pregnant was one of disbelief. Although she had done the work of a grown woman for years he still looked on her as a child, just as he looked on Tom and Lizzie as children.

Now he pushed back his plate (for Mistress Pearce knew that bad news is best heard on a full stomach) and stared as if at a stranger at the tall fair-haired girl who stood before the open fire. Almost for the first time he noticed her well-developed breasts and the generous curve of her hips.

When her step-mother began talking, Margaret, as though to distract herself, had picked up one of the cats, a bad-tempered tabby fighter by the name of Achilles, and she was stroking him thoughtfully, with that distant, slightly troubled expression she often wore.

'Surely this is not true, Margaret. Surely . . .'

She rubbed the cat behind the ears and bent over slightly to nuzzle his fur before saying, 'I don't know . . . it could be . . .'

John Pearce banged his fist down on the table. 'I won't have it! I won't have a bastard child in my house! How dare you do this! You go off whoring when my back is turned – how dare you disgrace us all in this way!'

His wife let him continue until the first of his bewildered rage was exhausted before saying, 'Now we must plan carefully. The damage is done already, nothing to be gained by fretting.'

He scowled. 'Well then, and what is to be done?'

'She must be married, and the sooner the better, or the child's a bastard and your daughter's ruined and the rest of us disgraced. There's no other way.'

'Hmm. That's the way, true enough. Who is it, then? I'll go settle this with him at once.'

Margaret made an indistinct sound.

'What was that?' straining to catch the words. 'What was his name?'

'I asked her this morning but she would not say.'

'She had better tell me.'

'I can't, Father.' For the first time Margaret turned to him in direct and frightened appeal. 'He'll not marry me so there's nothing to be gained if I tell you and I gave my word, I promised.'

John Pearce looked at his daughter in utter disbelief. To be pregnant and unwed was a crime of folly only, an error that in time would no doubt be forgiven. But to keep a secret from him – and such a secret! – that was open defiance, a challenge to his authority as her father and as head of the household that could never be overlooked.

He stood up. 'You will tell me,' he said in a low voice.

'I cannot.' In her fear Margaret clutched the tabby Achilles so tightly that, with a howl of alarm, he leapt out of her arms and streaked towards the kitchen door just as John Pearce raised his hand and struck his daughter a blow across the face which almost knocked her to the ground.

'Father, please . . .'

'Name the man.'

She shook her head.

'Then you give me no choice.'

John Pearce took no pleasure from what followed. He had never been considered a violent man and he could not remember when Margaret had ever given him cause for anger before – but that only made her present betrayal worse. Tom, coming in from the yard to see what all the commotion was about, ran off howling to see his beloved Mattie beaten and was comforted by a trembling and baffled Lizzie.

It was quickly over.

'For the last time, Margaret, tell me the name of this man and it can still be settled somehow.'

Sobbing and choking, Margaret could only shake her head.

John Pearce looked at his daughter with contempt. 'Then thank the Lord your poor mother is not alive to see the disgrace you've brought us,' he said and, turning on his heel, he strode out across the yard.

The afternoon was long and bitter for John Pearce and he purged his anger cutting brushwood down by the stream. He did not regret his harsh treatment of Margaret, far from it, for he had only done what any father of a wayward daughter was bound to do. On consideration he thought it was probably his earlier lack of firmness that had brought this trouble on him now.

Yet the conflict had left a bitter aftertaste. She had not named the man and he guessed there was nothing he could do would make her. He might break her body but from now on there would always be a secret part of her that was hidden from him. It had been the same with her mother, whose body he could possess whenever he wanted but who had become more remote with every year that passed.

He had no wish to think of her mother, but images, memories, coloured his brain as he hacked at the brambles and willow that were spread from the banks of the stream.

'Cat will after kind,' he thought bitterly. No doubt her mother had been no better than she should be. He had never known, really, anything about her. But if Margaret was turning out bad then he did not doubt it was the mother's blood betraying her for there was little enough of that sort of thing among his folk.

The first time he had seen Margaret's mother she had been seated by the fire in fisherman Truscott's cottage above Porthew. John Pearce was a young man then. Strong and dark and with a swagger in his walk he was considered locally to be a fine-looking lad and was much in demand among his neighbours' daughters. That morning he had come to hear news of the ship that had gone down in the night.

The young woman was the only survivor. She would no doubt have died with the rest had not Susannah Truscott, a local fishwife as strong as she was broad, stood guard over her through the night, swiping at any who crept too close. Whether it was the young woman she was guarding, or the bale of cloth she had clung to as the ship went down, none chanced to find out, but there was no doubt that the stranger owed her life in equal measure to Susannah Truscott and a bale of cloth.

She was in a state of profound shock. She knew no English, and no one could make out a word of what she said, so she quickly ceased to say anything at all and looked around her with terrified eyes.

From that first sighting, John Pearce could think of nothing else. It was not that she was beautiful. Her features were too sharp and her pale hair, unknown among these dark-haired Celts, aroused interest but general disapproval. It was her air of mystery and helplessness that won him. He would rescue her and she would be grateful to him.

And, for a while, it was so.

As no one could make out her name, or repeat it when she said it, she became known as Francey. But when Sir John Sutton's guest, who was said to speak fluent French, came to talk with her, he went away shaking his head in mystification. Too late it was discovered that the ship had been carrying among its cargo a small group of refugees from the Low Countries who were hoping to escape religious persecution in America. What sect they belonged to, or where exactly they were planning to settle, no one ever knew, for by the time Francey had mastered sufficient English to tell her story, there was no longer anyone who cared to listen.

They were married before the summer.

His family were, of course, appalled by his choice. The girl brought no land with her, no property: she did not even have a name that anyone could understand and you could tell by looking at her that she was ill accustomed to hard work.

They could not speak to each other much that first summer, but they achieved a communion of another sort in their rough and tender love-making. She was grateful, as he had hoped, and he still revelled in her helplessness and felt himself grow in manhood with each passing day.

He neglected his few acres of farmland. He loved to come up to her as she worked and bury his face in the softness of the back of her neck. He loved the pallor of her skin, her hair the colour of ripe corn, the smoothness of her flesh beneath the shift she wore at night.

He was delighted to teach her his language, and she was quick to learn. Long hours they spent together, lying on the cliff-top at the far boundary of the farm, sharing the softness of the sea-fined grass and their own young bodies. He would look down at the beach.

'They gather seaweed for the fields,' he would say, and she repeated, 'They gather seaweed for the fields,' only from her lips the words were distorted like images in a pond and became magic, dancing.

By the time the autumn came she could talk quite easily about everyday matters. She mentioned one day that hers was a different church, but he scowled at that and told her

85

it was of no account. The truth was that it troubled him to think that she had had a life before she met him, a life she might now be looking back to with regret. He preferred to think her story had begun on that grey morning when she had shivered by the Truscotts' fire and waited to be rescued by him.

That first winter was an uneasy time for them both. In smiles and looks and touch their love had been secure, but now that she could understand his words he frequently felt that she was disappointed by what he said. In the beginning he had chattered to her freely enough. Now, too often, he felt tongue-tied and uncouth, and he could not see the reason for it at all.

Little by little his confidence gave way to doubt. Often, it seemed to him the words he had so delighted to teach her were now used to criticise or even to mock him. She became fretful. Sometimes she tried to talk to him about her life before the ship was sunk, but he always stopped her roughly. She took refuge in bitter silences. More often than not, that winter, they were both hungry.

The following autumn Margaret was born. For a few months Francey rocked the cradle and nursed her daughter and a kind of harmony was restored. When Margaret was nearly a year old, John Pearce set off proudly for Porthew on St Ewan's Day with his wife and daughter. Among the drifting fair-day flotsam were half a dozen fair-haired sailors who spoke in a language no one could understand. Francey turned pale when she heard them speak and, when her husband was engrossed in watching the wrestling, she slipped quietly away. When he found her again, she was down by the harbour wall and talking with the fair-haired sailors in her native dialect and her eyes shone with a joy he had never before seen. In a panic of possession he told her to come home with him at once. She stared at him, as though he were a stranger. He repeated his command and then, instinctively, he snatched the baby from her arms and, standing a little distance away, he told her he was returning to the farm and taking the child. She wavered, bowed her head and followed him without a word.

It was at about this time that she took to going to the cliff-top at the end of the farm in the evenings when her day's work was done. John would see her sometimes as he came back from the fields, her tall figure outlined against the rolling clouds to the west; gazing, always gazing at the wide sea from which she had come. He began to think she was searching for a ship to take her back to that home he knew nothing of. Too late to ask about it now.

That was when he began to count the cost of marrying her. The land was too stony and windswept to support them without endless struggle. Had he followed the path that had been intended for him he would have married Ellie Roberts, the three fields to the north would have been joined with his and he would not have been driven by hunger to seek work from the Suttons. Such thoughts were bitter in his heart when he came home to a dismal hearth and his cold, unsmiling wife.

Their second child was a lively boy. Though John no longer had any pleasure from his wife, he delighted in his two bonny children. It was a grim day for them all when young John caught the fever and died before the night was out. John Pearce was beside himself with grief but he thought his wife had lost her wits. She seized the little corpse and ran out with it to the sea's edge and screamed abuse in words he could not understand to the crashing waves. He was frightened of her then, frightened of her unknown language and the past he knew nothing of. His fear made him brutal and he followed her down to the sea and knocked her down and dragged her back to the farm. He thrust her into an empty shed and barred the door and did not let her out until her demented wailing had ceased. By then the child had had a Christian burial and John Pearce had forgotten he ever loved the woman who was washed ashore in the storm.

He did not remember until she died, some four years later. He had sat beside her through the long night, stroking her damp pale hair and moistening her lips with a rag dipped in ale and as the first light spread across the room her harsh breathing faded to an endless silence.

And now that her eyes no longer looked at him with scorn and her bitter words were silent, he dropped his head on her breast and sobbed for the woman he had loved and lost, the woman he had never really known at all.

For two days he stayed there and would not allow them to take the corpse away. For two days he sobbed for his lost dreams. Then he dried his eyes, followed the coffin to the churchyard and, still in his best clothes, set out to court Ellie Roberts, the girl he should have married years ago and who was recently widowed herself. She agreed, as he had known she would, and she brought with her not only the three fields that had been her portion but also half of her late husband's lands as well. That had been six years ago. During those six years he had worked hard, and Margaret had helped him, doing those jobs his new wife was often too poorly to attend to. And now the girl's foolishness threatened to make a nonsense of all he had struggled to achieve. He hated her for her frail woman's body and he scythed and cut his anger against the undergrowth beside the stream until the day grew dark and a sliver of a moon rose into the sky above the farm.

'Ambrose Treloar,' said Ellie Pearce as soon as her husband came into the room. She had been waiting in the darkened bedroom for his return. He pulled off his shoes and breeches and climbed into the bed beside her. His hands still smelled of earth and bracken and the sap of cut willows.

'Ambrose? Why did she not tell us, then?'

'No, no, he's not the father, more's the pity. He's had his eye on the girl for months.'

'I never noticed.'

'You never do see what is happening under your very nose.'

John Pearce grunted. Experience had taught him that his wife, despite the isolation of her illness, was as well informed as any woman in the district.

'So what about Ambrose?'

'He's the one shall marry her. He'll agree to it, I'm sure, if we handle him right. Then the child will have a father at least and your daughter a husband. You must talk with his family tomorrow.'

He lay in silence for a while, staring at the pale square of sky visible through the little window. 'Do I speak of the child?'

'Best to do it straight away. I will think of something will make it not so bad. And then Margaret must talk Ambrose round. It's the girl's best chance.'

The next morning, as soon as the sun was up, John Pearce saddled Juno and set off for the Forge at Porthew. When, several hours later, he returned to the farm, he was well pleased with his morning's efforts.

'His parents are none too taken with the idea,' he told his wife, 'but Ambrose is delighted and it seems he makes his own decisions nowadays. He will visit this afternoon to talk with Margaret himself.'

Mistress Pearce squeezed the vinegar water out of the damp cloth and patted Margaret's face gently. The girl's lip was misshapen and a bruise had half-closed one eye.

'You'll have to win him over with words, no one is going to be seduced by your pretty face, not for a while at least.'

'*Must* I see him today?'

'Certainly, if that's what *he* wants. And you must tell him that the man forced you, that it only happened once and you couldn't fight him off. You know how to make it sound convincing.'

'But it's not true.'

In her annoyance Mistress Pearce dabbed more fiercely than was necessary at the bruised cheekbone and Margaret winced.

'Just now that has nothing to do with it. All you need to worry about is getting yourself a husband before news of this baby is all over the district.'

'But why Ambrose? I don't care for him at all.'

'Have you anyone better in mind?'

Margaret was silent, then, 'But suppose I lose the baby?' she asked.

'Suppose, suppose . . . there's no time for supposings now. The sooner you do something, the better for everyone.'

'But why? Can't I just stay here like I've always done? I'll always work hard, you know I will. Why must it all be different now?'

'Because it *is* different, that's why. Lose your name and there's nothing left. Jenny Prosser went east to have her baby but word came back and her father was named. She'll never find a husband now, even though the baby died. Or would you rather the church courts got word of this so you can enjoy a spell in the House of Correction in Penryn? Did you know all the midwives are under oath to get the father's name if they can? I've heard of a young girl dying because they were slow to give help. And how will it be for Lizzie and Tom when word gets around that their sister is a strumpet with a bastard child? Sometimes I truly believe that for all your book-learning you must be the most foolish of them all. Now is the time for you to make use of all that famous cleverness of yours. Talk Ambrose round – and the sooner the better. It's your only chance.'

'It's not fair.' But Margaret said the words under her breath. Everything her step-mother said was true and she honestly intended to persuade Ambrose to marry her. Though the prospect of a life with him was bad enough, the alternative was infinitely worse.

A brisk wind was blowing off the sea as Ambrose urged his horse along the track that led to the farm. His hopes were as high and bright as the white clouds in the sky above him.

He had been fascinated by Margaret ever since the day when she first appeared at Dame Erisey's little school: a small thin girl with yellow hair and an ill-fitting dress. Like the other children he had laughed at her in the beginning, but they discovered soon enough that she already knew how to read and write and was willing to help them with their work. Before long she was allowed to join the little group of boys who studied with the parson in the church porch.

Even then Ambrose, for all his huge size and his strength, had been slightly in awe of her. His awe had increased as she changed from a thin child into a tall and shapely young woman. He grew tongue-tied and clumsy whenever she was about, and though in his dreams he was all-conquering and she yielded to his strength as easily as a young willow, he had no idea how to transform his dreams into the stuff of daytime reality.

But now all that was changed. In theory, of course, like any other man, he had expected his future wife to be a virgin, or at least to have known no man but him, but now he found the fact that Margaret had been with a man and was in all probability pregnant as well, far from putting him off as might have been expected, only increased his desire to possess her. Some of the mystery, the remoteness, that had always surrounded her, was now gone for ever. She was no better than she ought to be (though her father had hinted vaguely at rape) still, she was liable to the same accidents and misfortunes that befell other more ordinary girls who could not write whole sentences without a pause or read in Latin. For all her learning and foreign-seeming ways, she was as weak as any other female. And, what was more, she needed him.

The more he considered their altered circumstances, the better pleased he was with what had taken place and he dug his heels into his horse's sides and cantered along the narrow lane that led between pale fields of stubble and hedges strung with rose hips and ripe blackberries to the little farm at Conwinnion, determined to win her undying gratitude and love, and make her his wife.

She was waiting for him by the orchard gate. In her hand she held an old and fragile copy of Catullus that had belonged to her mother. It had fallen open, as always, at the familiar page.

Nulla domus tales umquam contexit amores,
Nullus amor talis coniunxit foedere amantes.

She repeated the words like an incantation: no house ever held such loves as these, no love ever joined lovers in such a union.

No other house, no other love . . . she cherished the words for the certainty they offered; she cherished them above all because they revived an image of her mother as she liked best to remember her. Not impatient or despairing as the woman so often was, but brought to eager life by the magic of poetry. Only when one of her precious books was in her hand and she was interpreting the words to her little daughter did she seem content. They became accomplices in the pleasures of escape. Small wonder that the child had developed a passion for books.

Nullus amor . . . and now her high hopes and childish

ignorance had brought her to this, the suffocating knowledge that her best hope for the future was to marry Ambrose, a life with no possibility of love.

Hearing the horse's hoofs she closed the book and composed herself as best she could. She told herself what a sturdy, hard-working husband he would be, that he came from a family well respected in Porthew, that there was, anyway, no one else . . . but all she could see as he swung down from his horse was the great brute strength of him, his ginger hair rough and curling and his face reddened by the sun and the fire in the smithy, his hands large and coarse, and his broad, unthinking grin.

He looped the reins over the gate post and came towards her.

'Well, Mattie,' he said, 'you're in trouble now and that's a fact.' And then, noticing, 'My God, girl, whatever has happened to your face?'

Embarrassed, Margaret turned away.

Ambrose considered. Although his father clouted his own mother often enough and he considered it all part of the natural order of things, yet somehow the sight of Margaret, with her face bruised and misshapen, was something quite out of the ordinary, a kind of unexpected nakedness. He found it disturbing in a way he could not have explained to himself had he tried.

'Your father had reason to be angry, I suppose,' he said, his voice softened by doubt, 'but still, he didn't have to . . .'

Margaret gave a small hiccuping sob. His were the first words approaching tenderness she had heard since her troubles began.

'We can be married, you know, Mattie,' said Ambrose, 'and then it will all be right again.'

It was not what he had intended to say. He had intended to hold off, let her be anxious for a while as to what his decision might be; he had intended to revel, if only for a little while, in all his newfound power, but he was so perplexed by her sudden vulnerability that the words were out before he had considered best how to say them.

'Yes,' said Margaret. Her face was still turned away, perhaps to hide the bruising, and he could not see her expression.

Ambrose scratched his head and stared. Nothing was turning out as he had expected. Surely she had just now agreed to marry him, so why was she still as distant as she had always been? She should be in his arms now, loving and submissive, that was the way it was done. He wondered if perhaps he had missed something.

'You will marry me, Mattie, won't you?'

'Yes, I'll marry you.'

'Hmm.' He shifted from one foot to the other. 'That's it, then.'

Still grinning with the newness and perplexity of it all he stepped forward and put his arms around her shoulders and kissed her awkwardly. Margaret, her body rigid with the effort not to break away and run, closed her eyes and allowed his lips to cover her mouth. His cheeks were badly shaven and the rough stubble scratched her skin. She flinched in panic but his huge arms, arms that had cracked Robert Trelyn's ribs at the Feast Day, held her firmly and she could no more have escaped his grasp than a prisoner can shake off iron manacles. I'm drowning, she thought as she inhaled the smell of leather and sweat and the mingled odours of the smithy, dear God please help me for I'm drowning now . . .

He drew back, releasing her. 'That settles it, then. That's better. Let's sit down for a while, and talk.'

The embrace had made him more confident. She was so weak, after all, just like everybody else, no match for his great strength. He was amazed that he had allowed himself to be in awe of her for so long – but now all that was changed for ever. She was going to be his wife. She would be his own thing.

At the far end of the little patch of ground that was graced with the name of orchard there was an old pear tree that had blown over in the previous winter's gales; some of its roots remained in the ground and this summer it had blossomed and borne fruit as well as ever. The lower part of its trunk made a convenient seat, and it was here that Ambrose and Margaret sat down.

'We shall be married, then. That's good.'

'Yes.' Margaret's voice was very soft.

'You'll have me to take care of you from now on, you'll

see.' He put his arm round her waist as though to remind himself that she now belonged to him. 'I shall take good care of you.'

'Yes.' Almost inaudible.

'So what's all this I hear about you and some other fellow? Your father said he forced you, some stranger. How was that?'

'It doesn't matter now, Ambrose, leave it go.'

'But I want to know.'

'If my father says a stranger took me against my will then that must be what happened.'

'But I want *you* to tell me about it.'

'It's better to say nothing, Ambrose, really it is.' She turned to face him and spoke in a low, hurried voice. 'We want to start afresh, you and I. The past has nothing to do with our future together. I'll be a good wife to you, Ambrose, I promise you that. I'll work hard – you'll never have any reason to regret marrying me and . . . and . . .' forcing herself, she ended up, 'and I'll always be grateful to you, Ambrose.'

'Hmm. Yes. Well.' He scratched his upper arm thoughtfully. 'I should think so too. It's not every fellow would marry a girl in your position, you know. And I want to do what's right. I'll find that scoundrel and beat some sense into him. I'll make him sorry.'

'But that's just why, don't you see?' Margaret seized her opportunity, 'For then everyone will guess what has happened and the story will be all over the district, but if we say nothing at all, people will believe the child to be yours. You'd much rather people thought that, wouldn't you?'

This possibility had not occurred to him before. Ambrose was embarrassed, then pleased with himself.

'They will, won't they?' he queried, blushing through his freckles.

'That's right.'

He smiled broadly for a few moments, considering how his reputation locally would rise. But then he frowned again. 'Even so, I think you should tell me – I promise I won't touch the fellow. I'll just talk to him a bit, just warn him not to try anything in the future, let him know I know . . . it's only right.'

'But it would never work like that. You'd be sure to lose your temper and forget your promise. Much better to forget all about it.'

Ambrose considered, frowned, grew irritated. 'It doesn't seem as though I can forget about it, Mattie, that's the whole trouble. Was it Ned Williams? He got a girl in trouble over Mullion way and would not marry her.'

An exasperated sigh. 'If I tell you who it was *not*, Ambrose, then soon enough you'd discover from my silence who it *was*. And I'm bound not to tell anyone. I promised.'

Try as he might, Ambrose could not follow her down the logic of this statement. He grew restive. 'I can't see why you said nothing at the time. After all, if some stranger fellow came and forced you against your will I'd have thought you'd say something.'

'I was not forced.'

'What? But your father said –'

'Oh Ambrose, for God's sake let it drop. I promise you I'll be a good wife and you'll never regret marrying me, but you must promise never to speak of this again.'

'I don't see that I'm the one should need to go making promises at a time like this. You're the one in trouble, Mattie, not me. And what kind of wife has secrets from her husband?'

'There'll be no secrets once we are married. Forget about it . . . please . . .'

Her voice was so soft, so pleading, and she touched his cheek so gently with her finger, smiling as she did so until he grew light-headed with desire and, murmuring, 'All right, I promise,' he bent down and kissed her once again.

'There,' she said, as though soothing a child, 'that's better –'

Ambrose smiled. 'Poor Mattie. Your face is so bruised.'

'Oh well. Any father would have been angry.'

There was silence. Ambrose was staring thoughtfully at his broad palm. After a while he said slowly, working it out, 'But if you were not forced then you must have been willing. I just can't figure it out.'

'Oh, for pity's sake, Ambrose, I thought you promised not to fret about it any more.'

'I'm not fretting. But I have a right to know.'

95

'You have *no* right to break your promise. How can I ever trust you if you go back on your word so soon?'

Ambrose was thoroughly bewildered. He felt vaguely that he had said or done the wrong thing, yet he was certain that for once in his life it was Margaret and not he who was at fault.

'You mustn't go accusing me of things,' he said, 'and you must always do what I tell you. I'll be the master in my own house, you know.'

Margaret smothered a sigh. 'Of course you will, Ambrose,' she said gently, adding after a moment, 'and you might as well know that I never loved the man . . .'

Her voice trailed away and Ambrose looked down at her. 'I don't understand it at all,' he said.

'No more do I,' Margaret smiled, 'but I do know that if you really wish to marry me, then we can put all of this behind us and learn to care for each other as a husband and wife should.'

'Yes, that's it.'

He pulled her towards him and kissed her again, and all his doubts dissolved in the softness of her lips and the feel of her warm body crushed against his own.

Margaret freed herself. 'We should tell Father now,' she said.

'Yes.' Ambrose stood up, but he was still uneasy. He had the suspicion that Margaret was once more in command of the situation and he wanted to find some way to reassert the authority he had believed himself to possess when their conversation began. He considered whether to pick her up and carry her the short distance to the farmhouse but, tempting though that idea was, he feared it might make him appear foolish.

'Mattie, wait . . .'

As she turned towards him he reached out and placed his hand over the curve of her breast and felt the warm dome move under her dress. He grinned, sensing the ease of physical possession. Just that act, the same brief sequence that he had on occasion enjoyed with the woman who came sometimes to help his mother with the washing, would be enough to prove his mastery and destroy for ever those strings of words in which he was so hopelessly entangled.

96

It was in his mind to take her there and then, right here in the orchard, put his seed beside that other fellow's. His hand cupped her breast, then gripped it and his eyes were so clouded by desire that he did not notice an expression of disgust pass over her face as she twisted deftly away and said in a choked voice, 'Later, Ambrose. There'll be plenty of time.'

She stooped and picked up a book that was lying on a low branch and began to walk briskly in the direction of the gate. Catching up with her in a few long strides, Ambrose grabbed her arm.

'What's that, then?'

'Oh, it's nothing. Just a book of Latin verses that belonged to my mother.'

'Give it here.'

Margaret did not appear to have heard him.

'I said give it here,' he repeated roughly and snatched the book from her hands.

'Ambrose, what in God's name are you doing?'

He was holding the book aloft and the pages fluttered helplessly, white against the blueness of the sky. He looked at the black patterns of print with loathing. 'No need of this nonsense now we are to be married. You'll have plenty of other things to keep you busy from now on . . . no time for Latin and all that foolishness. I never saw why your father allowed it – and it's done you no good at all, you have to admit that now.'

'Give me back that book at once!' Her voice was unusually shrill.

'No! You must not tell me what to do. I shall be the one to tell *you* what's what from now on. And I don't hold with learning in a woman. It's not natural, everyone knows that.'

'Ambrose, wait . . . we don't have to quarrel over a book. You'll never see it again, I promise you, only . . . Ambrose, you mustn't tear it! No!'

The book was old and fragile and with two twists of his powerful hands Ambrose had broken its back and the pages were scattered like spent blossom in a wind.

At once Margaret was on her knees, gathering the fallen pages. 'Oh, you great fool!' she exclaimed. 'Why did you ever have to? Now look what you've done. The poor book is ruined.'

'And a good thing too. Look, it's only paper, you can use it in the privy.' He caught her by the arm and hauled her to her feet. 'Leave them where they lie, they're no use to you now.'

Fury gave Margaret strength and she wrenched herself free. 'That was *my* book. It was my *mother*'s book! You had no right to spoil it. What does it matter to you if I like to read occasionally . . . it's no business of yours.'

Ambrose was not to be foxed by words again: now was the time to assert his authority over Margaret once and for all. 'No wife of mine is going to spend time book-reading!'

'Then I'll not be your wife! I always knew you were an ignorant fool, Ambrose Treloar, but I did not believe you'd be so cruel. Why must you destroy something simply because you don't understand it? Why?'

Ambrose caught her by the arm again and this time he did not let go. 'Who are you calling a fool?' he roared. Such a confusion of rage and desire boiled within him that he did not know if he wanted to beat her or make love to her, so he shook her back and forth like a terrier with a rat, repeating, 'Who's a fool, eh, tell me that! Just tell me that if you can!'

'Let me go, you great oaf! My God, I must have been insane to think I could marry you. I'd rather die . . . it would be like dying . . . oh, let me go, for God's sake!'

'Then I'll not marry you neither!' he said, but still he held her arm, waiting for the apology, the submission, that was sure to come.

'Thank God for that,' was all she said. 'Let some other poor girl suffer your pig-headed ignorance.'

'You shouldn't talk to me that way. It isn't right.'

'I can talk to you how I like since I'm not to be your wife.'

Ambrose felt like a fisherman who sees the catch he had thought firmly on his hook break free and swim gaily away. 'You'll be ruined,' he growled. 'No one will marry you now. You'll come to a bad end just like all bookish women do, just you wait.'

'So? And what do you know about it anyway?'

'I know what I know. Yes, I do. But if you came begging

to me now, begging,' he paused here, waited hopefully '. . . I'd not marry you after the things you've said.'

'Then you'd best go away at once, hadn't you? There's no more to be sàid.'

Baffled, Ambrose released her arm and Margaret began at once to gather up the torn pages of the book. He kicked the trunk of an apple tree.

'It's only a book,' he complained. 'I don't see why you get so hot and bothered over a stupid book.'

She didn't even reply.

'You think you're so fine and clever and all because of a few fancy books,' he went on, 'but you're just the same as any other girl except that most ordinary girls have more sense than to open their legs to some fellow who won't marry them, and get a baby in their belly and then chuck away the chance of a good marriage. I'm not the fool you think I am, Mattie, I know that much.'

Having retrieved the last of the torn pages from a clump of nettles, Margaret grew calmer once again. 'I did not mean to call you a fool,' she conceded, 'but you had no right to spoil something that wasn't yours.'

'You should have listened to me. It's all your fault, you know.'

'Maybe, maybe so . . . but it wouldn't have done, anyway; we would only have made each other wretched. Better to find that out now, don't you think, rather than after, when it's too late.'

Ambrose did not know what to think. He was filled with anger yet he could still feel the round shape of her breast against his palm: he had discovered the ease of physical possession, and yet now she was more distant from him than ever before.

'You'll be sorry.'

To his amazement she actually laughed. 'Not nearly so sorry as I would have been if . . . Go on home, now, Ambrose, I must try to mend my poor book.'

He wavered: rage, frustration and disappointment – a furnace of confusion was burning within him. Surely now was the moment when she would mend their quarrel with soft words, but no – she had seated herself once more on the trunk of the fallen pear tree and was smoothing the yellow sheets of paper against the fabric of her skirt.

'I'm going now,' he growled, still waiting, and then when she made no move he burst out, 'Just don't say I didn't warn you, that's all! No one will want you now, you and your damned bastard child!' and, yanking his horse away from her feast of fallen apples, he swung into the saddle, clapped his heels into her sides and clattered off down the track that led to Porthew, with never a backward glance at the farm, nor a word for John Pearce who ran out at the sound of horse's hoofs, ready to congratulate his future son-in-law.

Margaret lingered in the orchard, arranging the pages of her book with meticulous care. She could hear voices raised in bewilderment – 'Why did he go in such a hurry?' 'Where's Margaret to now?' 'What has happened between them?' – and she knew she should be afraid of the storm that was sure to break about her head, should be anxious for a future that was now bleaker than ever. There was bound to be trouble, worse than before. She knew she had been an empty-headed fool to throw away the chance of marriage to a respected neighbour. But just for the moment, even as she caught sight of her father, red-faced and furious, blundering across the yard towards her, she revelled in the sweet relief of not being betrothed to Ambrose, and she clutched the pages of the book to her chest and prayed that her foreign mother, whose book had so unexpectedly ruined her chances of a respectable but altogether desperate marriage, would at least have understood the necessity for her folly.

3

By the time Margaret set off for church at Porthew the following Sunday, the news of her disgrace and the certainty that she was not, after all, to marry Ambrose Treloar, was all over the district. The young lad who worked the bellows at the forge had overheard Ambrose trumpeting his disappointment to his father (Ambrose's voice was so loud when he was angry it was a wonder the fishermen out at sea did not hear him) and had wasted no time in passing the information on to his father's aunt, the same Mistress Calwodely who had given the girls the fine knitted stockings on fair day, while she in her turn was quick to tell every old woman of her acquaintance and anyone else who would stop to listen.

Margaret's calamity offered a satisfying mixture of bawdy, moral and mystery. The outrage was caused not by the fact that she was pregnant and unwed – plenty of brides went to the altar a good deal plumper than they should have been and no one thought the worse of them for that – no, what outraged local convention was that Margaret appeared to have no intention of either naming or marrying the father (and there was no lack of speculation as to who he might be) nor, since she had rejected the eminently suitable Ambrose Treloar, anyone else either.

Opinion was divided. There were many who attributed Margaret's fall from grace to her foreign mother. It was well known that all foreigners were shameless and wicked: Spaniards were said to eat live babies and to do unmentionable things to their own mothers, so Heaven alone knew what a Dutch heretic was capable of. With such parentage, Margaret's eventual ruin had been only a matter of time.

Others in the village, while not denying that bad blood played its part, preferred to emphasise the importance of her superfluous education. After all, a girl who recited Latin in public and read heathen texts that no one else could understand was bound to absorb ideas that were not at all fitting to a female. A girl had no business being interested in such things and John Pearce had only himself to blame for having allowed her dangerous education to continue.

Margaret, usually unaffected by the opinion of others, could not fail to notice the hostility which greeted her in Porthew that Sunday. The same people who had been so friendly at the Feast Day now ignored her greeting or turned away, whispering. Lizzie, who had chosen to accompany her, was almost in tears by the time they reached the church and Margaret was heartily glad that Tom had stayed at home. Her father had refused to attend, saying the shame of it would kill him, and Mistress Pearce hardly ever visited Porthew since the journey was torture for her painful joints.

The two girls took their places in a pew towards the back of the church and after a little while two elderly sisters who spoke only Cornish and lived in a farm so remote that gossip seldom reached them, took the empty places beside them. Margaret held her head high and tried to ignore the faces turned to stare, the whispers just loud enough to be heard – 'No better than she ought to be for all her cleverness,' 'And Ambrose such a fine great lad,' 'It only goes to show you can never trust a foreigner' – but she wished she could hide the green and yellow bruising on her face, wished she could creep away and hide herself altogether.

The beginning of the service was delayed by the late arrival of the Suttons. Parson Weaver, anxious and vague, fidgeted at the front of the church, opened and shut the huge black-bound Bible, exchanged a few words with the three musicians who were to accompany the singing of the psalms, scowled his disapproval at his own chattering brood of children.

Loud voices in the churchyard and the clatter of horses' hoofs heralded the arrival of the Suttons. Now, at last, attention was distracted from Margaret and Lizzie. Sir John Sutton, grey-haired and frail, entered first with his new wife, the woman who was said to have used witchcraft to snare him. Tall and ungainly, she had a strong angular face and a masculine way of walking: Margaret recognised her at once as the mother of the gaunt-faced Richard Treveryan.

102

He, however, was not in the party, although Nicolas Sutton, making no attempt to lower his voice as he entered the church, came in accompanied by two young ladies and a younger boy. When all the Suttons, their guests and hangers-on, had settled themselves in the three front rows, the service began. To Margaret, isolated and anxious as she was, it seemed to last for ever.

Clouds had gathered over the sea and people were talking of rain before nightfall when the good folk of Porthew, with Parson Weaver's exhortation to charity still ringing in their ears, followed the Suttons' party from the church, and stood around in chattering groups before going their separate ways. Only Margaret and Lizzie stood alone. Not far away, Ambrose Treloar's ginger head emerged above a close group of family and friends.

'Let's go home now,' said Lizzie miserably, 'there's no sense in staying here.'

'You go on ahead. I'll follow later.'

'I'll not leave you here alone.'

A woman's voice, shrill and emphatic, drifted over from the cluster of people around the Treloars: 'I reckon you were lucky to escape, Ambrose – always better to stick to one of your own,' and another, 'Repent at leisure – someone will learn the truth of that before long.'

Lizzie slipped her hand into Margaret's and held it very tightly.

At that moment Meredith Hocken, the dizzyingly handsome Mr Hollar by her side, caught sight of them and hurried over.

'Mattie! Lizzie! I've been looking for you everywhere.' Her voice was raised so that all around could hear. 'I was half-afraid these wicked harpies might have torn you limb from limb by now, but here you are, safe and well as ever,' and she put her arms around Margaret and hugged her.

Margaret would have gladly died for Merry in that moment. Her friend's plain, moon-shaped face seemed almost beautiful, transformed by warmth and defiance. She turned to her cousin.

'William, you remember my good friends Mattie and Lizzie from Conwinnion. They are very fussy about the company they keep in this paltry town, but I know they'll make an exception for us.'

William Hollar inclined his head in the echo of a bow and said with careful courtesy, 'I'm delighted to hear it, since I remember them well. I'm hardly likely to forget a young lady who taught me that there is love of learning to be found even in a place such as this.'

Margaret, receiving the gift of his unexpected smile, allowed herself, just for a moment, for the first time that day, to relax. She said ruefully, 'Love of learning and foolishness go hand in hand, I fear,' but he only looked puzzled and she guessed that, being new to the neighbourhood, he had not yet heard the scandal. She felt a twinge of disappointment, having briefly hoped that this stranger was more charitable than the people she had always known.

Merry spoke in a low voice. 'Come back with us and have a bite to eat and we can talk.'

'Later, Merry. There's someone I must see first. Take Lizzie home with you – she's already had enough to suffer on my account – and I'll follow as soon as I can.'

'Come along then, Lizzie, we'll answer them look for look. Copy my expression, like this, I'm sure we can outscowl anyone,' and Merry, who was not as a general rule overfond of Lizzie, put her arm about her waist as if they were the oldest of friends and guided her through the crowd. William Hollar, with a brief farewell to Margaret, followed them, and his elegance and smiling courtesy were the very things to take the sting out of scandal. Lizzie was so relieved to have found friends at last that her eyes filled with tears and she began to chatter incessantly about nothing in particular and Margaret saw her brown curls bobbing with animation.

When they had gone Margaret slipped away unnoticed and went to wait at the far side of the church.

It was Parson Weaver's habit, when the service was over, his congregation dispatched and the musicians paid off, to spend a few moments alone in the church before returning to the dubious delights of his family. His fiddle was kept wrapped in a cloth in the vestry, also a pitcher of ale with which he liked to fortify himself both before and after the long service. On this particular Sunday he lingered rather longer than usual before coming out and closing the door behind him. Just over thirty, thin and with dark hair, he had a face that fell just short of handsome. All the ingredients were there, but there was something sketchy, almost unfinished in his appearance, as though whoever had fashioned his face had begun with high ambitions but lost interest in the job before it was all done. He noticed Margaret, sitting alone on an old tombstone and walked over to her at once.

'Hello, Margaret,' he said, 'are you waiting to see me?'

She turned to look at him and for the first time he noticed the ugly bruise on her cheek. 'Heavens, child, what's the matter? Have you been fighting?'

'Can I talk to you privately?'

Parson Weaver's face was troubled. 'Of course you may, my dear. Come into the vestry.'

Margaret rose and followed him along the path to the church. The vestry smelled of damp stone, candlewax and whitewash. Margaret looked about her thoughtfully. By the far wall ladders and leather buckets were stored for use in case of fire and beside them were the vast books in which the church wardens kept their detailed records of parish accounts. Many of her happiest childhood hours had been spent in this sparse room beside the church, studying and reading Latin with her teacher.

Puzzled by the sadness in her face, Parson Weaver put his arm about her shoulders and said gently, 'Tell me, Margaret, it's not like you to be in a brawl. What have you been up to?'

'I wasn't . . . it's not . . . my father was . . .' She was floundering, unable to find the words – and then they tumbled out in a rush. 'I'm nearly three weeks late, Parson. I must be carrying your child.'

'What? It can't be . . . damnation!' Quick as an eel he strode over to the door and shot home the bolt, then looked into the church to make sure it was empty. He came back slowly. 'Are you sure of this? Easy enough to make a mistake, you know.'

'Pray God I am wrong. This last week I've been sick every morning. But I know you can help me.'

'Wait, wait, give me a moment,' and he turned from the look of absolute trust that he saw in her eyes. 'This is so unexpected . . . I never . . .' He paced up and down, took up his tankard to drink some ale, put it down again untouched, paced some more. Finally he stopped pacing and glared at her.

'An attractive maid like you has many admirers, no doubt. It must be hard at times to be certain which of them is responsible.'

She stared at him. Her expression of trust gradually turned to one of incredulity, angry disbelief. 'Parson, you know full well there was none but you!'

'Hush now, don't grow excited. I did not mean to say – only that – here, calm yourself, take some ale. Hush now.'

He put an arm about her shoulders and guided her to the bench; above all he was terrified lest she run out with her story into the churchyard and the village beyond. To think that only an hour ago he had been lamenting, as he did almost every day, his dreary existence as parson of this godforsaken parish. Suddenly the monotony of the daily round seemed a precious blessing indeed, and one which could all too easily be forfeited by scandal. Yet even as he put an arm around her shoulder he felt the warmth and softness of her, and desire rose up in him like a flame. God curse her for a wanton child, he thought; was it any wonder that he had been led astray by her winning ways?

'Have you –' he hesitated, 'mentioned my name?'

She shook her head wearily. 'Of course not. I had given you my word. But my father was angry that I would not tell him.'

The parson's relief was so intense that an icy sweat covered his body. 'You poor child, what you must have suffered. But you know I never doubted you.'

She gazed at him, troubled, but still trusting. Her face had all the freshness of childhood and for a moment he felt a surge of hope: it seemed impossible that her young body was ripe enough to bear a child; surely this whole episode would prove to be only a false alarm, something they would doubtless laugh about in a week, a month. No longer afraid of betrayal, already half-convinced the danger was passed, he began to feel that familiar surge of longing course through his body. He put an arm around her shoulders once again, as though to comfort her, but this time his hand was trembling. His earlier fears were swept away by the warm sweet smell of her and his fingers stumbled over the coarse fabric of her dress to touch the soft skin at her throat.

She twisted away from him and rose slowly to her feet. 'Parson, can't you see the trouble I'm in? You always said you would be able to help me and I have no one else to turn to now.'

He stared at her helplessly. 'What do you want me to do?'

'I thought you would have an answer.' She frowned. 'My father says that since I will not tell him who is responsible I am to be turned from the house. But I don't know where I can go.'

Go? Parson Weaver hardly saw the frightened girl standing before him in her grey dress and her heavy shoes; instead he saw the petal softness of her skin, could almost feel the dark warmth of her yielding and he knew only that he must not lose her.

'My wife needs help at home,' he said, 'no doubt we could arrange for you to live with us. As her maid . . .'

'And as your mistress by night?' He had never seen her angry before, leastways not with him. 'Are you gone mad, Parson Weaver? You always said that you could help me but now you have only dreams and insults to offer! And I have always trusted you!'

Her reproach hit its target. 'Margaret, wait —' A long pull on the ale and the mist in his head began to subside. 'Of course, I have it now. First we must take steps to clear your good name.'

She drooped, her sudden anger evaporating. 'I fear it is too late.'

'No no, not at all, I can . . . a husband, you must get a husband, a man who can claim the child for his own. If it is arranged now and you — you allow him liberties, he may well believe himself the father. Yes, yes, that's it.'

Her grey eyes were very wide, staring at him. 'You mean I should trick him?' she asked.

'Not exactly trick, of course not,' he was beginning to be irritated by her obtuseness, 'I'm trying to be practical,

Margaret, for your sake. Have any of the young men around here shown a particular interest in you?'

'I'll not marry Ambrose Treloar,' she said sullenly, 'no one will make me marry him.'

'Ambrose, the very one. He's had his eye on you for years. Come now, don't look so downhearted. He'll suit you well enough, in the circumstances.'

She shook her head. 'It's no use. He's asked me already and I said no. I won't change my mind.'

Now Parson Weaver was hissing with vexation. 'Don't be such a fool, Margaret. What in God's name induced you to turn him down?'

'I meant to say yes, really I did. Father went to see his family and it was all to be arranged. But . . . then we were talking and he tore my mother's book, for no reason except he's too stupid to understand it. He tore it! I'd rather die than marry him.'

'A fine mess you've made of things. I've a good mind to wash my hands of this entirely. Good heavens, girl, whatever possessed you to go quarrelling with Ambrose when he would have had you? Plenty of time you'll have to think of your damn pride and your books when your father turns you out of doors and you've a howling infant to consider. You were happy enough to get yourself into this state –'

'Would you pretend I did this alone?'

'That has nothing to do with it, as well you know. What's done is done and there's nothing to be gained by idle recriminations. It's hardly my fault that you saw fit to quarrel with Ambrose and let him slip through your fingers. I can't be blamed for that, can I?'

He heard his voice rising in a high whine. Good God, he thought, I am ranting on like my own accursed wife – and he almost hated Margaret for being the cause of his self-disgust.

She was staring at him, as if seeing him for the first time. Her face was pale, drained of all hope. 'If you cannot help me, then I don't know what I can . . .'

Her voice faltered, faded into silence and the parson felt his rage vanish. He had no weapons against her helplessness, her long habit of trust.

'I will help you, Margaret, I promise.'

He put his arm around her and drew her close to him, a

father and protector once again, as he had been through all her childhood. Margaret sensed the difference in his touch; she let her forehead rest against his shoulder and her body shook with harsh dry sobs.

'I'll think of something,' he assured her again, 'trust in me, Margaret, I promise you I'll think of something.'

And Margaret clung to the tatters of her old illusions because there seemed to be no choice: without the parson, she must face the future utterly alone.

When Margaret, somewhat reassured, had pulled her shawl about her shoulders and set out to join Lizzie at Mistress Hocken's house, the parson returned to the vestry and stayed there a long time, his head in his hands.

'Look after my child . . . don't let these ignorant fools make her one of them. Teach her . . . take care of her for me.'

Was it only six years ago that the dying woman had whispered her last request to him? He was new to the parish then, and had still nursed hopes of bringing some light and comfort to this remote and desolate corner of a remote and desolate county.

'I'll look after her, Mistress Pearce. And I'll teach her as long as she wishes to learn.'

As promises go, it was easy enough to keep. The girl was so quick and eager that their lessons were a constant pleasure to them both. Would that his vows of ordination had been as easy to keep. Before the end of his first year in Porthew his early idealism had been corroded by the realities of parish life. He had imagined himself bringing solace to the sick, comfort to the dying . . . but he had not reckoned on the stench of the hovels where so many of his parishioners suffered and died like abandoned animals; the putrid smell of fever and gangrene and soiled bedding. The awesome beauty of the service for the dying decayed into nothing more than a meaningless jumble of words in the squalid sickrooms of the poor.

During the years of disillusion his only solace was the young girl, Margaret. From week to week their lessons together were the bright moments that made his life tolerable.

'Take care of my child . . .' It had been only too easy; she hungered for knowledge, revelled in the discoveries the texts revealed.

But it was not only knowledge that she hungered for. After her mother's death there had been little tenderness for her at home. It was not that her father was deliberately unkind, simply that in his weary struggle for survival it never occurred to him that his daughter required more than food on the table and a bed to sleep in at night. Only Parson Weaver recognised her craving for affection, her pleasure when, as they were studying, he might put his arm around her waist, or stroke the long pale hair that lay across her shoulders.

The habit of touching . . . how slow the changes and how natural they seemed . . . he could not tell by what progression it had occurred but he only knew that one day, one bitter morning during the last winter when the wind howled in the yew trees and Margaret arrived half-dead with cold and wet and he took her on his knee and put his arms around her to warm her as he had so often done before, he became aware that it was a woman's body he was holding in his arms, that the girl who leaned against him so trustingly was round and full-breasted, ripe as a summer peach.

He pushed her away and she was distressed by his sudden coldness. He was strict and formal in his dealings with her and sent her home early. But his imagination burned with the taste of her lascivious innocence and at night in his dreams he thought of Margaret and his hands caressed his wife with a tenderness she had believed was gone for ever – yet in the morning he was angry and restless and thought of nothing but Margaret and found numerous reasons for visiting the farm at Conwinnion.

Their lessons became an agony for him. When he endeavoured to be formal and remote, Margaret, baffled and hurt, used every means to coax him back to his former easy familiarity. He almost convinced himself that she knew his mind – and wanted the same. His resistance did not last long.

'Don't be afraid, Margaret, trust me . . .' he had groaned as he lost himself in the morning newness of her body. And she trusted him as she had always done – but afterwards

110

she barely spoke, returned to her home and did not come again to their lessons for a full three weeks.

Those weeks had been a kind of torment for him. By night he yearned for her and by day he cursed her for a wanton temptress, but in the end he could stand it no longer and he rode over to the farm to enquire if she was ill.

'It was a mistake, Margaret, nothing more . . . come back at the usual time, there's a good girl. Everything will be just as before.'

She was doubtful, yet she longed to believe him . . . she had missed his tenderness and his need of her just as much as she had missed the learning.

How many times had he possessed her? Three or four at the most. God knows, he had tried hard to resist, tried to recapture the old sweet innocence of their friendship but it was vanished for ever.

And now the damnable fecundity of women had trapped him once again.

Oh, if only Margaret had not been so trusting, if only she could have had an ugly cast in her eye or some disfigurement which would have made her less desirable, if she had not so tempted him with that loveliness, half child, half woman . . . God knows, he was frail flesh and blood, not stone.

God knows . . . Parson Weaver was not unduly troubled by his Lord's omniscience. The God he worshipped was, by and large, a kindly and forgiving deity. Never one to cast stones himself, if he could avoid it, Parson Weaver did not expect his Heavenly Father to bear a grudge against him either. His flock, however, was a different matter altogether. He had little hope of forgiveness from the good people of Porthew. If this affair should ever become public . . .

His bowels turned liquid with fear at the very thought. Oh, there were clergy, he knew, who kept mistresses for years and got away with it – but for him it was not even a possibility. If he lost his standing in this community, if he was to see scorn in the eyes of these people he had for so long despised, if he lost his self-respect, he would lose all. He must act at once to find a husband for Margaret, to see her tidily settled before this business destroyed him. What a fool she had been to reject Ambrose Treloar! But he could still arrange it – he had some influence over the local families and if he promised Margaret to keep her books safe for her then she could still visit him from time to time . . .

It was the only sensible course. When he left the vestry that Sunday his mind was quite made up – and yet the days passed and still he did not visit the Forge. In his imagination he could see Ambrose and Margaret on their marriage bed, he saw the young blacksmith's huge and calloused hands touching her where only he had touched before . . . and each day he found some fresh reason to do nothing.

Superficially at least, the routine of Margaret's life continued unchanged. She washed and scrubbed and baked and tended the animals; but all the time she was weighed down by a sense of betrayal, and a gnawing fear of the future.

'Trust me . . .' the parson had said. And she had trusted him as she had trusted no one else. He was the only person with whom she could talk freely and keep the memory of her mother alive. Her lessons were for her a mark of loyalty towards the foreigner whom everyone else was only too eager to forget. She considered herself fortunate that the parson, whom all the parish treated with respect, was prepared to be her teacher. Why should she doubt him? He told them that Moses stretched out his hand and the waters of the sea drew back to let the Israelites pass through – and they believed him. He told them that Jonah lived for three days in the body of a whale and no one dreamed of contradicting him. It was his voice that read the words of the royal decrees, telling men what they must and must not do. He had taught Margaret almost the whole of what she knew and if he said, 'Trust me,' then she trusted.

She knew now that her trust had been misplaced . . . Perhaps she had always suspected it but had closed her mind to the problem. She did not choose to forgo the rich delights of her studies with the parson, and besides, she too had grown used to the feel of his hand upon her hair, the habit of touching had been a familiar pleasure for too long, making it hard to believe that changes so subtle – the altered pattern of his breathing, his lips against her mouth, rather than her cheek, his hand sliding down from her shoulder to her breast – could mark the step from innocence to corruption.

Hard to believe . . . because she had not chosen to believe. She had only spoken the truth when she told Ambrose that she had never loved the father of her future child; the parson had for long been the window through which love could be glimpsed in the words of a poem, but him she had seen only as a friend and a teacher. His caresses had never ceased to be tender and the sensations they aroused in her, although disturbing, were not altogether unpleasant. She was confused and unhappy – but life without her lessons was a more dismal prospect still.

'Don't be afraid, nothing will happen . . .' And she had been lulled into believing that the man whose voice could save a newborn infant from the eternal torments of damnation could protect her from the consequences of his desire.

He could not. When she spoke to him of her pregnancy he had been as fearful as the most ignorant ploughboy caught in his crime.

And now she was trapped.

Those days of late September and early October were slow and strange. Margaret felt herself to be in a kind of limbo, a state of half-being, a stillness of waiting like the heavy calm that precedes summer thunder. About a week after her meeting with him, Parson Weaver rode over to the farm and she ran out eagerly to greet him. 'Have you thought of anything?' He shook his head and told her to be patient. But after he had spoken privately with her father and Mistress Pearce, no more was said about turning her out, and she was grateful at least for that.

Afraid, she yet longed to escape. Her imagination teemed with the tales of the heroes, their journeys and adventures . . . and here she was with nothing but a loveless marriage to look forward to – and so far, not even that. At times she was almost on the point of running away to make a new life for herself – surely somewhere a place existed where she and her baby could find a home – but she had heard too many stories of unwed girls being hounded from one parish to the next, because no one would take the burden of a bastard child, and she knew from the tales the sailors told that the whorehouses of Plymouth and Fowey were full of women who had once been girls like her, girls with a desperate hope and nowhere else to go.

Only at night was it possible for Margaret to clutch at remembered happiness. Ever since Ellie Roberts and her daughter had come to live at Conwinnion, Margaret had loved the hours of darkness. No more the loneliness of her single bed, now there was Lizzie, warmth and giggling. And later, when Tom grew too big for a crib in his parents' room, he was given a truckle bed beside their own, but seldom had reason to use it. For if he was cold, or frightened by thunder or had had a bad dream, or if he simply wanted company, then he scrambled in beside his two big sisters and listened to the stories they loved to tell.

Lizzie, from her mother, knew the gossip from generations back: who had killed his eldest brother to inherit the land and in which well the body had been hidden; who had lost her wits because she had been forespoken and who had entered a pact with the fairy folk and would never grow old, nor bear children neither; who was a thief and who a fool. From her mother and her grandmother, now dead, Lizzie knew the old stories from the time when Cornwall was peopled by giants and elfin folk, stories of the little men who lived in the mines and the strange music that the tinners heard at Christmastime; the stories of ghosts and witches and riderless horses on the moors on moonlit nights; of young girls whose drowned lovers returned to lure them to a salt-sea grave . . . and of infants who died before they could be baptised and wandered the earth in torment of spirit causing mischief wherever they went.

Margaret told the stories, perhaps more ancient still, of the heroes of Greece and Rome. Like the Cornish, theirs were tales of love and war, betrayal and a restless hunger for land and power, the ties of families and tribe . . . but the stage on which they acted out their dramas was so much grander, and made mysterious by distance. Zeus with his thunderbolts could destroy cities, and Poseidon's rage or whim might overturn a whole fleet of ships.

And as the children grew more drowsy and their voices could hardly be heard above the sound of the rain falling

114

on the thatch above their heads or the wind in the elms at the far end of the meadow, so their stories began to mingle and blur: King Priam in his palace began to resemble Sir John Sutton in his fine new house, the sacred grove of the ancient Greeks was none other than the copse on the edge of the moors which no traveller would willingly pass through at night, and Ambrose Treloar's grandfather, he of the ox-defeating fame, who had once pulled a full-grown tree up by its roots, gradually assumed the short tunic and sandals of Hercules himself.

One morning early, when the fields were white with dew, Mistress Pearce bestirred herself and set out with a small basket over her arm, returning some time later with a selection of green leaves and stalks. All day she was busy by the pot over the fire and the kitchen so reeked with pungent smells that John Pearce was obliged to take his midday meal in the yard. In the evening she was finished: she handed Margaret a mug filled with a warm and greeny liquid. 'Drink this,' she said, and Margaret did so, although the taste was more foul than any she could have imagined. All through the night she vomited, and her step-mother observed with satisfaction, but in the morning, though her throat burned and her guts ached, she knew, with the growing instinct that was binding her to the life within her, that the child had not been shifted. No more was said between them.

A few days later, as John Pearce led Juno homewards by way of the headland from a visit to Dawkins Mill three miles away, he saw a sight that made him pause, and shiver with an uncanny remembrance. He almost thought it was his first wife standing there, that tall figure on the cliff's edge, clothes billowing in the wind that blew off the sea. Beyond her, huge black clouds were building up in the west and the sea was restless, stirring, like ripe blackberries in a cauldron.

He paused, thinking to go and speak to Margaret in her loneliness and distress, but then he knew that he would not be able to find the words he wanted and he remembered the shame she had brought him, so he walked on back to the farm and pushed the thought of her from his mind.

4

A rabbit, motionless in the short grass in the middle of the meadow. Crouched, seeking refuge in stillness. Dun brown against the brown dead stalks of grass and weeds.

The horseman saw it first. On his wrist the hawk remained heavy, unfocused. Then the change . . . that faint but powerful alteration in the pressure of her talons on his gloved hand, an eager tension that throbbed a message of elation through his veins, heightening his own awareness, making man and hawk see and respond as one. Steady now . . . the bird was still young and lacked experience.

A slight movement of his wrist and she stretched and raised her wings and then she was away and the man's heart flew with her as she swooped down to skim the tips of the bracken. And in the same instant the rabbit broke from its stillness as if from a trance and raced away towards the shelter of some gorse. Rowing with powerful wingbeats the hawk was gaining on the rabbit. '*Le rameur*' the French called their goshawks – oarsmen, rowing birds, and it was an apt description.

The goshawk was almost over the rabbit and lowering her talons for the kill when suddenly the animal flicked its body in mid-bound, doubled back and hurtled towards a low hedge. Taken by surprise the bird lost her rhythm for a moment, shuddered and all but landed, but then she swerved, regained her speed and followed her prey once again. Then, just where the weeds grew out from the hedge, her talons struck home in a turmoil of feathers and fur.

Richard Treveryan had dismounted and was running across the open meadow. The rabbit was large and kicking and the young bird was unaccustomed to the kill. She watched his approach with huge yellow eyes. He pulled a knife from his belt and plunged it into the rabbit's skull, skewering it to the ground. It kicked once, twice – and then

116

was motionless. A sweet relief flushed through Treveryan's body as he scooped out a choice morsel of warm brains to reward the bird.

Footsteps on the grass behind him, a man's voice breaking the spell. 'That was well done: the bird will prosper now, right enough.'

Treveryan turned slowly, as though waking from a dream, and stared with empty eyes at the young groom who came forward from the nearby copse where he had stood to watch the sport.

'She will get her confidence now,' said Treveryan, speaking almost with difficulty. For a brief span of time his spirit had flown in such harmony with the bird that he had forgotten he was a man; he had shared the terror of the victim, had known what it was to be a winged killer, all his being fixed on one cruel and deadly purpose.

Only slowly, and with huge reluctance, did he return to consciousness of his own body, two feet planted in the damp grass of the meadow and an old hunger in his belly.

He became aware that Mark, the young groom, was watching him, and waiting.

'Shall we go on?' Mark spoke eagerly. His duties had been all pleasure since Treveryan arrived with his dedication to hawks and hunting, and for all that the young gentleman was considered strange and unpredictable, Mark found he liked him well enough.

'No.' The word was a sighing acceptance of present reality. 'You are far from home and it is late. Take her . . . and be sure she quietens slowly. I shall go on alone.'

Mark took the goshawk on his wrist and with his free hand scooped the mess of rabbit into the leather pouch that hung from his waist.

Frowning, Treveryan watched the thickset figure of the groom trudge across the meadow and disappear into the woods beyond, then walked back slowly to his waiting horse.

When he was hunting, all thought and energy was dedicated to a clearly defined end. Each time he traced a peregrine in her cloud-high circling, or threw a merlin to catch a lark, or, as now, when he shared in the ruthless pursuit of the goshawk, there were no questions or confusion in his mind: his energies were purified, almost as though the sport produced some transformation similar to the alchemist's art.

But now the bird had killed, the spell was broken, the alchemy was all undone.

He mounted his horse and set off along the track without bothering to consider where he was or where he might be going. He had no wish to return to the house his mother now called home. The sun was already low in the sky and a smattering of rain was blowing in from the sea. A south-westerly wind was rising, a buffeting wind but not a cold one. He could ride all night or find shelter in a hay-rick somewhere . . . either prospect was more attractive than the odious constrictions of Sir John Sutton's house at Rossmere.

For a long time he rode on, all unaware of his surroundings until, just as the sun had begun to sink behind huge banked-up clouds in the west, he recognised the tiny cluster of buildings he was approaching.

He decided to explore.

Jennie Treloar had just settled to her spinning when the stranger rode up to the farm. Hard work and poverty had aged her much beyond her twenty-five years; her features were blunt and homely and when she smiled – which she did surprisingly often, considering the circumstances of her life – her pink gums were all exposed above her sturdy teeth. She did not smile now as she said anxiously, 'Someone's come.'

Her husband looked up from his loom and then frowned as the stranger, scattering children and chickens, splashed through the mud and into the yard.

'Treveryan,' he muttered. 'I was wondering how long before he showed his face.'

Joseph Treloar reached for the sticks that were propped against the wall by his loom and struggled to his feet. Like all the Treloar men, like his younger cousin Ambrose, he had massive shoulders and powerful arms. But in him the strength was a kind of mockery. His legs had been crushed in a boyhood accident when a cart laden with beach stones had overturned and pinned him to the ground; by the time he was freed he was considered lucky to escape with his

118

life. He could walk, after a fashion, but in a world that was challenge enough for the able-bodied his life since had been a relentless struggle. Though his eyes were honest, his lips were a hard line, stubborn, refusing to give way to pain or hardship . . . and the arrival of Richard Treveryan filled him with unease.

Jennie, going to the doorway to stand behind her husband, watched the newcomer with interest. She had heard much about the Treveryan family in the years since her marriage but she had never seen one of them before. She had heard tell of Richard's father and his grandfather, both hard men, and drinkers too. But this evening she saw merely a tall youth with untidy dark hair and bony, irregular features, nose and chin too large, cheekbones prominent and shadowed, eyes watchful and restless, a mouth that twisted now into a kind of reluctant greeting.

'Welcome, Mr Treveryan.' Joseph had a voice that boomed deep from the vast cavity of his ribcage. 'We had been expecting to see you. Johnnie, take the gentleman's horse and look after her for him.'

A small boy, no more than nine or ten years old, ran forward as Richard swung a long leg over the saddle and slid to the ground. The young boy, gazing at the mare with eyes that shone with wonder, stepped forward and took the reins as though afraid they might break. He had never touched a real fine horse before, only nags and donkeys, still less been given charge of one.

'Walk her for a few minutes,' said Richard, 'and give her some water – clean water, if you have it.'

Gently, very gently, the boy led the mare away.

'Won't you come in, Mr Treveryan, sir,' said Jennie, 'I can find you something to eat.'

Richard glanced beyond them through the low doorway: the room they lived and worked in was cramped and dark, with little furniture beyond the loom and a couple of stools. There was a smell of chickens and stale food and the old sour smell of poverty.

'We can talk in the fresh air well enough,' he said coldly. 'Perhaps if you have some bread and cheese . . .'

The woman's face lit up with a smile of anxious pleasure and she disappeared into the house. From within came the sound of children's voices: 'Mother, who is that gentleman?' 'What's he come for?'

In the yard, the two men maintained an uneasy silence.

Huge shoulders and shrunken legs: there should have been something grotesque about the cripple who stood before him and looked up suspiciously from under heavy brows, but in fact it was his dignity that Richard noticed most, dignity and pride.

Perhaps that was what made his opening words sound awkward in his ears. 'You were late with the rent again at Michaelmas.'

'I was,' Treloar's gaze was unflinching. 'I paid it all once I was able. This has been a hard year for everyone, corn the price it is and no one paying proper money for cloth. Jennie works all the hours God gave and would work more but we often have a hard time just to find a meal for the children each day. It's not for want of trying if we're sometimes behind with the rent, you can be sure of that.'

There was no whining in his voice, no pleading – just a simple statement of fact. This misshapen man commanded respect.

Richard said nothing.

'Do you want to look around, Mr Treveryan? You were but a lad when you visited last.'

A shrug of the shoulders indicated his landlord's agreement.

There was pitifully little to see: a few outbuildings, a hovel for the pigs and sheep, a muddy pond, half a dozen twisted fruit trees. And among the scarcity, the signs of Jennie Treloar's hard work: a neatly stocked vegetable patch, fresh hay for the animals, even a few late flowers growing beside the house.

'We do what we can,' said Joseph simply.

'You no longer use the old Hall, then?'

'Only to shelter the animals. The roof collapsed in my father's time but by then it had been empty for years. Too big, too cold. The little house suits us well enough.'

The Hall, all that remained of the original dwelling, had been built in the old style from grey stone: four square walls, narrow windows, a single high-beamed room inside.

Now the walls were crumbling, the rafters were open to the sky and pigeons skirmished in the curtains of ivy.

'It must have been a fine place once.' Richard was thoughtful. Even on a grey-shrouded October dusk such as this the place had an air of serenity that somehow took him by surprise. He could understand now why this, alone among his father's properties, had been in some way his favourite, the only one, so it turned out, to have been neither mortgaged nor sold. From here the land sloped down to the sea, just over a mile away, and the path of a stream that ran down the valley was marked with alder and willow. There hung about the place a sense of journey's end.

'A good location,' Richard commented.

Joseph was watching him closely. 'You'd not be thinking of selling, would you?'

'I don't think so. Not now. Who knows, I may want to live here myself, one day?'

Joseph was about to reply when Jennie, a troop of children following and peering round her skirts at the mysterious stranger, came along the path towards them. He said nothing, but watched his landlord with uneasy eyes.

'Here's food.' Jennie was smiling anxiously as she spoke and her pink gums were revealed. 'It's not much I fear, but –'

The shy eagerness of her manner touched Treveryan. Her offering was so pitiful after all: a wooden platter with a hunk of black bread, a piece of cheese pale and past its best, a mug of ale that looked little better than brackish water, a couple of pitted apples.

He noticed the woman for the first time, her kind eyes, her careworn face. What kind of life must she have here, he wondered, marooned with a pack of children and a crippled husband? He smiled down at her for the first time. 'Thank you, goodwife Treloar. This is most welcome.'

Jennie beamed. Why, she thought, when he smiles like that you can see that he's hardly more than a boy, this ogre we've all lived in such fear of.

She was about to speak when her husband said roughly, 'Take the children back to the house. Mr Treveryan and I have business to discuss,' and when he was certain his wife

121

was out of earshot he said in a low voice, 'You know my father got this place for three lives, Mr Treveryan. It goes to my son after I'm gone.'

Richard, eating hungrily, made no sign that he had heard.

'You wouldn't be thinking you could turn us out, would you?'

'I haven't considered yet what's best to do.'

'This is my home, Mr Treveryan. My home and my family's home. God knows, it's hard enough as it is, if we were to lose this place, then . . . but our right is legal. We've the evidences to prove our title to the land. I can show you –'

'You can keep your scraps of paper, Treloar. I've no interest in them.' Suddenly bored, Richard threw down the platter among the brambles that grew beside the path. At once, half a dozen scrawny chickens seized the scraps. Without another word Richard strode past the old Hall and back towards the yard, too fast for Joseph's painful hobble to keep up. 'Hey, boy!' he shouted. 'Bring me my horse.'

Joseph came into the yard just as Richard swung up into the saddle, and Jennie ran out to stand at her husband's side.

'It's money that matters, Treloar, not bits of paper. Make sure you've the rent in full by Lady Day or –'

But the last of his words were lost in the noise of his horse's hoofs and the evening wind that was blowing now through the oak woods behind the house as he rode from the yard.

At a little distance from the farm the track curved sharply and Richard, glancing back for a last look at the old Hall and the valley that stretched down to the sea, found himself looking instead at Joseph and his wife. She had put her arm around his waist as though the effort of long standing had been too much for him, and his arm lay across her shoulders. Their heads were inclined towards each other as together they shepherded their little group of children back into the house.

They were gathered in the doorway when the fire within flared briefly and he saw them all silhouetted against its warm glow. Not understanding the source of his sudden anger, Richard rode on through the darkening woods.

*　　*　　*

The wind that had chased Treveryan's parting words from Joseph Treloar's hearing blew also around the walls of Sir John Sutton's house at Rossmere. A fine October wind, south-westerly, crooning the year's lament at summer's passing, it shook brown leaves from the elm trees and the sycamores and chivvied the skirts and chased the hair of the serving-girls as they ran across the courtyard from kitchen to hall with huge platters of food for their master and his family and guests.

The food was served with exaggerated solemnity, the flushed faces of the maids forced into expressions of unnatural composure. Usually they chattered quite unaffectedly as they handed round the food, but on this particular occasion there was a constraint in the atmosphere which warned them such freedoms would be ill received. They assumed it was the presence of the guests, Sir John Arundell of Trerice and the two ladies from Camborne way, that made everyone so puritan-solemn. So they pursed their lips and avoided each other's eyes and burst into fits of giggling as soon as the heavy doors had closed behind them.

Sir John Sutton, seated at the head of the long table, eyed his plate with dyspeptic suspicion.

'This venison is not cooked.' He looked accusingly at his wife. She did not appear to have heard him. Seated at the far end of the table she was half-listening to something that Sir John Arundell was saying – but she also had the expression of someone who is listening, waiting . . . and in some dread of what might be heard, what might appear.

Nothing made Sir John Sutton so instantly peevish as to be ignored. He tapped his knife against his plate and his voice was edged with irritation as he repeated, 'Isabel. This venison is not cooked.'

'Then try a little pie. These quails are most tender.'

'I particularly wanted venison. It's not too much to ask, I should have thought, just sometimes to be served a plate of well-roasted meat in one's own home.'

Lady Isabel Sutton met her husband's gaze, then quickly lowered her eyes again. Although she remained outwardly calm, her inner spirit raged. How those milky, plaintive eyes had deceived her. She had believed herself to be marrying a genial invalid. Now she saw his greying hair and delicate features, his unceasing concern with his stomach and his bowels, as a gross deception to hide a ruthless will.

She laid down her knife. 'I'll send Joan for some more.'

'You'd best fetch it yourself.'

'I'm sure that Joan –'

'You.'

He smiled at her almost humbly as she stood up and his guests thought, poor old man, how gentle he is.

He said, 'I did expect an *old* wife would have learned how to manage the kitchen properly. I do so hope you'll try harder in future, my dear.'

Isabel Sutton took her husband's plate and, with a flick of her wrist, tossed the offending venison to a couple of hounds which were waiting by their master's chair.

As she walked to the door his voice continued, still gentle and confiding, 'The gossip in Porthew, so they tell me, is that my new wife is trying to poison me. If the food continues in this manner I shall begin to think they are right. Heh, heh, heh,' and Isabel heard his humourless wheezing laugh as she stumbled across the courtyard in the dark.

Poison him, she thought, grinding her teeth in a fury, my God, if only I could.

She had been so thankful to achieve this marriage, had thought herself so lucky – but heavens, how bitter luck could prove to be. When Christopher Treveryan, her late and not at all lamented husband, had died of a seizure in the spring, she had been looking forward to a well-deserved and tranquil widowhood. Galling indeed had been the discovery that she was virtually penniless. She could still taste the bile that had risen to her mouth on that gleaming April day when the lawyers gave her the news that blighted all her hopes: their home in Bodmin and all the eastern farms mortgaged and no money, no money at all to redeem them; their western lands all sold to raise money for the Newfoundland venture – the Newfoundland misadventure as it turned out to be – all her hopes of independence now rotting somewhere as food for crabs and fish on the Atlantic sea bed.

And for Richard, their only surviving child, nothing remained but the farm at Trecarne, still being worked by that useless cripple Treloar – and the rent from that wretched heap would not provide the boy enough money to keep a decent horse, let alone live as a gentleman's son should. Not that she had wasted much sympathy on him: her own situation had been at least as desperate. She had two choices: either she could live with her brother in Plymouth and be for evermore at the mercy of his spoilt wife or she could marry again before the prestige that attaches to a gentleman's widow had been all swallowed up in the general news of her poverty. She chose to marry – and she worked hard to persuade Sir John that she was the best person to provide those comforts he had so sorely missed since his first wife's death.

At least, she had thought grimly, in those weeks before their marriage, as she began to glimpse the steel will hidden in the sickly body, at least those comforts will not include those of the marriage bed. Ever since the pain and violence of her first wedding night she had had a horror of the sexual act and had done everything in her power to endure it as seldom as possible. Their home near Bodmin became famous for the prettiness of the serving-girls.

Disillusion swiftly followed her second marriage. Not only was her husband potent but, what made it much worse, he considered himself to be a religious man, of the Puritan persuasion, and was not to be distracted by the charms of the servants. Isabel quickly came to dread the nights at Rossmere, the boredom and the ridiculousness of it all, the uncoordinated dance of their withered flesh. During the day she had only to breathe a hint of his old-man's smell of patent medicines and sweats to be overcome with disgust.

'Your venison, my dear.'

He hardly heard. He was telling his guests the story of his part in the Cadiz venture. Already, Isabel thought, I must have heard that story a hundred times.

She resumed her seat at the other end of the table but her appetite was gone. She took a glass of wine and, as she replaced it on the oak surface of the table, she noticed that her hand was trembling.

Sir John Arundell, seated on her right, enquired politely, 'And has your son returned to the university? I had expected to see him this evening.'

125

'He's here. He's . . . hunting.' Isabel paid scant attention to her guest. Above the noise of the wind she thought she heard horse's hoofs, a single horse. Her fingers gripped the stem of her glass.

Far off, a door banged in the wind.

Nicolas Sutton, his face flushed with wine, and handsome in the candlelight, was listening too. 'I thought that might be Richard.'

'Yes.'

He eyed his step-mother curiously, noticing her pale face and taut mouth. 'You have surely warned him already?'

'I thought . . . he left so early. No.'

'You mean then that he's no idea?'

'None, unless you told him.'

Nicolas let out a whistling breath. 'And I thought he knew. Now there'll be the devil to pay.'

Isabel Sutton sat very straight in her chair. Her long face was grim. 'I doubt he'll come back tonight,' she said. 'He may stay away for two or three days. He often does.' And inwardly she prayed, three days, please God as long as possible. Not him as well.

'There's a rough surprise waits on his return,' said Nicolas cheerfully. 'I find I am almost sorry for him.'

But Isabel Sutton did not feel sorry for her son, and never had done. He would look out for himself, as he had before, and survive too, as he always did, even if others, more precious than he could ever be, perished in the process.

Richard Treveryan awoke in that hour before dawn when there is light in the world but no colour. Somewhere in the branches above his head a thrush had just begun her morning song and a bunch of sparrows squabbled through the brambles that spilled out from the hedge. There was a gnawing hunger in his belly and his limbs ached with the cold and damp.

For a short while he lay there, propped on one arm, listening to the birdsong and the distant booming of the waves. The wind had dropped during the night: there was a scent of mist in the air and the promise of a mild October day. An old dog fox, tired after a night's hunting, padded slowly across the meadow, not noticing him at all.

Slowly, a remembered contentment crept through him, warming his body like the glow of a turf fire. At some stage during the night, as he lay and watched the clouds and the stars and tried in vain to banish that image of Joseph Treloar and his wife as they stepped across the threshold of their home, he had reached a decision. He smiled and lay back on his arms, the cold and hunger all forgotten. Today, tomorrow at the latest, he would set in motion the events which would create around him that closed circle of loving he had until now only glimpsed at from outside. The only question that remained was why he had waited so long.

A great rush of energy coursed through his veins and he stood up and ran down to the stream, hunger and cold all forgotten. He splashed his face and drank some water, which was numbing cold, and his mare whinnied a greeting from across the meadow.

He was smiling as he set off, riding down narrow lanes while the sun rose like a huge opal among the scattered clouds in the east. He called a greeting to the labourers who made their sleepy early-morning way to the fields and, just below the downs, he passed a group of vagrants, Irish by the look of them with their thin faces and their rag-tag children, and instead of the curse they had expected, he threw them a coin.

His mare sensed his eagerness, her ears flickered and there was a lightness to her gait; when they reached the downs, Richard gave her free rein and she galloped into the morning sunlight.

Richard could not remember a time when he had not known Alice Laniver. The families that made up the Cornish gentry were not numerous; all were known to each other and most were related. Alice maintained that the four-year-old Richard had tipped her from her cradle in a fit of rage. He had no memory of the incident. He did remember taking a small dark-haired girl to the edge of the cliffs near Stowe to spy out a pair of nesting peregrines on a ledge below them; he also remembered the beating which followed (their host, Bevil Grenvile, had himself wielded the whip) when the child mentioned to her nurse how she had passed the afternoon.

The growing friendship between the two children seemed

more often than not to result in trouble for either or both. When Alice insisted on joining the boys in their games it invariably led to disaster. If Alice was stranded on the apex of the stable roof, too terrified to come down, it was Richard who was blamed for having led her into mischief. Not that Alice was slow in his defence, wailing loudly at the injustice and cruelty of it all. Her loyalty often led to fresh misfortunes. On one occasion, when Alice had fallen into the horse pond and Richard, being blamed, had been confined to his room with no food, Alice had, at some considerable risk, climbed along the outside of the building and in through his window and, sobbing with anguish at the thought of his near starvation, had smuggled him copious supplies. But had then been too panic-stricken at the drop from the window ledge to the ground, to make her escape. When he was discovered to have lured the girl to his room, Richard was sent home in disgrace.

And then, eighteen months ago, Richard had returned to Cornwall after an absence of nearly two years, to discover his childhood accomplice on the brink of womanhood and, miraculously, as ardent in her devotion as ever. Nothing in his life so far had led Richard to expect devotion from anyone; at first he was wary. Gradually, however, his resistance had crumbled in the face of her avowals of undying love. He did not mind that her words went far beyond what was correct in a young woman not yet betrothed: he cared only that her sincerity was revealed by every look and touch and smile.

By common instinct, perhaps because their earlier alliance had always brought down the wrath of their elders, they took care not to make their growing feeling for each other public. In the spring Alice had begun to press for a formal betrothal but Richard had hung back. Partly it was his natural love of secrecy. Whatever ties there were between him and Alice in those early days of courtship they concerned no one but themselves. Later, of course, there must be lawyers' talk and money arranged, all the paraphernalia of two families joining: he knew this and accepted it but – not yet, not yet. For just a little longer let there be only the simplicity of their tenderness for each other.

Now, as he rode back towards Rossmere, he knew that

the time for secrecy and waiting was past. In the next day or so Alice and her mother were to visit Sir John Sutton: this time the whole world must be told of their happiness.

Richard was smiling as he reined his mare to a halt above Rossmere, its rooftops glinting in the early-morning sunshine. Over the past hundred years each generation of Suttons had added to the original few buildings and the result, although it had emerged without plan, was harmonious and graceful, as much a part of the landscape as a grove of trees or an outcrop of granite rock. Richard, looking down now, appreciated it with a stranger's eye – to Nicolas, he knew, these few acres of stone and field and wood were dearer than any human ties.

Richard's mare whinnied and stamped, impatient now to be home. 'Very well then.' Richard slackened the reins and she leapt foward and cantered down the hill and between the avenue of newly planted limes towards the stable-yard.

As he passed through the archway Richard slipped from his horse and Mark, the young groom who had gone with him the day before, caught the reins and led her away to be rubbed down and fed. The other men were intent on examining a dainty bay mare, a horse he did not recognise at all. They paid scant attention to Richard's arrival. The young man had spent so much time with the stable hands and the farm labourers that they almost regarded him as one of themselves – an error frequently shared by the gentry.

'Whose mare is that?' asked Richard. 'I've not seen her before.'

'Mistress Laniver's. Went lame on the journey over.'

'Then Mistress Laniver is here? Already? And her daughter too?'

'That's right, sir. Arrived yesterday, towards evening . . .'

But already Richard was bounding up the steps that led into the back of the house, through the kitchen snowy with goose feathers and across the courtyard that led to the hall where visitors were generally received. Disappointment that he had already missed some precious hours of her visit mingled with a surge of pleasure that she was here already, in this house . . .

He burst open the door into the hall with such energy

129

that the pistols and calivers rattled against the wall and the two women seated by the fireplace gave little startled cries of surprise.

'Why, Richard.' His mother had turned pale at his entrance and the expression on her long and bony face was almost one of fear. She was a tall, angular woman and her movements were mannish, awkward. Both strong and nervous at the same time she appeared often to be on the verge of an exasperated outburst.

Her companion was also in her early forties – but there all similarity ended. Round and smooth as a pat of butter, all was softness and curls, lace falling over ample contours, rings on fat fingers, a perfume of lavender and violets. Like Lady Sutton, the visitor displayed alarm at Treveryan's entrance.

Isabel Sutton was the first to recover. 'How dare you enter so abruptly?'

'Where is Alice? I thought she wasn't expected until later today.'

'Their plans were altered suddenly and they arrived last evening. But you have not greeted Mistress Laniver yet.'

Richard smiled down at his future mother-in-law, a lady who had always reminded him of a sleek and plump little duckling with her large brown eyes and dark curls greying somewhat – so like Alice and yet so utterly different.

'Good day, Mistress Laniver. And where have you hidden your daughter?'

'Well, I haven't, of course . . .' Mistress Laniver's voice was soft and droning like a bumblebee on a summer day – and given the chance it flowed on almost as continually. 'She's . . . I . . .' For once at a loss for words, she glanced an appeal to her hostess.

'Really, Richard,' his mother chided and her voice was harsh, unmusical. 'You are always so impetuous. And where on earth have you been? Sleeping under a hedge, by the look of you.'

'How very perceptive of you, but never mind that now. Where is Alice?'

'I do declare there are leaves still on your coat. Are you mad to come bowling in here, hair mussed up like a tinker boy's? I can't imagine what –'

'Mother, will you stop your confounded twittering and tell me where I can find Alice?'

Both women fidgeted, said nothing. Richard burst out, 'For God's sake, she's not ill, is she? She's not –'

'No, no, certainly not.' Mistress Laniver laughed her plump little duckling laugh. 'She's very well indeed, never been better in fact.' She laughed again and glanced nervously at Lady Sutton.

'Good. Where is she?'

But the women's anxious glance towards the door that led into the adjoining room told him what their words would not.

'Why then –'

As he strode towards the door Isabel Sutton leapt to her feet and tried to block his way.

'Richard, wait! She isn't –'

Impatiently he pushed her aside and threw open the door. 'Alice.'

A pleasant room, south facing, filled with sunshine and with fresh strewn herbs scenting the floor. Miss Alice Laniver was seated on a settle near the window and Nicolas Sutton was at her side. They looked as though they had been alone together for quite some time.

'Alice!' With two steps Richard was in front of her and, catching hold of her hands he had pulled her to her feet. 'I'm sorry I wasn't here when you arrived but Nicolas has been taking care of you, I'm glad to see. How are you? The way they spoke, I thought you must have been ill. But you look pale. Alice, you're trembling . . .'

Staring up at him with huge eyes Alice moved her lips but did not speak.

'Richard –' Nicolas began.

'No, let me.' Lady Sutton had entered the room behind her son and now she seized the chance to intervene. 'I should have spoken sooner and this wretched muddle is all my fault. Dear heavens, I don't know how to say this for the best.'

Treveryan, smiling down at Alice Laniver, was oblivious to his mother's agitation.

Her confusion was making her angry. 'Richard, for the love of God will you pay me some attention when I'm speaking to you. You can't . . . there isn't . . . oh, the devil take it; Alice is to marry Nicolas –'

Without letting go of Alice's hands, still smiling down at her, he replied coldly, 'Don't mock me, Mother. Your teasing is in bad taste.'

'It's God's own truth, I swear it. 'Tis all arranged. Nicolas and Alice. Sir John wished it so, and Alice's family too. No one wanted to tell you in case you made trouble while the final details were being settled and anyway, if you will go out hunting from morning 'til night and never tell a soul where you are going or what you're doing –'

'Stop babbling, woman.' His black eyes flickered and instinctively he tightened his grip on Alice's hands. 'Is this insanity true, Nick? Did you know of this?'

'Everyone knew except you. It was only . . . and let go poor Alice's hands. Can't you see you're hurting her?'

'And what's that to you? I could break every bone in her body and you wouldn't . . . you've never cared for her at all. My God! Alice,' and still he gripped her hands, 'Alice, for mercy's sake, say something. Tell me this isn't true!'

But Alice seemed quite unable to speak. She glanced helplessly at Nicolas, then down at her imprisoned hands.

'Richard,' it seemed to Treveryan that Nicolas's voice was reaching him from a huge distance, 'release her at once. You have no right . . . and if you ever did it's too late now. There's nothing you can do.'

Richard flung down the girl's hands and banged his fists down on the table, making a pewter jug leap into the air. 'My God, I don't believe it!' But a babble of women's voices rose around him like a cloud of flies and told him it was true.

His lips were drawn back in a strange and crazy grin of disbelief as he turned abruptly and stepped the brief distance to the window. 'I should have guessed . . .' he muttered, 'I never imagined . . .' He fell silent, controlling himself.

Mistress Laniver laughed nervously. 'Well, that's all settled, then. No harm done. I always thought, Isabel, that you were exaggerating the –'

'Can someone get that tiresome baggage out of here?'

132

'Well, really!'

'Richard, you shouldn't speak –'

He turned swiftly. 'Alice, oh Alice,' the girl was trembling as he took her gently by the shoulders, 'how have they made you agree to this? Only trust me, what's done can be undone.'

Nicolas burst in angrily. 'Leave her alone. Everyone is perfectly happy with the arrangements; it's nothing to do with you any more.'

'Get out of here. Alice and I must talk – alone.'

'You cannot –'

'Get out, I say!' Suddenly Richard was all energy, bundling Nicolas and the two women towards the door. 'Get out at once and let me speak with her. Damn you all, get out!'

'Don't push me!' Nicolas blazed back. 'How dare you tell me what to do in my own house! I won't let you speak with her alone, not now she's –'

'Get out, Nick, you've done enough damage already.'

'No!'

Richard caught hold of Nick's sleeve to thrust him through the open doorway but Nick flung his arm up, evading his grasp and the next minute they had tumbled into the hall, struggling and punching.

Mistress Laniver screamed. 'Help, someone! Call Sir John! For mercy's sake, Isabel, he's killing Nick!'

'Leave them be. They'll have to settle this eventually.'

The settling did not take long, for Nick was no great fighter at the best of times and Richard was in an unholy rage. He flung his opponent down on the floor and would have set upon him again had Isabel not restrained him.

'That's enough, Richard. Quick now, talk with Alice if you must, but don't imagine you can change anything – their marriage is all arranged.'

Nicolas was groaning. 'Oh my poor head, I think my jaw is broken. You must be mad to attack me in my own house.' He looked up spitefully. 'You're only tolerated here, you know. I should have you thrown out now. And then where would you go? You've nowhere to live, nothing. Nothing! My God, you even look like a vagrant. And you really expected to marry Alice? And take her to live at that hovel at Trecarne, I suppose. Ha!' He began to pull himself up painfully. 'Fists and fight is all you have left, Richard. Alice is for me.'

'No!' Isabel dragged at her son who was about to lunge at his opponent again. 'Don't be a fool. Talk with Alice while you have the chance. Go on, she's waiting. And maybe she can make you see some sense.'

Richard was staring at Nicolas and his expression was murderous. Gradually his features softened, his harsh breathing grew easier.

'Alice, yes.' He spoke in a low voice, distracted. Then, with a last contemptuous glance at the red-faced figure still crouched on the floor, Richard went quickly into the other room and closed the door, pushing the bolt home behind him.

5

Alice Laniver was standing by the empty hearth, her head tilted at a defiant angle; a beam of October sunlight that slanted through the window touched her brown curls with a shimmer of red. No one had ever called her a beauty, although her figure was good – slim yet rounded with high firm breasts and a slender neck. She had dark eyebrows and her eyes had always been richly expressive, yet her mouth was clumsy, upper teeth protruding slightly to rest on her lower lip and her manner had always been awkward and impetuous. Richard realised, in the brief moment of silence that filled the room once he had secured the bolt in the heavy door, that until now he had considered it almost an act of generosity on his part to allow this gawky girl to lavish her affections on him.

He cursed himself now for an arrogant fool. All that he had ever desired was standing there by the carved mantelpiece. She was wearing a dress of rose-coloured cloth, fine lace at wrists and throat and her brown eyes, which avoided his, were huge . . . frightened? defiant? excited? And so beautiful. Richard thought that he had never truly loved her until this moment.

'Alice, tell me this isn't . . .' He broke off, the words sticking in his throat.

Her chin jerked a little higher. 'You should know better than to fight with Nick,' she said imperiously. 'You will have to learn prudence, Richard.'

'Prudence, is it?' He fell silent a moment, considering. 'You never used to talk me of prudence. What has happened to you, Alice?'

'I am to marry Nicolas Sutton.'

'Don't mock me.'

'It's the truth.'

'Then it's a shabby truth, Alice, since you know full well

you don't care for him at all. Your family have decided on this marriage – and we always knew they loathed me. Somehow they have forced you –'

'No!'

'How then? And why am I the last to be told?'

'You were away so long that I couldn't . . . and anyway, you're wrong. No one forced me.'

'No? Not with whips and locks maybe, but there are other methods just as effective. Oh Alice, was it really so easy to forget about me?'

'I thought that *you* had forgotten. You hardly ever wrote.'

'But you knew my feelings would never change.'

'Your feelings? How was I to know what they were? But it's too late now, even if I wanted –'

'No! It's never too late, at least, not yet. Oh, if only you had got a message to me somehow. But there's still time for us to be together as we were before. Oh Alice, surely you remember how it was?'

At his question a strange noise escaped her, somewhere between a sob and a groan, and though she hung her head and turned away, Richard saw that her lashes were damp. In an instant his arms were about her shoulders and he pulled her to him.

'Don't be afraid, Alice. I'll never let them force you against your will.'

She raised her head to look at him and her brown eyes were swimming with tears.

'There,' he said, 'I'm with you now,' and he bent and kissed her tenderly and an energy flowed between them. Yes, he thought, this is it, this closed circle of loving, our future filled only with each other inside this space where no one can reach us. 'My own sweet Alice –'

'Oh Richard, if only –'

'Don't speak.'

He pressed his lips against her mouth and sensed the resistance draining from her and in its place was the passion he had known, her craving and her pleasure. But then her body seemed to slide from his arms, like water, like something he could never hold – and he watched, not understanding, as she prised herself away from him.

'Richard, I can't . . .' she was quivering from head to

foot, 'I must not . . .' With a huge effort she dragged herself across the room and went to stand once more by the fireplace. Her face was flushed and her eyes were glistening.

'Alice –' His arms ached to hold her again.

'No, don't come near me.' She spoke in a low voice. 'Whatever might once have been between us, it is now at an end. You *must* understand that I am to marry Nicolas –'

'Why?'

'My father desires it. And my mother. I cannot oppose their wishes.'

He laughed bitterly. 'And what of your wishes? What of mine? Do they count for nothing?'

Unable to control the gesture any longer, she stamped her foot. 'Oh, why did you have to return now and spoil everything?'

'*I* spoil everything?' Richard's face was strained but he spoke in the steady tones that the stablemen used to quiet a highly strung animal. 'Listen to me, Alice, they have made you agree to something that you know in your heart will only make you wretched. But now I'm here with you again and we can untangle this together.'

'It's too late, the arrangements have all been made,' and then, as if remembering something, she added soberly, 'it is my duty to God to do as my parents wish.'

Richard snorted. 'Good heavens, girl, do you honestly believe the Almighty cares a twopenny damn for anything so trivial? I'll tell you this, though, it would be a sin against love and against God if you were to marry Nick, you know you have always despised him.'

'Stop! I think Nicolas has many fine qualities.'

'Indeed? So why did you used to tell me you thought he was conceited and spoiled? Odious even?'

'Oh, you're so good at twisting everything I say for your own advantage. You'll do anything to make me miserable. How can you talk of the time when we were ignorant children? Can't you realise that everything has changed?'

'Everything?' A gleam came into Richard's eyes and his voice was suddenly very quiet. 'What exactly do you mean by everything?'

'You know my brother died in March.'

'Yes?'

'He was my father's heir, may God rest his soul. Now that he is . . . no more, I am to inherit all my father's wealth.'

Richard frowned, still not understanding. 'All the more reason, surely, why you may now suit yourself. Alice, when you said just now that everything was different, I thought perhaps you meant to say that you no longer love me.'

Alice did not answer and a waiting stillness filled the room. Outside, from the hall, came the sounds of gathering commotion, voices raised, fists pounding against the door.

'Well, Alice, and do you love me still?'

She turned away. 'Not in the same . . . I mean, you know I . . . all right then, yes. Yes, I do . . . But it's different now –'

'For pity's sake, have courage now. All our future happiness depends on this. Alice, look at me.'

'We can't talk now, Richard, they're breaking down the door.'

'Let them batter down the house.' He tilted her face and saw the panic that glittered in her eyes. 'Very well then, but we must talk properly together soon. I'll wait for you this afternoon at the mews. Will you come?'

'No, I must not.'

'Why so timid?'

She put her hands over her ears. 'They're making such a noise. We must let them in –'

'Then say you'll meet me this afternoon.'

'No, I can't . . . oh, I don't know what . . . yes, very well then, I will.'

'At three o'clock.'

'Yes.'

He smiled then, and briefly stooped and kissed her. Again their mingled strength and hope, her loving gathered in his arms. As he breathed the flower-water fragrance of her hair and sensed her quickened heartbeat he knew he could not, must not lose her.

'We'll fool them yet, you'll see.' And then, still smiling, he strode to the door, pulled back the bolt and a tangled heap of servants who had been pushing at the door, tumbled into the room. Behind them stood Nicolas and Lady Sutton.

And Sir John, his eyes bulging with rage, brandishing a horse-whip.

'How dare you, sir, how dare you!' His voice was shrill and trembling. 'You should be whipped for such an outrage! To attack my son, and in my own house! A whipping, that's what –'

Richard plucked the whip from the old man's shaking hands and threw it into the corner of the room, narrowly missing a couple of scullery maids who had come to witness the commotion. To their astonishment he seemed to be in a high good humour.

'Your hospitality is most touching but I regret that I must decline the honour,' and he laughed as he made a mocking bow towards Sir John, 'and in the meantime God be with you all.'

He looks as though he might be seized by a fit of apoplexy, Richard thought as he strode out into the October sunshine. And good riddance if he is.

The buildings at the back of any country house, the stables and the mews, had always been Richard's preferred location. Here among the soft voices of the men at their work he could relax and discuss the real business of the day – a troublesome horse or an ailing hawk. As a boy he had only ever known real happiness with his father's servants: he loved the orderliness of a well-run stable-yard, the mingled smells of leather and hay, dogs and soap and dung. He had been quick to learn all the older men could teach him: how to coax a foal that would not nurse, how to mend a broken feather with an imping needle, how to know when a bird was ready to fly again after the moult.

And there were other lessons too, ones that were perhaps more important though he was hardly aware that he was learning them: he had discovered that the truly gifted grooms and falconers won all their battles through kindness and patience. A horse whose spirit was broken was of no use to anyone and it was common knowledge that a hawk will die sooner than submit to a cruel master. Children and servants might be beaten and, in his father's house, they frequently were, but animals – never. So the angry and rebellious boy learned to persevere, to remain calm in those

139

small hours of the night when his nerves screamed with frustration and lack of sleep and every muscle in his body yearned to thrash the bird who so obstinately refused to accept his mastery: he learned to be more obdurate than a mere bird could ever be. And he learned that his will could make him win.

His instinct told him that when Alice talked to him here, away from the restrictions of the house, she would be free to share his vision of their future.

Seated on an upturned barrel and watching a family of kittens at play in the afternoon sunshine, he began to understand how Alice had been persuaded to this alliance with Nicolas Sutton. Oh, it was easy enough to disobey family pressures in trivial things, to go out riding in the time allotted to sewing-work, to refuse to help her mother in the kitchen and the still room. But to rebel over their choice of husband, to contradict all the dictates of upbringing and expectation – that was another matter altogether.

He blamed himself. He had been so certain of her devotion that he had grown lazy. He should have ridden over to see her as soon as he returned from university following his father's death. No doubt she had interpreted his absence as proof of his dwindling affection – and that too had helped to weaken her resolve.

And the reason for his absence? There was his loathing of her parents' house for one thing, that monstrous gloomy edifice where she was watched constantly by her jealous father's servants and where there was never the slightest chance of time alone together. And he had never believed it necessary: her passion had been so sure, so strong, he never imagined it might fade – and if he did succumb to any doubts then they were quickly dispelled by her letters, tender, secret, constant in the love they showed. The last had arrived only the previous week.

Now, watching the three kittens as they chased at leaves and pounced on each other's tails, he forced himself to examine the possibility that her love for him had weakened. Certainly her words had been confused, but then he remembered the unmistakable message of her kiss, the passion in her eyes. No doubt that her feelings were as strong as ever.

It was clear that this was just another of those many occasions when Alice's boldness had evaporated suddenly, landing her in a situation from which she could not free herself unaided. Well, in the past he had caught her as she fell from the back of a half-trained stallion; he had guided her to safety from the heights of a summer sycamore. Surely now he could find a way to extricate her from this farcical alliance with Nick.

He was certain of one thing: Alice must never marry Nick.

It would be a vile travesty of love. She had never cared for him at all. As for Nick, whose first and only true love was his home at Rossmere, his attitude to his future bride could not have been more cynical. When his father had mentioned that they were considering approaching the family of a young widow from Saltash, Nick's only comment was that so long as she was rich enough to pay off the family's debts, then he would marry whomsoever they chose.

His eyes scanned the path that led back to the house. What could have delayed her?

He was on the point of returning to the house to search for her, when he caught sight of a woman coming down the grassy path towards him. Not Alice, however, but his mother, striding like a man, her greying hair streaming behind her from under her coif.

'Richard,' she said, a trifle breathless, 'thank God you're still here. Come towards the meadow gate where we will not be overheard. No, don't argue. Alice is not coming. She asked me to give you this.'

He stared at her.

'Go on, Richard, read it.'

Mechanically he unfolded the letter. His eyes scanned the page.

Richard, it grieves me more than I can say to have to write these words, but write I must. I cannot see you now, there would be no purpose in it. I am betrothed to Nicolas Sutton and there is no undoing what we have done. Nor would I wish it otherwise. This has been my own free act. You must try to forget the childish things that once we said and did – Alice L.

The paper shivered in his hand as Richard stared at it. Cold despair was inside and all about him.

'Who forced her to write this?' he asked in a low voice.

'No one did, I swear it. When she told me of your plan to meet here, I offered to help her, but she would have none of it. She said she had no wish to see you again. She asked me to bring this letter instead.'

'You're lying. You're afraid to let me see her because you know full well she'd never agree to this travesty of a marriage. Where is she now? I demand to see her.'

'It's too late. She is betrothed already. Even if she wanted to she couldn't go back on her word now. You've lost her, Richard.'

'Betrothed? But how?'

'Sir John called in witnesses at noon. It was all perfectly legal, you can be sure of that. The marriage will probably take place before the New Year.'

'And Alice . . . was she . . . ?'

'She was delighted. I know you're too stubborn to accept this, but she has been as much in favour of this marriage as anyone.'

'How in God's name can you expect me to believe that? When I know that she has always loathed Nick, and loves me still!'

'Does she? How do you know? Because of her letters? That tender one she wrote last week perhaps?'

Richard stared at his mother. 'What – ?'

'It was Alice herself who suggested she should continue writing to you while the final details of her marriage to Nicolas were settled. So you would be less likely to get wind of what was happening and make trouble.'

'That cannot be true.' It seemed to Richard in that moment that all the colour had drained from the world.

His mother regarded him dispassionately. 'Delude yourself if you must, Richard, but luckily Alice has more sense. Oh, I daresay she was fond of you, in fact she told me as much herself. But feelings can change, Richard, and if she's a girl not much given to strong emotion then so much the better for her. Surely even you can see that your marriage to her had become impossible.'

'Why?'

She sighed. 'When Nicolas said that you had nothing to offer a girl like her, he was only speaking the truth. You're a poor man now. Your father ruined us both and you must shift for yourself. Since her brother's death Alice is the sole beneficiary of her father's wealth, so she knows she can expect the finest match in the county.'

Richard's laugh was bitter. 'And that means Nick?'

'Who better? He has the Sutton name and in time he'll have Rossmere. She knows she's done very well for herself. Her family may have money but she can never forget that her grandfather was selling furze for a living while the Suttons were entertained at Elizabeth's court. She has good reason to be content.'

'Content?' Richard had a sudden image of a young girl, a girl as Alice had been not so very long ago, seated on a fine dark horse, her face radiant with laughter and courage. She faced him for a moment, then whipped her mount with the reins and set off at a gallop, away, away . . . the wisdom of childishness gone for ever. He rounded on his mother. 'Good God, woman, her mind has been poisoned by all your talk of pounds and portions and rents and God knows what else besides. What of her affections? Do they count for nothing at all?'

'Alice is under no illusions about Nick. She knows he'll settle down in time, and learn to shoulder his responsibilities.'

'Ah, my God, the way you talk. Responsibilities. And what about the wealthy widow he was so fiery keen to marry last month?'

'The lady from Saltash? Sir John hopes she will agree to marry Stephen. It is simply a question of altering the name on the arrangements.'

'Your husband appears to be in a damned hurry to see his sons married. Stephen is scarcely seventeen.'

'Sir John is anxious, yes. He worries about his health, you know. He wishes all to be tidily settled.'

'So he can die in peace?'

'It gives him peace of mind.'

'May he rot in Hell. Why should he have peace of mind when his sole aim is to wreck the lives of those around him?'

'That is no way to speak of the man who is now my husband.'

'You loathe him as much as I do.'

She shrugged. 'You have no power against him. Wait, Richard, just one word more. After your outrageous display this morning he is determined to throw you out –'

'I would not want to stay here anyway.'

'Try to think calmly, for once in your life, and consider your prospects. You have nothing, Richard, only the farm at Trecarne and that is as good as nothing. You must fend for yourself from now on; you could try your luck as a soldier on the Continent – or some say there are fortunes to be made in the Americas.'

'The Americas now? You're mighty eager to be rid of me.'

'That's right, Richard. You've made trouble enough for me in this house as it is. I don't know why I am helping you now except that it would humiliate me to see my own son flogged by servants.'

Richard's eyes narrowed. 'You are too soft-hearted. But what is this talk of flogging?'

Lady Sutton looked uncomfortable. 'I overheard Sir John . . . 'Tis lucky for you the servants are all away and he has been obliged to delay his plan. But you must leave before they return. Now, listen. My brother in Plymouth might help you. I've written him this letter for you explaining your situation. And here is some money. Enough at least to buy you a decent set of clothes. You'd be lucky to find employment as a stable-hand dressing the way you do.'

Richard was silent. Plymouth, the Americas . . . Why not the gates of Hell as well? It mattered little now that Alice was lost.

'It seems I have no choice. But first I must see Alice, just once more.'

''Tis impossible. She and her mother departed over an hour ago and Sir John has provided her with an escort – Matthias and Walter and a couple of the lads from the farm. They have instructions to see that she arrives safely – at any cost.'

'Does he fear she might try to escape?'

His mother returned his look steadily. 'Only that you might attempt some rash abduction. Walter has a pistol – and there is nothing would give Sir John greater pleasure than to know you had been killed trying to intercept their journey . . . I know you are tempted to try it. But wait – Alice asked me to give you this. She said you'd understand what she meant by it. It's a curious charm, I've not seen its like before.'

Richard took the pendant, an intricately worked piece in some silver alloy that he had purchased from a foreigner at Oxford. It lay now in his palm, extinguishing hope.

The final proof, if proof were needed, that Alice's rejection of him had been her own decision. That the armed escort was indeed to protect and not to imprison. 'This shall be our secret, yours and mine, ours together,' she had confided when he gave it to her, 'by this token we shall always be together.' He had never guessed that 'always' might have an end, might be, in fact, no more than a few brief months.

'So,' he said at last, 'she's gone.'

Numbed by loss, light-headed, he walked away towards the house, and as he passed through the stable-yard he commanded Mark to prepare his horse for his immediate departure.

The little group of riders entered Helston by late afternoon. For the first hour or so they had travelled at unusual speed but now, with a sense of danger passing, they allowed their horses a steadier pace.

Mistress Laniver, who abhorred any form of exertion at the best of times and who was now a mass of aches and pains, demanded of an unkind God why the simple matter of arranging a daughter's marriage should be such an unmitigated trial. Alice, however, sat proudly on her borrowed gelding and was quite oblivious to personal discomforts.

Their own two servants rode ahead, Timothy the groom and Giles, her mother's serving-boy. And behind them were four of Sir John Sutton's fiercest-looking manservants and one of them, the wild-looking fellow they called Walter, even had a pistol in his belt. If she had been in any danger of

145

doubting her newfound importance then this impressively armed escort would have quickly reassured her.

Of course, she wished no harm to Richard, loathed violence of any kind . . . Yet she half-hoped to see a solitary figure following them at a distance. It would add to the romance of her position. In her imagination the pistol was fired towards him (missing, of course) and perhaps one of the serving-men could be slightly wounded in her defence. So far the pistol had only been used to scare away a poor half-witted beggar who had wandered in front of their cavalcade on Goonhilly Downs.

But Richard Treveryan had most thoughtlessly failed to appear.

By now Lady Sutton must have given him the letter, told him of the betrothal, handed back the pendant. She felt a pang of real regret at forfeiting the necklace . . . but she consoled herself with the thought that she now had a Sutton family ring on her finger, an ornament of greater value by far, and one moreover which could be displayed in public with pride.

Alice's life had changed hugely in the six months since her brother's death. Her fortunes had prospered. Not that she was an especially mercenary person, far from it. She had always been devoted to her elder brother, and his sudden death from typhus had seemed to have deprived her of a part of herself. Poor Robert, always sensible, always conscious of his duty, sober and upright beyond his years. She knew how much her mischief and teasing had vexed him while he lived . . . so much heavier, therefore, was the burden of her responsibility now to adopt the unchanging values of family, land and position in the county which had coloured his every decision. And, in truth, these values were easy enough to subscribe to now that wealth and status had become hers.

Richard Treveryan, unfortunately, showed scant regard for wealth and none at all for status. At one time, such irreverence had thrilled her, but now she considered herself to be older and wiser and she perceived the wisdom of the traditional view.

Her brother's death had only set the seal on what was already inevitable – she would never consent to marry

Richard. She would have been at a loss to explain precisely why she knew this to be so – she told herself that he was unreliable, so foreign-looking, hardly a gentleman . . . but the simple fact was that in some strange way she feared him. The very qualities that had attracted her to him in the first place now drove her into retreat. She had been drawn by the mystery of him – but she shrank from the idea of marriage, knew she could spend every day for fifty years with him and never be able to read the expression of his dark eyes. He was a youth to flirt with, to fall in love with even, but to marry – never.

She remembered the summers when they had both been guests at the Grenviles' home at Stowe and he had seemed as out of place among that kindly, boring household as a raven who has strayed into a coop of domestic fowls. It was for that wildness that she had loved him – and that same untamed quality ensured she would never marry him.

His passions were so sudden and unpredictable: he laughed when she expected anger, raged when she would have wept; he was affectionate with servants and rude to those who might have been useful to him. She had loved the uncertainty of his company. At some times he was all energy, a driving flame of action, while at others he was moody and slow and spent long brooding hours alone.

Yes, she had loved him. Until he had taken her in his arms that morning she had forgotten how deep her love had gone. Those searching black eyes, his face gaunt and hard . . . and his lips that aroused such craving in her body that the colour rushed to her face when she thought of it now, she who was soon to marry Nicolas Sutton.

With Nick her future was as certain as anyone could hope for in this world where an adored elder brother could be fitted for a new suit of clothes one day and be dead from typhus before they were ready to be worn. Marriage to Nick was the first link in a predictable chain: life at Rossmere, children, social duties and entertaining friends, position and respect.

And love? Well, Nick was a handsome fellow, much better looking, as all were agreed, than Richard. Did it matter then that her heartbeat did not quicken when Nick tilted her chin and kissed her on the lips as their betrothal was witnessed that day? Did it matter that she was still half-hoping Richard might appear on the horizon behind them, that she might once again feel his arms about her waist, hear his voice speak her name. Alice . . .

Enough. She had laughed that noontime when Nicolas kissed her. He had smiled and so had all those present, relief mingling with satisfaction at the sight of such an eminently suited couple.

Yes, it was satisfying. Safe, predictable and satisfying. She had turned her back on the danger, the scent of unknown possibilities, on the intensity of passion that Richard had offered. And now she no longer looked behind her to see if a lone figure was following them in the dusk. As the twilight thickened around them she began to look out eagerly for the candlelit windows of Godolphin House where they were to break their journey. She anticipated their reception with fierce pride. For the future wife of Nicolas Sutton the best room would be made ready, the finest Spanish wines would be produced with which to drink her health, her little retinue would spread the news of her newfound importance through the servants' quarters.

Her eyes were sparkling with happiness and she looked prettier than ever in her life before, that evening at Godolphin House. Her mother, usually so talkative, was bruised to silence by two days' riding, so Alice was free to hold court like a grand lady. The Godolphins, man and wife, looked on fondly and when they retired to their chamber they praised God for an alliance that, while being eminently practical, was nevertheless such an evident source of joy to the prospective bride.

The stable-boy, Mark, had prepared Treveryan's horse for him but it was Nicolas who brought it round to the front of the house. His lip was slightly swollen and his head still hurt where he had fallen against the table but despite his earlier alarm about broken bones he was otherwise unhurt.

Richard, coming through the archway to the forecourt, saw Nick and paused. They had not seen or spoken to each other since their fight. He fingered the carved hilt of his rapier. If Sir John still hoped to avenge the humiliations of the morning then he would find him eager and ready to

148

defend himself. But Nick appeared to be alone. Richard walked forward slowly, dark eyes suspicious.

Nicolas too was uneasy, but all he said was, 'You are leaving already.'

Richard inclined his head. 'Yes.'

'Mark wished to accompany you.'

'I prefer to travel alone.'

'I wish it hadn't happened like this,' Nick cleared his throat and appeared to be uncomfortable, 'not that I'm sorry to be betrothed to Alice, of course not, but still . . . I'm sorry that you . . . well, my father has no right to turn you out in this manner.'

Nicolas Sutton apologising? Richard allowed himself a wry smile. 'Sorry' from such a source was like one of those portents the almanacs were so fond of, cattle born with two heads, winged horsemen galloping across the sky – something beyond the natural order of things.

'I was leaving anyway.'

'It's probably for the best. There's nothing for you here. And I'm . . . well, she's a fine girl.'

'You're a fool, Nick, and always will be. But you're right about one thing at least – there's nothing for me here.'

'You've always been restless. But you must come back and tell us of your adventures . . . we've been good friends in the past, Richard. No sense quarrelling over a girl.'

Richard almost laughed. 'Would you prefer us to fall out over a game of cards?'

'Don't twist my words, damn it. I simply meant . . . not worth spoiling everything because . . . oh, to Hell with you, you know full well what I'm trying to say.'

Richard's eyes narrowed, watching him. Then he looked away, over his shoulder, to the oak woods and the treeless hills beyond. Every nerve in his body flickered with the effort of not hitting the man. He betrayed no emotion. If Nick was too stupid to see that Alice was more to him than just another girl, then it was nothing to do with him.

'You're right,' he spoke at length in an impassive voice, 'no reason to fret over a mere girl. They're all the same under the sheets. I wish you joy of her.'

Nick grinned uncertainly. 'Then don't stay away too

149

long. I'll make sure my father relents soon enough. Come and visit us in the New Year.'

'When the danger is past? You'll be . . .' He was going to say 'married to Alice' but found that the words lodged somehow in his throat and could not yet be spoken, so instead he said, 'Maybe I will.'

He swung up into the saddle.

'Don't forget us, Richard,' Nick began, 'Alice and I will be –'

Treveryan winced. He fiddled for a moment or two with the leather strap that secured his few belongings to the saddle. Then he said in a low voice, 'I'll be back, Nick. But I'll never come begging to your father for his damned favours, never. And I'll return a rich man. Maybe all I have now is that hovel at Trecarne but before I'm finished that will be the finest house in all of Cornwall. You and – you and your wife will be my first guests.' He laughed suddenly, laughter harsh as a raven's cry, 'Let me give you my invitation now. Be pleased to dine with Mr Richard Treveryan at his new house at Trecarne at . . . three, maybe six altogether . . . Michaelmas, say, in six years' time.'

'We'll be there!'

'And while I'm gone you can have that young peregrine Mark's been training. And the goshawk too. Ah, damnation, here's my fond mother and your father too, come to shed tears over my departure, no doubt. If hypocrisy was a sickness there's two would be dead of it by now. But I'm through with play-acting.'

And with that he dug his heels into the mare's sides and cantered away between the two rows of Sir John's newly planted lime avenue.

Nick, watching him go, wondered when or if he would ever see his friend again. He was sorry to see him depart and his apology had been sincere. Richard Treveryan was the only friend he had ever really cared for: all the other young men he knew were characters cast in a familiar mould but Richard was different, and unpredictable. And what would happen to him now? Maybe he would return a rich man in time: it was not unheard of. Or he might be killed in the European wars, be snuffed out by the plague or drowned at sea. And Nicolas would watch for him – and then forget.

'Has that scoundrel gone at last?' A strong odour of patent medicines heralded the appearance of Sir John who stood now in the archway that led towards the stables. He had one hand over his heart, as though afraid any moment it might stop beating.

'Yes, husband, he's gone.' When Lady Sutton watched her son cantering away between the twin rows of saplings, she experienced once again that same intense relief that she had known when the apothecary pronounced her husband finally dead.

Sir John turned to her, offering his compassion like a gift. 'My dear, do not grieve to see him go. It is for the best. And if he should return –'

His wife cut him short. 'I pray God I never see him again,' she said, and strode away quickly, before she might be obliged to explain her most unmaternal sentiment.

Later that afternoon, while Sir John was in his chamber having a mustard poultice applied to his chest, he happened to glance out of the window and noticed a tall figure striding down the walks that bordered the garden. It was his wife. There was something fevered in her endless motion – although they would have been reluctant to admit any similarity, both mother and son were possessed of the same restless energy. Sir John assumed that she was grieved by her son's misfortunes.

He could not have been more wrong.

It was nearly twenty years since she had known what it was to feel maternal love for a child; and then she had been the mother of two boys. The oldest, Philip, was a sturdy lad of three when the younger, Richard, was born. Philip was all his mother had ever wished for: quick and strong and bonny, and he took pleasure in everything. His delight was infectious. When she was with her first-born child Isabel was happier than she had ever believed possible.

Her second child was a whining, plaintive infant and she had no hesitation in putting him out to a wet-nurse in whose care he was reported to thrive. When she herself fell ill of

151

a fever she was persuaded to send Philip to join him until all danger of infection was past.

She could still remember, as if it had occurred only the previous night, the fiendish dream from which she had awoken, washed with sweat and quaking with a terror that had nothing to do with her sickness. She found strength in panic. Taking only one servant, a sturdy old man called Joseph, she had the swiftest horse in the stables made ready and she drove him so fast he was ruined for real riding from that day on and Joseph, following on his steady mare, had been left far behind.

It was just after Easter. Sycamore buds were fat and pink and the hedgerows frothed with blackthorn flowers as she hastened through the morning sunshine to the lonely farm where the wet-nurse and her family lived.

She had half-fallen from her horse and threw open the door into the farmhouse.

Philip was there, lying on the settle, with a face so beautiful and innocent it broke her heart; brown curls and an expression of quiet serenity – a serenity that nothing, now, could ever disturb. He must have died in the early hours of the morning.

The nurse was there too, after a fashion. Unable to face the disaster that had occurred she had drunk herself into a stupor and hardly stirred at Mistress Treveryan's long howl of despair.

A long time had passed since that spring morning, but Isabel knew it would take more than time to erase the horror of that memory. The scene was still fresh-vivid in her mind. The drunken woman lay sprawled near the ashes of a spent fire and across her naked breast, as chubby and contented as an Italian cherub, lay her second son, scarcely out of babyhood yet in her eyes stripped for ever of a baby's innocence. He had his father's crow-dark hair and was ugly as an elfin child. His small hand caressed the slattern's breast and his cheeks were flushed and then, when his mother fell sobbing to her knees beside her dead child, Richard laughed.

That laugh still tormented her dreams. It seemed to her to be the laugh of a survivor, a laugh of triumph, and utterly without feeling for her grief. While the favourite son had sickened and then died this goblin boy had revelled in the drunken embrace of the strumpet whose neglect had killed his brother.

Isabel struck the wicked woman's face and as she leaned closer to her child she could smell the reek of alcohol on his breath. By the time old Joseph entered the room Isabel was hysterically beating her fists against the soft flesh of the wet-nurse, not caring that her infant was too young to crawl to safety and a good number of the blows fell on him.

Unable to restrain her, Joseph pulled the now screaming babe to safety and waited until the passion of her rage had exhausted itself.

The nurse was moaning feebly when Isabel at last drew back and turned to cradle the dead boy in her arms.

'Come, Philip,' she murmured through her tears, 'I shall take you home.'

'And what of the other lad?' Joseph had asked.

But Isabel did not even seem to hear the question for she made no reply, only stumbled out into the sunshine, her firstborn child held tightly in her arms.

For a long time she could not even bear to look at Richard and he was left to the care of servants who were sometimes kind, sometimes neglectful, occasionally cruel. And when Isabel's grieving for her eldest son was passed and she noticed the black-haired boy who played with the children of grooms and scullery maids, he was a stranger to her and sullen and uncomfortable in her company.

She had never ceased to feel, in some deep and wordless part of her, that his life had been spared at the expense of his brother's. She was glad now that he was gone. Contrary to her husband's conjectures as he watched her through the mullioned window, she did not mind at all, would probably consider it a blessing, if he never again returned to trouble her at Rossmere.

Richard Treveryan felt no emotion as he cantered down the track that led to the road across the downs. It was as if he had always known that the prospect of an alliance with Alice was an illusion, as much a chimera as any other glimpse of happiness had ever been. Somewhere deep within him a door had slammed shut and outside that door, where he was now and would always in the future remain, was a cold, harsh solitude. At least it was familiar: loneliness had been his companion for as long as he could remember – and now he knew it would be with him always, a despised but constant friend.

His tenderness for Alice had made him weak. Just as she was weak now, blindly plunging into a loveless marriage with Nick. He alone would remain free of the miseries of entanglement. Invulnerable.

The road became steep and his mare slowed to a walk.

Alone. There was a strange sense of relief in the fact of being alone once again, a relief so powerful that he was able to ignore the despair that ached within him like a sickness.

At the top of the rise the ground opened out into the wide bleak space of Goonhilly Downs. High above him against a pale blue sky a buzzard wheeled in wide, lazy circles. High and lonely, nothing can touch those birds: his heart went out to the buzzard in its steady flight. And gradually a kind of strength began to flow through him once again: there were no ties of affection to bind him, no loved ones to fear for him, no one to consider but himself alone.

The buzzard, high in its soaring flight, blurred into a haze. Appalled, Richard realised that his eyes were streaming with tears.

Savagely he whipped his horse to a gallop. No tears for Alice, she was not worth the trouble. None of them were. She and Nick were well matched – let them destroy each other. This much was certain: no one would ever have the power to destroy him.

When he had spoken to Nick just now and told him he would return a rich man he had meant nothing in particular – it had been only the spiteful boast of a hurt child. But now he saw that he must make it true. Wealth was power and power was stronger than anything, stronger by far than love or honour or family affections. He must become wealthy, powerful – or else resign himself to being a nonentity for the rest of his days.

And he knew that he could do it. He did not know how or when or how long it would take but he knew that he could do it. Energy coursed through him like a tide. He was young and strong and intelligent. He could learn to be ruthless and cunning if that was required; he could wait and endure; he could play any part, rise to any challenge. One day, one day when his love for Alice had become a dull dead thing of the past, Alice would discover the bitter folly of her choice today.

His horse jerked her head and swerved and, fine horseman though he was, his thoughts were far away and for a moment he lost his balance.

A young girl had stepped out on to the track in front of him and, seeing the horse too late, she attempted to retreat but slipped instead on a patch of damp grass. She fell awkwardly.

'Take care!' he shouted. 'You frightened my mare.' And then, when the girl did not respond, he asked roughly, 'Are you hurt?'

No reply. It was obvious that she had not fainted for she was supporting herself with her arms, head bowed. Dazed perhaps. She wore the rough sturdy clothes of a country girl, not a vagrant at all, nor yet a lady. Muttering curses Richard was about to ride away but his mare was more gentle and nuzzled the girl cautiously.

She looked up then and her grey eyes were clouded. He had seen her somewhere before. A maidservant perhaps? No. The Porthew fair, yes, that was it. He remembered that unusual pale hair, her broad and handsome face – it was the girl whose little sister had so nearly learned the arts of love from Nick. The girl who had baffled the crowd with her Latin speech and then smiled at him when it was done.

He slipped off his horse and said, more gently this time, 'Here, let me help you to your feet.'

'It's not much further,' she murmured, making no sense at all. He noticed then how much she had altered since their last meeting. His memory was of a girl tall and strong with a fine bold way of speaking and a ready laugh. But now her shoulders were stooped as though under the weight of an enormous burden, her cheeks were pale as chalk. He remembered how she had berated him in the little stable and felt a sudden pang of regret that her fire had been so soon extinguished.

'There now,' he said, with rough gentleness, 'you can

155

stand well enough, there's no harm done. Wait, I have some brandy with me. That will revive you.'

He unscrewed the flask and put it to her lips. Her face puckered as she drank the unaccustomed liquid.

'Ugh, no more. I shall be all right now.'

She looked at him then. Richard found he had forgotten how disconcerting the gaze of those grey eyes could be. He noticed too that she was trembling.

'Is your home far from here?'

She shrugged. 'It's not important.'

Richard was annoyed by the interruption and yet still he hesitated. She was obviously half-dead with exhaustion, an exhaustion apparently caused as much by a sense of utter hopelessness as by any physical cause. He turned and caught hold of his saddle as though to remount: his own raw wound made him unwilling to witness her naked pain. He told himself that she was nothing to do with him, but just at that moment a strutting group of magpies took wing and rose up cackling to fly above their heads and the thought flashed through his mind that the appearance of this strange girl at such a time as this was a kind of omen. He dismissed the thought at once. Such superstitions were for servants and old women and besides, what possible warning could their meeting imply? But still, the fleeting moment of hesitation had been enough. He turned to her once again.

'I can take you to your home, if you wish. My business is not so urgent.'

A half-smile hovered on her face. 'Where are you going?' she asked.

'Plymouth, first.' Until now he had not given his destination much thought but there was no alternative. 'And then, who knows? London, perhaps, or maybe the Americas.'

'The Americas –' She echoed his words with a fervour that took him by surprise. And then she added, 'Why don't you take me with you?'

'You must be mad.'

'Yes.' She swayed slightly as she stood. 'The Americas . . . my God, I wish I were a man. To be so free, to ride away . . .'

Her voice faded into silence and Richard saw that she

156

was no longer looking at him but beyond him towards the road that he would travel. Instinctively he took hold of her arm to prevent her from falling.

'I can take you home,' he said.

She shook her head. 'Thank you, but that is a journey I can make alone.'

'Well then . . . is it money you want? I do not have much but –'

Again, that despairing laugh that somehow wrung at his heart. 'Not money, no . . . but wings . . . to fly away . . .'

A small cloud blotted out the sun. For a fleeting moment Richard was infected by her madness and he thought, why not? Why not lift her up beside me and take her wherever we are to go? In that brief instant he knew the strength of her despair as though she were someone he had known his whole life through, and with whom he could have no secrets. The sun emerged from behind a cloud, a wren began to sing in the nearby gorse, the moment passed.

Releasing her arm, he drew away from her as though afraid she might be bewitched. 'Then I can do no more for you,' he said roughly. 'You'd best get home before dark.'

She nodded, but did not move. He swung up into the saddle and wheeled his horse around to face the open road.

'May your troubles be short-lived,' he said and then, when she still did not answer, he clapped his heels into his horse's sides, not wanting to see that her eyes were brimming with unshed tears, and galloped away without once looking back to see if she was still there.

For some while Margaret remained without moving until the sound of hoof-beats on the grassy track had long since faded into silence.

6

The tall narrow house at the top of the town which had belonged to the late Master Hocken was considered as grand as any in Porthew. From the street, the visitor entered immediately into the shop itself where the bolts of cloth were stacked in a honeycomb of muted colours against the wall. For the most part the draper had dealt in the materials for working clothes: fustian and baize, osberow and crimson phillip, Irish straights and common russets. But among the coarser items he had always a bolt or two of something finer – a shimmering length of striped tabby or a bale of sarcenet from the East which glowed even on the dullest day.

Margaret had always enjoyed her visits to Master Hocken's shop, and his tales of the towns with the magical names where the fabrics were made, almost as much as the time she spent with Merry in the room at the back of the house which served as parlour and kitchen together.

After his long illness and death Master Hocken's widow continued to sell the cloth, but she was too dispirited to buy in fresh stocks and the shadow of neglect dulled the brightness of even the glowing brocades. And once William Hollar was installed among the bolts of kersey, frieze and brown Holland, he made it quite clear that casual visitors, those in search of gossip rather than a purchase, were no longer welcome.

Margaret was relieved to discover the welcome at the rear of the house remained as generous as ever. Since the Sunday when Merry had championed her outside the church, the bond between them had grown still stronger. And, as September mellowed into the lingering days of a mild October and still no end to Margaret's dilemma appeared, Merry was the only person with whom she shared her troubles.

Walking over from Conwinnion one afternoon, Margaret found her seated under the apple tree at the end of the garden. It was clear that Merry had started out with the intention of gathering windfalls but had quickly become distracted and had lapsed into a contented reverie. (It was the general opinion of the town that Meredith Hocken could find more ways of doing nothing at all than any other girl born.)

Merry was no beauty. Short and thickset, she had mousy brown hair that fell in lank curls, and too small features set in a doughy-pale face. But when she smiled, as she did the instant Margaret pushed open the gate beside the little barn that bordered the lane, her plain face was at once transformed.

'Come and sit down,' she exclaimed, 'you're just in time to rescue me from the bother of gathering apples. Here, have one.'

'No, thank you. We've been eating nothing else at home for weeks.'

They chatted idly for a while. In the back lane behind the barn they could hear a farmer berating his over-laden pack horse as together they stumbled up the steep hill.

After a while Merry asked, 'Do you want to come in and have a bite to eat?'

'Is your cousin at home?'

'William?' Merry's eyes were dancing. 'And I was fool enough to think it was me you'd come to see! You're as bewitched by the man as all the other girls who pretend to be my friend!'

Margaret laughed. 'That's right. Didn't Lizzie tell you I've been heartsick and pining for a month? But tell me, has he decided if he'll stay?'

'Indeed he has.' Merry assumed an air of mock solemnity. 'He told us most graciously only two days ago that he might be persuaded to shoulder our burdens for us on condition that we agree to reform ourselves entirely.'

'Reform? How?'

'Oh, nothing much. Only that we must scour the house from floor to ceiling twice a day and three times on Sundays and prepare only those delicacies that he likes to eat. And he will have title to the shop and we must not interfere with his management in any way. Oh yes – and in time he rather thinks he will need an apprentice.'

'You've obviously not fallen victim to your cousin's charms.'

'If only it was that simple. I still don't feel as if I really know the man, even though he's been in our house for nearly a month.'

And she began to tell of an incident that had occurred a few days before when William, usually so controlled, had been distraught at finding a mouse drowned in a pitcher of milk. 'He can't abide to see the bulls baited. I can't make him out at all.'

'I admire his kindness,' said Margaret.

'And what of his blue eyes? Come in, anyway, and have a mug of ale.'

But Margaret suggested instead that they find somewhere where they could talk in private and Merry, hoping that at last her friend had decided to share her secret, willingly agreed.

There was a track that led southwards from Porthew towards the Lizard and the girls had often walked this way when they wished for privacy in the past. Today they walked briskly until they had left the last house of the town behind them, then they slowed to a contemplative dawdle, stopping every now and then to pick a late blackberry from the hedge.

Margaret sighed. 'Such a dismal time of year, I always think. All the world seems to be dying.'

'It's only the trouble you're in makes you so morbid,' Merry prompted.

'Morbid, yes, that's it.' Margaret fell silent.

Was that what it was, this heavy lump of dread that chained her former hopes to the weary ground of reality? More than once over the previous weeks she had been reminded of an incident that had taken place a couple of years earlier. A group of men from the village had devised, for their entertainment one Sunday afternoon, an elaborate maze of trenches and tunnels into which a sequence of rats had been introduced. Margaret, coming upon them by accident, had glimpsed a pair of bright and intelligent eyes before she turned from the scene in disgust: no matter how cunning the victim its only fate was to be skewered on a pitchfork and tossed to the yapping assembly of dogs.

'Is there nothing I can do?' she burst out suddenly, but even as she spoke, she knew the answer. 'I know, I know,' she replied impatiently to her own question, 'I can stay at home and bring shame to my family, or I can try and find a man fool enough to marry me.'

'You were right to refuse Ambrose, at least.'

'Was I?' Margaret nudged a stone moodily with the tip of her shoe, then glanced over the hedge to a meadow where a couple of bullocks were grazing some scrawny grass. Merry could not know the misery of her position now at the farm where she was daily reminded that she had become a burden and a disgrace. 'I wonder . . . sometimes I think I ought to tie a placard around my neck and stand outside Porthew church: husband required for –'

'Stop it, Mattie. You're only tormenting yourself. And heaven knows there's plenty of lads would have come courting you earlier only Ambrose always let it be known they'd have to settle with *him* first.'

'And now it's the scandal that frightens them away. You've no idea what it's like to feel such an outcast, as if I'm supposed to hide myself away like the poor lepers at Bodmin.'

'Good heavens, Mattie, you'd think you were the only unmarried girl who ever carried a child without a father to give it his name!'

But Margaret was determined to feel sorry for herself. 'You can't imagine what it's like to be so worried all the time, to see no way out at all.'

Merry placed her hands on stout hips and glared at Margaret. 'So I don't know what it's like, eh? And supposing I told you that last spring when Ned Roberts and I were courting I truly thought that . . . I was convinced . . . heavens above, Mattie, I count myself lucky every morning when I wake that I'm not swelled up as large as a house already!'

Margaret was so taken aback that it was a moment or two before she said anything, and then it was a grudging, 'You're only saying this to make me feel better.'

'No, Mattie, I'd not make up such a lie against myself, not even for your sake. It's the honest truth.'

'But why didn't you tell me at the time?'

'Oh well . . .' now it was Merry's turn to look away, 'you were always so busy with your books and your learning – I was afraid you would despise me if you knew.'

'Did I really seem so arrogant?' Margaret was silent, remembering now that she had noticed a difference in Merry that spring, but had assumed it was caused by her father's illness. 'I should have guessed. I'm sorry.'

They had reached a low bridge where the road ran over a stream, a place overhung with bare branches and rank with ferns and moss. Sometimes when they came this way they glimpsed the jewel-blue flash of a kingfisher, but on this October afternoon the scene was gloomy. They settled themselves on the parapet of the bridge and dropped leaves into the water while Merry recounted the story of her erratic courtship with Ned Roberts.

Although he had grown up not three miles from Porthew, he was a young man little known in the district: from boyhood he had been restless and had worked on boats up and down the coast from Penzance to Plymouth. But during the spring of that year several people had remarked on the fact that Ned Roberts had stayed home a week, a fortnight, six weeks . . . and that Meredith Hocken appeared to be the cause of his sudden liking for Porthew. But not even Margaret had guessed how serious it had been. Merry's voice grew languid as she spoke of him.

'I think I loved him for his laughter, more than anything,' she sighed, 'especially then, when my father was so ill and Mother half out of her wits and the whole place as miserable as a pest-house. I don't know how I would have endured the days if I hadn't known that as soon as it was dark I could steal out to the little barn and be with Ned.'

Margaret burst out laughing. 'You met him in your barn? Weren't you afraid you'd be found out?'

'Why me in particular? You don't know half the scandals that fill the town once the sun has safely set.'

'No wonder you always looked so tired.'

'Mm. And the glory of it was that everyone assumed I was worn out from looking after Father. "Poor dear Meredith,"' she imitated the drone of the village gossips, '"worn out, she is, caring for her father." "Oh, but Aunt

Calwodely, any girl would do the same." "Ah, Mrs Hocken, your daughter is a rare treasure." If they'd only known what their saintly girl was getting up to as soon as darkness fell!'

They both dissolved into peals of laughter.

'But surely your mother must have suspected something?'

'Why? You know she never sees what is right under her nose.'

'Then what went wrong?'

'I wish I knew. We quarrelled, of course, but it was such a petty quarrel I can't even remember the cause of it. Maybe he'd grown tired of me and was looking for a way out and like a fool I gave it to him. The last I heard he was chasing some trollop from Mullion.'

'Don't talk like that, Merry. We're no better. How do you think it is that we both grew up to be so wicked?'

'Oh, we've only been a little bit wicked compared to most people. The trouble is it's such a showing kind of sin. It was only after Ned had gone that I began to panic. By the time of my father's funeral I was frantic – Lord, how I sobbed –'

'Yes, I remember.'

Merry laughed harshly. 'Everyone assumed the darling daughter was grieving for her poor dead father –'

'Poor Merry!'

'And yet it must be worse for you. As it turned out, I was lucky. But if I *had* been carrying Ned's child there would have been no need to keep the father's name a secret. I daresay he might have married me, too. Whereas in your case –' Here Merry glanced sidelong at her friend. She had been hoping Margaret would match one secret with another and divulge the man's name. Like several others she guessed it might be one of the gentry, someone too well placed to consider marriage to a tenant's daughter.

But her hopes were disappointed by Margaret's brief, 'My case is not the same as yours.'

'Do you not trust me to keep your secret?'

'I wish I *could* tell you, Merry – but I made a promise.'

Merry was sceptical. 'And so did he, I daresay. I know Ned was very free with his promises in the beginning but we heard less about them as time went on.'

'The thing is,' Margaret pondered, 'that I seem to have

made a mess of so much recently that if I break my promise too then I don't know how I should live with myself. It's bad enough to have everyone else despising me without despising myself as well.'

'Everyone? Who for instance?' asked Merry angrily. 'Mistress Payne perhaps? I'll have you know that whey-faced Puritan went east to have a child a twelvemonth before she was married.'

'Oh Merry, you're making it up!'

'I have heard tell it was twins.'

Margaret burst out laughing, as Merry had intended, but this time her laughter was short-lived. 'It's no good, Merry, no matter what everyone else has been up to in the past I'm the one who's in trouble now. And I've thought my brain into a knot and I still can find no solution.'

'There is yet something you could try.' Merry couldn't bear to see her friend so downhearted, but as soon as she had spoken she regretted it, for Margaret seized on her words.

'What? I'm so desperate I'd try anything.'

'Forget it, Mattie. I'm sorry I mentioned it.'

'Why?'

'It's too dangerous.'

'Just tell me and I'll be the judge of that.'

'Have you heard of Father Pym?'

Margaret shuddered. 'I thought he had died long since.'

'It might have been better if he had. Oh Mattie, forget I ever spoke of him. Joan Little went to see him years ago and though her family swore it was dropsy everyone said she was with child.'

'And did he cure her?'

'No. They say that sometimes he can but at other times . . . Joan Little was raving for a week before she died, you could hear her screams all over town, her agony was terrible. After that her brothers burned Father Pym's house down and he fled . . . they say he lives on the downs but it isn't always possible to find his house because of the magic he uses to hide himself from ill-wishers.'

'And I'm sure there are plenty of those.'

'They say he won't do healing any more, though he can sometimes be persuaded to find lost objects. But what with fear of the church courts and fear of those he has harmed, he chooses to keep his magic to himself.'

'Does he live there alone?'

'He has a daughter but she's an idiot, no brain at all, just empty bone and that's God's punishment on him for his wickedness. Promise me you'll forget I ever spoke of him.'

Margaret smiled ruefully. 'I don't make promises any more. And anyway, this may just turn out to be a false alarm, as yours was.'

They stood up and began to stroll back towards the town. 'I hope so,' said Merry.

At the sawpits two old ladies were gathering sawdust into sacks. They greeted Merry, but turned in stony silence from Margaret. Merry linked arms with her friend.

'Pay no attention to any of them,' she said warmly. 'If I had a penny for every woman in Porthew who was already carrying a child when she made her marriage vows, I swear I'd die a rich woman.'

'What a shameless way to make money,' said Margaret, laughing.

They never spoke of Father Pym again. For when Margaret awoke one morning to the certainty that she must visit the old wizard who lived now on the moors, she knew also that this would be a journey into the shadows where silence would be the best protection.

She knew also that she must set off at once, before she had time to regret her decision. So she whispered to the still-sleeping Lizzie that she must manage the work alone that day, and crept out of the house while it was dark, leaving the two outraged dogs shut in the barn. She had decided not to take Juno, since she was more likely to attract attention on horseback.

As the sky began to pale in the east, she fought hard to keep her imagination in check. As is often the case when one is preoccupied with a subject, it seemed to Margaret that, since her conversation with Merry, the people around her did nothing but talk of Father Pym and his remarkable powers. Less than a week ago Lizzie had returned from Porthew full of the news of a woman from Coverack who had been forespoken by a neighbour and been afflicted with deafness until treated by the wise man. And only yesterday a pedlar who called at the farm and was invited in for a bite to eat by Mistress Pearce entertained them all with the story of his visit to the lonely cottage and the trio who lived there: man, woman and idiot child. It was from him, secretly, that Margaret had gained instructions how to find them.

The sun rose; the morning was unusually mild for October. Margaret had found recently that she tired more quickly than usual. As she went along she paused frequently . . . but never for very long. Always the fear nagged her: turn back. Don't take the risk. Remember Joan Little who died raving; remember the child with no brain; remember all those dead-of-night stories of devilish pacts and hauntings and prophecies of ill-omen. Remember . . . no, no. Don't remember. Don't think of it at all.

She walked on steadily, head bowed, looking neither to right nor left.

Towards late morning she climbed a slight rise in the ground and looked down on the little tuck in the hillside where the cottage stood – or rather, crouched. Even with her weak eyesight she could tell that it was more hovel than cottage: rough walls and a roof of furze – small protection against the winter rain and gales. But then, Father Pym had come here in a great hurry – to escape the rumours and the vengeance of their neighbours, so it was said.

Margaret stood quite still, looking down at the tumbled heap of a building. No road to the house, just this path. No sign of any other houses, no sign that anyone ever passed by the place. Just the huge blue dome of the sky and all around them the desolate yellow and black of a moorland landscape. Not a bird or a leaf or a flower anywhere.

Fear rose through her body like a white sea mist, numbing and chill. Despite the warmth of the morning, she found that she was shivering. What she was proposing to do was a sin and God would surely punish her as she deserved: the child would be born anyway and it would be a devil-child, a monster, like one of those terrifying figures in the paintings on the walls in church with burning eyes and a gaping hole for a mouth; her body would be ripped open by the birth; she would die raving and fall into everlasting torment; her womb would be consumed by flames. She would . . .

Stop. Stop thinking. God save me from my fear. She rammed her fist into her mouth and bit her knuckles. The pain was reassuringly real. She did not need to go on. She could turn and go home.

Behind her was the farm at Conwinnion, that comforting huddle of buildings and trees. It must be nearly midday now; she pictured Lizzie setting out the food for her father's meal while Tom and the two dogs clamoured for scraps.

Turn home. Go home.

But then? To continue as before? The whispers and the sidelong looks. Her father's face so hurt and defeated; his eyes that avoided hers yet lingered when he thought she was not looking – as though he hated her yet could not drag his eyes away. The endless waiting and fear of what might follow. Last Sunday she had heard talk of a girl from Lizard way who had been sent with her bastard child to the house of correction at Penryn.

Suddenly resolute, she picked up her skirts and hurried down the slope to Father Pym's hovel.

Margaret was so ready to be terrified of the old sorcerer that it was some moments before she realised how kind his face was, though suspicious. He had the smooth baby-pink skin that some men keep into old age, a toothless mouth and eyebrows somewhat pointed in the middle that gave him an expression of perpetual surprise. His clothes were ragged and it was evident that he lacked all but the most basic necessities – and sometimes, Margaret guessed, even those.

'Father Pym?'

He nodded.

'I came to see if . . . I need . . .'

'Wait a while. No hurry now. No, no.' He spoke in a fluting, bird-like voice. 'We can sit on this bench together and you can tell me slowly. Worn out, you look. But no promises, mind. You must understand that. No promises.'

He led the way to a bench behind the house where the sunshine was warmest. Margaret hesitated, afraid to seat herself beside a man who was credited with such varied powers.

He raised one pointed eyebrow and smiled. 'Sit down, my dear. Old Pym is only dangerous at the full moon. No, no. Not really. My humour. You've heard bad things of me. Don't deny it. I know what they say.'

Margaret did not know how to answer.

'Yes, yes. I know their slanders. You see, people always fear what they don't understand. All I've done is practise a little of the medicine my father taught me. I know the plants and a few rhymes that are useful also. And sometimes I can perceive things that are hidden behind a veil. Is that so very terrible?'

Margaret sat down. His voice was thin and reassuring. It rose and fell in a sing-song chant, like that of the old religion. She began to forget her fear.

'That's better. Much better. And you've an honest face. Perhaps I can help you. But first you must tell me what you want.'

'I must . . . It's hard to explain, Father Pym. I don't know what to do. I'm not married, you see, but . . .'

'You want a husband?'

'I suppose so but . . . not exactly. You see, I am expecting a child.'

'And the father of this child – ?'

She shook her head. Father Pym's little eyes shone with pleasure.

'Then I can help you. Yes, yes. I know a potion will make him change his mind. A very good potion indeed. I've had great success with it in the past, some of my most remarkable successes. One girl who came to me had such a face you'd think the moon had turned. No man would marry her. But with my potion she was wed within the year. And you've such a pretty face we'll have no trouble. Your man will change his mind, don't worry.'

'He cannot marry me. He has a wife already.'

'Hmm. I see. Less good. But someone else perhaps?'

She shook her head.

'There's someone, surely. A girl in your condition must be wed.'

'I thought perhaps . . . I might . . . that you might . . .'

He was frowning.

Margaret stared at her hands and said in a low voice, 'I thought that perhaps I might lose the baby. That it might . . . die . . .'

Her voice trailed away. Father Pym was quivering with rage and he sprang to his feet. His forehead puckered into a hundred tiny wrinkles and his eyebrows stood like arrow points above his eyes.

'You shameless girl!' He stabbed an accusing finger at her. 'You come to my house and dare to ask –! Do you know what they would do to me if they found out? Don't you know they're just waiting for their chance?' He began to dance from one foot to the other, jabbing at the air with bony fingers. 'Did they send you here to trap me, eh? No respect for Father Pym. I try to help but they bite back, yapping at my heels like a pack of dogs. I thought you had an honest face. I thought maybe you had lost something and I could help to find it. And a little money too when we've not a farthing in the house . . . But no. You want . . . You're nothing but a strumpet and the likes of you will ruin me!'

'I did not mean –'

'No? Then what did you mean? Hey?' Now, for the first time, he really did look like a wizard, dancing with rage while his tattered clothes flapped around his skinny legs.

And then Margaret saw the fear behind his anger – and at once all her own fear vanished.

'I mean you no harm, Father Pym,' she said in a steady voice, 'I've come here alone and no one knows of my visit. I promise you I can keep a secret – I've done it before.'

Something in her manner made him believe that she was telling the truth. He began to calm down. 'You've an honest face, I'll say that for you. And you say you've come alone and told no one. Well, maybe so. Maybe so.'

'I know full well that what I am asking is wrong, but I can think of no other solution. I've thought of nothing else for days and – and I'm prepared to take the risk.'

He glared at her and scratched his head. Then he walked away and stood for a few moments at a little distance, muttering to himself before returning to her once again.

'You say you can bide your tongue, eh?'

'I promised the man I would tell his name to no one and I've been true to my word. And always will be.'

'Hmm.' He sat down beside her again though his feet continued to execute little dancing steps from time to time.

'It's important. It is dangerous. When my potions work people thank the Lord and forget all about me. But the other times . . . then they come back soon enough and blame me and talk of witchcraft and Satan and goodness knows what else. No respect for the old ways, that's the trouble. It was better in my father's time. They listened to him. And they did what he told them. Now people get it wrong. They won't follow my instructions. And then they blame me. Chased me away – and my family too. Is it my fault if cows die sometimes? Cows must die. All die. And if a baby is born with crippled legs, am I to blame?'

'I give you my word I'll never tell anyone I came here today. No matter what happens. But if you know of anything that might help me, then tell me, please.'

'Hmph. Well. There is a powder. I'm not saying what sort of powder, mind you. Nor what it does. But you're in trouble and you've an honest face. I'd like to help you. Perhaps I can find the powder. Perhaps you can use it. Always too soft-hearted, that's my trouble.'

Still muttering and shaking his head he disappeared inside the hovel. Margaret could hear him shuffling about, moving things.

Suddenly she was very tired. Weariness like a great sea surrounding her. She leaned her head back against the rough stone of the wall and closed her eyes.

Perhaps she slept. Gradually she became aware that the huge silence of the moor had been broken by the sound of singing. It was a child's voice, pouring out song in a long pure ribbon of sound. The voice came closer.

She opened her eyes.

A child was standing in front of her, a girl who might have been about eight years old but it was impossible to be sure. Her hair was matted and her face filthy. She had coarse lumpy features and her father's pointed eyebrows. She was peering into Margaret's face with unabashed intensity.

'Hello,' said Margaret.

The child stepped back, blinking, as though astonished to discover that the stranger had the power of speech. Then, having obviously decided that Margaret was not dangerous, she came closer once again, still peering intently and, with a filthy hand, touched Margaret's cheek, then her hair.

'Sun,' she said, and her mouth hung open in a lazy grin, 'lovely sun.'

An involuntary shiver ran down Margaret's spine at the child's touch. The idiot child, God's punishment on the old man for past sins. No brain at all but empty bone. She forced herself to say in a steady voice, 'What's your name, child?'

The girl shook her head and then, without another word, she picked up the little bundle that Margaret had brought with her and opened it. She ignored the few coins that Margaret had brought for payment, but snatched as eagerly as a scavenging mongrel at the piece of bread and portion of cheese that she had wrapped in a cloth. Clutching the food close to her chest she ran a little distance away and began to eat. Margaret would have stopped her but the child was obviously famished. When the last crumb was eaten she returned and would have searched her clothes to see what other titbits might be hidden but Margaret pushed her away.

'Enough. There's no more food for you. Leave me alone.'

Far from being alarmed by Margaret's gesture the girl laughed out loud and, still gurgling with pleasure, she climbed on her lap and put her brown arms around Margaret's neck.

The smell of the child was appalling and Margaret was just about to push her away when the singing began, that strange, pure, eerie sound, a song without words, clear and mournful as the curlew's cry. The girl was rocking herself in Margaret's arms as she sang.

Margaret was both disgusted and strangely touched. The child was so odd, so trusting. The stench was so foul and the song so sweet.

Father Pym came out of the hovel and looked at the filthy child with great tenderness.

'Dorcas,' he said, opening wide his arms, 'come.'

She scrambled off Margaret's lap and ran to the old man, flinging herself in his arms and he swung her up into the air and caught her in the crook of his arm.

He beamed at Margaret with every sign of paternal pride. 'Did you ever see a maid so lovely? And she trusts you, she likes you, that's good. My little beauty.'

Margaret did not know how to reply. She stood up and brushed down her skirts.

'My little angel.' Father Pym kissed his daughter and she gurgled and crowed with pleasure like an infant. 'Whatever will become of my little Dorcas when I am gone? Who will take care of you then, eh? The Lord will provide, yes, yes. But will He know the things you want? I wonder. The lilies of the fields in all their glory, yes, yes. No harm will come to you, my child, no harm.'

He set her down tenderly. 'Now, be patient for a while, my little lady, while I give this stranger girl a powder for her stomach. She has an ache that must be made to go. Poor ache, away it goes. Now, Dorcas, run to Mother.'

A woman had appeared through the low door of the hovel. Every bit as unappealing as her child, she had a scowling expression. She looked at Margaret with the greatest suspicion.

'Are you sure she's come alone?'

Father Pym looked uneasy. 'She told me so,' he said apologetically.

'You should have sent her on her way. She'll bring us trouble. We've had trouble enough. Why should we help her? What do they ever do for us?'

'I promise I'll tell no one of this visit. No matter what happens.'

'Promises. Worthless all of them. How much is she offering to pay, then?'

Father Pym hung his head in shame, like a schoolboy who has forgotten to learn his lesson.

'Just as I expected,' the old woman burst out in a fury, 'you risk us all and then never even ask for payment. Well then,' and she rounded on Margaret, 'show us your money. What can you give us, eh? To make it worth our while?'

'I brought money. Here . . . it's all I have. I hope –'

Old Pym's wife snatched the coins as eagerly as her daughter had snatched the bread and cheese. When she had examined them thoroughly she appeared to be slightly mollified.

'It's more than some,' she said grudgingly, 'though little enough for the risk we run. You'd best give her the powder.'

172

Father Pym took a little paper packet from his sleeve and handed it to Margaret.

'Powder for the stomach ache. Put a little on your tongue tonight when the sun goes down. And then each evening at sundown for a week. Do you understand? But to make the ache go away altogether – see this paper? No, don't look at it yet. I've written some words there. Can you read? That's good, very good. Repeat the words every evening three times as you take the powder. And all the time wear the paper next to your belly and at the end of the seven days you must burn the paper and with the burning the trouble will go. Do you understand?'

Margaret nodded.

'Good. Now leave us. And never a word of this to anyone.'

'I promise.'

Mistress Pym was still suspicious. 'That's easy to say. You'll promise anything when you're in trouble. And then forget it soon enough and squeal for all to hear when the powder begins to burn. But take care, I can see what you do even when you are far away and I'll make you suffer if you try to betray us. Not only the burning in the womb –'

'Enough, wife, no need to scare the child.'

'Hmph. I'm warning her, that's all. To protect us all. Something you never think to do.'

'Poor ache,' the child, Dorcas, came over from her mother's side and placed her hand on Margaret's stomach, 'poor ache, go away.' And she smiled up at Margaret with that strange, slack-jawed smile.

Suddenly Margaret could not bear to remain for a moment longer. The very air around the hovel was corrupting; if she lingered any more she would surely breathe in their suspicion and their magic like a noxious plague. She would become vacant as the filthy girl, frightened like the mother, a sorcerer like Old Pym.

But as she walked away across the moor she heard the singing voice of the child, Dorcas, clear and wordless as some ghostly bird.

The way home was very long. Her food was gone and she dared not call at any of the outlying farms along the way for fear that someone might guess where she had been. Although it was October and the sun was already low in the sky, its brightness dazzled her.

She was very hungry. The hem of her skirt was heavy with damp from the long sedge grasses that grew beside the path. The flat moorland landscape shimmered unsteadily. A wavering giddiness threatened to overwhelm her. Her vision blurred.

I must rest a while, she thought. I'll be stronger then.

She sat down on a smooth lichen-covered stone. But then a fear possessed her. Perhaps this strange giddiness had a more ominous cause than mere fatigue. Perhaps some of the evil enchantment that surrounded the wise man's hovel was already beginning to work on her. Even as she sat here her brain was being emptied as the child Dorcas's brain had been emptied . . . she would be found raving, die babbling some wordless stream of nonsense.

She pulled out the packet Father Pym had given her. The powder was wrapped in a page torn from an almanac which was covered in strange words and even stranger symbols. Safe within it lay the powder, fine white grains looking harmless as salt . . . but which had the power to break the tentative life within her. Her hand was trembling so much she was in danger of spilling it. Carefully she refolded the paper, tucked it into her bodice. Then she examined the other piece of paper on which Father Pym had written:

Fire of Mary, Fire of Eve,
Take away this child I breathe.

She shuddered, refolded the paper and put it away. Such simple words, such terrible power. She remembered what Mistress Pym had said: 'You'll squeal for all to hear when the powder begins to burn.' Already she could feel a pain within her belly, like a white-hot fire. Her mouth was hot and dry and yet she was shivering with cold.

I don't have to do this, she told herself. I can throw away both paper and powder. I can forget this day entirely.

But then what? The same questions, the same agony, round and round and never an end to it.

Later, later I can decide. At home. Walk home first.

She stood up and began to trudge along the track once

more. For a little while she felt better, revived by the rest, but then the giddiness returned, worse than ever before. As if the ribbon of track that she followed led not across the moor at all, but across a moving yellow sea that tipped and swayed so that one moment her view was all pale sky, the next all land. She reached out a hand to steady herself but touched only air. A strange wavering cry sounded in the space around her but whether it was the plaintive call of the curlew or the wordless singing of the idiot child which had somehow followed her across the moor she could not tell. Her head throbbed and an empty sickness flowed through her belly.

And then, suddenly, there was no longer emptiness within. A child was there, so small, no larger than a thimble and with a wizened baby face like that of an old man, tiny, but perfectly formed in every detail. And his mouse-small hands were gripping the dark red rim of her womb, little fingers clinging, clinging, never to be dislodged.

Then Margaret knew that she was trapped for ever, trapped by this too fertile woman's body, by the instinct that drove her to accept any shame rather than destroy a part of herself. And she hated the tiny hands that gripped her from within, just as she knew that one day love would follow.

There was to be no escape. If she had been a man she could fight her enemies and be a master of her own fate but the only weapon she had now was that of endurance. She threw back her head as though to seek an answer from the skies: there was the smudge of a bird moving overhead. Her weak eyes could not focus on it clearly but she knew from the pattern of its movement that it must be a buzzard or an eagle. So free, so effortlessly soaring.

She stumbled on, light-headed with hunger and fatigue, hardly aware of where she was or where she was going. Instinct guiding her home.

She never heard the hoof-beats, only saw the huge dark shape as it reared before her. She tried to turn but her foot twisted on the damp grass and she fell heavily. There was a voice but she did not hear the words. She could only hear a voice within her that said, again and again, 'Trapped, no escape, trapped. For ever.'

A hand touching her arm. She looked up and saw the head and shoulders of a man, dark against the sunlight. He was familiar somehow though she could not remember why. She felt the cool metal of a flask pressed against her lips and then the liquid, a searing fire that burned her throat and made the tears start to her eyes. And then revived her.

The man was watching her closely and there was both irritation and concern in his expression. As though he was anxious for her in spite of himself. There was an air of urgency about him, of departure. Margaret noticed the pack strapped to his saddle and guessed that he was starting on a journey.

A sudden madness gripped her. She would go with him. And if he'd not agree to that then she would steal his horse, mount up and ride away. She could take her shame and her secrets and this parasite life within her, ride, ride and never return. Somewhere over the edge of the horizon in that country she had never seen, somewhere there must be a place where she could live her life in dignity and freedom.

But he had pushed her hands away. His foot was in the stirrup and now he was seated in the saddle, looking down at her with that same mixture of impatience and concern. She recognised him then: the youth whose rapier had slashed Ambrose's hand on the Feast Day. A rough-looking fellow but a gentleman, so they said, cousin to the Suttons.

Her hands fell limply to her sides. He was troubled, she had known that the first time she saw him, demons rode his back – but he was a man and he could ride away. He could escape.

Hoof-beats fading on the grassy track. A fine dark mare to carry him away. And for her? Only the long slow walk back to the farm, a baby to come and her family's shame, a fire to light in the morning, bread to be baked and washing to be done, the chickens and the cows, work and rest and sleeping, now and for all eternity.

Afterwards she could not remember the rest of her walk back to Conwinnion. She arrived just after dark. Lizzie and Tom crowded round her demanding to know where she had been all day but her step-mother said not a word. She looked at her once and then warmed her some milk and raisins, dipped in some bread and fed her as if she were a baby.

And when Margaret went to bed that night she found that the powder had all been spilled. The packet must have fallen when she tripped before the horse.

The next morning she took the paper with the magical rhyme written on it to the furthest edge of the farm and buried it in some soft earth beneath a hawthorn tree. All that day she could feel a burning sensation in her hands, where the paper had touched her skin.

7

On a bright morning in early November Parson Weaver
saddled his mare and rode over to the farm at Conwinnion.
For once not even the horse's constant shying at every leaf
that rustled in the hedge could ruffle his pleasure; he
shouted cheerful greetings to the men working in the fields
and hummed a psalm as he jogged along and reflected that
the Lord was a wise and beneficent father after all since a
solution to Margaret Pearce's troubles had so cleverly and
unexpectedly presented itself.

Margaret was lifting a bucket of water from the well.
She raised a hand to shield her eyes as she heard the
horseman approach, then, at the sound of his voice, she
frowned.

'Good day, Margaret. Are your family all at home?'

'Father is in the first meadow, Mother is indoors. What
brings you here so early, Parson?'

'All in good time, my dear. You'll hear the good news
soon enough.'

'Good news?'

He beamed at her, his face as cheerful as a schoolboy's
with a secret. 'Your troubles are over, I think. Didn't I tell
you I'd think of something? Now, take Sarah away and tend
to her and then fetch your father and this can all be done
properly.'

Margaret did as she was told without another word.
Sarah, a dark brown mare with a long neck and an irregular,
jerky gait, rolled her eyes suspiciously and laid back her
ears in protest, but Margaret spoke to her soothingly and
the mare condescended to be led away.

At length all was ready in the house. Parson Weaver was
seated in the best wooden chair with a glass of sweetened
canary wine in his hand. Mistress Pearce was huddled by
the fire, rubbing her swollen knees and every now and then

glancing at the parson as though she wished to read his mind. Margaret stood by the fire and stirred it to a blaze until her step-mother scolded her, and she picked up a black and white cat and nuzzled the fur behind its neck thoughtfully. Lizzie waited by the window and every now and then she opened her mouth to ask a question and then, catching sight of Margaret's warning eyes, she closed it again. Then Tom came in, laughing with pleasure at the unexpected treat of a morning visitor, and his father followed close behind.

'Good day to you, Parson,' John Pearce spoke with gruff pride, 'we don't usually see you so far from Porthew at this hour of the morning.'

'I saw no reason to waste time. I have good news for your daughter – for all of you, in fact.'

'Hmm.' John Pearce scowled at his daughter, who infuriated him further by continuing to stroke the cat and appearing to be lost in secret thoughts, quite unaffected by this present conversation. 'Then it's more than she deserves. She should be punished for her wrongdoings and though you say different, Parson, I cannot help thinking you are too easy-going on sinners.'

Parson Weaver was careful to avoid Margaret's eyes as he replied, 'Our Lord Himself commanded us to be merciful, John Pearce. Remember when He spoke of the woman who had been taken in adultery –'

'You reminded me of that when you visited here before – and that's the only reason the girl's been let off so lightly. But I'm still not happy with it. There are rules laid down in the Bible, rules that are quite clear. And if people can break them and get away with it, then everything is a nonsense, or so it seems to me.'

'The divine order of things can never be termed a nonsense,' said Parson Weaver coldly. His benevolent mood was giving way to irritation. There were few events he found so tedious as a theological dispute with one of his uneducated parishioners – and what's more, Margaret did not even appear to be listening to him.

'I only meant to say –' John Pearce began.

'For mercy's sake,' Margaret burst out suddenly, 'why must you waste your time in argument!'

'Mind what you say,' her father growled, 'or must I teach you manners too?'

But Parson Weaver was pleased by this evidence of her interest and said with a benevolent smile, 'Forgive us, Margaret. I'll keep you all in suspense no longer. I have found you a husband, Margaret.'

'But who – ?'

'I was visited last night by a young man who has recently come to the neighbourhood. He was considering approaching you, Mr Pearce, to see if you would permit your daughter to marry him, but he naturally wished to make some enquiries first.'

Mistress Pearce darted him an anxious look. 'But does he know – ?'

'He is fully aware of the circumstances, yes.' The parson smiled discreetly. 'He would appear to be blessed with an unusually charitable disposition, but then, as I have said, he has seen a good deal of the world. I daresay you have already guessed, Margaret, that I am speaking of William Hollar.'

No, she had not guessed. She sat down heavily. She remembered William Hollar as she had seen him first when he stood in the doorway of Mistress Hocken's kitchen. A modern-day Aeneas with his honey-coloured hair and his features so perfectly formed they might have been chiselled from a block of white marble. And now, when all the boys and men she had known since childhood would have nothing to do with her because of the scandal, this handsome stranger wished her to be his wife. But why?

She must have voiced the question, for Parson Weaver smiled and said, 'He can tell you that himself. I presume that in the meantime I may give him a favourable answer?'

Suddenly they were all talking at once. Mistress Pearce hastened to assure the parson that she considered it an excellent solution; although she had not yet seen the fellow she had heard nothing but good concerning him. John Pearce grinned and slapped his thigh and told Lizzie to fetch more canary wine since this was a cause for celebration and Lizzie brought the wine and poured it and kept saying, 'William Hollar! Whoever would have thought it! Oh my!' and her eyes shone at the thought of how Margaret must now become an object of envy.

It was some little time, therefore, before anyone even heard what Margaret herself was trying to say.

'What about me?' Her face was very flushed and her voice shook. 'What about *my* opinion? How can you all assume . . . just like that . . . and not even ask?'

John Pearce glanced at her scornfully. 'Whatever is the matter with you, girl?'

Margaret struggled to control herself. 'No one has yet thought to ask my views on this matter.'

'*Your* views?'

'The girl is surely mad!'

And Lizzie, seeing her dreams of a respectably married sister fade to nothing, wailed, 'Oh Mattie!'

'Yes, *my* views. You are all talking of the man I am supposed to marry but no one even considers my feelings. You all talk as if I was nothing but a block of wood or – or a carcass of butcher's meat!'

John Pearce rose slowly from his chair. 'Now see here –' he began in a voice of terrible rage.

But this time Margaret stood her ground. 'Father, you are wasting your time. You may threaten me all you like, you may turn me out, but I *will* not marry a man just for your convenience.'

Lizzie gasped, Mistress Pearce squeaked with fury, Tom plugged his thumb into his mouth and watched wide-eyed. In that moment of taut silence it suddenly crossed the parson's mind that Margaret, in the heat of a violent battle with her father, might disclose what she had hitherto kept secret. He decided it was prudent to intervene.

John Pearce seemed to be on the point of hurling himself at his daughter when the parson laid a restraining hand on his arm. 'Wait, don't strike her. Let me speak with her first.'

'I'll teach her to defy me!'

But he had hesitated for an instant and in that moment Margaret ducked past him and ran out of the kitchen.

'This has all been so sudden,' said the parson hastily, 'I expect it is the shock. Only let me talk with her alone and I promise you she'll come round,' and he followed her out into the yard.

He found her down by the duck pond. She was pacing up and down and when she saw him approach she exclaimed defiantly, 'I will not change my mind. They cannot make me.' She was shaking violently.

The parson had intended to speak sensibly to her, to explain the idiocy of her refusal, to point out that she really had no choice in the matter, that it would be madness to refuse William Hollar's proposal. He had been as angry as her father at her sudden outburst but now, as he heard the depth of passion in her voice, his anger vanished. He saw that the child who had given him so many sorts of pleasure existed no longer – and he found that he was curious to learn what manner of woman was taking her place.

He said, 'I did not know you disliked Mr Hollar so much.'

'What does that have to do with it? I never said I did not like him – how can I, when I scarcely know the man?'

'Then what is your objection?'

'I hardly know –' She glanced at him briefly, then turned away and walked to the rushy edge of the pond. The parson had sat down on the shaft of a cart and appeared to be absorbed in contemplation of his nails. Margaret had expected anger and argument; his apparent quiescence made her uneasy. She frowned, drew in a breath and let it out on a long sigh. 'My objection is not to Mr Hollar –'

'What then?'

'But if he wishes to – to marry me, surely he can ask me himself, surely *my* wishes are of some account.'

The parson thought he began to understand. 'I daresay,' he said slowly, 'that we were a little hasty just now. His offer seemed such a Heaven-sent opportunity that naturally I assumed you would see it that way too.'

She was silent, and Parson Weaver could not see the expression on her face. He said at length, 'And if you do not marry Mr Hollar? I doubt if I can persuade your father to be forgiving a second time.'

'No.' She stooped to break off a fat rushy stem and roll it between her fingers. Suddenly she remembered the old sorcerer on the moors, and his words as he lifted the strange child Dorcas in his arms. She said, 'I shall remember the lilies of the field . . .'

Her impracticality revived the parson's exasperation.

'Such talk does you no credit, Margaret. Our Lord did not intend us to interpret His teachings as an encouragement to fly in the face of common sense. From what you have already said, I understand that it is not Mr Hollar himself that you object to, only the somewhat impersonal manner of his proposal. Is that correct?'

'I suppose so.'

'Then I intend to return to Porthew now and tell him that although you see no reason to reject his offer, you would prefer to hear it from his own lips.'

Still rolling the reed between finger and thumb. 'Yes.'

'Hmm.' He was frowning, but then he grinned at her suddenly. 'For someone in such a desperate situation as you are now, you drive a hard bargain. But Margaret, before you speak with him yourself, consider well what the alternative would be.'

'I will.'

He glanced towards the farmhouse. 'I will talk to Mr Hollar but you must deal as best you can with your family. I daresay you will manage them admirably.'

They walked back together towards the yard. As Margaret led Sarah from her stable, Parson Weaver was about to bid her farewell but then he smiled and touched her arm. 'I did not know,' he said, 'that you were possessed of such courage.'

She answered his smile and at the sight of her wide mouth and dancing grey eyes the parson felt the familiar kick of longing deep within him. Then she was solemn again.

'It's not courage, Parson. Maybe my step-mother is right and I am mad after all. But when I heard you all talking in there I knew that if I didn't say anything, if I allowed this matter to be settled with no more thought for my opinion than for a heifer being got ready for market, then I would have lost the only thing that I have held on to these past few weeks.'

'And that is?'

She searched her mind for a few moments, then gave up. 'I do not know the word for it,' she said. 'Maybe it is pride.'

'Then I hope for your sake that your pride has not been dearly bought and Mr Hollar is prepared to play the part of the humble suitor. Good day to you, Margaret.'

And with that he mounted the ungainly Sarah and splashed through the puddles at the entrance to the yard – and Margaret heard him cursing the mare as she flattened her ears and swerved to avoid some feathered danger hopping through the hedge.

By the time William Hollar himself rode over to Conwinnion a couple of days later he had good reason, though he did not know it, to be grateful to his prospective sister-in-law. Lizzie had been more than half in love with the newcomer since St Ewan's Day and now that he had offered himself as Margaret's rescuer, it seemed to her quite obvious that this was the stuff of which fairy tales are made.

'He must have been taken with you the very first time he saw you,' she insisted as they churned the butter together and the hail rattled down on the roof of the dairy. 'I *thought* there was something unusual in the way he looked at you even then.'

Later that day as they sat plucking chickens in the doorway of the hay-barn, she warmed to her theme. 'Do you remember how he went out of his way to be friendly that Sunday after church when no one would speak to us? He was falling in love with you then, I'm sure of it.'

And the next morning, as they pounded washing in the wash-house, Lizzie had the whole business settled – at least to her own satisfaction. 'And that explains why he decided to remain in Porthew and look after Mr Hocken's shop. He's prepared to give up the grand life he's always been used to because he's head over heels in love with you and so he wants to stay. I can't wait to see everyone's expression when they hear the news, they'll be so angry!'

'What news? Really, Lizzie, you do talk endless nonsense. Parson said nothing of love . . .'

But though Margaret pretended to be unmoved by Lizzie's daydreams it was easy enough to let the illusion grow. She knew hardly anything about William Hollar, merely that he was kind-hearted, educated, that he had travelled – and that he had told Parson that he wished to marry her. He was a stranger and he was quite the handsomest man she had ever seen – and around the figure of his well-dressed person she found herself weaving a young girl's dreams. Lizzie's talk was all idle nonsense, of course . . . unless, just supposing, what if . . . ?

All the more galling, therefore, that when William Hollar did arrive at the farm Tom had just tumbled headlong into the midden while helping the tabby Achilles in his swift pursuit of a rat. Tom was wailing so loudly that she did not hear the approaching horseman and though she picked the child out of the mud as carefully as possible he was less considerate and clung to her skirts with filthy hands.

'Stop your fussing, Tom, there's no real harm done. Hush now and when you're clean I'll find you a sugared apricot.'

'I see you are busy. Perhaps I should come back later.'

Startled, Margaret looked up and found herself staring into the violet-blue eyes of Mr Hollar. Still seated on his chestnut cob, he was looking down on the scene with obvious distaste.

'Oh, Mr Hollar, I never heard you coming. Tom has just . . . well, you can see for yourself what has happened. There now, Tom, stop your wailing. We must see to Mr Hollar's horse –'

But Tom still howled and clung to her skirts and Mr Hollar suddenly looked as though more than anything in the world he wanted to clap his heels to his horse's sides and gallop away from the farm.

At that moment Lizzie appeared at the doorway, her hands floury with baking and her most delighted smile dimpling her face. She had no intention of dealing with the filthy Tom but she smiled up at their visitor most prettily and said, 'Won't you come in, Mr Hollar? We have been expecting you,' so that while Lizzie led him into the house, Margaret was able to take Tom to the wash-house and to clean him (and herself) as best she could.

By the time Margaret, less dirty now but damper from the washing, went into their little kitchen, Mr Hollar had already refused Lizzie's offers of ale, mincemeat tarts and almond buns and was, at Mistress Pearce's suggestion, sipping a little of the wine that had been got in for Christmas, though with no sign of enjoyment.

He glanced up and smiled as Margaret came into the room. 'I hope the child is not hurt?'

'Only his pride,' she said, taking heart from the note of gentleness in his voice, 'and that will mend soon enough.'

'Lizzie,' Mistress Pearce addressed her daughter without once taking her eyes off the stranger's face, 'Margaret can tend to Mr Hollar now. Go and fetch your father.'

'But –'

Her mother frowned and Lizzie, pouting, left the room.

Margaret sat down on a joint stool, fiddled a moment or two with the hem of her apron, stood up again suddenly and said, 'Mr Hollar, we can talk more privately outside.'

Mistress Pearce said, 'There's surely no need of that.'

But Margaret ignored her step-mother and waited for the visitor's response. Unable to meet her eyes, he glanced away briefly before saying, 'As you wish.'

Margaret led the way across the little orchard to a gate that led into a small meadow where their two cows were grazing.

She leaned her forearms on the highest rail of the gate and turned to look at William Hollar. 'You wished to speak with me?'

His eyes met hers for the briefest moment before he looked away, cleared his throat and began to speak. 'Parson Weaver has already told you of the reason for my visit. As you know, Mistress Hocken has asked me to remain at Porthew and take over the management of my late uncle's business. I stated what I considered to be reasonable terms and conditions and these she has seen fit to accept. I intend therefore to make my home with them. Since I am now in a position to settle down . . .' until now his words had been fluent enough but at this point his self-assurance began to unravel, 'it appears to be a suitable moment in my life at which to consider . . . As a man of some standing in the community it is only right to . . .'

Margaret suppressed a smile. This elegant stranger was as nervous as a tongue-tied schoolboy; obviously he was unaware that his hesitation was more persuasive than any eloquence could have been. Ever soft-hearted, Margaret felt obliged to help him out.

'Are you saying that you wish to marry me, Mr Hollar?'

'Yes.'

Really, she thought, if I refuse him now they might as well carry me away to Bedlam. 'Then I accept.'

She heard his sigh of relief.

'But why?' The question was out before she had considered it.

He answered promptly, 'Because I want you to be my wife.'

'Oh.'

Margaret thought briefly that if this little scene had been played according to Lizzie's designs, then he should now be declaring undying devotion; instead he gave the impression of someone who has just successfully completed an awkward business transaction.

He said, 'We should inform your parents.'

'Yes . . . but wait. First there is something that I must . . .' This time it was Margaret who was momentarily at a loss for words. 'You know, Mr Hollar, that I am expecting a child?'

'My cousin told me.'

'Yet you wish to marry me none the less?'

'I knew all the circumstances when I approached Parson Weaver.'

'That is good. But – but, I never wish to speak of it. I gave my word. It's in the past now but . . . I don't want you to ask me –'

'What's done is of no interest to me at all. Parson told me something of your misfortunes and he assured me that you will be an honest and loyal wife. On the few occasions when we have met I have reached the same conclusion. That is all I ask.'

'Thank you.' But even as she spoke, Margaret shivered. Really, she thought, I must be the most contrary person alive. Here he is giving me the very answer I wanted and yet it seems too cold, too distant. How strange to think that one day, perhaps not so very far from now, this chilly stranger will be as familiar to me as my own family. More so. Perhaps then we shall be able to look back on this odd courtship and laugh over it together. Man and wife. Blood of my blood and flesh of my flesh. She shivered again.

'You are cold. We should return to the house. But first

I have something for you. Here –' And he drew from his pocket a small volume. 'It is the story of Hero and Leander as told by Mr Marlowe.'

The gift was so unexpected and so hugely welcome that Margaret beamed with pleasure and began at once to pour out her thanks. William's eyes met hers for the first time and he smiled, a smile of great gentleness and charm. Suddenly Margaret dared to hope that her own life might one day be touched with that same magic that she had so often read about in books.

'Oh William –!' She touched his arm.

He drew back, retracting his head slightly like a snail retreating into its shell. He said, 'Now that you have accepted my offer I shall have the volume bound. I did not want to go to the expense until I was sure of your answer.'

She was amused by this evidence of his caution, but, fearing that her smile might annoy him, she began to leaf through the book, reading eagerly.

'See here,' she said, beginning to read, '"Whoever loved, that loved not at first sight?"' But as she looked up again he turned away coldly.

'I am not familiar with the poem,' he said, 'it was the parson who suggested the choice.'

He began to walk briskly back towards the house and Margaret, after a moment's hesitation, picked up her skirts and followed. He did not wait for her but stayed always a few paces ahead, picking his way carefully through the mud. Margaret walked more slowly, and took heart from the smooth pages of the book against her hand.

John Pearce was pathetically grateful to meet the man who was to save his daughter's reputation. He came in from the fields with his boots caked in mud and his clothes filled with the smell of animals and furze. By now Margaret was growing used to William Hollar's fastidious manner when meeting people, that backward tilt of the head, the way his hand nervously touched the clean lace at his throat.

As she followed him into the house and took her seat by the fire she found herself looking at their kitchen for the first time as he must surely be seeing it: the furniture serviceable but rough; their few items of pewter displayed on the shelf beside the window with her step-mother's beloved silver salt-cellar, the only item of any value they possessed. Until this moment she had only seen its warmth and familiarity; now, suddenly, she felt almost ashamed.

The conversation between the two men was brief and to the point. Yes, he wished to marry Margaret. Well, John Pearce had no objection to that. William thought a wedding before Christmas would be best? John Pearce was all agreement. There was the matter of a dowry to consider, and William must provide a portion. Her father was not wealthy but he knew when it was right to be generous. William Hollar likewise.

By noon the outlines of the agreement were settled. More wine was poured, a toast was drunk to the future couple, Lizzie and Tom were allowed in to share the celebration. Tom remembered suddenly that this was the man who had given him a penny on St Ewan's Day. His belief that Christmas was come early this year was confirmed when Mr Hollar obliged him with another coin.

'I am glad you'll marry Mattie,' said Tom generously, 'then you'll come and live with us and I shall have pennies every day of the year.'

William laughed, the first time he had done so that day, and pinched Tom's cheeks.

Margaret said, 'Don't be silly, Tom. Mr Hollar will not live here. I shall go to his house at Porthew.'

Tom stared at her in disbelief. 'But you'll have to come home again each evening.'

'No. My home will be with Mr Hollar once we are wed. I shall live there always.'

'But I want you to stay here!' Tom was furious.

'Lord help us,' even Mistress Pearce had forgotten her aching joints and was laughing that day, 'the boy's been at the wine when no one was looking.'

Tom's face was beginning to turn a curious shade of purple.

'Oh dear,' Margaret could not help laughing, 'I promise you I'll come back and visit whenever I can.'

'You must not go! I shan't let you! Stay here!' He was working himself into a lather of hysterics. 'Bad man, go away!' And before anyone could stop him he had hurled himself at Mr Hollar's legs with all the fury of a rabid dog and was beating his fists against the stranger's fashionably clad legs.

'You wicked boy!'

'Stop that at once!'

'Tom, don't –!'

But before any of the women could reach him, John Pearce had grabbed his son by the scruff of the neck and picked him up, still yelling and kicking and clutching at Mr Hollar's clothes. There was an ominous tearing sound. To their horror they saw that one of Tom's flailing fists still held a portion of fine boot hose.

'Oh Mr Hollar!' Margaret was torn between laughter and dismay, but, after the tensions of the morning, it was hardly surprising that laughter won the day and this time she was quite unable to hide her amusement. She could hear Lizzie vainly trying to smother her giggles while John Pearce walloped his son.

William Hollar had turned very pale. He gathered up his hat and gloves.

Tom was set down and ran to bury his face in his mother's skirts. She stroked his curls tenderly and said, 'You must forgive him, Mr Hollar. Margaret's always taken care of him when I was poorly and he's fearsome fond of her.'

'Then she should have taught him better manners. He ought to be whipped, damn him!'

His outrage damped their laughter at once. Silence followed, broken only by an occasional bubbling sob from Tom.

'I wish you all good day.'

Proud as a cat, William Hollar stalked from the room.

'After him, Margaret,' said Mistress Pearce, 'don't let him leave in anger.'

But when she caught up with him at the door of the shed where his brown cob had been stabled she found him more than ready to be placated.

'I daresay I was somewhat hasty,' he said, fingering the reins; 'I fear I am not much used to children.'

'Oh, Tom's mightily spoiled. You were right to be angry,' said Margaret easily, 'he's had three doting females to look after him all his life and he would like the same arrangement to last for ever. But I'm sorry that we laughed.'

'I do like children, you know. But still, it might be a good idea if next time we meet in Porthew.'

'I shall be at church on Sunday.'

'I look forward to seeing you again.' He paused. Margaret expected him to mount his horse and ride away, but still he lingered, not speaking, not even looking at her.

'Is there something more you wish to say, Mr Hollar?'

'Yes.' He pressed the tips of his pale fingers against his forehead, then, letting his hand fall once more to his side, he said, 'It may well be that when people learn of our betrothal they will think . . . it is after all only natural that some will assume . . . that since you are to have a child and I am . . . people will of course make their own judgements but if some should believe that I am the father –'

Margaret stood very still. She was searching his face intently. 'What then?' she prompted gently.

'You need not tell them different.'

'You wish it to be thought that the child is yours?'

'Yes.'

'But why – ?'

'I would have thought the answer was obvious. It will be much better for all of us, certainly better for the child.'

Margaret could see him very clearly, the flecks of gold in his violet-blue eyes, the Adam's apple high in his throat, lips parted over little white teeth, the honey-coloured hair that fell in fashionable curls over the white lace of his collar. At that moment, more than anything in the world, Margaret wanted to believe that she and William Hollar might one day love each other.

He raised his arm slightly, as though to shield himself from her gaze.

'I shall see you on Sunday. Good day.'

And with that he mounted the chestnut cob and rode swiftly from the yard, leaving Margaret staring, and wondering.

William, riding his misty way back to Porthew, wondered if his success today had indeed been cause for congratulation.

Once he had decided to take up his aunt's offer and assume the role of town draper and respectable member of the community, it seemed eminently sensible to do the job properly. A man who settles in a place is expected to take a wife; he had had no hesitation in choosing Margaret. She appeared warm-hearted and reliable, with some quality he could not precisely name but which no doubt was inherited from her foreign mother and which set her slightly apart from her fellows. He liked her. He felt sorry for her. He hoped she would be grateful. He wondered, now, if that was enough.

And, as he began the descent into Porthew and the sounds and smells of the little town rose up around him, he wondered in an agony of doubt, how he would ever learn to withstand the piercing clarity of her wide grey eyes.

The scandal-mongers were outraged.

Not only had their victim escaped her proper punishment, she had turned to laugh in their faces. After all their gleeful prophecies of doom it was heartless of the girl to prove them so completely wrong. Just look at her now, walking to church as proud as a queen and laughing with her sister as if she had not a care in the world. It all seemed to prove that there was no justice to be had this side of Judgement Day. And how could Mr Hollar have been so perverse as to choose a girl who read foreign books and was no better than she ought to be, when young Joan (or Susan or Mary or Tamsin, depending on which thwarted mother was speaking) had been a good girl all her life and couldn't even sign her name and would have suited the wealthy newcomer so much better?

A brief attempt was made to denigrate Mr Hollar. Surely there was something suspicious about the suddenness of his appearance from the middle of nowhere. And what did anyone know about his life during all those long years abroad? He had never been heard to speak of it, and he was quite unlike any of the local men.

But these attempts soon foundered. William Hollar was handsome, he was hard-working and his behaviour was impeccable. Half the women in the district were in love with him already and those that weren't could not help but be impressed by his character and appearance.

There were residual grumblings against Margaret. It was still accepted that she was sure to come to a bad end one day, but since the timing of the bad end had been incomprehensibly postponed, they had no choice but to bow to the inevitable. The future Mistress Hollar would be a woman of some standing in the community – and there was no reason to cross her now.

And then the gossip wavered for a short while, changed course, then surged full ahead on a strong tide of speculation. For if Mr Hollar was to marry Margaret Pearce didn't that suggest that he was the anonymous father of the infant she was carrying? Why else should his choice fall on her? There were other girls to pick from with wealthier fathers . . . but the conniving girl had snared him that very first day. Joan Dawkins hinted as much, though not quite in those words, when she was in his shop to buy some baize. He did not answer her directly but his smile told her more than enough: the suspicion was as good as confirmed.

The news was all over town before nightfall. Yes, certainly, he must have bedded her almost at once (another midsummer baby for St Ewan) and the only puzzle that remained was why he hadn't agreed to marry her as soon as the knowledge of her pregnancy became public.

By the beginning of December the last grumblings of disapproval and suspicion had died away. The same men and women who had turned their backs on Margaret when she went to Porthew with her face bruised from her father's beating, now smiled indulgently when they saw her with her future husband. It was perfectly obvious that he must be the father of her child. Anyone who saw the pair of them walk arm in arm down the street, both so tall and fair and handsome, could see that they thought the world of each other, were, in fact, head over heels in love.

A sombre blustery afternoon. The sea moving, restless; a dark swell coming in from the west. Tiny boats hastening to harbour ahead of the charcoal blur between sea and sky that told of the approaching storm.

Margaret, hurrying back from Porthew before the storm broke, saw the smoke rising from the farmhouse chimney and then, on a sudden impulse, cut across the field and went to stand on the cliff's edge as her mother used to do when she herself was a child.

Below her, between the cliff face and the sea, gulls soared and screamed. The smells of salt and seaweed were blowing inland on a heady west wind.

Just once more, she thought, to stand here alone, Margaret Pearce, my own name. My own self.

Darkness was spreading across the sea; another day was slipping away. Stop, stop, don't let the time pass so quickly. Only five more days before the wedding. Only five more days of Lizzie's giggles and the smell of woodsmoke in the kitchen, only five more days of Tom's tantrums and his sudden laughter; only five more days of familiar cats and the two old dogs and the rooks' constant squabbling in the elm trees; only five more days of this life that was suddenly more precious than any wealth could ever be.

Five more days. A shiver of excitement at the changes that were to come. A new life about to begin for her in the narrow house at the top of Porthew. A home for her child and a new sister in Merry.

Her courage grew as she thought of Merry. Her friend had been so pleased at the thought of Margaret coming to share her home that she had hardly stopped grinning all month.

Five more days. And then William. Margaret shrugged slightly and told herself for the hundredth time that she must give him time, that she was used to the rough and ready ways of the local men and that his manner, which seemed to her so cool and distant, was probably considered quite normal in those cities with the faraway names of which he sometimes spoke.

And yet . . . each time she was with him she found herself asking herself again the question that had come to haunt her: why had he chosen to marry her? Though he was courteous enough in public, every word and look made it clear that he was uncomfortable in her company. Lizzie's talk of secret love and adoration seemed more and more unlikely.

That afternoon Merry had dropped an unknowing hint and Margaret considered it now with a growing sense of desolation. Apparently William Hollar had been outraged when he had heard how badly Margaret had been treated when news of her pregnancy was made public and it was shortly after that that he had spoken to the parson concerning marriage. Margaret had to admit that he was a very kind man, a very generous one – but she was learning to her cost that pity is a humiliating suitor.

The sound of the wind and the gulls and the waves was so strong that she did not hear the footsteps approaching along the grassy track.

'Margaret.'

She turned around quickly.

'Father, I did not hear you.'

He had been leading Juno laden with two sacks of flour from the mill just as he had done two months before when he had seen her standing in this very spot.

This time he did not turn away.

His forehead was gathered into a frown, the anxious frown of a man who is grappling with problems beyond his understanding. His voice was gruff, as it always was when he was ill at ease. 'You have come from Porthew?'

She nodded. 'Mistress Hocken needed my help.'

'Did you see the parson?'

'There was no need.' Margaret had avoided him as much as possible during the past month.

'Then everything is arranged for Friday?'

'Yes, and my new dress is almost finished.' Her voice was suddenly tinged with pleasure. William had insisted that a length of sea-green cloth be used to make her a special dress for the wedding. He had given Mistress Hocken detailed instructions as to how it should be made and the finished result, though it seemed a little odd, was, he assured them, the height of fashion. Margaret was nearly as pleased with the new dress as she had been with her precious book.

But her father was still frowning. 'So you are satisfied with this present arrangement. With this marriage.'

'Everyone keeps telling me how lucky I am. And I suppose they must be right.'

'Hmm. I hope so.'

'What is it, Father?'

'I expect it's just an old man's foolishness but I dreamed . . . well, never mind what exactly . . . but it set me wondering . . . still, you're happy with it and that's good.'

Margaret was increasingly bewildered. 'What's troubling

195

you? I always thought you were more eager for this marriage than anyone.'

'Of course I am.' John Pearce appeared more uncomfortable than ever. 'But has he ever . . . well, you're not a maid so you must know . . . damnation, I should have got my wife to talk to you. Do you think you can be a proper wife to him, Mattie?'

It was the first time he had used her childhood name for many years, not since those far-off days long long before her mother had died. There was a constriction in Margaret's throat as if she might cry. Oh, to be a child again. To set down her burden and fling herself in her father's arms and bury her face in the worn leather of his jerkin and close her eyes and let her worries ebb away to nothingness in the gentle sea of his voice.

But the easy comforts of childhood had gone for ever. Besides, she could not forget that this man had beaten her when she yearned for understanding.

'I shall do my best to be a good wife,' she said.

'But if you feel you can't, if you want to change your mind . . . If for any reason . . . Well, I've been harsh with you since this trouble began. All I could see was the shame you'd brought us, but there are other things just as important and – well, if you felt you could not marry Mr Hollar, I daresay we'd manage somehow.'

Margaret was staring at him in disbelief. 'But what about the scandal? What about Lizzie and Tom? Why should they have to suffer because of my mistake?'

'There'd be a problem, certainly.'

'Then why do you even think of it?' Margaret searched his eyes for some hint of what had prompted this strange declaration but all she could see was the stubborn energy that drove him, the granite strength of the man.

He was scanning the simmering darkness of the sea. 'That must be the Roberts' boat,' he said, 'they'll be lucky to get home before the storm breaks.'

'Father, please, if you've heard talk, if you have any reason to think that Mr Hollar is not suitable, for God's sake tell me now. Don't leave it until it's too late.'

'No no. They're all full of his praises round here.'

'Then why are you talking to me now?'

'It's only . . . well, foolish of me even to mention it. I've never been one to set much store by dreams.'

'So what was this dream that troubled you so?'

'Tch. I can't remember the details now. It left a bad taste in my mouth, that's all.' He patted her shoulder, and it seemed to Margaret that the gesture was as much for his own comfort as for hers. 'But I see that I was fussing for no reason, so there's no more need be said. Come, we'd best get home before the rain starts; it's going to be a bad night. He's a good man, Mr Hollar, no doubt about it. God willing, you should do well together.' And with that he slapped Juno's rump and began to trudge down towards the farm.

Two days before the wedding was due to take place, William Hollar awoke with a burning mouth and throat. During the morning he collapsed in the shop while lifting down a bolt of cherry-coloured damask and Merry, running to her assistance, found to her horror that his face and hands were covered in a fiery rash. By evening the rash covered the whole of his body and smallpox was diagnosed.

Margaret spent the day that should have seen her married, in helping the apothecary who arrived from Helston with leeches and powerful emetics. William was delirious and did not even recognise her. The illness had struck with more than its usual severity and he was not expected to recover.

8

To travel from West Cornwall to Plymouth in the year 1630 was to move from a narrow community, enclosed in its own ageless rhythm of birth and death, planting and harvest, famine and plenty, to a city pulsing with vitality and new ideas: a city in constant touch with London and the sea ports of Europe; place of departure for the terrors and endless possibilities of the New World.

Plymouth was a city grown fat on the hoped-for wealth of the Americas, a city of merchants who counted their riches in tuns of wine and bales of tobacco, in stores of grain to provision the ships, a city of every trade associated with the sea, enough rope to girdle the earth, canvas sufficient for a winding sheet for the nation, a forest of trees sawn into planks daily, oceans of tar.

When Richard Treveryan entered its city walls in the driving rain of an October afternoon, bad weather had prevented any ships from sailing for over a week and the inns and hostelries were choked with travellers waiting to take ship and with seamen whose craft had been driven to seek shelter from the Atlantic storms. Plague had swept through the city during the summer but now, with the onset of winter, the number of new cases was declining. Only a few houses remained closed and the life of the town was returning to that degree of organised chaos which was generally considered normal.

The narrow streets were choked with the ebb and flow of an ever-changing population: plump merchants in their beaver-lined cloaks, their eyes eager for the next day's profit; sober-suited Puritans averting their gaze from the Babylon in which they must now abide and fixing their inner vision on the Eternal City and its earthly counterpart across the sea; craftsmen of every kind – and that huge assembly of human parasites who swarm around a rich sea port like flies over rotting fish: pimps and whores and pickpockets and tricksters; survivors of earlier tragedies, the blind and the maimed and the dying; charlatans and quacks to prey on men's despair – soothsayers and necromancers and purveyors of chalk pills to cure every ill. And the entertainers, jugglers and dancers, the Irish with their music, sailors with strange animals and tales of hardship and adventure.

And here the gossip had a cosmopolitan flavour – not just the endless tally of the sick and dying, the cuckolded husband and the bastard child, but reverberations from a wider stage. Here there was anger at King Charles's treatment of Sir John Eliot, that favourite Cornishman who even now was a prisoner in the Tower, and all for having dared to voice the opposition many shared; anger that the King's French wife was allowed to let her Papist priests loose in the country; anger too that the King continued to collect his revenues without the legal assent of Parliament.

Richard had little interest in politics but he threw himself with gusto into the turmoil of city life. In the taverns there was laughter and music and good company, wines from France and Spain and girls who were pretty enough by the light of a tallow candle for a passing pleasure. In little more than a week he was persuaded that he had forgotten Alice Laniver completely.

It was less easy to forget his ruined fortunes since each day his small store of money declined. He wasted no time in being fitted for a new suit of clothes of the utmost elegance and fashion – now that he no longer had the income of a gentleman, it was important to look like one.

He stayed at the house of his uncle long enough to know the accommodation was not to his taste. Matthew Dawlish, like so many of the wealthy townsfolk of Plymouth, had been infected by a new and virulent strain of Puritanism. Richard suspected that it was the financial advantages of the creed that attracted his uncle. The relative cheapness of modest clothes and an unostentatious lifestyle appealed to his natural parsimony and a liberal sprinkling of biblical references usually inspired a measure of trust in his business associates.

His dizzy-headed wife, Celia, had at first fretted against

199

the hated plain clothes and tedious family devotions but, by the time Richard arrived in Plymouth, she was beginning to recognise the advantages of her husband's certainty that they were the fortunate members of God's chosen few. Having been spoiled by her father as a child and by her husband as an adult, it seemed only right and proper that she should continue to be spoiled by the Almighty in the world to come.

It was instantly obvious to the divinely favoured couple that their nephew did not share their heavenly good fortune. The youth had the mark of Cain on him if ever a man did. Matthew Dawlish was impatient to be rid of his nephew: his presence was unsettling in a household of young children, and besides, he saw no reason why he should waste his hard-earned money simply because his sister Isabel had been foolish enough to marry a man who had squandered every penny he possessed. Celia was more tolerant. In fact she was fascinated to study at close hand such an obvious candidate for damnation. Since his arrival in Plymouth Richard had devoted himself with a single-minded zeal to drinking and whoring and occasionally brawling as well. Her imagination burned with images of how he spent his idle hours and during the long sessions that the household devoted to extempore prayer and readings from the Bible – sessions that Richard categorically refused to attend – she diverted herself by imagining poignant scenes during which she exhorted him with great eloquence to save his eternal soul. Sometimes, as she pictured their conversations, he was so impressed by the sincerity of her arguments that he declared himself to be overcome with love for her and had to be gently (and not always immediately) repulsed.

To Celia's intense chagrin her chances to examine, let alone to reform, the young reprobate became increasingly rare since after the first few days he was hardly ever to be found at home. She was quite disproportionately piqued when she learned from her maidservant that he was now always to be found at the Swan Inn, an establishment that was run, during the owner's long absences at sea, by his wife, Mistress Miriam Porter. Mistress Porter was reputed to possess a bed that had cost over a hundred pounds and it did not need the maid's suggestive remarks to tell Celia that her nephew was now sharing this expensive item of furniture with the woman. Her romantic daydreams ceased abruptly and she began to agree with her husband that it was high time Richard found gainful employment, preferably as far from Plymouth as possible.

Miriam Porter lay back against the heaped-up pillows and yawned. Although it was nearly noon she had not yet risen and the curtains of her room were still drawn against the commotion from the street below. As a girl she had been considered a beauty, with the black hair and pale skin of her mother's Spanish forebears. Hers was the kind of sultry loveliness that quickly fades: in a few years' time nothing would remain of her charms, but in the autumn of 1630, when she was not much older than the century, she had reached that point of overblown beauty when some things are at their loveliest, like a full-blooming damask rose at that fragile moment just before the petals fall to the ground. There was a husky ripeness to her voice and movements, ease and sureness in her manner.

Her dark eyebrows were now gathered to frown at the girl who was trying to convert damp sticks and hay into a blaze.

'Confound you, girl, can't you work any faster? I'm half-perished with the cold.'

The girl, a frightened mite who had only arrived from the country a week before, scrabbled anxiously with the flint and twigs in an effort at least to be seen to do something. Miriam cursed her briefly for an idle wretch and reached for the glass of wine on the table beside her bed.

There was the sound of a man's footsteps on the stair and Miriam's face softened with pleasure as Richard, knocking briefly at the door, came into the room.

'At last,' she said. 'Where in the world have you been all morning? I've been bored to distraction and now this clod-head has allowed the fire to die.'

'I've been visiting my tailor. See now –' And ignoring the unfortunate maidservant he threw back the curtains and as the light poured into the room Miriam gave a cry of amazement, then laughed aloud with pleasure.

'A transformation! My *lord*, such fine new clothes, how

201

very grand you look. I am honoured –' And she broke off, laughing.

'See here,' he came closer, 'the colour may look a dark red but the fellow assured me it was mulberry which as you know is different altogether. And how do you like the cut of my doublet? Five buttons below the elbow, and the same fabric, look, lining the cloak. Just as it is done at court. And the breeches, note carefully the length. And how about this great quantity of lace? I feel as if I've just stepped into a closet full of cobwebs but . . . there it is, fashion is a hard task-master.'

'And your boots?'

'The finest Spanish leather. I still squeak when I walk. The hat – well, I'm afraid you'll have to wait a little longer for that masterpiece. They had decorated it with a feather so large I might have flown away altogether. They are changing it now. By this evening my renaissance will be complete.'

'And what has become of the leather-coated country gentleman who arrived only last month?'

Richard gestured with his hand across his throat. 'Dead, ma'am. Murdered in the interests of commerce, or advancement, call it what you will. My God, Miriam, but I loathe these ridiculous clothes. I feel trussed up and foolish as a Christmas goose.'

'But a good deal handsomer. I never yet took a goose to my bed. And if they make you uncomfortable you can always take them off. Here . . .' he sat down on the bed beside her, 'tch, these buttons are so stiff.'

Suddenly she broke off, staring at him in mock horror. 'Lord above, just look at you. Such courtly clothes – and hair like a tar brush. That won't do at all. Hey, girl, what's your name . . .'

'Mary, ma'am.'

'Well then, whatever your name is, fetch me my scissors. No, not there, you fool. In the box beside the chest. And the brush. Now –'

She began snipping at Richard's rough hair, brushing and snipping, with an expression of intense concentration. 'It's a shame there's no curl to it. To be a proper courtier you need elegantly curling locks –' And she took a portion of

202

his wiry hair and let it fall in apparent despair. 'Still, if you just sit and let me trim a little more, we'll soon have a passably elegant head for your grand new *chapeau* to rest upon.'

'You'll turn me into a complete fop.'

'You? Never – but all the wealthy widows will be tripping over each other to lay their money at your feet. And then you won't have to go away and fight in Holland as you keep threatening. Stop twisting – or you'll lose an ear. Did you look in at the tap room on your way through?'

'I did. Your servants are all stealing from you and drinking your ale and the cook is asleep by the fire. In fact all is just as it was yesterday.'

'The scoundrels. The moment my back is turned . . . Look at that girl there, can't even light a fire properly and yet she expects to eat her fill with the others.'

'It's going now, ma'am.' The girl scrambled to her feet. Her pinched face was covered in soot and smuts.

'Lucky for you that it is. Now be off downstairs and fetch some Spanish wine – warmed and sweetened, Piers knows how it should be done. And no tasting it yourself, either. There now,' she declared as Mary scampered from the room, 'His Lordship's *toilette* is finished. How do you like it?'

Richard pulled a face. 'I preferred it before. Now I look like every empty-headed youth with his eyes fixed on advancement.'

'No,' Miriam was thoughtful, 'with those features you'll never look like anyone but yourself,' and she let her finger-tips brush the gaunt outline of his cheekbone, the arch of his nose, the smooth skin around his lips, twisted now into a smile of self-mockery. Her heartbeat quickened. This youth who had first attracted her attention by brawling with her ostler a week ago was altogether different from the idle young gentlemen or sea-coarsened sailors with whom she habitually diverted herself during her husband's absences. 'And anyway,' she went on, 'I thought advancement was the reason for this peacock display. Or was that just an excuse to mask your vanity?'

'Not at all. Ambition is my only motive, as it is for most men even if they do like to dress it up in fine words and call it public duty and working to the glory of God and Heaven knows what other nonsense. For myself, ambition is enough – and duty and the glory of God be damned.'

Miriam's smile was mocking. 'Oh, and don't you think you're a fine fellow to admit it and not be a damnable hypocrite like the others?'

Richard laughed and did not bother to argue. Despite her indolence this innkeeper's wife understood his weaknesses as well as anyone. He said, 'After a week at my uncle's house I'm an expert on hypocrisy.'

'Oh, your uncle's no worse than many others. So, tell me, how do you intend to make use of your grand appearance – apart, that is, from getting credit with tradesmen?'

'I've not yet decided. Perhaps I should follow your advice and seek out a wealthy widow.'

Miriam was sceptical. 'If they were that easy to come by there'd be no poor men left.'

'There's one in Saltash I know of already. She's young too, so I'm told. Apart from that I know nothing about her – except that my step-father intends her to marry his younger son.'

'Ah, now I understand her real attractions. Not only wealth, but the pleasure of thwarting poor Sir John into the bargain.'

'If only I could. His vexation at seeing a rich heiress slip away might well induce a terminal fit of apoplexy. But that's probably too much to hope for. I daresay the young lady is already spoken for.'

'Then you'd better hurry. Ah, at last, here's the spiced wine I ordered. Confound you, girl,' as the frightened Mary set down the tray, 'this is barely tepid. Can't you do anything right? No no, leave it here and get back to your pots. And leave orders we're not to be disturbed. Well then,' she turned her attention back to Richard, 'if you are planning to go widow-hunting then I'd better make the most of you now. Pull the curtains around the bed – that miserable fire is less use than a candle in a snowstorm.'

She poured the wine while Richard pulled off his boots. 'Oof, that's better. The old ones were far more comfortable.'

Miriam smiled up at him from her nest of white pillows. 'Old things often are,' she said. Richard brushed back the hair that fell across her shoulders and noticed the threads of grey among the black. He noticed too the puffiness around her eyes, the loose skin on her cheeks and jaw. What beauty she had once possessed was fading fast, its decline speeded no doubt by her habit of tippling wine from the moment she awoke in the morning until last thing at night. Sometimes he despised himself for having taken up with her at all but she was easy and convivial company and, as she herself had said, her body was as comfortable and pliant as a well-worn suit of clothes.

'Here,' she said, her night-brown eyes watching his every move, 'let me warm your hands.'

Her breasts were huge and formless, a sea of pleasure in which he had hoped at first he might lose himself entirely. But there was no surrender for him in their love-making. Even as he kissed her and heard her wordless sounds of pleasure, there was a part of him that remained detached, aloof. And that still separate part of him whispered, 'If this were only Alice . . .' and he had a vision of a girl's clear eyes and a body slim and firm and he was engulfed by a huge loneliness, that terrible isolation in being mortal which he could never quite obliterate. It was not Alice herself that he mourned, so much as the death of his dream that love might prove an end to isolation. The door that had closed.

And so Richard made love to the innkeeper's wife and drank her wine and seized on any pleasure or distraction that came his way – but even as he spent his energy between her silk-soft thighs the emptiness within him was growing to a huge cold cavern of loneliness in which he knew he must abide for ever.

'Positively no, Father. I will see no more messengers from Sir John Sutton.'

Ralph Jordan looked at his daughter with exasperation. 'Only meet with him, Kitty. He told me himself that this was an informal visit.'

'Since I have no intention of marrying Sir John's son, I see no purpose in wasting my time with his kinsman.'

'And what else do you have to do that is so much more urgent?'

Kitty regarded her father coolly. 'I plan to visit my

steward later this morning. He recommends selling some trees at the Barton.'

'Tch! That's man's work. You should let me deal with it.'

'We discussed all that when Edwin died. I plan to remain in this house and to manage my own affairs. And I will not let you dictate my choice of husband again.'

Ralph Jordan had to turn away to hide his irritation. It had been so much easier the first time when he had wanted to marry his fourteen-year-old daughter to the wealthy but elderly Edwin Sawle, late of Saltash. Two days in her room without food and the threat of a beating had been sufficient to bring her into line. Now here she was, a widow at twenty-two and mistress of her own house with three manors to her name and two ships now returning to Plymouth laden with cargo, and the damned girl had the notion that she could do as she wished – and the worst part of it was that she was right.

He turned again to face her. 'Come now, Kitty dear. Let's be reasonable. I'm only trying to guide you as a loving father ought. After all, since Mr Sawle's death you're all alone in the world. You should be settled, not worrying your head about rents and revenues and trees. A young husband, children –'

'I don't remember that you were much troubled by such considerations at the time of my first marriage.'

'Well. Maybe there were one or two problems between you and Mr Sawle. But the Suttons are one of the oldest families in Cornwall. Marry into that family and you can take your place in any company in England.'

Kitty eyed her father warily and, as she always did when agitated, she bit the skin around her thumbnail. She felt disorientated and found herself almost yearning for her father's usual threats and bluster. At least then she would know where she stood.

'First you marry me to a dotard and now you would have me wed to a beardless boy. If I do decide on a second marriage I want a man who can be a real husband, not some puny child.'

'There there. Boys turn into men soon enough. Perhaps this messenger of Sir John's will be able to tell you more about the lad. There's surely no harm in hearing what he has to say.'

Kitty said nothing.

'Only talk to him, Kitty. He's waiting downstairs now and he assures me he has an important message from Stephen himself. Please, Kitty, for my sake.'

'Oh, very well,' Kitty capitulated crossly, 'but I shall only speak with him for a short while. I plan to inspect that woodland while the weather holds.'

'That's my good girl.' Ralph Jordan rewarded his daughter with a brief kiss on the forehead. 'I'll tell him to come up at once.'

Well pleased with himself he hurried from the room to usher in the messenger before the wayward girl changed her mind.

Afterwards, he could think of nothing in his whole life that he regretted half so much as persuading his daughter to talk with Richard Treveryan.

She had a narrow face, not pretty at all. A flatterer might have said Kitty Sawle's features showed animation – but it was less the animation of high spirits than a kind of constant busyness which led only to the appearance of activity – seldom to any real achievement. If she was in company she talked; if she was alone she sought companionship. If there was no one else about then she bothered the servants.

She was small, not much above five feet tall. Her face was thin and sallow with a long nose and a mouth that drooped in perpetual discontent. Her only pride was her hair which was brown and curled most fashionably with hardly any help. She devoted a large portion of her day to her appearance. Now, in anticipation of yet another of Sir John Sutton's apparently endless stream of relatives and minions, she automatically went to a little mirror that hung by the fireplace and adjusted the curls about her face to exactly the positions that she believed most flattering.

'Kitty, my dear, this is Mr Treveryan. He's been telling me that his mother has recently married Sir John – so he and Stephen are as good as brothers.'

She had intended to ignore her uninvited guest: another of those legally minded family hangers-on, no doubt, some elderly relation hoping to ingratiate himself with the power-ful Sir John by winning over the wealthy widow for the family. She had raised the back of her hand to her mouth to draw attention to an ostentatious yawn but, catching sight of Richard, she paused, mouth still open, hand still raised: the yawn evolved into a little cough. She looked startled, stepped forward and extended her hand in greeting.

'A pleasure to meet you, Mr Treveryan.'

And, indeed, her surprise was a kind of pleasure. He was much younger than she had expected and had a vigour and energy that breathed a gust of fresh air into this old-man's house. She had lived all her life with people much older than herself: her father and his family, then the elderly Mr Sawle and his companions. She examined Richard carefully and noted with approval the fashionable cut of his clothes: perhaps the feather adorning the hat could have been a little larger, but still – the overall effect was far from displeasing. Like many women with more money than beauty, she had a formidable interest in dress. She decided that this interview promised more entertainment than she had anticipated.

'I regret that I cannot spare you much time, Mr Treveryan, but I am obliged to look over some woodland with my steward. And I fear that your journey here has been a wasted one.'

'Why so?'

'I must be honest with you. I cannot abide any kind of duplicity. I have absolutely no intention whatever of con-sidering marriage to Sir John's son.'

To her surprise the Suttons' messenger showed not the least dismay at her announcement. He merely shrugged his shoulders and said, 'Obviously you must make your own decision.'

Kitty found she was a little piqued. She had been looking forward to parrying his deft pleas on his cousin's behalf. 'No doubt, Mr Treveryan, you come armed with *all* manner of fine arguments in his favour: you've come to tell me what a fine young man he is and how well respected the family – et cetera et cetera.' And here she paused hopefully.

But 'No' was all his reply.

Ralph Jordan was fidgeting. 'Come now, man,' he said, uneasy but not yet angry, 'I thought you had a message from Mr Stephen Sutton that might perhaps persuade my daughter to think more kindly of him –'

Treveryan looked at him with disdain. 'Why should I trouble to do that? I am sure Mistress Sawle knows her own mind.'

'But . . . but . . . she knows nothing of the family, their standing in the neighbourhood.'

'Oh, that. They have lived a long time in the same place and own a good deal of property in the area: men are generally respected for such accidents of birth.'

'Have you come here, sir, to slander your own family?'

'Not at all. And young Stephen is a perfectly amiable boy. I'm sure that when he is older –'

'Then have you no message from him?'

'Oh yes. I have a message.'

'Tell her, then, for God's sake tell her!'

'Sir John bid me tell you, Mistress Sawle, that Stephen was made wretched by your indecision. Sir John asked me to tell you that one word from you would make him – though whether he meant the father or the son I cannot quite recall – either the happiest or the most miserable of men.'

'Surely Stephen gave you this message himself?'

'No doubt he would have done so but he was occupied with a game of skittles when I left and was not to be distracted.'

'You see, Father, he's just a child! First you make me marry someone old enough to be my grandfather and now you choose a boy hardly out of petticoats. I don't care if his family is as old as the Ark and as well respected as – as – as any other family. If and when I marry again it will be to a man of my own choosing. I will not be ruled by you. And it's no use trying to find another suitor to come courting me. This time I will decide for myself.'

'You have grown too headstrong!'

Kitty turned to Richard. 'How about you, Mr Treveryan? Is it headstrong to wish to make up one's own mind?'

Richard had been attending to her declaration with intense interest. He answered thoughtfully. 'Since all your future happiness depends upon it, Mistress Sawle, I do not in all honesty see how an intelligent woman could leave such a vital decision to intermediaries. But I also understand your father's concern: your position is vulnerable – and could easily be exploited by the unscrupulous.'

Kitty dismissed his words with a little laugh. 'I'm well aware of the dangers, no need to worry about that. And I've grown very clever at spying out the insincere. I know what they're up to, all of them. Another brace of pheasants arrived this morning from Horace Coome, Father. I shall thank him when I remember, but marry him – never!'

'I can see, Mr Jordan, that your daughter has a romantic disposition.'

Ralph Jordan eyed Treveryan suspiciously. 'She's not without friends or family, sir. You'd best remember that.'

'Father, what a strange thing to say. Mr Treveryan can hardly fail to see that I have a family.'

'He knows what I mean.'

Richard turned to Kitty. 'Your father believes I might be one of those unscrupulous suitors I was referring to just now. That I came here this morning with the express purpose of belittling my step-father's son and forwarding my own suit. Is that not right, Mr Jordan?'

'It could be, though I'm damned if I can work out exactly what you're up to –'

'Father! How can you be so suspicious!'

'Your father is merely trying to protect you, Mistress Sawle, and I must respect him for that. Unfortunately for his theories I must confess that, like you, I am one of those weak-willed people who could never marry where they did not also love. Oh yes, I know that property and family and all the rest of it are important enough, I'd be the last to deny that, but without the seal of mutual respect and affection they are merely . . .' Feeling that he was getting somewhat out of his depth, Richard cast around vaguely. Inspiration arrived. '. . . Merely sounding gongs and clashing cymbals,' he said, 'empty nothing. A mockery and a sham. But there, I'm sure you have better ways to spend your time than listening to my views on the subject of love and marriage. I shall leave you both in peace. Of course I am sorry that my cousin Stephen is to be disappointed, especially now I have seen for myself what a charming and high-spirited young lady he is losing. But, to tell you the truth, it is his father will take the loss hardest.'

210

Ralph Jordan could barely contain his rage. 'Good day to you, sir! I shall see you out!'

'Mr Treveryan,' said Kitty, 'wait. I am about to visit a manor of mine about five miles from here. If you've nothing else to do, perhaps you'd care to accompany me?'

'I'm sure Mr Treveryan has business to attend to in Plymouth.' Ralph Jordan spoke through clenched teeth.

'On the contrary, Mistress Sawle, I'd be delighted to come.'

'Kitty –'

'You must understand, Father, that now I am a widow I intend to do precisely as I please. And there is absolutely nothing you can do to stop me.'

As she swept past her father and led the way from the room, head held high, Richard, following, could barely restrain himself from bursting into loud and mocking laughter.

'You were right all along, Mistress Sawle, your steward clearly hopes to swindle you.'

'I thought as much,' said Kitty, trying to hide her surprise, for she had guessed no such thing. 'But tell me, how exactly do you think he plans to do it?'

'It's too soon to cut those woods down now unless you have urgent need of the money –' here Richard paused and looked at her curiously, but when she made no reply he continued, 'they've another ten years' good growth in them, perhaps fifteen. Which made me wonder why he was proposing their sale so soon. But when he told you their market value, I could see right away what he was up to.'

'And so could I.' Kitty frowned, wondering what Richard could possibly be driving at. 'He'd set the price too high –'

'Too low, you mean. You're absolutely right. They'll fetch at least a guinea a load more than he quoted you at the sawpits in Plymouth. The cunning rogue has found a buyer who has agreed to a paper price way below their proper value – and a generous donation to the steward on each one. That way the buyer gets cheap timber, the steward receives a handsome supplement to his wages – and the only loser is yourself.'

'The scoundrel!' Kitty's face, when angry, was

211

remarkably similar to her father's. 'How dare he try to cheat me like that! I shall send him packing at once.'

'That's for you to decide. But his replacement would likely be just as bad. Such types always think they can cheat a woman. Better by far to show him he must deal honestly with you or not at all.'

'Perhaps you're right.'

As it happened, Richard's advice was perfectly sound. He had seen at once what the old steward was aiming to do, and the man's carelessness made him guess that he had made a long practice of swindling, that the late Mr Edwin Sawle had been as blind to his trickery as Kitty was.

They were riding along a grassy track a little distance from the road itself which had been made almost impassable by the autumn rains. Kitty's manservant rode at a discreet distance ahead. Kitty wore a riding hat of such extravagant fashion that her face could hardly be seen: she appeared almost pretty.

'I shall ride out and speak to him again tomorrow. How dare he think he can trick me and get away with it!'

'You could tell him you are still undecided: it won't hurt to let him live with the fear of dismissal for a few days.'

'Or a month. I'd like to see him suffer. I'm not a vindictive person, Mr Treveryan, but I cannot tolerate dishonesty.' Kitty was still seething to think how she had been tricked. 'After all the help my late husband gave his family! A fine example of ingratitude!'

'Mr Sawle was a generous man?'

Kitty sighed. '*He* certainly thought so. He was for ever worrying what people thought and could hardly ever make up his mind.'

Richard noticed the exasperation in her voice as she spoke of her late husband. The plume on her hat wagged with irritation.

'He was a good deal older than you?'

'I was fourteen when I married, Mr Treveryan, and he was nearly seventy. I was married for eight years but –' she broke off, frowning.

'Now I understand your determination to make your own decisions. And, for what it is worth, you have my full support. Sir John Sutton wants a wealthy wife for his son; your father wishes for an alliance with an old family. The Lanivers put in a higher bid and are given the older son . . . it's a grubby and cynical business.'

'And if they had their own way I'd not even be consulted! Well, my father will see I intend to be the mistress of my own future. He finds that truly shocking.'

'He's old-fashioned, that's all. You can hardly blame him for that.'

'And do you also plan to marry for love, Mr Treveryan?'

'I certainly hope to love. Whether I shall marry or not is quite another matter.'

'Why do you say that?'

'I am not wealthy, Mistress Sawle. In fact, to be truthful, I have no fortune at all. My father brought me up to the life of a gentleman but by the time of his death, he had not only spent all his money but had borrowed large amounts so that virtually all our land had to be sold off to pay his debts. It's a sorry story – and one your father is no doubt aware of. Which accounts for his suspicions.'

'Oh, pay no heed to my father. He'll think I'm still an incompetent child when I'm a grandmother. I could never be one of those docile women who always do as they are bid. I'm far too high-spirited. Why, when I was only five years old my mother said I was more trouble than all my older brothers together. And when I was only seven . . .'

She rattled on. Try as he might, Richard found it hard to focus on her words. He was watching a kestrel which was hovering over a patch of open ground to the left of the road.

Kitty did not notice his inattention. She was delighted to have a young man to talk to and a constant stream of chatter issued from beneath the enormous hat. Her steward's trickery still rankled: she recounted several episodes that displayed her skill at outwitting would-be tricksters and then several others to reveal her kindness.

'. . . He looked so poor and thin, Mr Treveryan, that my heart quite went out to him, but I told him, "Now, look here, fellow, I'll not give you money because I know you'd only spend it all on drinks, but I'm a kind woman so here's

213

what I'll do. You chop that pile of wood over there and you can have as much food as you can eat while the job's being done." He was wonderfully grateful. And the wood was chopped cheaply for I told the cook only to let him have bread and vegetables: meat and cheese are always too strong for the stomachs of people like that. Why, one fellow I tried to help . . .'

Eventually they reached Saltash and Kitty's spacious home overlooking the estuary. Richard dismounted and helped Kitty from her horse. He was stunned by the volume of words that had poured round his ears during the journey home.

'You've a long ride back to Plymouth ahead of you, Mr Treveryan,' she said brightly, 'would you like to step inside and take a little wine before you go?'

Richard hesitated. He thought of Miriam, the rich caress of her voice and the blessed silence of the journey home. 'Unfortunately I have urgent business awaiting me in Plymouth,' he said. 'Besides, you do not want to arouse your father's suspicions.'

'The old busybody may think what he likes, I shall be mistress in my own home. But before you leave, Mr Treveryan, you must promise to visit me again: your advice has been most helpful. I look forward to telling you how events turn out with the steward.'

'I'd be only too pleased to come here again, but unfortunately this is a little out of my way. And I'm sure your days are very busy.'

Kitty looked wistful. 'Of course there are always a hundred and one things to do, but still . . . how about the day after tomorrow? I'm not to be thwarted, Mr Treveryan. When you know me better you'll understand that I can be most determined.'

'I don't doubt it. Very well, then, I shall make a point of calling on you again in a couple of days.'

Richard swung up on to his horse. 'Until next time –' he said.

Kitty turned pink with pleasure, and there was an unaccustomed lightness in her tread as she went up the steps to her house.

*　　*　　*

'You should have seen me, Miriam! It was the performance of a lifetime. If this falls through I intend making my fortune on the stage. The King's players are surely crying out for such formidable talent. I was every inch a gentleman, I even applauded her father's wish to protect her from a certain breed of unscrupulous suitor.'

'But did she not see through your insincerity?' Miriam was wiping tears of laughter from her eyes.

'Not for an instant. Mistress Sawle sees only herself, that's the whole beauty of it. My only task now is to persuade her that marriage to me will provide the best way to prove her independence from her father – and then my fortunes are assured. Just imagine what an opportunity those two ships could provide! I could turn her puny fortune into real wealth!'

'Are you so sure that is all you want?' Miriam leaned back in the settle. She and Richard were seated together by a blazing fire in the tap room: the weather had improved over the last few days and most of the travellers who had been packed into the inn had already been able to leave. She was wearing a loose-fitting tawny gown and every now and then she drew contentedly on a clay pipe.

'Wealth is what every man wants if you scratch deep enough. To be wealthy is to be in control of one's destiny, and nothing else matters.'

'But what is she like, your Mistress Sawle? Could you ever learn to care for her? To love her?'

'You miss the point altogether, Miriam. This is a financial transaction we are discussing. From what I saw of her this morning I believe her to be a silly and irritating woman: all her feminine charms are contained in her three manors and two ships. And the house at Saltash. All those I love already. Why do you look at me like that? You can hardly pretend to be shocked. This would be no different from all those other marriages the Church blesses every year – a purely practical arrangement.'

'So you keep saying – but you've not convinced me yet.'

'Love plays no part in my plans,' he said, 'it's merely a mask men use to hide their true motives.'

'You only say that because you've never known what it was to love.'

The merest hesitation before he agreed, 'That's true enough. I did once believe that someone cared for me but I was wrong, of course. She soon gave herself to the highest bidder.' He laughed suddenly. 'And by now I'm sure she believes it was love that made her choose so.'

'Ah, at last I begin to understand. You cannot have the love you hoped for so you are determined to marry where there is no possibility of love whatsoever. It's a dangerous strategy.'

'To wed for money? Everyone does the same, if they have the chance.'

'Many do, it's true. But I know you well enough to guess that you want more than that. The worst cynics are always those who were idealists to begin with.'

'I did not know you were such a philosopher, Miriam. Besides, I'm only being realistic. Not cynical.'

'Indeed?' Now it was Miriam's turn to be disbelieving. She gazed thoughtfully into the fire. So much troubled humanity passed through the Swan Inn – travellers, dreamers, whole families about to be torn apart for ever – that she had become something of an expert on men's secret hopes and fears. And she had already spent enough time with Richard to know that there was more to him than the callous façade revealed.

'You'll end up a Jesuit,' she concluded.

'An excellent idea. I shall enjoy sending heretics to the fire.'

'Piers! More wine!' Miriam began to be depressed. In a far corner of the room an old man who had fallen asleep against a barrel began to snore noisily. 'Perhaps she'll not have you after all.'

'I intend calling on her a few times more, then our affection for each other will grow naturally enough –'

'You flatter yourself.'

'– and then, that's it, that's what I'll do. I shall tell her that I must leave Plymouth at once, that my feelings for her have grown so far beyond those that are proper to friendship that I must travel far away, et cetera, et cetera.'

Suddenly laughing like a schoolboy he flung himself down on one knee before the innkeeper's wife. 'Beloved!' he exclaimed with great theatricality. 'To be near you these past weeks has made me happier than I would have thought possible – but to remain now would mean nothing but unspeakable torment. I must leave you. No no! Don't try to stop me. You are sure to forget me soon enough and I . . . but my feelings are of no consequence now. If you have any affection for me at all, then promise me only that you will forget me as soon as I am gone for I have nothing to offer which is worthy of your love: no wealth, no prospects, home or family. To throw in your lot with mine would be . . . and so on.' He dusted off his knees and returned to the settle. 'It's so ridiculously easy, Miriam, to play the passionate lover when you have not a single scrap of sincerity. It's the honest romantics who are always tongue-tied. Would you like to hear more?'

'Spare me, please!' She was laughing again, though a sadness lingered in her eyes. 'You treat it all as such a contemptible game.'

'It may be a game, Miriam, but it's one that I intend to win. Shall we drink to my success?'

It was a stormy day in mid-December and Ralph Jordan was once again visiting his daughter.

He was struck at once by how much she had changed. That thin face now glowed as though warmed by an inner fire.

He wasted no time in coming to the point. 'Has Treveryan made you any propositions? Has he talked to you of marriage?'

At her father's question Kitty managed to look both haughty and mischievous. 'Our conversations are really no concern of yours. But you can rest assured that you have no reason to be ashamed of me.'

'And what, precisely, am I to understand by that?'

'Our conversations are wide ranging. He is delighted to find someone who is intellectually his equal and he is constantly amazed by the breadth of my understanding. But marriage we have only discussed in the abstract.'

Her wistful confession confirmed her father's fears. 'I wish to God I'd never set eyes on him. He's playing a devious game.'

'He happens to enjoy my conversation, Father, and I really cannot see what is so surprising in that.'

'Have a little sense, Kitty. It's hardly conversation he's after.'

She flushed angrily. 'I'm perfectly capable of looking after my own interests.'

'If that was so, you would not be encouraging him.'

'I do not encourage him.'

'He has already visited you twice this week.'

Kitty darted him a furious glance. Her father was well informed. Which of her servants, she wondered, was in his pay? 'And what if he has? It does not follow that I must therefore lose my head and be seduced by him. A woman in my position attracts many admirers. You should have more confidence in me, Father.'

'How on earth can I have confidence when it is plain that his motives are entirely mercenary.'

Kitty stamped her tiny foot with vexation, all haughtiness and mischief gone. 'That is not fair! You assume all the world is as mercenary as you are.'

'He has not a penny to his name and you are a wealthy woman.'

'And must a man be for ever blamed for his father's misfortune? Besides, he told me he was penniless the very first time we met. I would have seen through any pretence straight away. He believes as strongly as I do in the importance of love between two people and that everyone should be free to decide their own future.'

'Aye, I'm sure he does.' Ralph Jordan regarded his daughter with despair. He could hear the echo of countless intimate conversations in her words but there was no denying her blazing sincerity. He said coldly, 'And did he also tell you that his coming here in the first place was itself a lie? That Sir John Sutton had never sent him with a message? That Sir John very sensibly drove him from his home with the threat of a whipping?'

Kitty faltered only for an instant. 'Richard has a very low opinion of Sir John. I would not waste my time on anything he might say.'

'Oh Kitty, don't you see how he is deceiving you?'

His daughter's eyes brimmed with tears of vexation. 'You seem to believe that people only want me for my money.'

'No no, it's not that. Ah, the hell with it; it's only Treveryan I don't trust. I had not meant to tell you this but . . . tch, it's a messy business. Do you know how he passes his time, this young man of yours with his fancy talk of love and honesty?'

'If you're trying to slander him –'

'Listen to me, girl. Do you honestly believe that when he leaves your house he spends each evening singing psalms with his uncle? The Swan Inn, that's where he goes. Free lodging in the landlady's bed. That bawd Miriam Porter has been his mistress since he arrived in Plymouth. I'll wager he's there at this moment and toasting you for a gullible fool.'

'Oh! How dare you make up such lies!'

'Save your anger for the one who deserves it. Treveryan's nothing but a liar and a scoundrel. He comes to you each time hot from that woman's bed –'

'No! I don't believe you – I won't –'

'Then find out for yourself. Ask anyone. Go to the Swan and see. They say she's a drunkard and slattern. Just the companion one would expect for a man of Treveryan's morals.'

Kitty had been clutching the corner of a high-backed chair. She was gasping as though she had been struck. Slowly she recovered and, drawing herself up to her full five feet and half an inch, she spoke with icy calm. 'Father, I have always known Mr Treveryan's circumstances, so your malicious slanders are wasted. For the last time, stop meddling in my life!'

And with that, fearing that if she stayed longer she might break down and betray how deeply his words had wounded her, Kitty stalked from the room.

A fine wind was blowing from the south as Richard stepped on board the ferry that crossed the Tamar to Saltash. The shortest day of the year. Pale sunlight flooded the vast expanse of water, catching the masts and gunnels of the ships, shining through the canvas sails which appeared, from this distance, as fragile and translucent as a dragonfly's wing. After less than two months in Plymouth, Richard was already experiencing the lure of the sea.

So many evenings passed in the company of travellers, men who talked of islands where fire broke through the icy ground and spring water ran hot as from a boiling kettle; countries whose rivers were laced with gold, lands brimming with perpetual harvest. It was the adventure that attracted him, the risks. The chance to win great wealth or to find an anonymous grave in the huge ocean. To discover the famed treasure of El Dorado or to be destroyed by savages.

He craved the challenge. He was sick of his fashionable new clothes and bored by the company of women. Yesterday his uncle's wife had tried to convince him of the need to save his immortal soul. He took refuge at the Swan only to find Miriam in a state of maudlin affection; she tried to persuade him to remain with her. Most of all he was tired of playing suitor to Kitty's boundless vanity.

He had begun to believe that Miriam must have been right and that his cynicism did not run so deep as that of other men who could wed a woman they disliked simply to gain possession of her wealth. The novelty of play-acting had quickly lost its appeal and he had no real liking for the part he had been called upon to play. He found that he despised himself for the ease with which he was deceiving Kitty. And he despised her utterly for being so easily taken in. It was a shabby business after all and he felt himself defiled by it.

But now a clean wind was blowing in from the Atlantic and ships were making haste to leave port while the good weather lasted. Barbados and Cathay, Newfoundland and the Azores – yesterday he had talked long into the night with a Captain Henwood, master of the *Esther*, and the captain had invited him to travel with them on a voyage to the Indies. Richard had been undecided: since he had no stake in the voyage there would be little profit in it for him. But this morning, with the tide running and the breeze blowing in off the sea, the prospect of adventure was more seductive than this tiresome landbound scheming.

His attitude might have been different if he had thought he was any closer to winning Kitty's heart and wealth but he had realised at their last meeting that she was quite content to let their courtship remain in its present state indefinitely. She delighted in the attentions of a young admirer and she was glad of his advice on the management of her lands but she also, as she never tired of repeating, valued her independence and intended to remain mistress of her own affairs.

When he had visited four days earlier he prepared to play his trump card. He had implied – though not in phrases quite so extravagant as those he had rehearsed with Miriam – that his feelings for her were developing beyond those proper to a friend and, since anything other than friendship was impossible between them, he had decided to quit Plymouth and seek employment elsewhere. She had attended closely to his words and, when he took his leave, she pressed his hand tightly and made him promise to return again as soon as he could, but apart from that – nothing.

He was glad. What had begun as a challenge had degenerated into a tiresome exercise. As he led his horse off the ferry and began the long climb up the hill to Kitty's home his spirits were higher than they had been for weeks – and all at the prospect of saying goodbye to the wealthy Mistress Sawle for ever.

As soon as he entered her dark panelled parlour, he knew that something was wrong.

Kitty was pale and her eyes appeared smaller than usual since the skin around them was puffy with weeping. She had hidden the signs of her earlier distress as best she could and Richard saw only her petulant expression.

'Is something the matter, Kitty?'

'Nothing. Nothing at all,' she answered in a voice that said quite clearly that everything was wrong. 'I'm perfectly all right and not in the least bit upset.'

Richard smothered a sigh. Kitty was tiresome enough in the best of circumstances, but Kitty nursing a grievance would be well-nigh impossible.

'You *are* upset. But if you do not wish to tell me –'

'And why should I confide in you? You have never once considered me . . . And to make such a fool of me. I *won't* be made a laughing stock.'

This time Richard made no attempt to smother his sigh. 'Since you will not tell me the reason for your anger, I

221

can only assure you that I have never wished to cause you grief.'

'No?' The single word was a yelp of pain and rage. She began to pace up and down. 'It's not the debauchery I mind so much –' still pacing – 'though Heaven knows that is bad enough. No, it's the lies and the deceit. All that talk of honesty, of truth. And love – oh! And all the time . . . I didn't believe my father when he told me. But when I sent my manservant and he told me . . . he saw . . . and now even the servants are laughing behind my back. I've never –'

Richard was unmoved. 'You grow incoherent, Mistress Sawle. I cannot imagine what has so upset you but clearly we are wasting each other's time. I only came to bid you farewell. I will take my leave –'

'Yes, go! Back to your whore at the Swan!'

So. That was it. Her father had done his fatherly duty and sent his spies a-spying and told her the truth about her eloquent suitor. Well, no doubt it was all for the best. Now that he knew this was to be their last meeting he found he had grown almost fond of Kitty Sawle.

'That's right, Kitty,' he said without emotion, 'for the time being at least. In a day or two I shall take ship –'

'Oh!' Quite suddenly Kitty's agitated dignity deserted her. The wealthy widow crumpled, sobbing loudly. 'And I thought . . . I was so sure you cared for me . . . for me . . . that you . . . oh, it isn't fair, it's not true! Tell me it's not true. Tell me . . . and I trusted you – oh!'

Her grief was genuine and total. Richard, watching her little body shuddering with sobs, loathed himself with a complete and utter loathing. So this was how his despicable game turned out: foolish little Kitty Sawle who had never in her life wished him harm, wounded where she was most vulnerable, in her vanity. At that moment Richard did not believe there was a single person in the whole world so contemptible as he.

'Kitty –' But the sound of his voice only made her sob the louder, 'Kitty, please don't cry. I'm not worth your tears, truly I'm not. You ought to be glad to discover the kind of person I am before you learned to care for me. Your father was right to tell you. Hush now –'

222

He was not even sure that she could hear him, so violent was her grief. He knelt down on the floor beside her and put his arm across her shoulder and wondered at the smallness of her body beneath the sumptuous fabric of her dress.

Feebly she attempted to shake him off. 'How could you, how could you!' she kept sobbing. 'And all the time . . . oh, how could you do this to me!'

'Kitty, listen. Stop now. Miriam Porter is nothing to me, only a convenience.'

'But I believed you, I trusted you!' Her tears seemed unending. 'And when you came last time and said . . . I thought you cared for me, really cared. And all the time . . . it was nothing. Nothing at all.'

'No, Kitty, that's not true. I meant what I said to you last time, I promise you that.' After all, he had lied to her so freely in the past, to stop now would have been worse than heartless. 'I have grown to care for you very much these past weeks, but it's hopeless. Surely you can see that.'

'What do you mean?'

'I must leave Plymouth. There's a ship sails in a day or two and I intend to be on board. I only came this last time to say goodbye.'

Quieter now she sobbed, his arm still around her shoulder. 'I hate you,' she said, 'I don't want you to leave so soon.'

'I must. I cannot stay here.' As he spoke he could see the *Esther*, decks scrubbed, hold crammed with stores for a long sea voyage, hear the jingle of her rigging in a fresh Atlantic breeze. Oh, to be aboard her now!

'You never cared for me.' And she flung herself away from him with a spasm of misery. 'All last night I was awake. Dear God, let him tell me it's not true, please God tell me it wasn't my money. But it was. That foul woman has been your whore all this time and you only came here because I was wealthy. Oh God, why can't I be loved for what I am!'

It was more than Richard could bear. He gathered her in his arms and kissed her gently on the forehead. 'Listen to me, Kitty, only listen. I do care for you, very much, you know I do. I've enjoyed this time with you, I swear it.'

'That's only words –'

'And it's because I care for you that I must leave now. Here, dry your eyes, no more weeping, please. I'm not worth it, believe me, Kitty, no one is. If I'd had wealth of my own then our story might have had a different ending, but as it is –'

'Why different?'

'Because . . .' Richard's only concern had been to calm her down and he said, without thinking, 'Why, then we might have married.'

She had stopped crying. Her red-rimmed eyes were suddenly very intense. 'Do you mean that you would have wished to marry me if you had only had wealth of your own?'

He hesitated. 'Yes. Yes of course I would. You must know that.'

'So it wasn't my money you were after. If you are leaving now because of that then it proves that you did care for me. Oh, tell me that I am right!'

Only the briefest hesitation this time. 'Yes, Kitty, you've been right all along.'

'Yes, yes, of course. I understand everything now. And you do love me, don't you? You must do –'

'But it doesn't matter how I feel, Kitty, since no good can come of it. We had best say goodbye now and have done with it.'

But Kitty did not appear to have heard him. She scrambled to her feet. 'Lord, what a state I'm in: there's dust on my skirt and my lace is all grubby. But no matter, nothing matters now except for you and me. As soon as we are married –'

'What?'

'Well, of course we must be married now,' and she laughed nervously. 'I know you love me and wish to marry me and would have asked me long since except that you have no fortune to offer. I always knew my father was mistaken when he called you mercenary and unscrupulous. He'll soon have to admit how wrong he's been.'

'But Kitty, consider what you are saying.' Almost for the first time Richard spoke sincerely. 'I'm not worth your affections. Everything your father told you is true. I've been living at the Swan with Mistress Porter –'

'No, no. I won't hear it.' She put her finger on his lips. 'Don't say another word. You love me, I know you do. If you had thought there was any chance of marriage then I'm sure you would have broken with her long ago. You can hardly be blamed for – for consoling yourself, can you now? I know a little of men's ways. After all, I was married before.'

'All the more reason not to be hasty now. Perhaps when I return –'

'No! Oh Richard, I could not bear it!' And she caught hold of his hand as though to restrain him then and there. 'I know you love me. You *must* love me. We shall be married –'

He took her face between his hands and kissed her mouth gently. 'Kitty, I never want to hurt you.'

She answered his kiss with a hunger that surprised him. 'Don't go, Richard. Never leave me. I could not bear it if I thought you did not love me!'

He kissed her again.

'Oh Richard, we must be married at once. And secretly. No, no, don't protest. I know that my father has been consulting his lawyers. How dare he interfere . . . we can be married tomorrow. I'll show him I'm mistress in my own house. Lord, I'm so dishevelled and . . . but wait here. I'll tidy myself and return – oh Richard, I'm so happy, aren't you?'

And in a flurry of excitement she was gone from the room. Richard was left alone revelling in the sudden silence. He strolled over to the window and looked out at the bleak winter garden and the grey expanse of the estuary beyond.

So, Mistress Sawle had lost her heart to him after all. She could not face the knowledge that she had been duped. Richard wanted to laugh but somehow he could not. If her father had not been so thorough in his duty, then Kitty would most probably have remained content with her suitor's apparent admiration and he would have been left free to depart with the *Esther*.

The *Esther*. He yearned to be standing now on the deck of that fine ship, gulls flocking round the rigging as she pulled away from land on a blustery wind. He could still go. But even as he considered the possibility, he knew that he would not. Kitty, in her folly, was offering him every-thing he had schemed for: power, wealth, opportunity – all that he wanted. He had vowed to be ruthless, to lie and dissemble. He had been lucky – and he knew that such chances do not occur twice in a man's life.

Sounds of turmoil on the stairs while Kitty, her voice musical as breaking glass, called orders to the servants. Her scurried footsteps were approaching the door. With a last glance towards the estuary, Richard turned and composed his features into an expression appropriate to an adoring suitor as his future bride, dressed now in dazzling yellow silk, burst into the room.

They were married, with only two lawyers to witness the event, on Christmas Eve. As Richard rode out of Plymouth that morning he saw the *Esther*, sails billowing in a strong south-westerly, pass from the shelter of the estuary into the heavy Atlantic swell.

Whatever lingering regrets might have remained were dis-pelled at once by the knowledge that when he did decide to sail from Plymouth harbour it would be as a master of his own ship. Kitty's ship, his own ship – the prize and the profits his alone. No man was ever so pleased with his bar-gain as Richard Treveryan on his wedding day.

The little church where they were married, about a mile from Saltash, was garlanded with holly, rosemary and bay for the Christmas season. The lawyers fussed briefly over the marriage settlement; the parson pocketed his fee with pleasure: it was larger than was customary since his dis-cretion had been important.

It was already growing dark when they returned to Kitty's home. She unlocked the front door and pushed it open slowly. An unnatural silence echoed through the house. Not having been able to discover which of her ser-vants was spying for her father, Kitty had sent them all off to watch the mummers in the town. Far away, across the stillness, the sounds of laughter and revelry drifted on the night air. In an upstairs room a mouse scuttled beneath the floorboards.

Richard suddenly realised that, almost for the first time since he met her, Kitty's incessant chatter had stopped. He drew her towards him and felt her whole body trembling violently.

'Are you cold, little wife?'

He lifted off her ridiculous hat and tipped her face towards his. Pale moonlight shone down the stairway and in that moment, her eyes glittering with eagerness and fear, Kitty was almost beautiful. Richard felt himself suddenly to be on the brink of an enormous sorrow. He kissed her tenderly.

She clung to him. 'Not cold,' she whispered, 'Richard, I never –'

He scooped her into his arms. Beneath the yards of cumbersome silk and trimmings there was scarcely any substance to her at all.

As he carried her up the moonlit stairway to her room all the bells of the town began to chime at once, ringing in the Christmas season.

And it gave Richard a certain wry satisfaction to know that, for the first twelve days of his married life at least, it was the Lord of Misrule who reigned supreme.

9

Even in the height of his delirium William still heard the bells of Porthew church. He heard the gulls too, which screamed and fought on the chimneys and rooftops of the town. Gulls and bells, bells and gulls. Sometimes the sounds became confused and the bells chimed out a peal of gulls' cries and at other times a huge grey and white bird opened its beak on the ledge beyond his window and somewhere far off a bell tolled its mockery. It was a whole pharaoh's plague of gulls which rang in the Christmas peal.

William was adrift in time. At times he knew himself to be very close to death. He was floating on a vast grey sea with a vast grey sky above, endless empty nothingness all around him. Once the clouds above him parted and death welcomed him like a friend. An angel stood before him, a young boy with hair yellow like the sun who smiled at him and shook his head. 'Not yet, William,' said the angel, 'not yet,' and he was overcome with sorrow at being turned away.

An endless expanse of time later he opened his eyes and saw the angel still watching him, but smiling no longer. The face of the angel was pale and anxious, worn out with worrying and lack of sleep.

'Margaret –' he tried to say.

The angel smiled.

It came to him then what he should do: one good deed to wipe out all the foul ones. Perhaps then the real angel would permit him to enter the kingdom of heavenly joy.

'Marry –' he said, 'we must be married.'

'Hush now, don't tire yourself. When you are well again –'

'No no . . . might die . . . do it now.' He gathered his strength. 'Your reputation . . . even if . . . must be safe . . . for the child.'

'He means it, Mattie,' he heard his cousin Merry's voice, 'we'd best send for Parson and see if he is willing.'

A speckled gull landed on the windowsill and laughed its raucous laugh. In the greyness where William was living the bells of Heaven rang out in celebration of his plan.

Parson Weaver, pleased to learn that William Hollar wished to marry Margaret without delay, hurried through the wintry streets to the draper's house to see whether the prospective bridegroom was in a fit condition to make his vows. To his dismay he found him once more delirious and apparently unable even to hear the questions he was asked. But towards evening he rallied once again: he demanded fresh sheets for his bed and clean linen for himself. Yes, certainly, he intended to marry at once. He did not wish the child to be born a bastard in the event of his own death.

Margaret's father came hurrying from the farm. Mistress Hocken fussed and lamented that she had no warning and was all unprepared for guests. Merry insisted that Margaret put on the dress of sea-green wool that William had provided for her wedding.

It was as strange a ceremony as Parson Weaver had ever performed. The bridegroom lay propped on a heap of white bolsters: the flesh on his face was so wasted that his blue eyes were unnaturally huge in the guttering candlelight. His skin had an ethereal, translucent quality and his arms were so thin, emerging from his shirt sleeves, that they looked too weak to lift his large hands.

Margaret stood beside him. She too had grown paler since she had exchanged the life at the farm for the stuffy tedium of the sickroom but even so she looked almost rudely sturdy beside the skeletal figure of the man who was to be her husband. Parson Weaver spoke in a subdued voice, all unaware that he read the marriage service in the hushed tones usually reserved for the consolation of the dying.

The spectators watched anxiously: John Pearce, Mistress Hocken, Merry and the two neighbours who had been brought in as witnesses. All observed the bridegroom closely, afraid that at any moment he might slide back into unconsciousness altogether.

But, though his voice was feeble, he spoke clearly and

229

with conviction and even managed, with a little help from Merry, to lift his hand enough to slip the ring on Margaret's finger. When it was done there was an awkward silence, no one quite certain how the occasion should proceed.

'Some wine, Mistress Hocken,' said Parson Weaver, beaming his official smile. 'A toast to the happy couple.'

John Pearce was looking proud and puzzled and pleased all at once. 'Give him a kiss, now, Mattie,' he declared, 'that's the way to do it.'

Margaret hesitated. Giddy with the unexpected swiftness of her marriage, she still half-believed that this candlelit ceremony might be a hallucination induced by extreme fatigue. Then she leaned over, a curtain of hair brushing her cheek and, very gently, as though he were fragile as gossamer, she kissed her husband of a few minutes on the lips.

Exhausted by the effort of the ceremony, William closed his eyes and turned his head away.

That evening, her wedding night, Margaret sat beside the big double bed that William had lain in throughout his sickness. Mistress Hocken and Merry had long since retired for the night. In the pale moonlight that filtered through the uncurtained window she could easily discern the features of her newly married husband, the features she had come to know so well during these long days and nights of nursing. Of William himself she still knew nothing.

What manner of man was he who took such pains, even when he knew he might be dying, to ensure that a stranger's child should not be born a bastard?

She sighed. Moonlight fell across his peaceful features and a wave of tenderness for this man washed through her. She reached out, wanting to touch his curling hair, the delicate shadows of his cheeks, but her hand hovered and then she drew back. So frail, so handsome – and now, she knew, so kind. She could almost imagine herself in love with him.

Some time after midnight, when Margaret was numbed to the bone with cold she stumbled along the passageway to the room where Merry was sleeping and climbed in beside her. The bed was deliciously warm.

Now we are sisters, Margaret thought. Merry, without waking, rolled over and put her arms around her and Margaret was instantly asleep.

A wedding, as everyone knew, was not properly done until there had been music and drinking and dancing – and frequently a hurling match as well. It was not until the beginning of March that William had recovered sufficiently for this most important celebration to take place.

Everyone who was a friend or relative of either Margaret's family or the Hockens was invited . . . and that was a fair proportion of all those who lived in Porthew and the surrounding farms. People had been looking forward to it for weeks: the twelve days of Christmas feasting and hospitality were long since over and these late winter days were traditionally the hardest of all. Mostly the sea was too rough for the boats to leave harbour; and when the fishermen did venture out, driven by hunger as often as not, the women gathered early by the harbour wall to scan the horizon for their return. At the beginning of February a St Keverne man set out one morning with two of his sons and never returned. Two bodies were washed ashore a few miles along the coast a couple of weeks later. His wife was left with nine surviving children to care for.

At this pinched and anxious time of year entertainment was rare and doubly precious: a chance to eat and drink and forget the fear and the cold and the hunger. No one now cared to remember that they had ever thought to criticise Margaret Pearce: even Ambrose Treloar let it be known that since her father was a cousin to his mother, he considered it only proper to attend.

Margaret and Merry were baking for a full week beforehand. Such a quantity of cakes and pies and sweetmeats and tarts that Margaret was worried at the expense but William insisted that everything should be done properly and in style.

Two days before the wedding party Lizzie was allowed over from the farm to help with the work. Margaret enjoyed hearing the news of home; since she left there was too much work for them to manage alone and their father had arranged with the overseer to take on an orphan lad from

Manaccan to help with the field work. He was also considering hiring a girl to help in the house. Mistress Pearce was confined to her room often these bleak wet days; the tabby fighter Achilles had disappeared for a week and come home again missing an ear and more fractious than ever.

It was not until the day before the party that the sisters were alone together and Lizzie was able to ask the question that was troubling her.

'Mattie,' she began diffidently, running her finger around the creamy lip of a bowl and relishing the uncooked mixture, 'why do you and Mr Hollar not . . . ? I mean, now that you are married I thought . . . and yet still you share a room with Merry.'

She thought at first she had not been heard. Margaret put another tray of cakes in the oven and poked the fire until the flames leapt up the chimney. When she turned to face Lizzie again her face was flushed from the heat of the fire.

'Such a quantity of food!' she exclaimed. 'You'd think all of Cornwall was coming to celebrate my wedding.' She pulled a pan of dough towards her and began punching the air out of it vigorously. 'William is still weak from his illness,' she went on in a low voice, not looking at Lizzie at all, 'the apothecary advised him to keep his own room until he is fully well again.'

'But he looks so strong and –'

'Really, Lizzie,' Margaret snapped, 'have you nothing better to do than stand around gossiping all day? Here. Divide this into portions for the rolls. Do I have to do everything myself, you stupid girl? I'm off to get more water. And some fresh air too.'

Margaret's anger was so rare and unexpected that Lizzie's eyes filled with momentary tears. And, when she blinked them away again, Margaret was gone.

Richard stood on the deck of the ship that was carrying him towards Porthew. The previous day they had docked at Fowey. Tomorrow the *Mary* was to continue to Penzance without them.

The wind was blowing strongly from the south and there was a heavy swell. From time to time the *Mary* dipped into

232

a trough so deep that the grey outline of the coast vanished altogether.

Richard watched the sailors at their tasks, talked with the captain and his mate, learned bit by bit the language of the sea. He revelled in the speed of the little ship, her combination of fragility and strength, the swift road provided by the water. It was just over a week since the first of Kitty's ships had returned to Plymouth and now he was more determined than ever that when she sailed again he would be her master.

Kitty was devastated at his decision. She had fallen on the floor and sobbed just as she had done on the day she accused him of deceiving her. But by now her tears only irritated him. He had discovered that each occasion when Kitty failed to get her own way was for her a total disaster calling forth hysterical tears. Her grief at the wrong finish on a new hat was almost as violent as her grief when she thought Richard was neglecting her. No doubt the elderly Edwin Sawle had been kept on a tight rein by his wife's tantrums but Richard, once he was certain there were no barriers to his control of her fortune, had no intention of being so restrained.

Kitty. She was below deck now, suffering in the throes of a mild attack of seasickness. Richard relished the respite from the constant stream of her high-pitched chatter.

Yet their marriage was not without its unexpected compensations. Their wedding night had revealed the interesting information that Kitty, though married eight years, was still a virgin. Evidently Mr Sawle had been persuaded to restrain his husbandly instincts when they were first married in view of her extreme youth – Richard guessed that Kitty, in her childish fright, had used a well-timed tantrum to advantage – and by the time she had reached an age when he might expect to enjoy some reward for his patience, the unfortunate husband had already been incapacitated by the illness that was to kill him.

Richard, in his mood of tenderness towards his little wife on that moonlit Christmas Eve, made love to her with gentleness and skill, with the result that Kitty woke up on Christmas morning head over heels in love.

If their marriage had been conducted entirely between

the sheets they might have got along well enough. Richard enjoyed her body as much as that of any other woman – and as little. Despite the physical pleasure his sense of isolation only increased as she surrendered herself to him. The gaping loneliness of love-making he was now resigned to . . . but Kitty's incessant babble, more often than not on the subject of her clothes and those of the ladies she knew, was quite another matter.

This journey had been planned in the wake of her hysterics at the prospect of his leaving. Earlier she had expressed an interest in seeing the only property his father had left him. Richard had no objection. He remembered his angry boast to Nicolas on the day he left Rossmere, that within six years there would be a new house at Trecarne, as splendid as any in Cornwall. He was curious to look again at the property and see if that idle pledge might one day be turned into reality, though he was certain it would not be possible so soon.

And he was vain enough to relish the chance to return in style to the house from which he had been so ignominiously ejected just a few months before.

He smiled to himself as he anticipated the annoyance of all at Rossmere when they learned the extent of his good fortune. And he was grinning still when he at last made out the spire of Porthew church, and the increasing detail of the houses that were clustered round the harbour.

Jack Pym was a monstrously hairy man. Long hair and beard and whiskers, thick hair on his chest and back and hands, hair everywhere, so it was said. Occasional jokes were made about his mother's probable choice of partner – but only occasional, for he was a kindly man and well liked in the town. Nothing gave him so much pleasure as to see people eating and drinking and enjoying themselves and the Hollars' wedding party made him happier than he had been for months.

The air in the single large, low-ceilinged room of his ale-house, a place as dark and warmly hospitable as a badger's set, was dense with the mingled smells of sweat and woodsmoke, stale beer and tobacco and the resinous aroma of freshly cooked meat. Jack Pym's eyes sparkled beneath the heavy thatch of hair as he went among the guests, filling tankards, exhorting them to forget their troubles and seize the pleasure of the moment. By the time the *Mary*'s passengers came ashore towards late afternoon, the gathering was coming to the very peak of enjoyment.

William Hollar clearly relished his duties as host. Although he was thinner and paler since his illness, the smallpox had miraculously left no scars to mar his features. If anything he had become still more attractive, for he now had an almost ethereal air about him which the women of Porthew, whose menfolk were almost exclusively of the earthy and robust variety, found completely irresistible, if sometimes a little puzzling. He moved among his guests, seeing to their needs and tending to the musicians with restrained courtesy, so much in contrast to the usual rough manners of the neighbourhood, that Margaret had swiftly been transformed into the most envied woman in Porthew. Even Dame Erisey, who had nursed a fondness for the girl ever since she first arrived at her little school ten years before, found herself dazzled by the splendour of the newly arrived William Hollar. And she wondered, as the bridegroom refilled her tankard of ale and complimented her on her lace kerchief, if the blessed Archangel St Michael himself in all his heavenly glory, had shown a face more radiant.

Of Margaret herself she was less sure. Certainly she was as lovely to look at as ever: but Dame Erisey could not escape the suspicion that the girl did not seem happy at all. She was very young, of course, only sixteen, and the changes had been swift in the past few months. But was that enough to account for the taut set of her mouth, the hurt expression of her eyes?

Dame Erisey was not the only wedding guest to comment on the bride's troubled expression when she first joined the celebrations – and as she had always been considered to have a cheerful disposition, those guests who did notice were baffled by her apparent discomfort.

But then, no one who was present in Jack Pym's ale-house that afternoon had witnessed the scene that had occurred earlier between her and the impeccable Mr Hollar.

They had been, for once, alone in the house, Mistress Hocken having departed with Merry and Lizzie laden with baskets and trays of food for the wedding. In the little back bedroom which she continued to share with Merry, Margaret put on the dress of blue-green wool which William had chosen for her wedding dress. She let her hands slide slowly over the soft fabric where it covered her hips, the now generous curve of her belly. There was a luxury in the touch that was new to her, a luxury she enjoyed.

Hesitating only for the briefest moment, she left her room, crossed the passageway, and knocked on the door of the best bedroom. 'William,' she said, 'can I come in?'

Silence, then the sound of footsteps, the lid of the wooden chest closing and the door opened slowly. 'What do you want?' A single cold blue eye, all that could be seen through the crack in the doorway, looked out at her.

'I wanted to show you my new dress. And to see for myself in your mirror.'

Grudgingly he opened the door. 'It looks well enough,' was his uneffusive comment. 'The appearance is somewhat spoiled now you are grown so large.'

Margaret stepped into the middle of the room. William was clad only in a shirt of fine cambric and a pair of breeches that, since his long illness, hung loosely at his waist.

She gazed at him. She had never known what it was to be shy with anyone in her life before and so did not recognise the unusual emotion which William inspired in her now.

To William it seemed that her long stare was a net cast out to entangle him, though he knew it to be a stare without artifice, the candid gaze of an interested child. He had never been able to abide the watchful eyes of children.

He gestured her away. 'There is the mirror. Go, admire yourself.'

But she remained standing before him. 'This is like our real wedding day, isn't it? You were so ill before, but now . . .'

And slowly, her eyes only leaving his face for an instant, she turned full about and her skirts billowed like a soft green sail.

William was unable to tear his eyes away and a muscle twitched beneath his eye. 'Margaret,' he began, 'please leave me, I must dress.'

She might have noticed the urgency of his request but at

236

that moment a burst of laughter and a jangle of music wafting up from the street below distracted her attention. Her face lit up with sudden pleasure and she caught hold of his arm and started to draw him towards the window. 'Look, William, the musicians have come to serenade us on their way to Jack Pym's.' And as she spoke the fiddler struck up a raucous tune.

'Leave me be, you fool!' He snatched his arm away.

Margaret was gazing down at the musicians and she replied without thinking. 'Lord above, William, whatever is the matter with you?' and she laughed out loud as she recognised the bawdy sentiment of the song. She turned, assuming that he must share her laughter – but when she saw the expression on his face her merriment was all snuffed out. 'What is it, William? Don't you like their song?'

'No. I don't like their song and I don't like your intrusion and I wish to finish dressing in peace.'

But Margaret had a great longing to enjoy herself and his obduracy annoyed her. 'What's wrong with you, William?' she exclaimed.

'How dare you!' Now he was quivering with anger. 'Get out of here this instant!'

'But why? Why are you always trying to get rid of me? Really, I don't understand you at all. I'm your wife now and yet –'

'Don't dare to say another word!' he interrupted her. 'I will not be plagued by your whining.'

'But William –!'

He caught her by the shoulders and his fingers dug so deep that her eyes stung with tears. 'Just look at yourself,' he said, steering her towards the mirror, 'that's what you came in here to do. So look. See how disgusting you are. You carry another man's child inside you and yet you dare to come in here and tell me . . . and ask me what is wrong with *me*! You are utterly loathsome, don't tempt me to despise you even more than I do already.'

His attack was so swift and unexpected that Margaret could only gasp; for a few moments it seemed as though he might hurl her at the clouded glass of the mirror and Margaret was suddenly amazed by the strength of his frail body and terrified by the hatred in his eyes.

'William . . . no . . .'

He released her suddenly and walked to the window, closing it fast against the musicians' song. Margaret watched him.

'I don't understand,' she began in a low voice. 'What have I done to make you hate me so much? I thought you cared for me. I hoped –'

'Spare me your self-pity, Margaret.' He spoke without emotion. 'I do not hate you. On the contrary . . . but you are very young and foolish and must learn to abide by my requests without questioning my reasons.'

'Why? William, you have no right to be so cruel!'

He shrugged. 'Save your breath,' he said, almost wearily, 'I am your husband, or have you forgotten that already? You cannot speak to me of rights.'

'But –'

'Listen to me, you stupid girl. I had expected gratitude, not reproach. Do I beat you? Do I make your life a daily hell? No – but I could do and no one would raise a finger to protect you, you know that as well as I do. Your family were only too glad to be rid of you – you ought to be on your knees every day in prayers of thanksgiving that I saw fit to rescue you from your shame.'

She recoiled. 'Then you should have left me where I was. I never asked for your cruel charity and you have no right to –'

'Never speak to me of rights. You know full well that as my wife you have none. Your foreign mother should have taught you that much, at least.'

'Ah –' All the colour drained from her face. Margaret sank down on to the wooden chest and pressed her hands against her face as though to blot out the memories that flooded through her brain.

'Margaret, get up and leave now. I wish to finish dressing.'

She gave no sign that she had heard him. She was remembering now what she should perhaps have remembered sooner: that day when the men came to the farm to bear away the body of her little brother. A wife can outwit her husband through quicker intelligence, she can cajole and persuade and woo but in an open contest of strength she

238

will always be the loser. Her mother had been pushed out of the way and the door bolted behind her while John Pearce, granite-faced, supervised the removal of the child and ignored the animal howls that came from behind the barred door. No one had helped her mother then and no one had noticed the terrified child who tried to whisper consolation through the cracks in the door. William was only speaking the truth when he said a wife had no rights against her husband.

'Margaret, can you hear me?'

She seemed to be waking from a kind of trance. She stared at him, as if seeing him for the first time. She had not noticed before that his eyes were set close together, giving him an almost foxy appearance, that his mouth had a pinched and anxious look.

William turned away, unable to endure the expression he read in her eyes, and fiddled with the trimmings on his doublet, which was laid out on the bed, until he heard the door close quietly behind his wife.

The kitchen was empty but for the grey kitten which slept by the fire. Lizzie had brought her from the farm two days before, knowing her sister's fondness for animals – and knowing also that the kitten would be drowned otherwise like the rest of the litter. Lizzie disapproved of her sister's habit of giving all the animals outlandish names and told her firmly that Tom had named the kitten Mouse. This seemed to Margaret such a ridiculous choice, yet at the same time singularly appropriate since there was something so mousy about the curious little face and whiskers, that the name had stuck.

Alone now with Mouse, Margaret busied herself with unnecessary work and fought back the tears that threatened to engulf her. No, William would not make her weep on her wedding day, she was too proud for that. She had known shame and despair before – and survived it too. But this was different. William's contempt and loathing made her feel dyed so deep with shame that she feared it would never be washed away.

If she had been able to comprehend the reason for his disgust, she might have found it easier to dismiss. But why had he struggled from the very brink of death to marry her, only to punish her now that he was recovered? Was it some error on her part that had brought about this change? She searched her memory for an occasion when he had had cause to fault her, but found none.

'Come, Margaret, our guests will be waiting.'

He spoke in the brisk tone of voice he often used when eager to cut short Mistress Hocken's mournful ramblings. Immaculately dressed in a doublet of crane-coloured velvet, he was waiting for her at the doorway. Margaret felt sick with the pretence.

'Go on alone, William. You may tell them I'm not well. Perhaps I will follow later but . . . I do not have the heart for merry-making.'

'Nonsense, girl,' he plucked a speck of dust from his sleeve, 'this is our wedding celebration and you must attend.'

'I said I might come later.'

'We will go together.'

'I cannot –'

'You must.'

It was an unequal contest from the start. William was quite clear about his wishes and Margaret, at that moment, was not clear about anything at all except that she was bitterly unhappy and confused.

'I don't understand,' she said hopelessly; 'what is happening?'

Sensing her capitulation he took a step towards her and said, in an almost friendly voice, 'Don't be such an innocent, Margaret. You have gained what you wanted, a father for your child. We are both respectable now. And it is only proper that we go to our wedding celebration together. What do you want your worthy family and neighbours to think of us? Now, look, your kerchief is not spread quite right. Here, so, like this. And the coif, just a little further back on the head, so . . .' Rapidly his hands made the necessary adjustments to her appearance. And as his cool fingers flickered over her shoulders, her hair, her throat, Margaret thought, this is the only time he ever touches me, when he is preparing me for public display, like a doll or an image in a papist's church.

'There,' he said when he was satisfied, 'now we are ready. Come, my dear.'

And as they passed through the shop and into the street he took her arm and inclined his head towards her as though in intimate conversation and Margaret, the most envied woman in Porthew as she walked the brief distance to the ale-house, felt herself to be crossing a thick dark sea, a heavy swell of falsehood.

The waiting guests broke into a loud cheer as Margaret and William walked into the ale-house. The warm smells that enveloped them were to Margaret like a suffocating cloth held over her face. She was no actress and she did not know how to play the part expected of her. But Merry, seeing her hesitation, stepped forward and hugged her with an easy laugh of welcome, and led her to the place of honour beside her husband.

Trestle tables had been set up, and benches. William had insisted that their entertaining must be lavishly done and even he was pleased with the resulting display: huge joints of pork and beef and mutton had been roasting on spits since morning. There was goose and pheasant, capons and duck, quantities of oysters and fish and pies of every description as well as countless platters piled with sweet-meats, tarts, buns and marchpanes.

The guests' enthusiasm at their arrival had been at least partly because this heralded the beginning of the serious business of eating.

The newly wed Mr and Mistress Hollar were seated at the centre of the long table that ran the whole length of the room. Their immediate families and those guests of some importance in the community such as Parson Weaver and Robert Payne, fish merchant and the wealthiest man in Porthew, were seated near them. At the far end of the table was a large and noisy contingent of Treloars. Ambrose's red hair showed above all the others; Joseph and his wife Jennie ate with hungry gusto but their children were almost too awed by the occasion to touch their meal.

At first Margaret thought the food would surely choke her. William heaped food upon her plate like the most attentive of bridegrooms and she began to wonder if she could have imagined their recent conversation. All around her were rosy and contented faces – why should she alone be miserable? Gradually her spirits began to revive. There remained a core of pain and confusion but in time she was able almost to forget that the man beside whom she was sitting, the man with whom she was united for ever and ever amen, appeared to regard her with nothing short of loathing and contempt. She would not let him see that he could spoil her pleasure entirely. She forced herself to laugh and joke with the rest (taking care always to avoid her husband's eye) and only the most astute of her guests noticed the air of strain underlying her apparent enjoyment.

When the door of the ale-house was thrown open and the strangers stepped into the room, Margaret was flushed and laughing at some new scandal Merry had dredged up and looked every inch the radiant bride.

There was a lull in the conversation as all heads turned to examine the intruders, a well-dressed couple followed by a small retinue of servants. William Hollar was on his feet at once. He quickly discovered that the lady and gentleman were newly arrived from Fowey and had hoped to rest at the ale-house until horses could be fetched from Rossmere. Jack Pym was in a quandary and his furry eyebrows were gathered in a frown: his little ale-house was bulging at the seams as it was with the wedding party and there was not an inch of spare room anywhere.

William, whose interest had increased at the mention of Rossmere, hit on a solution at once: if the gentleman and his wife would consider themselves as his guests he would be only too honoured; nothing too much trouble; the pleasure all his; in fact, as it was nearly dark and the lady appeared fatigued by her journey (this was diplomatic of him since Kitty was a delicate shade of green and could barely stand) a ride to Rossmere was surely out of the question. William's hospitality was boundless: would the gentleman and his wife consider themselves his guests for the night? Although his house was far from grand . . .

And so it was arranged. A bewildered Mistress Hocken was quickly ousted from her seat and dispatched with a couple of the gentleman's servants to make her home ready for their guests. Beaming with delight at the grand prize he had netted for his wedding, William led the elegant pair to be introduced to his wife.

They had been no more than a blur to Margaret as they conferred with William and Jack Pym by the door and it was only when the tall man in the coat of midnight blue had been led over to stand beside her that she recognised the gaunt features beneath the immaculately tailored hat.

A shadow crossed her face as she rose to her feet. 'Mr Treveryan,' she said solemnly, 'I did not expect to see you again so soon.'

William, who already regarded the Treveryans as his own personal property on this occasion, was nonplussed by this evidence of his wife's prior acquaintance. 'You have met before?'

'Only once or twice.' Margaret found that she did not care to remember either meeting – but thoughts of the events in Robert Payne's stable made her glance quickly at Lizzie, now safely wedged between young Tom and an elderly female relative.

But Richard merely commented, 'We meet now in happier circumstances. Allow me to introduce Mistress Treveryan,' and his expression was inscrutable.

Margaret found herself looking down and greeting the most immaculately dressed little lady she had ever seen. She would not have believed it possible that so much lace and trimmings, so much finely worked brocade, so much slashed silk and intricate embroidery could have been concocted around a single not very large personage.

'You are welcome, Mistress Treveryan.'

Kitty replied, 'We would not have agreed to remain in this tiresome place but the journey was slower than we had anticipated. Normally I am an excellent traveller and think nothing of hardships but today –' She did not appear to have the energy to continue with her sentence.

'When Mistress Hollar is not occupied by wedding celebrations,' Richard informed his wife, 'she keeps herself busy by haranguing crowds in Latin and tripping up unwary horsemen. And occasionally she throws buckets of water at people.'

Kitty looked anxious. William glared at Margaret and

insisted his guests sit on his left-hand side while his wife remained on his right.

Mistress Treveryan, who had been seriously wondering whether she might perhaps be dying of seasickness, began to rally as soon as she saw how much interest her arrival had caused. She found herself seated between the good-looking bridegroom and her own husband. Her earlier misery at Richard's woeful neglect of her while they were aboard the *Mary* was banished by the thought that he had agreed to this interruption in their journey out of concern for her condition (she rather thought she might be pregnant). In fact Richard had only agreed to spend the night at Porthew because of a sudden dread of returning to Rossmere. At the thought of having to witness the charade of Alice as contented wife he felt a hollow ache of misery in the pit of his stomach. Why on earth had he agreed to this folly? Not that any feeling remained for Alice, that was all in the past, but it was a cruel waste of time to rub salt in the wounds of old betrayals. Morosely he picked at a wing of goose – Kitty, he noticed, was already eating heartily – and reflected that this interlude might have offered more entertainment had he been seated beside the bride who, for all her youth, already had the rounded contours common to country brides, and who, unlike her obsequious husband, seemed quite unaffected by their arrival.

In fact Margaret was more interested in her guests than Richard knew, and she was especially fascinated by the dainty Mistress Treveryan. It was true that her face was somewhat pinched and peevish-looking but that was easily explained by the inconvenience of her journey. It was a busy face that peeped out from under the enormous hat; little eyes darting round the room, never remaining long on the person to whom she was talking. Her mouth was never still. When not eating, she talked incessantly.

William was fascinated by every word she uttered, and discussed with her the finer details of her costume and the provenance of the fabrics. Yet despite the richness of her clothes it was her hands that Margaret found herself looking at time and again that evening. Tiny hands, no bigger than a child's, but paler and more delicate than those of any child Margaret had seen before. Little milk-white claws, those hands had never been required to undertake any tasks more arduous than the display of jewels and rings or occasionally to divert themselves with a little embroidery. Margaret glanced ruefully at her own strong hands, long since roughened by hard work; the nails were chipped; there was the mark where she had scalded her hand on a cooking pot last week, there the scar where a knife had slipped while chopping cabbage. She had never really thought about her hands before, but now she wondered if William would like her better if she had hands as small and smooth as Mistress Treveryan's.

She thought wistfully that it must be a fine thing to be the owner of such pampered hands; a woman with hands such as those might marry where she chose.

Richard had grown impatient with the meal and found some pretext to slip outside. When he returned he watched the proceedings for a while from the comparative solitude of the doorway. This wedding celebration was so much livelier than the doom-laden affair Kitty had eventually persuaded her father to arrange for her. These country people knew how to seize on pleasure when the chance arose. Even the cripple, Joseph Treloar, and his downtrodden wife had managed to get here somehow and now they were enjoying themselves with a vengeance, quite undeterred by the sudden arrival of their landlord. Richard found himself almost envying them their gift for throwing themselves into the pleasure of the moment. Most of all, as he watched the toasts and the mock-solemn speechifying, he envied the bride and groom.

An affair of the heart, evidently – the girl's swelling belly was eloquent testimony to that. They were a well-suited pair at any rate, both so tall and fine-looking. He reflected that a genuine love-match must be easier for such as these – no talk of portions and dowries and contracts. A child on the way and the Church's blessing on their lust – a most commendable arrangement. He watched them both as they rose to their feet and smiled their thanks at the guests. The girl especially was radiant-looking, flushed with wine and happiness; hard to believe that he had last seen her draggle-tailed and miserable on the day he made his escape from

Rossmere. Well, her figure told her story plain enough: both her unhappiness then and her present joy. The fellow had married her after all, and not surprising either. Such a good-looking girl, he would have been a fool not to.

'A kiss, a kiss!' the guests began to shout. The bridegroom smiled at his audience, then put his arms around his wife. She flushed slightly, seemed to pull away, but it must have been in jest for Richard saw him close his eyes and kiss her. When he was done he patted her round stomach and grinned and the guests shouted and banged on the table and the musicians struck up a triumphant song.

10

Darkness fell and the flushed faces of the guests showed that all that could be eaten had been eaten; the remains of the food were carried back to the kitchen and the tables and benches cleared away to make room for the dancing.

Margaret sat in a small group with Merry and her family from the farm. Her father, mellowed by drink and enjoying the reflected glory of the lavish entertainment, sat with his arm around his wife. Friends and relatives came to join them for a while, and to offer their congratulations to the bride. The good wishes of some, especially those with marriageable daughters, fell somewhat short of whole-hearted sincerity: you are luckier than you deserve, was their unspoken reproach.

'The Lord's mercy is a mystery to us all,' said Robert Payne's wife, a sharp-faced woman who tended to the Puritan persuasion. 'We may none of us fathom His purpose but must pray for His grace. By your works shall He know you. Congratulations. Good night.'

'Hypocritical old beezum,' muttered Merry as the soberly dressed lady led her husband away before the sinful business of dancing began, 'she waters her good wishes just as her father watered down his milk –'

'Oh Merry, he didn't –'

Merry nodded. 'Famous for it. And her daughter is so dim-witted she believes that looking at the full moon too long can give you a child. And with a face like hers it's the only chance she'll –' Margaret was giggling but Merry had broken off, suddenly agitated. 'Mattie, look. Over there by the door.'

'You know I cannot see so far.'

Merry gripped her by the arm and a deep flush spread over her face as she exclaimed, 'It's Ned! I'd never have believed he'd be so brazen as to come here after what he's done!'

'But you told me to invite his mother.'

'Only because she had told me he was away to Ireland until the middle of next month at least. I hope he doesn't think I'm going to talk to him because –'

But talking to Merry appeared to be his sole purpose in being there. He waited in the doorway only long enough to greet one or two old friends and then, as soon as he had spied where she was sitting, he crossed the room to join them. Ned Roberts was a trim-built bantam of a man. His movements were quick and sure; every gesture showed his self-confidence. He had curling dark hair and blue eyes set in a neat and handsome face. Margaret had always thought that he and Merry were a strangely matched pair, but she could understand why her friend had been so attracted to him.

He was grinning as he greeted Margaret and congratulated her on her marriage. Then he held out his hand to Merry and said simply, 'Come, let us dance.'

Merry's breathing had grown suddenly very shallow and rapid. 'I'd not dance with you, Ned Roberts, if you were the only man left in this room.'

'If we were left alone then I'm sure we'd not bother with dancing anyway,' he laughed.

Merry looked furious. 'I was hoping to hear that you had been drowned at sea. Or butchered by the Irish barbarians.'

He was still grinning broadly. 'Come, Merry, we're wasting time. We can argue much more easily while we are dancing,' and he reached out and caught her by the hand and pulled her to her feet. Margaret had almost believed her friend's protests were sincere, but Merry hesitated only for an instant before allowing herself to be led away, still scolding him, on to the crowded dance floor. The next time they circled the room Margaret saw that they were both laughing; she saw the way Merry's body arched towards him, their instant oblivion to all around them, her delighted smile.

Margaret felt suddenly lonely. She tapped her feet restlessly, wanting to be part of the dance. She longed to be claimed for the dance, as Merry had been, if only by a scoundrel. She wanted to be able to laugh and to forget.

Lizzie took Merry's chair. She had been looking forward

to this wedding feast for so long that now she was grown anxious that the pleasure was passing so fast. She talked excitedly of Mistress Treveryan and the cost of the gold embroidery on her bodice. Margaret grew impatient.

A huge figure loomed above them, a haze of ginger hair, a freckled face, an aroma of soot and leather from the smithy.

'Well, Mattie,' Ambrose's deep voice boomed out over the noise of the dancing, 'you've done well for yourself now. No one can grudge you that. Best forget the past, eh? Then come and dance with me.'

Margaret frowned. 'Perhaps later, Ambrose. Not now.'

Lizzie bounced to her feet at once. 'Then you'll just have to make do with me,' she said prettily, new ribbons bobbing in her curls. 'These married ladies are all so dull. Come, Ambrose. And mind you don't tread on my toes; your feet are so large I'd surely be crippled for life.'

Margaret watched them as they too joined the press of dancers. Ambrose, who had to crouch to avoid cracking his head on the roof beams, shuffled awkward as a dancing bear while Lizzie hitched up her skirts and skipped round him like a kitten. Ambrose ambled into Merry and Ned's path, causing a brief accident in the dance; but they were so absorbed in each other that they barely noticed the interruption.

Margaret suddenly had the feeling that she was the only outsider at her own marriage party. She pulled her little brother towards her. 'Come and talk to me, Tom. How are you enjoying my wedding?'

Tom struggled to free himself. 'I'm dancing!' he shrilled. 'Watch me dance, I'm a spinning top!'

'The boy's eaten himself into a fit,' was his father's indulgent comment. John Pearce was pleased with everyone that day.

'Lord help us but he'll be seeing his dinner again before the evening is done!' And Mistress Pearce's huge frame rocked with laughter: plentiful wine and the infectious music had made her forget her pain and her swollen and twisted joints; her arthritic fingers tapped a rhythm on her knee. Tomorrow there would be a reckoning. Tomorrow could wait.

249

Parson Weaver, who liked a party as much as any of his parishioners and who had drunk a good deal more than most of them, approached Margaret, swaying as he walked. 'A dance, a dance. You must dance with me, Margaret. Your wedding . . . you should be dancing.'

'Not now, Parson. I do not care to dance.' Anxiously she searched the crowd for sight of William. She was gripped by the irrational belief that if her husband would not dance with her, then she must dance with no one else.

The parson leaned over her, sinuous and dark. 'Must dance, Margaret . . . only right. Tell her, Mistress Pearce.'

At that moment she saw William Hollar lead Mistress Treveryan into the dance and a familiar voice said, just above her ear, 'Well, Mistress Hollar, and does your condition prevent you from joining in the dance?' and glancing up quickly she saw Richard Treveryan, his dark eyes gazing down into hers. He had cast off his fashionable hat and his doublet was unbuttoned at the throat. For all his expensive clothes, Margaret noticed that his hair remained as coarse and unruly as before.

His question seemed more challenge than invitation. 'I am able to work still,' she said with a touch of defiance, 'so I might as well enjoy myself also.'

'Excellent.' There was a glimmer of amusement around his mouth as Treveryan reached out his hand and Margaret, hesitating only for the briefest moment, put her own, coarse-grained from hard work, into his. As she stepped past Parson Weaver she heard his faintly hissing breath, which no one but she knew to interpret as vexation, and she thought that perhaps it was only a malicious impulse to grieve the parson that had made her agree to the dance.

They began to move through the throng but Margaret felt suddenly awkward, and painfully aware of her own large belly and her clumsy, ill-fitting shoes. William, cool and unruffled, danced past them with a smile on his finely chiselled face. Mistress Treveryan had raised her voluminous skirts just enough to reveal a glimpse of daintily slippered feet. Her partner was holding her with a fixed concentration that showed his one aim was to see her safely through the crowds.

Treveryan was less careful. A pair of over-enthusiastic dancers lurched into Margaret's back and she stepped forward awkwardly on to her partner's foot. She righted herself quickly, a flush of annoyance and shame spreading across her cheeks. I must be lumbering like an ox. Margaret wished she had not agreed to the dance. Treveryan's eyes slid round to meet hers but when he spoke she was unable to make out his words above the noise of the drummers and the pipes and the shouting. 'I cannot hear what you are saying.' He must think me a turf-brained fool as well as clumsy, thought Margaret, her spirits sinking lower by the minute.

She was longing only for the dance to end so that her humiliation would cease. It seemed, perversely, that it lasted for an age. Then the rhythm of the music changed. Margaret had begun to curtsy her thanks and relief to Mr Treveryan when, with an impatient gesture, he caught her round the waist and pulled her towards him.

He said briskly, 'Our dance is just beginning.' The pressure of his hand was firm against her back, drawing her closer; the dome of her stomach was pressed against his doublet and her chin grazed the midnight-blue velvet of his shoulder. He was not so much taller than her, after all.

Kitty and William had withdrawn a little so that they could criticise the rustic gathering. Richard said to Margaret, 'Your husband is determined to monopolise my wife. I must make the most of the bargain.'

Margaret laughed. The rhythm of the drums and of dancing feet beating on the hard-packed floor pulsed through her body. She began to relax, coils of unhappiness slipping from her shoulders.

Treveryan grinned his approval. 'We'll make a dancer of you yet,' he said. And this time she heard his words quite clearly.

It had grown very hot in the ale-house and the doors were opened to let in the night air, causing the candles to flicker in their sconces. The dancers wove through the shadows and those who were tactful did not look too closely at the couples who were twined in the darker corners of the room. Margaret felt her forehead grow damp with perspiration.

Her partner's face was very close to her own: one moment so shadowed it was hard to make out his features, the next it was lit up and golden in a sudden flare of candlelight.

As they circled near the door Margaret caught a glimpse of Merry, sliding out into the darkness and she saw Ned Roberts wink at a friend as he followed. Ned's hand was around her waist, trailed downwards to caress her hips.

Treveryan's mouth was so close to Margaret's ear that there was no mistaking his next words. 'Does the worthy Mr Hollar know that his bride is the most beautiful woman in the room?' She seemed startled by the compliment, frowned slightly as though wondering how to reply, then threw back her head and laughed. Richard was intrigued by her response; in his head he could hear the predictable litany with which Kitty greeted every compliment. He shook his head, brushing all thoughts of Kitty aside – then wondered why that wine-loving parson was watching him with such animosity.

Margaret felt herself launched on a sea of music and dancing and a half-forgotten feeling that might even have been happiness. She was wishing only that this dance might last for ever. No matter that Treveryan's was the kind of meaningless compliment that such men scatter like coins to passing beggars; no matter that he would laugh later with his dainty wife when they went over the evening's events together in the privacy of their room; no matter that the worthy Mr Hollar who was busy sending for cushions for Mistress Treveryan's tiny back, did not consider his wife to be beautiful in the least, that on the contrary . . . but no matter. Not now. Now was everything.

And then all thought was gone and there was only the dance. All that she had ever wanted, today and always, in this moment with the strange man whom she had no reason to like but who yet held his arms against her and made her feel a woman.

Richard, who had been so prepared to be bored by William Hollar's wedding that it took him some time to realise that he was in fact enjoying himself, sensed a growing recklessness in her movements and gave himself up to the dance with a pleasure in the present moment that he had not experienced for a long time.

Perhaps the poets are right, he mused; it must be these simple rustics who have the secret of true happiness after all.

From where she lay in the back bedroom Margaret could see the starry sky through the window; a thousand thousand stars, more than man could ever count. No moon.

She could not sleep. Her limbs ached with fatigue but there was a pulse still beating within her which would not be quieted. She turned, threw back the bedclothes and was soon too cold; pulled them up to her chin and was then too hot again.

Oh Lord, make me a good wife and let me sleep.

Beside her lay Merry, warm and sated from her hours with Ned Roberts. She slept a deeper sleep than innocence.

Oh Lord, let William grow to care for me. Don't let him hate me.

Still her body burned with the rhythms of the music, the drummer and the pipes and the Irish fiddler. She had danced with Ambrose and had felt herself shrink in his huge embrace. She had danced with the parson and had turned her head from the expression in his eyes, an expression she recognised too well. She had danced with her father, who danced too slow, and with little Tom who danced too fast and then was sick and could not dance at all, and at some stage, when William had recollected the proper behaviour of a devoted groom at his wedding party, she had danced with her husband. Stiff and formal. He had smiled down at her and laughed as though at some private amusement . . . and she knew that his smile and his laughter were not for her at all but only for the benefit of his watching guests.

And if his smile had been for her alone? She no longer knew. Already she was half-afraid of his too handsome smile, his cold eyes in which she saw herself distorted and ugly.

Oh Lord, let me sleep.

But chiefly it was the dances with Mr Treveryan, whose gaunt features broke into unexpected amusement when their eyes met, that she remembered. His wife was obviously the kind of woman William admired. William had given up his own room to them and assured them that he was more than happy to sleep on the couch in the shop. Mistress Hollar could share a bed with his cousin for once . . .

Suddenly impatient, Margaret slipped out of bed and pulled a shawl around her shift. It was very dark in the passageway. She moved noiselessly, only pausing for a moment outside the best bedroom, William's bedroom. Mr Treveryan and his lady wife slept in the big bed tonight.

She could hear the steady rise and fall of sleeping breath. She imagined how Mistress Treveryan's fretful face must be peaceful now as she slept with her head in the crook of her husband's shoulder. Earlier, when Margaret had ushered them to their room, she had seen the expression on her face as she looked up at her husband and asked him if he thought they might contrive to be comfortable.

Stepping softly, so as not to wake the sleeping household, she went down the narrow stairs to the kitchen.

The fire had not quite died away and the room was full of shadows. There was the darker mass of the table, pots and pans glowing slightly in the dying firelight, the pale square of the window and the blackness of the oaken doors. And by the fireside the figure of a man sitting with legs outstretched.

'William?'

A man's voice answered but it was not her husband's. 'I believe he is sleeping in the shop.' It was Richard Treveryan.

'Oh –'

'I did not mean to startle you. I found I could not sleep.'

'Nor me –'

There was a brief silence. Treveryan's chair creaked slightly as he shifted his position. 'You were looking for your husband?'

'No. Yes. But I won't disturb him now.'

'Here –' He leaned over and pulled a chair forward from the shadows. 'Just as I was in danger of being overcome by dismal thoughts, you arrive to raise my spirits. It is very convenient.'

Margaret smiled, and hesitated only for a moment before sitting down on the other side of the fireplace and pulling her shawl more warmly around her shoulders.

Richard said, 'My wife and I have caused you a mighty inconvenience, I'm afraid. And on your wedding day too.'

'Oh no, we were married just after Christmas,' Margaret felt the need to explain, 'but my husband was ill at the time so the actual celebration had to wait until now.'

In the darkness she could see the splash of white linen at his throat and the whites of his eyes as they narrowed in a smile. 'I'm glad to see your fortunes have improved since our last meeting. I've never seen a maid so distracted-looking as you were then.'

'Yes.' Margaret saw no reason to deny the fact. 'And you were in a powerful hurry to leave too, if I remember rightly. As though you had demons on your back.'

He laughed softly. 'Nothing so poetic. Only the damned Suttons.'

'You can't imagine how much I envied you, even so. If I could have escaped . . . but it's always crueller for a woman.'

'Surely, Mistress Hollar, what you desired was waiting for you here all the time?'

Margaret was adjusting the logs stacked by the fire so that he could not see her face at all. 'Yes,' she said in a low voice.

Since she did not seem particularly inclined to continue the conversation, Richard picked up the book that he had found there earlier. He asked, 'Your husband is familiar with the Roman poets?'

'He may be, but that is my book you are holding.'

'May I –?'

She nodded. 'Of course.'

Since Ambrose had attacked it in the orchard, it was less a book than a collection of papers. Richard commented, 'You should take better care of your authors.'

'I was not the one who tore it.'

'Indeed?'

'There are men foolish enough to be jealous of what they do not understand.'

Richard asked, 'Does the estimable Mr Hollar object to your studies?'

'He does not care what I do.' Something in the dismissiveness with which she spoke, her brief glance towards the oak door that led into the shop, roused his curiosity.

'How old are you, Mistress Hollar?'

'I was sixteen last autumn.'

His strong hand cradled the book as he said with a smile, 'You have an unusual taste in literature. Who has been your teacher?'

'First of all my mother. That was her book. But since she died the parson continued to give me lessons when he could spare the time.'

Richard burst out laughing. 'The *parson* taught you this?'

'And what is wrong with that?'

'Don't be angry but – did your parson go through all the poems with you?'

'No, there were a few that he said I would not be able to understand.'

'I'm not surprised.'

Now it was Margaret's turn to be intrigued. 'Are you a scholar, Mr Treveryan?'

'One of the best.'

Ignoring the self-mockery in his voice Margaret reached on to the shelf behind her for a taper and, lighting it from the fire, she lit the two candles that stood beside the chair.

'Here,' she said, 'I shall find the page.'

'Is this any way for me to repay your husband's hospitality, Mistress Hollar? By introducing his bride to scurrilous poetry?'

'Let me fetch you a glass of wine.'

'By all means. I find that wine almost always undermines my scruples.'

'Good.' She set the glass of wine down beside him.

He added ruefully, 'Not that I am normally overburdened with scruples.'

'Good,' said Margaret again. The parson's reticence about some of the more potentially interesting poems had long been a source of annoyance. She began to leaf through the pages eagerly.

'My mother had been reading this one with me just before she died. It did not mean much to me then, but now I have come to love it too. I think it was her favourite.'

256

She began reading the Latin and Richard translated as she went,

> No house ever sheltered such lovers as these,
> No love ever united lovers in such a bond.

'Your mother was a romantic, then?' It seemed to Richard an unlikely poem for the wife of John Pearce to have favoured.

'I suppose she must have been, once. She was a foreigner, on a Dutch ship that was headed for America when it went down off Porthew and she was the only survivor. Her first husband was drowned.'

Margaret stared into the fire, the poem for the moment all forgotten. Richard remained silent; he might have known that this girl, this respectable draper's young wife, was only partly rooted here. He sipped his wine thoughtfully.

'I wish I could have asked her about it,' she said at length.

'"*Nullus amor*" – no other love. That much is simple enough to understand. Perhaps you and your husband will have the words carved above your door one day.'

Margaret turned her attention briskly back to the little book. 'I have been able to read that poem without help for years. I only showed it to you because . . .' She broke off, suddenly not quite sure just why she had stopped there, except that it had long been one of her favourites. 'Now, how about this one?'

Richard groaned in mock dismay. 'I was afraid you might choose that.'

'I hope you do not intend to let me down now.'

'Heaven forbid. That word refers to the male member.'

'I thought as much. And this phrase here?'

'Ah, yes.' Richard was silent for a few moments before asking softly, 'Do you know what is meant by the other kind of dying?'

In the silence that followed Margaret lifted her eyes from the page and gazed very steadily at him, neither denying nor agreeing that she understood. 'So?' she asked.

'Well then, Catullus is merely promising his mistress that she will die – in that other, pleasant sense, of course – nine times before they are finished. I expect like most poets he was an incorrigible braggart.'

Margaret burst out laughing, then clapped her hand over her mouth to smother the sound, but her eyes remained shining with amusement.

'You have the perverse tastes of every schoolboy,' scolded Richard.

'But I work a good deal harder than most,' she countered.

'Bravo. Is Catullus your favourite?'

'Sometimes, but sometimes I do not like him at all. He can be so cruel.'

'I think I know the poem you refer to. The woman whom he had loved more than himself, more than all his own, grew tired of him eventually.'

'And he accused her –'

'– of becoming a common whore. Can you not understand his rage and bitterness?'

'But we only know his account of what happened between them. Supposing she had been able to write poetry and her poems had survived? I'm sure then we would hear a different story. It is so easy for men to be scornful – they have so much greater freedom, so many different avenues to choose from, whereas women must make the best of impossible situations and very often have no choice at all in what they do.'

She broke off suddenly. Richard was watching her. She turned her eyes from his scrutiny and, with a sigh, returned the book to its shelf beside the fire. A shiver of sudden cold ran down her spine.

After a long silence Richard rose and crossed the hearth to stand beside her. 'Here,' he said, letting his cloak slip from his shoulders and placing it around her.

'Thank you.' He had returned to his chair. She avoided his eye, wondered if she should return his cloak, but it was warm and with a spicy scent that she had never come across before.

Richard fidgeted. 'Perhaps,' he said, 'you have inherited your mother's wandering spirit.'

'Maybe. But it is no use to me now.' As she spoke she leaned her head back and a great weariness seemed to spread across her face. Rousing herself with some difficulty she said, 'Your family will be mighty surprised at the change in you, Mr Treveryan. I scarcely recognised you when you came into Jack Pym's first.'

'That is my intention,' he said, and Margaret noticed the hint of bitterness in his voice. 'In part, that is the reason for our visit. Also my wife was curious since she still believes that all the county west of Fowey is inhabited by giants and fairies. Your blacksmith has only confirmed her fears.'

Margaret smiled. 'Ambrose is a big man.'

Silence then; only the distant murmur of the waves, the creaks of an old house in the stillness of the night.

'And how is your wayward sister? Keeping away from Nicolas Sutton, I hope.'

'Of course she is.' Margaret's answer was crisp. 'Since I left the farm to come here and care for William in his sickness she has been far too busy for any mischief.'

Richard leaned forward. 'Strange,' he teased, 'I never thought you were a hypocrite.'

'A hypocrite!'

'If I remember,' his laughter was mocking, 'you were fiercely determined that she should not discover the pleasures you must already have been enjoying.'

She knew she should have been angry with him but her laughter betrayed her. 'Surely, Mr Treveryan, you've seen enough of the world to know it is always a mistake to judge by appearances.'

'And what is that supposed to mean?'

'Oh –' She sighed and, in an unconscious movement, she placed her hand over the dome of her stomach. Then she smiled, as if at a secret source of happiness. 'I love to feel him move,' she murmured.

'Him?'

She did not answer. Of course it was a boy. Impossible to explain the image she had on her long walk across the Downs of the strange little homunculus, gripping with fierce fingers to the rim of her womb. 'He is so strong already,' she said softly.

Richard shifted in his chair. It was colder now without his cloak and he moved a little closer to the fire. It occurred to him then that she was sitting just within reach, that he could stretch out his hand and place it beside hers, that he too could feel the child move; that it would be an easy thing, but never a simple one, to take her in his arms.

259

A log subsided on the hearth. Margaret put on more furze and the fire crackled and sparked. She appeared lost in thought but gradually, though she was still gazing into the fire and watching the specks of flame dart up into the chimney, she became aware of his gaze on her. She turned slowly. Every detail of his face was clear in the yellow glow of the candles; the hawk-like features and the brooding troubled eyes fixed now on her. She drew back, yet there was triumph in her recognition of his stare. He was looking at her as a man looks at a woman for whom he has just felt the first stirrings of attraction. In his gaze she felt herself grow beautiful again.

She rose to her feet, and for the first time in weeks she stood up very straight and tall. 'Mr Treveryan,' she said, 'I have disturbed your solitude long enough.'

He shrugged. 'I find I'm not yet bored with the disturbance.'

'But still . . .' She turned and walked towards the door. 'Good night.'

'Good night.'

She turned suddenly and crossed the room to stand before him. 'I almost forgot – your cloak.'

The heavy garment slipped from her shoulders and landed in his lap. He grinned and stood up so that he could put it around him. Now that he was standing, his eyes were very close to hers. The smile faded from his face. He raised his hand and his palm brushed the side of her cheek.

She stepped back. 'Mr Treveryan, please make sure the fire is safe before you retire for the night. And that the candles are extinguished.'

'You do not wish to burn on your wedding night?'

She glanced towards the oak door that led into the shop. She said crossly, 'I'm sure you and your wife will want to be away early in the morning. We certainly have no wish to detain you.'

'Really? Your husband gave a different impression altogether. But then,' he added, talking now to her retreating back, 'I should have known that your wedding night would be unlike any other.'

* * *

The horses from Rossmere arrived an hour after first light. Richard and Kitty were seated in lone eminence at the kitchen table which had been spread, at William's insistence, with the best damask tablecloth. Mistress Hocken fussed and achieved nothing. William, showing no ill effects from his night spent on the apprentice's bench in the shop, was all consideration – nothing was too much trouble: some spiced wine, perhaps, before their journey? Margaret wished only that their guests would leave; the events of the night seemed as fantastical as a dream and much more disturbing. She took refuge in silence. Merry was still asleep. William was prepared to compensate for all his household's shortcomings.

'Some canary wine, Mr Treveryan? Or maybe your wife would care for some frumenty, more nourishing, I'm sure, and my wife has learned a passable recipe though maybe not as fine as you are accustomed to –'

Richard had slept badly and was out of humour at the prospect of revisiting Rossmere. He surveyed the choice remnants of the wedding feast which had been piled up on plates before them, enough for a whole month of breakfasts. 'Really, Mr Hollar,' he said drily, 'you are far too generous.'

William hovered, trying to interpret their slightest glance. 'Margaret,' he commanded, 'make some frumenty.'

'I don't believe they want it, William.'

He manoeuvred her into the back scullery where they could not be overheard. 'Why must you be so surly with our guests?'

'Don't you realise he's mocking you, William? He despises us.'

'You're such a clod-pole, Margaret. You don't understand such people. It's only his manner. Now –'

Margaret made the frumenty.

'I can't abide frumenty in the mornings,' said Mistress Treveryan, as Margaret set the steaming bowl on the table, 'far too heavy on the stomach, don't you agree, Richard? Now in the evenings a little may be taken with care, but milk is always risky, especially in the spring. Last Easter one of my scullions had frumenty in the morning and the wretched boy was doubled up and screaming for two whole days. I had to send him home.'

'And what became of the lad?' William was genuinely concerned.

'Him?' Kitty had been mopping gravy with her bread. 'Oh, I cannot remember; servants come and go so quickly, don't they? I think he may have died.'

Treveryan laughed. 'My wife is famous for her tender heart.'

Kitty helped herself to more pie. 'It's true, all true. I always send beggars away with the threat of a flogging for I cannot abide to see their suffering.'

'You see what I mean?' Richard directed his appeal to Margaret, but she turned away at once and put another log on the fire.

'You'll roast us all,' said William crossly, as the flames leapt high in the grate.

Merry wandered in, still yawning.

'Heavens above, what a feast,' and she made to pull up a chair but William intercepted her.

'Can you not wait?' he snarled.

'Why don't you join us?' said Richard. 'It's always better to eat in company.' Margaret guessed that he would have invited the town half-wit to join them if he thought it would annoy William.

But William was so pleased with his wealthy guests that he was oblivious to Richard's manner. He began, 'You do us too much –'

'Here are your horses, Mr Treveryan.' Margaret interrupted him with some relief.

Voices raised and a clatter of horses' hoofs in the lane behind the house confirmed her words. Nicolas Sutton was the first to enter. He was the very picture of good looks and health. His brown hair was ruffled, his cheeks glowing from the early-morning ride and his eyes sparkled with pleasure as he caught sight of his friend. Unable to bear a grudge himself, it had never occurred to him that Richard might still be mindful of the events of that last day at Rossmere. Ignoring everyone else, he strode across the room to where Richard was slowly rising from his chair and clapped his arms around him in a warm embrace. 'Richard, it's good to see you again. It's ridiculous how much I've missed you.'

Margaret had noticed the expression that had briefly shadowed Richard's face as his friend entered the room. She saw too how the shadow lifted at the warmth of Nicolas's words. 'Nonsense, Nick,' he said, embracing his friend, 'I've not thought of you at all.'

Nicolas laughed. 'You old misery. Heavens, but it's been dull here without you.'

'Dull? Is that the word of a newly married man?'

'Don't twist my words, you know full well what I mean. And I keep forgetting I'm married – but Alice is a good girl.'

Richard changed the subject swiftly. 'Let me introduce you to my wife: Kitty, this is my friend, Nicolas Sutton.'

'Ah yes, the –' Nicolas stopped himself in time, 'delighted to make your acquaintance.' He turned back to Richard: Kitty was not a woman on whom a man's attention often lingered.

But Kitty was not so easily dismissed. 'And I am equally pleased to meet you. In fact I am always pleased to meet someone from an old and respected family and I know that the Suttons are highly thought of – at least in these western parts of Cornwall. You must not think that my refusal to marry your younger brother was in any way intended as an expression of my low opinion of your family but sometimes –' and here she slid a meaningful look towards her husband, who appeared to be relishing her speech, 'but sometimes there are other considerations of greater importance. I'm sure you understand.'

'Ah,' said Nick, 'yes.' He cleared his throat, glanced a quick appeal to Richard who ignored it. Kitty, who had no experience of embarrassment herself, was unaware of the effect she often produced on others.

William also cleared his throat. He was hovering on the perimeter of their conversation, hoping to be introduced to the gentleman from Rossmere – whose wife might be encouraged to buy cloth from him in future.

Treveryan ignored him. Margaret grew irritated.

'Let us leave at once,' said Richard. 'There is nothing to keep us here.'

'And Alice is all eagerness to see you again.' Nicolas was helping himself to slices of goose and hunks of bread and cheese and did not notice the bleakness that once more touched Richard's face.

His mouth still full of food, Nicolas glanced up and looked at William Hollar for the first time. 'Does everyone in this town eat such enormous breakfasts?' he queried.

Delighted to have been noticed at last, William rushed in eagerly, 'Not at all, our needs are usually very modest. But yesterday was my –'

Nicolas was already leaving. 'Are your servants ready, then, Richard? Small wonder the social order is crumbling if townsfolk eat goose and pies at breakfast, eh?'

Margaret was wondering if Mr Treveryan and his wife would also leave without a word of thanks as she and William followed them down the path that led to the gate at the end of the garden where the horses were waiting. The narrow lane was crowded with horses, servants and a few neighbouring dogs and small children who had wandered from their homes to watch the spectacle.

Richard stopped suddenly and, taking a small money bag from his doublet, he asked William, 'What do we owe you for the night's lodging, Mr Hollar?'

William coloured slowly. 'Nothing at all, Mr Treveryan. We were only too honoured to have you for our guests.'

'Nonsense. If you play innkeeper, you surely expect some recompense. How much?'

For once William was speechless.

It was only with the greatest difficulty that Margaret managed to stop herself from boxing Richard Treveryan's ears. She said loudly, 'You must be a sad and mercenary man indeed, Mr Treveryan, if you cannot recognise hospitality that is freely given.'

His eyes met hers for a fleeting moment. 'Nothing is freely given, believe me,' adding, with the trace of a smile, 'not even lessons on the Roman poets.' Then his horse was led over and he swung up easily into the saddle. 'Very well then,' he had returned his money pouch to safe-keeping, 'but I hope you never expect us to return your hospitality.'

'I'd not wish your hospitality on a starving dog,' she snapped, 'and my husband and I would certainly never stoop so low.'

'Margaret, be calm,' murmured William somewhere in the region of her ear. But for once she sensed his approval.

Treveryan was laughing and Nick, who had wheeled his horse around and caught the end of their conversation, whooped with delight. 'There you are, Richard, didn't I tell you that girl was born to scold you? Do you remember?'

'She was deprived of her husband on her wedding night, thanks to our untimely arrival, that's why she's so fierce.'

'What's the delay?' asked Kitty, who until now had been busy with the proper arrangement of her safeguard. 'There, now I'm prepared for any amount of your Cornish mud. Why are we still talking to these people?'

Richard leaned down from his horse and spoke to William and Margaret in a low and confidential tone. 'You must excuse my wife,' he said, 'her rudeness is all instinctive whereas I must study to achieve mine.'

'A paltry waste of time. I never heard such nonsense.'

'I'm sure you must be right, Mistress Hollar. Perhaps I should reform my manners. Nick! I intend to change at once.'

'Heaven forbid. Alice might regret her choice if you become a courtier.'

'Really, Richard,' Mistress Treveryan's shrill voice could still be heard as the cavalcade of riders clattered away up the narrow lane, 'sometimes I think I don't understand a word you say.'

And the last thing they heard was Treveryan's laughter, 'That, sweet wife, is probably just as well.'

'How dare he be so rude!' exclaimed Margaret as she stumped back towards the house.

'You do not understand the ways of the wider world,' said William, following her, though he sounded less confident of his greater experience than was usual, 'he was merely indulging in a little irony. You must learn to distinguish when such people are being ironic.'

'Pray God I never set eyes on the ungrateful wretch ever again.'

By the time they reached the kitchen where Merry was enjoying the remains of the breakfast, William had rallied somewhat. 'Looking back, I can see that it was your surly manner that must have provoked him. He was always perfectly civil in his dealings with me.'

Margaret could not think what had provoked him. But later, when William had retreated to the cool silence of the shop and Mistress Hocken had gone down the street to see to an elderly neighbour, Merry leaned across the table and beamed at Margaret. 'Did you notice the expression in Mr Treveryan's eyes when he looked at you, Mattie?'

'I most certainly did not.'

Merry was not convinced. 'He may not be a good-looking fellow in the same way as Mr Sutton, but still, don't you think there is something most unusually attractive about the man?'

'No. I've seen conger eels with prettier faces.'

They both burst out laughing. Then Merry explained why she had decided after all to forgive Ned Roberts and Margaret told Merry her recent discoveries in Catullus until William, hearing their noise, poked his head around the door and asked if he was always to be the only person in the house to be usefully employed.

The Falling Years

London, October 1660

Some time during the quiet night hours before the day when he was to have a formal audience with King Charles II, Sir Richard Treveryan awoke suddenly from a troubled sleep. His conversation with that irksome daughter Perdita the previous day had worked on his sleeping brain like an elixir of discarded love. Margaret, her loveliness and her treachery, still wove her way into his dreams on these cursed nights and rekindled the age-old pains of loss. Meg . . . he murmured as he surfaced into waking . . . and would have repeated the word but he clenched his teeth and bit back the hated name.

'*Nullus amor* . . .' the dream voice had promised, 'no love ever bound two lovers so closely . . .' And he had remembered her expression of childish delight at glimpsing the forbidden knowledge of the words as he translated on that other night, so many years ago.

One of the rumours was that she had been killed in a brawl. At times such as this, when his dreams seemed haunted by such an unshakeable intensity, he wondered if hers might be one of those souls condemned, by reason of their violent and unhallowed deaths, to haunt the living in their quest for peace. In the daytime he laughed such ideas to scorn. In this mournful dark of night, when even the watch was slumbering in his booth, such fancies were harder to dispel.

'Idle nonsense,' he muttered peevishly, 'all nonsense.'

He rose from his bed and, by the light of a hastily lit candle, he found the Venetian potion that sometimes stilled his dismal memories.

The liquid burned his throat and then its fire started to warm his stomach. He began to relax.

He barely remembered that first visit to Rossmere with Kitty. He supposed he must have visited the farm at

269

Trecarne and shown Kitty the full magnificence of his landed estates. He supposed there must have been pain and anger at seeing Nick and Alice together, some satisfaction at returning a wealthier man than when he left. He did not care to remember.

Better by far, if he was going to succumb to the old man's habit of dwelling in the past, to remember those turbulent years when he had turned Kitty's small fortune into a large one. There had been disasters – one ship sunk in the Bay of Biscay with all the crew and cargo lost, another captured by Barbary pirates almost within sight of Plymouth and the crew all taken into slavery. But the rewards had been greater by far. He had learned to love and to respect the sea, and he had learned the many variations of the simple merchant's trick of buying at the lowest and selling at the highest price.

And he enjoyed the voyages for their own sake, found pleasure in exotic places and strange customs. On the North African coast he had met men whose passion for hawking matched his own: even now he could remember the beauty of the desert falcons ringing the high blue of the southern sky. They were expert traders too, these men of the Southern Atlas, and their main commodity was men. On one voyage Richard did well selling slaves to the New England settlers, but he found there was something about the trade that displeased him and he did not do it again.

After the first few years, when the urge for profit was no longer the only motive that drove him, he was free to devote time to the more leisurely occupations of the traveller. In Italy he met men of business whose interest in sculpture, painting and music was more highly developed than any he had come across before.

One man in particular became a close friend: Signor Gianfranco Carlotti of Amalfi who had amassed a fortune during a long and unscrupulous life and had spent a good deal of it on works of art – paintings and tapestries, exquisite items fashioned from silver and gold. Each time Richard visited the old palazzo which crouched on the cliff-top in Amalfi like a toad of weathered stone, there was something new and wondrous for him to admire.

And now the memories came full circle. It was an autumn evening and a sudden storm beat its anger against the outer

270

walls of the palazzo. A servant led the way holding a flare and, at Signor Carlotti's command, stopped in front of his newest purchase, a Madonna with lilies painted about a hundred years before. She wore that vacant expression sometimes characteristic of pregnant women and her long, boneless fingers were laid as if in benediction across her rounded belly. And as the Italian sang the praises of his newest treasure Richard found himself gazing into the Madonna's empty eyes and the wind beyond the walls of the palazzo became a voice that crooned, 'I love to feel him move – so strong.' And he remembered with a jolt that strange conversation by the firelight at Porthew. He had not thought of her in years, was not sure that he even remembered her name. On the few occasions when he lapsed into regrets for England, his thoughts only strayed to Alice.

But it was at that moment when he began to tire of his wandering life, and to plan his return to Cornwall.

Sir Richard Treveryan sat a long time in his high-backed carved oak chair, his head supported by his hand. Absent-mindedly he fondled the ears of the hunting dog which had thrust her head against his knee. He could remember every detail of that Madonna with the lilies to this day, but Margaret's face was obscured by some subtle alchemy of pain and he only glimpsed it occasionally as if through a veil of mist. He had no wish to recall her, anyway.

And yet he knew, even now, that her face bore no resemblance at all to the languid Madonna of the picture.

Cornwall, 1631

11

Margaret's son was born towards the end of May.

It was a day of early summer perfection: a soft wind blew from the south, land and sea both shimmered in the morning sunshine. Margaret and Merry, their routine tasks accomplished, had set off to the wood that spanned the top of the valley, to pick bluebells.

The wood was a tall church of dappled blues and greens. It was cooler there, cool and peaceful, a closed world untouched by the worries and concerns of town and farms. The two girls drifted slowly apart.

It was there, as she waded through the shimmering blue sea of flowers, that Margaret felt the first pains grip her belly. The flowers fell from her hand.

'Merry!' she called.

But Merry had wandered down to the bank of the stream where the flowers grew more thickly and the only answer that came back was the tumbling song of a mistle thrush in the green-hazy branches above her.

'Merry!'

The pain eased as abruptly as it had begun. But the tranquility of the morning had been shattered, leaving panic in its wake.

For almost nine months Margaret's condition had made her a target for every lurid tale of childbirth: tales of the women who died screaming while their child was cut from them with a butcher's knife; tales of babies born with monstrous defects, goblin faces, two heads, fishy fins instead of arms; tales of women who were driven insane by the agonies of labour, of others who survived only to be brought down by the fever that so often followed. Talk of changeling children and foul curses and the eternal punishment of Eve. In that instant the blue carpet and the flowers at her feet and the canopy of the wood all around her grew dim and unreal:

she had taken the first step along the road that for so many women led only to tortured death.

'Merry!'

A voice shrill and unfamiliar pierced the woodland – her own voice, transformed by fear.

'What in God's name are you squawking about now?' Merry appeared suddenly behind her and never, not even on that October Sunday when Merry had approached her after church, had Margaret been so glad to see her.

'The baby – it's begun –'

A fleeting glance of alarm was quickly replaced by Merry's broad smile as she gripped her by the arm. 'Is that all? I thought at the very least you'd seen the drowned sailor or a Turkish pirate. It's high time that child was born, anyway. I'm sick and tired of you lumbering about the house like a colossus. Let's get you home, then.'

'But the bluebells –'

'Here. Take the ones you dropped. You're surely not thinking of having the child here in the woods, are you?'

Margaret looked about her: at the high blue sky and the still brighter blue of the flowers at her feet, at the busy movements of the birds and the fresh young green of leaves and buds everywhere. 'Why not? Then the first thing he sees will be –' she swept her arms wide – 'all of this.'

Merry had gathered the fallen bluebells which she now thrust into Margaret's arms. 'Just because your labour's begun is no reason to take leave of your senses entirely, Mattie Hollar. Come along. I'm not letting you give birth to a wood nymph even if you . . . are you sure you can manage the walk?'

'Certainly I can. I'm pregnant, not crippled. And what did you have in mind anyway? Carrying me? I'm as big as a hill and twice as heavy.'

With a last backwards look towards the shadowy vault of the woods, Margaret allowed Merry to chivvy her gently back, to the town.

Parson Weaver was not especially partial to babies, newborn or otherwise. His own wife gave birth each spring with chronic regularity and her suffering each time appalled him. During her last confinement in March he had become con-

276

vinced that she was sure to burst open like some overripe fruit. As he paced the paths behind his house he could not believe a body could survive such torment, nor could he reconcile his image of an amiable God with the Creator who inflicted these horrors for all time on the hapless daughters of Eve.

So it was with mounting apprehension that he entered William Hollar's house that fine May afternoon. He had tapped on the kitchen door but, receiving no answer, he went in quietly. The kitchen was empty, nothing stirred except a bee against the windowpane. It seemed to him a most unnatural silence, but a silence that he knew too well.

As he stood by the kitchen door he was seized by a violent fit of trembling. He could picture the scene in the upstairs bedroom so clearly: the midwife, hands and clothing filthy with blood as she gathered up her few instruments of torture; and the woman or girl – the mother – but no longer any of these things, just a corpse, a useless heap of pale flesh, growing colder. It was at such moments when Parson Weaver acknowledged that other presence in the room, the dark shadow of Death himself, most greedy of apparitions. So often Birth and Death came visiting together, the warm hand of one crushed in the other's icy grip.

There was a movement on the stair. For an endless pause he saw the faint outline of Death himself, the old enemy made visible at last.

'Dear God, no!'

Not Margaret. Take anyone but her.

The spectre of Death melted, shrank, reassembled itself and bulged into the dumpy and anxious shape of Mistress Hocken.

'You startled me, Parson, but then, today everything is in a spin.'

'And Margaret?'

'Oh her, laughing and chattering with Merry as they always do. Now, what did I come down for?'

'And her labour?'

'Over and done with an hour since. But then Margaret is broad built and has always been a healthy girl.'

Relief had apparently affected Parson Weaver in the region of his knees. His legs folded beneath him and he sat down heavily on a stool – and even remembered to offer a brief prayer to his once-more kindly God, the God who had preserved Margaret. The only person in all the world – he saw this now as clearly as if it were written on the wall in front of him – he had ever really cared for.

He hesitated. But then – why else had he come?

'Let me carry that basin for you, Mistress Hocken.'

'So kind, Parson . . . these stairs, too much for old legs –'

She was so stout that, following her up the narrow stairway, he had a premonition that her spreading rump might one day become inextricably wedged between the walls. He almost burst out laughing at the thought – and then realised it was relief at Margaret's safe delivery had made him lightheaded.

Mistress Hocken waddled down the corridor. 'It's only the parson, Margaret, come to see how you are doing.'

A floorboard creaked as he entered the room.

He blinked his disbelief. A scene so calm, so tranquil, sunlight filtering through the window. Was this really a room in which a child had just been born?

The proof lay sprawled in Margaret's arms.

Her confinement had taken place in the back bedroom that she still shared with Merry. The furnishings were minimal: a curtained bed, a stool, a clothes press set into the alcove beside the chimney-breast. And now, in pride of place, a heavy wooden cradle. Merry was folding linen in the crib and Dame Watkins, the midwife, had paused in her work to refresh herself with a mug of ale. Parson Weaver had long since decided that those women in the neighbourhood who survived into old age either became very fat, like Mistress Hocken, or very thin. Dame Watkins was definitely of the thin variety: limbs like an assembly of broomsticks and barely enough flesh on her face to cover the bony cheeks and chin.

Margaret appeared to be dozing, her hair spread across the white pillows that supported her. The expression on her face and the weight of her resting limbs were suffused with that profound calm that often follows extremes of physical effort. The infant was sleeping too. He had been wrapped in the linen bands with which newborn babies were traditionally swaddled but he must have kicked his protest while he was feeding for one skinny leg had emerged to sprawl against the whiteness of his mother's cotton shift.

Sleep had overcome them together. Margaret's shift was open to reveal the circle of her engorged breast and Parson Weaver saw with fascination that the child's fist was clenched beside the nipple from which he had been feeding.

The next instant, as Margaret opened her eyes and recognised her visitor, Mistress Hocken had tweaked her cotton shift to cover the exposed flesh and decency was restored.

Alarm shadowed Margaret's face. 'Parson!' she exclaimed. 'Did Dame Watkins send for you?' For the swift arrival of the parson indicated a frail infant who needed instant christening to save him from eternal torment should he die.

Merry, who had been watching the parson closely, reassured her, 'No one told Parson to come. He only wants to see how you are.'

'That's all right then.' And she relaxed and shifted the weight of the sleeping babe against her arm.

'You are well, then, Margaret?' Parson found his voice at last.

'Yes, thanks be to God. And the child.'

Merry added, 'Dame Watkins said there never was an infant so eager to be born. Just look at him, Parson, isn't he beautiful?'

He took a step forward and peered more closely at the child. The small portion of face that was visible looked to him as grotesquely ugly as every other newborn infant it had been his duty to contemplate.

'He looks bonny enough,' he conceded, and then, as though to justify the speed of his visit he added, 'without wishing to alarm you, Margaret, an immediate christening is always best. Even the healthiest child can sicken suddenly . . .'

Margaret frowned and spread her broad hand across her son's back and drew him more tightly to her. 'He'll be safe enough with me for a day or two,' she said.

'That child is hungry for life,' said Dame Watkins. Her work for the day was almost done and she was beginning to pack away her things.

The parson asked, 'And the child's name?'

'I have given it much thought,' said Margaret. Which was no more than the truth, knowing as she did that all those who still doubted his paternity, especially her immediate family, were watching for any clues that she might drop.

'Luke,' she said finally.

'His father . . . Mr Hollar . . . must be a proud man.'

Margaret did not answer right away. Then, 'I daresay he will be, when he sees him,' she said softly.

Merry spoke up. 'As soon as we sent for Dame Watkins he left on urgent business – or so he said. He's not used to these things the way you are, Parson.'

He fidgeted. Something in the boldness of her manner was disquieting. He recollected the gossip that was circulating concerning her and Ned Roberts and decided he should tackle her on the subject as soon as he could.

The little pink scrap of a leg jerked against Margaret's chest and the bundle in her arms began to shudder into waking. 'Look, Mattie, he's waking again.'

Parson Weaver knew his departure was long overdue but still he could not tear himself away. He watched, fascinated, as Margaret cradled the infant in her strong hand and gazed into his unseeing blue eyes. And when she smiled, a smile so warm and serious, it seemed that all the heartache and tenderness and joy of loving was in her smile.

And for one delicious moment the parson wanted only to cross the room and kneel beside the bed and rest his head against her breast. Let everyone know the ties that bound them now, all three.

Merry touched his arm. 'She needs to rest now, Parson.'

There was a warning in her voice that pulled him back from the brink. Hardly aware of what he was doing, he turned and stumbled from the room.

The parson, as he performed his duties that day and the next in a kind of daze, would have been amazed if he had been able to catch a glimpse of the turmoil that lay behind Margaret's outward show of calm.

Although her labour had been almost indecently swift and easy in the opinion of all those women who had been less fortunate themselves, to her it had seemed arduous enough. This agony on the brink of new life . . . she clenched her teeth and refused to cry out, but she had no defence against the memories that skipped like tormenting demons across her mind.

Again and again she heard the cackling voice of the old Pym woman and her threat, 'You'll squeal for all to hear when the powder starts to burn'. Burning, yes . . . there was a red-hot fire between her legs, a searing pain that the warm liquid pouring from her body did not soothe at all. She had not taken the powder. She had buried the magical rhyme. Ah, but – she could not pretend she had not been tempted. And all her upbringing, every lesson she had ever learned, had told her that wrongdoing is always followed by punishment. She had wanted this thing dead that was tearing her apart: the child had been conceived in sin and sinners can never escape retribution.

Impossible to love a punishment. She heard herself give a mighty bellow, more like the roar of an ox as it is slaughtered than any human sound, there was a sudden blaze of fire between her legs and she felt the thing leave her body. She closed her eyes.

Dame Watkins cackled, Merry whooped with pleasure, Mistress Hocken was still anxious.

Margaret opened her eyes. She could see, but faintly, as if they were an immense distance away, Merry and Dame Watkins and the strange blue and bloody morsel of flesh they were busy with. So tiny and so far away, those two women, so far, impossibly far, that tiny thing that had come from within. Tears were mingling with the sweat that streaked her face.

She turned away and closed her eyes and groaned. After a few moments she heard Merry's coaxing and turned once more to find that the messy scrap of red and blue was now wrapped like a chrysalis in his white swaddling bands and most recognisably a baby.

'Your son, Mattie . . .'

Margaret stared. She expected to be flooded by emotion for her newborn child but all she felt was . . . nothing. Cold, hard, empty, mocking nothing.

How strange, she thought, he's my son but I don't love him at all. He came out of my body, he has turned my life upside-down for ever but I don't care for him at all. No love.

Another dot appeared on the horizon of the room: Mistress Hocken bearing a tray of warm spiced wine.

'Take a sip,' she urged, 'it will bring your strength back.'

It was true. She had not realised how cold she was, how drained, as though all the warmth of life had left her body with the child. She sipped the wine: it was weak and spiced and sweet.

And then she heard what seemed to her the saddest sound in all the world, sadder even than the curlew's lonely cry at the ebbing of the tide – her newborn infant weeping.

Poor child, poor helpless scrap . . . to have a mother who doesn't even love him. No love, nothing, she thought. I don't care for him . . . And now she was appalled by her own lack of feeling, by the empty space within her where a mother's love should be. Was there anything more wicked and unnatural in this whole cruel world than a mother who does not care for her child? How can I not love him? I'm Margaret, the one who is always so tender-hearted, the one who dotes on every runt and sickly animal at the farm, the soft-as-butter girl who can't bear to see a shrew caught by a cat or a sparrow with a broken wing, yet my own son . . . dear God, forgive me, for I must be the most unfeeling mother who ever lived. I cannot love my child.

'Mattie, what is it? Why are you crying?'

'I don't . . . I can't . . .'

Dame Watkins loomed over the bed. 'You'll be wanting to hold him now, Mistress Hollar.'

It was a threat, a judgement, a penance. There was much to-do about arranging the pillows and bolsters on which Margaret was supported. She fussed and said she was not comfortable, desperate only to delay the moment when she must hold her child.

'Here you are –' The white chrysalis was being lowered into her arms. A tiny face, exquisitely wizened. The pressure of her swollen breasts.

Her arms, her shoulders, her whole body, had grown rigid with panic: no, please, she wanted to beg them, don't put him in my arms, don't trust me with him. I tried to

282

kill him once already and I might – I could throw him on the floor and dash out his brains, I could – I'm wicked and don't deserve a child, I don't love him, I can't . . .

The weight was in her arms. She did not dare to move. She lay as stiffly as a wooden doll while Dame Watkins settled the child against her breast, pulled open her shift, cradled his head so he could seek out the nipple. He began to feed. The midwife watched them both for a short while and then, muttering her approval, she went back to the task of packing up the tools of her trade: the potions, knives and charms.

Margaret's arms ached. She was absolutely still, hardly even daring to breathe for fear that she might injure him. His mouth was warm and greedy at her breast. She noticed the gentle touch of his cheek against her breast, the moth-like softness of his breath.

I shall try to love him, she told herself. Maybe I am unnatural and wicked – but I can still try. And all the while, as she drifted into a kind of semi-sleep, her body was warming, responding to the urgent needs of the child. No love, no love . . . her thoughts drifted at random. Yet this feels good, this closeness and this warmth. Confusing, but still good.

It was then, as the evening sun poured in through the open window and the voices of children playing in the lane beyond the garden mingled with the endless sound of the gulls and the sea, that Margaret awoke from a sleep that was both troubled and yet infinitely contented, to see the parson gazing down at her from the doorway.

Later, much later, when Dame Watkins had taken her fee to spend at Jack Pym's ale-house and Merry, having asked Margaret a hundred times if she was sure she could manage, had been persuaded to join her mother in the other bedroom, mother and son were left alone together. Luke slept in the little wooden crib beside the bed. He was tightly wrapped and Dame Watkins had insisted on pinning his gown to the sides of the crib to stop the little people from stealing him away in the night.

Margaret lay back on her pillows and watched as the sky changed to the magical green of an early summer night. She had never imagined that it was possible to feel so troubled and so peaceful all at the same time. No longer alone, never alone again. Everything had changed for ever by this day, this birth.

Already she was trying to forget her first feelings of numbness and self-hate. Already a fierce possessiveness was growing. She told herself that she would willingly die for him now, and at that moment she would have welcomed the chance to show how much she loved him.

She vowed always to be a good mother to this sleeping innocent with the puckered face, whose conception had been so disastrous for her. She wept for her own childhood ending as his began.

And maybe, if her feelings for her son during those first hours and days of his life had been less troubled, young Luke might not, years later, have had the power to break his mother's heart.

Some time after midnight she awoke to see the flame of a single candle moving about the room. Her first thought was that the little folk had come to steal her son. She was wide awake at once.

'Who's that? You cannot take him!'

The candle moved closer to her face and with a sudden relief she recognised the shadowy features behind it.

'I merely came to see the boy.' And the candle moved once more and trembled over the crib.

William was gazing down on the newborn child with an expression of wonder and . . . tenderness. A tenderness so profound that it almost pained her to see his face so vulnerable. All the coldness, all the contempt, had vanished and his features glowed with love for the fragile scrap of a child who slept so quietly in his crib.

'William –' she began, but he placed his finger against his lips. Then he left, stealthy as a cat, noiselessly as he had come.

Silence and darkness once more and the distant whisper of the sea.

But like a boat that passes through the water without noise yet leaves turbulence in its wake, William had disturbed the peacefulness of the room. A sense of menace lingered long after he had gone.

284

Margaret could not sleep. After a little while Luke began to whimper and she reached out to soothe him.

The next day her whole family travelled over from Conwinnion to see the baby. Lizzie was awed, excited, jealous of Merry, filled with admiration for Margaret. Tom was awed and jealous, though if he felt any admiration or excitement he kept it to himself. Margaret's father was ill at ease among the women gathered in the bedroom and quickly went downstairs again to murmur embarrassed congratulations to William Hollar. But it was the arrival of Mistress Pearce, whose arthritis kept her always at the farm, that caused the greatest stir.

'They said all was well,' she said, when she had caught her breath after climbing the stairs, 'but I wanted to make sure for myself.'

Luke was sleeping and, instinctively, Margaret reached out to protect him, but Mistress Pearce brushed her hand away and, with heavy and painful movements, lifted him from his crib and laid him on the bed. He opened his eyes and blinked up at her crossly, like an owl surprised by daylight. She began to unwrap his swaddling bands; one by one the tiny limbs were exposed and examined. Outraged by this assault on his sleep he began to cry with an irritable high-pitched wailing.

'That's good,' said Mistress Pearce as, apparently satisfied, she handed him over to Merry to be clothed and pacified again, 'he shows no signs of harm.'

Merry looked at Margaret in mock amazement – but Margaret turned away and fiddled with the hem of her coverlet. She could almost smell the evil green liquid her stepmother had prepared for her: she too had feared the child might have suffered lasting damage and was relieved by his ten perfect toes, his lusty appetite and vigorous crying.

The child was crying still when Mistress Pearce nodded her farewell to Margaret and shuffled slowly from the room.

Two days later Margaret came downstairs for the first time and found William packed and ready for a journey.

'You are leaving?'

'Robert Payne has offered me a place on a ship of his that

leaves Fowey next week. It has been obvious to me for some time that I will never make a handsome profit unless I buy and sell the cloth myself in the markets.' He spoke briskly, forestalling Margaret's possible objections. But her only response was envy.

'Where will you go?'

'Holland. There's a market for our cloth there. And I can select the finer fabrics that are hard to come by and which carry a bigger profit.'

But Margaret was not thinking of profit. Through the open window she could hear voices from the lane behind the house: a dog barking; far off, a donkey. And then, as always, sometimes no more than a murmur, sometimes a thundering roar, the movement of the waves against the land, water and rocks and shingle; the sea, that endless highway that came almost to her door and on which she so desperately longed to travel.

She said wistfully, 'I always guessed that you were restless.'

'After my long illness I hope the change of air will be beneficial.'

'Oh William, if only I could go with you!'

He looked at her sharply. 'Your place is here.'

'Oh, I know that!' She was impatient. 'I know it is impossible for me to travel now but . . . Did you know that Holland was my mother's country?'

His expression softened. 'I had forgotten. Perhaps one day you will have your wish.'

The knowledge that he was soon to leave Porthew, though only for a few weeks, seemed to have a mellowing effect on William. Or maybe, Margaret conjectured, it was the birth of her child that had brought about this change in him. She found that it was a fine thing to be spoken to without contempt, to be consulted on matters concerning the management of the shop in his absence, to hear him talk of Antwerp and The Hague and the other European towns where he had lived. Margaret began to believe his earlier distaste must have been caused by the cuckoo child she had been carrying – yet William showed only tenderness towards the baby, and his face was never gentler than when he was contemplating her sleeping son.

On the morning of his departure, Margaret's own restlessness was almost unbearable. She had been down to the harbour, seen the *George* sail round the headland and drop anchor: she could not make out the sailors, nor the details of the boat, but she could smell the sense of adventure and movement that bristled in the early summer air. Robert Payne, impatient and important, was organising cargo, passengers and stores and a replacement for the seaman who had fallen the previous day and broken his arm. William too had a few small items of cargo to be loaded and he fussed over each bolt of cloth as it was rowed out to the waiting ship.

She stayed by the harbour as long as she could, only reluctantly tearing herself away when the time came for Luke to be fed. He was still sleeping on her return and, suddenly tired, she stretched out on her bed. She could hear barrels of fresh water being trundled down the street for the *George*. All movement flowed towards the harbour and the sea.

Light footsteps on the stairs, knuckles tapped against her door. 'Come in, William,' she said. Her husband was a scrupulous respecter of privacy.

'I have come to bid you goodbye.'

He glowed with the happiness of departure. His white cambric shirt was open at the throat and his moleskin doublet was draped over one shoulder. With his hair tousled by the fresh sea wind, his whole body was vibrant with energy and eagerness for change. Margaret closed her eyes for a fraction of time and wondered what it would be like if he suddenly stepped across the room and took her in his arms.

He stood quite still. And Margaret, who had been schooled by long months of rejection, said merely, 'God grant you a safe journey, William.'

'Thank you. And may you . . .' He broke off and went to stand by the crib. 'Take care of our son,' he said in a low voice.

Margaret did not answer.

William's hands were clenched at his sides. 'I know that I have not . . . I hope . . .' He was frowning. 'But when I return we may . . .'

The silence in the room was now grown so huge that she

almost imagined she could hear the heartbeat of her sleeping child.

'Yes, William?'

He struggled. 'We may yet learn to live together amicably. As husband and wife should . . . as friends.'

Margaret waited, then, 'I should like that very much,' she said.

He raised his face to look at her and there was an agony of dread and longing in his features.

'What is it, William?'

'Nothing . . . only . . .' He came and stood before her where she sat on the edge of the bed; hesitated only a moment before catching hold of her hand and raising it to his lips. His fingers were long and thin and cool, dry leaves against her hand, his lips merely breathed against her flesh. A shiver ran through her body.

She stood up slowly. Her eyes were on a level with his mouth and his lips were very slightly parted. The pink tip of his tongue emerged to lick them quickly. He took a step backwards. That recoiling movement of his head, like a tortoise retreating into its shell.

'William . . .'

Luke was snuffling, preparing to cry.

With clear relief he directed her attention towards the crib. 'He is restless, look . . .'

'Only hungry,' she said.

William watched while she lifted the baby from his crib and carried him to the nursing chair.

'He is a fine boy,' said William.

'Yes.' Margaret was beginning to loosen her bodice. Her breasts were pale and swollen with milk. Luke was nuzzling blindly into her shoulder and smacking his lips. Margaret hesitated. What was more natural than that William should stay and watch them, mother and child together? But when she looked up, William was already in the doorway and his eyes glowed with the excitement of the journey to come. He did not even look at them as he said, 'God keep you both safe until I return.'

He was gone. And Luke broke into a loud wailing.

William stood on the deck of the *George* and thought that

there was not a sound in all the world so satisfying as the slap of sails in a summer wind.

He raised a hand in dutiful farewell. Since the little knot of people on the harbour were too far distant to see his expression, he did not bother with a smile. How delightful to watch them grow smaller by the moment: he only wished they were always reduced to this most appropriate insignificance.

That short round speck was his aunt. Dumpy and colourless as a hedge sparrow. This trip would have been worthwhile simply for the escape from her endless wheezing and confused mutterings. He had no patience with her at all.

And there was his cousin Merry, scruffy and self-satisfied as a strutting starling. Probably her thoughts were all of Ned Roberts (a sleek blackbird, perhaps?) handsome enough close-to but now just another speck. He wished them joy of each other.

Only Margaret, his wife, was missing from the cluster of folk on the shore. William continued his feathered musings and then abruptly wished he had not. If Margaret reminded him of anything it was of a collared dove he had brought down with a sling shot when he was a boy. The bird's slow death had caused him to abhor killing for sport ever since. His young wife was the person he was most heartily glad to escape from and yet, paradoxically, of all those he had met in Porthew she was the only person he had begun to like. Admire even. She was honest and loyal. When he heard her sing at her work, or laugh with Merry, he was filled with a great yearning to be a part of her world. She had intelligence and courage. When he was ill she had nursed him. It was even possible that he owed her his life.

Yet still she was intolerable. Those grey eyes that stared at him, watching, hoping. Always hoping for what he could not give her. He was beginning to hate her eyes. Last night he had dreamed of blinding her, of gouging out her eyes with his nails. He had awoken shaking with horror and appalled.

The insignificant specks by the harbour side dwindled into nothing. Now it was the church and buildings that were shrinking, now they vanished behind a fold in the hills. Vanished, gone, no more.

William began to whistle softly between his teeth.

Away from land the breeze was cooler. His doublet was below decks, in the cabin he was to share with Robert Payne. He turned and crossed the deck towards the hatchway and was almost knocked down by a barefoot young sailor boy who was racing across the deck.

'Watch where you're going!' he snapped, but the boy only grinned at him impudently. He could not have been more than about twelve but William recognised at once the stamp of fresh-faced corruption so rapidly gained by young boys at sea.

'Captain's orders!' the lad shouted over his shoulder as he scampered away.

'Then take more care in the future,' William shouted, but his advice was only for the gulls and the salt breeze.

More pleased than ever that he had decided on this trip, William went below deck.

When Luke was once more sleeping, Margaret went to her window, leaned her arms on the sill, and gazed over the rooftops to the blue expanse of sea and sky beyond. She strained her eyes to see if that fragment of white might be the sails of the *George* as it melted into the haze of a summer horizon.

She drummed her fingers on the sill and told herself that this lightness that she felt now could not possibly be relief at seeing her husband leave. Perhaps when he returned . . .

'Mattie?'

Merry had come in and was standing just inside the doorway, as if anxious to leave again as soon as possible.

'We saw William away safely,' she said.

Margaret wondered if Merry shared her sense of lightness, but she did not ask her since the question alone sounded hopelessly disloyal.

'How is Luke?' Merry glanced dutifully at the wooden crib.

'Sleeping.'

'Are you all right?'

'A little tired, that's all.'

Merry hesitated, then, 'I met Ned down by the harbour. His cousin has loaned him a horse for the day. Well, a pony, really. He suggested we might ride over to see his cousin in Manaccan.'

'You'll enjoy that.'

'I only wondered . . .'

Margaret frowned, not understanding right away what Merry was driving at. Then she realised with a twinge of sadness that Merry was requesting her permission. Because she was William's wife and now head of his household in his absence? Out of reluctance to leave her alone on the day of his departure?

Margaret said firmly, 'You'd best leave at once. It's a good long way.'

'Are you sure? I can stay here with you if you like. Ned and I can always go another day.'

'Don't be foolish, Merry. Luke and I plan to rest and we can do that well enough without any help from you.'

'Mother is below if you need anything.'

'Go on. Enjoy the day.'

Merry beamed her relief and clattered off down the stairs quickly, as though afraid Margaret might change her mind. Margaret could hear her singing as she made ready for her outing, the tuneless contented song of a girl who is preparing to meet her lover.

Margaret thought wrily that they were unlikely to reach Manaccan. She very much doubted that the handsome Ned Roberts even had a cousin there since as far as she knew all his family were Coverack people.

Merry's singing ceased abruptly. There was a man's voice, laughter, then a door slammed shut and their voices faded on the summer air. An empty silence spread through the house. Silence as huge and lonely as the emptiness Margaret felt growing inside her.

For the first time in her life, she knew what it was to envy another's happiness – and the knowledge had a bitter taste.

12

Luke was a fretful baby. Never seriously ill, he was always sickly and complaining. Those brief midsummer nights while William was away were often sleepless for Margaret as she paced the boards with her baby or took him down to the kitchen so his cries would not disturb Mistress Hocken. Sometimes she was still awake when Merry stumbled into the house after a night spent with Ned in the little stone barn at the end of the garden.

One morning Merry, more asleep than awake, crept into the house in the greyness that precedes a summer dawn and found Margaret in the kitchen, still trying to comfort her dissatisfied child.

'Poor Mattie,' Merry was at once full of compassion, 'you look worn out. Here, let me take him for a bit and you can have some sleep.'

But Margaret was by now as frayed and irritable as her child. She hugged him tightly and, 'I can manage,' she insisted.

Merry wavered. She saw Margaret's weariness and longed to help, but she saw her crossness too and wondered if she condemned her nights with Ned.

'Just let me help, for once.'

'I was getting him settled.'

Merry yawned widely, then shrugged her shoulders and went on up the narrow stairs to her room.

The more Luke fretted, the more tiresome his grizzling, the more fiercely protective of him Margaret became. Some shadow of her first appalled rejection must have remained to make her prove the strength of her devotion day after weary day. When he cried, which was often enough, she would allow no one else to soothe him. Merry, who had expected them to share in his care, felt hurt by Margaret's exclusion of her. Then Margaret's possessiveness began to irritate her and gradually she ceased to feel any qualms about spending ever more time in the company of Ned Roberts.

Merry's suspicion that she was being judged could not have been further from the truth – but Margaret did feel her own loneliness exaggerated by the lovers' all too obvious happiness. Slowly, without either Merry or Margaret being able to name the change that was occurring, a coolness developed between the two friends.

Mistress Hocken was, as always, oblivious to the cross-currents that existed beneath the surface of her household. All her energies were absorbed in following the detailed instructions William had left her about caring for the shop. The bewilderment which had afflicted her since her husband's death increased daily, compounded now by her fear of William's possible displeasure on his return. Once or twice Margaret heard voices in the shop and, going in to see if Mistress Hocken needed help, found the woman all alone. She was carrying on a conversation with her dead husband and did not even notice the intrusion.

With Merry either thinking of Ned or absent altogether and Mistress Hocken inhabiting a world where the dead were more real than the living, Margaret found the narrow house at the top of the town an increasingly lonely place.

The days that summer were slow and hot. A stench of rotten fish and refuse hung over Porthew like a blanket of decay. There was talk of plague in nearby hamlets. Sometimes the air was so thick and putrid that Margaret thought she would surely choke if she stayed there the whole day. As often as she could she saddled up Samphire, William's chestnut cob, and set off with the baby wrapped in a shawl against her chest, while the early-morning freshness remained in the air. Sometimes she went back to the farm where she and Lizzie chattered together and played with the baby and Tom resorted to ever more outrageous tricks in his efforts to reclaim his position as centre of attention. But most of the time she simply rode.

She became familiar with the travellers on the early-morning highway: hired labourers setting out to work on the harvest, shepherds and stockmen, higglers and pedlars and the occasional frightened vagrant. One morning she heard the sweet music of a reed pipe and, half-afraid but drawn by the music, she approached quietly. An old man was sitting on a boulder at the edge of a spinney and playing music as endless and varied as the song of the lark. She listened for a long time and then, not wishing to disturb his song, she went on by a different route.

The following day she saw him again in Porthew. He was a miserable figure, frail and hungry. She gave him some food and money but she could do nothing to help him when, two days later, he was whipped from the town as a vagrant.

The darkness was alive with little sounds and Merry, stretched out on the loose hay in the barn, had grown to know and love them all. In the distance there was the rustle of a quiet sea against the shore which blurred into the soft sound of the breeze as it caressed the leaves of the apple tree by the garden gate. Samphire, tethered in his stable, shifted his weight from one foot to another and sighed his contentment as he slept. Half a dozen chickens, roosting in the rafters of the barn, churred occasional comments to each other as if sharing their dreams. From time to time there was the scratch or scramble of unknown creatures. Best of all, there was the rhythmic breath of Ned as he slept with his head pressed against her shoulder.

She wondered why she loved him so. She had heard the rumours – it would have been impossible to ignore them. She believed he told her the truth when he said he loved her, but she knew he lied when he denied the gossip about Dolly Namble and all those others. Sometimes it seemed that Ned was a sickness and she yearned to be cured of him. But never for very long; the pleasure of loving him was too great. He was a friend to laugh and talk with and a lover who could conjure up a hunger in her that became a kind of madness. And then, occasionally, as now, he became in his sleeping as vulnerable as a child and she wanted only to cradle him in her arms and protect him. And she could almost forget that in an hour or two he would stir, kiss her briefly on the lips and steal away into the dawn – and she would lose him once again.

*   *   *

One night, when an August thunderstorm hurled its violence across the sea and Porthew was suddenly awash in a downpour of rain, Margaret heard, above the noise of the thunder and the lashing rain, the tread of feet on the landing beyond her room. At first she thought it was Merry, creeping out to an assignation with Ned in the barn, but then she heard the sound of muffled whispers and laughter, the deeper resonance of a man's voice. And in the morning she discovered, as she had guessed, that the large four-poster in William's room had been slept in.

She found Merry washing cabbage leaves in a pail of muddy water.

'Have you gone mad, Merry?' she demanded. 'What in Heaven's name induced you to bring Ned into the house?'

Merry glanced up at her and laughed, that low throaty chuckle that reduced anxiety to a mere nonsense. 'Would you prefer me to catch my death of cold? Last night the roof of the barn was leaking so much we thought the watch had discovered us and was throwing buckets of water in our faces.'

'You should not make a joke of it. People are bound to notice and to talk –'

'So let them talk.'

'But Merry –'

'What about you, Mattie?' Suddenly Merry was no longer joking. 'Are you so disapproving of our pleasures that you want to ban us from your house?'

'But this is your home, not mine.'

'It is William's now – and you are his wife.'

Margaret turned away. 'I only worry for your sake, now that you are growing so indiscreet. What of the parson? If this should come before the Church courts then –'

Merry patted her shoulder affectionately with a damp cabbage leaf. 'Parson will not bother *me*,' she said with heavy emphasis.

'How can you be so sure?'

'Don't ask,' Merry grinned, and hoisted up the bucket of muddy water to empty it at the back of the house, 'and even if he did take it upon himself to poke his nose in where it doesn't belong, then he'd only be wasting his time. All the parsons and Church courts and busybodies in Cornwall can't stop me from seeing Ned if I want to.'

Still grinning, Merry went out into the back garden and carefully poured the bucket of water around a few small cabbage plants. Margaret watched her thoughtfully. She could not help being worried by her indiscretion. How could she be so sure that Parson Weaver would not see fit to intervene? But more than anything else, Margaret was filled with envy. She could only think it must be a fine thing to care for someone so much that you would risk everything for them, even if that someone was a scoundrel, and rumoured to be unfaithful.

A couple of weeks later, during a night in early September, Margaret was awoken in the small hours by Luke. Although he settled quickly back to sleep she found that she was unusually restless. The earlier sounds of vigorous love-making that had emanated from William's room had subsided into the gentle breath of sleep. In a little while she would hear Ned awake and creep off into the night. Gradually she ceased to rock the cradle; then she pulled a shawl around her shoulders and stepped softly down the stairs.

She lit a tallow from the embers of the evening's fire and Mouse, the grey cat Lizzie had brought her from the farm, stalked over and demanded that she fondle her.

William had been gone for nearly three months. He had been gone for so long that she had almost been able to persuade herself that she looked forward to his return. Being optimistic by nature she had endeavoured to forget his coldness and his frequent criticism, his baffling words on the day of their wedding party. Better by far to remember his kindness when they first met and he had tried to stop the badger-baiting, or his eagerness to marry her even when he thought he might be dying, his tenderness towards her child.

Her thoughts began to wander in the night-time stillness. Once before when wakefulness had driven her from her bed she had found an almost-stranger sitting by the fire. She retraced the contours of their conversation as she had done a hundred times before. She could not imagine how they had come to talk together so freely. As though a window had been opened between them through which the other could be seen quite distinctly. The old restlessness wove its patterns of discontent through her fatigue. She fell into a kind of dreaming. She could see Richard Treveryan standing on the prow of his ship and shielding his eyes from the sun as he searched the approaching land. The New World. A world of marvels.

The back door burst open and Margaret had barely time to think herself back into the present when a voice exclaimed, 'Margaret, what in Heaven's name are you doing up at this hour of the night?'

'William! I never expected –'

His face was pale, dark shadows under his eyes and his whole body was slumped with fatigue. 'We should have come in on the afternoon tide but the wind has been slack since Fowey. My God, but I'm tired!'

'Can I get you anything to eat or drink?'

He shook his head. 'And how is the boy?'

'Thriving.'

'That's good.' The ghost of a smile crossed his face. 'Just now I'm fit for nothing but sleep. I'll see him in the morning.'

'Your bed – oh William! Oh my heavens!' But he had already turned towards the stairs and did not notice her sudden panic. She tried to reach the stairs before him but was too late. 'William, wait, your bed is not aired, only let me see to it a moment before you –'

'No matter, Margaret, tonight I'm so tired I could sleep on bare boards.'

'But the sheets may be damp and I was not expecting you so soon and if I had known you were coming tonight I could have made sure that – oh William, are you sure you don't wish for a glass of wine?'

'Stop fussing, woman,' and he continued before her, muttering to himself as he went, 'I'll leave the bags till morning. Some fine cloth I've brought back – lace and silk and damask – all the gentry will buy from me now –'

'William, wait, please. There's something I must –'

He turned and patted her shoulder kindly. 'Don't worry me with trifles now. If you and Mistress Hocken have made errors in the shop then I daresay they're not as serious as you fear. It can all be dealt with in the morning. And I'll show you the fine cloth we are to sell. And there's a piece for you – a blue-grey wool that is just the colour of your eyes.'

'But William, stop, please –' They were on the landing now.

'Cease pestering me. Can't you see how tired I am?'

He pushed open the door of his bedroom and flung his bag on the bed – and stared in amazement as the bedclothes themselves seemed to move and to gather themselves up into an untidy mound.

'My God, whatever –!' He rubbed his eyes.

Merry's grumbles came from under the covers. 'Leave me alone, can't you?'

Margaret seized her chance. 'That's what I've been trying to tell you, William. The baby has been so wakeful that sometimes Merry has made use of your bed. If you just go downstairs and have a cup of ale we can have it all straight in no time at all . . .'

'Merry! In my bed! How dare you! Get out of here at once!' And he punched the heap of bedclothes before heaving them to the floor.

Ned Roberts sat up cursing. William leapt back as though the bed itself had suddenly sprung to life at his touch. For a few moments he was quite unable to speak, only stared open-mouthed.

Merry blinked up at him from behind Ned's naked shoulder and ran her hand through her tousled hair. 'William,' she said serenely, 'it's good to see you safe home again. How was your journey?'

William gurgled. Then, 'How – dare – you!' He leapt forward as though intending to drag Merry out by her hair but Ned scrambled from the bed and intervened to defend her. Then, suddenly recollecting his nakedness he clutched a pillow over his loins and warned, 'No need to upset yourself, Mr Hollar. We weren't expecting you so soon, that's all.'

'You scoundrel, how dare you talk to me like that in my own home! How dare you! I'll teach you both to make a fool of me, I'll –'

William, half-delirious in his fury, waved his arm at Ned who raised the pillow to protect his face, then, lowering it once again to protect his modesty, caught the blow on the side of his face. His black eyes sparkled with anger, he dropped the pillow altogether and lunged towards William.

Merry shrieked, 'Ned, no!' and, still clutching the bed-clothes to her breast, she sprang up to restrain him, only to catch her foot and fall between the two men in a tangle of sheets and counterpane.

Margaret had watched the whole scene with mounting horror but suddenly, at the sight of Merry upturned on the floor, her white buttocks shining like twin moons in the candlelight and William and Ned both staring down at her with a kind of appalled fascination, she could restrain herself no longer. A great bubble of laughter rose up inside that even William's anger could not smother.

'You – are laughing!' William hissed.

'Oh William – I did not mean –' Tears of laughter were streaming down her face and she could not finish her sentence. She could hear Merry choking on her giggles as she struggled to scramble into her shift.

'You turn this place into a bawdy house the moment my back is turned – and then you have the audacity to laugh about it!'

'No, William, only –'

But he had whipped around and caught her a stinging blow across her cheek with the back of his hand. 'Whores, all of you!'

'Don't go blaming Mattie,' Merry was pulling on her dress, 'we're the ones you should be angry at, not her.'

'Out, get out of my house!' William was shaking with fury.

'Don't shout so, William,' Merry was still making an effort to sound conciliatory, 'you'll only wake the neighbours and then –'

'Do you think they don't know already?' William picked up Ned's breeches and thrust them at his stomach. 'You bring shame on this house and shame on all your family! You'll do penance for this, you should be publicly whipped, you should –'

In all the pandemonium Luke awoke in the back bedroom and began to cry. Even Mistress Hocken emerged from her bedroom. She was convinced that the house had been invaded by Barbary pirates who were attempting to carry off prisoners. 'I'm a poor widow!' she wailed. 'Don't take my child, she's all I have left in the world!'

By the time Margaret had soothed both her and the baby and settled them back to sleep, Merry and Ned had vanished into the night. And the door of William's room was firmly closed against her.

When she herself finally drifted into sleep, her cheeks were wet with tears. But whether they were caused by anger at Merry's carelessness or chagrin at William's stinging blow, or whether they were still tears of laughter at the whole ludicrous scene in his room, she would have been quite unable to say.

Neither Merry nor Ned did penance, nor were they whipped. But they were married within the month, William saw to that.

Ned capitulated with a kind of grudging bravado. Valuing his freedom, he was opposed to marriage on principle – but since it was bound to catch up with him sooner or later, then he supposed it might as well be Merry: he liked her better than any other girl he knew, liked her in a different sort of way – and besides, her father had settled a small sum of money on her to be realised when she married.

Merry herself was subdued. Not that she loved him any less than before, but perhaps she had hoped to be cured of loving him in time, so that she would have been free to choose a husband who might offer her a better future. She might have spoken of her fears to Margaret, except that she was proud and Margaret, in the month after William's return, had worries enough of her own.

William's rage that night was not dispersed by the morning. He told her that he held her responsible, that she had shown herself to be weak and easily led: at one time he might have expected better things of her but now he had been bitterly disappointed, that she had betrayed his trust and that he would never be able to have faith in her again. At first Margaret tried to defend herself: how could she be expected to tell Merry what to do in her own home? But eventually, in the face of William's implacable anger and knowing that every husband and father in Porthew would have shared his view, she found herself reduced to tears and asking him to forgive them both. He had dismissed her coldly.

From then on his wrath had settled into an implacable rejection. Merry had been dispatched to her aunt's house in Coverack until her wedding and Margaret, alone in the house with William and Mistress Hocken, was lonely and bewildered. She was annoyed with William for his lack of compassion or humour, but after a few days she found his unyielding silence unbearable. She was too generous and warm-hearted by nature to remember an injustice against herself for more than a day or two – and she would have forgotten any number of cruel words if only to live in harmony with those around her.

William, it soon became clear, was made of sterner stuff. All her attempts at reconciliation were repulsed. He was never again angry – though Margaret often thought anger might have been preferable to this endless contempt. Her hunger for warmth and affection was so strong that she could not believe him happy in his silent enmity. She wavered between anger, despair – and a determination somehow to make him change.

Her desperation led her to consider her appearance for the first time in her life. She had always known she was attractive, but had never attached any particular significance to this. Now she found that whenever William looked at her she was filled with shame, without knowing the reason why; in her misery she began to consider the way other men looked at her. Could it be that William's rejection was somehow her fault? Was there something wrong with her that he had detected?

Others did not seem to share his distaste. They looked at her with approval. She resolved that one day soon William must learn to see her as other men did.

As the date of Merry's wedding approached, Margaret began to fuss over the details of the dress that was being made from the length of blue-grey wool that William had brought for her. Still as publicly generous as ever, he had insisted that it be cut and stitched by the best seamstress in Porthew. Margaret fretted over every particular, as if somehow the dress held the power to dissolve the enmity that lay between her and her husband.

By the afternoon of Merry's wedding, as she slipped on a dress so elegant that surely even Alice Sutton would have been proud to put it on (or Mistress Treveryan – Margaret had never forgotten that tiny lady so garlanded with embroidery and lace), even Margaret's high hopes were satisfied. She knew now with the certainty that her new self-consciousness had taught her, that the effect would be stunning. She stood very tall and straight; although her breasts were still swollen with milk, she had otherwise regained her former figure. She brushed her hair until it shone like the sun, damped her neck and hands with flower-water. She even allowed Mistress Hocken to take charge of Luke and to carry him ahead of her to the church.

'Do I not look fine?' she asked Mouse as she waited in the kitchen for William to join her. Mouse purred a reply that seemed to be affirmative. Absentmindedly she picked up a book of poems the parson had lent her earlier in the week and began to read.

When William came down the stairs into the kitchen she was standing in a pool of sunlight that streamed through the open window. Without having to look at him she knew that he was appraising her with that same expression, reserving judgement, that he had when examining a length of cloth. What she no longer knew, in that slow moment of his contemplation, was whether she now liked or hated him. Only that she would not let him ignore her any more.

After a long silence he stepped forward and took her hand in his, raising it to his lips. 'I have the handsomest wife in Cornwall,' he said, brushing a kiss across the tips of her fingers. His hand was icy cold, and trembling slightly.

He was wearing a doublet of cream-coloured velvet, his face was still bronzed from his travels that summer and his whole body was glowing with health and vitality. Margaret offered him the smile that she had learned most men found irresistible, then flinched as his grip on her hand tightened, crushing her fingers.

'Only do not force me to hate you,' he murmured.

And then, before she had a chance to respond to his words, his face was wreathed in public smiles as he led her through the shop and out into the street and the soft October sunshine.

Merry's wedding was a good deal less decorous than Margaret and William's had been. The Roberts' were a large and improvident tribe; the food was neither plentiful nor good but there was all the ale that anyone could drink – and no gentry arrived to introduce unnatural restraint. The atmosphere in Jack Pym's ale-house quickly became hot and stuffy and the descent into drunkenness was swift.

The effect of Margaret's dress was impressive; she could tell as clearly from the peeved expressions of the other women as by the reactions of the men. Merry was only half-joking when she chided, 'Really, Mattie, must you eclipse me on my wedding day?'

William for once was watching her every move. As they entered the ale-house he had whispered in her ear, 'Take care, Margaret, that you do not provoke me too far.'

Briefly, Margaret faltered. She was half-sick with apprehension but still resolved to play her part to the full. When the dancing began Ned caught her round the waist and tried to tease from her a wedding kiss, and Margaret, laughing as if she was without a care in the world, could see how Merry's eyes followed them across the room. Later it was Parson Weaver who held her in his arms and slurred out the words, which she both welcomed and despised, that he had never cared for anyone but her. And later still it was Ambrose who fended off her many admirers and ploughed around the room holding her to his massive chest while he bellowed his verdict, 'Always said you were the best, Mattie!' and Lizzie pouted and tugged at her curls with annoyance.

And through all her desperate gaiety, Margaret was conscious of William's eyes watching her and she thought, surely now he must recognise that he has a wife he should admire.

Certainly he was changing. He seemed as determined as any man in the Roberts clan to drink all he could. Despising the rough ale provided by the host, he had installed his own exclusive supply of French wine. Soon his cheeks blazed a fiery red, his eyes sparkled, his lips were slack and moist.

As the wedding guests jostled for Margaret's attention he pretended to be talking to Miller Dawkins, but she knew he was aware of her every move. His gestures became more extravagant, his voice shriller, his laughter ever more strident.

Suddenly Margaret's heart began to race. William had stood up, he was crossing the room towards her. Thrusting Matthew Erisey aside, he caught her by the wrist.

'Come, Margaret,' he insisted as he pulled her on to the dance floor, 'our dance is long overdue.'

Merry had enjoyed enough ale and good company to forget her own worries, but she felt a sudden tinge of anxiety for her friend when she saw her step on to the dance floor with William. He moved through the crowd of people with the same precision and elegance that he brought to any task; fair and sleek, he was like a streak of precious metal through the dross – and Margaret was a worthy partner. Merry had been piqued earlier when Margaret had seized the centre of attention, but her irritation had passed quickly, and now was all forgotten.

She loved Margaret. She loved her because she was clever and kind and generous and different from anyone else she had known. They had always been friends, but when Margaret's pregnancy became common knowledge she loved her all the more for her mistakes and her muddle and her strange, proud secrecy. And she took pleasure from watching her, as now, because she was beautiful.

Merry knew that as long as she had remained in the house, William had never been a husband to his wife. Margaret had always refused to talk about it. But Merry knew too that many of the most sturdy marriages were those with slow beginnings, and since she had left for her aunt's house in Coverack, Margaret had hinted that this situation had changed, though Merry thought it was probably pride talking, not honesty.

Watching them now as they danced together, Merry tried in vain to solve the enigma of their strange marriage. She had never seen a couple so totally absorbed in each other as they were now, almost as if they were alone in the room, or as if all the other dancers and the musicians had become suddenly invisible. Both were flushed and taut like two people waiting for something that was about to happen. The dance had taken on the appearance of a duel.

As the candles were lit around the walls, Merry searched Margaret's face in an effort to read her thoughts. She was laughing, her eyes were bright with a recklessness that seemed to Merry to be a kind of despair. And then, in a brief flare of candlelight, Merry read the look in William's eyes and she was seized with dread. Her one certainty about her cousin had always been that he was a kindly man; he had always shown compassion (except towards her and Ned – but that would have been unreasonable to expect) and gentleness. She had never before seen him intoxicated. She had never before seen him cruel.

Now she saw with horror that cruelty was spreading like a poison across his face. Had Margaret seen this too?

Merry searched around for a reason to stop the dance but Luke, for once, was content with Mistress Hocken. She stood up – and immediately Ambrose approached and invited her to join the dance.

They had not taken more than a few steps when there was a brief pause in the music. Merry, glancing across at Margaret and William, saw that Ned had swaggered over to separate them and an argument was brewing.

'This is *my* wedding,' Ned asserted, rocking slightly on his feet, 'come and dance with me now, Mattie.'

Margaret blinked, as though surprised to see anyone else standing with them – but William had snaked his arm around her shoulders and pulled her close to his side.

'How dare you insult my wife.'

'Don't be daft, Mr Hollar . . . only asking for a dance.'

William's voice was raised theatrically high. 'She only dances with me.'

But Ned, growing annoyed, refused to be put off.

'Just one dance,' he persisted.

William jabbed his fist in the direction of Ned's shoulder. It was a gesture, rather than a blow, but in Ned's uneven state it was enough to send him crashing down in the midst of a group of old women who had been watching the scene with interest. William peered down at his victim and whinnied derisively.

'See how I vanquish all rivals!' Then he turned to Margaret and demanded, 'Does this satisfy you?'

The old woman into whose lap Ned had so unexpectedly plunged shook him off and crowed with laughter. He struggled to his feet. He seemed to be debating whether it was worth resuming the fight and, since he had been annoyed by William's high-handed manner over the past few weeks, he was just deciding that it probably was, when Merry came and said in a low voice, 'Leave them, Ned. This is nothing to do with you – only look at them.'

He looked and saw, without understanding, that what Merry said was true. William was gazing at his wife and hissing, 'Does this satisfy your trollop's pride?'

Margaret recoiled slightly, but he only gripped her arm more tightly and said, 'You'll surely not shrink from me now?'

The music had begun again but no one seemed inclined to dance. Margaret was watching William with wide eyes, like someone still sleeping or in a trance.

Merry felt a sudden urgency to wake her up. 'Mattie –'

But William interrupted. 'Come, wife, I shall take you home.'

Merry said, 'Mattie, you can stay with us if you wish. William will be himself again in the morning.'

'And what would she do with you on your wedding night? You have always been a slattern, Meredith, but your influence over my wife is ended.'

Merry gasped. 'Don't dare to say such things.'

'William – please!' Margaret was appalled.

'William, please, oh William, please,' he mimicked, and then, suddenly vicious, 'but isn't this what you've been trying for all this time? All your preening and prancing and ogling and acting like a common drab?'

'Oh!'

'How can you talk to Mattie like that? How dare you!' Merry tried to pull her free but Margaret, seeming suddenly to awaken from the misery into which she had plunged, said, 'No, Merry, we must finish this between us.'

'Well spoken, wife,' he sneered, 'my *lady* wife, the most respectable Master William Hollar and his much esteemed wife. Shall we leave this rabble, dear wife?'

Avoiding Merry's protests, Margaret nodded her agreement. A more serious fight had broken out at the other end of the ale-house between Bob Dawkins and his brother and several of the younger members of the Roberts clan. Merry was briefly distracted by the pandemonium – and when she looked again, Margaret and William had vanished into the still October night.

The moon was up and approaching the full and they could see their way quite clearly as they crossed the town. As if fearing that she might try to escape, William kept a tight hold of her wrist as they hurried along the cobbled street but his precaution was unnecessary. Margaret sensed that their long charade was over; she was both curious and afraid.

William pushed open the door that led into the shop, but no sooner had Margaret followed him into the darkened room than he turned suddenly and, catching hold of her shoulders, rammed her back against the wall.

She struggled to be free of him but, 'Wait,' he insisted and, forcing the full weight of his body against her, he pressed cold lips against her mouth. A slime of revulsion coiled through her stomach as his teeth crushed hers in an action too vindictive ever to be called a kiss.

She tried to twist away but was amazed by the strength of his slim body that pressed her against the wall. Quite suddenly he released her, stood back. She could hear him fumbling to light a tallow. Usually all his actions were crisp and efficient, but tonight his hands were clumsy and the task took longer.

And then there was a pool of light. William held the tallow aloft and stared at her. 'You seem sad,' he spoke without pity, 'why's that? I thought this was what you had been craving all this time.'

Margaret could not tear her eyes from his face. In the dim light she felt as if she was seeing him for the first time: his eyes were more close set than she had realised before, his mouth and chin weak and ill defined. As the shadows flickered across his features she could suddenly see how his face would look when he was an old man. She shuddered.

He said, 'You are not grateful, that at least is clear.'

'Why?' The question that had tormented her for months now demanded to be answered. 'Why – ?'

He winced. Then, still holding the tallow level with his face he took two steps towards her. 'Why?' he echoed. 'Ah yes, the reason, there has to be a reason.' He considered for a while and then said in a low and steady voice, 'Because I find you are already corrupted, Margaret, and so, regrettably, you are repellent. There, that is your reason.'

'But you knew, you always knew! And you said it made no difference.'

He shrugged. 'Then I was wrong, that's all.'

She turned away in despair, but suddenly he caught hold of her full woollen skirt and twisted a handful of the fabric between pale fingers.

'William, stop!'

He had lowered the candle until it was only inches from the bunched-up cloth. 'You are disappointed; you wanted a fine hot lover like the father of your bastard and instead you have only . . . don't try to deny it, I can see it in your eyes. Damn your eyes, woman, they follow me all the time. But I will not let you mock me, I will not suffer your scorn. I will not be made a laughing stock by your bawdy tricks, do you understand me, Margaret?'

'Stop it, William, have you gone mad?' For indeed there was a madness in his eyes as he waved the tallow ever closer to her skirt. At the sound of his braying laugh, fear shivered between her shoulder blades.

'I too have suffered disappointments; had you considered that? I thought you might be different from others of your sex but now I find you share all their frailties. Can you imagine my despair? But perhaps there is a remedy after all.' That shrill laugh once more. 'There are many people, many wise people, so I'm told, who believe that man's sins can be wiped clean by fire, did you know that? Even the most unrepentant heretic will ascend to heavenly bliss when his mortal carcass, our loathsome prison of flesh and bone, has been purified by burning.'

'No!'

'Oh yes, Margaret, yes. In Spain I saw a good Protestant housewife burned at the stake, did I ever tell you that before? It was an unforgettable sight, shall I describe it to you? She had put on a dress of grey taffeta perhaps because she believed that it would burn more quickly but, poor woman, she was horribly mistaken. In fact –'

'Stop it!'

'Her screams seemed to last for ever and the smell –' But at that moment, perhaps because his hand was shaking so much, the tallow scorched the bunched-up cloth of her skirt that he held in his hand and Margaret sprang backwards. There was a tearing sound. William dropped the candle and pounced on her as the room was plunged into darkness. Margaret twisted and struggled and had almost managed to free herself when he hooked his foot around her ankle and hurled himself against her as she lost her balance and fell to the floor, his weight on hers, pressing the breath from her lungs.

He spread his hands over her face and his nails dug into her skin. One of her hands was imprisoned behind her back but with her free hand she struggled to pull his wrist away; he only clung the tighter, almost as though his aim was to wrench her face away. She could not speak or breathe or see.

'I *told* you not to provoke me, I *warned* you, God knows I gave you fair warning. Why didn't you listen to me? This is your fault, this is all your doing, you stupid stupid girl. Why must you force me to hate you and to hurt you? Why? Oh God, it's the wine I drank and this wretched town and I loathe them all and despise them too and my God but I wish I was free of you all, my God how I wish –' His voice cracked and broke. His fingers released her face. He raised himself slightly and Margaret gulped in a shuddering breath.

From the kitchen came the sounds of Mistress Hocken returning, and Luke crying for his food. The sounds might have emanated from another world.

'Don't weep, damn you,' for Margaret's body was shaking with sobs, 'this is your fault, can't you see that? Oh God, I might have killed you and I never meant to hurt . . .' He sat up slowly. Margaret curled herself away from him. 'Wait,' he said, and then, as she stayed motionless in the darkened shop, she heard his body slump against some bolts of cloth, 'no, don't stay. Get out of here and leave me be. For God's sake, woman, just leave me be.'

She stood up slowly, but as she reached the door there was a sudden movement and she found her way barred.

'You will never talk of this to anyone. Never, or –'

But no threats were necessary. Margaret went through the door that led into the kitchen and her whole body ached with shame.

'Why, Margaret,' said Mistress Hocken, 'there is blood on your face.'

'I fell,' said Margaret, not troubling to search for a better lie as she took the howling child into her arms.

A little later, when she opened her bodice and cradled Luke's head against her bruised and swollen breast, she was surprised only that her son did not also turn from her in disgust.

During the next few days it seemed to Margaret that she had barely the energy to tend to Luke and to perform her household tasks. Merry was gone to her new home with Ned Roberts and the house was quiet and lonely. William avoided her, and she was happy to give him a wide berth. She neglected her appearance, was reluctant to leave the house or to talk with anyone. The hems of her skirts were often caked with mud as she no longer bothered to lift them free.

On the fourth day, William scolded her. 'I did not marry the finest looking woman in Porthew just to watch her turn into a common drudge.'

'Isn't that what you consider me to be?' she answered bitterly.

William, in silence, retreated to the shop.

Gradually Margaret's resilience reasserted itself. Although for some time her courage and optimism were utterly crushed, she could not remain in that state for long. She began to attend to the chatter of the other women, to enjoy caring for her son and to notice that the ever-changing sea was as beautiful and mysterious as ever.

But her old spontaneity had gone. She was grown reserved, mistrustful. She was learning to watch William and his moods, to know when to avoid him and when he was most likely to agree to her requests. She was learning to be devious.

On a windy day at the beginning of November William returned from Helston late one afternoon and, instead of going at once into the shop as was his habit, he came into the kitchen where Margaret was tending a song thrush which had been brought to her a few days earlier with an injured wing.

'I have something for you,' he said after a few moments.

It was a small hand mirror. He gave it to her saying, 'You must never forget that you are beautiful, Margaret.'

She raised her eyes to his face but he turned away at once and his expression was cold.

'Thank you.' She set it down. Then carefully lifted the speckled bird from its basket.

'Is he making progress?' asked William.

'He's fit and well as ever he was.' The bird was showing his gratitude by pecking her hand. 'I was going to release him.'

'Best to do it now, then, without delay. Before the captivity destroys him.'

She rose and walked towards the back door and William opened it for her as both her hands were folded around the bird. She could feel its feathered heartbeat against her palm.

It had rained during the day but now the dark clouds were breaking up and yellow shafts of light were piercing through in the west. In the apple tree at the end of the garden a blackbird was pouring out his evening song.

Margaret raised up her hands and spread them wide. For a little while the bird sat crouched on her palm as he looked about him. Then he ruffled his feathers, stretched out his wings and flew off into the twilight shadows.

They stood together in silence and stared at the place where he had been.

William said, 'It is better to be free.'

Margaret was frowning. 'Amen to that.'

She turned then, to try and read the expression on his face, but already he was walking back towards the house and his own impenetrable reserve.

311

13

By the time Ambrose and Lizzie were married in the autumn of 1633 Margaret, now nineteen, had become an expert in the dubious art of hiding her true feelings. When William once again offered her his arm to lead her from church to ale-house, she walked beside him as proudly as the happily married woman the world thought her to be. She laughed with Ambrose and told him she was delighted that he was marrying Lizzie. She joked with the parson and told him that she loved a wedding above everything. She laughed at every crude joke that revolved around Ambrose's great size and the smallness of his bride.

For Ambrose, in the years since his victory over Robert Trelyn on St Ewan's Day, had grown to physical maturity. Long hours working in the smithy had developed his puppy fat into hard muscle; he now moved with the slow grace of a man who knows his own strength and sees no need to squander it on trifles.

Beside Ambrose, who even in his wedding finery looked for all the world like a last survivor of those giants who had lived in Cornwall before the coming of mankind, Lizzie appeared dainty as an elfin queen. She was wearing a new dress of leaf-green frieze. William had given them the material and Margaret, who was a dismal seamstress, had laboured long and painfully over it until William, exasperated by her slow progress, had insisted that Dame Erisey be paid to finish it, thus sparing Lizzie the ignominy of appearing at her wedding still bristling with as many pins as a hedgehog. Thanks to Dame Erisey the finished product was more than passable – and Lizzie at any rate was delighted.

That day everything delighted her: the new dress, her own prettiness, Ambrose's reputation, the music and the crowd and the fuss. She even appeared to relish the more than predictable wedding-day jokes which provided an unusual gloss on the idea of a camel's ability to pass through the eye of a needle.

When the first of the food had been consumed the guests began to drift on to the patch of rough ground in front of the ale-house to watch the beginning of the hurling match. As was traditional at weddings, the guests had offered to take on all comers and a small group of hopeful players had already arrived and was standing around drinking ale and boasting of past successes.

Hurling to the country, the variation that was practised in the west of Cornwall, was a sport demanding almost as much energy from spectators as players. The goals were set at least three or four miles apart and the players were mostly uninhibited by rules as they endeavoured to carry the silver ball to victory. Often the sport came to resemble a full-scale military campaign as troops were deployed at all strategic points to intercept and ambush their opponents. Sleight of hand and a minute knowledge of the terrain were as important as speed and strength. Injuries were taken for granted.

The day was overcast, but mild for late October with a damp wind blowing from the south-west; soon the men and boys who intended to take part had stripped down to their breeches and shirts. William, standing as usual a little to one side, watched with faint interest. As soon as politeness permitted, he would retire to his solitary haven in the shop. Little Luke, now a wan and busy two-year-old with his mother's pale hair and an expression that was all his own, was eager to participate.

'Me too, me too,' he insisted, stumbling over to join the men.

'Not yet,' Margaret caught hold of his skirts and restrained him; 'when you are older.'

Tom, who had been allowed to join the wedding team as a rare treat since this was his sister's wedding, watched with the lofty scorn of a nine-year-old as Luke began to yell his protest.

Lizzie, hearing the din, skipped over, taking care to lift her green skirts out of the mud, and scolded him with mock ferocity. 'Shame on you, little Luke, how dare you be such a sour-face on my wedding day. Enjoy yourself, you little rogue, or your Aunt Treloar won't love you any more. And here's another marchpane to make you see sense and don't you dare tell anyone I gave it you. That's better.'

For Luke had gulped down his complaining and was regarding his pretty aunt with awe. Margaret was always surprised that Lizzie, who had not the least patience with small children, could invariably bend them to her will.

The two sisters hauled Luke to sit between them on a bench that stood against the ale-house wall. 'Look, Luke,' said his mother, 'we can watch well enough from here. The game is about to start.'

For indeed the milling crowd of men and youths was beginning to separate into two teams of roughly equal size.

'Me too,' Luke repeated mechanically, but his mouth was so stuffed with sweetmeats that his complaint was little more than a routine motion of his jaws.

'Have you spoken to Merry today?' Lizzie asked.

'Not yet,' said Margaret, 'I tried to earlier but she's been with Ned all the time.'

'She clings to him worse than a limpet. It's pathetic. Ambrose says she even tried to persuade him not to take part in the hurling. She'll drive him away quicker than ever if she carries on like that.'

'What do you mean?'

Lizzie looked at her scornfully. 'Everyone knows,' she said.

Margaret searched the crowd but saw no sign of Merry. Ned was plainly visible as he discussed tactics with the wedding team; he was quick and clever and a valued player in any match.

'She's so pale recently. And today she doesn't look well at all.'

'No one could ever have described her as pretty.' Lizzie patted her shining brown curls and added, 'I often wonder what Ned saw in –'

She broke off. They both caught sight of Merry in the same instant. Everyone did.

There was a shriek from the edge of the crowd; mocking laughter and voices raised in anger.

'You –! You –!' Annie Dawkins, the mill-owner's black-haired daughter, was gasping and spluttering her rage.

Merry stood four square in front of her and the empty tankard in her hand, together with Annie's dripping clothes and hair, told the whole story.

'You're lucky I don't drown you!' Merry blazed.

Annie flew at her, and the next moment they were fighting and scratching and tearing at each other's hair like a couple of wild cats and would have knocked each other down if Ned had not raced over to pull his wife clear while Ambrose pinned Annie Dawkins (who was a cousin on his father's side) to him with a single powerful arm.

Ned shook Merry furiously. 'What's got into you, woman!'

'You should know!'

'Have you no shame?'

'Oh –! For you to talk of –!'

'I'll teach you not to make a fool of me!'

Margaret reached them just in time to seize hold of his arm and prevent the blow. 'Ned, don't!'

'Keep out of this, Mattie, damn you. It's time she learned a lesson.'

'No, Ned, not . . . oh my heavens, look, both of you, look!'

Margaret had never expected to welcome the sudden arrival of Nicolas Sutton. Splendidly dressed in a new buff coat and feathered hat, he cantered on to the scene on a tall grey mare accompanied by two manservants. At once all attention switched to the newcomers.

'I heard there was to be a hurling match,' he grinned down at them cheerfully; 'if I'm not too late then here's three more for the outside team. Where are the goals to be set?'

'You are welcome to join us, sir,' growled Ambrose, still clutching the dripping Annie to his chest. Although he had little liking for the gentry in general and Nicolas Sutton in particular, it would have been unthinkable to turn down the young man who was after all his landlord's son. 'As you know, we always take on all comers.'

'Excellent.' Nicolas swung down from his horse and handed the reins to the nearest available person (John Pearce as it happened, who was somewhat bemused by his sudden transformation from step-father of the bride to

315

ostler). 'Then I accept your challenge. I and my two men here. Where are the goals to be set?'

'You're to reach Peg Truscott's – if you're able.'

'Simplicity itself. And tell me, Treloar, do you intend to run with this bedraggled young lady under your arm?'

Everyone laughed. Everyone, that is, except those most closely involved. Ambrose pushed Annie away and Ned released his wife with a warning. Margaret seized the chance to hurry Merry back into the ale-house and as the players began to prepare in earnest for the match, the incident was all but forgotten.

Merry poured herself a mug of ale and slumped down disconsolately on a settle by the fire. After a while she glanced up at Margaret and commented ruefully, 'I did make a fool of myself just now, didn't I?'

Margaret, not knowing how to answer, put another log on the fire and watched the sparks whirl up into the chimney.

'I should have killed her. Oh – I don't know. Nothing seems to make any difference.'

'Can I get you anything?'

'No.' Merry kicked the toe of her shoe against the floor. 'I wish it had been boiling water, not ale.'

'Oh Merry –'

'I'm pregnant again.'

Margaret was silent. Then, 'That's good.'

'Is it? I don't know any more.'

'I thought that was what you wanted.' Merry had miscarried twice since her marriage, each time at about two to three months.

'I suppose so.' Her voice was listless.

'Merry, tell me –' But Margaret was unable to complete her question. The hurling match had begun with a shout from all the onlookers and since the players had immediately scattered through the town, those of the guests who were too old, too young, too lazy or simply too well fed to follow the game, began to drift in ones and twos back into Jack Pym's. In a corner of the room the fiddler started to play a thoughtful tune.

Lizzie came in laughing and deposited an equally contented Luke into his mother's lap. 'Oh Mattie,' she began, ignoring Merry altogether, 'you'll never guess what happened while they were waiting to begin the game. Nicolas Sutton walked over to where I was sitting on purpose to talk with me, I'm sure. "You must be the bride," he said and I asked him how he could tell and he answered . . . well, all nonsense of course. Oh and you should have heard his compliments about my dress –' she paused briefly to flounce her full green skirts, 'and when I told him that you had sewn it for me he said it was as fine as any worn by the ladies at the King's court in London.'

'Heavens, Lizzie, how can you believe such idleness?'

'Why shouldn't I? He sounded most sincere.'

Margaret surveyed Lizzie's simple gown of leaf-green wool that had caused her such trouble already in the making of it – and then she remembered the concoction of embroidery and lace that Mistress Treveryan had been wearing when she appeared so unexpectedly at her own wedding and she thought of the rich fabrics that Alice Sutton had purchased from William for her elegant attire and she said ruefully, 'It's nothing but flattery, Lizzie. You know what Nicolas Sutton is like; besides, I don't suppose he's been anywhere near the King's court so how should he know?'

'Of course he has, he's a gentleman, isn't he?'

'You're a married woman now,' Merry interjected bitterly, 'you must accept compliments from none but Ambrose and be a good little wife. Of course *he* may do just as he pleases but there is nothing, absolutely nothing at all, that you can do to stop him –'

'I don't see that you have much to teach me about the duties of a wife, Merry Roberts. You've made a fine spectacle of yourself today.'

'Lizzie, that's not fair.'

'Why should I be fair if she makes trouble at my wedding?' And, without waiting for an answer, Lizzie whisked away to talk with some late arrivals to the celebrations.

Luke, huddled in his mother's arms, was growing drowsy. After a while Margaret suggested, 'Shall we walk down to Ia's Bridge, Merry? Like we used to? Mistress Hocken can mind Luke for me and we might catch sight of the hurling match if we're lucky.'

317

'That's the best idea I've heard in days,' said Merry, rising to her feet at once.

By the time they were half-way to Ia's Bridge their sombre mood had begun to lift and long before they arrived Merry was laughing at herself for her hot-tempered actions.

'What a waste of good ale! Next time it'll be slops, I promise you – though God knows Ned is hardly worth the effort!'

'No husband is!' Margaret agreed warmly.

Merry slid her a curious glance. 'Do I hear Mistress Hollar being disloyal to her husband for once?'

'Oh well –'

From the woods at the head of the valley came the occasional sound of men's voices raised to halloo the progress of the chase. A little earlier Matthew Erisey had raced past them, half a dozen opponents following close behind. But he had winked at the girls as he passed and they guessed that he was leading the men on a false trail and that the ball was somewhere else entirely.

Merry waited to see if Margaret was about to elaborate on their theme but when she remained thoughtfully silent, Merry continued, 'I'm sure William cannot be half so bad as Ned. When Ned is away on the boats I miss him and know he is up to no good, and when he is home again we argue so that I wish him away again. It is hopeless.'

Margaret considered the chasm of silence that lay between her and William and said, 'We never argue. It might be better if we did.'

'How can that be?' But even as she spoke Merry thought of their brief moments of reconciliation, the countless times that Ned had told her the other women were nothing to him and she had believed him and loved him as fiercely as ever and she grinned and said, 'It's a great puzzle, isn't it?'

'The biggest.'

'Perhaps when we are both toothless old crones we'll begin to understand.'

'Maybe you and Ned will get along better when your child is born.'

'It could hardly be much worse. Is William fretting for another child? Luke will be three next year.'

'Oh well . . . you know . . . of course, one hopes . . .'
Steering a course between the curious enquiries of her
neighbours as to when her next child might be expected
was an almost daily trial for Margaret. Merry had been
scrutinising her closely; now she patted her hand.

'It's all right, Mattie. Don't tell me anything unless you
want to. But if ever you decide to share your load, remember
I can be as discreet as . . . well, at least as discreet as the
parson.'

Something about the way she stressed the word 'parson'
made Margaret look up quickly, then, reading Merry's
intention only too clearly she looked away again as the tell-
tale colour spread across her face and neck.

'What do you mean?'

'You know perfectly well.'

Silence, then, 'How did you know?'

'It was in his eyes on the day Luke was born.'

'Oh Merry, if you only knew how much I've longed to
tell you!'

'So why didn't you?'

Margaret answered slowly, 'Everything has always been
such a muddle – *I've* made such a muddle of everything.
My promises have always seemed to be the only sure thing
I could hold on to. Besides, it's not so easy to tell –'

'Do you want to know what your problem really is,
Mattie? I'll tell you. You've spent your whole life protecting people who would never lift a finger to help you. Why
don't you learn from me? I love Ned, half-wit that I am,
but that doesn't mean I have to keep his secrets.'

Margaret did not answer straight away. There was a pain
at the base of her throat, a tightness of words and tears held
back.

She said, 'Oh Merry –' then stopped. A rustle of leaves,
a twig snapping in the copse behind them. 'Did you hear
something?'

'Just a bird.'

'Are you sure?'

'There's no one else about.'

Margaret drew in a deep breath. 'That's good, because –'
But at that moment Nicolas Sutton appeared around a
bend in the road, clutching something under his arm and

319

running towards Porthew. His two manservants were following at some distance, unable to keep pace with his long stride. Just as he was approaching the little bridge, Ambrose erupted from a thicket beside the stream and, with a roar of jubilation, leapt on to the parapet with such driving force that Nicolas was knocked clean into the water.

There was pandemonium. Nicolas appeared to be injured and yelled in pain. Ambrose, who had fallen on top of him, floundered for some seconds before he could regain his footing. The two manservants watched in horror. The ball, which Nicolas had indeed been carrying, had vanished into the water. By the time Nicolas had been dragged on to the bank of the stream and Ambrose, dripping water like a giant spaniel, had said for the hundredth time that he had meant no injury to the young gentleman, the roadway was swarming with players who had been alerted by the din. Tom raced on to the scene, his cheeks aglow, and Merry, who had recovered the ball when she waded into the stream to help Nicolas Sutton, passed it to the boy without anyone seeing, though he ran off with such speed and happiness that a couple of players followed him just in case.

By the time everyone had regathered at the ale-house, Ambrose was well pleased with his afternoon's work. To injure Nicolas Sutton while making it appear to all the world an accident seemed to him the height of cunning, and the violence had fuelled his courage like a tonic wine. Hard to imagine now that earlier that same day he had felt confused and awkward beside his dainty bride and filled with a bashful timidity at the prospect of the night that lay ahead. Now all his doubts were swept away.

So what if Lizzie shrieked with feminine horror at the sight of his torn clothes and muddy, sodden appearance? He only laughed and picked her up in his arms and hugged her to him; and when he set her down again her face was streaked with blood from the scratch across his cheek and her precious dress of fancy green wool that had inspired those vacuous compliments from young Sutton was crushed and grubby with earth and mire.

The winter that followed was long and harsh. A few warm days of spring were followed, at the end of March, by high winds and a driving, cruel rain. It was the time of year when old people and children were most vulnerable to sickness and the gravediggers were among the few men with extra money to spend at the ale-house.

Parson Weaver fell into a kind of lethargy: it seemed to him that the days of urging his horse knee-deep in mud to yet another scene of poverty and disease would never end. When he fell asleep at night he could still hear the rain drumming against his house and the sound of his own children coughing in their crowded beds. A little way up the coast a French ship was driven on the rocks and its crew drowned – but its cargo of bay salt and spices was all ruined and there was little besides gashed timbers to be gained from the wreck. The voracious sea emerged the only winner.

The days were long and tedious for Margaret. She and William had long since settled into a habit of avoidance; as a rule he was courteous, but the moment she allowed her guard to slip, he lashed out with sudden cruelties. Mistress Hocken seldom emerged from her private twilight world and was often confined to her bed with illness. Luke suffered constant minor ailments which kept him cooped up in the house and fretting to be allowed more freedom. Margaret, having no other outlet for her energies, heaped all her love and hopes on her son – but already he seemed to be striving to escape her too possessive grasp, preferring William's company in the shop, Mistress Hocken's and her friends or to visit Lizzie at the Forge; or best of all Tom at Conwinnion and all the activity of the farm.

From time to time Margaret made use of the hand mirror that William had given her. In the unthinking confidence that preceded her marriage she had hardly considered her appearance at all; now she searched the cloudy reflection to find what it might be that set her apart from other men's wives.

She comforted herself with the promise that in the spring, after Merry's baby was born, she would confide her worries in her friend. Several times during that winter she had been on the verge of continuing the conversation they had begun at Ia's Bridge, but each time something had made her hold back. Merry had been working at Robert Payne's fish cellars through much of the autumn and since then there had always been some obstacle that had come between them – but it did not much matter. The knowledge that Merry was there, that she had somehow guessed the outlines and needed only to be filled in on the details, was a rich solace.

'I never knew you were so vain,' said Lizzie when she visited one afternoon. Margaret laughed and put down the mirror at once.

Fond though she was of Lizzie, she would never have spoken to her of anything that touched her deeply. Besides, that rainy afternoon, Lizzie was too full of her own news to attend to anyone else.

'I'm to have a child in the autumn,' she announced with pride. 'Ambrose is so pleased he's been grinning like an idiot all day and his parents are making plans for us already. I do think that this summer we may move into the larger bedroom and they must have ours and if they will not give us their feather bed then we must have our own one made.'

Margaret hugged her sister and congratulated her and Lizzie continued to provide details of the continuing campaign between her and her mother-in-law for domestic dominance at the Forge. Margaret, knowing Lizzie's determination, did not rate Mistress Treloar's chances very highly.

Luke scrambled on to Lizzie's lap and enquired whether she had brought any treats for him.

'The best treat of all, you little rogue – a younger cousin to tyrannise and make a fuss of when the mood suits you,' and she hugged him.

'Luke follows Tom around like a shadow. If yours is as lovestruck with Luke then the three of them will be like three ducklings in a row.'

They burst out laughing and Luke was on the verge of indignation at being called a duckling when a voice could be heard approaching through the garden shouting, 'Mattie, Mattie, come quick!' and the next moment the door burst open and Ned Roberts, dripping with water from head to foot gasped, 'Mattie, oh thank God you're here.'

'What is it Ned? Come in, sit down –'

'No . . . must hurry . . .'

'Why? Is Merry –?'

'It's much too soon. She wants you . . . I'm on my way to fetch Dame Watkins.'

'I'll go at once. Don't worry, Ned, she's –'

But he was out of the door before she finished her sentence and he was away, splashing through the rain-soaked garden.

Lizzie smothered a momentary sense of pique that Merry had once again stolen the limelight and helped Margaret while she fetched a bag and packed linen and food. Yes, of course Luke was welcome to stay with her at the Forge until Merry's baby was born though as Merry had always been a strapping great girl and not delicately built like her, she was quite sure there would be no problems.

Pulling her heaviest cloak about her shoulders Margaret set off through the driving rain. Although Merry's home was less than a mile away, Margaret was soaked to the skin by the time she could make out the steeply thatched roof of the Roberts' cottage over a rise in the hill. Water was streaming from its roof and cascading in brown torrents down the uneven road.

Merry and Ned had lived since their marriage in two little rooms that had been added to the side of the house, but when Margaret pushed the door open she found them empty. Out into the rain again and she spotted the flicker of firelight in the main part of the house. The door opened before she had knocked and Mistress Roberts pulled her into the living room.

'She's upstairs in our bed. Their rooms are so damp . . . here, take off your wet things, warm yourself.'

'How is Merry?'

'She's doing well.' Ned's mother spoke in a tone that declared her determination to make it so. 'And mighty eager to see you. Come along –'

Margaret hardly needed to be guided to the room where Merry lay: the gasping cries were all she needed. At the foot of the stairs she paused and a shiver of dread ran down her spine. She told herself sternly that it was nothing but a trickle of rain on her neck, reminded herself of Merry's robust serenity when she herself had panicked in the bluebell woods. She climbed the stairs.

Upstairs the noise of the rain was thunderous on the thatch and the bedroom where Merry lay was small and dark with a low ceiling that sloped almost to the floor. The air was fusty with the smell of old apples, mice and dust.

When she saw Merry her fears fell away. The animal panting had ceased and the face on the pillows blossomed with smiles.

'Lord above, Mattie, look at the state of you. Did you walk here or swim? You're like something just emerged from the bottom of the sea.'

'It's obvious that there's nothing much wrong with you. I might just as well have stayed at home and saved myself the trouble.'

'Well, you'll be going home again soon enough so don't go fretting yourself about that. This infant clearly intends to join us as quickly as he can – two months early and impatient as a demon. Hold my hand, Mattie. My heavens, you've as much human comfort in your skin as an old fish. Oh – here it comes again . . .' and her voice merged with her rhythmic rasping breaths. When she was finished she pushed Margaret away, calling her a mermaid midwife and added, 'I don't see what all the fuss is about, truly I don't. Just a little pain and then . . . really there's nothing to it.'

'What did I tell you? Easy as shelling peas. You'll be over it all by nightfall.'

But Merry was not to be so lucky. All the rest of that day, and all through the night, Margaret sat beside her bed, holding her hand when the pains gripped, chatting, dozing, joking. Ned, who was doing his best to put a brave face on his anxiety, returned and said Dame Watkins was busy with Jennie Treloar and that she'd come as soon as she was free. Margaret reassured him and told him to rest for an hour or two.

Towards dawn Merry awoke from a few minutes' sleep and gripped Margaret's hand in a spasm of pain. Her face was drained of colour and there were dark shadows around her eyes. 'Why doesn't it stop?' she wailed when the pain had passed. 'It's gone on so long, I'm tired. When will it stop?'

'Hush now, don't fret. It won't take long.'

'Where is Dame Watkins? Why doesn't she come? Oh

Mattie, I'm so frightened. I don't want to die. Don't let me die, please, Mattie, please . . .'

'Stop it. Don't talk nonsense. No one's going to let you die.' Margaret held her hand tightly. 'You know it often takes a long time.'

Merry clung to her like a frightened child and Margaret stroked her hair and soothed her and did not allow herself to be afraid. 'Not much longer,' she murmured, 'it won't be long now.'

Merry was in labour for three days. Three days and three nights during which the storm passed and the sun came out and the birds perched in the bare trees and sang to welcome the spring. Dame Watkins came – Jennie Treloar's sixth child was a boy – and tied charms to the bed and dosed Merry with syrupy potions and massaged her swollen belly. There were others, Mistress Roberts, Merry's cousins, who came and went – but Margaret hardly dared to leave her side. To her those three long days and nights were an eternity, a time out of time, as though they and the stuffy room under the thatch had dropped into a limbo where time no longer existed and they moved uneasily through a dark sea of pain and fear and dread. She could not imagine that in nearby Porthew people were working and eating and following their daily rounds and all as if this slow drama was not being played out in the attic bedroom.

On the second day Merry raged. 'No! No! I can't stand it any longer, I won't have it! Cut the baby out, get rid of it, kill it, kill it! Before it kills me. Oh God!' But by nightfall she did not even have the energy for anger. Now she no longer tried to hide her fear and when the pains came she howled like a wounded beast until her voice gave out and she could only whimper, 'Oh Mattie, help me, do something, oh God, don't let me die . . .'

Ned was frantic. He could not stay and witness her suffering yet to be away from her was torture. He stood at the foot of the bed, his eyes blazing, glaring at her as if he could transfer his own strength into her body and bring her agony to an end. Then when she screamed he turned and fled the room. They heard his heavy boots clattering on the stairs, the front door bang shut. Through the tiny window just above the floor Margaret watched him as he strode down the road that led away from the house. Then, as quickly as he had left, he was back again, treading quietly, hoping to find them peaceful, the waiting over . . . and then his features collapsed into disappointment to see the torment unchanged.

The child was born, a girl, as the darkness of the third night of Margaret's vigil paled to a misty dawn. 'Thank God,' whispered Merry, as she slid into merciful sleep, 'thank God . . .'

When Dame Watkins handed Margaret the infant she could not see it for the tears of relief that poured down her face. Ned knelt down beside the bed and pressed Merry's hand to his cheek and sobbed like a boy. The child cried, a thin, reedy cry like some distant marsh bird and Dame Watkins frowned and said, 'Send for Parson, Ned. Quickly now.'

The girl was named Abigail because that was the first name that came into Ned's head. Parson Weaver came and christened her but he spoke so fast it was hard to make out the words.

Ned dried his tears. 'Look at her, Merry,' he said, 'I swear she has your nose.'

'Poor mite,' whispered Merry.

The parson left without a word.

The child died within an hour of the christening. Dame Watkins was grim as she wrapped the tiny corpse for burial and she muttered to herself, angry, gibberish-sounding words. Ned and Margaret watched her actions, their faces blank.

'How can I explain it to her, Mattie?' he asked woodenly. 'I can't figure it out, somehow. Merry only wanted a child . . .'

Margaret hugged her arms to her chest. 'She's come through, Ned,' she told him, 'at least Merry is safe.'

Dame Watkins went to the bed. The morning sun was streaming in through the windows and dust motes were dancing in the sunbeams. Dame Watkins seemed very tall, very gaunt as she stooped over the sleeping girl and the sunlight revealed all the weary lines of her face. It was only then that Margaret noticed the wheezing rhythm of Merry's breathing.

326

'At least Merry has come through,' she said again.

Dame Watkins did not answer. Her efforts over the past few days seemed to have turned her suddenly into an old old woman and then she turned on Margaret and Ned a look of such rage and such compassion that Margaret felt as though the floor had dropped away and she herself was floating and spinning through the emptiness.

The midwife turned away. 'She's worn out,' she said, 'there's nothing more I can do for her.'

Ned stared. 'She's a strong girl,' he said, 'she'll soon be up and doing again, you'll see.'

'You fools,' said Dame Watkins, 'can't you see she's slipping . . ?' and she went to her bag, pulled out a flask of something stronger than ale, and drank.

'No!' Margaret's shriek of denial burst across the room as she clasped Merry's hands, rubbing them between her own. They were cold, so very cold, and she must warm them.

'She's tired, I reckon, that's all.' Still Ned did not move.

Margaret was rubbing Merry's arms now. 'You can't give up now, Merry, not after all this. Don't leave me all alone!'

Merry's eyelids lifted slowly. Her eyes were dull but all the fear had left them and she gazed up serenely.

'That's right, Merry. Rest now and get strong again. Ned and I will take care of you. It's over now, no more pain . . . and soon we'll be able to go for walks together and talk. Oh Merry, there's so much that we can talk about!'

Merry stared back at her. Smiled. After watching the tranquil face for a while longer, Margaret turned to Dame Watkins in triumph. 'There, what did I tell you? She can sleep now and when she wakes –'

The old woman tried to drag her away with bony fingers. 'She's gone, Margaret. It's no use, her strength was all used up. Here, take a mouthful of this, it may help.'

'Ned, tell her Merry's sleeping.'

His face was empty of expression. 'Well then,' he said stonily, 'she's right, I suppose. I reckon it must be God's will and we just have to accept . . .'

'What?'

Looking down on the bed as if from a great height Margaret saw that they were right. Although she had been watching her closely all the while somehow Merry had slipped away from them, sloughing away her worn-out body as a snake casts off his skin. And now it was a tomb-cold stranger that stared up at her from the pillows.

Margaret turned to Ned. His jaw was working oddly as if he was trying to speak but no words would come. Margaret sank down beside the bed and stroked Merry's forehead. This cannot be, she thought.

'Merry,' she pleaded, 'don't go –'

'Get on home now, Margaret,' said Dame Watkins, 'I'll walk back with you. There's no more we can do here, neither one of us. Ned, you'd best tell your mother. I'll call in on Peg Harries on my way and tell her to come and lay out –'

Ned groaned aloud. He swayed, and Margaret rose to support him but he only glared at her and raised his arms, then brought his fists down with a fury against the door, splintering the wood, before he vanished down the stairs.

Margaret stood for a few moments, staring at the dark stairway. Then she said, 'You don't need to waste time worrying about me. I shall be all right.' And her words were as much for Merry as for anyone.

Mistress Roberts came into the room with a couple of female neighbours and the room was at once filled with their cries and lamentation. Margaret began to tidy the litter of three days and nights of sickness.

'Leave this,' said Dame Watkins.

They walked back to Porthew together. Raindrops glistened on every branch and twig and the road was chequered with puddles reflecting back the blue sky. Blackthorn bushes were starred with white flowers and primroses grew thickly beside their path; lambs were bleating for their mothers and all the world seemed busy with spring. As they passed the church, the old woman glanced up at the tower and her mouth twisted in a vinegar grimace. 'Lies,' she said, 'it's nothing but lies. He's a cruel God, no matter what they tell you. Sometimes I hate Him and I don't care who hears me. Cruel, cruel . . .'

Margaret was shocked – and also, oddly, comforted. At

Jack Pym's the midwife stopped. 'Come on in and join me,' she said, 'it's the best way sometimes, believe me.'

But Margaret shook her head and, bidding her goodbye, she stumbled up the road to her home.

As she entered the house by the back door, Margaret supposed that she must be simply too exhausted for grief. Numbness surrounded her like a cocoon: it was comforting and she hugged it to her tightly.

The kitchen was empty. She realised that Luke must still be at the Forge. She set her bag down on the floor and then wandered about the room touching the table, chairs, cup shelf, a pot of sweet geranium that stood on the window ledge – as though surprised to see these familiar objects still in their accustomed places.

Every nerve in her body was humming with weariness and yet rest eluded her. Though her body felt numb, thoughts hopped through her brain like hungry sparrows. Merry, the baby, Ned, don't die, no strength, all alone, slipping away, the baby . . .

She pushed open the door that led into the shop. William was standing motionless by the open window, a length of watered silk in his hands. Its wild-rose sheen seemed to be part-made of sunlight.

'William –'

He turned to look at her and his cheeks were damp. 'I know,' he said.

Still the restless thoughts hopped through her head. In desperation she went on, 'She's . . . the baby . . . Dame Watkins said . . .' Suddenly her teeth were chattering as though the room was packed with snow.

William frowned. 'I heard the news just now.'

Margaret stared at him helplessly. All around her the blessed cocoon of numbness was unravelling, drifting away like thistledown on a breath of air and there was no shelter anywhere from the cold blade of grief that sliced through her heart.

'And Merry too. We couldn't . . . she couldn't . . .'

William neither moved nor spoke.

Dry eyed, hoarse, Margaret could only stammer. 'Oh William, God help me but Merry is dead!'

'She was my cousin, Margaret, and I share your grief. But now you must be tired. You had best go to your room and rest.'

One word of comfort from him and she could weep, the healing tears her body was aching to release. 'Oh William, hold me. I'm so cold, so . . . please hold me.'

He raised his hands. For a moment it seemed that he would reach out in a gesture of compassion but as Margaret took a step towards him he held up his hands, warning her to stay back.

'You are overwrought.' His voice was clipped.

'Oh –! How can you be so cruel? It is not human, you're a monster! What is wrong with you? Merry is dead and all you can say . . . I don't understand you, William, I don't! What is wrong with you, for God's sake tell me!'

He stretched out his arms to her then, but only to thrust her from the room before his self-control crumbled altogether.

He did not push her hard, he certainly had no wish to injure her, but in her weakened state it was enough to make her lose her balance. She faltered, stared at him in disbelief and then her legs gave way and the walls and the many coloured bolts of cloth, the bright sunlight pouring through the window and William's agonised face all dissolved and curved away from her. The stone flags of the floor rose to smash against her face and then dispersed like a shower of sand.

Stunned by the fall, she did not see William crouch down beside her and cover his face with his hands before lifting her gently in his arms to carry her to her room. For some time she was only dimly aware of what was happening around her. She only knew that the thoughts which had hopped like hungry sparrows through her mind were now all flown away and there was nothing left but an empty roaring, the sea-echo of a traveller's shell held to her ear.

In the midst of the roaring, she slept.

Merry was buried, with the tiny bundle that had briefly been her baby, three days later. Margaret, moon-pale and hollow-eyed, was sufficiently recovered from her exhaustion and the mild concussion caused by her fall to attend the

330

funeral. Dry-eyed and silent she stood between William and Ambrose and watched while the coffin was lowered into the earth. Only when the first rattle of earth fell on its lid was she seen to sway slightly. William reached out to support her but she turned from him and put her hand on Ambrose's massive arm.

It was then that Ned appeared. No one had seen him or knew where he had gone from the moment when he fled the upstairs room. He was wild-looking, more like a vagrant than a local man. Mistress Roberts went over to comfort him but he shook her away and vanished again before the service was over.

Parson Weaver spoke the awesome prayer-book words and hoped that they brought more comfort to his flock than he could derive from them. He watched Margaret, recognising the half-crazed expression of someone whose grief remains locked away. When the service was over he tried to speak with her but she avoided his eye and fobbed him off with borrowed phrases. 'You don't need to worry about me,' she said calmly, 'I shall be right enough in a day or so. It's Merry's mother we must think of now.'

And she walked back to her home alone.

That night she could not sleep. There was no moon, the wind was still and the sea did no more than sigh upon the shingle. Her head ached and her mouth was dry. She lowered her feet to the floor, stood up – and discovered with interest that her legs felt as feeble as a newborn calf's. She put her hand on the windowsill to steady herself, paused for a moment, and it was then that she saw the movement, the flicker of shadow on shadow, at the end of the garden.

She barely hesitated, sensing that this must have been what she had been expecting after all, before pulling a shawl around her shoulders and stepping softly down the stairs, through the kitchen and out into the night.

The slate path was smooth and chill against her bare feet and the cool air touched her cheeks. When she reached the stone barn she found the door slightly ajar and it creaked in the silence as she pushed it open. Inside was inky darkness and the familiar smells of horse and chickens and hay; there were the myriad small noises of the night-time, and there was the sound of a man sobbing.

'Ned,' she whispered, 'it's me, Mattie.'

Guided by the noise of his racking sobs she crouched down beside him and clumsily, not being able to see what she was doing, she put her arms around him. At first he shrank away from her, stifling his tears, but then he crumpled like a child and clung to her.

'Why?' he asked her again and again. 'Why did she die?' and Margaret had no answer for him, but, with his head cradled in her arms and his tears damp against her neck, her own sorrow was at last unleashed and she wept with him.

Crouched against the hay they talked of Merry and cried and remembered the things she had said and done and laughed together through their tears and cried again. They remembered the sound of her laughter, her mischief and her strength. Margaret told him of the time Merry had championed her when all the others were aloof and Ned said that was just like her, she would stand no nonsense from anyone. And they chuckled over the details of William's return from Holland, Ned defending himself with the pillows, Merry upended, not a scrap of dignity left to her, yet still laughing at herself. With Ned Margaret discovered an animal warmth and comfort and slowly the burden of her grief was eased.

Towards morning Margaret slept, her cheek crushed against his russet coat. And while she slept he eased her arms from round his body and slipped noiselessly away.

Though she often looked out for him on the nights that followed, Ned never visited the little barn again. A few weeks later she heard from the packet-boat captain that he had found work on a merchant ship that had sailed from Fowey at Easter. From others she heard that he had enlisted in the European wars. Whatever the truth of the matter, neither Margaret, nor any of his family, ever saw or heard from him again.

She learned later, from idle words exchanged between Mistress Hocken and a pedlar selling ribbons and needles, that Abigail, the name he had chosen for his daughter while Merry was dying, was the name of the girl from Penzance who had been causing rows between him and Merry that spring. Yet Margaret knew how strong his love for Merry had been: strong enough to half-destroy him when she died, yet not strong enough to keep him by her while she lived.

There was an apple tree at the end of the garden, beside the little barn where Ned and Merry had spent their happiest times. Often that summer, in the evenings when Luke was asleep and her work for the day was done, Margaret went to sit beside it, or to lean her arms on the warm stone of the wall beyond. From there she could see the blur of the sea beyond the rooftops lower in the town, watch the changing patterns of the clouds. Usually she took a book with her but, in that time, she did not often read. The words were an irrelevance; they jangled and did not console.

The old certainties were fading. She did not understand how Merry's death had come about. Was it God's punishment for her earlier transgressions? If so, then Margaret was inclined to agree with Dame Watkins, that He was a cruel God, not worthy of man's love at all. Nor did she understand how Ned and Merry's strong love for each other had brought them only sorrow. She did not understand how she herself could live her long days through with a man who had built a stone wall around his heart to keep her out.

She did not understand. Images nagged at her, filled her mind. She still searched for answers – it was an old habit and hard to break – but it was with ever less hope of finding any.

Of one thing only was she certain: on that bright March morning when the birds were singing in the rain-dazzled trees and the lambs were calling for their mothers in the byre, there was something else besides Merry and her baby, something deep and wordless and precious, some part of her own self, that had also been destroyed.

Part 2

Cornwall, 1638

14

All about the boy, the darkness lay soft as feathers, coaxing him back into his dreams; his eyelids were heavy, lashes glued around with sleep. If he only closed his eyes for a moment . . . Luke pinched the warm flesh above his elbow until his eyes smarted with pain, and forced himself to sit upright in the bed.

I am a blind man, he told himself; this is how blindness starts – and a shudder of delicious horror passed through his body. No, he was not blind; there under the paler square of darkness that was the window lay a sliver of something that glowed as if with its own light: the Cordoba dagger. His own dagger. The most beautiful object that had ever belonged to anyone in the whole wide world and it was his. Father had brought it back for him from his travels.

Luke lowered his feet to the floor, pausing only briefly to feel the smooth surface of the boards against his soles, then pattered over to the windowsill and ran the tip of his finger along the polished beauty of the blade ('Careful, Luke,' his mother's voice was always in his head, her caution only prompting him to greater recklessness – and fear). There was a familiar tightness in his chest. His palm slid over the haft and explored the bumps and ridges with which it was decorated: vines, Father called them, those plants that grow in hot countries and are turned into raisins and wine. Luke intended to visit those countries with Father. One day, when this endless tiresome business of childhood was over, then Mother would have to wave them both goodbye as they set off from the harbour on a ship with full white sails.

They might go first to Spain and Luke would wear his dagger proudly in the country where it was made. Ghislain had told him about Spain. Father had brought Ghislain back with him from France in the spring, to live with them and to work as his apprentice in the shop. Ghislain knew a great many interesting facts. He said that sometimes they burned good Christian folk in Spain and you could hear their screams for days and days and their skin broke into black blisters and huge boils and still they kept on screaming. Mother treated this information with suspicion.

Mother disapproved of anything that promised to be interesting or fun. Last year on St Ewan's Day a huge shuffling bear had been baited and the sport had lasted for hours – but though he had tucked himself in the very centre of the crowd Mother had found him somehow and had hauled him away home. The humiliation was almost worse than his disappointment.

The tightness in his chest increased. Sometimes Mother's endless restrictions made him so cross that it was hard even to breathe. Then it occurred to him that if he wore the Cordoba dagger in his belt on this St Ewan's Day, no one would dare to tell him what to do, not even Mother . . . the boldness of the idea caused him to gasp. But he knew it was madness; if anything went wrong, Father would never forgive him.

Mother was often cross, Father hardly ever. But it was Father's anger, implacable and lasting for days at a time, that he dreaded most.

He chuckled to think how angry Mother would be if she could see him now putting on the shabby clothes he wore for visits to the farm at Conwinnion, and ignoring the newly made doublet and breeches she had laid out for him the previous night on the linen press. 'You must wear your best for St Ewan,' she had told him. Yes, he had thought in bitter silence, and be laughed at by all his friends.

Mother's obstinate refusal to understand the importance of friends was one of her many shortcomings, as far as Luke was concerned. When she went to the well at the end of the street she simply lowered her buckets, hauled them up full and returned at once to the house, while all the other mothers stood and gossiped and laughed and complained about their husbands and their strange female ailments. His mother preferred to sit alone in the empty kitchen with one of those books the parson was for ever lending her. She wanted Luke to read them too but he wriggled and pretended not to understand and put on the stupid expression that always caused her mouth to set into a hard line of disapproval until finally she burst out, 'Oh! You try me past endurance!' and he knew that he had won. Then he was free to escape the house and the hateful book and her unhappy face and her stifling never-ending concern.

Escape. Ignoring the hurt look in her eyes as he slipped through the open door and into the sunlight.

He had won a major victory at Midsummer. Grandmother Hocken had been dead for over a year and Luke had pleaded daily to be allowed to move from the truckle bed beside his mother's to the infinite luxury of his own room.

'I want my own room now,' he announced.

'You're too young,' was Mother's reply.

'When will I not be too young any more?'

'When you are older.'

'Why not now?' He watched carefully while Mother cast around for a suitable excuse.

'Ghislain should have it,' she said.

'Ghislain is only an apprentice,' said Father quickly, 'he sleeps well enough in the shop.'

Luke wished passionately that Father would take his side; but he was remote and busy with the shop and travels and customers. 'Am I older now?' he asked at every meal.

'Don't be foolish,' Mother scolded.

'Am I older today? Why aren't I older today? You said we grow older every day.'

Until finally Father said, 'You can see how desperate he is. It will surely do no harm to give him the room.'

And Luke knew that the battle was all but over. Father gave him a scented ball to put with his clothes. He clearly understood the importance of the move. After all, Father had his own room too.

And Father had given him the dagger. Mother said such a weapon was unsuitable for a child – and, of course, that only made Luke love it more fiercely than ever. Fully dressed now in his shabby clothes, Luke caressed the dagger; the tightness in his chest had increased so much that every breath had become a painful effort. Steel from Cordoba: the incredible beauty of it tugged at him. He fully intended to put it back on the windowsill at once but first, just to test how it might feel tucked inside his belt, he slid it carefully against his side. It was as though it had belonged there always. He planted his feet squarely as he had seen Tom and the older boys do, and caressed the engraved handle. He must replace it at once – but as he stood there his arm had grown heavy, his hand appeared unable to move. If he just pulled his shirt out so . . . no one could possibly see it. But still, if Father ever . . . only until daylight. Where was the harm in that?

Quick as a thief he scampered down the stairs and out into the crisp night air. Early-morning air. Already the sky in the east over the sea was paler; soon Mother would rise to light the fire and feed the hens and shake the house into the activity of the day. And by then he would be gone . . .

Now the blackness separated itself into familiar shapes and shadows. He knew the lanes and pathways near the house so well he could have found his way in twice the blackness. His hands and feet recognised every bump and pot-hole, the texture of stone walls and the pattern of each door and gate. Besides that, there were the smells that guided him as surely as if he were a scavenging dog. There was the mild aroma of horse and chickens in the little barn at the end of the garden and the rich stink of Dame Perkins's privy over the wall. (Their own privy was kept so clean, at Father's insistence, that it hardly smelled at all.) Then came the yeasty floury smell of Tom Williams's bake-shop – Luke could see the red glow of the oven fires through the open door: when Parson spoke of Hell it was those oven fires that Luke imagined, but bigger by far.

He crept on up the steep lane that ran by the shambles and the patch of ground where cattle were baited before slaughter; here was a potent mingling of smells – blood and dung and piled hides. Mother never took this route unless she had to; she said you could smell the fear of the poor creatures. Luke sniffed cautiously as he went past, but the precise smell of fear had always eluded him.

And then he was out of the town and had only the scents of the hedgerows and ditches to guide him, bracken and rank nettles and blackberries. He had never been so far in darkness before and was amazed at the snufflings and scamperings all around him, a sudden guttural noise from behind a gate which reason told him must be the sound of a waking heifer, though imagination was quick to conjure up hobgoblins, changelings, spirits that had tumbled unforgiven from the gibbet . . .

A dark shape loomed ahead in the softening night and the scent of fire and metal told him he had reached the Forge. Only when he slowed his pace and heard his own rasping breath did he realise that in his fear he had been running for some time.

When Tom finally emerged from the shadowy kitchen behind the forge, Luke had been crouched for so long in his hiding place by the lilac that his limbs were stiff with cold and dew.

'Tom!' he hissed. 'Over here!'

His young uncle was so startled at being whispered at by a brambly bush that he jumped backwards and then, to cover his fright, said crossly, 'Leave me alone, pest.'

Luke scrambled to his feet. Tom Pearce was at least six years older than he was, but not all that much taller, being short and thickset like his father, with a square face, vigorous and self-confident. Sometimes he tolerated Luke's hero-worship – but not today. St Ewan's Day was too important to risk spoiling it with young children. When he had finished emptying his bladder against the trunk of an old apple tree he began to walk briskly back towards the house.

'Tom, wait!'

'Go on home. Mattie will be looking for you.' He walked on.

'Let me come with you!'

'No.'

'Tom, please!'

Tom came abruptly to a halt and turned around, causing Luke almost to run into him. 'I'm warning you, Luke, if you try to tag along today –' and he made a threatening gesture with his fist.

Luke saw his hopes for the day, this most important day of all the year, come crashing down in ruins. Desperation made him blurt out, 'Wait, Tom, listen. I've brought you something –'

'Show me, then.'

341

Suddenly Luke was breathless, found it hard to squeeze out the words. 'It's . . . I brought . . . you can hold . . . the Cordoba . . .'

At the mention of the Cordoba dagger, Tom was all interest. He could see that Luke was holding something under his shirt and staring up at him with an odd expression in his greeny-grey eyes. That was half the trouble with Luke, thought Tom irritably, he looked at you so oddly sometimes and you never did know what he was thinking.

'Let me see it.'

'It's here –' Luke gasped.

'You'd never dare.'

'If . . . if you want . . . if you let me come . . . you can have it today . . .'

Tom paused as if he was considering the matter, but in truth there was little enough to debate. He would cheerfully have sold his soul to Satan for the chance to flaunt the Spanish dagger. He said carelessly, 'So what? It's only a stupid dagger.'

But Luke knew he was unable to resist. 'Only for today, Tom. You must promise to give it me back this evening.'

'I might do.'

Luke drew the dagger from his belt and Tom snatched it at once. Luke tried to ignore the wave of horror that passed through him at the enormity of his act. If Father knew . . . if Mother . . . he closed his mind to all thought of them.

As soon as Tom had the dagger in his hand he whooped with delight and slashed the tops off several nettles, then tossed it from one palm to the other and then, with a flick of his wrist, skewered it into the earth between his boots.

Luke watched miserably. 'Promise you won't tell anyone.'

'You never said.'

But Tom was fair-minded and prepared to be conciliatory. Besides, Luke looked so wretched, standing there with his shoulders hunched up and his eyes with that odd look that they had when his wheezing attacks came on. 'Come on in and have something to eat. Lizzie won't mind.'

Luke wavered. He realised that he was indeed very hungry – but a moment's thought told him that Aunt Lizzie

342

was sure to guess that he was playing truant. And he had experienced his Aunt Treloar's stinging slaps often enough to be cautious.

'I'll wait out here.'

'Suit yourself. I'll maybe steal you out some bread later.' Tom began to stroll back towards the house. Then he paused. 'There's to be a cock fight later. You can come with me.'

Luke's spirits began to rise.

But as Tom went through the door into the kitchen, Luke saw his dagger being borne further and further away, and he was almost overwhelmed by a sense of impending disaster.

By the time Margaret had searched for Luke in all his usual haunts she was in a turmoil of worry and irritation. She returned home, hoping to find he had come back in the meantime, but instead she found Jennie Treloar, seated on the high-backed settle by the fireplace and fanning herself with a large cabbage leaf. 'The house was empty and I didn't want to disturb Mr Hollar,' she explained, 'and I knew you'd not mind if we set down here for a bit – the walk from Trecarne is so long.'

'You should have found yourself a bite to eat, you look worn out.' Margaret had hardly ever seen Jennie Treloar when she did not look exhausted – and small wonder. Anyone less resilient would have buckled long since and Margaret was only surprised that she still found energy to snatch at any chance for pleasure.

She busied herself setting food and drink on the table. 'Luke ran off before I was up. I was out hunting for him.'

Jennie eyed the food hungrily. 'Did you find him?' she asked politely.

'No.'

'He'll be happily up to no good, I shouldn't waste time worrying,' advised Jennie, adding, 'just be thankful you've only the one.' She herself was far gone in pregnancy, there was a toddler clutching at her skirts while a slightly older child sifted pebbles and dirt in the doorway. The rest were all gone to the fair.

'But he's so secretive –' Margaret began, then checked herself. By comparison with the Treloars' problems, her worries for Luke must seem insignificant. 'Here,' she gestured to the food, 'help yourself. And the children too, they must be hungry.'

Jennie helped herself to a portion of pie. 'And how is Mr Hollar?'

'Well, thank you. And Joseph?'

'Worried, as usual. No, he's worse than usual. Did you know Treveryan is expected to return any day now?'

'Indeed?'

'Francis Crane came out to the farm last week. He's for ever prying into our affairs. I can't abide the man.'

Margaret made a vague sound of sympathy and agreement. No one liked Francis Crane. He had arrived in the area two years before with apparently limitless sums of money to spend on behalf of Richard Treveryan. He had purchased land and properties, but his high-handed manner had alienated even those who were willing enough to take his money.

She asked casually, 'And he told you Treveryan was coming here?'

'Joseph has thought of nothing else for days. He has the notion fixed in his mind that Treveryan means to turn us off our land, though Heaven knows how he can do that when we have legal title to the place for three lives and the evidences to prove it. Even Mr Crane was forced to admit that they were as legal as can be.'

'Then Joseph has no cause to worry.'

'That's what I keep telling him. And why should a wealthy man need our house when he has so many finer places to choose from? But when Mr Crane left last time his parting words were that we must mind and not lose the evidences – and now Joseph will not leave the house for fear they might be stolen. He refused to come today. I swear he'd sleep with the strong box for a pillow if he could. He never lets it out of his sight.'

'Have some more ale. You know what rumours are like, I expect Treveryan is much too busy to come back here.'

But Jennie, revived by the food and drink, continued to pour out her troubles for some time. Margaret was a sympathetic listener and it was good to unburden herself before putting aside her worries and enjoying the rest of the day. She spoke of barren cows and stony fields and the high price of bread and the low price of cloth. And of their eldest girl who had been sent to work for a farmer's wife over Manaccan way though she cried fit to break her heart for a week and had run away twice already, only to be sent back again each time with a beating for her trouble.

But Margaret was only half-listening.

It was rumoured that Richard Treveryan was now a man of fabulous wealth, with fifty ships at his command and lands that stretched from Porthew to Plymouth. It was said that he was on intimate terms with members of the King's court, some said even that he was the confidant of King Charles himself. He had survived incredible dangers. She supposed he must have changed a good deal.

But in her mind's eye she still saw the young man with the rough dark hair and the doublet of midnight-blue velvet who had danced with her on her wedding day, and despite the unending gloom of Jennie's words, Margaret could not resist breaking into a smile at the memory.

As she wandered through the fair-day throng with Jennie and her younger children, Margaret continued to search for Luke and wondered if she might see the dark features of Richard Treveryan among the crowd. It had been on St Ewan's Day that she had seen him first; since then he must have travelled the world, seen exotic places that she could not even imagine . . . and all the while she had remained anchored to this narrow town.

Irritation with Luke mingled with her familiar restlessness. She found it hard to imagine how Porthew on St Ewan's Day had once seemed to her the most exciting place on earth. Now even the jugglers failed to amuse her, the Irish fiddler scraped most unmelodiously on the strings, the pedlars and chapmen were selling tawdry wares. Jennie and her children were eager to savour every detail and Margaret soon grew impatient and went on alone.

The town was crammed with its usual bustle of outsiders, but there were plenty of familiar faces too. She found Lizzie down by the harbour wall chatting with a couple of friends while her two small children tugged at her skirts. She was grown a little plumper since her marriage, but otherwise was unchanged. She had new ribbons in her hair and a new collar for her dress and was quite aware of her own prettiness still. But Margaret noted with approval that when Nicolas Sutton strolled past with his wife Lizzie frowned and looked over the harbour wall towards the sea, so that Margaret had to greet them to avoid seeming altogether rude. Mistress Sutton now bought all her cloth from William, and Margaret took care to be courteous to his customers.

She was continuing her search for Luke when a man accosted her.

'Good morning, Mistress Hollar. Are you and your family well?'

Margaret suppressed a sigh of vexation. 'Yes, thank you. And you?'

'Indeed I am.' Francis Crane fell into step beside her. He was a tall man with tufty brown hair on a small head and a stomach so incongruously round that he looked as though he had stuffed a cushion inside his doublet. His voice was high pitched and his up-country accent made almost every statement sound like a query. Margaret did not like him any more than did her neighbours, but she felt sorry for him and was polite to him, and he considered her a friend.

He talked aimlessly about the fine weather and the wrestling and the life of St Ewan and Margaret barely paid him any attention until a stray word made her suddenly attentive.

'What did you say?'

'I said that when Mr Treveryan returns he will soon sort the fellow out.'

'So the rumours are true.'

'What rumours?'

'That Mr Treveryan is expected.'

'To tell you the truth, Mistress Hollar, I did think he'd be here by now. He returned from the Indies over a fortnight ago and my instructions were to expect him as soon as the cargo had been dealt with. He must have been delayed.'

'He must be eager to inspect his new farms.'

'Certainly.' The usually garrulous Francis Crane fell silent. He was a conscientious agent, and never discussed his employer's affairs. After a pause he said, 'Are you going to watch the wrestling?'

'No. I hate to see men fight. And besides, I'm looking for my son.'

She was relieved when they parted company and he went to watch Ambrose enjoy his annual triumph on the wrestling ground. That was the year a Flemish seaman gave him a black eye and received a broken arm for his impudence.

The spectators at the wrestling ground were fewer than usual that year since a large group of people had gathered near the churchyard steps. Such a crowd in fact that Margaret wondered at first if a fight was brewing and went to search among the spectators for Luke. But there was no fight and no Luke either. All she could see was a single elderly man, slightly built, who stood in the shadow of the lych-gate. He wore a dark hat and his clothes were threadbare and dingy black. He stood quite still and used none of the tricks of emphasis that were common among preachers. And his voice was so quiet, no more than a normal speaking voice, that one might have expected only those at the front to be able to hear, but his words carried perfectly and not a syllable was lost. His rather pale, watery blue eyes had an almost transparent look. His audience listened spellbound.

He spoke of the two Churches that existed where men saw only one. There was the Church that all men knew, with its buildings and its ministers and congregations, its ceremonies and hierarchy. But he explained that it was a mistake to call this the True Church. God's own Church was made up of those saints, His elect, who'had been chosen by Our Lord Himself to do His work on earth. This was the only real Church, the Church that had endured down the ages. The Church which no man could destroy but which was, even now, in this very year of King Charles's reign 1638, in which they were living, confronted by its most ominous threat.

It was then that Margaret noticed her husband standing not far from her in the crowd. He must have left Ghislain to look after the shop while he took a turn to see the sights of the fair. He was listening to the old man's words with an extraordinary expression on his face that Margaret tried in vain to untangle. Was it contempt or admiration that had troubled his usual impassivity? She could not tell.

The preacher continued quietly. He told them that the True Church had been sorely tested in the dark days of the Catholic Queen Mary, but God's Church had triumphed over persecution. He did not dwell, as most did, on the hideous suffering of those who had been butchered for their faith. Rather he emphasised their joy, the joy of God's chosen few. What had been the words of the holy Latimer as he stood at the stake with his brother-in-suffering, Ridley, and waited for the flames to rise up around their feet? Did he condemn his persecutors? Did he weep and beg for mercy? The speaker paused. The crowd waited in silence. No. Latimer had turned to his fellow martyr and told him in a clear, calm voice, 'Be of good cheer, Master Ridley, and play the man. We shall this day light such a candle by God's grace in England as I trust shall never be put out.'

And so it was. The candle had never wavered and in time the martyrs were rewarded by the dawn of Queen Elizabeth's great reign. God's True Church had flourished and England had flourished also and English ships had defeated the larger forces of Catholic Spain. But now the darkness was closing in again: the King had a Catholic wife and London swarmed with popish priests and Jesuits who worked on the King to weaken his resolve and God showed His displeasure by granting victory to the Spanish ships once again. Papists were rewarded in England now while godly men suffered persecution for speaking out the truth.

'I was there,' and now the old voice trembled with emotion, 'when Satan corrupted the Court of High Commission last year and the worthy William Prynne, the Reverend Henry Burton and Dr Bastwick were mutilated in the public pillory by order of that court. Yes, their ears were cut off as they stood there and prayed but their faith in God and love for Him never faltered. And now I ask you this, how much longer will Evil hold sway in this land of ours, how many of God's loyal servants must be cut by the Devil's knife, how many of Our Lord's children must be driven into exile before this Romish abomination is cast out from the land?'

'Who is he?' Margaret whispered to the man standing beside her.

But he did not know.

Parson Weaver watched the elderly speaker with some unease. None of this was new to him: it was the common fare of Puritan divines up and down the land and had hardly changed since the days when he himself was a student.

In recent years the Puritan voice had grown more shrill. All over Europe their brothers in religion were being slaughtered by the thousand and many believed the sword of persecution now hung poised to fall on England too. The King had little liking for their doctrines and was devoted to his Catholic wife. As the preacher said, Jesuits and Papist priests were welcomed at court while honest Englishmen were mutilated for their faith.

The parson agreed with most of what the man was saying; this Fletcher Grey who had arrived last night at the invitation of Robert Payne. It was not the man's message that troubled him, so much as the likely impact of such obvious conviction on his parishioners. It was bound to lead to a tiresome outbreak of piety, and demands, at least for a few weeks, that his ministry should be more rigorous.

Look at Margaret Hollar. She was listening with rapt attention. He knew that she was just the sort to be most vulnerable to the wandering preacher's magic. She was restless, lonely and searching for some purpose for her life. He had long recognised the taut mouth of an unhappy woman.

Well, that marriage of hers had been the best way out of a bad situation and he had no cause to regret his role as go-between. The preacher was forgotten as Parson Weaver continued to gaze at Margaret Hollar.

At first glance she had barely changed from the young girl (had she been only fifteen?) who had come to him in the vestry all those years before. She was far more elegantly dressed, of course, and so tall and straight that the simplest clothes became her. Today she was wearing a dress of fine tawny wool with a wide collar of white cambric. A few strands of pale hair had escaped from under her coif to blow across her face and she brushed them aside with the impatient gesture of a young girl.

349

The parson sighed. If his intention, in arranging that marriage, had been to preserve her just as she had been on her wedding day then, to a superficial observer at least, he had succeeded. Parson Weaver knew his original estimate of William Hollar had been correct; he knew also that his scheme had failed: it was a chemistry more subtle than the drudgery of childbirth and toil that was working to corrode Margaret now. There was such a reserve now in her eyes that sometimes he found it hard to remember the amazing candour of her former smiles.

He knew that since Meredith Hocken's death she had searched in vain for something to fill the void that was left. From time to time he had tentatively offered himself as her confidant – and he even believed he would have been content to remain just that – but she always rejected him. 'I am not such a fool, Parson, that I must make the same mistake twice over.'

A few months after Merry's death she had channelled all her energies into the house: for a while there had not been such a diligent housewife in all Porthew. From before dawn until after dark she worked, almost, he thought, as though she hoped to exhaust herself into oblivion with her endless baking and washing, cleaning, scrubbing, polishing and mending.

Her enthusiasm died down as swiftly as it had arisen and a state of almost dreamlike lethargy took its place. Little Luke went out in grubby clothes, cobwebs spread unheeded through the house, dust settled and drifted in piles. Parson had often seen her walking slowly on the cliff paths, her head bowed in thought, and on more occasions than he cared to remember he had called at the house only to find her gazing into an empty fireplace with an unread book lying open on her lap.

Mistress Hocken's last illness had rescued Margaret from this apathy. She nursed the old woman with an eagerness that betrayed her need for occupation and after the old woman died the parson, fearing she might lapse into her former melancholy, suggested she help Dame Erisey in the school. Margaret was reluctant at first but soon became an enthusiastic teacher. Not a child so dull-witted but she had them reading clearly and able to sign their name by the time their parents considered them old enough to stay home and earn their keep.

She delighted in her odd assortment of pupils and it often seemed to the parson, who was quick to cuff any boy stupid enough to make a mistake once he had graduated to his own lessons in the church porch, that her patience was limitless . . . or almost limitless. Only Luke had the uncanny knack of pushing her tolerance beyond its limits.

He was a strange child, pale and anxious and often unwell, but with a determination unusual in a boy so young. In his lessons with Margaret he stumbled over the simplest words (deliberately? the parson could never be sure) and made a point of showing his boredom. He resented the attention Margaret lavished so freely on her other pupils – yet rebelled when her focus turned on him. Margaret was by turns protective, puzzled and, with increasing frequency, irate.

About six months ago, around Easter, the parson had noticed that Margaret was becoming more attentive in church, but when he tried to question her she rebuffed him swiftly. 'This is my own affair, Parson. You've blocked the way for me too long.' And, since he knew only too well what she meant, he had no choice but to let the matter rest.

He sighed again. Her face was turned slightly towards him and even now he could not see her profile, that high forehead and straight nose, the wide mouth and the sweep of her jaw, without a jolt of – what? A bittersweet combination of remembered pleasure and anticipation . . . but he told himself there was nothing to anticipate.

Lord forgive me for my sinful thoughts, he said to himself – and was thankful that these had recently grown less intense. Margaret was no longer the blossoming child-woman he had craved so fiercely at the time of her marriage. Still attractive, yes, still tender-hearted to a fault. But . . . he could not ignore the fact that there was something crabbed, spinsterish even, in her manner. Her large spirit was being starved by her cramped existence.

And now here she was, inevitably fastening on to the fanatic words of the preacher – who *was* a fanatic, Parson Weaver was sure, for all the man's quiet voice and humble demeanour. His words had the unmistakable ring of the all-or-nothing believer.

'It says in the Scripture, if a man takes away your coat, let him have your cloak also. Give to him that asks . . . Resist not evil.'

Several heads nodded sagely at this injunction and the parson wondered cynically if any understood more than a tenth of what the fellow was saying. Men who were no more capable of returning evil with good than they were of taking wing and flying from the church steeple. And no reason why they should. Our Lord's commands were necessarily impossible to obey – or where would be the need for faith?

Parson Weaver had heard enough. With a last glance at Margaret, still absorbed in the preacher's spell, he retreated from the crowd and, smiling benignly at anyone who noticed his departure, he hurried off to Jack Pym's ale-house.

Seated high in the leafy world of Dame Erisey's plum tree, Luke decided that so far at least the day had been more than satisfactory. Tom had generously insisted that the older boys treat him as an equal in all their activities, and Luke responded by volunteering for all the most dangerous feats. When someone was needed to steal eggs from Master Calwodely's hen coop so that they might pelt a sleeping vagrant, it was Luke who wriggled through the gap in the fence. When they gathered turves to stuff down Dame Harries's chimney, it was Luke who crept over the steep roof – and joined the older boys who were hiding in some bushes just in time to see her whole family and their friends come choking out of the house as smoke filled their kitchen.

Tom, who had expected Luke to be a nuisance, was surprised by his daring; for all that he was a whey-faced whiner at times, Tom felt quite proud of him. And now Luke was sitting in Dame Erisey's precious plum tree in full view of the road and lobbing the juiciest and ripest of the fruit down to the assembled boys. And everyone knew that though Dame Erisey herself would never raise a hand to anyone, her son, who lived with her and was partially deaf, had been known to thrash plum-stealers with an ash staff kept specially.

Luke was well aware of the risk. But he had always yearned to be accepted by Tom and his friends and when he wanted something he longed for it unreservedly and it would have taken more than the threat of a beating to make him forfeit the delights of being the centre of attention. 'Luke, to me!' 'Luke, over here!' It was wonderfully satisfying to hear them jostling below for his favour, as he aimed the ripe fruit down towards their upturned faces.

Every now and then he caught sight of the little Cordoba dagger sticking out of Tom's belt and a shadow of anxiety checked his fun: if Tom should lose it, or forget to hand it back . . .

Needing to distract himself from futile worries, Luke shouted, 'The best are all at the top! I'm going higher!'

It was just as he was hauling himself up to the next branch that he heard a commotion from the boys below. 'Quick,' hissed Tom, 'he's coming!'

'Who?'

But Tom and the others had already scattered, over walls and through hedges, and Luke could see the burly figure of Matthew Erisey striding up the hill towards him.

The preacher spoke for over two hours by the church clock before allowing Robert Payne to lead him away for refreshment. It then became apparent how frail he was, his skin yellow and sickly, his hands trembling, his walk little more than an invalid's shuffle. But while he was talking one noticed none of this; one noticed only his power.

Margaret, needing solitude, walked past the harbour wall and up on to the higher ground beyond the town. She felt moved as never before, not so much by the man's words as by something beyond words and impossible to explain: he was possessed of an inner stillness as though he had already glimpsed the Heavenly Kingdom and had only been persuaded with great reluctance to remain a little longer on earth and share with them the glories he had seen.

She felt herself transformed. His speech had raised her to a place of harmony and inner peace.

Until that moment she had not realised how distracted her life had become: a busy, irritating tangle of concerns over which she had no control – Luke's waywardness, the lonely lie of her marriage, her own unceasing restlessness, anxiety for Jennie Treloar and her hopeless poverty, the unease she had felt at the apprentice Ghislain's sudden arrival a few months before, a sense sometimes of being a stranger in her own home.

And now, all these worries were forgotten – no, not forgotten, but reduced to the unimportant scurryings of mice in a cellar, while she herself had been raised to a high place and could regard them calmly from her lofty distance.

She had reached the summit of the cliff that overlooked the town. Her eyes could not make out the details of rooftops and walls, people and animals, though the noise of the fair day could still be heard above the softer sound of the waves breaking against the shore. But she could see the late summer gold and green of gorse and bracken and the opalescent blue of sea where it blended into a hazy sky. She could hear the hum of insects and the songs of the birds and she could feel the softness of the September air against her face.

She felt as though she was sensing her world for the first time in years. As if she had been moving through greyness for a long long time but now everything was breaking into a brilliant shoal of colour. Life was simple and joyous after all. She was at peace.

When she walked back through the town a little later, Margaret's radiant mood was unbroken. She intended going to Robert Payne's house to see if she could hear the preacher again, but first she looked in briefly at her own home, in case Luke had returned, and her great love for the child might be satisfied.

As she stepped from the garden into the kitchen she did not see her son, but the room was far from empty.

There was a man standing in the alcove by the fire, a thin, evil-looking fellow with sallow skin, lank hair and a ragged appearance. He looked as hungry and dangerous as a gypsy's cur and, as he caught sight of Margaret, he pulled a crude knife from his belt and said roughly, 'Hand over your money and you'll come to no harm.'

On a normal day Margaret might have screamed, attempted to flee or berated the man for a rogue and a thief. But not this day. For, from the heights to which the preacher's words had transported her, she saw not a terrifying criminal but a man half-starved and afraid, and she did not hesitate for a moment.

She beamed at him. 'You poor fellow, you look famished. Sit down and rest for a moment and I shall find you something to eat. How about a piece of bacon and some bread? There is cheese too if you care for it. Here, take this chair.' She noticed then that he held a shirt of William's over one arm. 'And that shirt of my husband's will not do, but there is a doublet upstairs that will serve much better.' ('If a man takes away your coat, let him have your cloak also.') Later, when the radiance of that moment had passed, Margaret did wonder if she would have followed the preacher's words so faithfully had it been her own clothes that were to be sacrificed. But William's wardrobe was so extensive and he took such a peacock pleasure in his appearance that there was satisfaction in removing a few bright feathers.

The stranger followed her every move with wild eyes. Every now and then, when she passed by the door in her preparations for his meal, he raised the knife as though to lunge at her, but she continued unperturbed. 'There,' she said soothingly, as she set the food in front of him, 'and now a little ale to wash it down.'

Bewildered now, and somehow more panic-stricken than he would have been if she had run screaming from the house – which was what he had expected, not being a very accomplished thief – the stranger was persuaded to pull up the best chair and eat.

As Margaret had suspected, he was ravenous and tore at the food with filthy hands. Margaret considered that she had probably never before seen such a repulsive sight as this verminous vagrant, and Mouse, coming into the room to be fed, was clearly of the same opinion for she backed off, hissing, the moment she saw him.

'A little at a time,' said Margaret gently, pulling the plate away from him. Again the knife was raised in warning and one side of his long, thin face was convulsed by a massive twitch which made him look more sinister than ever, but Margaret reassured him, 'You may have a little more later on. Rest here for a moment while I see what clothes of my husband's will do for you. You'd best wash first. I'll fetch water for you later.'

Half-dead with exhaustion and the first curdlings of nausea, the thief succumbed to her gentle bullying. He feared trickery, and kept a firm grip on his knife, the only thing in the world that remained to him. It struck him that she must be touched with madness, this woman whose eyes gazed at him with an expression so luminous that he could not return her stare and had to look away. He even wondered if perhaps he had died at some time during the previous night and that this unknown house in this unknown town by the sea might even be the gateway to Heaven itself.

William, when he returned a little later, tended to subscribe to the former theory, that Margaret had in fact gone mad. He found as evil-looking a man as he had ever set eyes on – for though Margaret had provided soap and water the grime of so many years was not easily washed away – seated in his chair and wearing his clothes, eating his food and drinking his ale. Although he was used to his wife's tendency to collect waifs and strays, on this occasion he was too astonished even to be angry and, seeing the beatific expression on her face he guessed, quite rightly, that anger would have been wasted.

'Get rid of him, Margaret,' he said, 'his problems are nothing to do with us.'

The man gazed at him mournfully, and then the whole side of his face was disfigured still further by a sudden spasm.

'He can sleep in the barn until he is well again,' said Margaret. 'These September nights are not yet cold.'

William stared at her in disbelief, then snatched up his plate of food and took it into the shop to eat in solitude.

News of the latest addition to Mistress Hollar's collection of lost causes spread with its usual speed and soon there was a small audience of neighbours thronging to her kitchen to watch and to offer advice. Parson Weaver had dropped in to tell her that Luke had been seen several times that day with Tom and a group of older boys, but when he saw her most unwholesome guest he was torn between amusement and concern.

'Isn't that William's doublet?' he asked. 'I'm sure Fletcher Grey isn't accustomed to being taken so literally. What do you intend to do with this fellow?'

Margaret shrugged. 'There'll be a solution.'

'Your faith is an example to us all,' said the parson drily and then added in a low voice, 'make sure you bolt your doors well tonight, Margaret. A rogue like that thinks nothing of cutting throats for a few pence.'

The stranger looked startled, but Margaret only smiled her disbelief and poured fresh ale for all her guests.

The moment Luke came into the house, the vagrant was quite forgotten. The boy's face was streaked with dirt, he had been crying and, though he fought back the tears, his shoulders still shuddered with an occasional sob. Tom steered him into the room and looked as though he would rather be a thousand miles away, anywhere at all but in his sister's crowded kitchen.

'Whatever is the matter?'

For answer, Luke flung himself against his mother's skirts and allowed her to take him on her knee and soothe him, something he had scorned for years. Between Luke's grief and Tom's shame the truth was some time in emerging, but as it did, Margaret's expression slowly turned from concern to fury.

In their haste to escape Matthew Erisey's wrath – and Luke too had managed to plummet down from the tree and over the wall just in time – the boys were separated. Tom, scurrying down a narrow alley near the ale-house, had pitched headlong into a group of tinners from the north of the county and by the time he escaped their clutches he was missing the exquisite Cordoba dagger.

Hence Luke's misery and Tom's mortification. Hence Margaret's rage.

'It's no use blaming the boy!' she exclaimed, for already voices were being raised in condemnation of Tom. 'Surely he can walk the streets of his own town without fear of being robbed. And he had the courage to come back here and tell us himself.' Tom cast a grateful glance at his sister, having struggled long and hard with his conscience before returning with Luke. 'It's those thieving tinners I'd like to lay my hands on. Which way did they go?'

After some consultation there was general agreement that they had been seen leaving by the Helston road. 'But so drunk and quarrelsome they'll not reach home tonight.'

Margaret tipped Luke from her lap and stood up.

'You're never thinking of going after them yourself, are you? The watch can raise a group of men –'

She shook out her tawny skirts with a gesture indicating her opinion of the watch. 'Yes, and by the time they're organised it will be the middle of next week and Luke's dagger will be gone for ever. You know as well as I do they're all too busy drinking toasts to St Ewan by this time in the day to be any help to us. And I don't intend to let those thieves escape.'

Parson Weaver sighed. 'Then we'd best come with you. You cannot go alone.' But at his words the narrow kitchen began mysteriously to empty; suddenly all the neighbours who had been so interested in discussing the newcomer, remembered pressing obligations that forced them to take their leave.

Parson Weaver smiled at Margaret and raised a sardonic eyebrow. 'Brave champions every one,' he commented. 'You'd best tell William.'

But at the mention of his father, Luke broke into loud wails of protest: his father's displeasure was what he dreaded most of all.

'Oh, never mind about William,' said Margaret, 'he'll be no use anyway. We're wasting time. Tom, you stay here and keep an eye on Luke for me and –' She broke off as her eye fell on the stranger. He was still seated at the kitchen table and he appeared to be undergoing some kind of inner struggle. He turned away from her gaze, looked down at his hands, the side of his face twitched a couple of times and then he stood up awkwardly.

'I shall come too,' he offered roughly.

'Wonderful,' Parson Weaver raised his hands in mock despair, 'in that case our problems are at an end.'

'For Heaven's sake,' Margaret exclaimed. 'I'm leaving. And anyone who wants to help can come and welcome.' And with that she swept out of the house.

The parson saw that there was little choice but to accompany her and he had to hurry to catch up. He was still not happy to have the foul-smelling vagrant loping along at his side.

'Where are you from?' he asked.

The man mumbled something deliberately incoherent.

'And your name?'

He said his name was Paul Viney.

At that moment Parson Weaver saw one of his more nimble, though timid parishioners, and he had an idea.

'Find Ambrose Treloar!' he shouted. 'And tell him to go with all speed to the Helston road to help Mistress Hollar.'

And then he had to save his breath in the effort of keeping up with Margaret who was running at full tilt through the fair-day crowds.

It was a source of eternal regret to Ambrose that he did not arrive on the scene in time to break the heads of the thieving tinners and rescue Margaret from their murderous clutches. It was small consolation to discover that it appeared the tinners had been the ones in need of reinforcement. The exact details of the encounter varied with the teller: there was general agreement that the thieves had stumbled to a halt somewhere near Ia's Bridge, to piss and drink and wonder why the trees that arched above their heads seemed to tip and sway as though the road was the deck of a ship in heavy seas. There were four of them, men who passed so much of their lives in digging beneath the earth that they seemed almost a race apart, unaccustomed to the ways of men. Certainly they were unaccustomed to the ways of a woman who, though dressed like a lady, set about them in a fit of fury that would have done any screeching fishwife proud.

'You should be ashamed of yourselves, all of you, to go and steal from a child not old enough to defend himself!' she exclaimed, and prodded the ribs of one of the men who had lain down beside the road and had rather thought he was asleep. He grunted and lurched to his feet with a snarl of rage.

'Leave me be!'

Margaret whirled about her. 'Where is it? Give back the dagger and you'll come to no harm.'

The four men milled around, uncertain whether to fight

or run. Beneath the fog of alcohol lurked a dim idea that to brawl with a woman was a more serious misdemeanour than the theft of a knife (and several other small items that had come their way also) but the ale, and a growing suspicion that this woman was making fools of them all, encouraged them to fight. One, more pot-valiant than the rest, gave her a shove that almost knocked her to the ground.

'Get on back where you came from,' he growled, 'don't you meddle with us!'

'How dare you!' Margaret blazed back. 'Thieves and cowards all of you! Give back the dagger at once!'

The youngest of the group, a scrawny youth who looked as if he had been born with a vicious grin on his face, produced the Cordoba dagger from inside his jacket – but with no intention of handing it back.

'Damn you, woman, this'll teach you not to go screeching at us,' and the dagger glinted suddenly as he raised it to threaten her.

Margaret then did something that neither he nor any of his fellows had ever seen an opponent do before. She raised her hand and snatched the knife from him by its blade. Had the youth been expecting such a manoeuvre then no doubt he would have held the shaft more tightly and could have kept it easily, but as it was, Margaret's movement, which he had thought was to protect her face, took him by surprise and he lost the dagger. A mass of blood appeared on her hand as the blade sliced her palm.

The parson had been watching from a short distance since, as he was careful to point out later, the encounter was more likely to end peacefully if Margaret handled it alone. But at the sight of her bleeding hand he momentarily forgot to be prudent, and hastened to join her.

'Begone, all of you, or you'll be up before the justices in the morning. Are you badly hurt, Margaret? Here –'

'I have the dagger,' she gasped, ''tis all that matters,' and she kept a tight hold of the dagger in her left hand while Parson pulled off his white neck-band and bandaged her right firmly to staunch the flow of blood. Viney continued to watch the proceedings with an attentive but otherwise impassive face.

360

The tinners meanwhile were muttering and swaying and generally building up their courage to regain their prize when the parson said, 'Praise the Lord, here comes Ambrose.'

The sight of the mighty blacksmith, pounding towards them like all the Four Horsemen of the Apocalypse at once, decided the tinners instantly in favour of flight. They turned tail and sped off down the road, drunkenness and the dagger all miraculously forgotten. Ambrose, who had heard only that the parson required him to rescue Mistress Hollar, was not so easily thwarted of glory and so took it upon himself to assume that Paul Viney had been the menace.

'Villain!' he roared, clutching the vagrant round the throat with a single massive hand.

'Oh Ambrose, no!' As Margaret's anger and fear turned to relief, she burst out laughing. 'Leave the poor fellow, he only came to help.'

Ambrose pretended not to hear. Viney's eyes were popping like a rabbit's and his hands clawed ineffectually at the imprisoning arm.

'He'll not frighten you again, Mattie!' Ambrose tightened his grip and his victim began to make strange gurgling noises.

Margaret, fearing that Viney might actually lose his life, stopped laughing at once. 'Ambrose!' she commanded. 'Let go of him at once!'

Whenever Margaret used that tone, Ambrose had no choice but to obey, and he did so now, only watching with mild regret as the man stumbled to a safe distance, gagging and massaging his stringy neck.

'The tinners who took Luke's knife are probably half-way to Helston by now, and good luck to them. This poor man came to help.'

'Where are the poxy thieves? I'll –'

Parson Weaver said, 'It's too late, Ambrose. I doubt they'll ever come back this way again, not after the fright you gave them.'

Ambrose slapped his fist against his thigh with vexation.

Unnoticed by anyone, Viney was retching into an elder bush.

'We've got Luke's dagger back,' said Margaret, 'nothing else matters.'

Now that the frenzy of the encounter was ebbing, she was acutely aware of the pain in her hand. But, as she set off once again in the direction of Porthew, the thought of Luke's pleasure on her return made it easy to ignore the throbbing of her damaged hand.

That night Luke wanted to sleep with the dagger laid beside his pillow but his mother said, nonsense, that was far too dangerous. She placed it instead on the chest that stood beneath the window. But after she had bid him goodnight he tip-toed across the room and carried his treasure back to his bed, meaning only to gaze on it, touch it for a while before restoring it once more to its rightful place. In the fading light the silver blade shone as though it had distilled the essence of the crescent moon.

Luke's mouth, which so often drooped in a pout of unspecified discontent, kept breaking into a wide grin. He could not remember such celebrations as there had been in their kitchen that evening. His mother was flushed and looked happier than he had ever seen her: the blood that continued to soak through the linen on her hand was most impressive, he thought, but she insisted that it barely hurt at all. Father had hovered for a little while on the brink of displeasure, but was quite unable to withstand the onslaught of excitement. So he brought out wine and raisins to add to the food that Mother had already set on the table, and even offered some to Tom. By now Tom was informing everyone that the tinners had threatened to kill him and that even so they had had to fight him long and hard before wrenching the dagger from him – so, from being a villain he was well on the way to becoming a minor hero: this untruth was the only shadow on Luke's enjoyment.

Parson helped himself to liberal quantities of Father's wine and his face was creased in smiles as he asked teasingly, 'Tell me, Margaret, what is the precise theological distinction between the theft of your husband's clothes and that of your son's dagger – you showed such a contrast in your response to both events.' But Mother only laughed and said she was not yet such a Christian that she could stand by and see her son robbed. Surely Our Lord did not intend us to be bad mothers? And Father had handed her a glass of wine and told her she would not know how to be a bad mother if she tried.

Uncle Ambrose was there, drinking wine in plenty and roaring about what he would have done to the thieves if he had only caught up with them, in a voice so loud it seemed that all Porthew must hear the story. Then Aunt Lizzie arrived and scolded Tom for being out so late, and scolded Ambrose for drinking so – and then she scolded Mother and said she must have been out of her mind even to think of chasing those men on her own.

But Parson Weaver said she was not out of her mind, only too brave for her own good. It had never occurred to Luke that his mother might be brave: in fact, he had never before heard her praised and it was a new and wholly satisfactory experience that gave him a warm glow, inside, like wine in his stomach. 'Lion-hearted,' Parson Weaver said she was. 'William Hollar, you should be a proud man; your wife is lion-hearted.'

Luke had only a very sketchy idea of what kind of a beast a lion might be, or how its heart differed from that of other animals – but such ignorance was a mere detail. Lion-hearted was a thought to lull you smiling into sleep.

15

A sky like smoke, drifting across the sun.

Since daybreak a salt wind had been blowing from the east, a cruel wind that heralded approaching winter. Margaret had been restless since first waking: Luke was fractious, ran off before she could set him to his books; Ghislain jeered – he had been encouraging the boy to mutiny; William told her sharply to stop fussing and leave them all in peace.

She left the house abruptly and walked to calm her anger through a landscape of soft russets and greens, the diluted colours of late September. The sun was white above the veil of cloud-haze, and a flock of starlings, winter migrants from the north, were flung like a swooping net across the sky. As she walked Margaret tried to recapture the serenity she had enjoyed after hearing the words of Fletcher Grey – but without success. In fact the memory was such a contrast to her present discontent it seemed a kind of mockery.

Margaret's impatient steps soon brought her to the Forge – for no better reason than that Lizzie was there and that she could not endure the thought of passing the day at Porthew. Briar, the Treloars' old brown and white dog, rose to his feet and shuffled over to greet her. As Margaret paused to fondle him she realised that there was something unusual about the place today, but she could not, just at that moment, put her finger on the cause.

Lizzie was dressed in her Sunday finery, the leaf-green worsted she had worn on her wedding day, and as she flung open the door in response to Margaret's light knock, she was all laughter and smiles . . . but her gaiety faded at the sight of her sister.

'Oh. It's you.' She stood aside to let Margaret into the kitchen but the deep frown between her eyebrows was anything but welcoming.

'Were you intending to go out?' asked Margaret, puzzled. 'Where is Ambrose?'

Lizzie began to tap the toe of her shoe against the table leg while she told Margaret in a bored voice that Ambrose and his father had both gone to Trecarne where their cousin Joseph was for ever fussing about his title to the land. Although the family had paid a small fortune to a lawyer to check the evidences, yet still Joseph clucked and fussed like a broody hen when the fox is near. 'And now that Treveryan is returned,' she said, 'the man frets more than ever. I hope I never hear talk of evidences again in all my life.'

'Treveryan is back?'

'He arrived at Rossmere yesterday.'

Margaret said nothing. It occurred to her then that the house was unusually quiet.

'How is William?' asked Lizzie dutifully.

'Well, thank you. And Ambrose?'

'Well.'

Again the silence, that silence which was beginning to make Margaret feel uncomfortable.

Lizzie said, 'I trust you've got rid of that thief you took in on St Ewan's Day?'

'He still sleeps in the barn. But he makes himself very useful.'

'I hope your hand is better.'

'It's healing nicely.'

'And the work on the new room of your house?'

'Slow, but – Lizzie, what is it? What's the matter?'

Lizzie turned away crossly. At that moment a volley of barks could be heard from the front of the house, shattering the silence.

'Where is everyone?' asked Margaret. 'Where is Mistress Treloar? The children?'

Lizzie sighed, as though Margaret's questions were really very irksome. 'She's gone over to Coverack for a few nights. Her sister has been poorly ever since the twins were born last month. And the serving-girl has taken the children to visit her mother for the day. She likes to return home sometimes – and *I* enjoy the peace and quiet.'

Margaret was on the verge of saying that in that case she would disturb her no longer when there was the sound of horse's hoofs, and part of a horse's flank, with a man's well-booted leg across it, appeared beyond the tiny window. A masculine voice could be heard above the noise of the still-barking dog.

'Be quiet, damn you, Briar! Stop your noise or you'll frighten my mare!'

Margaret thought she recognised the voice and, peering through the window she exclaimed, 'Heavens above, it's Nicolas Sutton. He must be looking for Ambrose, how very annoying he's not here.'

There was a loud rapping at the door. Slowly, and with apparent reluctance, Lizzie went to open it. 'My husband is not at home,' she announced at once in a voice that was pitched just a little too loud.

Nicolas Sutton, stooping to avoid hitting his head as he stepped through the low doorway, said cheerfully, 'I should hope n—'

'But my sister is here,' Lizzie interrupted swiftly.

Margaret emerged from the shadows by the empty fireplace.

'Mistress Hollar,' said Nicolas coldly.

There was a long silence. Lizzie, who was fidgeting with the handle of the cooking pot, said at length, 'I believe that pick axe you brought last week is mended now. I can look for it in the Forge.'

'Thank you,' said Nicolas, suddenly polite, 'I am sorry to have missed your husband. There are several items I should pay him for.'

'Lizzie, aren't you going to offer Mr Sutton some ale?'

Still examining the handle of the cooking pot with undue interest Lizzie asked in a manner that was almost surly, 'Mr Sutton, would you care for some ale?'

'Thank you.'

She fetched the ale and handed it to him without once lifting her eyes above the level of her hands. Embarrassed by the awkwardness and the silence, Margaret said, 'I understand Mr Treveryan is staying with you at Rossmere?'

Nicolas nodded. 'Since his arrival he has been entertaining us all with tales of his travels. My wife has been agreeably terrified with stories of pirates and shipwreck and man-eating natives.'

'Did his wife come with him?'

'She remains in Plymouth.' Nicolas took a mouthful of ale, glanced quickly at Lizzie and then asked, 'Are you fully recovered from your encounter with the tinners?'

'My hand is almost healed.'

'A bad business. I only wish they had been apprehended; then I could have dealt with them as they deserved.'

Lizzie's foot twitched with impatience. 'Mr Sutton,' she said, 'if you have finished your ale –'

'This very instant, Mistress Treloar. You can find the mended pick axe for me?'

Lizzie swept out of the kitchen and Nicolas Sutton, with a brief and amused smile of farewell to Margaret, followed. They were gone for some time, time enough for Margaret to conclude that in this instance at least, two and two almost certainly made four.

After a while she heard murmuring voices, low and conspiratorial, outside the house, hoof-beats fading into the distance – and then any doubts that might have remained were swept aside by the expression on Lizzie's face when she finally came back into the kitchen.

'Lizzie, how can you be so foolish!' she exclaimed at once.

Lizzie tilted her head defiantly. 'What are you so hot and bothered about? You know I always look after customers if Ambrose is not here.'

'Have you lost your senses, Lizzie? And Nicolas Sutton of all people! If Ambrose ever found out, he'd kill you both for sure, you know he would!'

Lizzie's defiance began to waver. 'Ambrose is too stupid to see what happens right under his nose. He'll never suspect . . .' Her voice faded into uncertainty.

'I hope to God you're right.' Margaret stared at her sister, frowning. 'Oh Lizzie, what in Heaven's name induced you to take such a terrible risk?'

Lizzie slumped down on a little stool, wrapped her arms around her chest as she had done when she was a child and something had made her unhappy. 'Don't think badly of me, Mattie, please don't. I couldn't bear that.'

'But why – ?'

'I never intended to . . . It was pleasant to be flattered but that was all. And then, one time, when I knew no one could ever find out and I thought, there's no harm just once. Ambrose will never know. But I am very discreet, no one will ever find out.'

Margaret said nothing.

'Oh, it's all very well for you to stand there and look so disapproving. William is practically a gentleman himself and though you never talk about it I'm sure he's gentle enough and knows how to please a wife –'

Margaret ignored this.

'And Ambrose – ?'

Lizzie looked away. 'He's never deliberately unkind. But he has no idea . . . And there's such a strength to him that sometimes he frightens me, though I'd never let him know that he does. Last week he killed a dog with a single blow of his hand and all because its yapping annoyed him. Have you ever noticed Nicolas Sutton's hands?'

No, Margaret had not.

Before she left she endeavoured to convince Lizzie that she was not disapproving, only worried at what might happen if her liaison ever became public knowledge.

'Don't worry about me,' said Lizzie, as they bid each other goodbye, 'no one will ever find out about us. I'm not so besotted that I'd risk everything for the fellow even if he does have a fine way with words.'

'And a gentleman's hands,' added Margaret with a smile.

But as she walked away from the Forge she was more puzzled and restless than before. Not yet ready to return to Porthew, she decided to take the long road back to town, the route that led past the crossroads by the holy well.

Margaret was not the only person to be muddled that September day when clouds trailed like smoke across the sun. For Dorcas Pym it seemed the world had ended abruptly three days before (though she herself had no way of reckoning the passage of time).

The only world she had ever known was small enough: the shack on the wide moors under the still wider and ever-changing sky. Sometimes it was a warm and friendly world and she lay on her back and listened to the crickets and sang to the skylarks overhead; but at other times the rain and the wind beat against their home and Mother fussed and Father fretted and water poured in through the roof and there was no food to eat. On those unhappy days Dorcas huddled in her corner and pulled her patched coverlet up to her chin. There was no warmth in the coverlet, but it was always a comfort.

On the morning Father did not wake up, even her coverlet lost its power to make her feel safe. Dorcas pinched Father, and shouted in his ear, but when Mother came over she made a noise like a gull's cry and told her he was dead. Dorcas did not believe her for a long time. Then Mother told her she must put him in a hole in the ground.

Dorcas did not want to dig the hole.

'I'm tired,' she complained, 'I won't dig any more.'

Her mother's sharp fist punched her in the back. 'You must,' she said, 'before They find him.'

Dorcas glanced anxiously over her shoulder and dug until her hands were blistered and her shoulders ached. Her life had been haunted by terror of Them – though who They were, or what They might do, she did not know. She did know that They had once forced her father to move from his home, that They blamed Father for every mishap, a child's sickness or a barren cow. She could not remember what They looked like. In her imagination They appeared as part men, part huge black crows, and often she would stand watching the wide rim of the horizon, fearful that a flock of huge crow-men would come striding over the yellow moor grass and pluck out Father's eyes with their beaks. Once she had seen a grey-headed crow pulling out the eyes of a young lamb. She must dig the hole so that Father's eyes might stay in his own head.

So the hole was dug and Father, no longer looking like Father any more and smelling strangely, was placed inside and then there was more work to be done to cover him up. And all the while Dorcas moaned because her hands and shoulders burned and because it seemed so strange to be throwing earth on those staring eyes, into that grinning, toothless mouth.

'Now I'm hungry,' announced Dorcas when the job was done.

'There's nothing for us here,' said her mother, 'my sister's boy will have to help us.'

Dorcas was more confused than ever when her mother told her they must leave Father alone in the ground and go somewhere else. She had never known that Somewhere Else existed and could not imagine it. She stood and watched and rubbed her coverlet against her cheek thoughtfully while Mother gathered up various items and wrapped them into a bundle. She wanted Father to get up out of the ground and be himself again.

'We'll come back soon,' she said hopefully, as Mother thrust a bundle into her arms and told her to get moving. Mother only grunted.

Dorcas did not much like to walk, but whenever she tried to slow down or stop her mother poked her with a stick. Dorcas looked behind her and the shack had disappeared. It seemed to her that it had been swallowed in the yellow mouth of the moor and she was frightened.

Towards evening they reached another house. Dorcas had never seen any house but theirs and she examined this one with interest. It was very big and had a proper chimney.

They slept that night in a hay-rick and in the morning a man came with a dog and chased them away. Dorcas found walking easier that day because Mother no longer took long steps; instead she shuffled along like a hobbled pony and Dorcas ambled contentedly beside her.

Now there were trees growing beside the road, green fields and more and bigger houses. 'We'll try here,' said Mother and Dorcas noticed that her voice had grown softer too. After Mother had shuffled up to the door and rapped her bony knuckles against it, a woman came and peered out at them. She had red hair and a cross face and when Mother spoke to her she looked even crosser and gestured to them to stay outside. She vanished for a few moments and Dorcas was busy watching a couple of black beetles lurch over the stony path when she came back with a pitcher of milk and some bread. The woman shook her head when she saw how Mother and Dorcas were so hungry they both tried to drink from it at the same time, and told them to go away and leave hard-working folk in peace.

The bread and the milk had made Dorcas's middle feel so strange that she wanted to sit down for a while but Mother prevented her. When they had walked a little further along this road that seemed never-ending, Dorcas glanced behind her and saw that someone was following them. It was a man with red hair like the woman who had given them food. Dorcas thought he might have bread and milk for them as well so she looked back over her shoulder and smiled.

He smiled back and rolled his eyes at her as if he was trying to tell her something. Then he lengthened his stride and caught up with them at a place beside a little wood where two roads met.

Dorcas hesitated, wondering which road her mother would choose, and the young man with the red hair caught hold of her arm. 'Come with me,' he said in an odd sort of voice, 'I'll get you food.'

Dorcas was brightening at the word food and expected her mother to be pleased as well. But instead the old woman gestured him away angrily. 'Leave the girl be!'

The man wasn't frightened of Mother at all and laughed at her. 'Come with me,' he said to Dorcas again, and began tugging at her arm. This time, when the old woman intervened to stop him, he pushed her so hard that she sat down suddenly on the ground. He laughed again at that – and Dorcas laughed too, without knowing exactly why. Her mother was struggling to rise, but her legs seemed suddenly as weak as straw and she sat helplessly on the damp turf while the youth with the red hair continued to pull Dorcas towards a gap in the hedge.

She found herself stumbling into a field where a few sheep were cropping the grass placidly. 'Food?' queried Dorcas hopefully, but the man's smile no longer seemed so friendly and his hands dug into her shoulders.

'You do as I say,' he told her, and then he pushed her on to the ground.

'Mother?' asked Dorcas, but he told her roughly to stop her noise. Then he tore her dress so that her skin was exposed to the cold air and Dorcas was more frightened than ever and wished he would go away, wished she had her coverlet and could pull it over her head and block him out altogether. Wished she was back in their house on the moors with the skylarks and the friendly sea of grass.

Not understanding what had gone wrong, Dorcas began to whimper, but the man jabbed his fist against her mouth and told her to stop her noise. Then he was on top of her, squashing the air from her chest and one of his hands pulled her skirt up and her legs were cold. Then he pushed something hard and painful into the hidden place between her legs and began to rock and grunt and Dorcas grew so hot and muddled that she forgot even to be afraid. She shut her eyes and tried to pretend that she was at home again.

She had no idea how long the rocking lasted. She only knew that he suddenly squeezed her shoulder so tightly that it hurt and at the same time he made a sighing noise as if all the air had been suddenly whacked out of his body, the moving stopped and it was quiet again, so that she could hear the sound of her own faint moaning and the sheep snatching at the short grass near by.

The burning thing that he had pushed up between her legs, right into her body, fell out, went away and the red-haired man sat up and adjusted his breeches. Dorcas remembered that he had mentioned food earlier, and the thought was so cheering that she almost forgot the fiery soreness of her body.

'Food now?' she asked.

He stood up and, when he looked down at her now, his smile was no longer friendly. 'Just a whore,' he said, 'that's all you are.'

'Yes,' said Dorcas, not understanding.

He laughed. 'I'll be back,' he said, 'I'll bring you food.' And with that he turned and strode away across the field, whistling cheerfully.

Dorcas, following him with her eyes, could see in the distance a church spire and beyond that something that glittered strangely. A vague suspicion came to her that she must have reached the end of the world.

The pounding in her chest and the hot muddled feeling in her head were beginning to ebb away when Dorcas stood up. There was that sticky feeling between her legs that she had when the bleeding came. She went back through the gap in the hedge and found her mother, still sitting where they had left her, beside the road.

'Help me up.'

But no sooner had Dorcas hauled her mother to her feet than the old woman began hitting her head and shoulders and shouting at her that she was bad and wicked. Dorcas stepped backwards with a howl.

'Don't ever do that again, d'you hear me? Never, never, never! You must stop them, fight them, tell them no. Don't ever let them do it again. Do you understand that, Dorcas, do you?' And her mother would have hit her again to make sure the lesson was well learned, but Dorcas ran out of reach just in time. Gradually her mother's anger subsided into a steady stream of muttering, and Dorcas could no longer make out the words and soon she ceased to listen altogether.

Perhaps Mother was waiting for the red-haired man to come back with food. Perhaps Father had stopped being dead and was on his way to find them and take them home again. Perhaps . . . Dorcas's head buzzed with unknowns until it ached. Then she lay down on a patch of grass and pulled the coverlet over her head and pretended she was safe in her corner and that when she woke up she would find Father had caught a rabbit for them to eat.

Loud voices roused her eventually. Their harsh sound frightened her, like the cries of black crows, like Them, and she pulled the coverlet more tight around her head, but it was snatched away and suddenly there was a dazzle of light, and laughter.

She tried to laugh too. It was the man again, the one who had hurt her and promised food, and Dorcas was hopeful and frightened all at once. But now there were two other men with him, young men, not much older than she was, and they were all red-faced and laughing and behaving strangely. They carried flagons in their hands.

'Food?' Dorcas scrambled to her feet.

A small man with heavy black eyebrows and missing teeth stepped forward. 'Here,' he said, 'drink this,' and he put a thin arm around her waist and lifted the flagon to her open mouth. But he tipped it so wildly that the ale poured over her neck and chest before she had a chance to drink any and she drew back, choking.

They all laughed uproariously at this. Dorcas reached out her hands to hold the flagon for herself and try again, but then she caught sight of her mother and every thought, every emotion, was wiped clean from her mind.

Her mother was standing very still, a little distance away.

She seemed somehow to have grown taller, so that she arched over them. Spikey and tall as a solitary winter tree. And her tiny eyes were filled with the malice and hate of a whole lifetime of injustice and she unleashed a stream of curses on the men.

She cursed them with boils and plague, every kind of disease, aching joints and broken bones, fevers and agues and never-ending misery. She was wishing their wives and sisters barren or else afflicted with all the torments that childbirth could bring and then at the end of it only malformed children to show for their agony, offspring with twisted limbs and swollen heads and every kind of monstrous defect.

Too stunned to move or speak, the three men stood motionless, and listened.

She wished hunger and destitution on their families, fire and flood to destroy their homes, every kind of calamity on their farms and animals and the everlasting torments of Hell in the life to come. She wished them madness and delirium, poverty and pain, and she told them that no matter how far they ran, no matter where they tried to hide and escape, her curses would find them out and reach into the four corners of the earth and to the end of their blighted days.

The little man with the missing teeth licked his dry lips. He glanced uneasily at his red-haired companion. 'You never told us about this,' he muttered, 'you never said nothing about the old witch.'

The third man, a shambling youth with watery eyes and a loose, lolling mouth, turned to go. 'We'd best leave them be, I reckon.'

But the red-head put out his arm to stop them. He was breathing quickly. He took a swig from the flagon he was carrying and then said, 'She's no witch. Just look at her. If she had any kind of magic powers she'd not have come so low.'

'It's not worth the risk.'

'What risk? All right then, watch me.' He caught hold of Dorcas and pulled her to his side. 'Show us your magic powers, then, old woman, stop me now if you know how.'

'Take your hands off my daughter or –'

'Or what? I've already laid a good deal more than my hands on your precious daughter and you could not stop me. She's just a whore and –'

'Don't touch her!'

The red-haired man only laughed and caught hold of the shoulder of Dorcas's dress and pulled it. There was a tearing sound, the dress fell, exposing one large, pale breast. The two other men laughed and seemed to be regaining their confidence. Dorcas looked around in panic and grinned, wanting to share the fun, afraid of angering her mother.

'There you are!' he jeered. 'No magic power, just a pile of talk. I told you not to worry. The girl is ours for the taking.'

At that Dorcas's mother barked like a wild dog and lunged towards him, arms raised as if to strike, but the red-haired man intercepted the blow and struck her in the belly twice in rapid succession and with such force that she crumpled on to the ground. The other two men cheered loudly and one of them even ventured a kick against her prostrate body.

An odd silence followed. The three men watched the old woman carefully, half-expecting sudden thunder or boils or griping pain, some sign that her curses had power after all. But she did not move.

'Dorcas?' she muttered faintly, staring up towards the cloud-hazy sky.

Dorcas started to go to her, but eager hands restrained her.

'She don't want you now,' said the small man, 'we'll take care of you.'

'Drink some ale. Forget the old woman.'

Obediently, Dorcas drank the ale and hoped for bread, but she found she could not forget her mother who lay so strangely on the rough grass beside the road and stared up into the smoke-veiled sky.

Margaret, coming over the brow of the hill and beginning the descent towards Porthew, heard the commotion before she could see its cause. Drunken laughter, cheering and a low whimpering sound . . . her first thought was that she had unluckily stumbled on an improvised badger baiting or a dog fight, but then she realised that the usual eager yaps and barks were missing.

As she approached the place where the two roads met, she stopped. Three youths and a girl . . . but the girl was grinning as though she was a willing participant even though they appeared to be dragging her towards a gap in the hedge: those vague moaning sounds could perhaps have been excitement as well as fear.

But then Margaret noticed the old woman, dead as a pile of sticks, lying on the ground, and she saw that the girl was struggling to escape the three men and go to the woman. And as Margaret stared down at the corpse, an old memory stirred: a shrill voice that had warned her, 'You'll scream for all to hear when the powder begins to burn,' the old man with eyebrows like little pointed hats and the miserable shack on the moors, their filthy daughter with nothing but empty bone where her brain should be. She remembered Father Pym's question as he hoisted the child in his arms. 'The lilies of the field, yes yes, but what will become of my child when I am gone?'

This, then, was the answer: his daughter was to be dragged into a field by three drunken youths while her mother lay dead and forgotten on the public road.

'Hoo, hoo!' said Dorcas. 'Mother! No!'

Margaret caught her breath. Pity and horror and anger gusted through her with such force that she was shaking. Perhaps it was her recent success with the tinners that made her decide to tackle the youths herself rather than go for help in Porthew. Most probably her shock and outrage were too powerful to allow room for fear.

'Bob Dawkins! Leave that poor girl be!'

He whirled round at the sound of his name and his companions, startled, paused in their struggle. But they did not release their grip on their victim.

'Let go of her at once!'

The fair-haired youth looked sheepish and his face flushed a dull red. The small man glanced questioningly at their leader. Bob Dawkins did not hesitate.

'Don't you go meddling in what doesn't concern you, *Mistress* Hollar. Get on home.' Then he turned to the others. 'There's no worry,' he told them, 'she's all alone. I'll deal with her.' And they took advantage of Dorcas's momentary distraction to pull her through the gap in the hedge.

The man with the black eyebrows put out his foot and tripped Dorcas, sending her sprawling sideways across the ground. He sank down with his knees across her chest and hitched up the fabric of her dress.

It was at that moment when Margaret remembered her name. 'Dorcas!' she said.

Hearing her name, Dorcas turned wild eyes in the direction of the voice. She heard the anger and assumed it must be directed at her for doing this strange thing that had made her mother so furious earlier. She struggled to speak, to free herself, but there was ale dribbled over her face and her tormentor was prodding that hot and sticky place between her legs; and she was muddled and fussed and wanted to giggle and to weep all at the same time.

'Let her go!' Margaret insisted, and tried to force her way past Bob Dawkins but he stretched out his arms to block her path and said, 'The girl's a half-wit, she doesn't mind. It's only a bit of harmless fun.'

For a brief moment his contempt made Margaret so angry she could not speak, but then she heard Dorcas cry out and, at the sound of her pain, Margaret put her hands against Bob Dawkins's chest to push him out of her way. 'How dare you treat her so, how dare –!' But before she could finish her sentence he had flung down the flagon he was carrying and caught hold of her wrists and drove her back into the road.

'Damned interfering busybody, you never know when to leave well alone, do you? It's time you learned not to go putting your nose in where it doesn't belong and spoiling other folk's fun,' he snarled. And his pinched face was so twisted up with malice that for the first time Margaret forgot Dorcas and felt a tremor of fear for herself.

'Let go my hands, Bob Dawkins!'

But he only tightened his grip and Margaret saw, too late, that he was very drunk indeed, too drunk to consider what he was doing as he called to his companion, 'Spence, leave the half-wit, come and help me teach this one a lesson!'

'Are you gone mad, Bob Dawkins?' she gasped. And then she realised that it was a kind of madness, worse than madness, he was oblivious to everything except a heady sense of power over those weaker than himself.

He was taunting her and pushing her backwards along the road. Margaret half-slipped in the damp grass, then he released her hands and she turned to escape only to find the fair-haired youth blocking her path and gazing at her with a slack-jawed fascination.

'Get out of my way!' she shouted, but he only laughed and pushed her back towards Bob Dawkins.

'Shout all you like, no one will hear you. Not here.' He wasn't angry any more; he was enjoying himself. 'You've become so proud now, haven't you, *Mistress* Hollar, but I remember you, Mattie Pearce, when you were no better than the rest and everybody knew it.'

'Stop it!'

He was smiling now. Margaret raised her arms to fight him off but they were caught from behind and pinned beside her waist by the other man. She could not see him but she could hear his gurgling laugh and on Bob Dawkins's freckled face she saw, to her horror, that same expression of fascination and anticipated pleasure that she had seen so many times before when there were badgers to be baited or when a dog fight was nearing its gruesome end.

'Stop!' she screamed again and tried to twist her face away but his hands gripped the sides of her head and forced her to look at him and his mouth was grinning and confident and very close to hers.

And the next moment there was pandemonium and a man's voice shouting and a noise like thunder and Bob Dawkins's face rose up before her like a freckled moon. He was grinning no longer. His mouth was a round O of shock as the rider dragged him by the scruff of the neck and then tumbled to the ground on top of him. Bob Dawkins was too stunned to fight back, he yelped with pain and tried to shield his face from the shower of blows until a brief lull in the onslaught gave him the opportunity to scramble to his feet and hobble away.

The second man had let go of Margaret's arms and, with a grunt of rage, he threw himself against the stranger, punching and kicking with all the force of thwarted pleasure. The stranger retaliated with a blow across his face with his riding whip which brought the blood pouring down over his eyes. The third youth, the wiry fellow with the black eyebrows who had been occupied with Dorcas, heard the general commotion and, assuming that they had been discovered by a large force of men, he fled across the open field, holding up his breeches as he ran.

The horseman watched their flight, an expression of disgust on his face. He was breathing heavily. Then he stooped to pick up his hat, dusted off its brim, and walked over to retrieve his horse which had been watching with startled eyes from a little distance away. Only when he had soothed his mare did he look across to Margaret who stood motionless.

'I thought I recognised you,' he said, walking over to her, 'it's not everyone I'd tackle three drunken rogues for. Are you hurt?'

She recognised his voice at once. His face had grown thinner in the eight years since she had seen Richard Treveryan last and the rebellious youth had been transformed into a brisk and confident man. Now that he was the master of six ships (not the fifty of popular myth) his fine clothes were no longer a matter of ostentation: he was accustomed to have always the best of everything.

At that particular moment Margaret was aware of none of this. She only knew that she had been humiliated and, now that the danger was past, extraordinarily frightened. Her whole body was trembling and there was a tightness in her chest that made each breath difficult.

'Oh!' she gasped. 'You didn't need to – always fighting – the only solution –'

The anger that she had felt for Dorcas's attackers was now diverted towards this man who had witnessed her humiliation.

His eyes scanned her face. He frowned. 'You surely didn't expect me to ride on past?' he queried.

'Oh, how dare you –!'

In an attempt to steady her, Richard put his hand on her arm, but his gesture had the opposite effect and she shook him off angrily. 'Don't touch me!'

'I only meant –' He shrugged and turned away. Sensing that Margaret needed time to collect herself he spent a little

379

while soothing his mare by stroking the soft velvet of her nose and murmuring the wordless sing-song phrases that grooms use.

After a while he said, 'Are you all right now?'

'I – I think so.'

'Good.'

'I did not mean to shout at you.'

'I forgive your wretched ingratitude.' He was smiling.

It was only then that he noticed the corpse lying in the grass beside the track. 'My God, what is that?'

Margaret took a deep breath and fought back the urge to scream and weep. 'I believe it is . . . I believe it was a woman called Mother Pym. Her husband is a wise man, some credit him with magic powers. They live on the moors so I do not know what . . . she must have died trying to protect her daughter.'

'Her daughter? Tell me slowly now what happened, and how you became involved.'

'Dorcas . . .' The sound of low moans coming from beyond the hedge brought Margaret back from the brink of hysteria. She went through the gap in the hedge and found the girl sitting with her legs splayed out on the damp grass. She had pulled her skirts down around her knees but had made no attempt to cover the upper part of her body; her dress was so torn that it would probably have been useless anyway. She was hugging her stomach, rocking herself backwards and forwards and crooning to comfort herself. Margaret stared at her, fascinated and appalled by the sight of those almost translucent white breasts, by something more vulnerable than nakedness. Dorcas glanced up then shrank away from the expected blow.

'I didn't want –' she pleaded.

Margaret slid the shawl from her own shoulders and laid it over the girl's exposed flesh. 'Come,' she said, 'they've gone now. You don't need to be frightened any more.'

Still Dorcas rocked. 'Mother –' she whimpered, 'I want Mother.'

Margaret reached down gently to help her to her feet but Dorcas shrank away from her with a squeal of fear.

'Please, Dorcas,' said Margaret, 'you can't stay here.'

Richard had come to stand in the gap in the hedge. After watching Margaret's effort for a moment he commented in disbelief, 'You took a risk for the sake of that creature?'

'They'd not have harmed me,' said Margaret firmly, 'it was only the girl –'

'You are too sanguine; they seemed to me to have every intention of doing you harm. But now that your efforts have saved the girl, I suggest you leave her alone.'

'Leave her?'

'Why not?' He peered at Dorcas, who turned to him fearfully and attempted a placatory grin. 'My God,' he murmured incredulously, 'they must have been at sea a year or more to set about such a drab.'

Margaret had a suspicion that it was the girl's vulnerability, her only too obvious weakness, that had been her main attraction. She herself found she was unsettled by the air of helplessness and misery exposed that hung about Dorcas as richly as her most potent smell. She turned away from her and, to cover her embarrassment, she said sharply, 'You ought to speak of her more courteously or you're no better than they.'

He laughed. 'I have never claimed to be better than anyone in my whole life.' He was watching Margaret carefully. 'I remember . . . I danced with you on your wedding day. Mistress –?'

'Hollar.'

'You read Catullus.'

'I still do.'

'You were expecting a child.'

'My son Luke.'

'And your husband was rather too hospitable.'

'And you repaid him with unforgivable rudeness.' But Margaret was smiling.

'Did I? I'm sure you exaggerate. But never mind, now I have repaid him by rescuing his wife from unspeakable horror so he should be for ever in my debt. If you are now sufficiently recovered, Mistress Hollar, I shall return you to the safety of your home.'

'But what about Dorcas? And her mother?' Margaret's smile vanished abruptly.

Richard sighed. 'The old woman is beyond earthly help.

381

We'll have to alert someone to deal with her body. And as for the girl, she can shift for herself somehow.'

'How can you be so heartless?'

'Heartless? And just when I thought I was being most considerate. Ah well, if you are seriously concerned about the girl, surely you can send someone from Porthew to deal with her. What about her family?'

Margaret turned to Dorcas and asked gently, 'Dorcas, where is your father?'

Dorcas was so alarmed at being spoken to directly that Margaret had to repeat the question twice more before she was understood. Then the girl bellowed like a frightened cow. 'Hoo hoo! In the ground! Father is in the ground.' Margaret tried to soothe her, but without success.

Richard backed off. 'There, you see, this is what comes of playing the good Samaritan. Leave her to the overseers, they can deal with her.'

Margaret looked first at his scornful face and then at Dorcas's abject misery. It occurred to her that if more strangers were to lay hands on the girl that day it was likely that her few wits would be destroyed for ever.

'I cannot abandon her now, Mr Treveryan. I am grateful for your assistance earlier, but believe me, I can manage this alone now.' She turned back to the whimpering creature huddled in the grass. 'Dorcas, listen to me, please listen. You cannot remain here, it will be dark soon and then . . . I shall take you to Porthew and there we can decide what is best . . .'

But the sound of Margaret's gentle pleading fanned Dorcas to wilder displays of grief.

'You see. Your kindness only makes her worse. Leave her.'

'Don't be ridiculous, I couldn't do that.'

'Why not? The country is full of such unfortunates.'

Margaret ignored him. 'Dorcas, please, try to get up and come with me.'

Richard watched her for a few moments before turning to go. 'If you insist on martyring yourself in such a useless cause then I shall leave you to it –'

'Good.'

'– I have plenty of better ways of occupying my time. But since I am going to Porthew anyway I shall stop by and

382

inform your husband that you might require some assistance –'

He had reached the gap in the hedge but with a sudden, 'No! Please –!' Margaret's urgent appeal brought him to an immediate halt. He turned.

'What is it?'

'There's no need to tell my husband. I mean . . . please don't talk of this to anyone . . . I don't want . . .'

'No?' He was intrigued by her sudden distress. 'But your husband, surely –'

Margaret gazed at him helplessly. 'Why? He would not . . . and it's over now. I don't see . . .'

She broke off. Richard drew closer. He saw that the very thought of telling anyone else of what had happened filled her with shame and dread, that she was suddenly on the verge of tears.

He put out a hand to comfort her but she turned abruptly and sank to her knees beside the girl. 'Dorcas,' she begged, 'Dorcas, please get up, you must . . .'

Dorcas howled louder than ever.

Richard hesitated for a few moments and then, raising his hands in a gesture of despair he said, 'This is hopeless, you'll never shift her that way.'

'What else can I do? I cannot leave her.'

'Here, I'll help you.' He leaned over Dorcas and took her by the shoulders. 'Now, you loathsome female, you must stand up and –'

'Do not talk to her like that! We don't need your help, Mr Treveryan. Leave her be, you are so rough!'

'Heaven help me, Mistress Hollar, I have no need of two hysterical females at once. Go and wait for me by my horse.' He gripped her hand and pulled her to her feet.

'But you must not –'

'For God's sake stop telling me what to do. If you don't keep out of the way while I sort this out I swear I shall use my horse-whip to make the girl see sense.'

Margaret stared at him in horror. Her reason told her that he was only speaking that way in order to shock her into compliance, but he was looking at her with such anger that she could not be altogether sure. Slowly she walked over to stand by the gap in the hedge and watched, ready at the slightest hint of danger to go to Dorcas's rescue once again.

'That's better.' Richard turned his attention once more to the wailing girl and caught hold of her chin, forcing her to look at him.

'Dorcas!' he commanded. 'Stand up, d'you hear me? Stand up or I shall send the goblins to stick pins in you!'

Dorcas had opened her mouth to wail afresh but at this she gulped, stared at him wide-eyed and, after only the briefest hesitation, she scrambled to her feet. Margaret's shawl fell to the ground; Richard picked it up and draped it once more over her bony shoulders.

'Now, Dorcas,' he continued grimly, 'although you are surely the most abject specimen it has ever been my misfortune to set eyes on, Mistress Hollar has taken it into her head to take pity on you. So you must do as I say and stay close behind me and not make a sound. Do you understand?'

She understood enough to nod her head vigorously and to follow so close behind him as he walked from the field that once or twice she actually trod on his heels.

'I think your methods are despicable,' said Margaret as he looped his horse's reins across his arm.

'They work.' Then he grinned. 'You're only annoyed because I succeeded where you were failing. Admit it.' When she refused to do so he said simply, 'You may ride behind me.'

She drew back. 'But what about Dorcas?'

'She must follow on foot.'

'But that's –'

'You surely don't expect my mare to carry three?'

Margaret was annoyed. 'Even you must be able to see the poor girl is on the point of collapse. Let her ride with you, then, and I shall –'

'If you expect me to share my horse with that creature you could not be more wrong.'

'Then you ride alone and I shall walk with her.'

Richard sighed with exasperation. 'Let this be a warning to me for attempting to help the most argumentative woman in the – Mistress Hollar, I find that my small reserves of gallantry are all used up.'

'And what about Mother Pym? We can't just leave her –'

'Why not?'

'Oh, you're impossible!'

This time Richard's annoyance was too strong for speech. He grasped Margaret around the waist and hoisted her up on to his mare. She was obliged to pull herself into a sitting position or risk falling back into his arms. He took the reins and led the horse to the stile so that he could mount up beside her, saying, 'Your contrariness has gained you the saddle at least.'

'I would much rather walk.'

He ignored her and turned to Dorcas who was staring up at him fearfully. 'And as for you, Miss Dorcas, make sure you follow close behind and keep away from my horse's hoofs. And if you stray from the road then all the hobgoblins from Hell will come and gobble you up.'

'Don't worry, Dorcas,' Margaret reassured her, 'he doesn't mean it. For some reason it amuses Mr Treveryan to play the monster.'

'Then be grateful for monsters, Mistress Hollar.' And he nudged his horse to a slow walk with a murmured, 'Get on, Sheba.'

They rode for a while in silence. Margaret was fuming – or at any rate, she assumed that her bothersome emotion must be anger; besides, she felt herself to be at such a disadvantage, seated in front of him on his high dark horse, that she bit back the angry words. Once or twice she twisted around to see that Dorcas was still following, but when she did so it was impossible to avoid noticing that Treveryan's face was only inches away from her own and that his eyes were ready to look directly into hers. After the second such occasion she resolved to keep her gaze firmly fixed on the road ahead.

Richard gathered the reins into his left hand and, with his right, he lifted her bandaged hand.

'You have injured yourself?' he queried.

'It was a knife wound. A . . . dagger.'

Without turning to look at him, she knew that the beginnings of a smile were spreading across his face. 'You lead an exciting life, Mistress Hollar.'

'No, my life is usually very dull. But on St Ewan's Day

some men stole my son's Cordoba dagger and since it was the most precious possession he has ever had . . .'

'Let me guess. You followed them and fought them single-handed and retrieved it for him, sustaining an injury to your hand in the process. Am I right?'

Margaret considered for a few moments but eventually, 'Well . . . yes,' she conceded.

He burst out laughing. 'Then thank heavens my business delayed me in Plymouth and I was not tempted to become embroiled in your adventures on that occasion at least. Are your days always so turbulent?'

Margaret could not help laughing too. 'I was such a fool,' she confessed, 'I took the dagger by the blade. It's a miracle I did not lose my fingers.'

He still held her hand in his. 'And the wound is healing?' He ran his thumb along the edge of the bandage and Margaret found herself tensing suddenly. 'You must be sure to keep it clean,' he said gently.

Margaret moved her hand away. 'I am most careful.'

'Careful? Is that how you see yourself?'

'You are not so cautious, Mr Treveryan. Your own knuckles are already badly bruised.'

'And all in your defence. Those country lads have uncommonly hard skulls.'

'I'm sure I'm not to blame if you insist on solving everything by fighting. You could have sent them packing without such violence.'

'Do you think so?'

'Yes.'

'Then you are wrong. Besides, I enjoyed thrashing them.' Margaret was on the verge of protesting but then she saw that this was said on purpose to annoy her so she stayed silent. 'As it is, they have escaped far too lightly. They should be properly punished.'

'I know. But . . .'

'If you do not want to report it in Porthew then I shall tell Nicolas Sutton. I'm sure he will deal with it discreetly.'

'But even so . . . I cannot bear the thought . . . I mean, I know the men, at least one of them and I'm sure they would never . . . if we could only forget about it and . . . and then my husband need never know . . .'

386

Her voice trailed away hopelessly.

Richard asked quietly, 'Are you afraid of your husband?'

'No, of course not . . . only . . . he would not . . .' Again her words faltered to a halt. She had no intention of telling him that her husband already despised her quite enough, that she did not wish to provide him with fresh cause for contempt. She ended lamely, 'But it would only make him worry, and where's the sense in that?'

Richard was silent for a few moments before asking, 'You said you know these men.'

'Bob Dawkins, the red-haired one, he is a local man. His uncle owns the mill but his family has fallen on hard times and he has always been a trouble-maker. Nothing serious until now. I believe the other two are from Coverack way.'

'All of five miles' distance, they are practically foreigners,' Richard mocked. 'Very well, if you insist, I shall deal with the rogues myself.'

'Deal with?' she queried in alarm. 'But you must promise –'

'I promise nothing and you, Mistress Hollar, are in no position to expect promises. But, if it makes you happy, I shall see first what can be achieved with words alone – and I'll only subject all three to slow torture and a lingering painful death if reason fails to have effect. Does that satisfy you?'

'Only because I know now you are joking about the torture and the lingering death. I half-believed you when you threatened poor Dorcas back there.'

'You must always believe me, Mistress Hollar.'

The reappearance of Richard Treveryan in Porthew after an absence of over eight years was bound to create a stir, especially since his agent had been buying up farms and manors all over the district for some time and he now had the reputation of a man of fabulous wealth. His reappearance with Margaret Hollar seated before him on his dark mare and with the draggle-tailed Dorcas scurrying in their wake, would have caused a minor sensation had Margaret not directed him to follow the narrow lanes that led to the back of her home.

She found she was almost sorry when their slow ride drew to a close: Sheba moved with a deceptively leisurely gait and Margaret gained a sense of gentleness masking great power and potential speed. Having never ridden anything but nags and ponies before, she was amazed by the lyrical rhythm of the tall horse's walk.

'This is my home,' she said, when they reached the low wall with the apple boughs reaching into the lane and the little barn with its roof of lichen-covered slates. 'You may set us down here.'

'Very well.' Richard reined Sheba to a halt and slid down from her back. He reached up his arms to help Margaret alight and she had just begun to tell him that she needed no assistance when he placed strong hands around her waist and swung her unceremoniously down.

'I've done with arguing with you today,' he said firmly. 'You can go inside and berate your unfortunate husband.'

'Come then, Dorcas.' For Dorcas was hanging back, too terrified by both Richard Treveryan and his huge horse to ease past them and join Margaret.

He scowled at her horribly. 'Remember, Dorcas, I shall be watching you always. Obey Mistress Hollar in every detail or the goblins will come in the night and –'

'Stop!' protested Margaret, as Dorcas squeaked with fear and fled past him to cling to Margaret's arm. 'Pay no attention to his bullying.'

Richard sighed. 'Get rid of her as soon as you can,' he advised, 'she'll be nothing but a burden to you otherwise. There must be someone who can find her work. Do you know which is her parish?'

Margaret was irritated. 'I can decide what to do without your advice,' she said tersely, but then, fearing that she had been too brusque, she added, 'though I am truly grateful for your help earlier.'

An almost imperceptible movement of his head, signifying his acceptance of her thanks. Margaret considered now that she should leave him and go into the house to deal with Dorcas but instead she said, 'Do you want me to bandage your hand so it is less painful on your ride home? Even though it *was* your fault for choosing to fight with them, I do feel myself partly responsible.' And now she found that

388

she was smiling, in spite of herself. 'You have been very kind, Mr Treveryan.'

'I am not often charged with kindness,' he said, 'I hope you will regard this as an aberration.'

'What nonsense.' She took her kerchief and wound it tightly around the knuckles of his right hand. 'How does that feel?'

'I do believe it hurts rather more than it did before.'

'Have I tied it too tight?'

'Maybe just a little.'

Richard was making the intriguing discovery that it was agreeable to be fussed over by Mistress Hollar. She looked up and met his eyes smiling into hers.

'Now you are teasing again.' She tried to push his hand away but he caught hold of her bandaged one and raised it towards his lips.

'With our twin wounds we are a well-matched pair,' he said. 'However, I strongly advise you to avoid all brawls until both our hands are completely healed.'

'I abhor fighting,' she said, pulling her hand away. 'Come, Dorcas, and I'll see that you are made comfortable. But first you must thank Mr Treveryan for having helped us both.'

Dorcas mouthed the words 'thank you' and Richard raised his hat in mock gallantry. 'Your most reluctant servant,' he said, and Margaret, feeling herself about to grow angry again, took Dorcas by the arm and propelled her through the garden gate without another word.

Richard watched until they had vanished into the darkness of the house before mounting Sheba and riding thoughtfully away.

William Hollar was not much interested in Margaret's explanation for her arrival in Porthew on Richard Treveryan's horse and with a half-clad simpleton in tow. She told him merely that she had found Dorcas being ill-treated by some wandering vagrants and that she had been in the process of seeing them off when Treveryan arrived and offered to accompany them back to Porthew. As various versions of events circulated the town, there was much tutting over the dangerous state of the roads and several husbands forbad their wives to walk beyond the town boundaries unaccompanied; but William Hollar was not inclined to offer his wife advice concerning her safety. Nor did he protest against the arrival of Dorcas, merely commenting that since Paul Viney showed no sign of leaving, he considered they had now taken on their full complement of strays.

In fact, the larger household suited him as well as it did Margaret; each was glad of any change that reduced their suffocating proximity. Now that the building work he had begun earlier in the year was almost completed, William considered it only fitting to have servants living on the premises. Paul Viney had swiftly made himself useful and William admitted that he more than paid for his keep. He had volunteered to help in the shop, but William insisted that Ghislain was all the help he needed. Margaret announced that since William had been telling her for some time to take on a serving-girl she had found Dorcas and intended to train her to usefulness. William, who was sickened by the girl's appearance, said Dorcas could work all she liked so long as he never had to watch her doing it. And he especially refused to allow her near him at meal times. Margaret was grateful for this ban when she discovered that the girl's only real talent was eating. No sooner had Dorcas recovered from the first shock of her new life than she began to eat everything within reach. Whole loaves disappeared into her mouth in the time it took Margaret to fetch water from the well at the end of the street. At first Margaret was amused by her gargantuan appetite: the poor girl must be half-starved, it was pitiful; but within a week she was driven to keeping the larder door locked at all times, simply to save back sufficient food for their own meals. One night Margaret awoke from a dream in which she had caught Dorcas in the act of swallowing Mouse, her grey cat, in one huge gulp.

Guzzling huge quantities of food was Dorcas's only accomplishment. Although she followed Margaret around like a puppy and nodded dutifully whenever Margaret gave her instructions, she quickly forgot what she was supposed to be doing. Margaret soon found herself devising tasks simply to keep her occupied.

As the balmy days of late September blended into the chillier mists and winds of a Cornish October, Dorcas was often to be found in Margaret's kitchen, amicably swatting at flies and wasps.

16

Richard Treveryan stayed at Rossmere for three weeks. When he was not occupied in assessing the farms that had been purchased for him in his absence by Francis Crane, or checking accounts and legal documents, he spent most of his time with Alice Sutton.

She bore little resemblance to the muddled girl who had rejected him for Nicolas Sutton. The freshness had vanished from her face and her figure was a good deal fuller. But if her former coltish charm was gone it had been replaced by the serenity, the ease of gesture of a woman with a nursery full of healthy children, servants at her beck and call, an amiable husband and an unrivalled position in the community. And to Richard that face with its black eyebrows and the teeth that protruded slightly to rest on her lower lip was still the yardstick by which all others were measured. In his eyes she would always be beautiful.

Not that he betrayed his feelings. He played the part of the returning gentleman of wealth. Families who previously might have been tempted to commit murder rather than allow him near their daughters now welcomed him as an honoured guest. Only the best wines and the finest bedlinen were good enough for Mr Treveryan who, it was rumoured, was rich enough to buy up half the county if he wished. Several people remarked that it was a pity his mother was not alive to witness his rapid rise in the world. She had died not long after his marriage, in the fifth month of her pregnancy and Sir John, who had found her on the whole an unsatisfactory partner, did not trouble to marry for a third time. Richard considered silently that it would have taken more than money to reconcile his mother to her only surviving child. Other than that, he hardly thought of her at all.

His wealth had made him acceptable . . . but it did not

cause him to be liked. Since most of the Cornish gentry suffered from a semi-chronic shortage of ready money, his rapid success was bound to provoke a certain amount of envy; besides, his manner was too reserved and scornful for popularity. He retained his former unfortunate preference for the company of serving-men, frequently leaving the table half-way through a meal in order to enjoy conversation and a pipe with the stable-hands.

As master of his own ships he had grown accustomed to command, and none among the easy-going local families cared to criticise him. Not openly. Behind his back several gave free rein to their suspicions: to have gained so much and so quickly pointed to dishonesty beyond the traditional licence of a privateer. If he was never quite accused of piracy it was because no one cared to offend Nicolas Sutton who, although as popular as any man in the county, let it be known that Richard Treveryan was his dearest friend and he would not hear a word against him.

Nicolas was free of all envy. He would have laughed at the very suggestion. Why should he begrudge Richard his manors and farms when he himself possessed all a man could possibly wish for? – or would do on his father's death. He knew there were larger and grander houses than Rossmere; he was even prepared to believe more beautiful ones might exist, but he doubted very much if anyone had ever loved their home as much as he did the house of his birth; the house where his own children were now born, where he himself would one day die and pass the fortunate inheritance on to his eldest son. Nothing could give him more satisfaction than to see his two fair-haired boys playing in the courts and lawns where he himself had played, riding their first ponies in the meadows where he too had learned to ride. After an absence no longer than two days, he had only to ride down between the avenue of young limes and catch a glimpse of the grey slate roofs, had only to hear that echo of hoofs as he passed through the archway and into the stable-yard behind the house, to know that he was the luckiest man alive.

Nicolas's contentment was the secret of his charm. He was happy, had always been happy, and saw no reason why he should not remain in a state of contentment until the end of his days – and it pleased him that others should share his delight in living. Just why he had always had such a liking for the morose and difficult Richard Treveryan was something of a mystery to his friends – but Nicolas never gave it a moment's thought.

Second only to his love of Rossmere was Nicolas's devotion to his wife. Some time during the eight years of their marriage he had conveniently forgotten that he had not chosen her but had merely fallen in with his father's mercenary schemes. He remembered vaguely that there had once been a time when he had considered Alice Laniver to be Richard's, but he thanked Heaven that all that muddle had been resolved long ago, as soon as Richard had the good fortune to find a wealthy wife of his own. Having married Alice, for whatever reasons, Nicolas soon believed himself in love with her; it would have been tiresome to share his life and home with her under any other conditions. Besides, she was everything he could wish for: amiable to look upon, mostly good-tempered and a sturdy producer of children. And if she was occasionally irritable and cold . . . well, at times like that it was a refreshing change to ride over to the Forge at Porthew and enjoy the different but equally delightful pleasures afforded by the smith's pretty wife. And there was the added satisfaction of cuckolding the young giant. Nicolas had all but forgotten his first disastrous attempt to seduce Lizzie, but some vague recollection of Ambrose's assault must have lingered in his memory. And he remembered only too vividly the occasion when Ambrose crushed him in the stream during the hurling match: more than once he had found himself wondering if that had really been the accident everyone supposed . . . whatever the truth, it was particularly gratifying (though hardly surprising) when Lizzie whispered to him that he pleased her as her boorish husband had never done.

Alice Sutton had long suspected Nicolas's infidelities, but since she had never expected faithfulness she did not regard herself as particularly wronged. She enjoyed him when he was there, but seldom missed him when he was not. It was not through any fault of her husband's that she occasionally found the rhythm of her days just a touch monotonous.

Until Richard's arrival. The youth she had rejected was

now transformed into a formidable man of the world. He had arrived with presents for them all – but more exciting than the presents were the tales he told: stories of deserts and magical islands, of the New World and the hardships of long sea voyages. And the manner of his telling heightened her pleasure; he was dry and understated and mocked himself as often as those strange characters he had encountered.

Alice was not to know that his gifts and his fine clothes, his ostentatious wealth and fund of droll stories were designed to impress her alone. Unless her brown eyes were fixed on his face, nothing would induce him to recount the tale of his meeting with the Indian chief. And it was only to see the way her gaze travelled over his costume, absorbing every detail of the rich fabric, expert tailoring and trim of gold and silver thread, that stopped him from reverting to his more comfortable buff coat and breeches.

Alice only knew that her days were crammed more full of pleasures than Christmas. She was even persuaded to go out riding with her guest, something she usually avoided when pregnant – her habitual and present condition. Richard made many visits to his new-bought properties and on fine days she eagerly joined him.

One particularly mild and sunny morning Richard interrupted her in her still room to announce that her chestnut mare was already saddled so they could ride together to visit a farm of more than usual interest. Alice barely bothered to protest that at this harvest time of year there was more than enough to keep her busy at Rossmere, and within half an hour they passed under the archway and between the long avenue of trees whose leaves lay scattered in their path like pools of butter.

Sheba was taut with energy and several times Richard had to pull her back to keep pace with Alice's slower mount. Before her marriage Alice had had the makings of a fine horsewoman and, though she now confined her horse to a walk, Richard still considered her to be at her most attractive when out riding. She sat very upright in the saddle, her cheeks were flushed, her eyes sparkled and a stray wisp of hair had escaped to trail across her cheek. She was wearing a jacket of faded tawny velvet, expertly darned at the elbows. Richard knew that Nicolas's love of Rossmere did not extend to a love of the financial dealings necessary to keep them solvent. He guessed that Nicolas intended to try and borrow money from him: he rather thought he would agree.

They rode for a while in near silence, only remarking every now and then on what they saw around them: a field of late corn not yet gathered in; a peregrine falcon spiralling into the high blue of the sky; a wandering beggar.

'The roads are grown more dangerous than ever,' Alice commented as the beggar scurried away from the horses. 'Only last week a Porthew woman was robbed and beaten by a group of Irish vagrants. They should all be sent back to their own country, don't you agree?'

Richard was nonplussed. Alice must be referring to Mistress Hollar, the facts of her ordeal having been distorted by rumour. He was disturbed by the realisation that he had at that very moment been deep in thoughts of Mistress Hollar himself. Ever since he had played knight errant to her damsel in distress, he had found that whenever his mind was idle, thinking of nothing in particular, an image returned to him, a memory of clear grey eyes whose message was not instantly readable, of a mouth that was one moment compressed in anger, the next breaking into a smile of sheer delight. He remembered the way her voice had caught as she pleaded with Dorcas, her annoyance when he had set her on his horse. He remembered the touch of her work-roughened hands as she wrapped the kerchief over his knuckles. He remembered that when he had mounted his horse and put his arm around her he had felt the rapid beating of her heart . . .

Small wonder Richard was annoyed now. He had no inclination to squander precious moments with Alice in thoughts of Mistress Hollar. He said curtly, 'I'm sure the story has been exaggerated.'

'Joan Treworgie said it was the draper's wife. Mr Hollar is a remarkably handsome man – have you met him? No one bothers to go to Camborne for cloth any more.' Alice slid a glance at Richard, to see how he had taken this remark, but he only frowned at the knuckles of his right hand and did not speak. They rode for some time in silence.

Towards midday they reached the brow of a hill and Richard reined Sheba to a halt. He was absentmindedly caressing her thick mane as he gazed ahead and his expression was inscrutable. Alice could see nothing of great interest: a long valley stretching down to the sea, scrub and willow marking the path of a hidden stream; a poor-looking cottage beside an ivy-clad ruin; a few fields where brambles and bracken were spreading from the hedges into meagre pastures.

'We have reached our objective,' he announced as he dismounted. He lifted Alice gently to the ground and added softly, 'One day soon all this will be my home.'

She burst out laughing. '*All* this? Richard, I'm not so easily deceived. You surely haven't become so wealthy simply to live in that hovel?'

The pressure of his hand still holding hers tightened imperceptibly and she saw that he was serious and had been annoyed by her laughter. She moved closer to him and added, 'But the situation is pleasant enough.'

Richard heard the conciliation in her voice, the fear of giving offence. He was gazing down into the valley. In his imagination he saw a fine house rising up where the ruined tower now stood, a house larger and more beautiful than Rossmere, stables, a mews, gardens laid out in the Italian style.

'That hovel, as you call it, will not be there much longer.' He was talking almost to himself.

Alice wished his attention once more directed on her and she tugged slightly on his hand. 'Why should you choose this –' she was about to say 'desolate' but she checked herself just in time – 'this remote place when you might pick any house in the county?'

Richard slid her a quick glance, saw from the eager expression on her face, her shallow breathing and the slightly parted lips, that the balance had shifted between them and that she herself was still all unaware of the danger into which she was heading. Voices drifted upwards from the farm. A woman came out of the cottage as he watched and began to spread washing on the hedge. Richard raised Alice's hand to his cheek, brushed it almost thoughtfully against his lips. He felt the sudden tension of her hand and

397

saw the slow blush of colour spread across her neck and face – but he saw too that she did not draw away.

'This godforsaken farm was all my father left me,' he said slowly. 'I came here once before when you and I were still . . . when I yet believed that you and I would marry –' Alice made a half-hearted attempt to withdraw her hand but he only tightened his grip. 'I imagined then that this would be our home. There was a magic here . . . can you feel it, Alice?' He turned to look at her once again and kissed the soft flesh of her palm. 'I find I must hold on to the old dreams when no new ones come to take their place.'

He heard her smothered gasp and paused, allowing time for her to pull back if she wished. But she remained quite still, her brown eyes shining. Very gently he curved his arm around her back and guided her towards him. A shiver ran the length of her spine as her body arched its welcome. 'Oh Richard,' she said lightly, 'you always talk in such riddles. Will I ever understand you?' But as she spoke she tilted her face, inviting his kiss.

Perhaps it was too easy, he thought as he bent his head to hers; perhaps he was grown too cynical, not cynical enough . . . but when he closed his eyes this pressure of flesh on flesh was awkward, a disappointment even . . . might almost, but for the silence, have been Kitty . . . Miriam. Anyone at all.

Her lips were dry and chapped and he ran the tip of his tongue over them as he kissed her. And knew from her response that she was unlikely to resist him now, whatever he suggested. A wave of depression washed through him. Suddenly he could have wept with sadness for them all, the endless futility of it.

Aware now that he was acting a part and unpleasantly conscious of the familiar onset of self-loathing, he held her more closely, caressed her dark curls and murmured, 'Alice,' before gently releasing her.

'Oh –'

She had never seen regret on his face, was relieved to see it now.

'We should not squander our present good fortune by wishing for what might have been,' said Richard.

Alice had not felt so giddy since she was a child and

played at spinning like a top. She smoothed the brown skirts of her dress carefully, and did not quite trust herself to speak.

From the valley below where they stood came the sound of a woman's voice singing. Richard took Alice by the hand and said, 'We shall come here again when my new house is built.'

Alice was still flustered. Uncertain whether she wished to advance or retreat she settled on diversion. 'Shall we inspect the place more closely and you can tell me of your plans?'

'Not now. I have no wish to encounter the tenant.'

'Who is that?'

'A cripple whose only talent is fathering swarms of wretched children.'

'Can you force him to leave?'

'Of course. The only question is how and when.'

Both were thoughtful as they rode back towards Rossmere. The sunny morning had given way to an afternoon sombre with cloud. Richard found it gratifying to know that Alice still responded to him, especially since he believed she had never been disloyal to Nicolas before. But he had no intention of following up his success; not so much out of loyalty to his friend, but because a clandestine affair had never been any part of his imagined life with Alice. From time to time he had imagined Nicolas dead, the widow turning to him for consolation, Kitty helpfully succumbing to a fever. To cuckold Nicolas now would only debase the lost ideal that Alice had once been. He knew her well enough to know that her earlier recklessness had now given away to alarm. As they rounded the last hill and saw the harmonious slate and stone world of Rossmere spread out before them, she gave him an anxious and questioning glance. Richard was quick to offer reassurance: whatever his feelings for her might be, his affection for her husband prevented him . . .

Alice was satisfied. And, as she plunged back into the evening turmoil of children and servants, even a little elated. By then she had persuaded herself that she would never have permitted more than a single kiss – but that fleeting moment of pleasure had been a welcome reminder that although she had four children and a frequently unfaithful husband, she was an attractive woman yet.

Later, while Richard was smoking a thoughtful pipe in the company of Samuel, the chief groom, he found himself wondering briefly if it had been the need to erase the troublesome image of Mistress Hollar that had caused him to take Alice Sutton in his arms.

Three days before he was due to return to Plymouth, Richard decided that he would, after all, pay a visit to Mistress Hollar.

His intention was to return her kerchief. This task could be performed equally well by a manservant but he told himself that it was only courtesy that prompted him to go – and at the same time he could tell her how he had dealt with her attackers.

To his dismay Alice, learning he was to ride to Porthew, offered to accompany him – and for once he was not swift enough to hide his feelings. Alice was duly piqued, and was hardly reassured by his claim that he must ride to Helford afterwards, the whole journey would take all day, was sure to be disagreeable and tiring. Alice said coldly that she had a glut of quinces to attend to anyway.

Richard was thoroughly irritated as he left Rossmere: this was the first time that he had ever lied to Alice and though honesty was not a virtue that had ever been especially important to him, he had always regarded his dealings with Alice as somehow different. He had loved her once. He did not know whether he loved her now or whether it was just that she reminded him he had once been a youth capable of love – in those years before he had married a woman he despised, simply because she had properties and ships and the opportunities for greater wealth.

He was annoyed with himself for the lie and he was annoyed with Alice for not accepting it as truth. Most of all he was annoyed with Mistress Hollar for having given him the kerchief which caused the lie. He did not intend to linger at her house.

That morning had been especially trying for Margaret and she had not weathered it well. The whole house had been at sixes and sevens since first light. As if the noise and chaos and dust caused by the workmen were not enough, Paul Viney, who could usually be relied on, had earned some money the previous day chopping wood for Dame Erisey and had spent it all at once at Jack Pym's ale-house. This morning he was nursing a sore head and a sick stomach and could barely stagger down the street to fetch water. Dorcas had upset a pan of cream and tried to mop up the resulting mess with her sleeve. And when it was time for Luke to be taken to school (the church was close and he could easily walk there unattended but, left alone, the boy followed such an erratic path that he generally arrived only when the class was finishing) he disappeared into the shop where she found him seated on his father's knee and resistant to all idea of school. Ghislain had been teaching Luke a phrase in French which was thoroughly scandalous, judging from their huge amusement as Luke innocently repeated the words. When Margaret told Luke sharply that he would be late for school, Ghislain said something to William that she could not understand (was he talking French? Half the time his English sounded so foreign that she could make no sense of it) but that made William quiver with laughter. Their merriment was all because she was excluded.

'Come, Luke,' she said coldly, but Luke clung to his father and refused to leave until William promised him he might help in the shop all afternoon if he did his lessons like a good boy. Only then did Luke slide to the ground and consent to leave with Margaret, pausing briefly at the doorway to deliver a final version of the newly learned French phrase. Margaret closed the door on their mocking laughter. It was the kind of event that happened daily, several times each day. Margaret could have accepted hunger and cold sooner than the knowledge that she was a stranger in her own home.

And then, when she had changed the fretful Luke into a clean shirt, she came down to the kitchen to find that the fire had gone out and that Dorcas, who was supposed to be tending it, had instead eaten an apple pie that Margaret had prepared for their lunch.

The class had already begun but Parson Weaver, seeing

Margaret's tight-lipped expression asked, 'Has Luke been misbehaving again?'

She shrugged her annoyance.

He said, 'Remind me later to lend you that book I told you about yesterday. I'm sure you'll enjoy it.'

'Don't bother. There's such a chaos in our house just now as leaves no space for poetry.'

Luke took his place among the other children and picked up his slate. His expression had that strange look, deviously ignorant, that he always adopted when confronted with his lessons. Margaret, feeling irritation boil up inside her once again, left swiftly.

Rather than go directly home, she walked down towards the shore, to the spit of land that was known locally as Gull Rock. A boat was leaving the harbour bound for Penzance. Pale birds wheeled and floated around its rigging; all was activity on the deck. Her heart ached to be on that boat, to be free and effortless as the birds, to escape on the silken highway of the sea. Even the parson's generously loaned books were a dangerous pleasure, increasing discontent. When she was a child books had held out the promise of a richer and more varied world than the one she knew at the farm; now she sometimes doubted if such a world of passionate intensity existed anywhere – and if it did, then she was certain that she would never taste it.

She had to force herself to return home. Her narrow world that morning offered the promise of cleaning Dorcas and offering Viney a cordial for his aching head while doing her best to avoid any further contact with either William or Ghislain. The last sight she expected as she climbed the lane behind the house was that of Richard Treveryan dismounting from his tall horse. She was not sure if she was glad or sorry to see that well-dressed figure, the incongruous shock of dark hair framing his sombre face.

'Mr Treveryan, I did not expect to see you again so soon.'

'I came to make sure you have recovered from your ordeal.'

'Oh, that.' As soon as she heard his voice Margaret had decided that, on balance, she was more pleased than sorry to see him. 'If you care to step inside for a moment, I can give you a full report.'

Richard inclined his head coldly and muttered something about pressing business in Helford. However, he looped Sheba's reins over the gate post before following Margaret between carefully tended beds of herbs and into the house.

Her kitchen did not present the well-ordered scene he had been unconsciously expecting. The girl Dorcas was poking half-heartedly at a wheezing fire. Although scrubbed and reclothed in a reasonable dress, presumably an old one of her mistress's, there was still no disguising her ugliness and she gave off a pungent smell of sour milk. Seeing Richard, she grew wide-eyed with alarm and grinned her hopes that he would not be angry with her this time. The only other person in the room was a sallow-faced man who was hampered in his efforts to lift a mug of small beer to his lips by the violent trembling of his hands.

Margaret briskly disposed of them both.

'Paul, go and tend to Mr Treveryan's horse. Dorcas, be off down the harbour and watch the boats. And don't come back until you see Eli return so I can buy some fish. I apologise for the noise,' Margaret had to lift her voice to be heard above the vigorous sounds of sawing and planing which came from next door, 'we must suffer for our future grandeur.'

Viney groaned and shambled out, Dorcas scuttled after him gladly. Richard, watching her, commented drily, 'You surely will not keep the drab?'

'She has nowhere else to go.'

'And your manservant?'

'Oh, Viney does at least work for his keep.'

'I did not imagine you had recruited him for any other reason.'

'Hmm.' Margaret was stoking the fire to a blaze. 'We did not exactly – recruit him at all.'

Richard, watching her, had already forgotten his urgent business in Helford and was smiling. 'I cannot believe that his honour was being threatened by rapists when you rescued *him*.'

'On the contrary,' she set down the poker, wiped the back of her hand across her forehead and turned to him with sudden amusement, 'when I found him first he was in the process of robbing us.' Seeing Richard's expression she explained hastily, 'Oh, he had not taken anything and the poor fellow was half-starved. He'd never steal from us now, I'm sure. In fact he is often quite useful.'

'He has the look of a drinker.'

'Only when he has the money, which is seldom enough. And anyway,' Margaret hesitated, not having confessed this to anyone before, 'he has always reminded me of one of my father's black-faced sheep, do you not see the resemblance? How could one ever be unkind to a man who looked like a black-faced sheep?'

'With the greatest of ease, I'm sure.' But Richard found that his amusement was stronger than his disapproval. Margaret's account of her methods of dealing with servants betrayed hitherto unimagined depths of incompetence. 'An imbecile and a drunken thief. Tell me, Mistress Hollar, what other paragons of virtue do you employ?'

'No one. That is . . . there is Ghislain, the apprentice, but he helps my husband with his business.'

'I only hope your husband has higher standards than you.'

'Oh, his standards are sure to be extremely high.'

Richard looked at her sharply: an unpleasant edge had entered her voice at the mention of her husband. She was on the point of saying that she did not know just what it was that made Ghislain so apparently indispensable since he often seemed to work even less than Paul Viney, but she merely compressed her lips in that tight, hurt line and added yet more sticks to the fire.

Suddenly Richard found that he could remember every detail of their conversation on that evening after her wedding when they had sat together by this same fire, the way her expression changed so swiftly from laughter to sadness, the way her hand lay across her swollen belly. He asked, 'Do you have other children, Mistress Hollar?'

She glanced at him swiftly, then looked away again. 'Only Luke,' she said in a low voice, 'my husband and I have not been . . . fortunate. And you?'

'My wife is childless.' The words were spoken without emotion.

The din from the carpenters in the adjoining room stopped suddenly and the kitchen was full of echoing silence. 'Thank heavens for that,' breathed Margaret.

'What are they doing?'

'A parlour. Mr Treveryan, did you talk to anyone about what happened the other day?'

'That was what I came to tell you. I –' But Margaret, glancing towards the door that led into the shop, motioned him to silence. The next moment the door swung open and William Hollar came in. As soon as he saw Richard his face broke into a smile of welcome.

'Mr Treveryan, what a great pleasure it is to see you here again. I had planned to ride over to Rossmere myself to thank you for your kindness in assisting my wife.'

Richard inclined his head coldly. William Hollar was not greatly changed, he thought; those ethereal good looks seemed impervious to time. But his manner was altered. More assured, less obviously ingratiating: this was now a merchant confident of his position in the community and accustomed to dealing with the gentry, if not on terms of equality, then at least with mutual respect.

But even as he appraised William Hollar, Richard could not help being aware of Margaret's reaction as her husband entered the room. Although there was no perceptible alteration in her expression her whole being had become at once guarded, isolated and remote.

William continued easily. 'Margaret, I hope you have offered our guest some canary wine; surely it is the least you can do after the trouble he has taken. I have often told my wife, Mr Treveryan, that her habit of interfering in other people's affairs will do her no good, but she is quick tempered and often muddle-headed. And I cannot keep an eye on her all the time.' His tone was bantering, affectionate. Richard looked at Margaret to see how she might respond but she was absorbed in contemplation of the fire and made no sign that she had heard. William placed his pale hand on her shoulder and smiled. 'I daresay that if our wives were faultless, we should not care for them half so much. Don't you agree, Mr Treveryan?'

Richard did not answer. He was wondering what strange alchemy was at work that made him know in his very bones how much Mistress Hollar resented and loathed her husband's presence.

With a barely perceptible movement of her body she was

free of his hand. 'I shall fetch the wine,' she said impassively.

'Do not trouble on my account,' said Richard.

William looked towards the adjoining room and frowned. 'Why have the workmen stopped, Margaret?'

'I have no idea.'

'If you will excuse me for a moment, Mr Treveryan, I must leave you in order to check their work. Next time you visit us I hope we shall be able to entertain you more elegantly in our new parlour.'

Richard said, 'It is unlikely I shall visit here again.'

As soon as William had left the room Margaret made sure the doors were firmly closed. 'Mr Treveryan,' she said in a low voice, 'I did not burden my husband with a detailed account of the events at Ia's Wood. I merely told him that some vagabonds were attempting to rob Dorcas and that I was trying to see them off when you arrived to help us.'

'Did it not occur to him that the girl possessed nothing anyone would wish to steal?'

'He accepted my story.'

'Perhaps, after all, I would like a little of your husband's wine.' Then he added gently, 'Do not worry, I shall not contradict your story. We have a secret, then.'

'Yes.'

She handed Richard a glass of wine. He was agreeably surprised to find it pleasant to taste, but then he told himself he should have known that William Hollar would always insist on the best. He said, 'I paid a visit to your friend Bob Dawkins.'

'He is no friend of mine.'

'And yet you insist on protecting him and his cronies.'

'No.' Her earlier merriment had vanished. She said hopelessly, 'I daresay it was only cowardice on my own part. I could not bear the thought of questions and interfering and always more cruelty. There is so much cruelty already.'

'Is justice cruel?'

She sat down by the fire, raised her eyes to meet his, then turned away again. 'Last week a vagrant girl was driven from the parish and all because she was expecting a child and no one wanted Porthew to carry the burden of it. Was that just?'

'I'm surprised you didn't offer her a place in your household.'

She did not smile. After a few moments she said, 'It is rumoured that one of them has fled the district, and Spencer Tully has been taken ill with mysterious pains to his stomach and no one can explain the cause.'

'I promise you I did no more than talk with them.'

For a moment her expression lightened, as he had hoped, then she was serious once more. 'Dorcas told me that her mother cursed them all before she died, terrible curses promising them all manner of harm. Dorcas believes she is taking her revenge on them now and that Spencer Tully is sure to die for his wickedness.'

'Most likely it is the man's own guilty conscience and fear of the supernatural that has made him ill.'

'Do you not recognise the power of cursing?'

'Hmm. I came prepared for Catullus and now you fling theology at me.' But then, seeing that she was still serious, he perched on the corner of the table by her chair and said, 'I have seen men die from terror alone while others survived horrific wounds. I have seen men walk barefoot over burning coals and emerge unscathed and all in the name of another God than ours. I have seen enough to be sure that there is a great deal we can never hope to understand.'

Margaret pondered this for a while, her chin resting on her hand, before she answered, 'You make a virtue of uncertainty.'

'It is the only truth I know.'

'Oh! I would give my soul to be able to travel as you have done!' With a sudden gust of impatience she stood up and paced to the window, then returned to stand before him. 'If you only knew how lucky you have been, to see and hear so much. Tell me, did you go to the Americas?'

'Yes.'

'And the Spice Islands?'

'Yes.'

'And the Azores? And Cathay?'

'Yes. And yes.'

'Oh!'

She sat down again. Richard burst out laughing. 'They do say that there are certain women who adopt men's clothes and seek out a sailor's life, though I have to say I have never knowingly come across any. But perhaps the next time we meet you will be dressed in a sailor's slops and with a cutlass between your teeth.'

She raised her eyebrows.

'But I'm afraid your figure would betray you.'

Her expression was hovering on the brink of a smile when William came back into the room and she was instantly sober again. Margaret examined her nails and asked him if the work was being carried out to his satisfaction.

Yes, William reassured her as he poured himself a glass of wine, the panelling would soon be completed. He told Richard that although these local workmen were not acquainted with modern styles and methods they were none the less progressing reasonably well under his vigilant tutelage. And Richard, seeing that to remain would be to enjoy the company of the husband as well as the wife, finished his wine and was on the point of bidding them farewell when a curly-haired youth came into the room from the shop.

'Mr Treveryan,' said William, 'before you leave, allow me to introduce my apprentice. Ghislain has heard of your famous travels and is all eagerness to meet you.'

The lad was young, with an intelligent face and the merest shadow of a moustache. Despite William's protestations, Ghislain did not look half so eager as his master, but he managed to say, in stumbling English, that he was honoured to meet the famous Mr Treveryan, though the smile that followed managed to be both surly and impudent at the same time.

'You have now met our entire household,' said Margaret as she walked with him to the gateway where Viney was dejectedly standing beside the tall mare. Sheba's vibrant health and energy contrasted with the manservant's sickly droop.

'Except your son.'

'Luke is at his lessons with the parson.' She took hold of Sheba's bridle and stroked her nose gently. 'You may return to the house now, Paul.'

For the first time Richard realised that her hand was no longer bandaged. 'Has your knife wound healed?' And he would have taken her hand to examine it but she quickly placed it behind her back.

'Yes, thank you. But my hands were rough enough before and the scar is very ugly.'

Her sudden confusion intrigued him, but she kept her hands firmly clasped behind her back until he was safely mounted on his horse. Only then did she step forward and say solemnly, 'Thank you for your help, Mr Treveryan. And your discretion.'

'Hmm. I've always been famous for my discretion. I'd like to tell you to be more careful in the future but I don't suppose you'd pay the least attention.'

'No.' And then, at last, she burst out laughing, and her laughter seemed to accompany him as he wheeled Sheba about and the big horse danced with the delicacy of a bird over the rough surface of the lane.

It was only when he had travelled about a mile from Porthew that he realised he had forgotten the very purpose of his journey. The white kerchief remained in his pocket. Less annoyed than he might have been by this further delay, he turned Sheba around and cantered back towards the town.

The laneway was deserted. From the privy came the sounds of Viney noisily paying the price of his evening's drunkenness. Resisting the urge to punish the fellow for his failings, Richard dismounted and slung the reins over the gate post once again before striding through the garden to the kitchen door. The sound of the workmen in the adjoining room was as deafening as ever, but when Richard looked into the kitchen itself he found it deserted but for a solitary grey cat stretched luxuriously on the settle by the fire.

'Mistress Hollar?' Richard tapped against the open door. A singularly useless gesture, he thought, considering the amount of banging and hammering to which the house was already being subjected. He stepped into the kitchen and looked about him. A book was lying on a shelf beside the fireplace – George Herbert's *The Temple* – and he set it down again with a gesture of distaste. A mending basket stood on the kitchen table. Richard picked out a child's shift and saw the place where she had begun to mend a small tear with clumsy and inexpert stitches. Clearly

Mistress Hollar was as bad at sewing as she was at managing her servants.

Richard was smiling as he went towards the half-open door that led into the shop and the sound of low voices. He had his hand on the latch and was on the point of pushing it open and announcing himself when he saw something that made him stop, his smile vanishing abruptly.

The French boy was seated at the desk, a ledger open in front of him. William Hollar stood beside him and was dictating words which Ghislain repeated as he wrote. Something about an order of worsteds and kerseys. William Hollar's hand was resting on the back of the boy's neck; his delicate fingers were absentmindedly toying with the long curls, caressing the pale neck where it was exposed. The jewel on his ring flashed briefly in a beam of light as his hand travelled to stroke the down on the lad's cheek. Ghislain paused, frowning at the page, then turned to ask William a question . . . and the expression of his eyes was unmistakable.

Richard turned. Dorcas had come in from the garden and was watching him anxiously. He pushed past her without a word, cursed Viney who had stumbled into the kitchen looking deathly pale, and hurried through the garden to where Sheba was once more waiting patiently. From Porthew he took the road to Helford and maintained a fast pace until concern for his mount forced him to slow down. A kind of anger was burning within him. A fury he could not have analysed if he had tried.

It was not that he condemned the merchant for his liking for good-looking youths. Though he had never been so tempted himself, he had been master of too many ships to trouble about how other men chose to divert themselves. It was the fact that Hollar was connected with Margaret that filled him with a sense of futility and waste. A thought echoed in his mind like a refrain: she had deserved better than that.

He remembered once when he was about fourteen years old and his father had been obliged to part with a young filly, a chestnut, the finest horse ever to have been reared in his father's stable. Richard had longed to possess the horse himself, had even curbed his pride and begged his father not to part with her, something he had never done before or since. But his father was adamant: the filly must be sold. Richard guessed now that the sale had been to repay a debt so his father had no choice in the matter but at the time he had assumed he was being thwarted deliberately. A beautiful horse she was, with the delicacy of the Barbary mares; a soft mouth and an eager intelligence – never had he seen a horse to match her. And she had been handed over to a crass farmer from Launceston: the next time he saw her, a couple of years later, she was already ruined, stiff-backed and awkward with a hard, tugging mouth and a neck like an iron bar. The sense of waste, the stupid cruelty of it all, had brought him almost to weeping.

But that had been a long time ago, when he was still a foolish and emotional boy. As the warmth drained from the October afternoon and Richard had done with his business in Helford, he found that his anger was already under control. He was able to remind himself that it hardly mattered to him if the fine-looking woman he had danced with on her wedding day had been unfortunate in her choice of husband.

He wondered idly what her story had been: hadn't he come across her that day on the moors when she was half-distracted and faint with weariness? Hadn't she wanted then to leave, to flee, to escape? Not that it concerned him in the slightest.

And yet . . . by the time he reached the brow of the hill and looked down on the orderly cluster of dwellings that made up the manor and barton farm of Rossmere, his anger had mellowed into something altogether more philosophical.

Mistress Hollar's unhappiness in her marriage had been obvious enough, even before he had stumbled on the cause. Richard had been sufficiently the product of a venomous union to be able to smell out misery even when the signs were not apparent to others. Perhaps now he could turn her misfortune to his own advantage.

It occurred to him that, if he was ever to spend much time in this quiet backwater of the kingdom, he might do worse than to amuse himself with the attractive and so obviously unhappy Mistress Hollar.

17

The first gale of the winter was ripping the leaves from the oak woods on the morning Richard Treveryan mounted Sheba and rode away from Rossmere. Nicolas embraced him and wished him a speedy return, and Alice found the few days following his departure almost unbearably tedious as she resumed her busy routine and heard the wind moaning in the chimneys.

Less than two weeks later Joseph Treloar's hay-rick caught fire. A brisk westerly was blowing that day and within minutes the blaze was spectacular, threatening to spread, and destroy the barn as well. Never before had Joseph so cursed his useless legs; Jennie and the older children raced back and forth with water from the well; there were not buckets enough, there was not water enough, the children were so small and frightened . . . in the barn the animals smelt the fire and clattered against the wooden door in panic.

By the time the first neighbours appeared on the scene the hay-rick was lost but the fire was under control and the barn and other buildings and all the animals were saved. Jennie stood in the yard, her face pale and smudged with soot, and shivered and wept with the horror of it all until a neighbour's wife put her own shawl around her shoulders and led her into the house.

It was there that they discovered a greater loss by far: the metal chest which held the evidences and other documents concerning their tenancy of the farm was missing from its hiding place under their bed. Friends and neighbours joined in an exhaustive search, but from the moment he saw the empty space beneath the bed, Joseph knew it would only be recovered by a miracle. And nothing in his life had taught him to expect miracles.

Suspicion naturally centred on Treveryan's agent, Francis

Crane. Only a week before the fire he had offered the Treloars a richer tenancy on the other side of Porthew if Joseph would give up his rights to Trecarne, but the cripple rejected him. Jennie feared her husband's intransigence was unwise but she knew he was nothing if not stubborn. It was his stubbornness had seen him through the hard times: he was too well schooled to learn compromise and flexibility now.

There was uproar for a time. Some people even claimed to have seen Richard Treveryan in the neighbourhood on the day before the fire. From that day onwards Francis Crane was careful always to have two men with him and was never seen without a pair of pistols in his belt. Nicolas Sutton, who had recently replaced his father as Justice of the Peace, promised to find the thief and bring him to justice . . . but he was known to be Treveryan's friend and, moreover, was rumoured to have recently borrowed money from him. As days and then weeks passed with no sign of either the metal trunk or the culprit, there was widespread anger and disgust and a growing resentment at the injustice.

None protested louder than Ambrose and his father, Robert Treloar. They let every caller at the smithy know that they would themselves kill the first man who attempted to evict their cousins from their rightful home.

Margaret was appalled by the incident; she could not believe that Richard Treveryan could be so callous towards Joseph and his family. She told herself that the fire could have been an accident, that it could have been coincidence that a thief happened to be passing and took the strong box assuming it to be full of money . . . She kept her theories to herself, knowing no one else would believe them for an instant; she hardly believed them herself. She wondered if Francis Crane might have acted without his master's knowledge: she did not really believe that either.

She did everything possible for Jennie Treloar and her children. No one was to know that it was a sense of guilt, as much as her usual generosity, that prompted her actions, as though she was somehow implicated in Treveryan's crime. Jennie was grateful and the friendship between them increased; Joseph occasionally responded to her kindness with grudging suspicion – but these days he was suspicious of every bird that blundered into the dark room where he worked all day at his loom.

The Treloars' grinding worries cast a pall over the remainder of the autumn. To Margaret's surprise her only entertainment, as Christmas approached, was provided by Dorcas. The girl's capacity for food was truly impressive: by All Hallows she had eaten herself into stoutness, a sturdy girl with red cheeks and a red mouth like a fledgeling's, always open for more food. By the middle of December she was grown positively gargantuan, jowls and breasts a quivering mound of flesh. Margaret began to wonder wildly when the process of enlargement would come to an end. Certainly Dorcas showed no inclination to stop eating. The only activity that could distract her from thoughts of food for more than a few minutes was attendance at church.

Until she came to Porthew Dorcas had known nothing of religion. Goblins and imps were all her supernatural world. On her first Sunday she sat towards the back of the church with Viney (who slept) and listened with open-mouthed wonder. She was both fascinated and terrified by the paintings on the church walls and insisted vigorously that Margaret explain the stories they depicted. She tended to confuse the Virgin Mary and Mary Magdalen and she was not much interested in John the Baptist but the idea of the Christ child excited her enormously. She never tired of hearing about the shepherds and the wise men and the manger with the star over it. Her excitement grew daily as Christmas approached. When Margaret was too busy to answer her endless questions she dispatched her to find Parson Weaver.

'Where will Jesus be born?'

'He was born in a manger, Dorcas.' The answer that she had already heard a hundred times filled her with such glee that she clapped her fat hands and whooped loudly.

On Christmas morning the parson was puzzled to see Dorcas weeping steadily throughout the service. 'What has upset the girl?' he asked Margaret afterwards, for Dorcas was nothing if not reliably even tempered.

'You had no Christ child waiting for her in the church,' Margaret explained with a sigh. 'She was expecting a real baby.'

Parson Weaver watched the vast girl as she waddled sadly from the churchyard. 'Except ye become as little children . . .' he mused, and then he smiled. 'If childishness is the key to the Kingdom of Heaven then your Dorcas will arrive there before any of us. It is a most sobering thought.'

Margaret agreed. Before she left she begged him never to mention the slaughter of the Holy Innocents in Dorcas's hearing. The prospect of steering her through the events of Easter was daunting enough.

Soon after the Twelfth Night revels were over, William left on a ship, the *Harry*, which was bound for France. Despite the heavy burden of ship money imposed by the King – and which the Cornish mostly paid – supposedly to strengthen the naval defences of the country, the sea had become so infested with Turkish pirates that summer journeys were now considered by many to be too dangerous to contemplate, but at this time of year the long light ships of the Turks were seldom seen off the Cornish coast. William told Margaret to expect him back within six weeks.

Ghislain remained behind. Margaret was surprised, then annoyed. She did not care for the youth, disliked having him in the house, and was quite certain she could have run the shop much better than he, if she was only given the chance. But, to her amazement, Ghislain's allegiance switched the moment the white sails of the *Harry* had vanished over the rain-dark horizon. Until then the lad had hardly spoken to her at all, he had stayed close to William as a shadow, would obey no order that did not come from William, took perverse delight in encouraging Luke to mutiny. Now all was changed. He accepted Margaret's authority without question, anticipated her wishes, encouraged Luke to do his mother's bidding. At meal times he was lively and amusing. Margaret was puzzled to discover that he spoke much better English than she had thought, though his accent was often strange. His status as an outsider, plus the impression he gave of hardly understanding a word that was said in his presence, had given him access to an abundance of gossip. And he had a way of telling his stories, half-scandalised, half-comical, that made even the most familiar tale entertaining.

Now, when they gathered round the kitchen table for a meal (the parlour was practically finished but Margaret never used it) there was laughter and talk, a vivid contrast to the silence that William had always insisted on. Margaret especially was grateful for the gift of laughter. Dorcas watched her face and giggled on cue without knowing why; Luke listened with that oddly intent look on his unchildlike face, as though storing up all he could remember for the future. Paul Viney was impassive as ever, only occasionally showing by a loud bark of laughter that he had been listening to every word.

Luke devoted less energy to vexing his mother. Although he missed William, he could not help being aware that the atmosphere in the house was more relaxed, that everyday life was suddenly fun. One evening, when Ghislain was telling them a highly embroidered account of how a Manaccan man had been tricked into buying a horse that died within a week of the sale, Margaret noticed for the first time what an attractive face the French youth had. Until then, seeing him only through a veil of dislike, she had considered his face sly and unpleasant. A small mouth, green eyes slightly aslant, a neat nose, somewhat pointed – now these added up to an endearing whole. The following day she noticed that his efforts to cope with the shop alone were running into difficulties. When she offered to help he accepted gratefully. For the first time since her marriage Margaret was free to spend time in the shop that she had so loved to visit when she was a child and Merry's father had held benevolent court among the dark honeycomb of cloth. Soon she had become familiar with every bale of wool, each length of silk and velvet, baize and canvas for working clothes, brocade and lace for the gentry.

Between helping Dame Erisey in her school, visiting Jennie at the farm and working with Ghislain in the shop, Margaret had never been so fully occupied since she left Conwinnion. She was almost happy. Customers began to drop in for a word or a gossip as they had done in Mr Hocken's time. And almost every conversation was prefaced by the courteous, 'Any word from Mr Hollar yet?'

No, there was none. He had said not more than six weeks but by the end of February there was still no sign of him. The beginning of March was mild, soft winds blowing from the south, winds for a ship to sail home on . . . but still no sign of William. Luke began to fret. Towards the end of March three Barbary ships were sighted off the Lizard and the fishermen, when they did venture out, stayed close to land.

The beginning of April saw high tides and heavy rain. William's horse went lame and Margaret was obliged to walk to Trecarne to visit Jennie and arrived drenched to the skin. She found that Jennie's children were all suffering from croupy coughs and one of them, a little girl called Mary, was gasping so for breath that Jennie was in terror of losing her. Their only cause for celebration was that Margaret's father, borne along on the general wave of sympathy for the Treloars, had given them Juno, his old mare. As soon as the roads improved Joseph would be able to get about from time to time in his little two-wheeled cart. It was a small comfort.

As usual their main topic of conversation was speculation about Treveryan's plans, ideas for resisting him, anxiety over money. Margaret was glad to escape and, as she hurried home through the driving rain, she found herself looking forward to the comfort of her home, dry clothes, a warm fire and Ghislain's colourful account of the customers he had talked with during the day.

The wind was beginning to blow quite strongly by the time Margaret trudged ankle deep in rainwater down the back lane to her home. A small boy pelted past her, heading up the hill.

Recognising one of her pupils Margaret exclaimed, 'Watch where you're going!' but the boy only yelled something incoherent and raced on.

When she went into the house, it was deserted and prematurely dark. She went through to the shop, but that was empty too. Beyond the window the street was full of people, all hurrying down the hill. She threw open the shop door.

'What is it?'

Two or three people answered at once, their voices barely audible in the driving wind and rain: a ship was in trouble.

Margaret at once stepped out into the street, and joined the crowds hastening down towards the harbour.

*   *   *

William, standing on the sloping deck of the *Harry*, felt his body to be a pure white flame of terror. He had just seen one man, a respectable French merchant who had beaten him at cards the night before, attempt to leap from the deck to the safety of some rocks. The man had said something to William before he jumped – 'God save me, m'sieur,' or some such – then crossed himself and sprang towards the shore. He landed safely, steadied himself – and then a huge wave surged around his waist. William saw the man's horrified face as his hands flew up, he was spun around, dashed against the rocks where his head split open and the receding foam was flecked with blood.

William clung to the rail of the ship: he would never let go. All about him was the shriek of cracking timber; the main mast had crashed with the sound of a giant tree falling; the hull of the ship was splintering right beneath the deck on which he stood; like the hideous roar of the underworld was the rolling, crashing, breaking of the barrels in the hold now open to the sea, the infernal endless wind and wet. Never let go. Hold on, hold on.

William could hear the water pouring into the hold. The fallen mast had created a perilous bridge to the shore and half a dozen sailors swarmed across and on to the rocks without serious harm. William, whimpering now, knew he could never follow.

Already it was almost dark. In the twilight the figures swarming over the rocks resembled a crowd of faceless maggots, clinging, feasting. Never let go.

A woman, the only woman aboard the ship, was about to clamber on to the mast. She was arguing, refusing to hand over her baby. Clutching the howling infant she attempted to crawl across the fragile bridge, but with only one free hand her attempt was doomed. As they fell the child's cries were swallowed in the louder wailing sea. Listen to me, God, wept William, not me too. Dear God, not like that . . .

The mast snapped.

A man pushed past him. It was the captain. 'Jump, man! If you stay there you're –' But William only stared at him wildly. The captain shook his head, jumped. The maggots swarmed. William did not see what happened.

The rocks themselves were moving, one moment spread out below him, the next higher than his face. Hold on. Too far. Can't reach . . .

Oh Lord, dear God, heavenly Father, save me just this one more time; don't let me die, not like this, not like that man, only let me live a little longer and I'll be for ever . . . no more sin, never again. Only save me, God, sweet Jesus save me and I'll follow Your path, do Your will, anything anything, only save me. No more sin.

He was sobbing. He screamed out to God but his voice was swamped by the louder screaming wind. God was not listening, God did not hear. He raged in anger. Damn You, God, listen to me, please listen, can You hear what I'm promising You? I'm offering You my life, my whole life, damn You, God, why don't You listen to me? The planks of wood beneath his feet groaned, parted. Black water boiled underneath.

Oh God, listen, can't You hear me, only hear me and I'll never sin again, Yours for ever, listen to me, God . . .

By the harbour there was pandemonium. Giles Erisey had tried to secure his boat against the fierce waves only to be crushed by its hull against the harbour wall and dragged across the shingle by the undertow. His brother and another man pulled him out, spewing seawater and with several bones broken.

Men and women poured on to the rocks to help the survivors: the *Harry* was a Penzance boat and many of her crew were known locally. Away from the modest shelter of the harbour, the noise of the waves was terrifying, a thunderous rage pounding against the land as though to destroy it, white crests of foam spraying high as a church tower above their heads.

Some men were more interested in the ship's cargo than its crew. They risked their lives to pull ashore a barrel of bay salt, a bale of canvas, a keg of wine. Men who could not swim and who had never ventured into the water in their lives before, waded waist deep into the white tumult of ocean. The current dragged at their ankles, pulling them from the shore, overbalancing them. They held hands and formed human chains to stay afloat.

Margaret paced up and down by the harbour wall. Her first thought, as always, had been for Luke. Where was he? She could not find him anywhere and in all the commotion no one even heard her desperate questions. At last she saw Ghislain, coming towards her over the rocks.

'Ghislain, where is Luke? I've been hunting everywhere –'

His face was ghastly, eyes wild with fear and shock.

'William –' He gestured hopelessly towards the remains of the ship. But Margaret turned away from him impatiently, not comprehending his distress; she could only think of Luke.

Not until she had found her son, huddled with Dorcas in the shelter of a doorway, overlooked by everyone and rather relishing the drama they were witnessing, did Margaret understand that it was the *Harry* that had foundered, that her husband was among the passengers and had not yet been sighted among those who had struggled to the shore, that some said he was still clinging hopelessly to the deck rail.

Parson Weaver, sleek and black as a cormorant, emerged through the deluge and put his arm around her shoulder. 'Have courage, Margaret,' his mouth seemed to be saying, 'God may yet bring him safe to shore.'

Margaret stared at him without speaking, then shook her head and began to walk towards the rocky headland. Most of the movement was now in the other direction: men slithering over the rough path with barrels on their shoulders, a few shocked survivors.

She reached the furthest point of land, the place where the rain mingled with spray to form a dense veil of water. And through that veil she could just make out the ship, the remains of the ship, and a single luminous figure pinned to the side, utterly helpless and alone in the storm.

'Margaret, for God's sake, don't watch.' Parson Weaver had followed her. 'Come back with me, there's nothing you can do.' He put his arm around her waist to guide her back to the harbour, but she shrugged him off impatiently. Stood there staring with huge eyes. Another wave broke and she saw that William was no longer standing on anything at all, the deck had vanished and he was clinging with white hands

420

and his mouth was open in a scream she could not hear. And something pale washed against his legs, pale and shaped like a long cocoon. A bale of cloth? Margaret saw that it was the body of a woman. She closed her eyes.

'Mattie, get back. The tide is rising.' Another voice. Ambrose. His huge bulk rose up beside her. 'Here, I'll help you.' And he would have dragged her back to the harbour but she pushed him away.

'No, Ambrose,' she was pointing towards the ship, 'it's William –'

Ambrose was staring over the top of her head into the white pall of spray. 'Oh no –' he groaned. William was insignificant as a wisp of pale seaweed washed against the tattered side of the ship.

'He can't –' Margaret began, then looked up at Ambrose but he was staring into the mist, an expression of deepening horror spreading across his face. When Margaret looked once more towards the ship, the pale wisp of a man who had clung so tenaciously to the ship's rail had vanished.

'God rest his soul,' muttered the parson.

Ambrose said, 'Get Mattie away from here.'

This time Margaret did not resist the parson's guiding arm, allowed herself to be led back along the rain-soaked path to the harbour. All at once she was intensely aware of the cold, her sodden clothes.

'I must go home and get dry,' she said as they reached the first house, and then had to repeat herself to be heard above the wind. The parson looked at her oddly.

Ghislain rushed towards her. His teeth were chattering so much that he could not speak but the question on his face was clear enough. Margaret stretched out a hand to comfort him. 'He's lost, Ghislain. There is no hope.'

He stared at her incredulously for a moment, his lips shaping a passionate 'No!' then he broke down, fell into her arms and sobbed like the child he had so recently been.

'Poor Ghislain,' she stroked his hair, 'you were a good apprentice.'

Still sobbing, he wrenched himself away and plunged into the darkness.

Parson Weaver's arm was very tight around her shoul-

421

ders. His hand was shaking. 'Come, Mattie, let me take you home.'

'Luke,' she was searching through the crowds, 'I must find Luke.'

News of William Hollar's death was passing through the crowd as if carried inland on the rain and the wind. Men looked at Margaret with that guarded, troubled look of grief observed; one or two of the women stepped forward and grasped her arm in silent sympathy. Dame Erisey hurried up the hill to prepare the draper's house for the widow's return. Dorcas and Luke were found, brought forward. Dorcas looked about her in terror, sure she must be in trouble of some kind. Luke realised only that he was the centre of attention without knowing the reason why. He was enjoying all the fuss, but felt a growing alarm at the mystery of it all, since no one would answer his questions.

'Mother, what is it, what's happening?' He caught hold of her hand and she gazed down at him with an expression he had never seen before. She seemed so strange, standing there in the half light with her drenched hair clinging to her cheeks and the rainwater running down her neck and her clothes like wet washing flapping in the wind. And Parson Weaver stood beside her and had his arm around her waist and his face was solemn and eager and strange.

'When we are home,' said his mother, 'I can tell you then.'

She took his hand and looked one last time towards the blackness of the rocks, shook her head as though puzzled by something that no one else could understand, before starting up the hill towards her house. Parson Weaver walked beside her. There were swarms of people everywhere, many carrying booty from the wreck. Margaret watched them with a strange detachment: that bolt of russet was surely William's.

As they reached the door of the draper's shop there was a mighty roar at the bottom of the street, a roar that could be heard even above the constant din of the storm. 'Mattie!'

She turned, but her eyes were too weak to make out the figure who stood at the bottom of the hill: Ambrose, his face bloodied, his shoulders hung around with seaweed like some huge and murderous Neptune.

The next moment he was striding up the street towards them, a man's lifeless body in his arms. Ghislain crab-skipped beside him and tried to hold the lolling head.

'It's Father!' Luke shrieked, only then understanding the full horror of what had occurred; and he would have run down the street to meet them but the parson held him back, murmuring, 'No, no, my son; it's only his corpse.'

Moving like a vast monster from the sea Ambrose came on up the hill towards them and all the while his eyes were fixed on Margaret. As he drew nearer she backed in horror into the shop. Dame Erisey, hearing the commotion, came in from the kitchen, holding a lighted tallow.

Ambrose carried William's body as easily as if it had been a child's. Parson Weaver gazed at him, appalled. 'Does she have to see it now?'

But Ghislain cried out, 'No, his lips are moving, I saw them, he's breathing, look, oh look!'

William was carried inside. Even by the light of the tallow his face was sickly pale as whey.

'Set him down in the kitchen,' ordered Dame Erisey, for Margaret could not speak, only stared, all the expression bleached from her face.

Radiant with triumph and never for one moment taking his eyes from her face, Ambrose said in a gruff voice, 'I saved him for you, Mattie,' and, fulfilling the ambition of a lifetime, he laid the tribute of his strength and love down at her feet.

The wind died down soon after dark. It had not been such a bad storm after all, even that winter there had been several worse. A barn roof blew off, a couple of small boats in the harbour were smashed, an elm tree fell across the road at Ia's Wood. It was bad luck and a moment's misjudge-ment that had driven the *Harry* on the rocks beyond the harbour wall. In the best bedroom above the draper's shop, William's bedroom, the distant roar of the still-mountainous sea was a dull blur of sound, almost soothing, drowsy.

By midnight they knew that William would pull through. All evening Margaret and Ghislain rubbed his frozen body with rough cloth while he switched from a deathlike stillness

423

to sudden bursts of delirium. 'Sin,' he muttered, 'God save
. . . no more . . . dear God, no . . .' And when his eyes
opened he did not see the familiar room, Margaret and
Ghislain bending to care for him; his blue eyes were huge
with remembered terror and he screamed and scrabbled at
the bedclothes with ripped and bleeding fingers. A few times
he vomited, grey seawater and bile.

While Margaret and Ghislain laboured to warm William
back to life, the kitchen was crowded with visitors. Ambrose
was the willing centre of attention and never tired of repeating how he had risked his life to plunge into the savage
water and pull the lifeless body to shore. He did not need
to stress the fact that any other man would have been sucked
down by the tide, dashed to pieces on the rocks, that much
was obvious to all who had witnessed the drama of the
disintegrating ship. Lizzie came from the Forge and kissed
his salt-whitened forehead and told him he was the bravest
husband in all the world; the *Harry*'s captain came over
from Jack Pym's especially to congratulate him. It might
well have been the happiest evening of Ambrose's life.

Before returning with Lizzie to the Forge Ambrose
climbed the stairs and peered in at the bedroom where
William lay. Crouched like a dancing bear he stood in the
low doorway and gazed on Margaret, who was sitting beside
the bruised body of her husband.

'I saved him for you, Mattie,' he said again.

She looked up at him in the glimmering light of the tallow, raised an aching hand to push back her hair. Too weary
even for gratitude she merely nodded. 'You did, Ambrose,'
was all she said.

He shifted from one foot to another, fingered the edge of
his leather jerkin. Surely this was the night when those calm
eyes would turn to him, brimful of gratitude and even love
. . . but her eyes were empty. No, not even empty. They
burned with a harsh and angry light.

'Well then, Mattie . . .'

A hard line appeared between her eyebrows and she
turned away with a gesture of impatience. Ambrose opened
his mouth, closed it again. She was too tired, too shocked
. . . perhaps tomorrow. Baffled, he turned and shuffled
away.

Gradually the house succumbed to silence. William was breathing peacefully now, the calmness of exhausted sleep. Ghislain smiled across at Margaret, allowed himself to relax, lean back against the bedpost. His eyelids drooped, then closed.

Margaret sighed, a barely audible sound but it seemed enough to wake William. He opened his eyes and stared at her with a sudden piercing directness.

'Then it is true,' he breathed.

'Yes, William, you are safe.'

Ghislain jerked awake and, seizing William's hand, began babbling with such a frenzy of relief that it was impossible to guess if the words were French or English or an incoherent jumble of the two.

William turned his head away. 'Make him go,' he fretted, 'don't let him near me. I cannot bear it.'

Margaret protested; it must be that in his delirium he did not recognise the youth, but he only became agitated. 'I loathe the sight of him! You *must* make him leave.'

In his dismay, Ghislain turned a silent appeal to Margaret. 'By morning he will be himself again,' she tried to reassure him. 'Leave him now, you need the rest.'

But when they were alone together, William took her hand and said in a voice quite free of all delirium, 'Today God has saved me for His work, and I must make myself worthy of His great trust. I shall be a true husband to you from now on. And . . . forgive me, Margaret, for . . . all that. Praise the Lord, henceforward we can work together to accomplish His great purpose for us. Praise God for that, Margaret, praise God . . .'

She stared at him, a slow horror spreading across her exhausted face. She withdrew her hand and stood up slowly.

'Sleep now, William.' She all but choked on the words.

He sank back on the pillows, tried to protest but slid almost at once into unconsciousness. She stared at him for a few moments more. Never before had she seen his face so tranquil, so perfectly beautiful as on that evening when he had been dragged back from the very doorway of death.

She covered her eyes with her hands. I am surely the most wicked woman in Christendom, she thought. When I saw the waves close over his head my heart rejoiced. For how many years now have I longed only to see him dead?

During the night the clouds rolled away and the following morning the sun rose on spring birdsong and a gentle breeze. Only the deep channels of mud running through the streets, seaweed and boulders cast up beyond the harbour wall, betrayed the tumult of the previous day. Was it possible that a ship had been dashed to pieces on those placid rocks where cormorants stretched their wings in the sun? And had that calm sea claimed five more victims?

Throughout the morning the bell tolled for the funerals of those who had died and whose bodies had already been washed ashore, among them the woman and the infant she had been clutching as she fell into the sea. The people of Porthew tended the survivors and searched the shore for anything that could be gained from the wreck; the sea was a capricious ally.

William listened to the mournful bell and smelled the soft air that wafted through his open window and a growing exultation rinsed the pain and weariness from his body. Those wretched folk had perished, had been sacrificed by God, but *he* had triumphed over death. God had heard his prayers; God had saved him; God had wanted him to live.

Far from regretting his hostility to Ghislain the previous evening, William was more than ever adamant. Margaret found herself championing a youth she had many times wished out of the house. 'But William, he's only a lad. Where can he go? He's done you no harm, William; only wait a day and reconsider . . .'

But her pleas only hardened his resolve. 'If that low creature is not gone from my house by the time I come downstairs, then as God is my witness I swear I shall throw him out myself. I promise you, Margaret, as your faithful husband, that I shall never speak or have any dealings with that vicious youth again.'

'Vicious? William, what has he done?'

'Ask me rather what he is. Only get rid of him, Margaret; he poisons the air while he remains.'

It was no use. And the fervour, the certainty that shone in his eyes like a kind of madness, terrified her. She went downstairs and broke the news to Ghislain: William would not see him or consider a reprieve. He must leave the house at once or suffer the humiliation of being thrown out by force.

'You can go to my sister's at the Forge,' Margaret told him, 'she will care for you and maybe William will change his mind in a day or so.'

Ghislain was seated on a low stool by the fire. He had been crying and suddenly he looked young, so very young, not much older than Luke after all. 'Your husband is a monster!' His voice cracked and broke. 'He thinks he can throw me off like a stray dog. Has he forgotten that I also can make *him* suffer! I'll make him suffer for this, you'll see!'

'Ghislain, whatever are you talking about?'

'I will make him sorry, I will make him wish he did not treat me so!' The boy leapt up and began pacing the room. 'He thinks he is such a grand gentleman and that all the world is fooled but I can tell them, I can start a scandal will ruin him for ever!'

Not comprehending his outburst, Margaret heard only the baffled anger and hurt behind his words. 'Poor Ghislain!' She stretched out a hand in a hopeless gesture of comfort. 'And I shall miss you so much!'

Ghislain stopped his pacing and was suddenly very still. He turned slowly to look at her and frowned. '*You* will miss me?'

'Yes.' Until she said the words she had not realised their truth. 'It's hard to explain exactly but . . . these last two months have been the happiest I can remember since . . . well, for a long time.'

He stared at her. 'Don't tell me that!'

'But it's the truth.'

'Ah –!' He raised his shoulders in a gesture of despair, then muttered under his breath, 'Maybe so . . . And there is Luke also.' He was silent for a long time. Eventually he said in a low voice, 'So, I see that I must pack my bags and go quietly. Mistress Hollar, I think your kindness has destroyed me.'

'What?'

He shrugged. 'Because if I punish your husband as he

427

deserves then you and your son will suffer also. Perhaps even more than he. And I find that, after all, I cannot do that. So, tell your monster husband that he has his wife to thank for the saving of his reputation. No, don't bother, there is no point.'

'Ghislain, what are you saying?'

For answer he took her hand and kissed it. And Margaret had the feeling that it was now a young man standing before her, no longer a child.

Luke had been standing by the scullery door. Watching and listening to every word.

Ghislain cheered up when he saw how much money Margaret had persuaded William to part with. As she packed food and clothes for him for his journey Margaret puzzled over what he had said and she came to the conclusion that he must have knowledge of some dishonest business transactions in which William had become involved.

Early the following morning Ghislain set off up the street that led away from Porthew with never a backward glance at the house in which he had lived for over a year. So he never saw the motionless figure who stood at the bedroom window.

William watched until he had disappeared into the hazy early-morning sunshine, and then he remained and watched the empty road. His hands were clenched at his sides, his mouth was a tight line of anger and his expression was remorseless.

But his blue eyes brimmed with unshed tears.

18

This time William was faithful to the promises that God had wrenched from him on the night of the storm. Not even Mistress Payne, the wealthy merchant's wife who had long been considered the epitome of Puritan virtue, was so rigorous in her devotions. He read the Bible for two hours every day, spent long periods on his knees in lonely prayer, and for an hour each morning and evening he led his household in worship.

By and large, they did not question the changes. Luke might have found it tedious had he not enjoyed the attention William now lavished on him and the knowledge (he had always suspected it) that they were superior to the common herd. 'God sent a miracle to save me for His great work,' William never tired of telling the boy, 'and Our Lord has chosen you to be my son. We must prepare and be ready when He calls.' For Luke the words echoed like a bugle's call to arms and every night, exhausted by long prayers, he fell asleep imagining the heroic deeds he was soon to perform at his father's side. Dorcas and Paul Viney had no reason to believe themselves specially chosen; William, when he mentioned them in prayer at all, referred to them as God's humbler instruments, but they accepted this without resentment and welcomed the enforced interruptions in their work. Paul learned to doze while still appearing to be awake and listening; Dorcas sucked her fingers and thought about the Christ child and food.

Only Margaret fretted under the new regime. In many ways her lot had improved: William was at pains to be courteous and patient; as master of his household he was without fault. It was his apparently privileged intimacy with all three members of the Trinity, Father, Son and Holy Ghost, that Margaret found intolerable.

Although she had never been able to recapture her vision

of harmony on the day of Fletcher Grey's visit to Porthew, she had treasured it as a remembered possibility. Occasionally, in the words of the Prayer Book, a phrase or image from the Bible, she had heard an echo from a wider sphere, one shaped not by the hard struggle for survival but by a consciousness of boundless love. Now all that seemed barred to her. There was no chance at all that William's God, the God with whom he was apparently so intimately acquainted and who had saved him from drowning, had any purpose for her at all, she who had only wanted to see this paragon dead.

'Praise be to God who delivered my body from the storm,' was William's daily thanksgiving; at first Margaret observed sourly that his rescue had been due to Ambrose's all too human strength, not divine intervention at all, but, confronted with William's unwavering certainty, her resentment only came to seem yet further proof of her own wickedness. To avoid an argument (which she was certain to lose, William being as convinced that he was in the right as she was of her own error) she learned to comply with the endless family devotions while inwardly detaching herself from them entirely.

Worse than the loss of belief was the growing estrangement from her son. William had always been affectionate towards the boy, but in a random, absentminded way. But now that Luke was to be his helpmeet in the great task God had preserved him for, his education was far too important to be left any longer to Margaret or Parson Weaver; William must now supervise it down to the last detail. Luke was thrilled to be considered so important. Having refused ever to enjoy the classical fables that meant so much to his mother, he became an eager student of the trials of the Israelites, the catalogue of Old Testament carnage that had become William's favourite reading.

Margaret tried every trick she knew to win Luke back to her side, but every day saw him slip further from her. After all, what could she offer the boy that might compare with the promise of eternal salvation?

During the late spring of 1639, while Margaret was grappling with the problem of her newly devout husband, ripples from the wider world began to disturb this western Cornish back-water. In far-off Scotland the people were perverse enough to rise up against the English king. To criticise King Charles was common enough, a habitual grumbling that all indulged in from time to time; to take up arms against his lawful government was another matter altogether. Even if the King had ruled for ten years without once calling Parliament, that did not justify rebellion. It was a symptom of changed times that Bevil Grenvile, who had always been content to pass his days in the quiet pursuits of a country gentleman, had decided to lift his dusty and old-fashioned armour down from its place beside the fireplace in the great hall at Stowe and become a soldier, an occupation that had hitherto been the preserve of his irascible younger brother Richard. Bevil threw himself into the task of raising and outfitting a troop of men to rally to his sovereign's cause.

Scotland was too far away to arouse much interest among the Cornish generally. A war with Spain, now, that would have been different . . . memories of glory and plunder in the time of Elizabeth were still vivid enough to obliterate the more recent memory of disaster at Cadiz. But there was no shortage of young men restless enough to flock to the Grenvile blue and white in the vague hope of adventure and chivalrous battle. Nicolas Sutton's younger brother Stephen left off the courtship of a Mevagissey heiress (she was not much interested anyway) and rode north, taking several of his father's tenants with him.

William Hollar was consumed with rage at the very idea of the King of England threatening to use force against the good Protestants of Scotland. Was it not enough that God's people were being persecuted by Romish armies all over Europe? Must England's own king do the Pope's devilish work here?

So, through that summer, while the children of Porthew scampered through the dusty streets and played at being Grenvile's men and hammered their imagined Scottish foes, Luke remained aloof from their games, and spent still more time at his father's side.

Towards midsummer of the same year, Richard Treveryan returned to Cornwall. As before, he lodged at Rossmere, but it was rumoured that he had come this time accompanied by a large retinue of servants, several of whom were more war-like than anything seen in Bevil Grenvile's troop of local warriors.

Within two days of his arrival Francis Crane rode over to Trecarne to talk with Joseph for the last time. Margaret heard the news next day from Lizzie, who had heard the news from Ambrose, who would talk of nothing else. The agent had informed Joseph that he had twenty-four hours to remove his belongings and his family from the farm; otherwise they would be turned out by force. Jennie had become hysterical but her husband still refused to compromise. Since then Ambrose and his father had abandoned the Forge and spent every moment drumming up all the men of the Treloar clan to support their kinsman.

Sick with foreboding, Margaret hurried over to Trecarne as soon as she heard the news. She was obliged to go on foot since William had ridden Samphire to Camborne that morning and was not expected back until nightfall. She feared that might be too late to help Jennie's family.

She found the farmstead in uproar. Ambrose was there, venting his rage on every scrawny chicken that wandered in his path, and bristling with energy for a fight. His father Robert, a big man, though not so large as his son, his dark hair and beard now brindled with grey, was every bit as angry, but his fury was calmer – and even more resolute. Two cousins from Manaccan had joined them already, Young Robert, as he was known to distinguish him from the smith, and his brother Roger both taciturn and kindly men (who had never been involved in a serious fight in their lives) but big men in the Treloar mould – and united behind Joseph in their hatred of gross injustice. Each time Ambrose roared his challenge to the tranquil summer sky, his father and the two cousins nodded their heads and rumbled a wordless assent.

When Margaret arrived the four men were crammed in the main room of the farmhouse, where Joseph still worked at his loom. She wondered then if the sounding of the Last Trump would be enough to distract the weaver from his ceaseless work.

432

'What right did he have to threaten you, that's what I'd like to know!' Robert Treloar thumped the table with his huge fist and the wooden platters leapt in the air. 'This farm will go to your son after you, everyone knows that.'

'Just let him try to throw you off your own land!' The veins stood out on Ambrose's neck. 'He'll soon discover his mistake!'

They were a formidable group. Margaret tried to comfort herself with the thought that Francis Crane would surely back down when he saw what mighty adversaries he had ranged against him, and some compromise would still be reached.

Jennie stood listlessly by the open doorway. Her latest pregnancy was already beginning to show, her face was pale and her eyes red-rimmed from crying. Joseph sat at the loom and worked the shuttle and said little enough, but his eyes blazed out black fury from under heavy brows.

'Tell me how I can help you,' said Margaret.

'We have mounted a guard,' Robert told her. 'We built a fire in the near meadow and at the first sign of trouble it will be ablaze. That will be the signal for Joseph's neighbours to joins us.'

'If Joseph can be thrown out of his home, then no one is safe,' declared Ambrose. 'Those gentlefolk think they have the right to treat us like animals but –'

Joseph interrupted him. 'Treveryan is no gentleman,' he growled.

Margaret shuddered, although the afternoon was warm. 'Will you show me the bonfire?' she asked Jennie, wanting only to escape the fighting talk.

Jennie nodded her agreement. She was so numbed with dread that Margaret might have suggested they leave at once for France and she would probably have complied.

It was a fine midsummer afternoon. Jennie's children, those too young to be affected by the martial atmosphere in their home, were playing contentedly in the chicken-scratched dust of the farmyard. From their wooden pen a trio of young calves looked out with huge eyes on the strange world. Although at this time of year the animals would normally be all out to pasture, they had been brought into the byres for safety, in case Treveryan's men should try to drive them off. Margaret paused by the little barn where Juno had been stabled. The old mare greeted her with a whinny of pleasure and Margaret reached in her pocket for a titbit and stroked her stringy neck. And wondered if she would have loved the animal half so much if she had not been so ugly-looking.

'Juno has been a blessing to us already,' said Jennie. 'It was mighty kind of your father to give her to us.'

'I'm sure he was glad to do it.'

They walked in silence to the meadow. Swallows were swooping under the low branches of the trees and skimming the muddy water of the pond; the air was laden with the scent of elderblossom and the gentle drone of insects. From the willows that bordered the stream, came the languorous call of a wood pigeon. Margaret, looking about her at the familiar fields and hedges, the trees motionless in the afternoon warmth, could not believe that such a calm midsummer moment could possibly be disrupted.

'Treveryan will never try to turn you out. He couldn't.'

But Jennie shook her head, afraid to allow the luxury of hope. 'He wants this farm, Mattie, Heaven alone knows why.'

'Maybe he'll change his mind.'

Jennie shrugged. 'I used to hate this place,' she said.

'What?'

'I was fifteen when they sent me here to marry. I must have cried every day that first year. But my father had died in a fall from the barn roof and my mother could not keep me. It was so lonely here, all alone with Joseph and . . . he frightened me then. Not that he was ever cruel, but he hardly ever spoke to me and never showed his feelings. And he seemed old to me then. It was only when Treveryan came here the first time, years ago it must have been, when Joseph first began to fear he wished to turn us out, that I realised I had grown to love this place. And Joseph too,' she added simply.

'No one will take your home from you.'

'Pray God you are right . . . And this has been the first year we've been able to pay the rent on time without borrowing. Now that the older children can do their share

– and more, often – we may even have a surplus at Michaelmas. If we are still here –'

Her voice cracked and broke and, blinking back the tears, she forced herself to smile. 'I'm supposed to be showing you the fire,' she said.

It was built of dry furze, the remains of last year's rick, and had been positioned just beyond the near-meadow gate. The smoke would be visible all through the valley.

'The children have hardly slept since Crane's visit. They take turns to watch from the top of the lane.'

Margaret looked down the valley towards the blue blur of the sea; it was a pleasant enough situation, but nothing out of the ordinary. What streak of perversity made Richard Treveryan single out this place when he had so many other manors and farms to choose from?

'Everyone knows you had the legal evidences,' she said, 'he'd surely never be so wicked as to flout the law.'

'Maybe you are right.' Jennie at last permitted herself a flicker of hope. She placed her hand on Margaret's arm. 'You're a good friend to come and help us now, Mattie.'

Margaret ignored the familiar twinge of duplicity and began to warm to her optimistic theme. 'Men always like to talk of fighting, but when the time comes they have the common sense at least to settle things without that. Why, what would be the point –?'

But Jennie was no longer smiling, no longer even looking at Margaret but beyond her, to where the road twisted up the hill above the fringe of oak wood. Her hand tightened on Margaret's arm.

'Jennie, what is it?'

All the colour had drained from her face and she looked on the verge of fainting.

'They're coming. Can you not see them?'

'You know my eyes are not so strong.' But she could see Jennie's terror plain enough. Above the line of the far hedge, her keener vision had spotted the heads and shoulders of several riders, approaching at a steady trot.

'We must warn the others,' said Margaret, since Jennie appeared suddenly paralysed. But at that moment a child's voice, shrill to the point of hysteria, echoed louder and louder down the lane. 'They're here, they're here! Hurry, they're coming, lots of them!'

'Light the fire, Jennie, quick, we must raise help!'

Jennie burst out in a wail, 'Oh Mattie, it's hopeless! How can we stand against them, there must be twenty men at least. Joseph will be murdered, I'm sure, they'll kill him! Oh Lord help us, what shall I do? What about my children? Oh Mattie, make him see sense, for God's sake tell him for he never listens to me, don't let them kill him!'

'Jennie, calm yourself. We must gather up your children.'

At the first cry of alarm Ambrose had rushed from the house and already the bonfire was ablaze.

'Come on then, damn you!' He bellowed his challenge to the tree-covered road that led down to the farm. 'We're ready, we're waiting for you!' And Margaret heard the passion in his call, the longing for a fight. Oh Lord, she found herself praying, let it be Francis Crane only. Don't let Treveryan be among them.

Jennie was sobbing with terror as Margaret dragged her back towards the house. Joseph had hobbled out into the yard and stood watching the spot where the track emerged from under the canopy of trees at the entrance to their farm. Behind him stood Robert and his cousins, all armed with a crude assortment of pikes, knives, axes and bars.

The sound of horses' hoofs, many of them, was coming steadily closer.

'Joseph, for pity's sake be reasonable,' begged Jennie, 'do what they want, don't let them kill you.' But her husband did not even seem to hear her pleading, but only watched, motionless, for the first sight of his enemy.

'Have more courage, woman,' chided Robert. 'Here, take a weapon and fight if you wish to save your husband's life.'

Jennie stared at him for a moment, then took the axe and with possession of it her weeping ceased and she went silently to stand beside her husband.

A man, breathless from running, leapt the stile into the yard; he was carrying a rusty sword and an axe. 'I saw the fire,' he gasped, 'Andrew and John are right behind.'

'Good men,' said Joseph.

'The rest will follow soon enough,' said Robert. 'Mistress Hollar?' And he offered Margaret a heavy knife.

'I cannot fight,' she groaned.

Ambrose glanced in her direction and his face softened for a moment. 'Mattie has always been uncommon tender-hearted,' he agreed.

'Or else too grand to help her own family,' growled his father, thrusting the knife into her hand. 'You can defend yourself at least,' he said scornfully.

She took the knife, but the weight of it was misery, dragging her arm to the ground.

From out of the black tunnel of trees the first horseman emerged into the sunlight. Margaret knew at once it was Treveryan. Sheba's dark flanks gleamed and she tossed her head proudly. For once Richard Treveryan had left off his fine garments and was dressed in a soldier's sturdy jerkin and breeches and his head was uncovered. More than a dozen men followed him in a tight bunch of jingling harness and flashing steel. Only Francis Crane was known, the others were all Plymouth men, cut-throats by the look of them, brought down especially for this task. No local man would help Treveryan now, no matter what reward was offered.

The group standing by the doorway of the cottage was too intent on watching Treveryan and Francis Crane to notice that three of the men had separated from the rest to go to the bonfire by the meadow gate. Margaret saw, but she guessed they planned to smother the flames and, since the signal had already served its purpose, she said nothing.

'Joseph Treloar!' Francis Crane's normally high-pitched voice was today raised to a squeak by his nervousness. 'We have this morning been given legal title from the Justices to evict you and your family from this property of Trecarne and –'

'Legal be damned,' burst out Joseph, 'my father bought this farm for three lives, as well you know.'

'Do you have the evidences to prove it? Bring them out and we'll trouble you no more.'

'You stole them!' trumpeted Ambrose, and would have dragged the agent from his horse there and then, but his father held him back, murmuring, 'All in good time, lad. Only wait.'

Francis Crane reined his horse back to the protective

shelter of Treveryan's tall mare. He licked his lips nervously and muttered something to his master. From the anxious look on his face Margaret guessed he was advising compromise, but Richard dismissed his pleas.

Too late, Margaret saw that the three riders who had paused by the meadow gate, far from attempting to smother the fire, had dipped brands into the leaping flames to light them.

The knife fell from her hand and clattered in the dust.

'Mr Treveryan,' she begged, walking across the farmyard, 'for mercy's sake, reconsider.' She caught hold of Sheba's bridle and the mare breathed a gentle welcome. Margaret took heart. 'You surely do not mean to turn my cousin from his home, you cannot be so cruel!'

Richard was looking over her head, his expression implacable. 'Get away from here, Mistress Hollar,' he said in a low voice, 'today's business is no concern of yours.'

'These people are my friends.'

His eyes met hers for only the briefest moment before he wheeled his horse around, tearing the reins from her hands, and called out, 'Do you hide behind women, Treloar? Or are you prepared to see sense at last and leave peaceably?'

'I'll see you dead first!'

Treveryan smiled grimly and, gesturing to his hired riders with a wide sweep of his arm, called out, 'Then set to work. We'll clear the place by nightfall!'

Suddenly half a dozen of the riders were carrying lighted brands: within seconds the hay-rick was alight and the straw in the cowshed and the barn began to smoulder. With a roar of rage Ambrose pulled two riders from their horses and before they had a chance to use their weapons against him he had smashed their heads together with a force that left them stunned. Jennie screamed and plucked her youngest child from the path of a riderless horse and whirled around in a panic, no longer knowing whether to stay or flee.

The other children were howling, too terrified to move. One of her sons, a whey-faced lad named Mark, seized a hatchet and sprang at a hired ruffian, who would have struck him down without mercy but Margaret plucked him from danger just in time.

'Jennie, help me get the children away from here!' she shouted, keeping a firm hold on Mark and catching a small girl by the arm. Jennie followed her and together they managed to herd the children to beyond the shelter of a stone wall. Mark was struggling and demanding to be allowed to fight.

'No! You must stay here and look after the little ones. Make sure they don't stray or God knows they'll all be killed. Do you understand me, Mark?'

He nodded and picked up his infant sister with a look of such misery and protectiveness as Margaret knew she would never forget. In the farmyard all was pandemonium. Young Robert and another man had dragged Francis Crane from his horse and were raining blows on his head and portly body. Smoke was pouring from the outbuildings and she could hear the animals racketing against the walls in terror.

It seemed to Margaret that it took an age to cross the yard. She could hear Treveryan urging his men on but she could not see him in the densely packed mass of men and horses. She managed to wrench open the door of the byre and the calves poured out in such a rush that she was almost crushed against the wooden door. But when she pulled open the door of the stable it was only a couple of roosters who flew out with a squawk of singed feathers past her face.

'Juno, Juno! Oh come out, Juno, or you'll be burned alive!'

Through the smoke she could just make out the darker shadow of the old horse, too paralysed by panic to make her way to safety. Margaret hesitated for only a moment before taking a deep breath and plunging over the smouldering straw to lead her out. She had caught hold of Juno's halter and was tugging her towards the open door, but as she put her foot down the straw burst into flame and she emerged once more into the fresh air, the horse at her side and unharmed, but the hem of her skirt a ring of fire. She beat at the flames with her hands and screamed as Juno cantered into the thick of the fighting, but her screams were lost in the tumult all around.

Then a dark shape loomed up before her and Richard Treveryan sprang from his horse and knocked her unceremoniously to her knees, stamping out the flames as he did

439

so. His face was bleeding from a cut above the eye and he was breathing heavily. 'Sweet Jesus, woman,' he exclaimed in a passion, 'will you never learn sense?'

She clutched him by the arm. 'Make them stop!' she yelled. 'Oh can't you make them – ?' But then she screamed again, this time in terror as she saw Ambrose knock another imported fighter senseless and race across the yard to set upon Treveryan himself. Warned by Margaret's cry, Richard just had time to mount Sheba once more and gallop the terrified beast across the yard, now a mess of brawling men and animals milling in panic.

But the combined fury and determination of the Treloar clan was more than the Plymouth men had expected: nothing, it seemed, could ever vanquish Ambrose's vast strength, nor his father's grim resolve, nor the insistence of the local men that outsiders would never beat them. The ruffians had expected an easy contest against a few feeble rustics, not this ferocious band of giants.

Richard sensed their waning enthusiasm for the fight. He shouted curses and encouragement and then, with a furious oath, he seized a firebrand and galloped to the open door of the farmhouse, throwing the torch inside.

'The loom, the loom!' Jennie shrieked and ran for water, only to have the bucket knocked from her hand by one of her opponents. Margaret picked up a shovel and ran towards the doorway but Joseph snatched it from her and hobbled inside the house himself, beating frantically at the flames.

'The loom!' Jennie sobbed.

A towering column of anger and fight, Ambrose pounded across the yard to throw himself at Treveryan's horse, and he would have knocked both man and rider down had not Richard, his face contorted with rage, pulled a firebrand from one of his men and plunged it into Ambrose's face.

His scream, the high-pitched whistling scream of a Michaelmas pig with a rusty blade in its throat, soared over the sounds of fighting and chaos. There was a hideous smell of burning flesh and hair and bone and Ambrose fell to the ground, clutching at his blazing face.

For a brief moment all those in the yard stood motionless. Despite the warlike assortment of weapons, despite all the talk of murder and dying for the land, there had been a kind of tacit understanding that this matter could be solved with fists and bruises, maybe a broken bone or two, but not this, this huge man writhing and screaming on the ground with half his face destroyed by fire.

The moment of shock passed. Robert Treloar wrenched his eyes from his son's agony and turned pure hatred on Treveryan. 'Murderer!' he groaned. 'I'll see you dead –!' And he lunged at Treveryan, driving his knife into his thigh and dragging him from Sheba's back as the wounded horse reared up in terror.

And now it was a different kind of battle. Andrew Roach, the neighbour who had joined them earlier, had been content to thrash the hired ruffian he had managed to unhorse. Now a kind of madness seized him: he took a blade and slit the man's throat, then laughed with shock and bewilderment as the red blood bubbled in the dust.

Margaret found herself carrying a bucket of water and pouring it over Ambrose's face, though she had no recollection of what she saw there. She saw Sheba rear up and gallop riderless away, the long knife wound streaking her neck and flank with crimson gore. She saw Richard Treveryan lift his sword and aim it at Robert Treloar's heart but the big man swerved and the blade sliced into his bare arm. She saw a man, kind-hearted Roger Treloar from Manaccan, hacking at Francis Crane's fat stomach with a hatchet and the blood poured like dark honey over his hand.

And then she saw Jennie wailing by the door of the farmhouse, no longer fearing for the loom; it was her husband's life that was in danger from the fire.

'Joseph!' she howled at the dark shadow that moved through the smoke and flames in the house. 'Joseph, it's no use, come out! Oh Joseph, save yourself!'

Then the threads of the loom caught and the flames leapt to the ceiling and then the whole room was ablaze, beams, walls and loom, and Joseph fell backwards through the door and Jennie caught him; and he buried his face in her shoulder, unable to watch as his home and his livelihood burned, unable to stop the tears of defeat and rage that poured from his smoke-reddened eyes.

Richard was mounted once more, though on a meaner

horse, Sheba having fled, and the ten men that were left to him regrouped by the entrance to the yard. The heat from the burning buildings was so intense that the water sizzled in the butt.

There was no longer any home or farm for the Treloars to defend, everything was now blazing in the summer heat; quite suddenly, as the roof timbers cracked and fell around them, the fight was over. Margaret found herself helping Young Robert put Juno between the shafts of the little cart, and three men lifted Ambrose and laid him, still uttering unearthly cries, but quieter now, inside.

Jennie hurried across the yard and gathered up Mark and the younger children from their hiding place behind the wall. Even the baby had ceased to cry, and a strange quietness came over them all, children, adults and fighting men.

Richard drew his pistol from his belt and rode over to Joseph, who was using his powerful arms to hoist himself on to the seat of the cart.

'You have until tomorrow morning to remove your possessions,' he told him, 'whatever then remains will be forfeit.'

Joseph took his time to settle himself on the seat and gather up the reins, while a couple of the smaller children were lifted up beside him. He turned slowly and took a last look at his blazing home. Only then did he look towards Treveryan and he shook his head in silence, his lips drawn back in something that was almost a grin of disbelief.

Richard wheeled his mount around and rode back with orders for his men to mount guard through the evening and brief night, but to allow the livestock and anything else that could be saved to be removed.

An elderly neighbour approached Margaret. His face was bruised and he made no attempt to hide the tears that were streaming down his cheeks. 'We'll gather up the animals,' he said, 'and whatever else can be saved. You'd best help the wounded, get them and the children away.'

Margaret nodded. She tore a strip of charred fabric from the hem of her skirt and bound up Robert's arm which was bleeding heavily from a wound just below the shoulder. Then she took two children by the hand and said, 'Come, we'll follow your father in the cart. It's over now.'

The group of riders who were waiting by the entrance to the yard parted to allow the cavalcade of horse and cart and people through on to the lane. As they passed, Robert Treloar stopped and turned to Richard and said in a voice that was calm, yet shaking with emotion, 'May you for ever rot in Hell for the work you've done today.'

Richard Treveryan did not answer. Margaret followed close behind the cart and never lifted her eyes from the wheels turning over the dry and rutted lane, and the sound of the creak and rattle of the cart was the sound of her own heart breaking. She dreaded to look on Treveryan. Besides, there was no need; she knew only too well how his face would be, ruthless and dark.

Shame and misery were dragging her down. Not so much for the violence she had witnessed that day, for Joseph's loss and Ambrose's injury, but rather shame at what she had glimpsed within herself, the truth she had tried so long to hide. Her grief was all because she knew now, had known in that split second of anguish and revulsion when she had seen Treveryan plunge the brand into Ambrose's face, that the villain who had done these terrible things was the man she loved, the only man in all her life she had ever cared for.

19

The casualties sustained in the fighting for Trecarne were a good deal worse than any suffered by the Cornish soldiers that summer in their battle against the Scots. King Charles made peace with his northern subjects before the two armies had done much more than wheel about and manoeuvre for position. Bevil Grenvile returned, having received a knighthood from His Majesty for his loyalty; several commented that he looked ten years younger after a summer spent adventuring far from the cares of mortgaged farms and a fretful wife. Stephen Sutton rode home full of enthusiasm for the soldier's life; he had seen the King on several occasions and now he alarmed his father by threatening to further his military career in the Continental wars. Nicolas was so inspired by his younger brother's exploits that for once he almost regretted having stayed at home. Another time, he said, not even his great love of Rossmere would prevent him from following the Grenvile colours into battle.

There was widespread fury at Richard Treveryan's mishandling of the Treloar eviction. By his actions he had damaged the delicate balance of society. Brute force was frequently used against vagrants and the landless, but the Treloars were a local family connected by ties of kinship with half the district and the use of hired cut-throats to turn them off their land was nothing less than a scandal. Feeling ran high, not only against Richard Treveryan, but also against those who appeared to be sheltering him; they were not to know that the gentry were almost as angry at the way events had turned out, as anyone else. However, Francis Crane had been brutally murdered, and if murder were allowed to go unpunished then a state of anarchy was the only result. A couple of days after the burning of Trecarne, Roger Treloar, whom all knew to be as law-abiding as any man in Cornwall, was dragged from his bed in the early

444

hours of the morning and taken in chains to Launceston gaol to await trial. Too shocked to understand what was happening to him, haunted by the image of his wife and two small children wailing on the doorstep in the dawn light as he departed, the man quickly developed a fever. Andrew Roach, Joseph's neighbour, went into hiding for several weeks but the authorities, anxious only to avoid further trouble, were happy to overlook the murder of Richard Treveryan's mercenary. No one had known his name and at some stage during that midsummer evening his body had unaccountably disappeared.

It was fortunate that Ambrose seemed likely to survive his injuries or Nicolas would have found it hard to resist the pressure to have Richard arrested for murder also. As it was, it could be claimed that he had acted in self-defence during the enforcement of a legal eviction notice. His wounds, and those to his horse, supported this version of events. But until the furore had died down, Richard was more disliked by the gentry than ever – and even Nicolas and Alice found themselves wishing he would return to Saltash.

But Ambrose did survive. For three days and nights the sounds of his agony allowed his household no rest. Parson Weaver called each day and reflected that the poor man's approaching death must surely be a blessed relief. Lizzie and Mistress Treloar mixed up a salve of hogs' grease and thorn apples and took turns to apply it to the mess of burns that covered half his face and neck. On the fourth day, Margaret happened to be talking with Lizzie in the kitchen when Mistress Treloar came running in and said that Ambrose had roused from his delirium and had asked for a sup of ale. They at once hurried to his side. When she saw his eyes soften at her approach, Lizzie burst into tears. Ambrose lifted a huge hand and gently touched her cheek. 'Don't weep for me,' he said, and his words sounded clumsy, coming from that misshapen mouth, 'I'll not die yet. I'll live long enough to see that scoundrel dead.'

Richard Treveryan was never mentioned by name at the Forge. 'That man', 'that devil', 'the scoundrel' – and everyone knew at once who was signified. And Margaret knew too, as she watched Ambrose brush the tears from Lizzie's cheeks and sensed the determination of the man, that it was his longing for revenge would give Ambrose the strength to recover.

Joseph and Jennie were lodged at the Forge. With no loom to occupy him, Joseph seemed suddenly shrunken, a hermit crab deprived of his shell. He sat alone for long periods of the day, in the little patch of garden behind the house or by the edge of the road, and threw an imaginary shuttle back and forth between his hands. Since the Forge was hopelessly overcrowded, Margaret took the two older children to stay with her in Porthew, though Luke resented the intrusion.

Local outrage and compassion took a practical form: each day gifts of food and ale were brought to the Forge. Parson Weaver set up a fund to help Joseph and his family, also for Ambrose and for the wife and two small children of Roger Treloar who, with the breadwinner in gaol, were threatened with destitution.

William gave generously to the fund, both as a good Christian and because, as a kind-hearted man, he was genuinely shocked by their tragedy.

Margaret would have given all she had.

That summer was a time of torment. She was convinced that the love she had felt for Treveryan as she shepherded the children behind the wheels of the cart, had been a moment of madness induced by the horrors of that afternoon. This powerful emotion that consumed her was surely hatred. She loathed and despised Richard Treveryan – how could she do otherwise? – yet she was unable to control the images which tortured her. She tried to wear herself out with hard work; but as she pounded washing in the barrel or worked in the fields at Conwinnion to gather in the hay with Tom and her father, she saw a man's face gaunt and shadowed, dark eyes looking out from beneath black brows. Sometimes the face was vicious and cruel and then she hated him freely. Worse by far was when she saw his imagined features crease into a grin of boyish delight. Worst of all was when that imagined face turned towards her with a change to gentleness that spelled a kind of welcome. Words echoed through her mind: 'You must always believe me, Mistress Hollar.' She heard him talking of the countries he had seen; she heard him recommending her to a man's disguise and a sailor's life – 'But I fear your figure would betray you.' She heard his laughter. She told herself she hated his laughter above all things. On those summer nights when she awoke from brief sleep in a sudden wordless terror she was sometimes sure he must be in the room, so clearly did she feel his presence. His dark energy was all around her, his boots stamping out the flames and as his voice shouted out for the hundredth time, 'Sweet Jesus, woman, will you never learn sense?' she heard the frenzy of concern behind his rage.

Despite her long practice at hiding her emotions, she was unable to mask her present anguish. She was grown changeable, one moment lavishing her affections, the next flaring up in irritation. She snapped at Dorcas at least once a day and made her cry, only to hug her a moment or two later and give her sugar tarts to show that she was sorry. She even quarrelled with William; she refused absolutely to join her household as they prayed together each day and listened while he read from the Bible.

Parson Weaver advised William that his wife was still shocked by the horrors she had been forced to witness at Trecarne. He recommended patience. But William had already quarrelled with the parson on several points of theology and dismissed his advice as yet another instance of his mealy-mouthed dithering in matters of religion and his reprehensible laxness. William's patience lasted only two days, after which he considered sternness was called for.

'What manner of wickedness has made you deaf to the comfort offered by Our Saviour's words? Only trust me, Margaret, trust in the Lord; together let us pray for the blessed solace of His healing.'

'William, stop. Your prayers would kill me for sure.'

He recoiled as though she had struck him. 'Evil woman! Surely the Devil is at work in your heart!'

And Margaret, who believed his words were truer than he would ever know, could only flee the house in misery.

It was a mercy of a kind that her father needed help at the farm. She was glad of the distraction and of the opportunity to quit Porthew. More than once, as she walked the dark green lanes of summer, she fell into a reverie – and when she roused herself she found that she had taken the road that led, not to Conwinnion, but to Trecarne. Appalled she turned back at once. She was quite sure she never wanted to visit the place again.

Richard Treveryan made no attempt to placate the local population. They might have forgotten his transgression sooner had he prudently lain low for a while. Instead he suddenly became a regular attender at church in Porthew. Each Sunday he rode up on a muscular grey stallion accompanied by a couple of manservants; immaculately dressed, his face impassive, he sat in lonely eminence at the front of the church, across the aisle from the numerous Suttons. If hateful looks and whispered loathing could hurt a man then the people of Porthew would have surely killed him that first Sunday . . . but he rode away unharmed, and returned as if to taunt them the following week. On the day at the beginning of August when Ambrose was sufficiently recovered to make the brief journey to the church for the first time, the tension in the church as Richard entered was almost tangible. Emotion remained high throughout the service and, although Parson Weaver offered thanks for Ambrose's continuing recovery, it was not gratitude, or Christian charity, that was uppermost in the minds of the congregation. Nicolas Sutton, sensing danger, walked out with him into the churchyard, but as Richard mounted his horse a stone whistled past him, narrowly missing the side of his face. With a common instinct the crowd closed over the culprit. Richard gave no sign that he had noticed either stone or crowd. As always Margaret took care to position herself as far from him as was possible and tried not to look at him at all, though her eyes seemed drawn to him as to a disfigurement. Never once did he look at her.

Every move she made seemed to demand a huge act of will. It was an effort to prevent her gaze from lingering on his face; it was an effort to drive all thoughts of him from her mind; an effort to visit Lizzie and the others who needed her comfort and assistance at the Forge; an effort not to turn from Ambrose's hideous wounds; an effort to maintain a semblance of composure in the face of his continued suffering.

She hardly dared to consider what was causing these

changes. It was bad enough that Richard Treveryan's image haunted her by day and night and seemed to engulf her in complicity with his crime. She, who had always recoiled in horror from any form of cruelty, now felt herself implicated in an act which all right-thinking people condemned. She assured herself that no one loathed Richard Treveryan more passionately than she. She remembered his nearness, his expression as she tied the kerchief around his hand. She feared the turmoil and the horror of it would make her lose her mind.

On a morning in late August, Margaret moved restlessly about her kitchen. She told herself there was a mound of work to be done but she could not settle to any of it. From behind the door of the new parlour she could hear William leading the household in their daily prayers, his voice throbbing with sincerity and punctuated by a straggle of 'amens': Luke's was high-pitched and eager, Paul Viney's emphatic enough to show that he was awake and attentive, Dorcas's shouted, ''Men!' always lagging a few moments behind the rest. William had that morning been so vexed by Margaret's refusal to join them that for a moment she had thought he intended to use force – but he checked himself just in time. That had never been his way.

His voice rose, sounding still more clearly through the closed door of the parlour. 'Forgive your erring daughter, Lord, teach her footsteps to walk once more according to Thy law, do not suffer her heart to be hardened . . .'

Seizing a light shawl, Margaret fled the house.

The day was sultry, heavy grey clouds seemed to press the heat back against the earth. The sea was sluggish and dull. In the harbour a fishing boat was unloading its catch and already several people had gathered around to select the choicest fish. She was about to join them, having no other plan in mind, when she heard a voice. 'And Roger Treloar is worse, so they say, and his poor wife doesn't know . . .' She turned away abruptly and walked on.

Soon she was above Porthew and walking briskly across the fields that bordered the cliffs. At the back of her mind was the notion that she might gather some early mushrooms to pickle for the winter, or perhaps some rosehips for conserve. She noticed the families working together in the fields to fetch in hay before the rain; she noticed the dusty greens of the hedgerows and the clouds of butterflies that rose up as she passed, but she never noticed that every step she took was bringing her closer to Trecarne.

Only when she reached the rise of ground that overlooked the Treloars' former home, before the track led through the oak woods, did she pause. Her heart was beating against her ribs, but this time, she did not turn back.

A man who was surely some kind of sentry was standing a little further down the lane. Not wishing to waste her arguments on sentries, Margaret climbed a stile and followed behind the tall hedge that bordered the meadows.

But as she walked across the last meadow, she thought for a moment that she must have taken a wrong turning on this route she knew so well: no trace of the farm or its outbuildings remained. Cottage, barn, sheds and byres – all had been levelled to the ground. Only the shell of the old hall remained, a tower of grey stone stripped now of its bird-filled cloak of ivy. Suddenly she found it hard to recollect just how it had ever looked before, hard to remember the precise shape of the farmyard, the arrangement of the buildings, the exact spot where Jennie's neat wood-pile had been. Stunned by the speed and thoroughness of the changes, Margaret walked ever more slowly until, at the edge of the first meadow, she stopped altogether. And stared.

The whole area was swarming with activity. There were several teams of oxen, more than she had ever before seen gathered in a single place, hard at work dragging stone, levelling the land. Already the muddy pond had vanished, hedges were being ripped up, earth and rubble shifted by the cartload.

A man was hurrying across the open space towards her. He was waving his arms angrily. His face was streaming with perspiration, his expression indicated that he had been harassed all day and the appearance of a female trespasser was the final straw.

'Begone and away from here at once! Get off this land, do you hear me?'

450

Margaret stood her ground. 'I have come to see Mr Treveryan,' she said simply.

'He's busy and not to be disturbed.'

'Tell him Mistress Hollar wishes to speak with him.'

The man swore. 'Do you want to lose me my job? I tell you, he'll see no one.'

'If it's his anger you fear, then you'd do best to let me see him.'

'I have orders to allow no one through.'

'Then give him a message. Tell him –'

'I have orders . . .'

Clearly the man was so afraid of his employer that he had lost the capacity for independent thought. Margaret was despairing of ever finding a way out of this stalemate when suddenly she caught sight of a man she recognised, leading a pair of horses towards the stream.

'Will!' she shouted. 'Will Stevens!'

He turned and, at the sight of her, he smiled and began to walk towards them.

'Thank heavens,' she breathed. 'Will, it is most important that I talk with Mr Treveryan and this man insists he will prevent me.'

Will Stevens had a shambling, lopsided face. 'What business do you have with him?' The question was apologetic.

'A message from my husband, an urgent message.'

'Ah, yes, a message from Mr Hollar, eh?' He turned to the first man who seemed to be on the verge of repeating that he had orders . . . 'I'll deal with this, you take the horses down to the stream. If Mr Treveryan decides to be angry, he can be angry with me. Go along now, I'll see you don't fall into any trouble.' The first man, looking just as harassed as ever but clearly deciding that this was the best way out of an impossible situation, took the horses by their halters and walked away.

Will Stevens grinned. 'Some of these folk live in such fear of Mr Treveryan I think they'd jump off the cliff if it was orders.'

'And you?'

He considered, then, 'Maybe a smallish cliff,' he said, 'if I knew there'd be no harm in it.'

451

Margaret smiled. 'I did not expect to find you working here,' she said.

'No more did I,' he agreed with a grimace, 'but a man must feed his family and there's good wages offered here, though he expects hard work in return. And it will not profit Joseph or poor Roger now if I turn down the chance of work and make my family go without. I reckon Ambrose will get justice for the Treloars soon enough. When he is ready.'

Margaret, following him through the crowds of hurrying, shouting workmen, suppressed a shudder. The belief that Ambrose would be revenged on the man who had maimed him, which provided almost universal consolation, only increased her sense of foreboding.

They found Richard Treveryan on a rise of ground a little apart from the centre of activity. He was seated at a table spread with plans, discussing them with a small, eager man with brown curls and a pinched and anxious face. Since the day was oppressively warm, his doublet was draped over the carved back of his chair and his shirt was open at the throat. He was bare-headed, dark hair as unruly as ever. But for the fine texture of his shirt, he could easily have been mistaken for one of his labourers. A large dog was sleeping by his feet.

Will Stevens cleared his throat. 'Begging your pardon, Mr Treveryan sir, but there's someone to see you.'

'I left strict instructions that I was not to be disturbed,' he said, without looking up from the plans.

Will threw Margaret an apologetic grin as if to say, what did I tell you . . . ? He tried again. 'Mistress Hollar here said it was urgent, sir.'

At the mention of her name Margaret saw his brown hand, which had been tracing a line on one of the sheets of parchment, hesitate for a brief moment before clenching into a fist. 'I thought I made it clear –'

Margaret interrupted him. 'Mr Treveryan, I do not intend to take up much of your time, but I must talk with you.'

Still he did not look up. 'I cannot imagine that we have anything to say to each other,' he said icily.

'She says it's an urgent message from her husband Mr Hollar, sir.'

'Indeed, then I am quite sure I do not want to hear it.'

Margaret took a step forward and placed both her hands on the table. 'You will hear what I have come to say. You must.'

'Then make it brief. You can see I'm very busy.'

'First you must tell these others to leave, for I will talk with you alone.'

'That is not necessary.'

'I insist.'

There was an ominous silence. Margaret, had she been aware of anything but the hostile face of the man who still had not raised his eyes to look at her, might have noticed that both Will Stevens and the fellow with the anxious face who stood beside Richard's chair seemed to be holding their breath in dread of the expected explosion of rage.

But it did not come. Instead he tapped his fist on the plans and then, as if he had reached a sudden decision, he sank back in his chair and glanced up at his companion with a bitter smile. 'Heaven preserve us from shrewish women,' he said. 'Go on, then, Thomas, leave us alone for a moment. I've had dealings with Mr Hollar's wife before and I assure you there'll be no peace for anyone unless she's humoured.'

The man he called Thomas had let out a sigh of relief that the moment of danger had passed, but now, on being dismissed, he tutted his annoyance and glared at Margaret as he began to gather up his plans.

'Let them lie,' Richard told him, 'this will not delay me more than a few minutes.'

The man retreated. Will Stevens had already made his escape. Richard slung one leg over the arm of his chair and looked towards the horizon, his face expressionless. A study in boredom.

Margaret's annoyance gave her courage. 'You have not wasted much time,' she said.

'On the contrary,' his voice was cold, 'I have waited nearly ten years to begin this work. Which is why I do not welcome interruptions now. What is the reason for your visit?'

'To talk with you.'

'Mr Hollar sent you?'

'No.'

'Well then, what is your business?'

'It concerns your former tenants. Since you turned them from their home –'

He interrupted her with a gesture of irritation. 'If you have come all this way simply to whine about that wretched family then you are wasting your time and the sooner you get back to your delightful husband the better.'

'But they are destitute! And their children –'

'That is no concern of mine.'

'It was your doing, you were responsible. You were the one who –'

'Enough!' Suddenly he swung round and was on his feet. For the first time that day he looked at her directly and his eyes, so close to her own across the table, were furious. 'Mistress Hollar, I'm warning you, if you think I'd have any scruples whatsoever about having you thrown off my land by force then you are quite mistaken. You had better leave at once.'

Margaret's heart was racing but she forced herself to remain quite still. And indeed, she could not have dragged herself away if she had tried. She said quietly, 'The lives of two families are in ruins because of what you have chosen to do and yet you try to tell me that it is no concern of yours. How can you –?'

'They will recover.'

'And Ambrose? What of him? You know full well he is disfigured for life, is almost certainly blind in one eye and –'

'Damn you, woman, I will *not* be subjected to this!' For a few moments they glared at each other and Margaret thought that she must have been insane to provoke him so, no good would come of it and he looked angry enough to throw her off his land himself. Then he dropped his eyes. 'Go on,' he said in a quieter voice, 'go on home. You are wasting your time.'

He turned and, as if dismissing her, pushed back his chair and walked quickly away. She hesitated only for a moment before following him and catching up with him at a place where a small gate led into the field which curved down to the willow-covered stream and the slowly moving sea.

'You are most persistent.'

'Because it is so important that you hear me out, just this once.' She laid her hand on his arm. 'If you only knew how much they have suffered, Mr Treveryan, you would not be so –'

'Stop,' he shook her hand off roughly, 'for once in your life, you meddlesome witch, you can listen to me. That cripple and his whole miserable tribe may die of slow starvation but it is no longer any business of mine. He was offered other farms, better ones and if the man is homeless today then the fault is his alone. His own pigheadedness and stupidity has been his downfall and I refuse to be held responsible. *Now* will you leave me in peace?'

Margaret was silent for a long moment, meeting his angry gaze. All around her she could hear the continuing noise of the workmen, harness jingling, shouted orders, a pack horse whinnying as it returned from the stream. Yet although everything around her remained the same, she had the feeling that the air itself was changing, that some transformation was taking place which she did not understand and had no hope ever of preventing.

She said in a low voice, 'You know that is not the full truth.'

'It is all the truth I care for.'

But Richard must have sensed the alteration too, for his voice was gentler, almost curious. For the first time that day he saw neither anger nor hatred in her expression. He was frowning as he asked, 'Now you may tell me the real reason for your visit. I cannot believe you came all this way merely to tell me what we both already know.'

Margaret could no longer meet his eyes. She looked at the ground and traced an arc in the dust with the toe of her shoe.

'Parson Weaver and Mr Payne have started a fund for Joseph and his family and . . . and the others that have suffered.'

'In that case we can forget about them with a clear conscience.'

Margaret drew another line, crossing the arc. 'Their

needs are great and the fund for their assistance is still pitifully small, although many have given what they could.'

'Well, I'm sure they'll be provided for somehow.'

'I thought perhaps –' She broke off, glanced up at him quickly, looked away again.

He said incredulously, 'You surely do not expect me to contribute?'

Silence. Then, 'Why not?'

'Mistress Hollar, you are surely mad.'

'Maybe so but . . . All that matters now is to raise enough money for a new loom for Joseph. Then he can begin to earn some money again and maybe in time they will be able to afford to find a home –'

'I am tired of hearing about him.'

'You are wealthy. You can afford to be generous.'

'But you misjudge me. I have no wish to be generous, least of all to a man who has caused me so much trouble.'

She was silent for a while, pondering this. And when she spoke her voice was so soft that Richard was obliged to incline his head to catch the words. 'You say these things and men believe you, and judge you for them. And yet I know you are neither as cold nor as cruel as you wish people to believe. I know . . .'

Her voice trailed away.

'Yes, Mistress Hollar?' Richard prompted gently. 'What exactly is it that you know?'

Whatever transformation had occurred earlier, Margaret only sensed the danger of it now. Her voice faltered as she replied, 'I believe you care more about what has happened than you admit.'

Richard, sensing her uncertainty, pressed home his advantage. 'My agent was savagely butchered,' he said, 'and another man in my employ murdered also. For all I know your friends threw his body to the flames to be rid of the evidence for their crime. But I do not expect for a moment that you are troubled about their deaths since they were not local men. Did it never occur to you that Francis Crane left a wife and four children? Do you really believe that it is only in Porthew that people suffer? For all your pretensions, Mistress Hollar, you are as narrow and petty in your vision as all the rest of your tribe.'

Margaret flushed. 'I never knew Mistress Crane, but if what you say is true, why then, I am sorry for her. But I can only help those who are close to me. And the fund for their assistance is still small.'

'So let it remain. Why should I lift a finger to help men who have done so much harm? Did you see the injury to my mare, Sheba? I would have given much to save her, but the knife wound went too deep. I had to put a bullet through her head myself.'

Margaret closed her eyes. She had seen his horse flee in terror, her dark flank gashed with crimson. And she had hoped the mare still lived.

Opening her eyes once again she searched his face. 'They are none of them vicious men, Mr Treveryan, as well you know. What they did was only to protect their home, what any man would have done. And they were mightily provoked.'

'And I was not?'

'Your business with them could have been settled peaceably, had you desired it.'

'That's what you said about those ruffians at Ia's Wood. I disagreed with you then and I disagree now, but for the moment we can let it pass. Tell me, Mistress Hollar, do you really believe your precious Treloars would accept a farthing from me?'

She considered for a moment. The scoundrel, that man. 'No. They would sooner die.'

'Well then?'

'If you were to give the money to the parson, anonymously. Or perhaps it might be better if it were thought to be a gift from the Suttons.'

'Nicolas? And why should he choose to shower charity on the smith and his family? Might people not consider that it was in the way of a debt repayment, or does your young giant still not know that his wife –'

'How dare you!' Margaret was so incensed her anger felt like a strong wind that must surely blow her over. 'How dare you! I never heard anything so despicable! They are right, everything men say about you is true and I was wrong to think . . . How can you speak of my sister, how dare you slander her after all they have been through, after all that you have done to them! I would have defended you. I wanted to believe the best of you, about the evidences and the farm and all the time . . . but you have no pity, you delight in other people's unhappiness, you are a monster, worse than a monster, you –'

'Mistress Hollar,' he seemed to be endeavouring to suppress a smile, 'you grow distraught –'

'Of *course* I am distraught. What in Heaven's name do you expect? I came to see you because I thought you might wish to make amends for all the misery you have inflicted, but instead you have only insults and mockery and –'

The day was close and humid. Margaret had walked a long way, and now her fury almost overwhelmed her. Suddenly her dress of sober grey seemed to be preventing her from breathing properly and the plain linen collar was constricting her throat, impossibly tight. Richard put a hand out to steady her, but she shook him off angrily.

'I am perfectly well,' she declared, gripping the top of the gate to prevent herself from falling.

'Good. I have no intention of arguing with you about anything at all. May I suggest, however, that it might be a good idea if you were to sit down? I can order some refreshments to be brought out, and, though I am not suggesting for a moment that you need reviving in any way, still it might be pleasant to rest for a little while and –'

'I shall leave you now, Mr Treveryan. I have wasted enough of my time.'

'No, don't go. Not yet. First I want an opportunity to show you that I can play the penitent sometimes. I *am* sorry for what I said about your sister, I had no right to be so insensitive and I cannot imagine what made me do it. Unless perhaps I derive some strange pleasure from hearing you provoke me. No, don't be angry again. I am perfectly sincere.' This time when Richard put his hand beneath her elbow Margaret did not shake him off and together they walked towards a rough bench that had been placed in the lee of an old and wind-sculpted yew. 'If you will just wait here . . . your request concerning the Treloars has taken me by surprise, as you can imagine. Now, rest for a moment and admire the view. I will not keep you long.'

He was gone. Margaret put her head in her hands and closed her eyes and in a little while the sensation of faintness passed. She sat up and looked around her, but the yew tree blocked off all view of the labourers and the ruined hall and all she could see was the empty field and the pale blur of the sea. She considered whether she should slip away now, before Treveryan returned. It had been an act of madness to come here in the first place; he would never forgive the Treloars, any more than they would ever forgive him. It was hopeless. Much better to leave at once.

But she remained seated on the bench. She told herself that having gone to all this trouble it would be senseless to leave now, while there was still a chance that he might contribute a few shillings to their coffer. Somewhere above her head a group of sparrows was squabbling among the branches of the yew.

The strangeness of it. She knew this spot so well, had sat here countless times with Jennie while her children played around their feet. She closed her eyes and tried to imagine that the Treloars were still at the farm and all was just as it had ever been, but it was no use. It was more than just the sounds of workmen and carts, pick axes and shovels, as though everything that was familiar, everything that she had ever known and been sure of, had vanished with the Treloars' shabby home.

A servant brought a tray laid with a pitcher of cool lemon julep and a plate of almond cakes, reminding Margaret that she had not eaten since early that morning and was hungry, as well as thirsty.

By the time she had eaten three of the almond cakes she began to wonder if Treveryan intended to return after all. It would be just like him to break his word about returning – why had she ever bothered to believe him? – and yet her sense of disappointment was acute.

'Good, I see you have been looked after.' Margaret had not heard his footsteps and his sudden appearance startled her. 'My architect can produce more complications in five minutes than any man alive. He especially requires me to be an expert in matters of drainage. Is the julep to your liking? Do you know, I think you must be the first guest I have entertained here at Trecarne.'

Margaret ignored this, not wishing to think of herself as Richard Treveryan's guest. She said coldly, 'Have you reached a decision concerning the Treloars?'

He did not answer straight away, but sat down beside her on the bench and helped himself to an almond cake. At length he said quietly, 'Tell me, Mistress Hollar, if you can, what makes you believe I would give a penny of my money to a group of people who, we both know, would like nothing half so much as to see my death?'

Half a dozen reasons occurred to Margaret, but she dismissed them all. She looked up slowly. He was waiting for her reply. 'Because *I* am asking it of you,' she said in a level voice, 'that is why.'

His eyes held hers in silence. His expression was stern, but at last he said, 'And that is a good reason, the only one I would have accepted.' He smiled, half to himself. 'And what do you consider an appropriate sum?'

Margaret had never considered this at all. 'Fifty pounds?' she hazarded.

He let out a whistling breath. 'An altogether ridiculous amount, as well you know . . .' He leaned back on the seat and seemed in no hurry to make up his mind. Margaret was wondering if she had spoiled the Treloars' chances by asking for too high a price. She was trying to work out the cost of a loom and materials for Joseph, six months' rent on a new home. Furniture and so on could probably be begged and borrowed for little cost. But her mind continually drifted back to this present scene, the field of yellow stubble in front of her and the sprinkling of rooks and gulls which were feeding there, black and white against the stalks of corn. And the silent man seated beside her. And the way she knew, without having to look at him at all, the moment he turned his head and the expression that was on his face as he watched her.

'You may tell your parson friend,' he said at length, 'that if he visits me here at this time next week I shall have fifty pounds ready for him to distribute as he sees fit. I assume he may be trusted with a secret? He can claim the ravens brought it.'

Margaret drew in a sharp breath. 'You are most kind,' she said.

'No, Mistress Hollar. I am not kind at all. I do not care twopence for the cripple or your maimed giant. I am only doing this for you.'

Margaret stared at her hands. 'I know,' she said in a low voice.

For some time neither spoke. The silence had become a kind of cloak, enveloping them both in its folds, creating a private world of silence which they alone inhabited.

She heard Richard shift his position. 'Another cake, Mistress Hollar?' She could sense his smile.

'No, thank you.'

A flock of skylarks rose up singing from the field. Richard, watching them, said thoughtfully, 'Now is the time for skylarks. Only when they have lost their summer plumage does a merlin have a chance of catching one. It's an elegant sport, one you might enjoy.'

'To see a skylark killed?' But Margaret's incredulity was more that she should be seated here with Richard Treveryan, when the pretext for her visit was gone.

'Not always. The birds frequently escape altogether. It is not always the hunter who wins, you must know that.'

She did not answer. Her hands were twisting and retwisting the hem of her shawl; her big hands, calloused with hard work. She looked down and hated them.

He continued easily. 'I intend to have a seat of wrought ironwork placed here soon. The yew will stay; it will form the apex of a garden in the Italian style, each path and bush of the utmost formality. And down in the valley where the stream widens I propose to have a pond constructed, a very fish-full pond, every modern contrivance. Do you see that branch where the heron is leaning?'

'I cannot see so far.'

'Not the heron or not the tree?'

'The woods are a blur. I could not see an eagle at half the distance.'

Richard was much intrigued by this evidence of her poor eyesight and spent a little longer trying to establish what she could and could not see. She answered his questions freely, but was disconcerted to discover that he was remembering the St Ewan's Day when she had delivered her Latin oration.

'That was so long ago,' she smiled, 'why should you remember that?'

But Richard would not tell her. 'Did you know I was watching from the side of the crowd? Could you see me?' he wanted to know. A memory had stayed with him, a memory of a girl in heavy boots and an ill-fitting dress who had seemed to reach out to him across the heads of the crowd and touch him with her wide embracing smile.

'I could just make out Sir John Sutton and his wife in the front row. No one else. My fear alone would have blinded me,' she added ruefully.

And he had imagined her smile to be for him alone. 'You always find ways to surprise me,' he said.

Margaret did not answer, told herself she ought to leave. But her limbs had become heavy weights, fixing her to this place. She could not drag herself away.

She turned to him and demanded, '*Why* did you have to do it?'

'Do what?' Though he surely knew the answer.

'Why build here when the cost has been so high? You have no shortage of properties that would have suited your purpose as well.'

'But I chose this one.' He leaned forward to caress the ears of the dog that had been lying at his feet. 'This is Chloe,' he said. 'Usually she travels with me but this time I must leave her behind. Your friend Will Stevens may care for her.' The dog's huge belly was all the explanation needed for her immobility. 'You'll have fine pups for me when I return, eh?' The dog thumped her tail and licked his hand carefully.

Margaret said, 'Can you do anything for Roger Treloar? He is due to stand trial for his life at the autumn assize.'

'I assume you are referring to the fellow who murdered Francis Crane. I may be wealthy, but I can hardly buy his freedom. And if I could . . .' He considered for a while, before continuing in a low voice, 'I shall tell you why I have chosen this place to build my home, why no other place would do. I came here once on an autumn evening; this farm was all that my father had left me. I had nothing else, not even . . .' He broke off, remembering Alice, then continued. 'I made a promise to myself then that one day

I would build a house here, a fine house. A man can die for lack of a dream to live for, you must know that. And the house that will soon exist here has always been my goal. It will be the grandest house in all Cornwall, and the most beautiful. I can show you the plans.'

'No, describe it to me.'

So he did. And as he spoke Margaret pictured the grey walls rising where now was only uneven ground; she saw the old tower restored and a second built in harmony with it and a long building, with porticoed façade and high windows, emerge between them; she saw a steep roof and high chimneys, a clock that chimed the hour and wide steps and a terrace, where peacocks strutted and pecked for crumbs. There was an arch leading to the stables and the mews, a driveway which swept through what had always been the Treloars' near meadow; within the house there was a hall whose high ceiling was decorated with leaves and flowers of plaster, a stairway sweeping in a wide curve, a library filled with books, parlours with paintings and tapestries and log fires blazing to keep out the winter cold; outside there was to be a dovecote, a cider press and malthouse, a buttery, gardens and orchards . . . And Margaret saw them all.

And she saw too that Richard Treveryan would return to this place and bring his little wife with the dainty jewelled hands and the dresses that sparkled with embroidery of gold and silver thread and together they would admire his wonderful new house and then, when they had seen it all, they would stroll over to this spot where the wrought-iron bench had been placed for their comfort and they would while away the August afternoons together, and she herself would never return to see his dream made reality.

She said, 'Others have paid dearly for your dreams. And it may be that you will pay a higher price than you had thought. Ambrose has sworn to be revenged – even when your home is built, you will have to be on your guard at all times.'

Richard shrugged. 'I do not fear the Treloars. If any one of them dares to set foot on my land I shall kill him myself.'

'No! For mercy's sake, hasn't there been killing enough already! Be careful, that's all. Don't underestimate

Ambrose. He may not be clever but he is determined and more cunning than most – and still as strong as six other men. And he will never forget the injury you have done him.'

'I thought as much, and I am grateful for your warning. But tell me, Mistress Hollar, why should you concern yourself for my safety?'

She did not answer. She might have asked him in his turn why he had risked his life to save her when she led Juno from the burning barn . . . but the ground on to which they were venturing was treacherous enough already.

They sat for so long without moving or speaking that a tortoiseshell butterfly fluttered down and settled on her hand. Richard was watching her intently. Her head was turned slightly away and all he could see was the curve of her cheek, just beyond the ear, the wide sweep of her jaw and the point where it touched her sun-golden neck, the pale hair that escaped in wisps from under her coif. He could see the rise and fall of her breathing. He moved closer so that he could see her slightly parted lips, the soft bloom of her skin.

Moving with the slow languor of a dream, he reached out and brushed the butterfly away, closed his hand over hers. She did not stir, but allowed him to open her palm and trace the line of the scar that crossed it with the tip of his finger.

'Margaret . . .'

She swayed slightly. A warm flush of colour was spreading across her neck and warming her cheek. He could not see, would never know, that the sound of her name was for Margaret a vast net thrown out to entangle her, that she was painfully aware of the filigree strands that were meshing her to this place, how she yearned for nothing in the whole world but to turn and face him and answer the look which she knew to be in his eyes.

She let out a sigh that was almost a moan and, staring always at a point some little distance in front of her, she dragged her hand from his. And then, as if it were the hardest task of her life, she stood up slowly.

'I must go.'

He stood up also. 'You will come again,' he said simply; a statement, not a question.

'No. That would be . . . impossible.'

Only then did she raise her eyes to meet his challenge.

'And yet I know that you will come,' he said, 'one day.'

She shook her head.

She turned and began to walk back towards the place where his grand new house would one day stand, and Richard walked beside her. He was telling her that he would arrange a horse and servant for her return journey to Porthew. 'I would accompany you myself only your reputation would suffer if you were seen in the company of the most hated man in Cornwall. How do you propose to explain your visit to me today?'

'I shall . . . think of something.'

At that moment she was thinking of nothing at all. Conscious only of the pressure of his arm against her own and the fleeting moments of his nearness.

The architect Thomas was standing by the table, still laid with plans, and he was none too pleased when Richard ordered him to arrange for a servant and a horse to escort Mistress Hollar to Porthew. While they were waiting, Richard showed her the plans of the house.

'I preferred the way you described it,' said Margaret after she had pored over them a little while. 'I imagined people and birds and animals, but these plans show only the buildings.'

Richard laughed and picked up Thomas's quill and dipped it in the ink. Quickly and inexpertly he sketched in the missing details, a rickety horse, a peacock that looked more like a turkey, a man and a woman walking on the terrace. 'Is that better?' he asked, and Margaret smiled her approval, though she would have liked to know the identity of the figures who were walking across the plan.

As her horse was led forward by a nervous-looking lad, Richard said, 'I shall send word when I have done as you request.'

He helped her to mount and she settled herself in the saddle, thinking suddenly of a hundred things she wished to say and ask. But the moment had gone.

'Goodbye, Mr Treveryan. And thank you.'

Then she nudged her horse forward and the serving-boy mounted his pony and together they rode through the bustle of workmen and oxen towards the cool darkness of the oak woods. Richard watched until the two figures disappeared into the tunnel of trees. But as he walked back to his much amended plans he was whistling softly to himself with good-humoured anticipation.

On the way back to Porthew the servant, a lad from Saltash by the name of Giles who had jug-ears and was homesick for his three older sisters and a certain friend of theirs called Mary, tried to engage her in conversation. He considered that Mr Treveryan was a man much maligned locally; he himself had never known his master to be anything but courteous and just. Margaret barely heard a word he said, and would not have known how to reply if she had.

The familiar journey had changed beyond recognition; now she felt as though she were travelling between two worlds, between reality and dream, though which was dream and which reality, she could not say. Despair and a fierce joy, almost exultation, were clamouring within her, so that she did not notice when the clouds that had been gathering all day massed in a grey swarm above the trees at Ia's Wood and broke into a steady downpour, drenching her to the skin.

20

Soon after Margaret's visit to Trecarne, Richard returned to Saltash to attend to his business there, leaving work on the new building in the charge of Thomas, the architect. He had sent no word to Margaret concerning the money for the Treloars, nor had he appeared in Porthew. Sometimes Margaret almost doubted that their meeting had taken place. Already that afternoon was assuming the strangeness of a dream memory.

It was a memory which troubled Margaret deeply and made her feel set apart from her companions in Porthew – but which she would not have changed for all the world. William was frequently vexed by her air of abstraction: often when he spoke, however sharply, she did not seem to hear him at all. Once or twice he found himself tempted to shake her just to gain her attention – a rare thing in a man whose distaste for violence was almost as strong as her own.

Ambrose continued to make slow progress towards recovery. His right eye could distinguish between light and darkness, but all detailed sight was gone. Never handsome, he was now grown hideous in disfigurement. So huge and so strong, so powerfully ugly, he had become a sight to inspire terror as well as pity. The kindness of friends and neighbours continued, but unknown to Ambrose mothers now threatened wayward children with a visit from the fearsome smith if they did not mend their ways.

Lizzie too was changed. Heavily pregnant with her third child, the one who was to grow up bearing a distinct but unnoticed resemblance to Nicolas Sutton, she moved always with a steady deliberation. Little trace remained of her childlike prettiness; most often now she was hollow-eyed from lack of sleep. Only the set of her mouth revealed her intention to steer her family through this tragedy. Although short tempered with the children who scampered through

467

the house – and Jennie's youngest were living with them still – she was endlessly patient with Ambrose. While he remained too weak to do much in the Forge, he sat for hours at a time on the mounting block by the side of the road, his hands pressed squarely against his knees, his face turned towards the road that led to Rossmere and Trecarne. Sometimes he glanced up at the hillside, now green with bracken, which he had watched that St Ewan's Day morning for a first glimpse of Margaret and Lizzie tumbling down the path, their little brother careering down happily between them. But it was not friends he was looking out for now.

On a chill September morning Margaret set out for the Forge as she had done three or four times each week since the fighting at Trecarne. Turning the last corner she tensed in anticipation of that first view of Ambrose as he sat and watched the road, his ginger hair framing the livid red of his damaged flesh. But he was not there. And, almost unheard of at this time in the morning, the smithy itself was deserted.

Suddenly apprehensive, Margaret forced herself to walk on briskly. In her basket were fresh linens for the children, savoury and mincemeat pies and some little cakes which Jennie's daughter had made with a good deal of help the previous day.

Going round by the back of the house, she pushed open the back door – and at once a mass of voices swept over her, all clamouring for her attention and she was carried into the kitchen on a joyful tide of Treloars. Margaret's amazement increased tenfold when she noticed Joseph seated at the kitchen table, a grin of pure happiness spread across his face.

'Have you heard the news?'

'What news?'

'Oh Mattie!'

With everyone trying to tell her at once it was some time before Margaret discovered that she had not been the first visitor at the smithy that morning. Parson Weaver had called soon after dawn and he had brought with him fifty golden sovereigns to be added to their fund. He had kept ten back, after some discussion, for the wife and children of Roger Treloar, but the rest, he assured them, was theirs, to use as they saw fit.

Jennie burst into tears as she explained to Margaret that Joseph could have a loom once again, more than that, they could now start looking for a new place of their own. The mystery was that no one had any idea where the extra money originated: Parson Weaver was adamant that their benefactor must remain secret. He had been seen talking to Nicolas Sutton only the previous day, but the Suttons had already given five pounds to the fund, why then should they suddenly contribute a further fifty pounds?

'Fifty sovereigns!' Jennie exclaimed again in disbelief. She had to sit down suddenly under the weight of so much money, but the next instant she jumped up again and hugged Margaret, then picked up a random toddler and cried briefly into his hair.

'Fifty golden sovereigns!'

The magical figure was repeated continuously, as though they were afraid at any moment the sum might vanish like a wisp of smoke on the morning air. But there they lay, the heap of golden sovereigns, a hoard of money greater than anyone there had ever seen.

'Oh, Mattie, can you believe it?'

Margaret nursed her secret and joined their celebrations. So, Richard Treveryan had been true to his word after all. She almost wished he had not – she had begun to convince herself that he was a bold-faced liar as well as a rogue. She had been working hard to hate him.

'It's wonderful,' she agreed warmly.

There was wild speculation concerning the identity of the donor: Robert Payne was a favourite, though he was known to be a skinflint; Mistress Treloar wondered if the parson perhaps had access to church funds, but Joseph commented sourly that he had never known the church keep a good deed secret. Jennie was firmly convinced that the King must have somehow heard of their calamity in far-off London and had donated the money from his own private fortune; she could not imagine anyone apart from royalty possessing such wealth. But in all the wild guessing that went on through that morning (and continued for days and weeks to come) the name of Richard Treveryan was never mentioned, except as someone who had been outwitted by their sudden reversal of fortune.

'I'd like to see his face when he hears about this!' gloated Ambrose's mother. 'Now he'll know Treloars can stand up for themselves!'

Ambrose's father fetched a flagon of their best wine, and they drank a toast to their future, to a new loom for Joseph and a home where the family could be together again. They drank a toast to Roger Treloar in Launceston gaol – surely his release was now only a matter of time – and to his wife and children. Margaret joined them gladly. And she joined them too, there seemed no escape, when they drank a toast to the eternal damnation of the usurper at Trecarne.

Amid all the excitement and noise, Margaret noticed that Lizzie appeared to be unnaturally withdrawn, an anxious frown interrupting her happiness. When Lizzie slipped out to fetch sweetmeats from the larder, Margaret followed her.

'Lizzie, what's the matter?'

She did not answer right away, but placed little tarts and sugar buns on a platter. When she had finished she handed Margaret the platter and leaned wearily against the slate shelf on which the milk and butter were stored.

'I was wondering . . .'

'Yes?'

Lizzie placed a thin hand on the dome of her belly and asked in a whisper, 'Do you think it might have been – Nicolas Sutton who gave the money?'

'But why should he –?' The question had slipped out before Margaret had a chance to consider what she was saying.

Lizzie flushed and looked at the floor and Margaret noticed then that her sister's eyes were brimming with tears.

'Because . . . he might think . . .'

Margaret said gently, 'I doubt he'd be so generous.'

'Ambrose is so happy,' Lizzie went on miserably, one huge tear spilling over and rolling down her cheek, 'and I want to be happy too but each time I look at him smiling I remember what I've . . . and I think maybe that was why . . . and I feel so ashamed, Mattie, you've no idea –'

'Don't, Lizzie. It wasn't Nicolas Sutton, I'm sure of it.'

'But how can I be sure?'

'If you don't believe me, why not ask him yourself?'

Lizzie was shocked. 'What? How can you even suggest such a thing? I'll never speak with him again as long as I live.'

'But –'

'I always knew you despised me, Mattie, for what happened between us,' Lizzie's whisper was grown hoarse with misery and outrage, 'but surely you know I could never see him again after what happened, after what his *friend* did to Ambrose?'

'Hush, someone is bound to hear you. I never did despise you, Lizzie, no matter what you think. And I can't bear to see you torturing yourself now. Believe me, I'm sure it was not Nicolas Sutton. You can enjoy their good luck with a clear conscience.'

'Do you really think so?' Lizzie wiped her tears on the back of her sleeve and Margaret handed her a clean kerchief, a sequence reminding them both so swiftly of their shared time together at Conwinnion that they both smiled at once.

'Tut,' said Margaret, 'and you a grown woman.'

'Oh well. I'll tell you one thing, I can't wait to see the back of Jennie and her family, this house has been a merry Bedlam. How do I look?'

'Fine. They'll all believe you're crying for happiness, anyway.'

'And so I will do. Now.'

The celebrations showed no sign of dying down when Margaret finally announced, towards noon, that she was leaving. Word of the Treloars' pile of golden sovereigns spread quickly and all through the morning people arrived in ones and twos to congratulate them and drink to their new prosperity.

As she was pulling her shawl about her shoulders, Ambrose stood up slowly. 'I'll walk with you a little way.'

'Please don't trouble yourself.'

Ambrose grunted that it was no trouble.

A fine rain was beginning to sprinkle the dusty road. Margaret, wishing for solitude in which to reflect the events of the morning, walked briskly, hoping to shake Ambrose off, but his massive legs might have been encased in seven-league boots, he strolled along so easily beside her.

As soon as they had rounded the first corner in the road, Ambrose laid his hand on her shoulder and said, 'You've been to Trecarne, is that right?'

'Who told you that?'

'One gets to hear most things eventually, in the Forge.'

'Folk should learn to mind their own business.'

'Then you did go, it's true.' His bass voice rumbled about her head, ominous as summer thunder. They had stopped walking, and when Margaret tried to shift away from the weight of his hand on her shoulder, Ambrose gripped her firmly.

'Why?'

Margaret calculated quickly that since there was little chance of contact between Ambrose and her husband, the old lie would still serve. 'William wished me to go on business.'

'Master Hollar is a fool to have any dealings with the man, but that is his affair. I'll keep your secret, Mattie, for now at least. Some of the others, Joseph and my father for instance, they might not see things the way I do.'

'What they think is no concern of mine.'

She twisted to escape his hand but he gripped her shoulder so tightly that she feared he might scrunch her bones as though they were no bigger than a rabbit's.

'Ambrose, let go, you're hurting me!'

But the days when he would listen to her, or to anyone else, were gone. He bent his head and Margaret averted her eyes.

'Pay attention to what I say, Mattie. Treveryan has regard for you. I daresay you haven't noticed but I saw it in his eyes that day at Trecarne. It seems that men can't help but pay heed to you.'

'You imagined it, Ambrose, there's nothing –'

He continued in his ponderous way, working it out slowly, letting nothing go. 'I know you hate him as much as I do. As much as anyone does. And I want you to know that the money we've received makes no difference, I'll never forget what he did to me. To me and to Joseph and to Roger there in Launceston gaol. No amount of money can bring back what is lost. He'll suffer for what he's done. First he'll suffer as I have done and then, when I'm ready, I'll kill him, even if I have to swing for it after.'

'Ambrose, no! Hasn't there been killing enough?'

'What is it, Mattie? Why are you crying?' His hand released her at once.

'I can't abide to hear any more of fighting and killing.'

'You always were tender-hearted. But I've always known I could rely on you. Don't be sad, Mattie. It may be that when the time comes, you will be able to help me.'

'What?'

'A trap needs bait, to be effective.'

Too appalled even for words, Margaret could only stare in horror as the slow, disfigured smile spread across his face.

'There's no justice in law. The gentry all stand by each other, and that is what we must do too. And if Treveryan has a weakness for you, as I believe he has, then we can find a way to work that to our advantage. So help me God, Mattie, I *will* be even with that man, no matter how long I have to wait.'

And with that, he bade her farewell, and strode back in the direction of the Forge.

Margaret was so wrapped in thought that it was some moments before she noticed the stranger sitting on the bench by her back door, and some moments more before she recognised the friendly face and jug-ears of Treveryan's servant. Luke was squatting on the path in front of him and playing with something that looked very much like a brindled puppy.

The young man stood up.

'Good day, Mistress Hollar,' he said respectfully.

'Good day.' Margaret discovered to her horror that her heart was thumping beneath her ribs. 'Is Mr Treveryan returned?'

'He arrived at Trecarne two nights ago. He asked me to give you this.' The young man, whose name, she now remembered, was Giles, handed her a letter.

'Wait here,' said Margaret, retreating into the privacy of her kitchen before breaking the seal and reading,

473

Mistress Hollar,

Your troublesome friends are today a good deal wealthier than they deserve. My generosity must, alas, remain a secret.

I returned two days ago to find that Chloe had mated with a mongrel cur. I ordered the litter destroyed but, remembering in time your strange partiality for anything worthless and abandoned, saved back the ugliest of them all. I send him to you with cordial respect, knowing that he will suit your rag-tag household admirably. He answers to the name of Puritan, but given your husband's sympathies, you may wish to find him another.

Tomorrow I return to Saltash,

Yours,

Richard Treveryan.

Margaret flushed with anger, then burst out laughing and read the letter through twice more before throwing it on the fire. Puritan indeed. Rag-tag household. Clearly this was one waif she could not possibly take under her wing. The puppy must be sent back to Trecarne immediately, there was absolutely no doubt about it.

Luke, who knew his mother well enough to realise the creature was sure to remain with them, had already decided on his name: Hedge.

'*Hedge!*' said Margaret later that evening as she sat with her sewing, Luke and the puppy crawling around by her feet. 'You cannot name a dog *Hedge*.'

'Yes I can. Hedge!' Luke stood up and fetched a saucer of milk from the pantry.

'If you feed the poor creature any more his stomach will burst for sure.'

'He likes it, look.' The boy set down the saucer and then lay down on his stomach and rested his chin on his hands and watched intently as the puppy, which seemed to have almost Dorcas's appetite, lapped greedily. Luke made lapping motions with his lips. Margaret reflected ruefully that the puppy was indeed quite remarkably ugly. He was of an indeterminate colour somewhere between soot and a kind of dusty brown, his feet were huge and his coat bristled like a hog's whiskers. Such ugliness in one so small was surprisingly seductive and even William was won over before the evening was out.

'Now I shall teach him to bark,' said Luke, and began to yap so convincingly that the startled puppy backed away and growled, until he suddenly decided that it was safe after all. He rushed forward, tail wagging vigorously, to lick the boy's ears, making Luke squeal that he was tickling, and they both rolled over together in a heap.

Roger Treloar lay chained to a damp wall in the bowels of Launceston gaol when he heard that his wife and children had been saved from destitution by a mysterious gift. He had been feverish for nearly a month and the news had little meaning for him. He had no very clear memory of that day at Trecarne. Sometimes in his sleep he imagined that he was hacking at a cushion of stuffed green cloth. Red blood spurted out of the cushion and blinded him, and when he awoke it was with the sensation that he was falling from a great height.

The other prisoners helped themselves to his rations.

Within two days he was dead. His wife, a great-niece of Dame Erisey's, had been lodging with his brother, Young Robert, since the day of the fighting at Trecarne. She heard of her husband's death with a spasm of grief which she was careful to hide from the man with whom she was now sharing bed as well as board. She had been grateful for the shelter for herself and her two young children, though Young Robert was not as gentle as his brother had been.

When Parson Weaver brought her portion of the money, Young Robert took possession of it at once, saying he had not expected his sister-in-law to bring with her such a handsome dowry.

For some time Margaret had been much troubled by nightmares.

Parson Weaver, believing that she still suffered from the scenes she had witnessed at Trecarne, advised quietness and rest. William was certain that the Devil was doing battle for possession of her soul and redoubled his efforts in prayer. And Margaret, who in her dreams was bait in the trap in which Ambrose and Richard Treveryan fought their final duel, could offer no explanation.

Several times she was awoken by the noise of her screams, only to see Luke standing in his pale shift beside her bed and shivering with fear. When she reached out to embrace him, he burst into tears and ran away. One night William awoke and came into her room carrying a tallow candle. He was very calm and sure and he took both her hands between his and knelt down beside her bed.

'Leave me,' said Margaret, 'let me alone.'

But William had the strength of his conviction and would consider no opposition. Convinced that the Devil visited her in her dreams, he allowed her no sleep but stayed by her bedside and prayed aloud until, as the dawn light began to filter through the little window, Margaret could endure it no longer; she had no arguments remaining, no anger to hold out against his insistence that she once more sit beside him through their endless household worship.

William, in triumph, spent the morning hour praising the Lord for having saved her from sin. Margaret could have shouted her denial aloud – but when she saw the expression of relief on Luke's anxious face, she regretted only that she had not given in sooner.

When scandal did visit Master Hollar's household that winter it was not Margaret, to her amazement, who was the cause.

Dorcas had been steadily increasing in size since Margaret had taken her in; her appetite was so gargantuan that no one looked further for an explanation. But one morning in late November Margaret came back from the harbour to find her squatting on the floor of the kitchen and tearing at her belly with a strange grunting noise. Towards midday an infant was born, but it appeared to have been dead for some time. Dorcas gazed at it without emotion as Dame Watkins wrapped it in a cloth and carried it away to be buried in unhallowed ground.

By early evening the house had filled with neighbours and church officers all demanding to be told the name of the father. William, tight-lipped with fury already, was further incensed to discover that several people appeared to suspect

476

him. Margaret's doubts centred on Paul Viney, who had been mysteriously absent since morning. However, once Dorcas had understood the questions that were being put to her, she began in a vague but wholly convincing way to name half the men in Porthew, as well as any number of transients. When she named the elderly uncle of one of the church wardens, and seemed on the point of naming his fifteen-year-old son as well, her cross-examination was brought to an abrupt halt.

It appeared that Dorcas, having once made the connection between the strange things men liked doing to her body and the consumption of food, had decided that to lie on her back in the straw of the barn in return for a custard tart, or to hoist up her skirts behind the slaughterhouse for a piece of meat pie, was an easy method of satisfying her endless hunger. Given Dorcas's obvious defects in understanding, the church officers were inclined to deal kindly. Paul Viney was clearly the more culpable: not only had he enjoyed Dorcas himself from time to time, he had also organised and profited from her enterprise.

Between them, William's servants had made him a laughing stock. Ever since the night of the storm he had presented an image of faultless piety. He had made no secret of his contempt for others less saintly than himself, had wrangled with the parson over the details of the service and was advocating a ban on dancing and music. Now this paragon was revealed to have lived in a bawdy house in foolish ignorance – or worse. Parson Weaver, hearing of his embarrassment, was unable to disguise his delight.

William blamed Margaret for his humiliation: she had introduced a common drab into his house – and provided the whore-master too. Clearly her sole intention was to see him ruined: he had a mind to turn her out with the two culprits. Margaret, who was still haunted by the thought of the innocent corpse lying cold and unhallowed beyond the churchyard wall, told him crossly that he might do as he wished, she did not care.

It was Luke who offered the solution.

When Viney returned, fortified against impending disaster by a daylong soak in ale, he found, instead of the beating he had expected, the cold fury of a master who told him he must pack his bags (he had none) and be gone by daybreak.

Viney's response was unexpected. He burst into a fit of loud weeping, declared that he had nowhere else to go, had never had a home but this one and, if he were thrown out, would go straight to the cliff-top and throw himself into the sea.

The sight of the always impassive Paul Viney blubbing like a child took even William by surprise. Margaret pacified him as best she could and persuaded him to wait and see if they could not think of another solution to this problem. Luke, seated as always on his little joint stool by the fire and watching the mysterious carryings-on of the adult world, said that if Dorcas's bastard child was the cause of all the fuss, then why did Paul Viney not marry Dorcas.

Just for the moment no one could think of any objection. Margaret pointed out to William that he could most quickly restore his reputation if he demonstrated that he could pluck good from a tangle of evil. As her husband, Paul would be responsible for Dorcas from now on. Margaret, seeing William waver, warmed to her theme: she was sure that this solution would give him the respect of a local Solomon. William gave way.

Through his fog of alcohol and tears, Paul Viney seemed to remember that he had in fact been married once or twice before, but decided that in the present circumstances it would be foolish to mention this awkward detail.

Dorcas was informed the next morning. She was also lectured, vigorously, on the vital importance of never, ever, lying down in the hay again with anyone but Paul, no matter how many honey cakes she was promised. Her future husband was assured that any backsliding by Dorcas would result in their immediate dismissal. Sober, he realised there was no hope for either of them except in the household of the eccentric Mistress Hollar, and in the bleak light of morning suicide did not present a tempting alternative. He therefore vowed to watch Dorcas's every move.

Only a handful of guests attended the wedding, but both bride and groom enjoyed themselves hugely: Paul Viney because he succeeded in getting roaring drunk at Jack Pym's afterwards, and Dorcas because she was allowed to eat a whole tray of currant buns.

Construction of the new house at Trecarne proceeded at a snail's pace throughout the winter. By early December heavy rains had turned the entire site into a sea of mud: carts loaded with stone were buried above the axles and the labourers fell sick. Richard paid a brief visit just before Christmas and dismissed all but a handful of skilled men whose main task, under the supervision of Thomas the architect, was to guard against sabotage. Real progress would have to wait for the spring, and drier weather.

But by the time the first primroses were starring the hedgerows Richard's attention, like that of all the nation, was deflected from his private concerns to events in London. After more than eleven years, King Charles had once again issued writs for a Parliament.

Richard had been a student at Oxford, confident in his studies and his assurance that his father would leave him the income and property of a gentleman, when Charles's last Parliament had been dismissed in anger and confusion and he had not then paid much heed to affairs in the capital. But he knew that the bitterness had lingered for a long time in Cornwall: in 1629 Sir John Eliot, a popular local figure and Member of Parliament for Plymouth had led the opposition to the King. As soon as Parliament was dissolved he had been thrown into the Tower of London where he proved himself the King's equal in stubbornness at least. He fell ill, but refused to acknowledge any wrongdoing and Charles was not inclined to be merciful. He weakened and died. The King rejected his young son's request to have the body brought home to Cornwall for burial. These hurts had not been forgotten.

Richard had no very clear memory of Sir John but he had reasons of his own to oppose King Charles. Heavy taxes hedged a merchant's business around with difficulties – especially if, like Richard Treveryan, that merchant was determined to avoid payment. Several times he had been obliged to pay nearly as much in bribes to corrupt officials as he should have paid in duties. Worse, the King's navy was failing to give protection against the Turkish pirates who grew bolder by the month. Only the previous year Richard had lost an entire ship, its cargo stolen and its crew taken into slavery. Such disasters made a mockery of the King's claim that ship money was being used for the defence of the English coast – it was common knowledge that he needed it for his personal struggle against the Scots. Only a few months before, cannons and ammunition, desperately needed to provide some protection to the Cornish, had been removed from Pendennis Castle, guarding the mouth of the Fal, to the north of England. The Cornish had no argument with the Scots – and now they were left more vulnerable than before.

All talk now was of the elections. Richard stayed at Trecarne only long enough to check the progress on the construction of the new tower before returning to the serious business of being elected as Member of Parliament for Saltash. Being wealthy and skilled in the ways of corruption he succeeded easily. He might well have been chosen anyway: his opposition to royal pretensions was well known and the electors desired powerful men to state their case.

Margaret, following events as best she could, tried to imagine the Member for Saltash taking his seat among the large contingent of Cornish MPs. She had only a very hazy idea of what a Parliament might look like or what took place there, but she thought it must be a fine thing to be close to the pulse of the country, to witness events as they occurred and not have to wait for days for muddled and conflicting accounts.

A fine thing to escape Porthew.

May Day, and the London apprentices were on excellent form. In most years their fighting high spirits were dissipated in running battles against their fellows but in May 1640 they united against a loftier target. Having raised expectations in the spring, the King and his ministers had terminated Parliament within a month of its opening and the people of London were furious. For once it was not the apprentices alone who rampaged through streets which had been decked with flowers and greenery to celebrate the coming of May; sailors too were up in arms and their anger was seasoned and more dangerous. For years the King had been sapping the navy of its strength and now their champion, the Earl of Warwick, had been placed under arrest in the Tower.

Rumours were spreading faster than plague in summer: the King had made a pact with Spain and Spanish troops were even now being shipped in to pacify the country; the King himself had turned Papist like his wife and before the year was out English Protestants would once more burn like torches for their faith as they had done under the Catholic Queen Mary; the Earl of Strafford was raising an army of heathen Irish so that his King might have such power as he need never call a Parliament again and all the ancient liberties of England would perish for evermore.

Fear and anger fuelled the mob. Within a few hours the apprentices' seasonal disorder had flamed into a bloody riot and then the crowd was breaking down the door of the Archbishop's Palace at Lambeth and the King called out the trained bands to restore order.

Richard had briefly joined the rabble. Such was the commotion in London that the appearance of a well-dressed but ruffianly-looking gentleman amidst the rioters was hardly noticed. After three weeks of frustrating inactivity in the chamber of the House of Commons he found it a blessed relief, if not, perhaps, becoming to the dignity of an MP, to hunt with the hounds and send the fat little Archbishop, a ridiculous fellow, in Richard's opinion, scuttling in terror for his life.

But after a couple of hours he had tired of the sport and began to walk back towards his lodgings. As he crossed the bridge, he caught a scent of the sea, that clean salty smell, unmistakable even among the rank stench of refuse and decay and close-packed humanity that was everywhere in London. And a huge longing to return to the West Country swept over him. He lingered for a while by the river, so lost in his own thoughts that he hardly noticed the distant ebb and flow of the rioters, the occasional apprentice slinking home to his master's wrath.

His brief contact with parliamentary life had been interesting enough but for his own sake he was not sorry it had been brought to such an abrupt conclusion. He had seen enough to know that King Charles was a man with whom

481

he would never wish to do business, a slippery pedant who so believed that God's right was on his side that he would stoop to any chicanery to achieve his ends – and believe himself virtuous to have done so. Richard reflected wrily that if there was indeed honour among thieves – which he had always doubted – there was perhaps a parallel infamy among kings.

He had also discovered that though opposing such a despot was no doubt an admirable cause, he himself had small patience for the task. The House of Commons was a seething nest of lawyers – and there was nothing that he found so wearisome as the intricacies of a legal mind. All their talk of precedent and long-forgotten statutes, when any fool could see the problem was simple enough: the King wished for money to be voted him without having to give anything in return. Richard doubted that any deal could be struck between King and Parliament so long as the Earl of Strafford remained to advise the monarch. Richard did not much like Strafford but he admired him. The King's Deputy in Ireland was a worthy adversary, clever and ruthless enough to show the King how to get what he wanted and the people's liberties be damned.

But the endless wrangling over details, so beloved by lawyers, had driven Richard to the verge of distraction. Now he wanted only to breathe the Cornish air again, to stand aboard his own fast ship and hear the chink of the rigging and the billowing sails, to see the fine house that had existed for so long only as an idea in his mind become at last a reality of stone and brick and timbers. Nor had he forgotten that he had once promised himself a liaison with Mistress Hollar. He had been furious to find her supporting the Treloars in their defiance, had believed his chances with her ruined. But since her visit to Trecarne the previous summer – so unexpected in every way – his hopes had more than revived.

On several occasions during the Short Parliament of 1640, when the Member for Tavistock had been dissecting an intricate point of order, one of the Members for Saltash had been distracted by thoughts of a tall woman who had sat beside him on a bench on a summer's afternoon, a woman with a scar on her hand who was more beautiful in her dress of sober grey than any of the court ladies in their gaudy silks and velvets. A woman who should by rights have hated him, but in whose wide and often troubled eyes he could find no trace of hatred, none at all.

With Richard's reappearance at Trecarne in the beginning of June work progressed at twice the speed. He dismissed the surveyor, who was a fool, and promoted a stone mason who had shown great good sense over a matter of drainage. Thomas, who was better at dreaming up houses than at turning his plans into reality, was much heartened to see the master of the place once more striding among the masons and the navvies, cursing and encouraging and allowing not the smallest detail to escape him.

Richard had turned his back on the nation's dramas. While Nicolas Sutton was busy browbeating his tenants into joining the levies required by King Charles for a new assault on the fractious Scots, Richard was absorbed in watching a second tower rise up, at a little distance, but similar in mass and appearance to the first. During the long summer days which his sovereign devoted to skirmishing in the north and striving to avoid humiliation from the rebels, Richard had the satisfaction of seeing the foundations laid for the central portion of his great house, that connecting the two towers. He was obliged to return to Saltash on business for a brief spell in August and informed Kitty, who was more jealous of his new house than she had ever been of his infidelities, that she would soon be able to visit Trecarne in comfort. Kitty shrank from the prospect of such a journey but she would not give Richard the satisfaction of knowing this. He was back in Trecarne by the beginning of September, so that while King Charles presided over the Great Council at York, Richard was entirely absorbed in the problems caused by subsidence in the area intended for mews and stables. And by the time the autumn storms brought renewed havoc to the builders' efforts and King Charles had agreed a truce with the Scots which fooled no one, except perhaps himself, Richard was ready to move from his temporary bivouac and spend his first night in the large first-floor bedroom of his newly built and beautiful tower.

Margaret saw his return to Cornwall as a deliberate assault

on her peace of mind. Just when she had persuaded herself that she had forgotten him entirely . . . she had long ago abandoned all hope of ever being a good wife to William, but there was still Luke: for her son's sake she would endure what she never could for herself. Her nightmares had become less frequent, her resentment of William's interminable preaching easier to hide . . . until those summer days when Richard was once more at Trecarne.

As if on purpose to increase her discomfort, he was a frequent visitor to Porthew. He attended church each Sunday with such regularity that his appearance no longer caused ill-feeling: there was a general understanding that Ambrose would deal with matters in his own good time and meanwhile folk had other business to occupy them. Once or twice he called on William Hollar in the draper's shop and discussed with him the need for such a quantity of furnishings for his house that William was convinced his fortune would soon be made. Richard Treveryan made a point, when the service was over, of lingering in the churchyard and chatting with the Suttons and on several occasions he singled out the handsome draper and his wife for a word of greeting. William was too conscious of the vast quantity of cloth that would be needed at Trecarne to mind that his hoped-for customer was the most hated man in Porthew.

The first time Margaret saw Richard approaching she tried to hurry William away. 'William, do not talk with him.'

'Don't be foolish, wife, it doesn't do to be rude,' and indeed it was already too late since Richard, wearing a short cloak with kingfisher lining, was greeting them with casual ease.

Margaret fidgeted and looked at the ground. William greeted him with a familiarity which made her squirm. 'Good day to you, Mr Treveryan. And how does the work on your new house progress?'

Afterwards William scolded her. 'This is purely a matter of business, Margaret. You must put aside your petty feelings concerning the Treloars. I fail to see how it will assist them if Mr Uren of Camborne is chosen to supply the fittings for the new house. You will be civil in the future, if you please, and hide your too obvious dislike for him.'

And was surprised by the baffled smile that spread across her face.

On the second occasion Margaret was standing alone by her mother's grave after church when Richard appeared suddenly at her side and asked in a low voice, 'How is young Puritan?'

At first she thought he must be referring to Luke and was on the point of offering an angry reply when she remembered the puppy's original name and had difficulty in suppressing a smile. 'His name is Hedge and he does well enough.'

'Hedge?'

'Luke chose the name. And the dog's nature is in no way Puritanical.'

'I knew he would suit your mongrel household.'

'Even your gifts are occasions for rudeness, Mr Treveryan.'

'Not always, I assure you. Will you bring him to Trecarne?'

'No.'

Richard was smiling. Margaret, looking away, saw that Ambrose was watching them. Though she knew he was not close enough to hear what was said, a wave of dread passed through her. William was hastening to join them, his expression radiant with goodwill.

On the third Sunday William was overjoyed and his wife dismayed when they were informed that they must visit Trecarne when sufficient progress had been made for Richard to consider receiving visitors. Margaret said firmly that she was sure that would not be for a long time – and was soundly rebuked later for her bad manners.

On the fourth Sunday Richard did not appear at all and Margaret told herself that she was heartily glad and hoped he was gone a year or more . . . yet was restless and discontented for days.

He reappeared on a Sunday just after Michaelmas and once again the Hollars were singled out for attention. His groom was already leading over his tall grey when Richard turned and, as if as an afterthought said, 'Visit me at Trecarne the day after tomorrow, Hollar. There are some matters concerning the choice of furnishings that can best be discussed there.'

'Certainly, Mr Treveryan. I have some Turkish damask new in which will –'

'And bring your wife,' Richard interrupted him without so much as a glance at Margaret, 'I particularly require a lady's opinion. Mistress Treveryan is expected later in the week and there are several matters I wish to have in hand by then. I shall expect you both at ten.'

With that he mounted up and rode away.

'I shall not go,' Margaret declared at once.

'Indeed you shall,' said William. 'Have you any idea of the money to be made by the man who supplies the fabric for a house so large? All I am asking of you, Margaret, for once in your life, is a little loyalty.'

The nightmares returned that night, and the next.

On Tuesday morning Margaret had little difficulty in feigning illness. After two nights of scant and distracted sleep she felt as wretched as she looked. She came downstairs to find William sorting cloth to take to Trecarne.

'William, I am not well. You must go alone.'

'Don't be ridiculous,' he replied waspishly, holding a length of silk to the light, 'I don't care if you are dying by degrees but you will come with me today. Mr Treveryan specifically requested it and I will do nothing at this delicate stage of the negotiations that might risk his displeasure, though the Lord knows, my own opinion in such matters is worth ten of yours. Make sure you agree with everything I say for I know which fabrics can be got easily and which bear the largest profit. Don't stand there looking sullen. And make sure you wear your newest dress.'

'William, please, don't force me to go.'

Her husband set down the roll of silk and took two steps to stand before her. His fingers gripped her chin. Margaret froze: it was so easy to overlook, the steel contained in his apparently delicate body.

'I insist,' he said coldly.

'But why? If you tell him I am unwell, surely he will understand.'

'Margaret, have you any idea what hangs in the balance of this meeting today?'

'Yes, William, I believe I do.'

'Then you will come.'

She succeeded in twisting away from his grasp. She was on the point of leaving when she turned to him with a little smile and asked, 'Are you quite sure you wish me to accompany you?'

'If you attempt to defy me now, I shall never forgive you.'

'So be it,' she said, and, closing the door quietly behind her, she went upstairs to search out her newest dress.

21

More than a year had passed since her last visit to Trecarne and, as they rounded the curve of the hillside, Margaret caught her breath in amazement. Even the route had altered: the lane through the thick canopy of trees had vanished and in its place there was a driveway, still rough from the constant traffic of carts and teams of oxen, which swept in a wide arc through the area that used to be the near meadow. Impossible now to remember the huddle of shabby buildings that had always stood there before. Margaret had heard rumours about the grand building that was under construction – but when Richard had described his future home to her on that August afternoon she had not imagined anything on such a scale. Bigger than Rossmere, bigger even than a whole street of houses in Porthew, bigger than any house she had ever dreamed of . . . surely even the King's palace at Whitehall would not be so grand.

The main part of the building was still obscured by scaffolding which, from a distance, reminded Margaret of the pins sticking out of a partly finished garment. The second tower was far more sumptuous than the old hall which had now been restored to something like its former grandeur. At the front of the tower were huge mullioned windows with hundreds of tiny panes of glass looking out over the valley and the sea: each window looked to Margaret larger than many a cottage front in Porthew.

As they drew to a halt on the rough ground in front of the house, William checked his entourage for the last time. Margaret was wearing a dress of pewter grey, a colour soberly denoting the wife of a man whom God had chosen from the sinful multitude. William was wearing a doublet of black taffeta with silver thread worked into a panel at the front – denoting a man who had been chosen by God but who also wished it to be known that he was by his own efforts a successful merchant and a man of discernment in matters of taste. The pack horse was led by a Paul Viney tortured by the wearing of his master's cast-off garments. Such finery, after the loose-fitting clothes he was accustomed to wear, itched and rubbed in all the wrong places. Luckily, not having troubled to look in a mirror, he was unaware that the tight-fitting velvet looked as ridiculous on his rangy frame as frills on a greyhound.

They stood in front of the house for a considerable while. Despite the huge numbers of people who hurried past them carrying tools and materials, no one seemed to be expecting them or to know where Mr Treveryan might be found. William fidgeted and grew irritable. A pedlar would have been treated with more respect and their presence had most particularly been requested. He snapped at Margaret, but she was sunk in such a strange and waiting torpor that she hardly noticed. Viney stood beside Samphire and ran his fingers under the rim of his too-tight collar. A robin sat on the scaffolding and sang to them.

And then suddenly Richard Treveryan strode through the empty space where the magnificent front door would soon be hung and greeted them with such a rush of energy and good humour that William's irritation vanished at once. Why had no one told him of their arrival? He had been occupied with a new goshawk since first light and had not known how late it was . . . their servant must be taken care of and one of his grooms would tend their horses. He himself insisted that they accompany him on a tour of the entire site; he was all eagerness to show them every detail, to explain the effect he intended to achieve.

William was delighted. He listened attentively to their host's every word and missed no opportunity to compliment him on the architecture, choice of materials, clever use of the natural features of the site. At the same time he was careful to stress that he was himself no stranger to grand houses: he made apt comparisons with several country houses in France and the Low Countries, letting it be understood that he had been on intimate terms with their owners.

Margaret followed in silence. She guessed that Richard's hospitality was not for William at all – he despised the merchant's pretensions – but all for her. Her guess became a certainty when he led them to the site of the old yew tree and William, slightly perplexed at being led so far from the main house to examine a comparative trifle, exclaimed over the fine workmanship of the wrought-iron bench that stood there now.

Annoyance simmered inside her. She thought of Ambrose and Lizzie. She thought of Joseph and his family, of Roger Treloar dying in Launceston gaol and his widow's resignation to her new life. She thought of Luke.

She raised her eyes to his face and said coldly, 'I'm sure a local man could have done the work as well, if not better. And the view from here is nothing special.'

William repaid her with an evil glance. Richard replied thoughtfully, 'I especially value the opinion of someone as keen-sighted as you, Mistress Hollar.'

William redoubled his efforts to praise the seat.

As they walked back towards the house, Margaret felt as if she were stepping back within a dream that she had entered a year before on that August afternoon. Or as if all the months in between had been the dream and she was only now beginning to awake.

She clenched her fists at her sides, refused to look at the tall figure who walked before her in his suit of tawny cloth. She would learn to hate him, no matter what the cost.

Richard showed them the hallway where William admired the exquisite workmanship of the newel post and the gently curving stairway. Richard asked Margaret if she thought the walls should be panelled or hung with tapestries and Margaret replied that she was sure his wife would wish to decide that for herself. William looked as though he would gladly tear her hair out by the roots and assured Mr Treveryan that nothing was so elegant in a hallway as the finest Bruges tapestry work – and obviously Mr Treveryan would only ever have the best of everything.

In the library William commented on the huge number of books that Mr Treveryan must be expecting to house, clearly he was a gentleman excellently well read. Richard said that indeed he had a liking for the Roman authors, Catullus especially: had Mistress Hollar ever read Catullus? Margaret replied that she had enjoyed the poet when she was younger but was glad to say she had now outgrown her childish interest.

Workmen were laying the floor in the parlour. Richard regretted the inconvenience but unfortunately they had to pass through that room to reach the two rooms of the new tower, which he was particularly anxious to show them; moreover he had ordered refreshments brought to his apartments there. Margaret said that for her part she was neither hungry nor thirsty and that they might go on without her. William's blue eyes darkened momentarily as he restrained the urge to strangle her there and then. Richard laughed easily and said he understood that Mistress Hollar was anxious about crossing the unfinished joists but that if she would only take his hand she really had no need to be fearful. In demonstration he took two steps across the floor supports and reached back to take her hand. Margaret hesitated. William, standing behind her, pinched her so fiercely just above the elbow that tears sprang to her eyes. She stepped forward and Richard gripped her hand in his and did not let go until they had gained the polished floorboards of the lower tower room.

Richard released her hand. 'You have the makings of an excellent sailor,' he said. 'Such a sure sense of balance is wonderfully useful in the rigging.'

William, concentrating on crossing the room without mishap himself, did not notice the look that was exchanged between them and he assumed that Richard must be addressing the remark to him. 'I have indeed spent a good deal of time at sea,' he said.

The lower room was sparsely furnished with an elegant oaken table and a few chairs.

'This is where I am obliged to make my camp while the building work progresses,' said Richard.

The table was laid with fine Italian glasses, a jug of spiced wine, a plate of cold meats and cheese, a loaf of bread. William could not have been more grateful if Richard had spread a banquet before them and he maintained a lively stream of conversation while Margaret picked at the food in silence and Richard dropped titbits to the dogs and appeared lost in thought. A log fire was burning in the grate. Margaret tried to shake off the sensation, which she could in no way explain, that she had visited this room, sat beside this very fire, many times before.

She yearned only for the visit to be over so she might make her escape.

But first they must see the tower bedroom.

Richard led the way up a narrow winding stair; there was a smell of fresh plaster and woodsmoke and strewing herbs. Margaret was last to ascend. She tried to fix her gaze on the back of William's soft leather boots but as she emerged into the open space she was almost overwhelmed by the dazzle of light that greeted her.

It was a large room, filling the whole span of the tower; its high ceiling was decorated with scrolls and vines of white plaster. The pale walls were bare of any decoration. On one side a large window looked out towards the oak woods behind the house; the window opposite gave a view of the valley and the sea. The day had been overcast but just then the sun broke briefly through the clouds and the whole room sparkled with gold.

It was scantly furnished, but in the very centre, opposite the fireplace, stood a huge four-poster bed of carved mahogany, hung all about with tapestries that glowed jewel-bright in the sunshine. William exclaimed in admiration.

'I have not seen such fine examples of Flanders craftsmanship since I returned to England. Look at the detail and the colouring! Mr Treveryan, I must congratulate you, these are splendid.'

'I'm glad you approve of them,' said Richard. Margaret saw a muscle twitch in his cheek and knew that he was losing patience with his over-appreciative guest. 'They depict the story of Paris and his three goddesses; I daresay your taste is more for biblical representations.'

'Oh no,' William lied, hoping that Richard had not noticed his dislike of the semi-naked figures, 'there is still much we can learn from the pagan authors, I'm sure.'

Margaret walked over to the window and leaned her cheek against one of the stone mullions. Clouds had blotted out the sun once more and the air that came in through the open window bore an autumnal smell of sadness and decay. A few shrivelled leaves were blowing across the ground in front of the house and in the distance was the grey blur of the sea. Richard crossed the room to stand behind her; even if she had not heard his footsteps she would have known from the energy that rippled over her shoulders like an unseen breeze.

'Mistress Hollar, you are very subdued. Is the tapestry not to your taste?'

'All your possessions are beautiful,' she said, 'you know that, without needing our opinion.' But he was standing so close beside her that she could not keep a slight tremor from her voice; without having to turn her head she knew that Richard had heard the tremor – just as William never had, and never would.

William saw only that she was in danger of displeasing their customer once again. He shot her an agitated glance and said, 'Come and look at these properly, wife, it will do you good to observe the achievements of true craftsmen, such work is rarely found in England.'

'Your husband is a connoisseur. Are you familiar with the story of Paris?'

'Yes.'

Margaret returned to the bed and listened in silence while William extolled the exquisite detailing, the harmony of texture and colour, the masterly rendition of the human form. She reflected that the three ladies, so pink and comely, looked as though they had never done a moment's work in their whole lives, but decided it was prudent to say nothing.

William picked up a corner of the hanging the better to examine the density of stitching.

'Take care, Mr Hollar,' Richard cautioned, 'the hangings were only brought in yesterday and have not yet been secured.'

But William was too intent on the texture of Paris's bare foot where it nestled amid a cornucopia of leaves and flowers and little dancing butterflies to heed the warning.

It could have been an accident, of course. Richard merely touched the hanging, could hardly have been said to tug on it, and the curtain rails were not, as he had said, properly secured. Hardly surprising, therefore, when the whole assemblage fell to the floor with a clatter of curtain rings and a whoosh of material and a barely audible grunt from

493

William. Barely audible because he was felled beneath the mound of Paris and his three beauties – helpless and invisible.

Margaret gasped with surprise, and then merriment welled up inside her and she was barely able to stop herself from laughing aloud. And then she knew that Richard was watching her; she raised her eyes to his face and his eyes were dancing with shared amusement as he quietly placed his foot on one corner of the muttering and writhing mound of tapestry.

The laughter was irresistible, breaking down the barriers of the years, drawing their eyes together as if such an incident, such a movement, had been inevitable from the beginning, only waiting for this impossible and wholly unexpected accident to occur. No power on earth could have stopped Margaret from swaying towards his down-turned and no longer laughing face. Briefly his arms circled her waist, briefly he pressed his lips on hers and she arched her body to meet his and surrendered herself, for an all too fleeting moment, to the magic of that contact. He caressed her hair, her neck, they pulled apart and then, more briefly even than before, they twined their arms around each other once again and kissed and Richard grazed his cheek against hers and murmured her name on a breath that was an almost silent groan of desire.

And then the next moment the grunting heap at their feet produced a white hand, a gasp of air, and they were apart again, exchanging a last unspoken message that all had changed between them.

Now a red face emerged from under the weight of tapestry and Richard reached out a strong hand and helped the discomfited merchant to his feet. William was anxious only that the tapestry was still undamaged; Richard's concern was all for his guest.

'A truly Athenian accident,' was his wry comment, 'but unlike the unfortunate orator you have been rescued in plenty of time.'

He was acting as if nothing had occurred. Amazed by his immediate composure, Margaret escaped to her former contemplation of the drifting leaves and grey sky beyond the window. Their contact had not even ruffled the surface of his serenity; perhaps it was the kind of event that happened frequently with him: a serving-maid, a merchant's willing wife, a pretty face at the smithy. She wanted to laugh, weep, push her husband from the room, tell him all that had happened, run from here and never return. Most of all she wanted to feel Richard's arms around her again, feel the firm pressure of his lips on hers.

Her heart was pounding. How could Richard Treveryan stand there so calmly and discuss with William the most suitable materials for linings for the offending tapestries? How could William be so blind to her present condition? She felt herself dishevelled, flushed, in every way altered from the sober wife who had reluctantly accompanied him on this visit. How did he not see?

The remainder of the visit was thoroughly businesslike and, by the time the horses were once more brought to the front of the house, William was well pleased with their achievement. He told Richard several times what an enjoyable and informative morning this had been.

Richard did not once look at Margaret. 'Mr Hollar,' he said soberly, 'the pleasure has all been mine.'

Torn between annoyance with William and an almost uncontrollable urge to laugh, Margaret turned aside and pretended to be busy with one of the straps securing the loaded panniers.

Richard said casually, 'Maybe we'll meet again at the play tomorrow. Nicolas Sutton was approached yesterday by a group of players requesting licence to perform at Porthew. These strolling actors are sometimes amusing.'

'I cannot approve of such frivolity,' said William.

'Mere harmless entertainment,' said Richard, 'perhaps more fitting to servants and children. Your wife might find it enjoyable.'

Samphire, over-excited by a generous feed of oats in Richard's stable, suddenly took it into her head to try to shake the panniers from her back, temporarily distracting William who was afraid all his precious fabrics were about to be pitched down in the dirt.

Margaret said in a voice that only Richard could hear, 'Servants and children? Is that your last insult for today?'

She was heartily glad that no one could see Richard's expression as he replied in a low voice, 'We have unfinished business, Mistress Hollar. Will you attend the play?'

'I shall try.'

Samphire was pacified. Richard helped Margaret to mount.

'Thank you, Mr Treveryan,' she said in a clear voice, 'I must confess that I do not share my husband's opinion of the theatre.'

Richard grinned. 'I'm sure Mr Hollar would not seek to impose his own views so rigorously on his household.'

'I daresay I should go anyway,' she said, 'even if only to keep an eye on Luke and the servants.'

'Luke will not wish to attend,' said William firmly.

They were ready to leave.

William was unusually talkative on the way home. Part of the time he spent in marvelling at the money to be made by supplying the materials for the new house at Trecarne. These happy thoughts were interspersed with grumbles towards his wife.

'Your sullen attitude was unforgivable. What, in the name of all that is holy, did you imagine you were achieving by your rudeness to Mr Treveryan at every opportunity? I was ashamed by your childishness. If you imagined that you were somehow demonstrating your continuing loyalty to the Treloars then all I can say is that you showed your petty lack of understanding only too clearly. Thank heavens he is too much a gentleman to be put out of countenance by such a display. Didn't Our Lord teach us to return evil with good? You should have followed my example in this matter, Margaret, but you are always too hot-headed and impetuous.'

His grumbling might have ceased sooner, but he was driven to fresh outpourings of irritation by the fact that no matter how he chastised her his wife continued to smile as if at some inward source of amusement. Try as she might, she could not mimic the penitence that she knew would defuse his anger.

'Really, wife, I fail to see the humour in my words.'

'I'm truly sorry,' she beamed.

But in fact she hardly heard a word of what he said. All she knew as she journeyed back towards Porthew and William fretted and grumbled beside her, was that the moment in the tower bedroom, the moment of laughter and the kiss, had unlocked a cage that had been too long tight closed within her. And a bird had escaped, a singing bird of freedom and happiness that even now was stretching its wings in the cool September air, a bird that would never consent to imprisonment again, that launched itself towards the open spaces – and flew.

The following afternoon Richard mounted his pale stallion and, with Will Stevens and young Giles in attendance, set off for the entertainment at Porthew. He was wearing a buff coat and a plumed hat and carried a rapier at his side; he had a pair of pistols in his belt. The day was cool, with an occasional smattering of rain. Their horses' hoofs made hardly any noise on the soft mud and fallen leaves of the track. Richard hummed tunelessly as they journeyed: he was in an excellent good humour.

He had thought of nothing but Mistress Hollar all day. Now that the prize he had promised himself was within his grasp he was all impatience to see her again, yet at the same time he found he was in no hurry to conclude their strange courtship. His patience surprised him. For years he had divided his time between Kitty and Miriam Porter, occasionally enjoying variety when it was offered but never bothering to seek it out. Yet now it was the very complexity of the pursuit that he relished, the need for strategy. How, in the crowded and close-knit community of Porthew, could he contrive such a liaison without discovery? How to trick the husband? Or was the truth perhaps that despite appearances, the draper's wife was skilled by long practice of infidelity? This he would soon discover.

The players had set up their stage on the raised mound where the Life of St Ewan was re-enacted each year and a good crowd was already milling around waiting for the drama to begin. Richard positioned himself on a slight rise towards the back where he was able to observe the audience as well as the stage. He told Will and Giles that once they had seen to the horses they were free to do as they wished until the entertainment was over. They set off cheerfully to seek out their friends.

Richard surveyed the mass of faces but Mistress Hollar was not among them. He frowned. Disappointment was not a possibility he had even contemplated. Had her pestilential husband prevented her from coming after all? But surely she could contrive some way to attend the play if she so desired. Perhaps the truth was that she had changed her mind.

A raddled-looking actor stepped on to the stage and announced the beginning of the play, his words reinforced by a blast on a sackbut and a roll of drums. Only having seen the occasion as a pretext for a meeting, Richard had not troubled to ask the name of the play itself. Now he learned it was one he had seen in London during the spring. He was surprised when the raddled actor turned out to be masterly in his portrayal of a king consumed by jealousy and a groundless mistrust of his wife.

The actor-king groaned aloud, tortured by his irrational doubts, 'I am a feather for each wind that blows,' he declared in a misery of malice.

But Richard had stopped attending; a tall fair-haired woman had appeared among the people standing a little to the right of the stage. Margaret looked agitated. He saw her eyes scanning the mass of faces, but though her gaze fell briefly on him it moved on at once, still searching. Richard was puzzled, then, remembering, he inwardly cursed her shortness of sight. He wondered how to move within her field of vision without drawing attention to the manoeuvre. After a moment he tipped his hat a little further back on his head and then, as if he wished to make it easier for those behind him to see the stage, he removed it with a wide flourish.

The gesture was enough. Margaret's eyes settled for a fraction of a second on him, though the anxious frown did not leave her face. There was no sign of her husband: at home, singing psalms, Richard had no doubt. Having satisfied herself of his presence, Margaret now seemed to be settling down to enjoy the drama which was unfolding on the stage. Richard grew impatient; she stood so tall and calm in her cloak of dove grey that he had a sudden urge to do whatever was necessary to see that composure all unravelled.

The jealous king was launching a vicious attack on his all too clearly innocent wife (played unfortunately by a youth who lacked the dignity and manners of royalty) when Richard at last saw Margaret turn and ease her way through the crowd. He at once pushed past the people who stood behind him and emerged into the empty space to the rear of the arena just in time to see a grey-cloaked figure disappearing down the alley that ran behind Jack Pym's alehouse. She was walking swiftly; Richard measured his stride so as to keep her in view while remaining at a discreet distance and followed her through a maze of paths until he judged they must be approaching the shambles at the far edge of town.

Sea mist was billowing in from the ocean, causing a premature dusk to fall. Droplets of water glistened on the fringe of thatch overhanging the lane and on the dying weeds that grew in patches beside the path. From the improvised theatre the noise of cheering and robust music signified the ending of the first part, but the sounds were distant now and muffled by the encroaching fog.

The lane narrowed, was become little more than a passageway. Never once glancing behind her, Margaret hurried around a far corner and out of sight. Lengthening his stride, Richard rounded the end of the lane and found himself in an open patch of ground that formed a kind of pen, slatted wood fencing and walls on every side. Instinctively his hand went to the hilt of his rapier; Mistress Hollar was nowhere to be seen and this enclosed space had the smell and feel of a trap.

He muttered a heartfelt oath; he remembered now that Mistress Hollar was not only the wife of the handsome draper, she was also sister-in-law to the maimed blacksmith and had sided with the cripple and his family when they made their stand at Trecarne. Like a fool he had not for a moment allowed for the likelihood that his quarry was in fact merely the bait in an elaborate ambush.

As he glanced all around him, assessing the potential advantages and dangers of this damp corner of the town, a kind of coldness entered him. Not so much fear of the danger he might be in – he relished the chance to settle with the Treloars once and for all – no, it was the chill of stumbling on bleak betrayal where he had come with a trust and hopefulness he had not known in years.

Blind fool, he rebuked himself, what in God's name did you expect?

A wooden slat swung slightly, creaking as it did so and a pale hand moved in the darker shadows beyond. His face grim, fully prepared for an attack, Richard drew his rapier and approached.

His first thought was that she did, after all, appear to be alone. She had pushed her cloak back from her head, she was breathing heavily and the anxious frown that he had noticed as she watched the players still shadowed her face. His second thought, as he slid through the space left by the broken timber, was that it had been madness to have doubted her for an instant.

She placed her hand on the pommel of his rapier, pushing it gently away. 'Why so fierce?' she queried.

There was no reply that would not have been an insult. He merely smiled and sheathed his weapon.

'What is this place?' he asked.

'They pen the animals here before market. And the bulls that are to be baited.'

'A curious choice for a tryst,' he smiled.

'It is little used, and cannot be overlooked.'

Richard was silent. In his eagerness to achieve this solitary meeting, he had never anticipated hesitation, but now his usual certainty was deserting him. What had been intended as a diversion was beginning to have an importance he had never expected. All at once he was afraid that if he made a wrong move she might step back, turn away altogether and reject him – and he discovered that the prospect of failure now was almost unbearable.

Her eyes were searching his face. 'I cannot stay long,' she said, in a low, quick voice, 'my husband expressly forbad any of his household to visit the play. I slipped out while he was occupied in reading his Bible but I must be back before he finishes. But I wanted to see you, to talk with you. You know that, already.'

'Mr Hollar is such a tyrant?'

She gave him a bitter smile. 'There are many forms of tyranny,' she said.

'Our time is short, then.'

'Yes.'

Still Richard made no move. Not since he was a lad of sixteen years had he known such a paralysing combination of yearning and doubt. The more he wished to take her in his arms, the more he dreaded a wrong move.

She had been smiling but now, as they stood facing each other in silence, her face grew solemn. Slowly she raised her hand and brushed the tiny droplets of water from his hair; her fingertips grazed the ridge of his cheekbones, the hollow beside his mouth. Then she drew his head down and kissed him.

Not briefly, this time. Richard wrapped his arms around her and crushed her body to him as though his craving would never be satisfied, and wondered only that her fierce hunger seemed to match his own. If he had feared resistance, he knew now there was none. He pulled back slightly and, still cradling her in his arms, searched her face to make sure his senses had not been mistaken.

She answered his smile.

But when he leaned to kiss her once again she placed her hands against his chest and pushed him away. 'Not here,' she breathed, 'not now.'

He frowned.

'I must return home,' she told him, 'before my absence is noticed. Besides, this place is far too well known.'

'Where then? We cannot always depend on travelling players and tapestry curtains. Does God's Fox guard you so closely?'

Margaret laughed. With his fair good looks and slightly close-set eyes, William resembled a fox exactly. 'He is . . . erratic. And today he is especially out of humour because he considers I was uncivil towards you yesterday.'

'Then tell him I insist you are always uncivil.'

'I shall do no such thing.'

'Margaret . . .' He slid his hands beneath her cloak and began to draw her towards him again but she shook her head.

'I must go.'

'Stay just a little longer.'

'I cannot.'

'Do you intend always to play the coquette?'

She laughed. 'You'll find out by and by.'

'When?'

She fell silent. Perhaps it was the mention of foxes that made her think of chickens and from there it was an easy step to the stone barn which had sheltered Merry and Ned.

'Well?'

'There is a little barn between our garden and the lane. Each evening at dusk I visit it to see my chickens are safe and bolt the door for the night.'

He raised a single eyebrow. 'A chicken coop, Mistress Hollar?'

'It serves for a stable as well. And there is a hayloft above.'

'A palace, obviously.'

'What's the matter? I thought it was variety you wanted, a diversion with a satisfying degree of risk. Am I not right?'

Richard was taken aback. He had not anticipated that she would understand him so well. He was not sure that he liked the terms of their meeting to be so starkly defined. But then he decided that it was better so, and his relief made it easier to overlook the present disappointment.

'Exactly,' he said.

'And now I must go. Can you find your way alone by the route we came? Wait until I've been gone a few minutes, in case anyone sees you.'

Richard agreed. Margaret twined her arms around his neck and kissed him once again, before pulling away with a gasp of impatience. Her cheeks were flushed as she drew her hood over her head and slipped out into the shrouds of mist. Richard waited for some time, lost in thought, before deciding that he might as well return and watch the rest of the play.

He was in time for the last moments: the jealous king, penitent now, was reunited with his all-forgiving wife and both discovered the daughter they had given up for dead, Perdita, the daughter whom they so nearly lost.

I must be mad, thought Margaret, to be making assignations with such a man. She almost wished she could be blind to

502

the folly of her actions. Richard Treveryan wanted only the kind of casual pleasure that Lizzie had offered Nicolas Sutton, while she, having lost her heart already, stood to lose everything. And for what?

'I am a feather for each wind that blows,' the actor-king had declared. She had never wanted to fall in love with Richard Treveryan, could see no way through this madness, but only deeper in.

Mistress Treveryan descended on Trecarne the following day. Fearing Barbary pirates, she was obliged to travel on horseback and the retinue of pack horses and serving-men and women that accompanied her was so impressive that the inhabitants of several villages she passed through believed they had witnessed Queen Henrietta Maria herself.

The admiration of a few ignorant villagers was all the satisfaction Kitty gained from her visit to Cornwall. She was grudging in her praise of the new house; it struck her as typically perverse of Richard to erect an ostentatious building in such a godforsaken corner of the realm that no one of any importance was ever likely to visit. For years she had pestered him to build in Devon; it was well known that as people rose in wealth they moved eastwards; no one had ever made a fortune only to squander it in the western wildernesses of Cornwall. But of course (as she knew well though she could not stop herself) her pleading only hardened his resolve.

Now that the main section of the house was more than half-finished she wished to claim ownership, to stamp it with her own character. As soon as she had recovered from the journey she made herself busy proposing improvements and alterations to the design. As usual Richard was by turns deaf and irritated by her interference – and ignored her suggestions. Kitty retreated to the first-floor bedroom in the new tower and thought she might be falling ill. Outside, the rain beat interminably against the windows and the ground near the house became a shimmering expanse of mud. Kitty lay in the huge four-poster and chivvied the servants into brewing warm cordials and listened to the wind and the rain and fretted that her husband neglected her.

All her miseries were caused by the lack of a child, she was sure of it; only let her produce a healthy son and she would not have to endure his terrifying silences, those eyes which, even when fixed on her, seemed to be far away, his caresses from which all tenderness had gone.

If she could but have a child . . . her desire for an heir had become an obsession. Over the years she had consulted every apothecary and wise man in Saltash and Plymouth and as far away as Exeter and Bristol. She had tried amulets and prayers, blood letting, potions and strange rituals; she raged against her endlessly empty womb. If she could only conceive, then Richard would attend to her as he had done on that starry Christmas Eve when he scooped her in his arms and carried her up the stairs to her bridal bed . . . but to remember was too painful. Instead she harangued the servants on their blundering, found fault with everything.

'This room is not elegant,' she complained to Richard on one of his rare visits to the new tower, 'silk or brocade is more suitable for bed-hangings than those tapestries I cannot imagine why you chose to hang such things around a bed. If you were to put them on the wall of the solar –'

But Richard interrupted her briskly. 'I will not hear a word against Paris and his three beauties,' he said, smoothing a hand thoughtfully against a fold of the curtains. 'I owe them a great debt and it would be gross ingratitude to repay them with banishment.'

On occasion Kitty's face seemed to shrivel with vexation. 'What nonsense you talk. How can you owe anything to a . . . you are speaking in riddles again on purpose to confuse me . . . you listen to nothing that I say . . . you never pay attention . . . ill and you don't care . . . stay and hear me out –'

'Kitty, you sing an old song. And God knows it was unmelodious when I heard it first.' And with that he turned abruptly on his heel and clattered down the stairs, calling Will to fetch his horse for there was work to be done on the estate.

More than once he was on the point of riding to Porthew at dusk to discover if Mistress Hollar would remain true to her promise. A secret meeting in a hayloft with the wife of a local worthy . . . the novelty alone would have been tempting, even without the attractions of the lady herself. But the driving wind and rain would have dampened the ardour of the most lovesick youth and Richard did not consider himself lovesick in the least. Besides, it irked him that she had set out the terms so callously. 'Variety and a diversion with a satisfying degree of risk' – whatever he had been expecting it had not been such a cool acceptance of the limits of their liaison. As he considered her words he began to think that she must after all be practised in adultery and, unreasonably, the thought annoyed him. Each afternoon he debated whether to ride to Porthew that day; each afternoon he put if off – but each evening as dusk spread out from the oak woods, he wished that he had gone.

Tiring of illness and the frustrations of living in a house where none of the resident servants would obey her orders, Kitty decided to turn her attention to social life. She had expected all the notables of the district to come calling as soon as they had news of her arrival, but so far only Nicolas had appeared. She suspected, quite rightly, that her husband had gained a reputation as an anti-social fellow. Nicolas told her his wife sent her apologies but having recently been delivered of a healthy girl even the short journey to Trecarne was too strenuous, but she hoped Kitty would honour them with a visit.

It took Kitty two days of packing and unpacking and reducing her servants to tears before she was ready for the journey. She grew hysterical at the prospect of going alone and Richard, eager now only to have her away from the house, agreed to ride with her and stay for at least one night. Kitty was pacified.

Her plan to make an impressive entrance at Rossmere was sabotaged by the implacable Cornish weather. Lashing rain and a north-easterly gale reduced her and her entire party to a collection of pitiful waifs. Richard, of course, found it all highly entertaining, but then he was never happier than when dressed in country leathers and riding his horse on the high ground to avoid the mud.

Kitty and Alice greeted each other like sisters. Alice was full of concern for Kitty's plight. Kitty, through rain-soaked hair and chattering teeth, said that in Saltash where the roads were at least civilised she always travelled by coach, and that hers was said by many to be the finest in the West Country.

That evening, wrapped in furs, she sat before a huge fire and recovered with the aid of hot canary punch. Sir John Sutton forgot that this was the heiress who had spurned his second son as soon as he discovered their shared interest in medical symptoms and the various methods for their alleviation.

Richard and Nicolas drew apart a little to talk of the new Parliament that was soon to gather in London. Richard was of the opinion that this could be no more successful than the last; the King wanted money to fight his war against the Scots but would never concede an inch of ground, nor need he, so long as he had the Earl of Strafford to advise him. Nicolas, more optimistic, said His Majesty's power would surely be checked because there was no other way out of the impasse: the King and his policies had grown so unpopular that raising levies during the summer had proved a near impossible task.

Richard remained sceptical. 'The King may appear to listen, may even make a show of giving ground – but he will never consent to be shackled by Parliament. And the Lord Deputy Strafford will give him the means to rule without need of Parliaments, and that is all the King wants. There will never be a compromise so long as Strafford lives.'

'But the King made no effort to defend Strafford when he was attacked at the Council of York.'

Richard could not believe King Charles would ever be so foolhardy as to sacrifice Strafford. 'No, this Parliament will be a repeat of the last one: the lawyers will squabble, the King will bluster and then it will all be over with nothing accomplished. I can think of many better ways to waste time than idling in Parliament. How is the chestnut mare I sold you in the summer?'

They fell happily to talking of horses and of their estates. Nicolas, like Richard, had no desire to follow the political life, but his reasons were different: he was so content in his life at Rossmere among his children and his farms and his local duties that he saw no reason to seek for anything else.

His wife was seated near the fire with her sewing. From

time to time she turned to gaze into the wooden crib beside her and an expression of softness suffused her face. Kitty became convinced that her hostess was deliberately flaunting her happily fecund state. From beneath her mound of furs Kitty let fly a constant stream of complaints: she had never found herself in such a dreary place, and she felt quite sorry for anyone condemned to such a monotonous existence. Alice, somewhat taken aback, countered that it was on the contrary an extremely pleasant life, if one had always known –

'*I* could never adjust to such tedium.' Kitty's shrill voice was adamant. 'The same few paltry neighbours, cut off from all news – ugh! In Saltash there is excitement every day. I've heard it said often that even London is not more cosmopolitan.'

It was some little while before Alice discovered that her best defence against Kitty's barrage of criticism lay with her lively brood of children. Once having realised what weapons lay within her hands, she used them without mercy. While Kitty patronised her hostess for her relative poverty Alice learned to extol the virtues of her children, the almost monotonous regularity with which she conceived, the rude health of her offspring once they had entered the world. Francis was the image of his father, Charles fearless on horseback, little Sophie already a mother to the younger ones.

'Nicolas rejoices daily in his boys. Only last week he mentioned to me how sorry he feels for poor Richard; to have worked so hard and made a fortune and yet to have no son to inherit when he is gone. That is a cruel twist of fate, Nicolas thought.'

The visit was not a success.

Kitty returned to Trecarne after only two days. Still the rain poured down and the weather was so impossibly bad that all outside work staggered to a muddy halt. The new chimneys did not draw properly and the rooms were smoke filled and cold. Kitty was sure her husband took a cruel pleasure in her discomfort and endured it as long as she could, but was infinitely relieved when he suggested they travel back to Saltash together.

Perversely, on the day they left, the sun came out at last.

At the head of the rise, Richard reined his horse to a halt.

'Look back, Kitty,' he offered, 'now do you understand?'

His wife, glancing behind her, saw only a huge and half-completed house set among acres of mud and brown fields. She saw scrubby trees that would never grow to full height because of the endless battering winds, a grey sea empty of ships and commerce, a bleak and desolate landscape. She did not see it through his eyes at all and was beginning to think he only liked the place on purpose to vex her.

'This whole landscape and its inhabitants are backward and odious. I hope I never have to set foot here again.'

And instantly she regretted her honesty because Richard burst out laughing and rode ahead, much cheered. Nothing she could have said about Trecarne could have endeared it to him more.

22

A dampness, part mist, part rain, had flung a veil across the night. Somewhere, high above the tranquil town and the softly breathing sea, a full moon was shining, its brightness suffused by the fine gauze of mist.

Margaret had no need of a lantern to light her way to the little barn at the end of the garden; she had trodden this path so many times before, would no doubt tread it many thousands of times again. Her skirts brushed against bushes of rosemary and sage, her feet knew every contour of the way – the stone that was still loose, Paul Viney having relaid it awkwardly, and which rocked slightly as it took her weight.

On her left, the privy, and beyond that the gate that led into the lane. Beside the gate was the stone barn. It was now the middle of March and in the six months which had passed since she made her assignation with Richard Treveryan he had not been seen in the district. She had long since abandoned hope that she would ever find him waiting for her; indeed, she told herself she must have spoken in a fit of madness, that she was glad he had lost interest in his fine new house and forgotten her entirely. Sometimes she thought their stolen meetings had never even occurred, had been merely the product of a corrupted imagination. Was it possible that he had taken her in his arms and kissed her while her husband writhed beneath the tapestry curtain? Had she really lured him to the bull pen and promised to meet him again in secret? Often the memory of those scenes was enough to bring a smile to her lips – and a lingering regret. If it had been a dream, then she had relished it and wished the waking world was half so magical. Maybe she would never again feel the pressure of his arms around her waist, his mouth pressed down against her own, but still, the evening ritual of checking on her chicken house had so worked itself into the fabric of her life that she could not stop now, even if the reason for it had faded to a half-believed memory. Without that ritual she did not know how her life would be bearable.

And it was often a lingering aftertaste of disappointment that caused her to follow the nightly visit to the barn with a stroll down to the harbour where the waves lapped unseen on the shingle, or along the road towards Ia's Wood, or sometimes, on clear nights, on to the bracken- and gorse-clad cliffs. If she could have no true companion, she reasoned, she must learn to make a friend of solitude.

'People will talk,' William often fretted, 'the way you wander the roads at night.'

'Then let them talk,' was Margaret's curt reply.

'You never consider our reputation,' he said, but he made no real effort to prevent her rambling: her restlessness that winter unsettled him and he was glad enough when she was out of the house.

This night, as always, Margaret pushed open the roughly made wooden door and heard the familiar creak of its hinges, but in this shroud of mist all sounds were subdued. She said softly, as she always did, 'Sleep soundly, Samphire, goodnight little chickens. God keep you all safe 'til morning.'

Somewhere in the darkness there was a ruffling of feathers, the sound of the horse shifting his weight from one foot to the other. Then there was a muffled sound and a voice, a voice that she would have recognised if it had called to her from the end of the world, said softly, 'Margaret!'

She stood absolutely still. 'You,' she whispered, her throat suddenly dry.

A shape moved in the blackness and pushed the door closed behind her. A shiver ran over her as she sensed his nearness. Every evening for six months she had imagined this meeting, what he might say and she reply, but now that the moment was come, all need for words had vanished. Her eyes were still unaccustomed to the darkness but she could hear his breathing was very close. His gloved hand touched her cheek and he murmured her name a second time and she heard the way his voice caught on the syllables.

He circled her waist with his arms and drew her to him and it was as if all the long winter months of waiting had never been and their last meeting had happened only moments before.

A brief giddiness washed over her; something so long desired, so often hoped for and as frequently despaired of, had caught her unawares and she half-expected to open her eyes and find that his voice, the moving darkness, had been nothing but another hopeless dream. The giddiness passed. The arms that held her so fiercely had substance and strength, the mouth that was seeking out hers covered her with kisses, hungry kisses that no phantom could ever possess. As she returned his kisses she felt herself to be stepping into a dark sea. His fingers slid beneath the soft fabric of her gown and she felt their cool tips feathering her breasts.

She was shivering, although her skin was hot as if in a fever. Suddenly she jerked her head back and pulled away slightly. She could make out his eyes now, and the gleam of white linen at his throat. 'Is it really you?' she murmured.

He brushed his lips gently against her cheek. 'Oh yes,' was his only reply, 'haven't we waited long enough?' And then, when she did not speak, he led her to the higher level of the barn where the hay was stored, and where his cloak was spread in readiness. They sank down on their knees and faced each other as they grappled with laces and buttons and ties and their clothes seemed to be briar thickets designed on purpose to thwart them. At last his hands drew her nakedness towards him and she clung to him, her palms holding the smooth angles of his shoulder blades as he pressed down on her where she lay on his cloak. She cried out as he entered her and he put his hand across her mouth, but gently, and she kissed his palm and tried to smother the sounds of her pleasure. Richard was too greedy, too hungry for her, to take his usual pains; he had not known how long and how totally he had desired her until the moment when he felt her softness open up beneath him like a warm flower.

It was only afterwards that he remembered the proper tendernesses of a lover, only later when she lay against him in the hay-drowsy darkness, that he kissed her breasts and stroked the smooth curve of her stomach.

'I have come courting you like a stable-boy,' he said at length, 'next time I shall remember the due courtesies of a gentleman.'

Margaret heard the two words 'next time' and wanted for nothing more. She assumed his apology was for the cloak laid on the hay and she said, 'This has suited me well enough,' not knowing anything else.

Some slates had become dislodged on the roof and through the gaps they could see the moon-pale mist of the sky. Margaret felt herself to be drifting in some strange place where words and thoughts no longer had meaning or weight. There was the slow rise and fall of his breathing, the feel of his heartbeat beneath her palm. No need for anything more.

When he sat up and began pulling on his doublet, Margaret reached up her hand to draw him to her once again. She dreaded the moment of his leaving, but feared to hold him back with words. Despite the darkness she knew that he was smiling as he bent once more to embrace her. This time he lingered in his caresses, wove a fine web of desire across her skin with his touch, and when he entered her a second time his body was slower, the earlier urgency already spent and this time, when she cried out, it was with a pleasure so intense it was almost like dying and he too was drowning and could only stifle her cries with kisses.

All desire spent, they sank down into the hay. He lay on his back and she rested her face against his chest. And when the fine lawn of his shirt grew damp he assumed it was their mingled sweat; nothing would have dragged from her the fact of her weeping; fierce tears of joy and grief and an emotion too strong to be contained in any word, an emotion so powerful it must burst out in weeping or laughter or drowning in a sea of love.

He propped himself on an elbow, kissed her tenderly and then slipped on his doublet. 'Mistress Hollar,' he said, 'I am your most devoted servant.'

'I am honoured, Mr Treveryan.'

'No more formality, not now.'

'Richard, then.'

'Hmm. Margaret . . .' he was caressing the nape of her neck thoughtfully, 'the name is still too formal.'

512

'My old friends call me Mattie.'

'Then I most assuredly will not. I do not intend to be confused with old friends. A new lover must find a different name.'

Margaret cared nothing for names, only for the knowledge that he planned to see her again. She sat up with a sigh and began to arrange her dress.

'You know I always visit the hens a little after dark.'

'From bull pen to chicken coop,' he mused.

'Are you complaining?'

'No. But I can offer you a fine four-poster with sheets and bolsters and every comfort.'

Margaret dismissed him scornfully. 'Such luxuries are only for people whose –' she was about to say 'love' but checked herself just in time – 'whose desire for each other is cooling.'

'Would you have me prove my devotion in a ditch?'

She laughed. 'Not yet, the roads are still too muddy.'

Reluctantly, they climbed down into the stable. On the cross-beam above them half a dozen chickens stirred and made their little conversational night-time noises. Moonlight was shining through the cracks around the door.

'Where did you leave your horse?' she asked.

'My groom Will Stevens is waiting for me by the little bridge.'

'The poor man will catch his death of cold.'

'But in an excellent cause.'

Their words were only an excuse to delay the moment of parting. As he moved to pull back the door, she placed her hand over his.

'Why did you stay away so long?' She could no longer restrain the question. 'I have been faithful to my poor chickens for half a year.'

'I took a ship to the Indies. We did not return until a week ago.'

'Oh. I imagined you in Plymouth.'

For answer, he raised her fingers to his lips and kissed them. Then said, 'I almost forgot. Here . . .' Reaching into his inner pocket he pulled out a fine chain with something heavy attached to it and slipped it over her head. 'It has been worked in gold by the natives of South America.

Mostly their jewellery is considered too barbaric and is melted down but I thought you might like the strangeness of it.'

His cool fingers were lingering at her throat. Margaret was entranced, not so much by the gift, which she could not see, as by the thought that even in the far-off Indies he had remembered her.

'Maybe it was made in El Dorado.' There was wonder in her voice.

'If such a city of gold has ever existed.'

'I shall wear it always.'

'And your husband?'

'He does not see what I wear.'

Richard was silent, pondering; he had been curious about God's Fox. He put his arms around her waist and pulled her close to him, pressing his cheek against her smooth fall of hair.

'Meg,' he breathed, 'my own Meg. Has anyone called you that before?'

'Never.'

'And do you like it now?'

'When you say the word, yes.'

'Then in my arms you will always be Meg.'

For a while longer they held each other close. Then, with a last kiss, he released her, pulled back the door and slipped away into the misty dampness of the night.

Will Stevens was waiting with the two horses in a grove of trees by Ia's Bridge. He was as miserable with the waiting as his master was pleased with the evening's activity. Their horses were eager to be home and made good speed in the moonlight. And it never occurred to Richard, as he cantered along the track to Trecarne and promised Will warm spiced wine on their return, that for once in his life love-making had not left him feeling empty and dissatisfied but that, on the contrary, he was filled with a sense of wholeness – and wonder.

Margaret did not return straight to the house. She stood for a little while at the gate and tried to make out the full moon above the mist. Her emotions were too strong for thought; she surrendered herself to the joy of the moment.

When she pushed open the kitchen door she saw Dorcas and Paul sitting near the fire, much as she had left them. William was in the parlour, reading his Bible by the light of a tallow. But he had left the door ajar and was watching for her.

'You have been wandering a long time,' he said, 'people are sure to talk.'

'Then let them talk,' she replied, as usual.

And then she laughed. William was startled. It was a long time since he had heard her laugh; he thought that he had never heard her laugh in quite that way before. It bothered him although he could not put his finger on the exact nature of his unease. And when he came to the door of the kitchen he discovered, more disconcertingly still, that she was regarding both him and their two servants with a smile of sheer delight, happiness radiating from her as indiscriminate as summer sunshine.

'Ours is a godly household,' he took refuge in the familiar phrases, 'remember our position, Margaret.'

And now there was defiance in her smile. '*Your* position, William. I shall never forget that.'

She picked up a candle from the table, lit it from his and, shielding the flame with her hand, she began to climb the stairs to her room. Even as she closed her bedroom door, he could still hear her laughter.

For a long time, Margaret sat by her window, the lighted candle on the sill, and listened to the familiar sounds of her household retiring for the night. At last all was silent. As if to convince herself that all that had happened was real, and not a dream, she had removed the chain from around her neck and the pendant lay on her palm. It was unlike anything she had ever seen before, so barbarous and strange it might almost have been alarming – except that on such a night she would have found beauty even in the head of Medusa.

When she could stay awake no longer, she pulled on her shift and slipped the chain and pendant once more around her neck; she fell asleep with the cool weight of it against her breasts.

Richard was waiting for her in the little barn on the following night, and the next, and the one after that . . . and every night until he thought he must be bewitched, so strong was the force that drew him back and back to the hayloft like some lovesick ploughboy. Each time he rode away from Porthew he told himself that for now his appetite was satisfied; he would not return for a few days more, a week maybe. But no sooner was he back in his own house at Trecarne than thoughts of Mistress Hollar began to buzz around his head like an unwanted song. When he awoke in the large four-poster he reached out, almost as though expecting to find her sleeping there beside him. Through the morning he often thought he heard her throaty laughter, her voice shaping his name with the soft inflections of the Cornish. By the afternoon he was yearning once more to feel the cool touch of her skin against his own, to press his face against her hair, to bury and lose himself in her warm darkness. Tomorrow, he told himself, surely I can wait another day. But by the time dusk was falling the urge to possess her once again had become intolerable; of course he could wait until the following day, but why postpone a pleasure so intense? As the light faded in the western sky he strode down to the stables, hallooed Will Stevens into activity, and galloped off towards Porthew once more.

'Meg, you are a witch, for sure,' he murmured one night as he held her in his arms.

'Praise God for that,' her laughter rose up from the depths of great content, 'I shall weave such a spell around you, Richard Treveryan, as you shall never in your life escape.'

But after a while, though still desiring her as much as ever, he began to grow impatient with their meeting place.

'When will you find a way to visit me at Trecarne?'

'Are you growing too fussy for our bed of hay?'

He laughed. 'No, not that. But this infernal darkness, Meg. I swear I shall soon forget what you look like altogether. I want to see your face in the light; I want to watch you when we are together.' As he spoke he traced the tip of one finger along the ridge of her nose, touched the curve of her cheek, her chin, her lips.

She bit his finger tenderly. 'You only have to attend church on a Sunday and you can see me plain enough.'

He groaned and hugged her to him tightly. 'To see you

and yet have to remain distant would be unspeakable torment. And I cannot visit you in daylight. The only remedy is for you to visit Trecarne.'

Unseen by him, she frowned. However many times she had taxed her brain to find a solution, she did not see how she could risk a journey to his home.

Margaret was under no illusions about her affair with Richard Treveryan. Had he come wooing her when first they met, when she was a girl of just sixteen, she might have deceived herself with hopes that he would learn to love her with the fierce undying love of the old tales and legends, to love her as she knew she loved him. But now she was a woman of twenty-six, she had seen and learned too much to allow room for fairy tales. She knew that Treveryan's affection for her, though intense enough at the present, was likely to be a matter of small importance to him; that in the end she would be only a diversion, as Lizzie had been to Nicolas Sutton. And the strangest part of it was that this knowledge did not trouble her at all, not now. It was enough, simply, that he took her in his arms and gave her his body's loving each night; enough that each time he vanished into the darkness she knew he would visit the little barn again. Once more, only once more – and each time that 'once more' satisfied her. If this happiness was doomed to be short-lived then she had no desire to tarnish it with future worries. She surrendered herself completely to the present, to the wonderment of loving him.

She was careful never to betray the strength of her feelings to Richard. Her instinct warned her that he would be wary of strong attachment, suspicious of an entanglement in which he might become trapped. She reasoned that a wealthy, much-travelled man like him must have enjoyed affairs with many women and therefore that the liaison which was turning her world upside-down was for him a commonplace interlude. At present she was too happy to waste time resenting this imbalance. She guessed his own marriage was a disappointment; she guessed also that he had never fully given himself to anyone.

Sometimes, in the heat of their love-making, or in the delicious lethargy that followed, he began to murmur the endearments of a lover. 'Come with me, Meg . . . we must be together always . . . there has never been anyone like you . . .'

But each time she stopped him. 'Hush, don't speak,' and she pressed her hand against his lips. 'Isn't this enough? Don't spoil it with false promises.'

He protested that she wronged him, and once or twice he was annoyed that she refused to match their physical passion with words. But later, when he rode away, he was always glad of his freedom.

One night, when the rain poured down on the roof and the drips splashed noisily around them, Richard wrapped his cloak around them both and complained bitterly. 'Mistress Hollar, I'll have you know I am the master of eight ships. I have an interest in half a dozen companies. I am in the process of building what is intended to be the largest house in all of Cornwall. I have a house in Saltash, another in Plymouth and half a dozen manors in Devon. Every one of them graced with a fine and sturdy *roof*. Meg, I tell you, they are *dry* houses . . . so why must we suffer like the meanest vagabonds in this damp and leaky hovel?'

'You moan on like a child,' Margaret chided him, 'and besides . . .' for the spring downpour had reminded her of that other rainy night, when Merry and Ned had scampered laughing into the house and tumbled into the comfort of William's empty bed, 'this barn is hallowed ground.'

His arms stiffened in their embrace, so that his grip was almost painful. 'Why, Mistress Hollar, have you always entertained your lovers here?'

She was silent for so long while the rain drummed on the roof above them that he almost imagined she had fallen asleep but when he shook her gently she said, 'Richard, believe me, you are the first.' And the last, she might have added, but she checked herself.

There was a strangeness in her voice that he had never heard before. She was thinking how lucky it was that he could not see her face, or he would have read her thoughts too plainly. Richard was pleased by her avowal but at the same time, illogically, he chose to assume it was a falsehood, a sop to his masculine vanity, because to believe her would have been to recognise that their affair had already grown deeper and more dangerous than ever he had planned.

Fearing that their conversation was becoming too serious, Margaret told him of Dorcas and her wanton enterprise in search of food. Richard laughed and forgot his irritation at the leaking roof. Before he left that night he took her in his arms and told her solemnly, 'Meg, if ever you are mistress of my household, I absolutely forbid you to hire my servants. I will not be responsible for cretins and wastrels, not even for you.'

He did not hear her stifled gasp, only felt her hands as she pushed him away. After a moment she managed to say in a teasing voice, 'What nonsense you talk sometimes, Richard Treveryan.'

Her coolness disturbed him and he was seized by a sudden urge to know that he could hurt her. 'Come and live with me, Meg,' he said fiercely. 'Leave Porthew, turn your back on your life here and we can be together always.'

He heard her mocking laughter. 'Always, Richard? You'd be tired of me before the year was up.'

'And would you tire as easily?'

'No!' But then she added lightly, 'I'd maybe manage a couple of years, who knows?'

But later, when he had vanished into the darkness, Margaret remained a long time alone in the barn, tormented by his words. Always . . . the word circled through her mind. We can be together always.

And later still, when her household was in bed and she found she still could not sleep, she returned to the barn with a horn lantern and a little knife and shooed the startled chickens from their beam.

'*Nullus amor talis coniunxit foedere amantes*,' she scratched in slow and awkward letters while the chickens sulked on the lip of the manger. No love ever joined lovers in such a bond.

By the time she finished she was exhausted. Richard would never see the words, since he only visited at night, but somehow the effort had satisfied her. It seemed to sum up all her wonder and despair at what was happening, and what would never be.

Will Stevens, victim of too many solitary nights in the copse by Ia's Bridge, took to his bed with a racking cough and a

519

fever. Richard was furious. He recruited the stable-boy, Giles, to stay with the horses while he paid his nightly visit to Porthew. Giles endured the damp and the cold for three nights but on the fourth, having gauged the length of time his master was detained by his mysterious business, the lad took the two horses into town and warmed his feet by Jack Pym's fire. By noon of the next day all of Porthew knew that Mr Treveryan was courting a local woman, though her identity remained uncertain. Several candidates were suggested; all denied the charges vigorously. Margaret's name was not among them.

On the fifth night Richard was waiting by the bridge as Giles, singing cheerfully, ambled back from the ale-house. Richard promised him a thrashing but, as they trotted back along the track towards Trecarne, he reflected that Margaret would no doubt want the fellow rewarded for his disobedience. He let the boy off with a warning. Two nights later Giles repaired once more to the ale-house and this time he was punished. He did not disobey again. Richard found it unnecessary to mention this example of the perversity of servants to Margaret.

Instead he tried to devise ways to see her at Trecarne. 'Could you not tell your husband you are visiting your family? I could have a horse waiting for you at the edge of town.'

'People are gossiping about you as it is,' Margaret was worried, 'I am taking risks enough.'

'Then I shall order cloth from your foxy husband and insist that you deliver it.'

'A brilliant scheme,' she said drily, 'you know full well he'd bring it himself. And how long could you keep him under a tapestry curtain a second time? He'd be on his guard.'

'I'd have him hung in chains from the tower if that meant I could have you to myself for a whole night.'

Laughing, she covered his face with kisses. 'Just the way to keep the gossips quiet. Poor William suspended from your roof . . . no one would suspect a thing!'

He rolled on top of her and pinned her arms to her sides. 'Admit it,' he urged her, 'you'd like it as much as I would. You want him out of the way too.'

'But not dead, poor man. If he would only consider a sea voyage . . .'

Nothing, however, was further from William's mind that spring. The seas were infested with pirates and besides, the news that came from London almost daily was too absorbing for a man who expected God's Holy Church to be established in England during his own lifetime. The Earl of Strafford, the most powerful man in the kingdom under the Crown and the sworn enemy of true religion and the ancient liberties of the subject, was standing trial for his life.

Margaret cared nothing for Strafford, nor for the King and his Parliament, nor the endless talk of rights and statute and treason. The only treason she cared about was the sweet treason of her hours with Richard and, try as she might, she could not think how to extend them.

Already William was growing suspicious. One evening Dame Calwodely called at the house just as Margaret was about to leave. William, who was suffering with a heavy cold, was seated by the fire, Luke on his joint stool by his side, Hedge snoozing in the rushes on the floor.

'I'm glad to see you're stopping in at nights now,' said Dame Calwodely, 'it used to worry me to see you walking in the dark, night after night, like a lost soul.'

Margaret, poised by the back door with her shawl over her shoulders, was about to speak when William said, 'I fear my poor wife is not yet cured of her evening rambles.'

'Mother's walks grow longer and longer,' Luke piped, 'sometimes she is gone for hours at a time.'

Margaret felt her cheeks flaming with colour and she took refuge in anger. 'What busybodies! Surely when I've done my work I may walk a little if I please. If I decide to stay at home or not is no one's business but my own. Or would you like me to draw you all a map so you may see the route I plan to follow?'

Later, when they were lying together on their bed of hay, she told Richard of this conversation and he slipped his hand between her legs and stroked her thighs. 'And what map did you have in mind for your worthy neighbours, Mistress Hollar? What record of your evening's occupation can you offer them that might put their minds at rest?'

'Our beautiful map would give them gossip enough for a whole year,' she sighed. But when she was with him Margaret gave no thought to the scandal-mongers of Porthew.

Three weeks, and he had visited her under cover of darkness each night and still they were undiscovered. Margaret knew such a miracle could not last, but in the drugged wonder of those spring nights, she never gave a moment's thought to the consequences of discovery.

Providence intervened in the unlikely shape of a bolt of brown fustian.

William had been busy in the shop since his early devotions, sorting through a consignment of goods that had been delivered by sea the previous day. Of all his tasks, this was his favourite: he loved to handle the various textures of the cloth, the almost metallic smoothness of satin, the rough luxury of silk, the heavy opulence of brocade. On such mornings as this he permitted no help or interruption but must sort and stack and note down each item in the huge ledger by himself. Even Luke was banished to the kitchen where he whiled away the time teasing Hedge and picking raisins from the dough his mother was mixing.

They were both startled when, well before the hour of their midday meal, the heavy oak door swung open and they saw William standing oddly in the doorway.

'Whatever is the matter, William?'

His face was constricted with pain. 'My back –' he winced. His body was tilted sideways like a broken branch. It had been the bolt of fustian, no heavier than any other, but still . . . a careless twist, an awkward lift – and the damage was done.

Margaret did not pretend sympathy but said briskly, 'Sit there by the fire and I shall fetch you some liniment.'

'I cannot sit.'

'Then lie down.'

But he could not lie either; nor could he walk or stand, both movement and inactivity were agony for him. Luke was all concern for his father; Margaret saw his injury as a nuisance until the real reason for his anxiety was revealed.

'But what of the cloth for Mr Treveryan? I was going to

ride to Trecarne today and take it to him. Now I'll have to make do with a servant and I particularly wanted to show him the quality of the silks myself.'

Margaret began to poke the fire with such vigour that the flames leapt high in the chimney. Not looking at her husband at all she said, with an attempt at nonchalance, 'Then I shall have to go instead of you. Such an errand is far too important to leave to servants.'

'But you are busy here. I'll send Viney.'

'And let him drink himself witless in Treveryan's kitchen and come home roaring fit to wake the dead at midnight? It's out of the question, I'm afraid. Since there is no alternative, I shall go to Trecarne in your place.'

William found he did not like having to be grateful to his wife. 'Well . . .' he agreed grudgingly, and then, 'I know you don't like the fellow, but for Heaven's sake, Margaret, at least try to be civil.'

'I promise I shall do my best,' said Margaret, stifling her laughter in a pretended cough.

Never had Margaret known a day so beautiful as the early April afternoon when she set off with Samphire along the familiar road to Trecarne. It had been raining in the night, but since dawn the clouds had cleared away, all but a few, high and fluffy and white. Raindrops sparkled on fresh green buds; the hedgerows were speckled with primroses and pink campion and the shy blue of violets. Wisps of steam rose from a newly ploughed field and everywhere there was a smell of growth and life and damp moss warming in the sun. Margaret wanted to run the entire way, so eager was she to find Richard and tell him of their good fortune; the next moment she dawdled, lingering over every singing bird and shimmering green leaf so that this most delicious of all journeys might last for ever.

Several times she had been on the verge of screaming with impatience as William supervised the loading of the panniers: this was the silk lace he had ordered for cuffs, not identical to the last batch he had bought but in many ways superior; and this damask was also to be had in a green (Margaret must find the green and examine it carefully so that she could describe it to Mr Treveryan) but William was of the opinion that the blue would suit his purpose better . . . of course, he might choose to buy them both, in which case . . . perhaps Margaret should take samples of each to make sure . . .

'Let me just take the blue today, and if need be I can visit Trecarne again,' she offered.

'Confound it, why did my back have to trouble me today of all days? Viney, unless you fasten that strap properly, you idiot, the whole heap will end up in the mud. Ah yes, here is some cut velvet I wanted him to see; it would make an excellent doublet, or the lining for a cloak, I'll maybe send a sample . . . gracious, Margaret, why ever are you in such a hurry?'

Impatience was a demon, an all-consuming flame. And then at last she was on her way to Trecarne; and now she rounded the side of the hill and could see the mass of the new house looking out over the valley. Even with her poor sight it was clear that the main building work was almost done: the roof was complete (a fine dry roof!), the scaffolding removed, the long elegant façade between the two towers revealed in all its porticoed splendour. And, miracle of miracles, there was Richard Treveryan himself walking towards the wide sweep of steps at the front, pausing and turning to look in her direction, striding across the rough ground to greet her.

His face displayed such a mixture of incredulity and pleasure that she was afraid at first he meant to take her in his arms right there in full view of the house and the dozens of workmen and servants who were labouring near by. She stepped backwards slightly and said in a loud clear voice, 'Good day to you, Mr Treveryan. I have brought the cloth my husband promised you should see.' But she could not hide the delight that sparkled in her eyes.

He checked his pace, stood four-square before her. 'Meg, you clever witch,' he said in a low voice, 'how have you managed this?'

'Unfortunately Mr Hollar met with a slight accident this morning. Since he is unable to call on you himself –'

'You have ground black antimony in his broth.'

She answered in a whisper, 'There was no need. He only lifted a bolt of fustian and now he can neither sit nor stand. To ride a horse is altogether out of the question.'

'Then praise the Lord for fustian! I shall order a dozen lengths in gratitude.' His dark eyes burned with his fierce longing to take her in his arms, the wretched impossibility of doing so in a public place. 'My God, Meg, at last I can see you plainly, in daylight. And I had almost forgotten –'

He broke off. Giles and a couple of servants were hovering at a discreet distance, awaiting orders concerning the pack horse.

Recollecting himself, Richard was once more the master of Trecarne. He ordered Samphire to be unloaded and attended in the stable-yard, the packages to be delivered to the lower tower room, refreshment fetched for Mistress Hollar who was surely fatigued by her errand.

Silently, the servants led Samphire away.

Richard led the way into the house, loudly proclaiming his regret at Mr Hollar's indisposition. 'How kind of you to come in your husband's stead. Please offer him my sympathy and my hopes that he will make a speedy recovery. I am sure that even in his afflictions he is much comforted by your kind assistance.'

Margaret feared he was exaggerating the pretence to the point of ridicule, but her efforts to maintain the doleful expression of a woman whose husband has been most unfortunately struck down were not altogether successful. Richard led her through the downstairs room where, on her previous visit, she had been obliged to take his hand and regretted only that the floor was now securely in place and she must therefore maintain a discreet distance. Striding ahead, he flung open the door into the large high-windowed room that occupied the ground floor of the new tower. Two silent manservants carried in the bundles of cloth while a third brought in wine and refreshments and laid them on the oaken table.

'A little wine, Mistress Hollar? You must be thirsty after your journey. Ah, I see your husband has sent the cut velvet he mentioned, excellent fellow . . .' Lifting the fabric he took it to the window to examine it in the light. 'Ah yes, good quality, just as I thought. That will be all, Daniel, tell the staff that we are not to be interrupted for Mistress Hollar and I have important business to discuss. Now, what did your husband say would be the price of –?' The door closed quietly and they were alone. Richard flung the velvet to the ground and at once crossed the room to take her in his arms.

He kissed her lips, her hair, the downy skin of her neck. 'Thank God,' he murmured, 'at last . . . I was afraid we were doomed to be for ever moles, meeting always in blind darkness. Shall I show you the dry warm bed I have been keeping for you in my dry warm room?'

She twined her arms around his neck. 'Are there no chickens to watch us? No horse?'

He shook his head solemnly. 'We must learn to do without such refinements. Will you mind so very much?'

But she was already unfastening the buttons of his doublet.

The tower bedroom, with its many windows and its pale walls, was a globe of sunlight, dust motes dancing in the luminous shafts of gold. Richard went to the bed and pulled back the tapestry curtains while Margaret circled slowly in the centre of the room, her arms outstretched as she revelled in the space and airy light.

'Look, Meg,' he teased, 'now we will have sheets and pillows and a counterpane. Do you consider this a sign that we are growing weary of each other?'

Her pirouetting ceased, her arms fell to her sides. 'No,' she answered simply, never for a moment taking her eyes from his face.

'No more do I.' He had been continuing to unbutton his doublet, but now he paused; suddenly he was looking at her as if he had never properly seen her before in his life.

'I had forgotten, Meg . . . now let me feast my eyes.'

Like the moment when a cloud passes in front of the sun, their bantering mood had shifted. In the darkness of the hay-barn their expressions had been hidden from each other, their feelings secret – only the hunger of their bodies had spoken. Now, in the brilliant light of the tower bedroom, he could no longer miss the passion shining in her eyes.

'I want to see you . . .' He reached his hand to her bodice, began to push back the fabric, but suddenly she raised her arms as though to protect herself, moved away from him.

'Meg, what is it?'

'I . . .' For a moment more she held back, afraid of the new intensity that was building up between them. But then she saw the expression on his face and her fears were washed away. 'Let me –' she said, unfastening her dress and letting it fall from her shoulders to the floor. Within a moment all her clothes lay in a little pile and she was standing, quite naked, in a pool of yellow sunlight, so that Richard could barely make out her face, only the circle of gold in which she stood. He sank down on his knees, caught hold of her hands and kissed them, then kissed the pale curve of her stomach. Smiling again, Margaret ploughed her fingers through his hair. 'Stand up, Richard,' she chided, 'what foolishness is this?'

He pressed his cheek against her flesh. 'In your hay-barn I have wooed you like a ploughboy,' he said, half-mocking, half-serious, 'but you deserve better than that.'

Standing once more, he gathered her in his arms and carried her to the bed, laying her down gently. As she sank into the soft luxury of the deep feather mattress and the lavender-scented sheets Richard said, 'You are a queen, Meg. Why do you squander your time with an ugly brute like me?'

'Hush, Richard, such a question does not even deserve an answer,' she rebuked him, 'only kiss me, do not speak.'

Their love-making was long and slow; their new-discovered solemnity filling it with a resonance that had been missing before. And afterwards, as they lay in each other's arms, Margaret turned her face away so he should not see the tears that rolled down her face. Tears of joy, tears of sadness . . . she no longer knew the difference, only that she would gladly die at such a moment as this if it meant that she could seal up their great happiness for ever.

On her return Margaret found William no better. He was, however, interested to know that Mr Treveryan, though quite satisfied with the new silk lace for cuffs, had requested to see the damask in the green as soon as possible. 'Tch, what a nuisance,' Margaret sighed, 'I shall have to take it to him tomorrow.'

'Viney shall go this time, he can surely manage a length of damask.'

'I wish I shared your faith in the fellow. But I know I'd only worry the whole morning that he'd botch the errand somehow. Don't fret, William, if I set off early I can be back in time to join you for morning prayers.'

'You are grown conscientious, wife,' said William, and sounded almost peeved by her reformation.

That evening, finding the stone barn empty of all but Samphire and the chickens, Margaret walked down past the harbour, taking great care to pass by Dame Calwodely's window twice.

On the following morning she left Porthew while the town was still in sleepy darkness; mist was lying in the hollows and in the hedges the first sparrows were beginning to cheep themselves into wakefulness. As she drew closer to Trecarne the sky began to pale and she dismounted, pausing to pick primroses, so many of the pink-stemmed flowers that she made a basket of her apron to carry them. The sun was just emerging above the sea as she came down the hill and rounded the corner in front of Trecarne. A handful of sleepy husbandmen were ambling to their work in the fields. On the driveway she met a tousled Giles, who took Samphire and let her into the house by a side door. The master, he told her, was not yet awake, but he would call one of the women from the kitchen to attend to her. Margaret told him not to trouble.

To her relief the parlour was deserted, as was the lower tower room, still scented by the ashes of the previous night's fire. Hardly making a sound Margaret climbed the winding stair that led into the tower bedroom. The first rays of sunshine were slanting through the latticed window and the curtains were still drawn around the four-poster. Paris, as always, was offering the apple of discord to Aphrodite while the rejected goddesses looked on with blank dismay. Margaret paused for a moment, then slipped off her heavy shoes and placed them behind a little coffer before padding across the floor. Pulling back the tapestry slightly she gazed on Richard as he slept.

His face was still brown from his winter voyage and against the snowy linen sheets his dark skin and hair looked almost swarthy. She could not imagine, now, that she had ever thought him anything but the most handsome man in the world. While sleeping, his face was stripped of its habitual reserve, the tension of a man who is ever prepared to believe the world his enemy. In the nakedness of sleep she saw his weakness, and the ache of love that swelled under her ribs was almost unbearable.

He rolled over and flung one long arm across the pillow. Without opening his eyes he murmured, 'Set the coffee down, Hester, I shall drink it by and by.'

Climbing on to the bed, Margaret knelt over him and shook the primroses on his face. 'And who is Hester,' she scolded, 'that she has permission to visit you in your bed? I swear I will allow none but boys and old crones to wait on you.'

Wide awake in an instant, he sat up and shook the flowers from his hair while his face broke into a broad grin of welcome. 'Hester *is* an old crone, you fool,' and he pulled her down into his arms. 'And why in God's name have you brought half the hedgerows with you?'

She rolled on her back beside him. 'I thought I should bring something of the open air to prevent you growing too dainty in your grand four-poster.'

'Queen Meg, my queen, queen of the flowers,' he teased, 'you'll never be content, will you, until I have had you in a ditch? I swear it is your perversity.'

'Then my perversity is your pleasure.'

'*You* are my pleasure. Now I can almost imagine that you have lain here with me the whole night long.'

'Then I warn you I shall mount a strict guard over your dreams, no Hesters –'

She broke off and stared at him, wide-eyed with horror as they heard the sound of the door opening and feet moving across the floor towards them. Silently Richard pulled the coverlet over her head, then he made a theatrical yawning noise and said, 'Set the coffee down, Hester. And leave the curtains this morning.'

'Good day to you, Mr Treveryan. And I hope it *is* a good day for you because it has certainly started off as bad as can be for me and my knees were troubling so in the night I scarcely slept a wink and now that new girl we got in for the buttery has fallen ill and –'

'Spare me, Hester,' Richard groaned, 'your dawn chorus

never changes and I've no patience for it now. Just set the coffee down and begone.'

But such a brisk sequence was apparently quite beyond Hester. She moved the little table, adjusted the items on the tray several times and carried on with her litany of complaint until Richard threatened to throw the coffee pot and its contents all over her if she did not take herself off. At that there was a loud cackle of laughter and they were at last left in peace.

'You are safe to come out. Hester has gone.'

'She has the voice of a young woman.'

'And the face of an old witch. But I shall dismiss her at once if you wish.'

'Good Lord no, that would be cruel. I'm sure there is plenty of work she can do without coming into your bedroom. Whatever is that foul-smelling brew?'

'Try some, it is coffee. In time I daresay your fashionable husband will be drinking it. I bought it from a Greek in Plymouth.'

'Ugh,' Margaret wrinkled her nose in distaste, 'surely you do not intend to drink it?'

'You have a true countryman's dislike of novelty, Meg. How do you expect me ever to turn you into a woman of fashion? Probably I shall have to kidnap you and carry you away from this backwater. When you have travelled you will become more broad-minded. How would you like that, eh? We could go to Italy and Greece, I would rename my ship the *Queen Meg* and we –'

'Stop it, Richard, don't mock me like that, not even in fun. You cannot imagine how much I –' She broke off, frowning. His teasing had stirred up such a wealth of impossible longing that for a moment she felt quite breathless. Then, forcing herself to be cheerful once again she said, 'What a slugabed you are, Mr Treveryan, I never thought to find you still asleep at this hour.'

'While you, no doubt, like a dutiful housewife, are always up at four – and busy with all the tasks those servants of yours are too idle to bother with. My excuse is that I was riding half the night. I found that I missed my evening visit to your chicken coop after all and could not sleep.'

'Nor I.'

But when he kissed her she complained of the foul taste of coffee on his lips. 'You're used to men who breakfast on raw onions,' he said ruefully as she pushed him away. 'So how else can I entertain you? I know, we can ride together and I will show you my plans for the farm.'

Margaret sat on the little coffer and watched while he splashed water over his face from the basin of water by the window. Then she assisted him as he dressed. It was the details of his life that fascinated her now.

They breakfasted on bread and cheese and then went down the wide steps at the front of the house where Giles had two horses waiting for them. Richard helped her to mount the smaller of the two, a sturdy bay.

Margaret, who was accustomed to the placid Samphire and had learned to ride on the almost comatose Juno, took a little while to gain control of her present more spirited mount. Richard rode beside her in silence for a while, not wishing to distract her and content to enjoy the fresh sounds and smells of the spring morning.

'What is her name?' asked Margaret at length. 'I should know how to address her when I'm scolding the poor creature.'

'Gossip,' answered Richard, 'a good name for a woman's mare, don't you think?'

Margaret's eyes were sparkling. 'And what is yours called? Bluster? Boaster? Slander?'

Richard laughed and then, 'Ajax,' he said firmly, 'he is a strong sensible beast and never breathes a word to anyone.'

Ajax flicked his ears, appreciating the compliment, and then instantly disproved it by whinnying to a group of mares beyond the hedge.

Margaret said thoughtfully, 'We had a hen once called Ajax.'

'A *hen*?'

'We thought she'd be a rooster but she proved us wrong.'

Later they paused beside a stream to let the horses drink. Sheltered from the wind by a grove of willows, the air was warm as summer and a few early butterflies flitted among the stalks of grass. Birdsong cascaded all around them, a waterfall of sound, and the warm bank was sprinkled with primroses and violets and the tender young green shoots of bracken.

Margaret was not, after all, home in time for morning prayers.

23

Parson Weaver surveyed his congregation. Try as he might to concentrate on his sermon (he was reading it from a book) he found his eyes being repeatedly drawn to the tall figure of Mistress Hollar who was sitting next to her son and her husband in their accustomed fourth pew.

Wearing a costume of simple grey worsted, she sat demurely enough beside her son. But sackcloth and ashes would have failed to mask the radiance which now shone from her like a beacon fire. Even when she was a girl he had never seen her looking like this; alone among the congregation her whole manner of being was a shout of joy and triumph. And Parson Weaver had been a student of human nature long enough to guess the cause; despite the dutiful grey of her dress, despite the hair demurely covered by a coif, the sensuousness that emanated from her as she looked at him and did not see him at all, was unmistakable.

Parson Weaver's stomach curdled with jealousy; he told himself it was only that he was anxious for her welfare. Knowing her so well, having watched her for so long, he had little doubt that she had at long last found an outlet for her generous and loving nature: that she had a lover.

The parson glanced at William – but he was as sure as could be that the husband was too absorbed in the contemplation of his own soul to notice anything so trivial as a suddenly joyous wife.

As he reached the end of the sermon, closed his book and stepped down from the pulpit, Parson Weaver scanned the rest of his congregation. Nicolas Sutton, who had passed the time during the sermon in playing a surreptitious game with his little fair-haired son, was seated in the front pew with his plump wife and their happy brood of children. The parson considered . . . there had been rumours a while back about Sutton and Margaret's sister. Well, maybe . . . but somehow he doubted whether the easy-going Master Sutton, gentleman though he was, would have captured Margaret's heart.

As the congregation trooped out into the gusty spring morning, the parson observed Margaret again, but she seemed to single no one out for particular attention. He had no doubt he would discover the truth soon enough. In a place the size of Porthew nothing remained secret for long.

Parson Weaver was not the only person to be struck by the change in Margaret. Without either of them being consciously aware of it, her relations with her son were in the process of transformation. Ironically, now that she no longer strove to centre all her hopes and affection on him, she became suddenly a desirable companion to the lad. All his life he had taken her almost obsessive love for granted and it startled him when she sometimes seemed to forget even that he was present. He began to demand to spend time with her, especially since her present happiness made her the best of companions.

During that spring Luke found himself relishing the hours they spent together. When he spoke to her of the thoughts that troubled him, the gruesome visions of God's wrath and punishment with which his imagination had been fired, she only laughed and tousled his head.

'God is loving,' she said easily. 'Why should He create us to be frail and sinners, and then punish us for being what He made?'

Luke found he had no answer to this. He had plucked up the courage to question his mother on a balmy afternoon when they had walked up on to the cliffs above Porthew. They were sitting together on a patch of rabbit-cropped turf while Hedge hunted with great noise but little hope of success in the brambles and bracken behind them. Sky and sea were soft as blue gauze and the air was full of the busyness of nesting birds. Margaret swept her arm in a gesture that encompassed land and sea and sky and her own great happiness as she asked, 'Why should Our Lord have made the world so beautiful and then not want us to enjoy His gifts?'

Luke pondered for a moment before saying anxiously, 'But Father says –'

'Oh, William says a great many things and I'm sure some of them are true. But remember, even your father is only a poor foolish mortal like the rest of us, and therefore certain to be wrong some of the time.'

Luke leaned back on the grass and felt the warm spring sunshine bathing his face. His own fallibility was not something his father had ever mentioned and Luke found the idea that William might be capable of error occasionally both alarming and, in some strange way, a relief. Although he still revelled in the certainty that he and Father were saved and therefore special, he had recently found that it was occasionally restricting, almost claustrophobic. Now his mother seemed to be offering a glimpse of escape. It was all most puzzling and really he did not know what to believe, but just at present he delighted to hear the joyful cadences of his mother's words.

'So you are wrong sometimes too,' he teased.

'Oh, I'm bound to be wrong most of the time,' she conceded. Luke, watching her carefully, saw her lapse into one of those abstracted silences which had become so common with her recently – and which he resented. In order to regain her attention, which was his by right after all, he broke off a stalk of feathery grass and stroked it across her cheek. At once she turned to him and to his relief her eyes were once more filled with laughter and tenderness.

'But this much I know for sure,' she told him as she pulled the grass from his fingers, 'if your father's God cares for you one hundredth part as much as I do, He'll never let you come to a moment's harm.'

'Good,' declared Luke, rolling on to his back. He stuck one foot into the air and watched the way the light shone on his boot. Then he squinted sideways at his mother. 'And will He care for you as well?'

I hope so, thought Margaret swiftly. 'Of course,' she said.

She stretched out on the turf and for a little while they remained without speaking. Luke was struggling to reconcile his mother's God, who seemed to be a part of the sunshiny contentment of that afternoon, and the vengeful and demanding deity his father worshipped.

It was a dilemma he would never wholly solve. On that particular occasion his musings were interrupted by the sound of hysterical yapping from a brambly thicket some-where just above them at the edge of a field.

Luke scrambled to his feet. 'Hedge has caught a rabbit!' he exclaimed.

Margaret watched him as he ran up the hillside. She saw how swiftly his childhood was passing, how fast he grew; already he was taller than other boys his age. And although his expression was often preoccupied, making him seem older than he was, he still moved with the loose-limbed awkwardness of a child.

William's back continued to trouble him and Richard Treveryan continued to require items delivered to Trecarne. Inevitably the day arrived when Luke petitioned to accompany his mother. Richard had sent word that he wished to discuss cloth for the livery of his servants; he would have visited Mr Hollar in Porthew to discuss the fabric most suitable for such a commission, but unfortunately he regretted that pressure of work detained him in his home . . . he must once more impose on Mistress Hollar's time.

William fretted. 'Another week only and I might have been able to ride over there myself. Maybe I should per-suade him to delay such an important decision until we can discuss it properly.'

'Surely you won't risk going against his express wishes,' exclaimed Margaret, genuinely concerned. 'He might be offended, William, and take his custom to Mr Uren of Cam-borne, and then you know you'd never forgive yourself.'

'But it must be such a trial for you to have to deal with a man whom you cannot abide.'

Margaret turned away and began to rearrange the wild-flowers that stood in a jug on the table. She did not like it when William showed concern for her, his hostility was much easier to bear.

Luke, who had been following their conversation with his usual attentiveness, chipped in, 'Can I come with you to see Mr Treveryan? Aunt Treloar says he is the wickedest man alive. I've never met a truly honestly absolutely wicked person in my life.'

'It's very wrong of Lizzie to call anyone wicked,' snapped

Margaret, but Luke, who was fascinated by all aspects of wickedness, was not at all deterred.

'Let the child go with you,' said William, 'it will make a pleasant change for you to have company.'

Though the change would in fact be anything but pleasant, Margaret could think of no way to justify her desire to go alone and so Luke was duly mounted on Samphire between the samples of cloth and they set off together along the road to Trecarne, the road which had become so familiar over the past three weeks that the horse no longer needed any guidance.

Primroses had made way for bluebells and the first lacy heads of cow parsley. Margaret could never see the woodlands with their spring carpet of blue without being reminded of the day she and Merry had gone bluebell-picking together and Luke's birth had begun. Happiness at the memory was mingled as always with a brief sadness that there was no longer a Merry with whom to share her pleasures and sorrows.

'In another week you will be ten years old,' she said. 'Is there anything special you want?'

Luke looked down at her from his lofty perch. He had had to resist the urge to scramble down and run along beside his mother; opportunities to ride Samphire were few and far between and he was determined to arrive at Trecarne in style. He was considering her question; with that quizzical look, half ignorant child, half wise old man, it was impossible to guess what he was thinking.

'Well,' he began soberly, 'I do, but maybe it's a sin to want it.'

'What?'

'Well . . . I have tried Sam Huxton's and he said I had the gift but . . . if I mentioned it to Father then he might think . . . but then if it was only used for holy music there'd surely be no chance of sinning, so . . .'

'Lordy, Luke, whatever are you rambling on about?'

'A fiddle.'

'Ah.' Margaret walked in silence for a few moments before saying firmly, 'All music is holy if it is beautiful.'

'Really?'

'I'm quite certain it is.'

Luke reflected that his mother had become very definite in her views of late. On the whole he liked her way of looking at things but he had an awkward suspicion his father would disapprove. He was learning, however, to regard his parents separately and so to accommodate the views of both, however contradictory.

On their arrival in front of the new house at Trecarne (House? A palace, Luke thought) he was gratified when Mr Treveryan, striding down the steps towards them, greeted him with a suitably wicked scowl. With his furious expression, dark eyes and unruly hair, the man appeared every inch the unregenerate sinner.

'Why in God's name did you bring the boy?' Treveryan made no attempt to lower his voice so that his most unflattering question might not be overheard.

Luke's mother looked cross and bothered and answered truthfully, 'Because he wished to come.'

There was something casual about their exchange that jarred on Luke's ears, but before he had time to consider why this might be, Treveryan was ordering someone called Giles to take him to the kitchen and occupy him there. He said he and Mistress Hollar were not to be disturbed as they had important business to discuss concerning cloth for the liveries.

Luke had not expected to be parted from his mother so soon after arriving in the den of iniquity, but Giles had a reassuring grin and chatted to him cheerfully about nothing in particular as they went through the echoing hallway and down a long passageway that led to the kitchen. Luke was amazed by the kitchen which seemed to him to be about as big as the church at Porthew and humming with activity: a boy of about his own age was turning a spit which had a huge piece of meat on it and from time to time fat dropped off and sizzled in the glowing ashes of the fire; a woman with arms that would have done one of the Treloars proud was pummelling dough on a huge table; a skinny man with the face of a ferret was skinning half a dozen hares while a couple of large dogs followed his every move. Luke was so intent on watching what was going on that he hardly noticed when Giles brought him some small beer and a plate of sweet cakes and told him to eat as much as he wished.

The cakes turned out to be quite remarkably good, but by the time Luke had eaten two he began to notice things that made his appetite fade away entirely. The first thing he saw was the way the woman with the large arms smirked and looked at him from under heavy eyebrows when Giles told her that Mistress Hollar was with the master and on no account must they be disturbed. Then the man with the ferret face winked at Luke and said his mother must be an excellent businesswoman and wasn't his father proud to have a wife who was such a help to him in every way. Especially good at pleasing important customers, said the big-armed woman and at that they all laughed and looked at Luke in such a way that he felt himself grow angry and ashamed without having the faintest notion why he should feel either. The incomprehensible mockery continued, and Luke found that he hated them more and more and grew more and more confused until he could stand it no longer. He flung down his plate and ran out through the half-open door.

When he had blinked back the shameful tears he saw that he was at the entrance to the stable-yard. He wondered where his mother had got to, wondered how he would set about finding her now. He was kicking his toe against the mounting block and fighting back fresh tears when Giles found him.

'Pay no heed to them,' said Giles kindly, apparently having forgotten already that it was he who had started the hateful joke, 'come along with me and I'll show you the Barbary foal that was born two days ago.'

The Barbary foal, all peach-coloured fur and tottering stilts, went a little way towards mollifying Luke. By the time they had seen the peacocks (newly arrived and still in a narrow pen until they were used to their new home, but Giles assured him that when the male spread his feathers it was the prettiest sight in all the world) and the inside workings of the newly installed clock, and the cider press, Luke had decided that although he never intended to return to Trecarne again, Giles was certainly a very decent fellow.

The good-natured groom was about to take him down to look at the newly dug fish pond with its ingenious arrangement for both salt and freshwater fish when Treveryan and

Margaret Hollar found them at last. Luke felt a quite ridiculous burst of relief at the sight of his mother's solemn-smiling face; even the ferocious Treveryan had ceased his scowling.

'Did Giles take you to the mews?' he asked, and when Luke said no, Treveryan said cheerfully, 'Then you have missed the best of all. Come, I'll show you myself.'

Luke looked uncertainly towards his mother, but she appeared to have no objection and so the three of them strolled down the grassy path that led to the building where the hawks were housed. For a wicked man Mr Treveryan was remarkably patient, Luke thought, as each bird in turn was described and shown off. Treveryan showed him how to hold his arm crooked upwards and had the falconer bring a hobby to set on his wrist. 'That's the best hawk for a young gentleman such as you to fly,' said Treveryan and Luke felt a thrill, quite unlike anything he had ever experienced in his life, pass up his arm and somehow lodge in the region of his heart as he felt the weight of the bird. He stood absolutely still, hardly daring to breathe for fear of upsetting the creature.

'And now the finest jewel of all,' Treveryan told him, motioning to the falconer, 'and without a doubt the finest bird in all of Cornwall.'

Luke shivered as the bird was brought forward and set on Treveryan's wrist. Without knowing the reason, he could see at once that this was a hawk of a different order. Treveryan explained that this was what was called a passage hawk that had been bought for him at the great spring fair in Holland the previous year.

'All the others were taken from their nests as fledgelings so they have never known what it is to fly free of man's control. But a passage hawk is one that has been trapped when already adult. He remembers what it is to be at liberty high above mountains and forests. See how he scorns us, how proud he is, and fierce. No matter how long he is fettered, he will never completely lose the beauty of his wildness.'

Luke gazed with wonder at the opaque black eyes of the hawk and almost imagined that he could see in that round darkness the huge spaces and wildernesses of Europe, a memory of freedom. Luke was so absorbed in listening and watching as Richard Treveryan handled the hawks and talked about them that he forgot his humiliation in the kitchen, forgot absolutely that this was the wickedest man in Cornwall, had eyes only for the savage beauty of the birds.

Treveryan touched him briefly on the shoulder and Luke looked up, smiling. 'Next time you come,' the man said, 'I shall show you how they fly.'

Margaret seemed suddenly to remember something and she took Luke by the hand. 'I would rather he did not learn that cruelty,' she said.

But Treveryan only laughed. 'Look at the lad's eyes, Meg,' he told her, 'only look into his eyes.'

Richard Treveryan was seated at a large table, the surface of which was almost entirely obscured by documents and letters, all the business he had contrived for six weeks to ignore. Kitty's letters had grown increasingly frantic: she was being pestered hourly for decisions she was uncertain how to make. The captain of the *Elizabeth* was suspected of having become an incorrigible drunkard and loading for her next voyage was taking twice the time it did normally and numerous items were going astray. There was the problem of the new tenant for the farm at Gunnislake and an Exeter merchant was still avoiding payment of an old debt and seemed likely to die before it was paid.

Richard pushed the papers away angrily and paced to the window; it was a tiresome heap of petty concerns and he knew he could sort them all out in a matter of hours – if he was only there in person. Why were stewards and managers so pusillanimous that they could not decide the simplest matter without quaking at the knees for fear of mistakes? Francis Crane had been a good man, as ruthless and efficient as he could wish, but those cursed Treloars had killed him and Richard had never found another so reliable. And now, this morning, Kitty had written yet again with her usual catalogue of worries, adding that by God's good grace their prayers had at last been answered and she was certain she was with child; however, such was the pressure of all her present anxieties that she feared she might miscarry if he did not return at once to Saltash.

Richard tapped moodily on the windowsill. Through the glass he could see workmen levelling the ground at the front of the house. Slow, tedious work. There were to be lawns there and a fountain and an intricate pattern of box hedging. Thomas had a mania for box hedging. Richard knew he would always prefer to look beyond the formality near the house and let his gaze linger on the line of alder and willow that bordered the stream, or to look beyond them to the grey of rocks and sea in the bay.

Kitty was not pregnant, of that much he was sure. Whether she believed herself so or not was another matter entirely. Several times in the past she had convinced herself that what she had longed for was now come true. As usual her stratagems only alienated him more than ever – but this morning there was a new dimension to his annoyance.

When Margaret had brought her son to Trecarne the day before, he had at first been angry. It had seemed to him as though she was attempting to intrude her everyday concerns into the brief magic of their solitude. He had seen the pride with which she introduced her boy, her absolute love of him, and he had experienced a wrench of jealousy, as fierce as it was unreasoning. No sooner were they alone together than his anger made him cruel: he told her that another time she might leave her whey-faced brat at home, that he did not wish his servants to waste their time entertaining other men's children, that he himself . . .

At first Margaret tried to dismiss his ill-humour with teasing but when she saw how serious he was she listened in growing disbelief. Then disbelief gave way to anger and when still he would not be reasonable she told him fiercely that she would not squander her time on a man who could be so put out by a mere child.

'Go then,' exclaimed Richard, 'and take him with you!'

But when she turned to leave the room he could not abide to see her leave in anger. He overtook her and banged the door shut and caught her round the waist, pulling her towards him, pressing his lips savagely on hers. There were tears of anger in her eyes as she struggled against him; she raised her hands to push him away but he caught hold of her wrists.

'Don't go, Meg, not like this.'

She heard the catch in his voice and her struggling ceased.

'Oh Richard,' she murmured and circled her arms around his neck, smothering his anger with the strength of her loving. And when their passion was all burned up and they drifted together in that wordless place between sleeping and waking, the knot that joined them was grown still more tight.

Remembering, Richard clenched his fist. He had come looking for entertainment and had found instead a honeyed trap. He could not shake off the image he carried of the look in Margaret's eyes as he showed the hawks to her son. Her obvious pride, her happiness at seeing man and boy together. Luke had a quick intelligence; Richard had become absorbed in telling him the nature of each bird, their temperament and aptitude for hunting. Reflected in the boy's face he had perhaps seen something of himself as a youth – that hunger for learning, lips slightly parted in an admiration for the birds that trembled on the verge of awe . . . yesterday Richard had realised for the first time the joy he missed in not having a son to be apprentice in the rigours of falconry.

And now Kitty wrote and said she was with child. He crunched the letter in his fist, then stood stock still, staring into space. When, in his imagination, he had seen a son standing at his side, it was Margaret's boy who stood there, his son and Margaret's – not a legitimate heir.

Ridiculous dreams. Worse, they were dangerous dreams . . . dreams that threatened to undermine all the strengths he had learned and lived by for so long. Solitude and freedom from all ties were his only proven friends; it would be criminal folly to let Margaret seduce him from the path he had chosen. He had no intention of entrusting his well-being to another, no matter whom.

But still . . .

Lost in thought, he did not at first notice that the door had opened and a man had joined him in the room.

'Richard,' exclaimed Nicolas, flinging his hat down on the nearest chair, 'have you heard the news?'

Richard looked up and focused slowly, as though awakening from a dream. Nicolas's face was flushed from the exertion of the swift ride from Rossmere and his boots and breeches were splashed with mud. His eyes were sparkling with the excitement of a drama.

'What news?'

'From London of course.'

'It must be momentous if it has dragged you all the way from Rossmere so early in the day.' Richard smiled. 'But no, I have heard nothing. Can I order you some wine?'

'I thought as much. You must be the last person in the whole kingdom to hear, you've grown such an incorrigible hermit. How do you manage it?'

'As usual, you exaggerate, Nick, but still, you'd best tell me this momentous news that everyone but I heard long ago – and then we can get down to proper conversation.'

'Well then,' said Nicolas, 'three days ago the Earl of Strafford was executed by order of Parliament.'

The smile faded from Richard's face. 'You are mistaken, surely.'

'No. The reports are true enough, I swear it.'

'It's impossible. The King would never consent to it.'

'He did, Richard. The death warrant bore the royal signature.'

Richard let out a long sigh of disbelief. 'It seems incredible. Strafford, of all people, I had thought he was invincible. And yet . . . if this is true then everything is changed.'

He lapsed into brooding silence. And Nicolas, who had never seen the Earl of Strafford nor sat in Parliament, now felt as though a shadow had fallen across his life, so ominous was Richard's reaction. Their shared silence was a requiem for the clever and ruthless man who had towered over the political arena for so long that it was difficult, now, to imagine the changed landscape without him; difficult, above all, to imagine the man who had subdued the impossible Irish and had appeared not so very long ago to have the potential to do the same to his fellow countrymen, being led out before the mob, having to unwrap the folds of linen from about his throat and lay his naked neck on the executioner's block.

Nicolas said, 'He was an evil man, God knows, and England is a safer place without him. But the King's enemies will not stop with Strafford; from now on His Majesty will have need of loyal friends.'

'Friends?' Richard laughed bitterly. 'The Earl of Strafford was the most loyal and clever friend the King could ever hope for – and yet now you tell me the death warrant bore the royal signature. For my part I would not wish to be the friend of such a faithless fellow, king or no king.'

'By all the accounts I've heard it seems that His Majesty had no choice; there was serious rioting in London for days, his palace was under threat and he is virtually a prisoner of the Parliament. Many people are convinced it will end in fighting.'

Richard frowned. 'I did not know their quarrel was grown so serious.'

'Where have you been hiding, Richard? For the last six weeks there's been talk of nothing else. Alice has forbidden all mention of the King and his troubles at table, since she claims such talk ruins a good meal – and needless to say, all her dinners have been spoiled for a good long time.'

'That shows her good sense; I have no time for these London squabbles either.'

Nicolas flung himself down in Richard's high-backed chair and looked up at him. 'That's because you've been too busy with the draper's wife to notice anything else.' He laughed. 'Don't scowl so, Richard, I'm hardly about to condemn you for your whoring and Mistress Hollar is without doubt an extremely good-looking woman.'

Richard clenched his fists and resisted a sudden and almost overpowering urge to take Nicolas by the throat and throttle him. He said coldly, 'I had no idea my business was so well known.'

'You know how servants gossip.' Nicolas settled himself more comfortably in his chair and crossed his feet on the edge of the table before continuing amiably, 'One or two other candidates were mentioned, but as soon as they mentioned Mistress Hollar I guessed she must be the one. As I remember, you had a liking for her years ago. I should commend you for your fidelity.'

'Commend me nothing.' Richard walked back to the window and looked out. The day was grey and overcast; the horizon misty with approaching rain. A familiar bleakness was spreading through him, the conviction that in this life at any rate the good things never last and the only certainty is grim self-reliance. The only difference, this time, was that he had not felt this way in weeks. On the terrace in front of the house a couple of sparrows were squabbling over a thread of dry grass for their nests. Richard sighed. He had not realised, until Nicolas burst in with his news of Strafford's death and the King's perfidy, how enclosed his world had become: this house, this valley that he loved, and Meg . . .

Under his breath he murmured, ' "She's all states, and all Princes, I, Nothing else is." '

'What was that?'

'Nothing. Just a poem.' Richard returned to the table, lifted a pile of papers, let them flutter down again on to the polished surface. 'So,' he said at length, 'the Earl of Strafford is dead. I had not thought such an event possible, and now you tell me there are great changes abroad . . . and Kitty's letters grow shriller by the day and my business affairs are all neglected. It seems one cannot keep the world at bay for long.'

'I never imagined for a moment that you wanted to.' Nicolas had been watching him carefully. 'Heavens above, Richard, I've never seen you so distracted. You must be half in love with the woman.'

Richard glanced at him sharply, then turned away with the barest shrug of his shoulders. 'Only half, Nick. The time is long since past when I could play the lover's part with conviction.'

'So long as the lady herself was convinced.'

When Richard did not answer, only continued to stare moodily at nothing in particular, Nicolas amused himself by folding one of the many papers that were heaped in front of him into a paper dart and aiming it towards the fireplace, but without success. 'If it does come to fighting – and pray God such madness can be avoided – will you support the King?'

'I've not given the matter any thought, but no, I don't think so. I do not see how I could take up arms to defend a man for whom I have so little respect. In my opinion King Charles is an arrogant fool and his troubles are all of his own making. Let him deal with them.'

'Such treasonous talk, Richard. Say that in London and

you could find yourself with your ears sliced off. But if the King is broken by those Puritan fanatics in Parliament, we'll soon find ourselves following the Scottish example and losing bishops – and heaven alone knows what would happen then. You surely would not take *their* side, would you?'

'The choice is not so stark as you describe.' Richard was thoughtful for a few moments but suddenly his face broke into a grin. 'But I tell you this much with certainty, Nick: if war does break out between the King and his Parliament then my ships will be worth their weight in gold. I shall fight on my own side and profit all I can from the abject folly of this most unnecessary quarrel.'

'Folly, eh?' Nicolas aimed another dart at the fire and this time it landed in the grate and curled up in flames. 'You mean you will devote yourself to your fair mistress and close your eyes to what is happening all around you.'

'If only it was that simple . . . or I could carry her away to the Indies where we might devote ourselves entirely to pleasure and by the time we heard the news from England, all would be over. But no, I rather think the time has come to finish with Mistress Hollar. Tomorrow I shall return to Saltash and when I have detailed reports of all that has happened I can decide how best to take advantage of all this talk of fighting.'

'Come and dine with us tonight, then. Alice is most put out that you have ignored us for so long. I told her you were busy with all your building work but I don't think she was taken in for a moment – especially since one of your grooms is courting our laundry girl.'

'Then please give Alice my apologies and tell her that when I'm next in Cornwall I shall attend her daily. But this time, since I have work to do, I must disappoint her . . . though if you carry on like that, Nick –' for another well-constructed dart had just landed in the fire – 'I shall never get my affairs in order.'

'Paperwork is the very devil.'

Richard said nothing. Just at present he realised he was in no position to lecture his friend on the importance of keeping proper records but it worried him that Nicolas was so indolent with regard to financial dealings that he had already spent the money Alice had brought with her, and would have fallen into difficulties if Richard had not lent him money on more than one occasion. He considered it a weakness to have done so, since there seemed little prospect of it ever being repaid.

Richard walked with Nicolas to the stable-yard, but just as his friend was about to mount, Richard touched him briefly on the arm and said in a low voice, so that no one else might overhear, 'Keep an eye on her for me, Nick, when I am gone. This has been a good few weeks and I'd not have missed it for the world.'

Nicolas was on the verge of making some light-hearted retort when he checked himself in time, having seen the intensity behind Richard's words.

'You sentimental old fool,' he said, embracing him affectionately, 'but don't worry. I'll see she comes to no harm.'

'Good. Remember me to Alice and the children.'

'God's speed to you, Richard.'

'Goodbye.'

Nicolas swung up into the saddle and clattered out of the stable-yard, turning once to wave to Richard with his large plumed hat and Richard, grinning, watched until he had disappeared from sight and then returned briskly to the house, determined to have made sense of his mound of neglected papers before nightfall.

That night, Richard was waiting for Margaret when she pushed open the door of the little barn. He had thought at first it would be easier to ride away without seeing her, send word of his departure by a servant and thus avoid the pain of parting. But as dusk began to fall he ordered a disgruntled Giles – it was raining – to saddle up his horse for one last visit to Porthew. It was not only consideration for Margaret that persuaded him to break the news himself; the urge to gather her in his arms just one more time was too powerful to resist.

'Meg!'

Laughing and eager she tumbled into his arms, covering his face with kisses, exclaiming at the dampness of his doublet . . . but something in the tension with which he held her, alerted her to danger.

'What is it, Richard? Are you angry?' She pulled back.

'No, not angry.'

'What then?'

He hesitated. Waiting for his answer, fearing what it might be, Margaret felt a cold dread spreading outwards from her heart.

'Tell me, Richard,' she prompted gently.

He had not meant to tell her until later but now, with an almost inaudible groan, he realised that secrecy was impossible. 'I leave for Saltash in the morning, Meg. Already I have stayed away too long. If I ignore my proper business much longer I shall surely be ruined.'

He spoke lightly, almost flippantly, his tone warning her that this was to be no solemn parting.

Margaret heard the warning but just for the moment the blow was too sudden and too devastating and her usual self-control deserted her.

'So soon,' her voice broke on a sob, 'I had not thought . . .'

'You knew it could not last.'

'Oh yes, I knew . . .' But there are different ways of knowing, she might have added. So many different ways of knowing what one does not want to know.

Suddenly impatient he wrapped his arms around her and drew her close and she made no effort to resist him. 'I should have left you long ago,' he murmured, 'before you had the chance to weave your magic in my brain. And then this parting would not be so hard to do.' And he tightened his grip as though he would crush her in his arms, squeeze out the huge and wordless feelings that he had for her.

And when they climbed on to their bed of hay and made love for the last time it was as if they had already parted. Though his hunger for her was undiminished she was remote, almost passive in his arms. Richard began to feel annoyed. He could not know that the great effort of hiding her true feelings from him was bleeding her dry of all emotion and he imagined that she was turning from him already.

Later, when they had lain together for a little while in silence and Richard was preparing to depart, he turned to her and said, 'Will you miss me at all, Meg?'

He had been wishing he could see her face, but when he heard her reply, 'More than you will ever know,' and heard the pain behind her words, he was grateful, after all, to the sheltering darkness.

He said, 'We've known such happiness this past few weeks, let's not spoil it now with grieving for what cannot be. It's your laughter I shall miss, Meg, as well as other things. Let me hear your laughter as I leave.'

There was a long silence, broken only by the gentle stirring of the chickens, Samphire shifting his position with a sigh. After a while he heard her sniff and tell him, 'Then you must find something amusing to say.'

He considered this while buttoning up his doublet. 'You are the most beautiful woman I have ever known,' he said at length.

'That is hardly intended to make me laugh.'

'But it's the truth, Meg. My own Meg. Queen Meg –' He reached over to kiss her again but she turned away.

'The time has come for your queen to abdicate.'

Though she spoke with an effort at levity there was no mistaking the tremor in her voice and, quite suddenly, Richard found her attempts to be cheerful were more than he could bear.

'I must go,' he said.

'Yes. Go quickly.'

But when he raised himself to go down to the lower level she caught hold of his sleeve and asked the question that had been pulsing through her mind since first he told her he was leaving. 'Will you come here and visit me again when next you return to Trecarne?'

He hesitated, prised her fingers from his sleeve. 'Oh, I daresay. And if I find you have taken another lover in the meantime I shall probably break his head for him. So best be warned.'

'I shall stay faithful to my chickens.'

At the doorway of the barn he turned and took her in his arms, kissing her briefly. She barely responded. But when he had drawn back the bolt and was about to step outside into the rain-dark night she suddenly flung her arms around his neck and kissed him fiercely.

'Take care, Meg, we shall be seen.' He caught hold of her wrists and pulled them down to her sides.

'That hardly matters now.'

550

He held her tightly and thought what a simple thing it would be to hold her so for ever. The fanciful picture he had described to Nicolas that morning no longer seemed far-fetched. Why should they not sail away from this damp and scandal-mongering island and seek out a haven where they need never be parted? The very vividness of the image alarmed him and he disengaged himself.

'Now let me hear your laughter as I go,' he said.

She shook her head and did not speak.

Quickly he turned and went through the gate and into the lane. Margaret stood without moving as she heard the sound of his footsteps fading on the track. At the top of the rise a dog was barking. Only when she was quite sure that he had gone did Margaret allow herself to fall to her knees on the rough floor of the barn and, watched only by the chickens and the placid horse, she wept.

24

August foundered on a cold wet wind.

At Rossmere, all were at sixes and sevens. Alice's famous brood of healthy children succumbed to a succession of minor ailments, nothing that placed them in any danger, but enough to make them fractious. Alice herself was pregnant again, and short of both breath and patience. A scullery maid was pregnant also, cause of bitter words between husband and wife. Nicolas, however, had other worries which troubled him more: his work as a Justice had been complicated recently by the changes imposed by an over-zealous Parliament. The old ways had been far from perfect but at least they had been understood. And the problems were growing just as the means of dealing with them faltered: the levies had been disbanded earlier in the summer and the highways and ale-houses up and down the county swarmed with former soldiers causing a noticeable increase in lawlessness. Nicolas now took his duties seriously and it grieved him to see tenants and neighbours harassed and frightened and to be able to do so little about it. In one of the remoter farms an elderly man was beaten and his wife and daughters assaulted by four men who might once have been in the King's service but who were unlikely ever to be apprehended. Obliged to witness the family's distress when he visited them next day, Nicolas reflected angrily that it was high time the King and his Parliament settled their differences and returned to the proper business of maintaining order in the country.

At Conwinnion John Pearce took care to lock and bolt the doors each evening. His wife was now almost permanently confined to her bed. Bess Treloar, Jennie's eldest daughter, was employed to tend her and to keep house for father and son. She was a sturdy, good-natured girl, the image of her mother, and Tom, now a susceptible fifteen, could think of nothing else. She teased him and told him she was too old for a lad like him (she was eighteen, she thought, or there-abouts) but she was often lonely at the farm and aware that it might be pleasant one day to be mistress of Conwinnion, so she allowed him the occasional fumbling kiss.

John Pearce saw none of this; he saw only his fields and his crops and his animals. He did not notice that his son was head over heels in love, nor that a clash was threatening in London, the echoes of which would soon be heard all over the land, nor that it was more than the pain in her swollen joints that confined his wife to her bed. Nor that it was nearly six months since his eldest daughter had visited him at the farm.

Margaret paid no visits that summer. At the Forge Lizzie noticed her absence – and was secretly relieved. Although she threatened to slap the face of any woman mean-spirited enough to mention a word against her sister, she could not remain deaf for ever to the rumours, the drifting innuen-does, the sudden tell-tale silences. Jennie Treloar, now comfortably settled with her family in a farm above Coverack, had also tried to fend off the rumours. For weeks she had championed Margaret against slander until one Sun-day, as she watched her walk into church beside her hus-band, she saw the unmistakable proof that the gossip and rumours were not malicious after all, but true.

By the middle of August everyone knew. Almost every-one . . . Dame Erisey, in whose school Margaret still worked, saw only her perseverance with the children. Half-blind, half-deaf, and totally loyal to Margaret, she remained in a state of blissful ignorance. An ignorance shared only by William Hollar himself. He was too absorbed in the battles being fought by God's True Church, by his own determination to discover God's purpose for him in His great plan, to observe the changes that were taking place in his wife's body.

For, as everyone but Dame Erisey and William knew, Margaret was carrying Richard Treveryan's child.

She marvelled at her husband's ignorance – and knew it could not last for long. She marvelled too at her own folly; how could she have been so reckless as to go time and again to Trecarne with no better excuse than a fardel of cloth that any servant could have delivered? She marvelled – yet she did not regret her actions for a moment; if she had that spring to live again (the very thought of reliving those few weeks was a pleasure so intense it was a kind of pain) she would not alter a single moment.

She was aware now that the wolf-pack eyes of the town were fixed on her. The servants at Trecarne were no more discreet than servants anywhere; she had been childless ten years and now was pregnant; she was known to have walked abroad after dark; Richard Treveryan was known to have a mistress in town; she had visited Trecarne many times and hardly troubled to be discreet – proof enough to damn her ten times over. Yet still no move was made; it seemed that everyone was holding back, waiting only for another to speak first, somehow restrained by William's apparent blindness.

She barely gave it a moment's thought. It was only further proof of her foolishness, she knew, but she still felt herself to be protected in a silken cocoon of her own weaving just as she had been throughout the spring. As though some of the happiness she had known during those weeks was stored inside her body with the unborn child. Richard's voice filled her thoughts as though she had heard him yesterday, would hear him again in the evening; she had not forgotten, could not imagine ever forgetting, the press of his lips on hers, the touch of his hands, the hot movement of his body, his strength and tenderness. The memory was pleasure and the loss was grief . . . after such a loss she did not fear any wounds that might be inflicted from outside. What could anyone do to her that was half so agonising as the ache of missing him? Always, the raw burning in her chest, the yearning so fierce it was almost beyond endurance. He was gone. She seldom allowed herself the indulgence of pretending that Richard would return to her; when she awoke from those sweet daydreams she must suffer the pain of parting as if for the first time.

She was strong and she was proud. She had rich memories to sustain her and the future would be decked out with the strong new life growing within her. And she had Luke.

Her son was in and out of fights all summer but Margaret never asked him in what cause he had gained his bruised face and swollen knuckles. She bathed his injuries and Luke was soothed, as much by the gentle scolding and the touch of her rough hands against his cheek as by her salves and ointments. He observed that her mood had grown sombre since the spring, and that troubled him. He had loved her laughter and her robust certainty. Now he must try every trick he knew to bring a smile to her face, and even then he was not certain of success. She who had always suffocated him with her affection was now altered; there was a part of her which would be hidden from him always.

One afternoon towards the end of August, Luke was hurrying home from Conwinnion with a treasure clutched in his fist which would make his mother happy for sure. A ring, a ring, he thought as he took the short cut across the Dawkins' new-cut hay field, a ring is a gift cannot fail to please. A magpie peered down from the branch of a solitary elm and Luke held the precious ring more tightly and whistled to Hedge who had plunged into a rabbit hole and was barking underground. The magpie flew away.

He had been paying a visit to Tom when unexpectedly summoned by his Grandmother Pearce. Luke hated having to enter that gloomy bedroom. It frightened him to think that huge blob of diseased flesh, with the bright little eyes peering out from behind mounds of wrinkled fat, had once been a running skipping child as he now was. He had edged forward, all the while avoiding those too perceptive eyes. Strange gurgling noises were audible under the piled-up bedclothes.

'Are you a good boy to your mother?'

'Yes. I mean, I think so. Well, sometimes.'

'She had trouble enough with you at the start, God knows, though she brought much of it on herself.' Since this made no sense to Luke at all, he quite sensibly ignored it. 'Here, boy,' and he saw that she was tugging at a single swollen finger joint, 'if I leave this any longer they'll have to cut it from my corpse,' and she wheezed a laugh that made Luke shudder. 'Take this back to your mother. My Lizzie will have all the rest, but this belonged to the foreigner once, your real grandmother though you never knew her, and by rights Margaret should have it when I'm gone. Don't fidget so, boy, you'll not have to listen to me much longer.' And she wheezed a final laugh as Luke fled.

He did not wonder, as he hurried home, why his grandmother should be apportioning her jewellery; all he cared was that he had a present for his mother.

Red-cheeked and out of breath, Luke pushed open the gate of the back garden and passed Viney who was chopping wood and stacking it by the barn.

'I've a present for my mother,' Luke could not resist saying as he sauntered past, Hedge following at his heels, 'but it's a secret and I'll not tell what it is.'

Paul Viney glanced up and sniffed. 'There's trouble for her now, I reckon. She needs more than presents.'

Annoyed by this disappointing reaction Luke went on into the kitchen where he found Dorcas dozing on the settle, a fly circling her face as though trying to decide the best spot to land.

'Dorcas,' Luke prodded her awake, 'I have a present for my mother.'

Dorcas rubbed her eyes. 'Is it food?'

'I'm not telling. Where is she?'

'Out.'

It was then that Luke noticed men's voices coming from the shop. Something in their tone warned him that this was not the usual haggling over debts and prices and, since the door had been left ajar, he crept forward to listen.

His father was in there with two men, but they did not seem to be customers. One of them was Matthew Erisey, the big man whose plum tree Luke had raided one St Ewan's Day. He was one of the few men in Porthew who tended to William's views in matters of religion and he had recently been appointed church warden. Usually William lectured him on points of doctrine; today he seemed to be hectoring William on quite another matter entirely.

'Everybody scorns a cuckold, William,' he was saying, 'and your wife has put horns on you good and proper. If you become a laughing stock in this town then Our Lord's holy cause is mocked as well. You know well enough how folk are always watching to see godly men falter.'

'Strong measures, Mr Hollar, you must take strong measures.' This time it was the second man who spoke: Walter Dyer was a poor fisherman much given to pulling at his nose when agitated. He had gained undeserved respect by his intimacy with William Hollar and Matthew Erisey, and that alone was enough to make him favourable to the Puritan cause. 'Only strong measures will stop the slanders now. Show them how a man of God deals with sinners.'

'He's right, William. Let the people of this town know that you will not stay your arm against wrongdoing. May the God of vengeance and justice strengthen you –'

Luke had been straining every nerve to make sense of their talk. Now he pushed accidentally against the door which swung a little way with a loud noise of complaint. Matthew Erisey stopped, mid-sentence, and the silence was total as three pairs of eyes turned to look at the boy. Afraid, without knowing the reason for his fear, Luke said, 'Where is Mother?'

No one answered. William was trembling and all the colour had bleached from his face. All his life Luke had been in awe of his father; now, for the first time, he saw his vulnerability and his heart went out to him. What could have brought about this terrifying change?

Wanting only to ease the pain visible in his father's velvet blue eyes, he caught hold of his hand and begged, 'What is it, Father? What has happened?'

William shook him off and barely seemed to recognise him. 'All women are irredeemably wicked,' he muttered as though in a trance, 'they are born in sin and they live in sin and all they want is to drag men into their own cesspool of corruption. They are of the Devil's own stock, heads, hands, hearts, minds and soul all evil, evil, evil . . .'

'Father, please, what are you saying?'

'What?' turning to him at last. 'You ask me what? Stay free of womankind, Luke, do not be tricked by their seeming softness. Even your mother, perfidious woman –'

Matthew Erisey had been nodding his encouragement. 'That's the truth, William. And now you must show the town that a man of God's True Church knows how to deal with such matters. I know this doesn't come easy to you, but Our Lord Himself told us to chastise and punish –'

'We'll stand beside you, Mr Hollar.' Walter Dyer tugged harder at his nose in his eagerness. 'A Christian husband must not shrink from his duty –'

'Peace, man,' William raised a trembling hand to silence him, 'I think I hear the woman returning.'

'Stand firm, William,' Matthew Erisey stood four square to demonstrate the principle, 'do not allow your natural gentleness to deflect you from God's chosen tasks –'

'My ways are not your ways –' William was looking about him in turmoil '– and yet if I must . . . Luke, go tell your mother I will speak with her.'

Luke was shivering. 'Why, Father?'

'No questions. Do it now.'

Luke looked at the three men, then retreated.

In the kitchen, Dorcas was still dozing and the fly was crawling over her cheek. Margaret had pulled off her coif and was unpacking mackerel from a basket; sea-light still glistened on their scales.

'Father wants you in the shop,' said Luke timidly.

'When I am finished,' replied his mother, not noticing his tone, 'and have washed these fish scales from my hands.'

'Matthew Erisey and Walter Dyer are with him. They are all angry, I think they are angry with you but I could not make out the reason.'

Her hands paused in mid-air. 'So . . .' The word was little more than a breath, a sighing recognition that the inevitable moment had come. Then she carried on with her tasks, lingering by the bucket of cool water. She laid the fish on a plate and covered them to keep off the cats, dried her hands carefully. Usually her movements were brisk and sure but now she was slow, as though suddenly old.

She smoothed her hands on her apron. Seeing the gesture reminded Luke suddenly of the treasure that he still had clutched in his fist. 'Mother, wait, I almost forgot. I have a present for you.'

She smiled ruefully. 'A new reputation perhaps?'

He did not understand. 'Grandmother wanted you to have her ring. She said it used to belong to my foreigner grandmother.'

He held the pale circle of metal in his palm. She stared at it for so long without any sign of pleasure that he was at first disappointed. And then he saw that her eyes were filled with tears.

'I thought this would make you happy,' he wailed, 'don't you like it?'

'Oh yes. Thank you, Luke, it does . . . And today especially I have great need of my mother's talisman.'

'But you're crying!'

She roused herself quickly and wiped the tears from her eyes. 'But not because of them,' she declared, 'they will never see me cry.' Then she slipped the ring on her finger and held it out to catch the light. 'Now why should I fear anyone when I have my mother's ring?'

So saying, she opened the door into the shop. Luke followed, close as a shadow, but when Margaret saw the two men standing beside her husband, she pushed him back into the kitchen. 'Stay out of this, Luke,' she commanded in a low voice. 'Go and help Paul stack the wood and I'll come and find you as soon as I am finished here.' And she closed the door firmly behind her, shutting him out.

Twisting the ring nervously, she lifted her chin in defiance of the men's accusing stares. But William was not looking at her face; his gaze was fixed on the round curve of her belly.

'It's true,' he muttered, 'I thought perhaps they mistook, but no, the stink of corruption in my very house. Foul harlot born in sin, creature of Satan –'

'William, I am sure you do not mean to talk to me so in front of these men. Tell them to leave and we can discuss this ourselves –'

'These men are my friends, while you are . . . nothing!'

'But this is none of their affair. Bid them go.'

Walter and Matthew moved a little closer to her husband. 'Tell the truth, Mistress Hollar – if you are able.'

'Only when you have gone.'

'Speak now, woman, these men are my witnesses. Are you with child?'

'Praise the Lord, yes.'

'No blasphemy!' burst out Matthew Erisey.

William was muttering like a man in a fever. 'Yea, Lord, the works of the flesh are manifest – adultery, fornication, uncleanness. For he that soweth to his flesh shall of his flesh receive corruption –'

'Can a married woman not conceive without being

slandered in this town?' she blazed. She was holding herself very straight. Perhaps William would support her rather than face a scandal. 'William, we should be rejoicing at our good fortune, not –'

'That child is a base-born bastard!' he hissed.

She flinched as though he had struck her. Still she did not give up. 'Is this what you want, William, do you really wish us to be at the mercy of every gossip and scandal-monger for miles around? Why, William? What is to be gained?'

William hesitated. Matthew Erisey leaped in. 'The truth, woman, God's holy truth will not be mocked.'

'Indeed?' She turned on him scornfully. 'Master Erisey, you are a hypocrite and have no right to stand there and accuse me –'

He raised his hand as though to strike her. 'Enough! Name the man, name your seducer at once!'

'William, are these men to be my judge and jury? Surely this is a matter for us alone to settle.'

But he did not seem to have heard her. He was murmuring, as if to reassure himself. 'But this I say, brethren, the time is short, let they that have wives be as though they had none.'

'Answer my question, Mistress Hollar!'

'Leave my house this instant, this is none of your concern!'

'The time is short,' repeated William, 'the time is short. Let they that have wives be as if they had none.'

'William!'

Matthew Erisey was shouting louder, 'The man's name!'

'Get out!'

Walter Dyer leered and tugged at his nose. 'Richard Treveryan,' he announced gleefully, 'all the world knows that.'

Margaret rounded on him. 'Then why ask me if you have the answer already?'

'Have you no shame?' Matthew Erisey, who had fathered bastards himself in his youth, was relishing his role as guardian of morality. 'You were seen in his very room, you visited him daily, in the light of day his servants saw you together, you flouted your corruption for all the world to see with no thought of the shame and degradation you were bringing to your family –'

'Shame?' She threw back her head and almost laughed at the church warden's outraged face, and Luke, his ear pressed against the door, wondered at her boldness. 'Why should I be ashamed of what I would gladly do again?'

Like a man awaking from a drugged sleep William started suddenly, stared at her in horror as if seeing her for the first time, and struck her across the cheek.

'That's the way, Mr Hollar!' Walter Dyer grinned his approval.

'William, no!'

'Silence! Is this how you repay my kindness to you? By making me a laughing stock and dragging me down to your own stink of corruption? I should have known when I rescued you the first time that you would never cease your whoring, but I took pity on your youth. I hoped that with God's help you might find salvation, but no, you were too deep-dyed in sin ever to join me on God's true and righteous path. The Lord knows, I tried, Margaret. Only the Lord knows how long I have prayed and fought to save you from Satan. I have been a righteous husband to you, Margaret, you have had no reason for complaint. I have always been a good husband –'

'No, William,' she interrupted him, 'you have never been a husband to me at all.'

Her statement stopped his tirade, as she knew it must. A moment's silence, a gasp of astonishment from Walter Dyer, a rumble of anger from Matthew Erisey – and the next moment William had picked up his wooden yardstick and brought it down across her shoulders. Margaret made a dash for the door, but when she pulled it open Luke tumbled into the room and clung to her in terror. Matthew Erisey pulled him off while Walter Dyer threw himself against the door blocking her escape.

'How dare you slander me!' William shrieked, picking up one of the boards on which the Irish cloth was wrapped. Margaret raised her arms to protect her face and the board crashed down on the knuckles of her right hand. Luke howled out as William raised the board for the second time.

He hesitated, the board raised high above his head. Then he flung it away in disgust.

'Go to it, Mr Hollar,' urged Walter Dyer.

'Let go of the boy,' suddenly William was on the verge of tears, 'get away from this house and leave us be.'

'You're only doing what a husband should,' said Matthew, relaxing his grip on Luke.

The boy flung his arms around his mother's neck where she had fallen against a stack of cloth, and sobbed. William stretched out his hand to comfort him but Luke screamed and shrank from his touch.

William turned on the two men bitterly. 'Matthew, Walter, leave us be. I must deal with this in my own way, not yours. Now, for the Lord's sake, leave us.'

'You are too tender-hearted, Mr Hollar.'

'Go.'

A few days later Alice Sutton was sitting before a good fire and wondering why pregnancy must always cause her feet to be cold. September rain beat drearily against the windows; the harvest this year was almost certain to be a complete disaster.

She picked up her sewing and frowned at the pattern of leaves and fruit which she had been working on earlier; in her boredom she had let the stitches grow long and clumsy and she now saw that the last petal must be undone and worked again. She threw it down in irritation. In her wooden crib the baby sneezed, smacked her lips together twice and then settled down again. Alice sighed. Idleness did not agree with her, she should be busy in her still room, there were a hundred different tasks to be attended to, but since her August illness, she did not have her usual energy.

From the hall she could hear the sound of Nicolas ordering his horse to be made ready. She heard his footsteps approach her door, then pause, turn away and vanish into silence. She frowned. Until a few months ago he almost always came to bid her farewell, tell her his plans, ask what she intended to do during the day ahead. Now that easy intimacy had gone. It was the business with the scullery maid had caused the change. He could not understand why she should object to this affair when she had turned a blind

562

eye to so many others, and Alice had not known how to explain that she could hardly ignore what occurred under her very roof. But Nicolas did not consider her feelings; no one did.

Suddenly restless she stood up and walked to the window. Always before, when Nicolas had been distracted by a pretty face, Alice had been able to console herself with the thought that in Richard Treveryan's eyes at least, she was still beautiful. She had found that a married woman whose husband is often unfaithful likes the attentions of a former admirer; it helped her to forget that she was plumper and dowdier than she had been before the birth of her children. But this spring Richard had barely visited Rossmere at all, and when he had, he had paid her scant attention. Richard's neglect had made it harder for her to overlook her husband's unfaithfulness.

She was annoyed with everyone. Her suspicions were wide-ranging. Almost as though it were an accident, she wandered from the window to the table where the pile of letters was stacked, waiting for the carrier. Nicolas had mentioned that there were one or two in there for Richard in Saltash. She turned and paced the short distance to the window once again. The letters were really none of her concern.

The rain was showing signs of easing up. Nicolas, handsome as ever in a new buff coat and mounted on his favourite chestnut gelding, clattered through the archway from the stable-yard and crossed in front of the house. For a moment it looked as though he meant to turn and bid her farewell and Alice, suddenly eager, raised her hand to wave. But then he thought better of it and rode off between the dripping lime trees with never a backward glance.

Her hand fell limply by her side and she remained for some time by the window, hating the interminable rain, hating Nicolas, wanting desperately that he should notice her unhappiness for she loved him too. Only when the sound of horses' hoofs had faded into silence did she return her attention to the pile of letters. She turned one or two over casually, as if only mildly interested.

Twice now she had observed Nicolas talking with the draper's wife after church. Alice's maidservant had told her that Mistress Hollar was expecting a child and that, since there had been no children in ten years of marriage and since Mr Hollar had beaten her when he discovered her pregnancy (Walter Dyer and Matthew Erisey had thought it prudent to exaggerate their accounts of his ferocity) it was generally assumed to have been conceived out of wedlock. Alice reflected angrily that it was extremely rash for any married man to be seen in private conversation with a woman who bore such a weight of suspicion and it was hardly surprising if several people were tending to name Nicolas himself as her possible seducer. Alice's maid was quite certain that on the occasion of their second meeting, she had seen Mistress Hollar hand over to Nicolas a letter or packet . . . some such item.

Alice flipped idly through the pile of letters. There were not many. Surprisingly, however, there were two letters addressed to Richard in Nicolas's clear bold handwriting. Why should Nicolas want to send him two letters? Why, more particularly, should one be addressed to Richard Treveryan Esq., 'for his attention only'?

She set the letter down, walked swiftly to the window, paused a moment or two then walked back to the table again. The house seemed suddenly very lonely. Pausing only to glance quickly around the room, she broke open the seal. The letter itself was written in a hand she did not recognise. Two spots of colour appeared on her pale cheeks as she read,

My dear Richard,
Mr Sutton told me that if I wrote to you he would see you had the letter safe. Well then, I never meant to write to you, but I am now so set about with troubles that I do not know where else to turn. Praise God, I am with child, your child. But my situation in this town is very difficult and it is better I should not stay here. You know I never asked you for anything for myself before and wish I did not have to now. If my Luke and I could only leave this place, if I could only have the child where I am not known, you know I would never wish to be a burden to you and in a few months I'm sure I could support myself. Please help me if you can. I can-

not write more since the injury to my hand is not yet healed.

Ever your loving Meg (crossed out and)
Margaret Hollar (written underneath).

(And then, scrawled all across the bottom as though in haste) Oh my dear dear heart, if you did know how much I miss your laughter and your loving.

Alice's first reaction was one of relief that this at least was one infidelity in which Nicolas was not directly concerned. But her relief soon gave way to a mounting anger and she began to pace the room, the letter still held tightly in her hand.

Her rage was all for Mistress Hollar. A wanton scullery maid was bad enough but for a respectably married woman to carry on no better than a common drab was unforgivable. And, to make it worse, she now had the audacity to drag Nicolas into her squalid problems and use him to demand money from Richard. How dare she! William Hollar was a handsome man, why should his wife go poaching other women's husbands? She should be flogged! And Nicolas was scarcely less culpable. He ought to be overseeing her proper punishment, not helping her in her attempts to trap Richard. Of one thing only was Alice certain in her turmoil as she paced the room. Richard must at all costs be protected from the machinations of such an unscrupulous hussy. Were gentlefolk to bear the blame and pay for every mistake that others made?

She read the letter through twice more and each time her sense of outrage increased. Maybe Nicolas had forgotten the true loyalty due to a friend, but she could still defend dear Richard's interests. Almost scorching her fingers in her eagerness, she thrust the letter into the hottest part of the fire, and stood back to contemplate in triumph as the flames curled round it, destroying it completely.

As it happened, her malice was superfluous. On that same September day that she threw Margaret's letter on the flames, Richard lay in a dark furnace of a cabin while a tropic sun blazed down on his stricken ship and he too ill to know or care.

The captain whose condition had caused Kitty such concern in the spring was indeed a drunkard. After serving Richard impeccably for five years he had lost his left hand in an accident with a musket and in consequence had taken to drink, first of all to ease the pain and later, out of habit. Rather than substitute an unproven man at such short notice Richard had decided to voyage with him. He intended, by supervising him closely, to see if he could restore the captain to his former sobriety. The journey might also serve to cure him of a continuing restlessness, a yearning to see Margaret Hollar once again.

It was one of those voyages so jinxed from the outset that the ever superstitious mariners were soon talking of Jonahs and ill-omens. The men began falling sick almost before they had passed the Hoe. Within two days they hit bad weather and the drinking water was mysteriously contaminated. The crew were even more surly and quarrelsome than usual. One seaman was killed in a fight and two others injured. Richard had the culprits flogged but he could not deal with them more harshly since he was already short of men. In Barbados he had only poor prices for his goods and several men absconded. Their replacements were worse than useless. And then, only a week into the journey home, Richard fell victim to fever. He drove himself on until on an afternoon of searing heat he collapsed on the deck and was carried below. He was delirious, and so he remained. He never noticed the storm that blew up, he never noticed that the captain was once again too drunk to make proper provision against the wind with the inevitable result that the sails were now in ruins and one mast broken.

Sensing disaster, the captain drank himself into oblivion. From time to time he stumbled down the ladder to see if his master had either recovered or died. The little cabin was hot as hell, and stank. In the dim light he could just make out the gaunt features of the man on the bunk; his eyes were open, but they were opaque, like those of a blind man – or of a corpse. A young lad was sponging brackish water against his lips. Sometimes, in his fever, Richard Treveryan babbled long and frantic streams of words . . . but they made no sense at all and even if they had, there was no one there to listen.

* * *

Whenever William was troubled in mind, as during that autumn of 1641 he was more often than not, it soothed him to arrange and tidy the contents of his shop until not a whisker of fabric was out of place. The affairs of the nation might be in turmoil, his own household a nest of iniquity – but at least all the damasks were folded and refolded and stacked with perfect precision in harmonising degrees of colour; the silks and velvets likewise; at least his ledger was filled in with an exquisite hand (his own) with every last farthing itemised and accounted for; at least his shears, the yardstick, balls of string were all arranged and in their exact position on the cutting table.

If only everything in this world was so readily ordered. The news from London told of the daily battles between Good and Evil. In Parliament the upholders of God's True Church had made good progress since the death of the tyrant Strafford, but their achievements remained vulnerable. At any moment the King might regain all that he had lost. Robert Payne, with whom he discussed these matters, shared his hope that the bishops and all the Romish hierarchy of the Church might be destroyed before another year had passed – but equally they knew that the King might find Spanish or Irish troops who would enable him to rule like a despot.

At the beginning of November the first reports began to trickle into Cornwall of a bloodbath in Ireland. At first the news seemed scarcely credible. The native Irish rabble had risen up against the English settlers and with each passing day the tales of carnage grew more horrific: godly Scots farmers driven from their burning homes, children and newborn babies skewered like suckling pigs and thrown screaming on the flames. William could so clearly imagine that wild country of mists and bogs and a still-wilder race of men who wore the skins of animals and ate raw flesh and whose womenfolk were said to be a swarm of savage beasts from Hell. He shuddered to think of such a force unleashed against the hardworking Puritan settlers; shuddered anew to think that the King might be intending to let loose these Catholic Irish hellhordes against the godly folk of England.

William deprived himself of sleep so that he might spend longer hours in prayer; all the portents indicated that the hour for which God had saved him from the storm was fast approaching.

It grieved William deeply that he had not been able to keep the forces of evil from his own house. All his prayers had been in vain. His wife remained a sinner and unrepentant. William was well aware that the general opinion in Porthew was that he had been too lenient, but he had little stomach for physical violence. Moreover Luke's horror when he saw his mother struck still haunted William, and seemed to have created a barrier between father and son. His main concern now was for the boy's welfare; above all William dreaded that Luke might become infected with his mother's sin and daily he prayed for guidance to protect the child. Sometimes he thought it best to leave this country altogether and take Luke with him to join one of the communities of saints in America. But this prospect was so appealing that William feared it could not be the hard and stony road that God had prepared for him. It followed, therefore, that the work he had been chosen for must lie closer to home.

In that case, William had devised a second plan to deal with the scandal of his adulterous wife.

William Hollar was by no means the only man in Porthew to be following anxiously the events that were unfolding in London that autumn. Parson Weaver watched the signs of growing hysteria and extremism with gloom. Being himself a follower of the middle way in all things, he could see the time approaching when he might himself be crushed between the twin grindstones of the fanatics. He hoped passionately that a compromise might still be reached. He dreaded to think that men like William Hollar and Robert Payne and Walter Dyer might gain the upper hand and force others to sing their most unmelodious tune. But the parson knew he was not the stuff of which martyrs are made; if he must change his theology in order to keep his position, and to keep his family safe, then change he would.

He was pondering these topics morosely one dank day in late November as he rode to the farm at Conwinnion where he had been summoned, almost certainly for the last time, by Mistress Pearce. Attendance at countless sickbeds over the previous two decades had given him an instinct at these times. Last night black crows had winged their way through his dreams and now, as he approached the farm, he could almost smell the greedy presence of his old enemy. How Death must be gloating in these unsettled times: all the talk now was of the possibility of fighting – Irish against the settlers, Scots against the English. In Europe the slaughter had continued for a generation and now, it seemed, Englishmen were preparing to take up arms against their own brothers and only Death would be the victor. Each Easter the parson preached the same message, that Christ's resurrection had vanquished death and sin for all eternity – but on a cold bleak November afternoon like this all conviction faltered in a desperate mire of suffering and doubt.

He was roused by the sight of Tom Pearce running across the yard to take his horse. A sturdy lad, thought Parson Weaver as he shook rainwater from his cloak. Mistress Pearce had reason to be proud of him. Despite the youth's cheerful greeting, it was obvious that he had taken refuge in the farmyard in an attempt to hide the fact that he had been weeping.

In the farmhouse kitchen, dark and crowded and smelling of damp clothing and woodsmoke, Lizzie Treloar made no such secret of her grief and chattered incessantly through her tears. John Pearce stood by the fireplace and stared with a dazed expression at his boots. Margaret, tall and stately as a full-sailed ship in her pregnancy, stood a little to one side, only the restless tap of her fingers on the windowsill betraying her emotion.

The parson was pleased to see that the injury to her right hand appeared to be healing well. He had no quarrel with William for the way he had treated his wife; to do less would have been to earn the lasting scorn of the neighbourhood. When he heard the news Parson Weaver had himself been shocked (what perversity had made Margaret seek solace with Richard Treveryan, of all men, when he himself might have –?) but the parson believed that there was a proper time and season for all things and after punishment should follow harmony. So he made a particular point, as always, of paying his respects to Margaret. She acknowledged his courtesy with an oblique smile; she knew that without his unspoken protection her situation could have been much worse.

John Pearce said gruffly, 'My wife expects you, Parson.'

He sighed and made his way up the stairs to Mistress Pearce's room where he found the invalid wheezing under a heap of bedclothes, Bess Treloar attending her. He hesitated . . . in the shadows and the floating dust of the room he could make out the figure of Death himself.

At first the parson thought she was unconscious but then Mistress Pearce opened her eyes and saw him.

'That's good,' her voice was faint, but still distinct, 'now, Parson, say me a good prayer.'

He obliged as best he could, while Bess smoothed the bedclothes nervously and his mind strayed to the cup of warm wine that would be waiting for him downstairs.

When he had finished Mistress Pearce nodded her satisfaction, then gestured to Bess to leave. 'Go on now, girl, leave me talk alone with the parson –'

Bess Treloar, who had been ordered to stay by her mistress's side, glanced at the parson and he said kindly, 'I shall tell you when to return, don't worry.' Gratefully the girl left the room, closing the door behind her.

'Parson . . . listen . . .' She broke off and for a few moments fought for breath. The parson fought down the urge to bid her hurry with her confession while he wondered what perversity so often compelled the dying to sully their last moments on earth with memories of their most shameful acts; he had lost count of the times he had had to endure the recitation of some best-forgotten error – a passing infidelity, a brother mistreated, some petty instance of swindling. But Mistress Pearce, he soon discovered, was not thinking of her own sins.

'Parson –' though faint her voice was gaining strength, 'Luke's father –'

He leaned a little closer to catch the words. 'Yes?'

'You –' Her accusation was little more than an outgoing breath but her meaning was unmistakable. The parson glanced quickly towards the door.

He cleared his throat. 'Did Margaret ever –?'

'No, always stubborn . . . she'd never betray a secret . . . but I always guessed. No one knows.'

Thank God for that, thought the parson. He said, 'Can I do anything more for you, Mistress Pearce?'

There was silence for a little while. By the way her eyes were filming over he doubted there was much chance of her mentioning his secret to anyone else. Just as he was about to leave and call for Bess Treloar, the old woman whispered, 'She has need of friends, Parson . . . the girl's a fool but deserves better than . . .'

Her voice trailed into silence. He waited for a little longer before saying a couple more prayers, as much for his own conscience's sake as for the dying woman since it was difficult to know if she could even hear him now. Her spirit seemed eager to be free of the imprisoning mound of flesh.

As he was about to leave a shaft of late afternoon sunlight suddenly lit the bedroom with a sulphurous yellow. A chill passed through him then as he remembered the last time he had stood in this very room by the side of a dying woman, the foreigner. He had been a young man then, an idealist who still hoped to bring the peace and love of God to his parishioners. 'Look after my child . . .' that other woman had begged him. And now, for a second time, a dying woman commended Margaret to his keeping.

Well, she had not been an easy girl to help: too dangerous, for all her calm and thoughtful manner. Too dangerous by far.

After sitting for a while in silence, the parson went downstairs and accepted the cup of sack that Margaret had ready for him. As he spoke to her and tried to gauge what lay beneath her apparent calm, he reflected that Mistress Pearce's exhortations had been unnecessary, after all. Over the years Margaret had so twined herself around his heart that he would always care for her; he had no choice.

It could have been the rare November sunshine, or maybe it was the generous quantities of ale that were provided to ease the progress of the coffin bearers, but Mistress Pearce's funeral was jollier than most. John Pearce had been downcast as the little procession left his home, but the coffin was so heavy, Mistress Pearce having been a large woman, and the journey to the church was so arduous, that many halts along the way were necessary. And each time the men paused to refresh themselves they insisted John Pearce share their ale, so that by the time the spire of Porthew became visible the bereft husband was no longer feeling the least bit bereft and young Tom, who was accompanying them, was positively light-headed.

In fact, John Pearce was not especially saddened by his wife's death; but one funeral always brings others to mind and he had been thinking, earlier, of his first wife, the foreigner. Now he had mercifully forgotten them both and, as he stood beside the open grave and listened to the words of the burial service and the eternal squabbling of the gulls, he noticed only that Bess Treloar, who stood now at Tom's side, was a strong, good-looking girl. He wondered how easy it would be, once a decent interval had elapsed, to persuade her to consider marriage to an older man.

Margaret stood alone and, as always these days, a little apart. She was aware that most people were uncomfortable to be seen with her. Lizzie, who stood sobbing at the graveside with two children by her, did not turn away from Margaret in judgement, but rather in bewilderment (which was worse) that her sister could have given herself to the man who was their enemy, the man who had half-killed her own husband. It felt to Lizzie too much like a deliberate mocking of Ambrose and his terrible disfigurement. It was not that Lizzie could ever cease to love Margaret, only that at present her love was too muddled and painful for comfort. It was easier for them both to remain apart.

And Margaret preferred to stand alone. She could not explain it in words, for she still cared for her family and her friends as much as ever before, but she no longer felt herself to be any part of that little cluster of people by the graveside. For Luke's sake, and for that of the unborn child, she would fight to regain some position in this town: for her own sake she hardly cared. Since the spring she had felt separate, in spirit at least, from all the people of Porthew.

She knew only too well how difficult the months ahead would be and, since there had been no reply to her letter to Richard, she was resigned to facing them unaided. She no longer allowed herself to think of Richard – it was too painful. Instead, more and more during that autumn, she had found that it was Merry she yearned for. If she could only have heard her robust laugh, her contemptuous voice as she declared, 'Hypocrites every one of them. Why, Mattie, did I never tell you about Matthew Erisey and the widow from Mullion –?' How much easier this outcast pregnancy would have been with Merry beside her.

The burial service over, the mourners gathered in little groups and prepared to round off the ceremony with a drink at Jack Pym's. Margaret paused only to say a couple of words to her father before leaving, still alone. Parson Weaver caught up with her by the lych-gate.

'Are you not coming to the ale-house?' he asked her.

She shook her head. 'They will enjoy themselves more easily without me,' she said without rancour, 'and besides, I left Luke at home with William.'

'Is he not well?'

'Never better. But William feared the funeral might distress him. Luke was going to come anyway but at the last minute a man arrived from Plymouth on business and William promised he might join in their discussions. Luke was flattered.'

A light breeze had sprung up. It blew Margaret's hair across her cheek and dragged at her skirts, accentuating the swell of her stomach.

The parson could not resist saying, 'Your condition becomes you, Margaret.'

'Thank you, Parson.' Compliments were so rare these days and the parson was almost the only person, apart from Luke, with whom she felt at ease.

'And are you feeling well?'

Just the ghost of a smile. 'I am in excellent health.'

'And are you –?' He was going to ask if William was reconciled to the child yet, but the reserve in her eyes warned him that intrusion would not be welcomed, so he said only, 'I am glad to see that your hand has healed.'

'Thank you, Parson.'

He watched with a mixture of annoyance and admiration as she walked quickly away: the days were long gone when he had been able to guess at her thoughts, longer still since she had confided in him all the trust of a lonely child. Did she still pine for Richard Treveryan? Had she cared for him or wanted a child only? Did she expect his return? Was she content or did she weep in secret? She kept her own counsel, did her work adequately and allowed not a glimpse of her inmost thoughts and feelings.

Wondering if she would ever take him in her confidence again, he walked slowly towards the ale-house.

Parson Weaver might have been disappointed if he could have read Margaret's thoughts as she walked home from the churchyard. Her mind was filled with a more immediate concern – Luke's all-consuming desire for a violin of his own. Ever since he had told her of his wish, hardly a day had passed without him finding a way to bring the topic up. For some months now Sam Huxton, the elderly servant at the ale-house, had been giving him lessons in secret and there was no doubt that Luke showed a singular aptitude – but the problem, as always, was William. He regarded all music with suspicion; even if Luke had promised to play only religious music (which seemed to Margaret a terrible waste of good melodies) it was likely his father would ban him from playing if ever he found out about it. And now Margaret had heard of a violin they could buy if William would only be reconciled to the boy's wish. She was contemplating now what was the best way for Luke to raise the subject with his father.

As she pushed open the kitchen door, her heart sank. Dorcas was sitting on a stool with her apron over her head and howling as only Dorcas could howl, that strange hooting noise like some heartbroken sea-mammal. Paul Viney was chewing thoughtfully on a wad of tobacco.

'Whatever is the matter, Dorcas?' she asked wearily but, neither expecting nor receiving any reply, she patted the shuddering mass of shoulder and said, 'Never mind, I'll see if I can find a sugar cake to cheer you up,' but at this normally uplifting prospect Dorcas only stamped her feet and hooted more loudly than ever.

There was a sudden movement in the parlour and William, his face strained and anxious, peered around the door at her. 'Back already, wife? I had not expected to see you so soon. I thought the mourners were sure to go to Jack Pym's.'

'And so they did but I chose not to join them.'

'I really thought you would be gone longer.' For some reason William appeared put out by her speedy return.

'Why, William,' she said coldly, 'I never expected you to be so eager for your wife to idle away her time in ale-houses. Besides, I thought you had business to discuss with the man from Plymouth.' She had been in the process of putting fresh furze on the fire but now she straightened, suddenly realising what it was that had bothered her as she came in. 'Has he left so soon? Where is Luke?'

'He's –' William glanced over his shoulder and then came into the kitchen, closing the parlour door firmly behind him. 'Come upstairs, Margaret. I have something to show you.'

When he placed a hand on her arm to encourage her to accompany him up the stairs, Margaret noticed he was trembling. Her mind was still so full of the problem of Luke's longed-for violin that her immediate thought was that William had discovered the boy's secret lessons and was determined to punish him. Since the best hope for Luke lay in first humouring William, she preceded him up the stairs without further questions. In the kitchen below Dorcas's wailing rose to a fresh crescendo of misery.

'What is it you wish to show me, William?'

'In here –' He pushed open the door of her bedroom, stood aside to let her pass, but, as she stepped into the middle of the floor and looked about her, half expecting to see the villainous fiddle on the chest by the window, William suddenly darted back and slammed the door shut behind her. There was the sound of the bolt shooting home.

'What are you doing?' Uselessly she went to the door and pressed her hands against it.

'You're not to come out –' His voice was shrill and very precise. 'Not until tomorrow at the earliest. I shall go downstairs but . . . you must stay . . . mustn't try to follow . . .'

'But William, why are you doing this? What is it?' And then, with a despairing groan, 'Oh William, no! Where is Luke? What are you doing with my son?'

'He is *not* your son, not any more, not ever again. He's gone away from here. I've sent him far away, where he'll be safe from you. Luke is a child of the Lord and must be raised in holiness and purity by God's own people. You can have Treveryan's bastard, stay here and rot in filth with your bastard child, but Luke is *my* son and will follow God's holy path of righteousness. The Lord has given the boy to my keeping and I must do the Lord's bidding and you will never see him again –'

Margaret heard the sound of her own cry echo around the room, the cry of someone demented, and she rammed her fists against her mouth and said, 'William, you cannot do this. Where are you hiding him? Only let me see him –'

William's voice had become a hypnotic chant. 'He that loveth father or mother more than me is not worthy of me, saith the Lord, and he that loveth son or daughter more than me is not worthy of me, saith the Lord. The child has found favour with God and I have found favour and been appointed to keep guard over him and yea, when the time comes that the Lord has chosen, we shall shake the dust of this evil kingdom from our feet and walk with the Saints of the Lord in the New World –'

'No! Oh God, please no!' Margaret sank sobbing against the door, hot tears of rage and frustration and despair pouring down her cheeks. 'Oh William, no, you cannot do this, not Luke, not Luke –'

But on the other side of the door his voice continued, assuring her that Luke was gone and she would never see him again. As the full horror of what William was telling her sank in, Margaret forced herself to be calm. Think, she told herself, think clearly. Where could Luke be –?

The man from Plymouth, that was it. He had come from Plymouth 'on business' but in fact William had intended all along that he should abduct her son. There had been no ships in harbour that day so they must be travelling by land. They could not have been gone long. She must escape, take the horse . . . the parson would surely help her if she could get word to him.

Kneeling beside the door she could still hear William on the landing proclaiming his faith in the Lord.

'William,' moderating her shaking voice as best she could, 'William, listen to me, please. Luke has gone, I accept that now, there is nothing I can do about it. But please, only let me out of here, don't leave me caged up like some animal, let me be about my work –'

'Kneel down, wife, kneel down and we shall pray together –'

'Yes, William. But open the door and we can pray together as a husband and wife should –'

'Praise the Lord that He has seen fit to humble you and bring you to His service –'

'Yes, yes, but first you must open the door.'

Silence while he considered this. Then, 'Today you must reflect on your sins in solitude. Tomorrow you may join me in my prayers. The Lord will hear your prayers here. Join me now in prayer –'

Margaret stifled a scream of fury. William was too cunning to release her while Luke remained within reach of the town. She stood up and paced the room, hunted wildly for means of escape. There was only the window.

She returned to the door. 'William, can you hear me, I'm just on the other side? Kneel down with me now, William, and let me hear the comfort of your prayers. Don't leave me all alone, not now.–'

She held her breath while he shuffled to his knees in the narrow passageway, then, as soon as she heard his prayers begin, she tiptoed to the window, all the while setting out her plan. She would not take Samphire, he was too slow – though perhaps she should take him anyway to delay William if he should choose to pursue her. The parson's Sarah was a swifter mount, and more reliable. She could find him in the ale-house and he would help her. With any luck William would remain a long time at his prayers and she would have a good chance to catch up with the runaways before they had made much progress on the Helston road. Never before had she so relished William's passion for long prayers. Let him remain in prayer the whole night long while she and Luke . . . What would they do? Richard had never answered her letter – did that mean he would refuse to help her now? Well then, she must shift for herself somehow. But these were problems for later, first she must escape this house, find Luke. Once they were together again she was sure all else would be swiftly solved. One thing at least was certain, once she had her son safe with her again, she would leave Porthew behind her for ever.

Being tall and far gone in pregnancy, she had a hard time

squeezing through the little window. There was a pear tree growing against the wall: she doubted it could bear her weight entirely but perhaps if she eased herself slowly . . .

She was doing well enough, and thinking gratefully of her childhood practice of robbing magpies' nests, when Dorcas emerged from the house and bellowed her amazement at the sight of full skirts descending through the pear tree.

'Dorcas,' she hissed, 'Dorcas, hush –'

But the distraction was all that was needed for Margaret to miss her footing. The branch that she had been holding snapped in two, her hand grasped wildly at the air and she fell, not far, but awkwardly.

'Oh –!'

The memory of a man's voice floated into her mind as Dorcas opened her mouth to wail. 'Dorcas! One more sound from you and all the hobgoblins in Cornwall will come and stick pins in you!'

Dorcas clamped her mouth shut at once. Margaret lurched somehow to her feet. Nausea was washing through her in icy waves and a sticky chill covered her skin. As she steadied herself against the trunk of the little pear tree she tried to ignore the dizziness and the sensation that was not quite pain but something more sinister still, a sick wrenching in the pit of her stomach. She forced herself to stand up straight, then began to walk, slowly, painfully, one foot in front of the other towards the barn. Never had the path between rosemary and lavender and bay seemed so long, impossibly long. Her palms pressed against the door of the barn, but her relief turned to panic as she found herself enveloped in inky darkness. She turned back towards the daylight and all was blackness there as well, sudden night all around her. She blinked, clutched at the door frame, opened her eyes and could just make out the dim form of Samphire watching her from his stall. The darkness had been that of sudden blindness; outside, the pale November sunshine was still bathing the garden.

She barely had the strength to unhitch his halter and lead him to the gate. There the blindness swept over her again and she could not even see the latch, could only feel with icy and trembling fingers the spot where she knew the latch must be. The waves of nausea were growing worse, surging up through her body and her legs felt flimsy as fronds of grass. The pain in her belly was acute, but mercifully far away. If she kept her thoughts on Luke, on reaching Luke, she must find him, then the pain and sickness would not overwhelm her, she could get away, she must . . .

A warm dampness was trickling down between her legs. At last the gate was open; if she leaned against Samphire then she could walk, the horse would support her, Parson Weaver would surely help . . .

But now there was a hand on her arm, a weight holding her back and a man's voice ringing around her head. William. William's voice.

'Viney, send for Dame Watkins. And the parson, quick now. Margaret, lean on me.'

'Don't touch me!'

'Woman, you're ill.'

'Then leave me die.'

'It's in God's hands. Come, you've lost him, you're too late.'

'No, oh no!' And then, as she fell, a piercing cry, 'Luke!'

Her shriek echoed far away, but Luke had already travelled further still.

Later that evening Luke, his precious Cordoba dagger tucked in his belt, arrived at the inn at Truro and could barely sleep for thinking of the adventures that lay ahead. His father had promised they would join him soon and in Plymouth a violin would be waiting for him. He fell asleep that night, his head full of happy thoughts of the future, while in Porthew his mother struggled against delirium to give birth to an infant too early and too fragile to survive at all.

25

While the rest of the nation debated the relative justice of
the King's cause and that of his Parliamentary opponents,
the inhabitants of Porthew tended to divide on the more
local problem of the Hollars' marital strife. Once Margaret
had miscarried Treveryan's child, her friends rallied to her
defence with renewed vigour: it was cruel of William to
have sent Luke away; small wonder that she had sought
comfort elsewhere when her husband was such a cold fish
and had not even given her a child, not since Luke anyway,
and his paternity, now that people came to consider it, had
been shrouded in uncertainty. Now that they could forget
the hated Richard Treveryan, Lizzie and Jennie were glad
to defend her as energetically as ever; they visited as often
as they could and brought sweetmeats to speed her recovery.
Even Ambrose sent word that she was welcome at the Forge
as soon as she was well again; that for his part he thought
it a senseless act to have taken away her only child and
that he had never cared for William Hollar anyway. Parson
Weaver brought her books but was troubled to observe that
she seemed to have lost all interest in them. He asked her
if she had considered a legal separation from her husband;
she begged him to find Luke before it was too late, before
William spirited him away to America; nothing else mattered. The parson made enquiries among his clerical
friends.

William was miserably aware that his household had
become the focus of all attention. He who had only married
because he craved respectability now found himself floundering in a stinking swamp of scandal. His foul wife was to
blame. Her perfidy, her sin deep-dyed . . . more and more
hours were passed on his knees in prayer; no longer pet-
itioning for her to be forgiven, but for divine judgement
and retribution. God's wrath had destroyed the base-born

infant she had been carrying – by what caprice of the Lord's had the mother then been spared?

His only consolation was the fact that most of the towns-folk took his part in the quarrel. Not surprisingly, since he was evidently much wronged. His wife had never had cause for complaint against him: he was prosperous and decent; he did not drink or beat her (except under extreme provocation) or chase after other women. And yet she had carried on a blatant affair with the most hated man in the district. It had to be remembered that her mother had been a foreigner and that she herself had shown an unnatural aptitude for learning – little girls who showed an interest in their brothers' books were quickly set to sewing, for fear that they might turn out like the wayward Mistress Hollar.

On the first day that this example of the corrupting effects of book-learning was well enough to resume her work in the house, she prepared a large and succulent mutton pie. The aroma of cooking meat and rosemary and cinnamon that wafted from the oven threw Dorcas into an ecstasy of hunger. Margaret set Paul to guard the food while she went out to invite Robert Payne and his wife to join them in their meal. 'William would be glad of your company,' she told them, 'he has been much burdened by the scandal of our quarrel.'

Mistress Payne examined her severely. 'I thank the Lord that He has seen fit to open your heart to receive His truth at last,' she said. 'My husband and I will join you in food and prayer.'

Margaret smiled an odd and secret smile and returned to the house to finish her preparations.

The meal was to be served in the new parlour and the prayers that preceded it were longer and more fervent than usual, William being anxious that none should accuse him of wavering in his duty. Margaret sat very still, watching him closely although she did not appear to be attending to the words. She was grown thinner and very pale – but any alteration in her appearance was attributed to her recent illness, and therefore to be expected. When at last William's prayers had finished, Margaret rose and brought the food to the table; William slit the pie crust with a knife and the steam that filled the air was so fragrant that Viney and

Dorcas, who had been banished to the scullery, moaned faintly with anticipation. A large portion was loaded on to each plate, Margaret served the vegetables and William carefully poured out four glasses of sweet white wine.

Robert Payne raised his glass. 'Mistress Hollar,' he said, 'here's wishing you a full and speedy recovery from your recent misfortunes.'

'The Lord has indeed been merciful,' his wife added sternly.

'Thanks be to God,' said William.

They then began to eat with relish and it was a little while before they noticed that Margaret had not touched a mouthful.

'Wife, are you not eating?'

Margaret drew in a nervous breath and fingered her mother's ring before slowly pushing back her chair and rising to her feet. 'William,' she began, but her voice was unsteady and she tried again, more forcefully this time, 'William, for the last time, in front of your two friends, I am begging you, on my knees if necessary, to bring Luke home where he belongs.'

William twitched with annoyance. 'Sit down at once! How dare you even mention the boy. Did you plan this meal on purpose to humiliate me in front of my guests?'

'If need be, yes.'

'Will there never be an end to your wickedness?'

Mistress Payne leaned slightly towards him and said in a low voice, 'You have indeed a heavy cross to bear.'

'I never expected sympathy from you, Mistress Payne,' Margaret flushed and glanced at her quickly, 'nor from you, William . . . only that you will hear me out this once.'

'Enough. I'll listen to no more.'

'But you must! Just once more, hear me out, and then I'll hold my peace, I promise. For ever if need be. William, look at me; I have no weapons against you. Night after night I have lain awake and tried to think how I might find my boy again, for he is my boy, not yours, as well you know. I have no money to go searching for him; the world is a large place beyond Porthew, and besides, I am haunted by the fear that if I leave he might return one day and find me gone. William, I know you love Luke in your own way, but surely you can understand that he is everything to me now and I *must* see him again, you *must* tell me where he is, or . . . or . . .'

Much moved, in spite of himself, by her too obvious unhappiness, Robert Payne said gently, 'Only trust in the Lord, Margaret, and He will –'

'No! I care nothing for your Lord, I care for nothing at all unless Luke is brought home again.'

William glanced at his guests in nervous triumph. 'See how she blasphemes against Our Heavenly Father, yet still expects to snatch the child from the godly household in which I have placed him for his own safety –'

'But he is *my* child!'

William stood up too and faced her across the table and his breathing was rapid and shallow. 'Listen carefully to what I say. Luke is the Lord's child now, not yours. And you will never set eyes on him again as long as you live. On God's holy book I have sworn it and I swear it again in front of these witnesses. That boy is dead to you from this day henceforth; he has been born again in the Church of Jesus Christ.'

At his words Margaret swayed slightly, closing her eyes and passing a hand in front of her face as if to brush away some substance that was oppressing her. Then she opened her eyes once again and, clenching her fists tightly by her sides, she said in a low voice, 'Is that truly your last word?'

'Yes.'

She nodded. 'So be it. But I tell you this, William Hollar, that until the day when Luke is home with me again, no morsel of food will pass my lips. You kill me by taking away my only child. Very well then, watch me die.'

And, never for a moment taking her eyes from his horrified face, she slowly lifted her plate and let it fall with a crash on the floor beside her chair.

Mistress Payne uttered a little cry of shock, Hedge leaped forward and began to eat greedily, Dorcas and Paul were watching from the doorway. William let out a snarl of rage and attempted to seize her by the arm but she shook him off.

'Save your strength, William, I've said my piece. Now

I'll leave you all to finish your meal alone – and by heavens I hope it chokes you.'

She swept from the room. For a few moments no one moved. William was the first to collect himself. He bundled Paul and Dorcas from the room, kicked a yelping Hedge after them and slammed the door closed before returning, with an attempt at normality, to his seat at the head of the table.

He picked up his knife. 'She was bluffing, I assure you. The godless creature thinks to gain sympathy for herself and force me to weaken in my resolve, but I tell you I will not falter in God's work.'

With great difficulty he managed to swallow a mouthful of food, Robert Payne and his wife still watching in shocked silence. William smiled nervously and said, 'Do not waste time worrying over her. I know my wife. I'm sure she planned this long ago and has food enough in her room for a week's siege or more.'

By nightfall news of Margaret's self-imposed fast had spread throughout the town.

To begin with, people assumed that William was right and that his wife was simply bluffing in order to frighten him into returning her child. But after little more than a week it was apparent to all who saw her that the threat was in deadly earnest. Already weakened by her miscarriage, she grew frailer by the day.

Lizzie alternately scolded her and pleaded, Jennie Treloar wept, John Pearce was summoned from Conwinnion to order her to see reason, Parson Weaver promised he would redouble his efforts to trace her son if only she would leave off her foolishness and eat again but Margaret, although obviously in great discomfort, was adamant. After a few days Nicolas Sutton was informed, since self-murder was a crime and punishable in law, but after consultation with the parson he made it clear that he would take no action against her. He offered to talk with her himself, if that might help, but the parson considered any reminder of Richard Treveryan might only increase her troubles, so Nicolas agreed to stay away.

Everyone had their own theories as to how William should act: some recommended that he beat her into submission;

others that he should restore the boy; still others that Margaret should be left alone to die and good riddance. As Margaret had known it must be, the humiliation was torture to William; he yearned to escape the gloating and superfluous advice, yearned to flee the town altogether and begin again elsewhere, but by now he was so locked in this final battle of wills with his wife that he could not drag himself away. Mistress Payne visited Margaret after ten days and informed her that since the taking of one's own life, *felo de se*, was a sin against God, she would be buried in unhallowed ground. Eyes burning with a fanaticism as fierce as ever her husband's had been, Margaret swore that she cared not where her body was laid since any place without Luke was an empty Hell. She forbad Mistress Payne to visit her again.

By the second Sunday of her fast, when Margaret was too weak to drag herself to church, rumours began to spread around the town that she was dying. In three days it would be Christmas. Too frenzied even to tidy the cloth, William paced his little shop and listened to the footsteps of Margaret's friends echoing on the stairs. He vowed that she would attend church on Christmas morning and lay the ugly rumours to rest, even if he himself had to drag her every inch of the way.

Returning to Plymouth after an absence of nearly six months, Richard was ignorant of events in Porthew. He had recovered from his fever and his broken ship had limped back to port, though without the captain who had died one night in a drunken fall. The joke in Plymouth was that the ship was too wretched a prize to merit the attention of pirates, and had therefore been left alone.

Kitty welcomed her husband with her usual mixture of eagerness and trepidation. He was grown thinner since she saw him last and the flesh of his face was yellow as parchment. He was pleased with the way Kitty had managed their affairs during his long absence – and furious with himself for having suffered so long only to lose money on the voyage.

As soon as the business of landing the cargo was completed, Richard announced his intention of travelling west to review the progress of work at Trecarne. Kitty was disappointed and had a brief and pointless fit of hysterics. She wondered through her tears if it was perhaps a woman who drew him so speedily back to the West Country. Richard ignored the hysterics, but assured her the only rival she need fear was the house itself; he told her she might accompany him if she wished. Kitty was tempted, but only for a short time: the foul December weather and a vivid memory of her earlier visit were more than enough to decide her in favour of a comfortable if lonely Christmas in Saltash.

Richard had only spoken the truth when he told her it was the house that drew him westward, not a woman. Somewhere in the heat and stench of his tropic cabin, his longing to be with Margaret had been driven from him with the violent sweats of fever. And when, during his recovery, he had reached out for a single memory to give him the strength to purge himself of sickness and return to England, it was his determination to stand in the tower room again and hear the damp wind in the oak woods that had sustained him, to see the grey waves breaking on the rocks in the bay and to feel the living Cornish air. If Margaret had played any part in his delirious ramblings then, once the danger was over, that part was all forgotten.

But the urge to return to Trecarne was a hunger, a constant craving; the emptiness, something beyond despair, that had haunted him through all that ill-fated voyage and which haunted him now, would only be healed when he felt the damp earth of the West Country under his horse's hoofs and rounded the hill to look down on his fine new house and the valley leading down to the bay.

And so he set off for the west. Giles accompanied him, a couple of manservants were to follow more slowly with the pack horses. Kitty was concerned that a gentleman should be seen to travel with more style, but Richard had no patience for the delays imposed by the trappings of wealth. He and his servant passed a brief night at Grampound and the following evening, as the December dusk was spreading outwards from the woods, they arrived at Trecarne.

The greater part of that first evening was spent with Thomas who was eager to show him the new long gallery with its elaborate plasterwork and wood carvings almost finished, and the completion of the stables and the buttery and cider press. Then there were reports from the estate manager, a visit to the mews and a talk with the grooms and the falconer, routine matters that pleased Richard most because they connected him with the place he had thought he might never see again.

News of his arrival had spread quickly. Just as he was about to retire for the night a messenger arrived from Rossmere: Nicolas insisted that he visit them without delay, the very next day in fact. There were a few further items of news: the latest addition to the family was a boy who had been christened Richard in his honour, he was as healthy as all the rest and Alice's spirits were much improved since her confinement. Nicolas had instructed the messenger to avoid all mention of Margaret Hollar: he assumed that since Richard had not replied to her letter he now wished to forget the whole affair, a sentiment he himself understood perfectly. Richard gave the messenger a brief reply thanking them for their invitation and promising to ride over and inspect his young namesake in the morning.

He was exhausted when Hester finally pulled the tapestry curtains around the bed and he felt the cool touch of the linen against his skin. From beyond the tower windows came the unending murmur of the wind sighing in the woods, the sound he had longed a thousand times to hear. Yet now he found it was not enough. Despite his fatigue and the knowledge of journey's end, he could not sleep. His yearning to be home again had been a delusion once again, as all else had been before. That emptiness, that bleak despair that ran like a hidden stream beneath his everyday and practical self, was never-ending; no hope for any change in this life, then.

And, he reflected ruefully, for him at least there was unlikely to be much chance of improvement in the life to come.

He was sleeping still when Hester grumbled her way into his room in the morning to light the fire and serve him his morning coffee. Her litany of complaint was familiar and hardly varied. Usually Richard silenced her with a sharp word but on this first morning of his return he found the sound of her unchanging lament almost enjoyable.

'There'll be more rain later, so Will says, and my

shoulders are aching enough for a downpour. But what does anyone care about my troubles? There, I've set your coffee down – just how you like it, I made it myself. Mind you, I have to do everything myself if it's to be done properly. The fire in the kitchen will not draw when the wind is from the south and the scullions are so idle they bring in damp sticks on purpose to vex me, but that's of no interest to you, I'm sure.'

'Not in the slightest, Hester. Have you no other news?'

'Merry Christmas, Mr Treveryan, though I'd almost forgotten it *was* Christmas since there's work to be done like every other day. More, in fact. Lord knows how I'm supposed to get it all done *and* find time for church, not that anybody cares if I fall into pagan ways.'

'Don't worry, the Devil would never put up with your moaning for more than a day.'

She watched him with her shrewd black eyes. 'I daresay I'm lucky compared to some. The draper's wife has trouble enough, so I'm told, though as you know I never listen to gossip.'

'Mistress Hollar?'

'I believe that is the woman's name.'

Richard frowned and propped himself on his elbow. 'Well, what is this gossip you never listen to but are so obviously itching to tell me?'

'I hardly know where to begin and I'm sure you're not interested anyway, but her life has been a sorry tale of woes since she lost the child and now that her husband –'

'What child?'

'Why, the child she was carrying. Would have been due in February, so I'm told. The story is that she fell trying to escape from Mr Hollar and that brought her labour on too soon and the poor mite was born before its time and . . . but if you want my opinion I think her husband was partly responsible for if he hadn't beaten her so . . . now look, Mr Treveryan, coffee all over the sheets, I'll go and make some more –'

'Hester, you are a malicious old witch and should be roasted over a slow fire. Damn you, woman, stop fussing over the sheets! What else have you heard about Mistress Hollar?'

'Nothing that would interest you, I'm sure.'

'Tell me anyway and I can prove you wrong.'

'Well then, they do say her husband sent their son to live abroad because he said she was not a fit mother for a Christian –'

'The cringing hypocrite!'

'– and that since then she has vowed to starve herself to death unless she sees her boy again. People have talked of nothing else for a week or more, but I daresay the scandal will soon be over. Will Stevens's sister works for Mistress Payne and she said the draper's wife is already too weak to stand and is sure to be dead before the New Year –'

'Enough! You cackle on like an old hen. Where are my clothes? Is this true about Mistress Hollar?'

Inscrutable black eyes stared at him. 'There has been such a wealth of scandal around the woman since you left, Mr Treveryan, that I hardly know what to believe. But I do know that to throw away the life God gave us is a wicked and unholy act –'

'Damn her!' Richard left the bed and strode across the room to the wide window that overlooked the valley to the sea. He beat his fist on the sill. 'Damn her for a headstrong fool,' he muttered again and then, turning to Hester he commanded, 'Fetch me my clothes. No, don't bother, I will be faster alone. Find Giles and tell him to saddle me a fresh horse –'

'Giles is sleeping like the dead, sir, after yesterday's ride –'

'Then wake him, woman! And tell him to have two horses ready by the time I am dressed or I'll skin him alive.'

'Will you take your breakfast downstairs?'

'No breakfast, hurry!'

Hester decided it was prudent to withdraw.

Richard dressed hurriedly, or as hurriedly as was possible without assistance and while striding furiously up and down the tower bedroom. But by the time he had pulled on his leather boots, still stiff with mud from the previous day's journey, he was beginning to think that his first reaction had been too hasty. And by the time a dishevelled Giles ran round to the front of the house leading two horses by their bridles, Richard had definitely decided that there was no real cause for alarm. Local gossip was notoriously unreliable and the rumours concerning Margaret had surely been much exaggerated in the telling. At this very moment the Hollars were probably sitting down together to a hearty Christmas breakfast, their earlier disagreements all forgotten. Besides, he himself had promised to visit Nick and Alice today; why should he inconvenience them because of some garbled rumour? Much better to leave off visiting the draper and his wife for a day or two; her pregnancy had perhaps been no more real than the many Kitty had imagined.

He descended the steps thoughtfully, but instead of mounting his horse he said to Giles, 'Go on back to the kitchen and get yourself a bite to eat. And tell Hester to bring me food in the winter parlour. We'll visit Rossmere later – there's no cause for hurry.'

The morning air was mild. Following an old instinct, Richard walked down to the mews; as always, he found the company of the falcons had a soothing effect. He had always valued their pride and independence; they would accept food from man, could be exhausted into accepting man as their master, but some part of them remained always free and aloof. While handling the hawks and talking with the falconer, Richard found his former agitation give way to a more philosophical approach. If Margaret Hollar was in trouble, what did that signify after all? He had finished with her more than six months before; he had never deceived her, the terms of their liaison had always been quite clear. If she had needed his help, she would surely have found some way to get word to him, or Nicolas would have let him know – but there had been no message, no request for assistance. Presumably that indicated she no longer considered him as a part of her life. Maybe she had even taken a new lover. Whatever bond had existed between them in the spring existed no longer – and it was better so. Loneliness was the only strength he had ever known. The strength he had learned long ago from the hawks.

As he walked back towards the house and the breakfast that Hester had prepared for him, he struggled to ignore the continuing unease that nagged at him; a lifetime's habit of withdrawal was fighting with an instinct deeper still, an instinct which he did not understand, never having experienced it before.

An hour later he and Giles were mounted on fresh horses and setting off in the direction of Rossmere. But at the top of the rise Richard reined his horse to a halt and said suddenly, 'We'll go by way of Porthew. It's still early and the detour will not delay us much.'

Gloomily Giles resigned himself to riding in circles for the rest of this Christmas Day and he considered himself lucky at least to have a good breakfast under his belt. The air was mild and a soft drizzle was falling. Somewhere above the gauze of cloud a milky sun was struggling to break through. A flock of skylarks and yellowhammers rose up singing as the two horsemen cantered by.

The rain had eased and a feeble sunshine was filtering through the mist by the time Richard reined his horse to a halt by the entrance to the churchyard. The draper's house had been deserted, apart from Hedge who had greeted them with a volley of excited barking; only then did Richard remember that it was Christmas morning. Now from within the church he could hear the sound of the final carol, lustily sung as the congregation no doubt thought of their dinners and the days of feasting that lay ahead. He told himself he would wait only long enough to see for himself that the rumours were ill founded, and then forget the whole business and enjoy a day among old friends at Rossmere.

The Suttons were the first to emerge after the service, as befitted their rank. Sir John seemed a little more shrunken and pale, but otherwise as well as ever; Stephen, Richard observed, now moved with the spare, almost austere gait of the soldier, which made him seem in many ways older than his brother. Nicolas was a little fuller in the face, his hair grown fashionably long and he looked every inch the country gentleman in his coat of gunmetal blue. Alice, cloaked in velvet, was detained near the church porch by the youngest of her accompanying children, a tow-haired lad still in skirts who had somehow contrived to trip on a tussock of moss, but Nicolas strode down the grassy path to the lych-gate as soon as he saw his friend.

'Merry Christmas, Richard! It's good to see you

again – even if you do look as though you slept in your clothes.'

As Richard dismounted and embraced his friend warmly, he realised that in his hurry that morning he had dressed in the same garments in which he had travelled. He grinned. 'Will Alice allow such a muddy guest at her table?'

'Oh, Alice is always pleased to see you, as well you know. She has been hard at work ever since she heard you were joining us. Prepare yourself for gluttony.'

'And my namesake is well?'

'The very best. And the little fellow seems to have healed matters between Alice and me, which is a blessing.'

'I'm glad to hear it.' Nicolas still had his arm around his friend's shoulder and now Richard lowered his voice and asked, 'Is it true what people are saying about Margaret Hollar?'

Nicolas shrugged. 'That woman has attracted such a swarm of rumour recently that I'm not sure what you have been told.'

'That she has lost a child, has been in trouble.'

'Yes, that's true.'

'Then why in God's name did you not tell me?'

'I arranged for her to write to you. Surely she told you all this herself in her letter.'

'What letter?'

They stared at each other for a few moments before Nicolas swore softly. 'Listen, Richard, I've done my best to protect the woman but she seems hell-bent on her own destruction. When we are at Rossmere we can talk this over in private and decide how best –'

But already they were interrupted. Alice, trailing a wake of children behind her skirts, was hurrying down the church path to greet him. 'Richard!' she exclaimed, her brown eyes shining with pleasure. 'What a Christmas present it is to have you safe home again. But you're as yellow as a Chinaman, we heard you were ill, you must tell us all your news.'

'My sad adventures would bore you into fits.'

'Nonsense, Richard, you could never be boring, you don't know how.'

'Merry Christmas, Alice,' he smiled, 'and thank you for my namesake.' He stooped and placed a kiss on her upturned cheek and Alice remembered the time when they had ridden together to Trecarne and he had kissed her in an altogether different way, and her heart began to flutter slightly and just for the moment she couldn't quite think what to say.

But Richard never noticed the warm flush that spread across her cheek. Over her shoulder he had caught sight of a tall figure emerging from the church. There were dark shadows under her eyes and she was supported by Ambrose Treloar and the way she moved, like an old woman, or a dying one, tore at his heart.

Alice saw his expression change, saw the muscle jump under his right eye as he murmured, 'God damn them all, it's true!' And then he took her by the shoulders and moved her out of his way as though she were no more than a child, and took a first hesitant step towards the church.

To Margaret, during the joyous Christmas service, it had seemed that the eternity of Hell had begun already. She was too weak to sit or stand or kneel without difficulty, too proud and stubborn to accept the aid of the man who stood beside her and who had insisted that she accompany him at this time of celebration to stem the prophecies of her dying. It had required a monumental effort on her part to follow the service without faltering. The weakness and the pain she was learning to endure, but the cold, the dreadful cold of hunger, was something she had not anticipated. It was as though the chill of death had already begun to spread from her feet towards her body and now it was the lonely cold of that unhallowed grave beyond the churchyard wall that she feared most. *Felo de se*, self-murder, the final sin in a life which had somehow been laced all around with wrongdoing though God must surely know it had never been deliberate. Now, wrapped in her warmest cloak, she shivered, and marvelled to hear the universal comments on the mildness of the winter's day, as if others in the congregation were already breathing a different air to that which chilled her to the marrow.

William stood beside her, his face impassive as stone. He felt himself to be carved from marble, one flicker of human warmth and he would be undone. Last night, as every night, he had heard her calling out in her sleep for Luke, and he had dragged the bolster over his head and shouted prayers to God to drown out the sound of her suffering. And now he was frightened, frightened by the weakness of her flesh and the unrelenting strength of her spirit. In this final battle of wills she was beating him down, slowly but inevitably; in another day he must either send for Luke or leave this town for ever, but he could not remain and be witness to her slow death, so help him, he could not.

His relief equalled her own when the service was at last concluded. Ignoring his offer of help, she edged her way slowly from the pew. Between them was the empty space where Luke had always sat.

Lizzie and Ambrose, who had been sitting with their family a couple of rows behind them, hurried forward. Lizzie caught her by the hand and Ambrose reached his hand about her waist.

'Lord save you, Mattie,' he exclaimed, feeling only bones and skin, 'if you were a chicken I'd not think it worth while even to wring your neck!'

'Hush, Ambrose!' scolded Lizzie.

But Margaret could not help smiling. 'You have a strange way of comfort,' she said, 'but thank you.'

There was a side of Ambrose's face that was always a ferocious mass of damaged skin, but when he was touched, as now, the unaffected side of his face seemed all the gentler by comparison.

'Surely you can see for yourselves,' said William, 'that your sister will recover soon enough. She has only to give up her wickedness.'

'You're a fine one to talk of wickedness!' snapped Lizzie as she and Ambrose drew Margaret towards the door. 'Come home with us, Mattie, we've a fine goose cooking and you know how the children love to see you.'

'No, Lizzie.'

At the entrance to the church Parson Weaver was waiting for her, tall and solemn in his black robes. 'Margaret,' he urged, 'this is a day for rejoicing and new beginnings. For God's sake, leave off your folly – I cannot call it wickedness for I know what the boy means to you.'

But she only said, 'Then make William fetch him home.'

She moved out into the churchyard. The pale sunshine seemed bright to her eyes and she raised a hand to shield her face; her wrists were grown very thin. Little huddles of people had gathered on the path and among the grassy graves to wish each other a merry Christmas, to talk, and to observe Mistress Hollar's slow progress from the church.

Her pace was made all the slower by the few friends who made a point of greeting her: Dame Erisey, Jennie Treloar . . . and she did not at once notice the dark-clad figure who was standing under the lych-gate and watching her every move. It was Lizzie who saw him first; she gave a little cry of alarm and Ambrose tightened his hold on Margaret's waist.

'What is it, Lizzie? What's the matter?'

A man's voice reached her then, a single word, an agonised 'Meg!' and at the sound she cried out and her legs buckled under her. She recovered quickly, forced herself to stand straight once again.

Ambrose rumbled like a cornered beast, 'Get away from here, you've caused trouble enough already. Leave us in peace or by God I'll see you dead!'

Nicolas stepped forward to put himself between Ambrose and Richard. 'Don't make trouble, Treloar . . . he has as much right to be here as you do.'

'I'll give him rights!' Ambrose lunged out, and would have attempted to seize Richard by the throat, but Lizzie flung her arms around his neck with a desperate shriek that set all her children howling with terror.

'Ambrose, no! Not now, not here, for mercy's sake, you'll hang!'

The smith cursed, but his fury had been checked and his children were clinging to him like flies; he fell back, muttering threats.

Too shocked for speech, Margaret was staring at the man who now took another step towards her. 'Meg?' he said again, more gently this time.

The parson hurried up and caught Margaret by the arm just as she seemed about to collapse. He shook an angry fist at Richard and said, 'Ambrose is right, Treveryan. Haven't you caused her trouble enough already? Why must you come back now and make everything worse?' His rage was real – but its reason was the expression he had seen in Margaret's eyes as she gazed on her former lover.

Now it was William who hastened to join the group standing by the lych-gate. He was desperately aware that the eyes of the town were on him and in his panic and humiliation his voice emerged thin and reedy. 'I command you to come home with me now, wife, and cease this public exhibition.'

Still unable to believe her eyes and ears, Margaret shook off his restraining arm and took a step forward, but hesitantly, as though expecting Richard still to disappear like some twilight will-o'-the-wisp. For several days she had been light-headed and her senses had been playing tricks on her: twice now she thought she had heard Merry speaking in the next room, once it had been her own mother; most frequent and most difficult to bear were the times when Luke's voice rose up among those of the other children playing in the street below. And now she heard Richard . . . and if she reached out she would surely touch him.

A dry sob rose to her throat. 'Oh Richard! They stole my boy from me and he was all I had!'

'Meg, believe me, I did not know until this morning.' He raised his hand. 'Leave this stinking den of hypocrites and come with me now. How have they brought you to this?'

Spitting with rage the parson exclaimed, 'You're responsible for this, man, no one else. We have only tried to help – now leave her be!'

'Is that what you want, Meg?'

She shook her head. Above them gulls were wheeling and calling through the drifting sun and mist, but within the churchyard itself a muffled silence had fallen as the whole town watched for the outcome of this meeting. Somewhere at the back of the crowd a small child could be heard enquiring about his dinner, but no one paid him any heed. Then someone spoke, an anonymous word of slander, and the whisper was taken up, a hiss of accusation simmered through the crowd.

Margaret caught a word and she almost laughed. 'Listen to them,' she mocked, 'if they only knew how proud I was to be called your whore.'

Richard's eyes were burning with anger, as he stepped forward and caught her by the hands. 'Come with me now,' he said again, but she could not speak for the tears that were streaming down her face as he folded her in his arms and pressed his cheek against hers. 'Oh Meg, Meg . . .' As Ambrose stepped forward, and then the parson, Richard lifted warning eyes and told them, 'Stay back, all of you – your claims were forfeit long ago.'

Giles, who had been watching all that took place from the roadway, now led the horses forward. As Richard lifted her on to his tall bay he was appalled to feel the lightness of her body. He had mounted up behind her and was about to ride away when Nicolas caught hold of the bridle.

'Richard, you hot-headed fool,' he exclaimed, half jesting but half in earnest too, 'what in God's name are you playing at now?'

Richard looked down on him scornfully. 'I don't play, Nick, but you've never understood that.' Then, as he wheeled the horse about, he caught sight of Alice, standing beside the lych-gate, her face like a vinegar poultice. 'My apologies to your wife,' he said, 'but you'll have to enjoy your festivities without me.'

He was beginning to walk his horse slowly away when Master Payne caught William by the arm and exclaimed, 'Don't just stand there and do nothing! You must make her stay!'

But William could not move. For a brief moment he forgot that he was God's chosen servant, forgot that he had been fighting that proud woman, fighting to the death. He saw only that Margaret was so engulfed by love for the man that she was oblivious of all else. He remembered suddenly that of all the people in this town she was the only one he could ever have cared for, the only one with whom he could have contemplated sharing a life, though it had led them both to disaster. And now as he watched her ride away it was not anger that he felt, not shame or humiliation, though these would follow sure enough. It was envy. In that moment he could only admire her courage, the courage to love where she chose and the consequences be damned, the courage that had failed him utterly on the day he sent Ghislain away. If the Lord Jehovah had appeared in a column of fire to command it, William could not have condemned her then.

Richard rode slowly up the street that led away from the town; he did not think Margaret had the strength for a faster pace. She let her head rest against his shoulder. Pale sky and the trees, the stony road and the familiar row of houses were a jumble of moving shapes, a blurred maze. She closed her eyes and let her senses drown in the smell and touch, the press of Richard's arm around her waist, the rise and fall of his breathing . . . if this was an illusion, if this was the madness that precedes death, then she thanked God that it was easier than ever she deserved.

A sudden intake of breath and the horse swerved to a halt. Opening her eyes she saw the huge bulk of Ambrose filling the narrow road in front of them. He must have cut through by the shambles; he was out of breath and the puckered skin of his face was glossy with sweat.

Richard said quietly, 'Stand aside, Treloar, and let us pass.'

Ambrose ignored him. He took a step forward. 'Mattie, for the last time, come back with me. Stay with your own people.'

She raised her head slightly and said, 'My life here was already over.'

'You heard what she said,' Richard told him, 'now stand aside.'

To their surprise, Ambrose did as he was bid, but as the horses passed him he shouted after them, 'Not this time, Treveryan, not yet! But one day I swear I shall kill you – or die in trying.'

Then die, you fool, thought Richard, but he said nothing for fear of disturbing Margaret. For some reason Ambrose's sudden acquiescence troubled him more than if they could have fought it out right then.

He said no more for the rest of the journey and Margaret fell into a kind of waking sleep. She was afraid to drift entirely for fear that when she regained her senses she would find herself once more in her Porthew prison.

Their arrival caused consternation at Trecarne. Giles was obliged to relate the story of all that had occurred at the churchyard a dozen times before he could take off his boots and settle to a drink of Christmas ale by the kitchen fire. Richard lifted Margaret down from his horse and carried her to the tower bedroom. Hester was dispatched to fetch sweetened bread and milk and a scullery maid revived the fire and heated a warming pan for the four-poster.

Richard was pacing the room in a fury of anxiety at Margaret's weakened state, but when the food was brought she turned her head away. 'They took my child,' her voice was little more than a whisper, 'I swore I would not eat until I had him back again.'

Hester was holding a spoonful of food in mid-air and she turned to Richard in exasperation, but he took the bowl from her and set it down, ordering her to leave them in peace. When she had gone he warmed Margaret's hands between his own and told her, 'I'll find the boy for you, Meg, I swear I will. I shall send spies into every nest of Puritans in the country, and into the Americas too if I must. Believe me, I'll bring him safe home to you however long it takes, I promise. But you must be strong and well to greet him on his return. So now you must eat.'

'And will you truly find him?'

Richard grinned at her suddenly. 'It will be a pleasure to outwit God's Fox.'

Margaret nodded, and sipped a mouthful of the food – and almost choked on it.

That night Richard watched by the large four-poster until he was certain Margaret was sleeping. Only then did he slide between the cool sheets, but carefully, as though fearful of disturbing her. He lay for a while and listened to a tawny owl calling in the woods – and he wondered what events had been started in motion by his actions that day at the churchyard.

Margaret's sudden cry roused him just as he was lulling into sleep.

'Luke!' she shrieked. 'Luke, no!'

He reached his arms across to comfort her. 'Hush now,' he soothed, 'you're dreaming. Remember we are going to find him.'

'I thought he was . . . drowning.'

'It was a dream.'

He wrapped his arms around her and within an instant she was asleep again, but Richard, conscious of the fragile weight against his shoulder, remained awake a long time.

Beyond the windows the wind was caressing the oak woods and the sea was a distant sigh. And Richard realised then that the emptiness and bleak despair that he had thought would be with him always, had vanished, and he did not yet know how to name the strange and growing emotion that had taken their place.

26

It snowed in Cornwall that winter of 1642; an unusual event on the extreme southern coast of the county and one which was later thought to have heralded the huge changes that the coming year would bring. In the meantime, men cursed the extra work: water froze in the butts and the short days were entirely taken up carrying food and water to the animals, keeping the weaker ones from freezing. The wind blew the snow into drifts between the hedges and all the roads and tracks were blocked; foxes driven to desperation by hunger stole chickens in broad daylight and the birds as often as not were too stunned by cold to fly away.

While housewives and husbandmen grumbled at the unusual weather, Margaret welcomed it. For over a week Trecarne was cut off from the rest of the world, no one could leave and no one could reach them. For a merciful week at least even the supply of news from London, where the struggle between King and Parliament was getting more vitriolic by the day, was curtailed – the muffled silence of the snow created at least an illusion of peace. For the first time since she left Porthew six weeks before, Margaret felt safe, completely safe. So long as the snow lasted Richard would not leave and no intrusion from outside could break the spell of their solitude.

It was during the week of snow that her recovery was completed. In the kitchen and the stables there was much grumbling at the drudgery of it all, but Margaret in her tower room was learning the charms of luxury: a servant to light the fire before she arose, another to fetch hot water and warm scented towels, another bringing a tray of delicacies to tempt her appetite. Later would come the seamstress Richard had hired to make her clothes. He had dismissed her suggestion that she might have her own clothes fetched from Porthew. 'No more greys and blacks,' he insisted, 'while you are in my house you will wear only rainbow colours,' and Margaret had laughingly agreed. It was not the clothes themselves that were important, but she loathed any reminder of Porthew.

The snow made it even easier to slip into the pretence that Trecarne was an island; she loved to imagine that she and Richard were alone in the world, marooned and unreachable. The clear snow light that washed the walls of the tower room increased her sense of unreality. It was pleasant to admire the intricate frost patterns that formed on the windows, and to look beyond them to a landscape transformed by snowfall. And if the changes that had occurred in her own life were to be as transient as the changes brought by the snow, well then, she was determined to enjoy both to the full for as long as she could.

It was on the third morning after the blizzard that Margaret, having bathed and breakfasted and dressed, realised that the final remnants of her weakness had gone at last. Richard had been occupied outside since daybreak; suddenly eager to use her newly restored energy, she wrapped herself in a warmly lined cloak and went outside.

The air was iron cold against her cheeks and she walked briskly in order to keep warm, in the direction of the yew tree and the bench. The sky was grey, and so weighed down with snowy clouds that it seemed to have moved a little closer to the earth. The snow was criss-crossed with the footprints of birds and animals.

It was these snowy signatures that gave her, as she walked back towards the house, her idea. Fetching a broom from the kitchen she chose a smooth patch of ground in front of the tower and dragged the broom up and down to make a large 'N' in the snow. One of the serving-maids, sent by Hester to check the fire in the winter parlour, was startled to look through the frost-feathered window and see Mistress Hollar, skirts raised clear of the snow, writing in huge letters 'NULLUS' and just completing an 'A' to follow. When she reported the strangeness of it to her companions in the kitchen one of the scullions went to look and came back with the news that the words 'NULLUS AMOR TALI' had appeared in the snow; this information was greeted with foreboding. The words, not understood, had a strange alchemical ring to them. It seemed likely that Mistress Hollar was resorting to the shadowy arts, perhaps to influence Richard Treveryan, or to regain her son, or, more alarming still, to harm some member of the household who had inadvertently displeased her. For the rest of that day the servants were much on edge, wondering on whom the ill-fortune might fall.

Richard, returning to the tower room at midday, could have laid their fears to rest at once, if he had known of them.

'*Nullus amor tali . . .*' he read, standing at the window, the snow falling from his boots and making a small puddle on the floor, 'but what has become of "*coniunxit foedere amantes*"? Was there not snow enough?'

Margaret laughed and came to stand beside him, slipping her hand through his arm. 'There's plenty of snow for a whole sonnet, if I wanted. But my hands were turning blue and besides, I knew that you could easily fill in the missing words, great scholar that you are.'

'No love ever joined lovers in such a bond. No house ever harboured such lovers as these . . . But why choose such a fragile medium for your poem? The snow will all be gone in a day or two.'

'Would you prefer me to have the words inscribed in granite?'

'Why not?'

His question sounded flippant enough, but there was a challenge there as well. Margaret hesitated, feeling a shadow fall across their former joking mood. During the six weeks that she had spent at Trecarne, no mention had ever been made of future plans. '*While* you are in my house,' Richard had said, 'as long as we are together . . .' To look forward was to look towards uncertainty and she preferred this present happiness. She knew full well that Richard had invited her to leave Porthew that Christmas Day on an impulse, that he had never planned their life together. He had returned from his travels to find her friendless and without hope, most probably he had felt sorry for her, perhaps in some way responsible. She could not imagine that his feeling for her would ever match hers for him. All in all, it was better not to speculate on the future.

So she turned to him at length and said lightly, 'Granite words are for tombstones, much too solemn for my taste. And the snow is so beautiful.'

Richard was about to tell her that she should have more faith, but instead he took her in his arms and kissed her; whenever they were together like this, ringed all around by whatever it was that made him feel that the pair of them were complete within themselves, there was no need of words to define the magic. Words were become superfluous, a gaudy trimming, after all.

But by nightfall her writing had been blurred into illegibility by a ruffling wind.

Unknown to Richard or Margaret, the young scullion who had been employed since Christmas to help in the kitchens and who now worked so diligently and well, was in fact a cousin of Ambrose's on his mother's side and was more than happy to provide his kinsman with information concerning Treveryan's movements. So it was that Ambrose learned, once the worst of the snow had passed and communication was resumed between Trecarne and the surrounding area, that the master of the house had fallen into the habit of riding each afternoon to the various farms on the estate, and that he was invariably accompanied by Margaret Hollar.

Ambrose received the information with no show of emotion. He was careful not to let Lizzie know of his dealings with the scullion. Not because he feared she might betray his intention to Margaret, far from it. Never for a moment did he doubt his wife's loyalty and he was certain she had had no contact with Margaret since Christmas. But he knew that she would do her utmost to dissuade him. On several occasions already, she had found him staring down the road that led towards Trecarne and she had tried to make him promise that he was no longer thinking of revenge.

'Forget about Treveryan, Ambrose,' she scolded gently, 'what's done is past and cannot be changed. I know how much you hate him – God knows, I hate the fellow myself – but you must think of me and your children and keep yourself from danger for our sake.'

Sometimes Ambrose stroked her brown curls and told

her not to fret, he would come to no harm, but sometimes he hardly seemed to hear her or to know that she was there. And when Lizzie woke in the night to feed her youngest child, vague fears clawed at her mind and they would not be stilled until she was once more curled up beside the immovable bulk of her gently snoring husband.

Ambrose was far from relinquishing thoughts of revenge – but he no longer felt inclined to die in the attempt. He remembered the subtlety of his attack on Nicolas Sutton during the hurling match and wished he could repeat that strategy: revenge masquerading as an accident, Treveryan dead and the murderer a free man still. But there was a problem, even here. Ambrose had sworn that he would make Treveryan suffer for what had happened, but if he met with an accident, and no one knew Ambrose was responsible, how could he let people know that he had fulfilled his vow? This was the conundrum that taxed him through the snowy week when the sparks from the smithy fire rose up brighter than ever against the whiteness all around.

When he thought of Lizzie and his four children, he was almost tempted to bow to the inevitable and give up all thoughts of retribution. But when he caught sight of his hideous reflection in a pail of water, or saw the fear in children's eyes as they watched him covertly at his work and wondered at his disfigurement, or when he thought of Mattie whom once he had loved and who was now an outcast and all because of Treveryan, at times like that, he was convinced that revenge would be sweet at any price.

He knew, however, that all things come to the man who is patient, and he was prepared to wait, comforting himself in the meantime with the knowledge that when the opportunity arose, he would be ready.

The interlude of snow was soon replaced by the more customary rain and wind of a Cornish winter. And one morning, as she knew he would, Richard announced that he could remain at Trecarne no longer but must return to his business in Saltash.

'Why so gloomy, Meg?' he asked. 'Though I hardly expect my dear wife to greet you with open arms, there are

605

plenty of other lodgings to be had in Plymouth. We do not need to be much apart, even there.'

It was the moment Margaret had been dreading. They had been breakfasting in the winter parlour. Now she stood up and went to the open fireplace and dropped a sycamore log into the flames. Resting one arm on the mantelpiece she watched for a little while as the fire gently licked the wood.

At length she said, 'I cannot come with you, Richard.'

'Nonsense, Meg,' he dismissed her statement briskly, 'I know how much you have always longed to see what lies beyond these few square miles. Besides, I want you to come with me.'

'And that is what I want too, you know it is, but –'

'But – ?' His expression hardened.

'But I cannot leave here until Luke is found again.'

In his relief Richard almost laughed. 'So that's the only problem. I wondered if perhaps you were regretting having thrown in your lot with me.'

'Never that.'

'Excellent. Then we shall leave together tomorrow as I planned. It will hardly help find Luke if you remain moping here. My guess is that he is hidden somewhere in Plymouth and you'll see him all the sooner for being close by –'

'But how will he find me? How will he know where I am? Supposing he manages to run away from wherever it is William keeps him? Supposing he finds his way back to Porthew and I am not there, only William, and the chance is gone for ever?'

Richard stood up slowly. 'Are you telling me that you intend to return to Porthew?'

'No, I can never go back. But here at least I am close by, and Parson has promised to get word to me as soon as he is sighted. And it may be that since I left his house William will send for Luke again. And if Luke did return and I was not here to see him, I do not know how I could endure it.'

'But you can endure the prospect of being parted from me?'

'Yes, if I must. Only because I know you will come back.'

Richard drummed an impatient rhythm with his fingers on the surface of the table. 'Surely the parson can get news to you in Plymouth.'

'But that is a three-day journey, a week for news to travel there and back. And much may happen in a week. I cannot risk it.'

'Hmm.' Richard was silent for a while. 'You've always been stubborn as a mule, Meg. Is there nothing I can say will make you change your mind? You know I've had men employed since Christmas in hunting for him, they are sure to succeed soon.'

'Pray God make it so, and then I will surely join you.'

He was frowning. 'I wonder,' he mused. Occasionally it occurred to him that Margaret might only have come to live with him because she realised that his wealth offered her the best chance of finding Luke. More occasionally still he wondered if there was not something a little too intense in her devotion to the boy. He dismissed the thoughts as irrelevant, for now at least; if she was crazy then it was a madness that he loved, though he had never told her so. Indeed, he found it difficult enough even to admit it to himself.

He asked, 'Do you intend to remain here?'

'If you agree.'

'Why should I agree when I want you to come with me? How will you occupy yourself?'

'I shall be miserable and miss you.'

'Good, it's only what you deserve.'

But already she had seen the beginnings of his smile. She was examining his face, every hair and crease, the flecks of gold in his eyes, the way annoyance fought with tenderness and the warm animal smell of him, as if she could store up the sense of him to see her through the empty weeks ahead. And then, for the first time, she told him, 'I love you, Richard.'

His eyes held hers; perhaps he too was hoping for an image to sustain him. He said, 'But you love your son as well.' It would have been so easy for him to be angry with her just then, but to his surprise he found it was easier still to understand. He slipped his arm around her waist. 'So I suppose I must learn not to be jealous of the boy because you love him too.' And he kissed her gently.

Later, because she had liked the sound of the words the first time she spoke them, Margaret repeated, 'I love you, Richard.'

'Words are easy,' he teased, the shreds of his old wariness still remaining behind the smile, 'if you love me as you say, you will be waiting when I return.'

'If . . . if . . . always if,' she chided, 'why can't you accept what I say?'

'Will you be lonely?'

'Yes, but not in the way I was in Porthew. How soon will you return?'

'In a month. Sooner if I can.'

'However long it is, I will be waiting.'

Margaret was waiting for him when he returned at the end of March with a cage of singing birds and the news that King Charles had been driven from London by hostile crowds and that his Queen had taken ship from Dover to raise money and troops in Holland for the royal cause. On the question of Luke he had less to report and Margaret did her best to hide her disappointment, as she knew he was doing all he could. In fact, he was doing more even than he told her since some of his less orthodox methods, such as the hiring of petty criminals to intercept and rob any hapless traveller from Porthew who was suspected of carrying a message from William Hollar, were likely to meet with her disapproval.

She was waiting for him still when he returned at mid-summer. This time the news was worse: Members of Parliament were returning to their homes knowing they could no longer put off the decision as to which side they supported. Richard was adamant that he intended no part in the quarrel and Margaret persuaded herself that they might somehow remain untouched by the approaching conflict.

During the summer nights that they spent together in the tower bedroom, windows open to the breezes from the sea, she could almost imagine that their life together could remain an island as it had done during the week of snow. And one night, in the dark privacy that followed their love-making, she was able to tell him of her confusion during her years with William, the shameful belief that there was something wrong with her that had led to William's rejection. How was it, she wondered, that Richard did not feel the same?

He did not reply at once, only stroked her shoulder thoughtfully before saying, 'You poor ignoramus, Meg. God's Fox would not have lusted after you if you'd been Helen of Troy herself. His tastes are of a different nature.'

'Different?'

'Do you remember the French youth?'

'Ghislain –?' Even as he spoke, Margaret felt herself to be swimming upwards towards the light of understanding; so many old lies, self-doubt, the burdens of not knowing, fell from her like broken fetters. She was not to blame after all, praise God, she was not to blame. But as soon as the first wave of relief was passed, she became angry at having been duped for so long.

'Then why in the name of heaven did he marry *me*?'

'To be respectable, probably.'

'Respectable!'

'Can you blame him? Good Christian folk are merciless towards men of his persuasion. Men convicted of unnatural acts can be punished by death, remember. Though God and most of the nation know well enough that if the law were ever enforced our King would lose the best part of his navy, and a good deal of his court as well.'

'Of course, of course, how could I have been so blind? What a fool I've been!'

'Yes,' agreed Richard, kissing her tenderly.

But when Margaret had worn herself out in exclaiming at her stupidity, her woeful innocence, the blindness of family and friends, Richard asked in his turn, 'Was he ever a true husband to you, then?'

'Never.'

'So he's not Luke's father after all?'

'No.'

'Then who –?'

'I made a vow never to tell anyone . . .' She fell silent, pondering. The girl, half-child, half-woman, who had given the promise with no hesitation at all, had long since ceased to exist. And now any secrets kept from Richard felt like a form of obscenity. And so she told him. To her amazement Richard found her confession extremely funny: she was further amazed to find that his gust of laughter was a fresh wind, blowing away all the old dusty burdens of secrecy and guilt that she had for so long believed to be hers alone.

'My poor loyal stubborn deluded tricked and put-upon Meg; the parson, of all people! I dread to think what arguments he used to convince you to become his mistress.'

'He was my teacher, everyone looked to him for knowledge of right and wrong. He told me to trust him.'

'And you did?'

'Maybe because I wanted to . . . Promise you'll never tell him that you know.'

'Why? When he's caused you such unhappiness I think I'd enjoy making him suffer in his turn. But on balance I suppose I should be grateful to him after all. If he hadn't driven you into marriage with your Ganymede-chasing husband, you'd never have looked to me for escape.' He kissed the bridge of her nose, her eyelids, the pulse that beat on the curve of her neck. 'You have been most unfortunate in your choice of menfolk.'

'Until now.'

'Hmm. I wonder . . .'

'Wonder then, if you must. I know.'

And Richard, holding her in his arms, was also convinced of the strength of their love, though he never spoke of it. But when, as he did each time, he tried to persuade her to accompany him to Saltash and when, as she did each time, she told him she could not leave Trecarne until Luke was found, his doubts were rekindled. If she loved me as she says, he sometimes thought as he rode away, she would not allow her anxiety for her son to come between us. But he found he was ashamed to tell her this. So all he said each time was, 'If you love me, you will be waiting when I return.'

And she was waiting still when he returned at the beginning of September with the news that the King had raised his standard at Nottingham, both sides were busy raising troops and attempting to gain control of militia and ammunition, and nothing, it seemed, would now prevent armed conflict. Margaret heard the news with a tremor of anxiety, but in those first moments of their reunion, wars and battles seemed of little consequence to either of them.

Nicolas wasted no time in riding over to Trecarne as soon as he had news of Richard's return. The two men were alone together for some time and Margaret, passing under the window of the lower tower room on her way to her herb garden, overheard the sound of voices raised in argument. And a little later, when Nicolas left, it was without first embracing his friend as was his usual practice. Margaret guessed, rightly, that Nicolas had been trying to persuade Richard to join the King's cause, and she was glad of their quarrel since it meant Richard was sticking to his earlier intention to remain aloof from a conflict which seemed to him to be a result of stubbornness and mismanagement on both sides. During that first evening she and Richard had much to talk about, and none of it was concerned with politics or fighting.

Anger was not an emotion that Nicolas was especially familiar with and in consequence his ride back to Porthew after his meeting with Richard was not a comfortable one. With the whole nation being swept forward on a strong tide towards war, Nicolas did not understand how Richard, always the most combative of friends, could still insist that it was none of his business. Eighteen months ago Richard's neutrality had seemed a harmless eccentricity, but since then the whole landscape of Nicolas's life had been transformed and he felt, in some obscure way that he could not quite explain, that he himself had been insulted by his friend's refusal to take sides.

He wondered if Margaret Hollar was to blame; he was quick to dismiss the occasional rumours that she practised witchcraft, but still, he had to admit that there was something unnatural in Richard's lack of interest in the outside world. Since she had moved to Trecarne, Margaret often made Nicolas feel uncomfortable. He had liked her well enough before, had even been prepared to help her and did not condemn her for what she had done, but it made him uneasy to find her assuming the role of mistress of the household. For one thing he did not know what sort of manner he should adopt with her: Richard seemed to expect her to be treated with the courtesy proper to a wife, but that, to Nicolas, would be a travesty, an insult to lawful wives in general. Nicolas was nothing if not conventional, and according to his view of the world a mistress was a diversion merely and it was a bad mistake to take one seriously.

Besides, he felt sorry for Kitty, who, for all her faults, had done nothing to deserve this shabby treatment. Small wonder, he thought, that Alice had been so outraged by Mistress Hollar's move to Trecarne.

For the next couple of weeks, Nicolas was too fully occupied in raising a troop of men and equipping them to fight with him in the blue and white colours of Sir Bevil Grenvile's Cornishmen, to have any time left for worries concerning Richard's irregular household.

During September, Richard continued his former habit of riding out each afternoon with Margaret. It was tacitly agreed between them that they would avoid her old haunts, but there remained wide tracts of countryside to cover. Whether because she was now a more accomplished horsewoman, or whether because Gossip had become a more obliging horse, the two of them now got along very well and those rides along the cliff-tops and the valleys were some of the happiest times.

As they approached the edge of the estate on an afternoon overcast and with the threat of rain, Richard said, 'Tomorrow I must leave for Saltash. And before you insist that you will not come with me, hear what I have to say. This quarrel between the King and his Parliament cannot be settled now except by fighting. With luck it will all be over by Christmas, but if not . . . well, civil war is an ugly business. Nicolas and the others are fired with enthusiasm only because they have little understanding of what is to come. In Europe I have seen how war destroys the land – destroys everything, not just the soldiers who take part but the whole population, trade wiped out, farms and villages ravaged. Meg, once this fight begins it will not be safe for you to remain alone at Trecarne. I want you near me.'

Margaret heard the urgency behind his words but try as she might, she could not share it. The lane along which their horses were walking so placidly on slack reins was one of the prettiest on the estate, especially at this September time of the year. Overhung by a canopy of oaks, the hedges were threaded with blackberries, rosehips and the jewel-bright beads of traveller's joy. She had grown so accustomed to their island retreat at Trecarne that she could not imagine how events in the world beyond could possibly touch them.

So she said at length, 'Surely no one will bother with a backwater such as this.'

'I have many enemies, Meg. Old scores are often settled under the cloak of war.'

She shivered, then went on, 'I would rather be in danger in your house –'

But he interrupted her, 'That's only words, Meg. And I can't promise there'll be no danger if you're with me, only that I'd rather we faced it together.'

This time she did not answer, finding his arguments unusually persuasive.

After they had ridden in silence for a little longer, Richard said, 'Is it only because of Luke that you insist on remaining here?'

'What other reason could there be?'

'That is what I want to know.'

'Only Luke. Once he is safe –'

'Yes? What then? God knows, Meg, you can hardly accuse me of being impatient, but this begins to seem more stubbornness than devotion. If you come with me tomorrow I can leave Will Stevens with instructions in case of Luke's return. Surely you trust Will?'

'Yes.'

'So?'

'Give me time to think this over, Richard. We can talk of it again tonight and –'

Her sentence was never finished. Just ahead of them there was an explosion of sound which made Gossip rear up in fright and Margaret, taken unawares, promptly fell to the ground. Landing with a thump she was winded and it was a moment or two – one of those moments that seem an age but are probably no more than the wink of an eye – before she was able to absorb what had happened. Both the horses were fleeing in panic. Whether Richard had fallen or had been dragged from his horse she did not know; what was certain was that Ambrose, bigger and stronger by far, had clamped Richard in his massive grip, and was slowly, and with obvious huge enjoyment, intent on crushing him in his wrestler's inexorable grip. The power that for years had entertained the crowds each St Ewan's Day was now dedicated to revenge. This time he would not stop until he had crushed out the life of the man who struggled helplessly in his deadly embrace.

'Ambrose, no!'

He did not even hear her. The muscles on his neck were bulging purple but the side of his face which could still show expression was smiling, almost tenderly, as he muttered odd snatches of words to his victim: 'Always swore . . . thought you were safe . . . respect the Treloars . . .'

She could see Richard struggling to reach his rapier but his arms were pinned so tight there was nothing he could do in his defence and already the air was being squeezed from him so he could not even cry out. Margaret scrambled to her feet and, without any very clear idea of what she intended to do to save him, only that she must, somehow, she began to run towards them.

The sound of the shot was a burst of light in her head. Looking down the track she saw Giles a little way off just as he raised his second pistol in the air and shouted out some incoherent command. He had aimed high for fear of injuring his master as the two men twisted and turned on the road, but the action had the desired effect since Ambrose, who had been expecting no interruption, was startled into relaxing his grip. It was only for a split second, but that was all Richard needed to grasp the hilt of his rapier and pull it free. Ambrose would have gone for him again, but then he caught sight of Giles hurrying closer with the pistol and, with a roar of rage and disappointment, Ambrose turned. Leaping the stile from which he had launched his ambush with an agility surprising in such a big man, he set off running across the open field.

Giles was already asking Richard if he was hurt but Richard, still unable to speak, brushed his questions aside and took the pistol from his hand. Ashen-faced and trembling he set one foot on the stile and rested his hand on his knee to steady himself as he took aim at the figure of the blacksmith, zigzagging in his flight. As he cocked the pistol Margaret felt a huge 'No!' screaming up within her and she lunged forward. She struck his hand just as he pulled the trigger and the bullet sailed harmlessly into the air. Ambrose vanished among some trees.

Richard turned to look at her. His eyes were black with horror and disbelief. For a few moments he could not speak, only stared, but then, 'Damn you, Meg –' he gasped, before he slumped into unconsciousness on the mossy granite of the stile.

That evening Nicolas took time off from the business of raising troops for the King's service in order to investigate the attack made earlier on his friend. Not surprisingly, Ambrose was not to be found at the Forge, nor in any of the other places searched; but with a family as widespread and tight-knit as his it was easy enough for a man to remain hidden for days, or even weeks, at a time.

'Most probably he'll next be seen in one of the armies marching east,' said Nicolas thoughtfully. 'No one will ask questions of such a valuable fighting man. I'll not cease searching for him, Richard, but I don't hold out much hope. The whole world is turned on its head and violent men are much sought after for their skills.'

Richard said bitterly, 'By rights that one at least should be dead already. It's only thanks to Meg's misplaced charity that he's living still.'

Margaret said nothing, only thought miserably how wretched it was not to be able to comfort the man she loved. Despite his anger now she did not see how she could have acted differently. When she saw Ambrose fleeing in terror across the field she had had no choice but to try and save him. In his clumsy way he had championed her since she was a child; Lizzie and her children had no one else to depend upon and besides, the immediate danger to Richard had passed. Even now, as she heard Richard and Nicolas talking, she was glad to know that he had escaped punishment. She could not explain to Richard that this in no way meant she cared for him the less, she could barely explain it to herself. And so she sat in miserable silence and waited for his anger to diminish.

Nicolas glanced across at her, then patted Richard on the shoulder. 'At least you're safe,' he said.

'Thanks to Giles. I owe that man my life.'

It transpired that Giles had grown suspicious the previous day when he had overheard the scullion, whom he now recollected was distantly related to the Treloars, telling another lad that he was sure Ambrose would seize his chance soon, before Treveryan left for Saltash. With all the population absorbed in preparations for the coming fight he reckoned his chances of escaping punishment were much improved. Knowing that Richard would dismiss his warnings, Giles had decided to follow him in secret when he left the shelter of the house and immediate area.

'And thank God he did,' said Richard.

Still he had not looked at Margaret, barely acknowledged that she was there.

When it was time for Nicolas to go, Margaret went with him through the long gallery since Richard still found any kind of movement painful. Nicolas walked briskly, as if wishing to shake her off, and he was frowning. At length he turned to her and said, 'I understand your husband has declared his intended support for Parliament. Will you ally yourself with him?'

'That depends,' she answered coldly, 'on how Richard decides. My allegiance is all to him.'

'You have a strange way of showing it.'

'If you're referring to this afternoon –'

'Of course I am, Mistress Hollar.' They had stopped walking and were standing now face to face at the far end of the long gallery. 'Surely this has illustrated all too plainly that your loyalties will always be divided, that when it comes to a real decision you have never really left Porthew.'

'Because I wanted to protect Ambrose?'

'Come now, Mistress Hollar, it wasn't the smith you were protecting.'

'Then who – ?'

'Why, your own self, of course. You know full well your time here is limited, that sooner or later you must return to your former home. If you had stood by and seen Treloar killed you would have earned the undying enmity of all his family and friends – and you know better than I do how numerous they are. Now, when the time comes to return –'

'But that is where you are wrong, Mr Sutton, I shall never return.'

'Don't delude yourself, you're too old for fairy stories. Richard is sure to tire of you sooner or later –'

'Stop!' Margaret wanted to sound indignant, outraged, and yet a leaden feeling in the pit of her stomach told her his words might well be true.

'It's inevitable, you know it is. And by heaven, if you continue as you are doing now, it's likely to be sooner rather than later.'

'What do you mean?'

'For one thing you insist on staying here. Presumably you know he has another mistress in Plymouth?'

Margaret was shaking. 'Stop it, keep out of our business.'

'I'll keep out of *your* business, and gladly, but I'll not keep out of Richard's. We've been friends all our lives and will continue to be friends long after you're forgotten. No need to look so miserable, I daresay when the time comes Richard will see you well provided for, he's not ungenerous, but everyone knows that unhallowed unions such as yours are always fragile.'

'You know nothing about us. But tell me, Mr Sutton, why do you hate me so much?'

Nicolas looked genuinely surprised. 'I don't hate you. Perhaps I'm angry with you now for letting Richard down today but apart from that . . . And I daresay I've grown impatient with the pretence.'

'What pretence?'

'That your liaison will last. Oh, I daresay Richard has said all sorts of things to you in the past, made all manner of promises. Maybe he even believed them at the time, I know I have done the same myself – but in the end such words mean nothing, nothing at all.'

Margaret, doubting if she would be able to control herself much longer, said coldly, 'Good day, Mr Sutton.'

And he, with an exaggerated flourish of his hat, departed.

Both Richard and Margaret, separate and lonely in the large four-poster, spent a wretched and almost sleepless night. Richard found that the potion he had taken to ease the pain of his chest had only succeeded in making his head feel fuzzy. He was badly bruised and at least one of his ribs was cracked; the ride to Saltash, which he could postpone for a day at the most, was sure to be torment. He was furious that Treloar had escaped, furious with Margaret for her

617

betrayal of him, furious with himself for ever having been so weak-minded as to trust her.

The next day he was irritable and found fault with everyone. Several times it occurred to him that he might as well ride away at once, that the agony of his cracked ribs was nothing compared to the misery of being cooped up with a woman who had shown by her actions how meaningless her words were. But as the day wore on he found he could not ignore the fact that her wretchedness was at least as great as his own. And though he told himself he should rejoice to see her suffer, in fact it had the opposite effect.

It was not until the evening when she sought him out. She found him in his library where he was putting some papers in order. He glanced up at her coldly, tried to ignore the kick of emotion that he always felt as she walked into a room.

She stood watching him for a few moments before saying in a low voice, 'Richard, I cannot bear us to part in anger. Surely you can see it was impossible for me to stand by and let you kill Ambrose? If he had been fighting you, maybe, but he was running away and –'

'Has it ever occurred to you how dangerous your so-called tender heart might be? When Treloar returns a second time and there is no Giles keeping watch, how will you reflect on your actions then? If he kills me in the future will you not wonder if you had a hand in –?'

'Richard, stop, that's not fair. In God's name you know that I would die for you gladly if I could, a hundred times over – but I could not stand by and see murder done.'

'I might find it easier, Meg, if you at least pretended some regret. Instead you stand there and try to justify what happened. And then you tell me we should not part in anger –'

'Why should I pretend regret? I have never pretended with you before, Richard. I do not ask you to agree with what I did, only to try to understand –'

'But that's just it, I cannot understand.'

She looked at him hopelessly for a few moments before going over to stand by the fireplace. Richard made a show of returning to his papers but his concentration was gone. Out of the corner of his eye he could see that she had draped one arm across the mantelpiece in a characteristic gesture. She was wearing a dress of deep blue satin, cut low to display her throat and the pendant he had brought back for her from the Americas and which, as long as she remained at Porthew, had been kept hidden beneath her Puritan greys. Her shoulders were slumped in dejection. Abstractedly, he knew, she took a log from the pile and dropped it on to the fire, watched for a little while and then reached into the basket for another.

'For God's sake, Meg,' he snapped, 'do you want to set the house on fire?'

'I'm sorry, I wasn't thinking –' She turned towards him, dropping the log back into the basket.

Richard felt the last of his anger draining away. Slowly he rose to his feet. 'So help me, Meg, I must be as crazy as you are. I believe I do understand you after all. I wish to God I didn't.'

Later that night, when they lay together and listened to the wind soughing through the woods, Margaret remembered Nicolas's words, and this time she smiled. At that moment at least, their fragile and unhallowed union seemed as enduring as any that had been sanctified in church.

Part 3

May 1643

27

Margaret stretched herself on the warm turf and let the golden sounds and scents of an early summer afternoon wash over her: a cock crowing in a distant farmyard; lambs bleating on the hillside and everywhere the drowsy murmur of insects and the tumbling song of skylarks high in the misty blue.

A book lay open on the grassy bank beside her but she scarcely glanced at its pages; the words, that she and Richard had read together during his last stay at Trecarne, had burned into her memory,

> That is my home of love; if I have ranged,
> Like him that travels, I return again.

The words hummed through her mind. Every now and then she shielded her eyes from the sun and searched the road that led north from Trecarne. Richard was expected home that day.

> As easy might I from myself depart,
> As from my soul . . .

Richard had asked her, that half-smile on his face, if she was claiming the words for her own. 'Of course,' she had told him, but when he left the next morning he had said only, 'If you love me, Meg, you will be waiting when I return.'

If, always if . . . his perennial doubt was always in the background, ready to cast a shadow over even their greatest happiness. Often he seemed to treat her love for him like a kind of sickness, from which she must surely one day be cured.

Faint scratches on the gleaming surface of her content. A content that was all the more surprising since it encompassed even the continuing pain of Luke's absence. Even now, while the sun's warmth caressed her face and her heart beat like a maid's at the prospect of Richard's return and happiness was a golden river carrying her headlong into an unknown future, even at this moment of great joy, there was a hard fist of hurt beneath her ribs, a physical pain which would never be erased, she knew that now, except by Luke's return.

From time to time the pain spread like a discolouring ink through her whole being. A few days ago she had heard the servants' children playing beneath her window and a falling cadence of laughter was so absolutely that of her son – it must be Luke, he had returned and sought her out and been caught up in the children's game – that she had sped down the stairs and into the spring sunshine, half-blinded by her eagerness, searching, searching, and not finally convinced of her mistake until all the startled children were assembled in a row, round faces and pointed ones, curly hair and straight, but not one of them her own irreplaceable and still-missing Luke.

And today was Luke's birthday, the second they had spent apart and (if he still lived, though his death was not a possibility Margaret could bring herself to consider) in whatever corner of the land he was now hidden, he had today reached the age of twelve. Margaret spent long hours wondering how he might be changed: she had a fierce dread that she would not recognise him on his return. She dreamed sometimes that a stranger approached her and claimed to be her son – a hideous old man, a drunkard, once it was a leprous vagrant – in vain she screamed her protests: Luke was still a child, was not yet a man, such a transformation was not possible. But the loathsome creature twisted his mouth in a grimacing smile and reached out a deformed hand. 'Mother –'

She shrugged off the nightmare image. So many nightmares still remained but now, mercifully, only when she was sleeping. Sometimes when she looked back on her years in Porthew it seemed as if the whole of her life with William had been a single, unending nightmare.

For over a year her terror that Luke might return and find her missing had kept her almost as much a prisoner in Trecarne as she had been in William's house.

Until today. This May birthday when Richard was due home. Over the past months she had learned that she could not only survive without her son, she could also be happy. At first she had felt ashamed of a happiness that excluded Luke. Recently her refusal to leave Trecarne had been prolonged simply because she found it so hard to accept her ability to contemplate a future without her son. And now that last tie had been broken. When Richard returned she would tell him at once that this time she was prepared to leave with him, to go with him to the ends of the earth, if that was his wish. It seemed to her that Richard had given her all the great happiness she now enjoyed and it was time to offer something in return. She was now ready, eager even, to leave. And she sat on the grassy bank and entertained herself by planning how she would tell him of her change of heart. She imagined his surprise, his pleasure, the moment when he took her in his arms and murmured her name.

Faint hoof-beats approaching on the driveway. She gathered her skirts and rose quickly to her feet but her eagerness was short-lived. Even at this distance she could tell that the sorrel nag with drooping neck and ears was the parson's Sarah. Its rider raised a black-clad arm in greeting and Margaret walked, with her easy, long-legged stride, to greet him.

'I am flattered, Margaret. Were you watching for me?'

'No, Parson. Richard is expected home today.'

He dismounted and walked beside her towards the stable-yard. Margaret had to slow her pace to accommodate his weary walk. Seeing him only occasionally as she did, Margaret was more aware than most people of the change in him over the past year. His hair was thinning and grey, he was becoming stooped, his face lined, almost haggard. Margaret thought that perhaps some of the change was because he missed Luke too, and their shared sadness created a bond between them.

Although she knew, already, from his expression, what his answer was sure to be, she asked, 'Is there news?'

'Of Luke, no. I'm sorry.'

And even though she had been expecting it, the all too familiar pain leapt up to torment her afresh.

'It's as though he's dropped over the edge of the world,' she exclaimed in anguish.

'It's a large place beyond Porthew,' he told her.

Yes. And soon she would learn some of its secrets with Richard. She fixed her thoughts on future adventures and gradually the pain became bearable, diminished, retreated to its accustomed place.

During the months she had spent alone at Trecarne, the parson had been Margaret's only link with the life she had left behind. From him she had learned that William was preparing to close the shop (leaving Paul Viney to care for the house – and Dorcas) so that he could move to Plymouth, where support for Parliament and the Puritan faith remained stronger than ever before. She learned too of the local men who had left their homes and farms to fight in the royalist cause: Robert Treloar of Manaccan, Bob Dawkins, Jack Thomas, John Erisey. He told her that his own two boys, Andrew and Peter, had set off as gaily as if they had been leaving to visit a nearby fair and that their light-heartedness had somehow affected him more deeply than if they had wept at parting. And he told her when her brother Tom put on the Grenvile blue and white and departed with the others. Rumour was that he had been eager for the fight only because his father was soon to marry Bess Treloar and Tom could not bear to stay at the farm and see his first love in his father's bed. When she thought of Tom now, marching east with his father's musket on his shoulder, it was not the sturdy youth she had last seen that her mind conjured up, but rather the tousle-headed child who had flown at William and torn his boot hose when he knew his Mattie was to leave the farm. Parson Weaver told her that so many men and boys had left to join the fight that Jack Pym's ale-house was a doleful place of an evening, and church half empty, the singing out of balance now that so many tenors and basses were gone.

Almost all were fighting in the King's cause. Had they been offered a choice most, being conservative, would doubtless have followed the King's standard anyway – but Sir John Sutton was their landlord, Nicolas their Justice of the Peace, and once the Suttons had shown themselves for the King, the rest of the area followed without question.

And those, like William, and like Matthew Erisey and Master Payne, who hoped for the victory of Parliament and the ushering-in of the rule of the saints, tended to keep their opinions to themselves while making plans to join those of like minds in Plymouth.

Although Parson Weaver kept Margaret as well informed as he could, the news that filtered down from the east of the county was blurred and often contradictory. What was beyond doubt was that the ill-equipped and amateurish rabble who had ambled from their homes in the autumn of 1642 were now a battle-hardened and formidable force, the best in all the royal army. A race of men made hardy by the unceasing struggle against the sea and the wind and the need to grasp a living from the thin and rocky soil were united under local leaders. A few small victories had fired their enthusiasm: with such soldiers at his command it was hoped the King might bring the rebels to heel in time for the men to get home for harvest.

Margaret listened to what the parson told her but she loathed all news of the fighting. It exasperated her to think that grown men – such as she assumed the King and his Members of Parliament to be – could devise no better way of settling their quarrel than by the slaughter of their fellows. It was small consolation that Luke, wherever he was hidden, was too young to be recruited into either army. If she looked forward to the parson's visits it was less for news of fighting, or local gossip, than for the chance to talk about her son. Their son.

By leaving her husband Margaret had made herself an outcast from the world in which she had lived. In her present happiness she hardly gave it any thought; she did not even miss Lizzie very much. If Merry had lived she might have regretted . . . but then she reminded herself that Merry would never have allowed scandal to interfere with friendship. Only Parson Weaver was still loyal; for all his faults he had remained steadfast, and he alone seemed to understand what Luke's absence cost her. Richard became impatient if she mentioned him too often; only with the parson could she indulge herself without restraint. 'Do you remember when the tinkers stole Luke's dagger?' 'I wish I'd not chivvied him so about his lessons.' 'Does he have a fiddle yet? I wonder.'

From time to time Parson Weaver said with a sigh, 'He was the only one to share my love of music . . .'

But on this bright May morning Margaret did not want to dwell on thoughts of the child she was now preparing to leave behind, and the parson's mood was sombre. 'This war grows bloodier by the day, Margaret,' he said wearily, 'all my life I have tried to follow the middle way, I had believed Our Lord to be a bringer of peace, but I am afraid that by the time these quarrels are ended there will no longer be a middle way to follow.'

Margaret did not hear the warning, only the fear, and she took his hand. She guessed he was thinking of his two boys, Peter and Andrew, and wondering if they would survive the conflict. She could hear Hester shrilling her wrath on some wretched maid, geese cackling down by the brook, men calling to their workmates in the fields. She could not see, as the parson did through every waking moment, the dark-feathered wing of Death hovering over the sunny landscape. But she knew that his wife, always frail, was now suffering a wasting illness and had no milk to feed her youngest infant, and she guessed that Parson Weaver was troubled by remorse and an awareness of the fleeting years. She had no words with which to comfort him, but he smiled as he held her hand, then raised it to his lips and kissed her upturned palm.

'You'll never be a lady,' he said, seeing the scar that still seamed her skin, 'look at your working hands.'

She touched a jewelled ring thoughtfully. 'I've never pretended to be anything other than what I was born,' she said, 'I only dress like a lady because it gives Richard pleasure.'

They stayed together a little longer. On his first visit to Trecarne, the parson had been struck by how little Margaret was altered by her new rich clothes. If his own wife, thin and pale as an autumn reed, had ever been draped in such finery, she would surely have been transformed. But Margaret was ever the same, whether clad in the rough clothes of a yeoman's daughter or the sober greys of a Puritan wife or, as now, wearing a gown that shimmered all the colours of mother-of-pearl and summer seas. It was always her eyes and her wide mouth one noticed, never her dress.

*　　*　　*

Richard was in an excellent good humour as he rode the last few miles to Trecarne and his high spirits burst out in song. Like all his songs it was quite without any semblance of a tune and Giles, who was of a musical bent himself, kept as much distance between them as he could and, from time to time, grimaced at his master's most unmelodic back.

For over a year Richard, in common with some other Cornish merchantmen, had interspersed his usual trade with that of privateer. Since Parliament had gained control of the navy at the outset of hostilities, Richard's ships were busy plundering their cargoes whenever possible and passing them on, for a small consideration, to the West Country Royalists. Beyond this, Richard still refused to commit himself: in his opinion the King was an arrogant muddler bent on tyranny while his opponents were lawyers and religious zealots who would have the whole nation a joyless psalm-singing Puritan conventicle if they had their way. And though he might enjoy the danger and profit to be found in war, more and more his thoughts turned to the possibilities beyond the sea. Let this old country eat out its heart in the barren struggle over rights and religions – for him there was a new life beckoning in the Americas.

He would have left long ago but for Margaret: her stubborn refusal to quit until her son was found was the cause of their only quarrels. Of course, there was nothing to prevent him from leaving without her – a small house could be found for her somewhere, regular payments made, these things were easily arranged, he had done it before – and yet . . . He told himself it was simply that it suited him to be with Margaret, that for some reason he had not yet grown tired of her – on the contrary, his eagerness to see her again, as he rode down lanes choked with bluebells and pink campion and the first white stars of cow parsley, was as intense as on those evenings when he had first left Will Stevens shivering in Ia's Copse and made his stealthy way to the stone barn. What infuriated him most was his awareness of Margaret's own longing to travel: she never tired of hearing of the exotic places he had visited. He could imagine no greater pleasure than introducing her to the islands and cities he had already seen himself. And then, somewhere, perhaps in the Americas in some part that had not been tainted by the chill breath of Puritanism, he could set her free of the constraints by which she would always be bound in this narrow, petty England.

For a few months or years, at least.

If he had analysed his thoughts on the subject, which he was careful not to do, he would probably have asserted that he was not the kind of dewy-eyed idealist who needed to deceive himself with the prospect of enduring love. He would have said that he found it easy to ignore Margaret's protestations of her love. Such was the stuff of which the poets sang and Margaret, in her lonely existence at Porthew, had had time for much poetry – and doubtless it was easier for her to justify her present outcast state if it was beribboned with the amorous language of the poets. In his more cynical moments he assumed that she had chosen to live with him only because he had the resources to help her find her missing child. But, though he was not aware of this himself, Richard's cynical moments had grown increasingly rare, of late.

Never was cynicism further from his mind than on the May afternoon when his horse, scenting home, cantered down the driveway and into the stable-yard. And there was Margaret, running to greet him and Richard sprang down from his horse and caught her in his arms and in that moment when the long ache of absence was washed away by the press of her body against his, her arms around his neck, all his doubts and reservations, all thought even, vanished, and there was only the heady release of her smell and touch and taste.

'Oh Richard, I was waiting all morning for you by the orchard and now you have come just when I was in the kitchen with Hester. You must be tired. Are you hungry, are you well? Do you want wine? A bite to eat? I can't wait to tell you my decision, you'll be so pleased, I know . . .'

'Later, Meg,' he laughed, curling his arm about her waist, 'first you must listen to the news I've brought.'

'News?'

'Only let me take my boots off and find a measure of wine . . . patience, Meg, I want to tell this right.'

Will took Richard's horse by the bridle and then paused,

a baffled smile on his face, to watch them as they walked towards the house. The man had pulled off his hat and tossed it aside, his boots and breeches and coat were pale and spattered with dust and mud from the journey; the woman's shimmering gown was already absorbing its share of the grubbiness, but both man and woman were so lost in the pleasure of reunion they were oblivious to all else. Never before, he thought fondly, had he seen such a pair of turtle doves; a musket could have been fired beside them and they'd probably not even notice.

The household, which had been preparing for days for his return, now sprang into efficient action. Food and wine were placed in the lower tower room, water for washing, towels and fresh clothes were laid out, the stewards, falconer and groom all took up their positions in readiness for the time when the master would see them and hear their reports. But first, they knew, he required time alone with Mistress Hollar.

Within the tower room Richard had kicked off his boots, unbuttoned his doublet, kissed Margaret several times and was savouring the excellent wine.

'Meg, what is it? You're as fidgety as a cat.'

Her eyes were shining. 'I've made up my mind, Richard, that's what I wanted to tell you –'

'But you must hear *my* news first.' Richard found he could restrain himself no longer. 'Meg, my dearest, your troubles are over. I've found your son –'

'Luke –!' she gasped, and sat down heavily on a low chest.

'He's safe, Meg, I've seen him with my own eyes and – Why, what's the matter? I thought you'd be so . . . here, let me, the shock is too much –'

But Margaret, though suddenly as pale as ice, had sprung to her feet again and began pacing the room, wringing her hands in a frantic gesture that brought a lump to Richard's throat. 'How can you be sure?' she exclaimed, striding towards him, swinging round, hurrying to the window, turning again. 'Perhaps it was a mistake. No, that would be too cruel. Did you speak with him? Ask him? There are many lads who look like . . . he must have changed . . . it would be so easy to . . . you had only seen him once before and that was . . . Dear God, if this is true –!'

'Meg, stop, I can't bear it.' Richard set down his mug of wine and intercepted her frantic pacing. He held her very tightly. 'It was Luke, it was your son. I'd not lie to you on such a matter. Yes, I did speak with him, briefly, but it was enough. Here, don't cry, Meg. Let me tell you the whole story.'

Richard had been so delighted by his success, so intrigued by the irony of finally discovering the lad in his uncle's house, that he had not paused to consider how Margaret might be affected by the news. She who had always been so stalwart in adversity seemed now quite unravelled by relief. His story, which had seemed brief enough when he rehearsed it, was an age in the telling since Margaret interrupted him a hundred times, testing every statement, still unable to believe in the miracle.

He had happened to visit his uncle, on a day when Matthew Dawlish was away from Plymouth. 'When I visited the stables late one night to check my horse which had a swelling above the knee, I heard the sound of a fiddle coming from a store room and I was curious. I saw the lad seated on a bale of hay. As soon as he caught sight of me he tried to escape . . .' Richard paused, remembering the unusual intensity of the lad's expression, something between anger and timidity and a kind of animal wariness. 'I gather his music-making is only tolerated if he confines himself to pious dirges and he lives in daily fear that his violin will be taken from him –'

'He was afraid?'

Richard hastened to reassure her that the boy had been more cautious than frightened, that he seemed to be in excellent health, had grown like a weed, was on the verge of tumbling into a man's voice but now struggled with a comical croak.

Margaret was not to be pacified. 'How tall? As tall as me? To my shoulder maybe?'

Richard had learned from one of the ostlers who had once been employed by him in Saltash, that Luke had been in Master Dawlish's household only since Candlemas. He went by the name of John Pearce and Mistress Dawlish was said to dote on him.

'I asked him if he wished to see his mother again and he

said yes indeed, he was tired of waiting for her to join him as he'd been promised –'

'My poor boy –!'

'But he was cautious. First he wanted proof that you had sent me.'

'Did he not recognise you?'

'I believe he did. Yet he was wary.'

'I will go to him at once. You must be tired after so much travelling, but I can take a servant. If we ride fast –'

'Meg, wait, be patient. Plymouth is under siege and all who come and go are carefully watched. My uncle is as zealous in his religion as your husband ever was and I've no doubt the two of them are thick as holy thieves. If it was known that you were anywhere near the city the boy would be spirited away at once.'

'Oh, you're right, sweet heavens, what can I do?'

'We'll send Will Stevens. You trust him, don't you? Good. And in the meanwhile you and I will remain here as though nothing was happening until Luke is safely home again. I'll send Jack Jenkin as well. He's a handy fellow in a brawl though I doubt it will come to that. They'll need some token to show him they come with your authority.'

'I shall write him a letter and . . . they must take this ring. It belonged to my mother the foreigner and Luke is sure to recognise it.'

It seemed to Margaret to be a form of torture to have to wait at Trecarne when she knew at last the whereabouts of her son, but 'We shall not have to wait much longer,' was Richard's reassurance.

And then he added, only half in jest, 'Will you still want to stay with me, Meg, now that I've found your boy for you?'

Overwhelmed by happiness and an almost unbearable suspense, Margaret caught hold of his hands and laughed. 'But that was what I wanted to tell you when you arrived, only you insisted on telling me your news first. That's what I had decided in the last few days, I would have left with you next time anyway, Richard, with or without Luke.'

His mouth twisted in a kind of smile. 'It's easy to say that now . . .' he said.

But she wrapped her arms around his neck and held him

tightly. 'Don't doubt me, Richard. Not now. Any time but now.'

He could feel the rapid beating of her heart, her face still damp with tears of happiness and relief, the roughness of her hands on his cheek. He caught a glimpse of her eyes, her pale lashes and then with a groan he surrendered to the certainty of that moment as his lips pressed down on hers with an urgency that was close to anger and he was swept, like a ship venturing into uncharted waters, into a new place where, after all, there was no space for doubt.

Of all the people and habits Luke had left behind in Porthew it was the luxury of sleeping alone in his own bed in his solitary room that he still missed most acutely. In Matthew Dawlish's household he must share a bed with the master's two youngest sons, James and William, a snoring, farting, giggling pair who resented him nearly as much as he did them. In other houses it had been even worse and at one establishment he had shared an attic with half a dozen apprentices and students. To give himself some little space alone each day he had trained himself to waken early: the moment before the stars began to fade in the night sky was a time too precious to be squandered in sleep.

He had recognised Richard Treveryan as soon as he entered the stable, though he had not betrayed his surprise; he was grown expert at masking even the strongest emotions. As he sat on the bale of hay and pretended to ignore the dark-haired man with the strange, almost frightening face, he had to fight to suppress the memories: that morning when he and his mother had visited Trecarne; his shame and fury at being left in the kitchen while the servants whispered and smirked and made fun of him; the awesome beauty of the hawks with their cruel eyes; his longing to see them released, soaring through the open sky, away, away . . . 'You must return and I will show you how they fly,' the man had told him. Well, that was in the time before Luke learned how easily men lie. He'd never believe such a careless promise now.

The strange-looking man had talked of his mother. (What right had he to talk of her?) But if his mother had wished to see him all this time then why had she abandoned him for so long with not even a letter to comfort him? 'Your mother and I will follow you to Plymouth,' Father had said, 'this parting is only for a brief time.' Was a week a brief time? A month, a year? Father sent messages from time to time, variations on the theme of 'trust in the Lord; this parting will not be much longer' – but from his mother there had been no word. Surely the truth must be that they had wanted him out of the way for some reason and now they had forgotten about him altogether. From scraps of conversation overheard among the apprentices he had learned that such callousness was common.

Luke hardly ever thought of Porthew now. Only sometimes, when he was absorbed in playing the fiddle, the old images crept unbidden from the corners of his memory: the way the light fell across his bedroom ceiling on a summer's evening; the solemn beauty of his father's voice reading from the family Bible; his mother sitting by the fireside on a winter's night and straining her eyes to read the book the parson had lent her; Dorcas hunting for fleas on Hedge's pale neck; Aunt Treloar and Ambrose and Paul Viney, and the rooks clamouring in the elm trees at Conwinnion . . . At first these memories had seemed to him more real than the muddled present he found himself in. But now he had learned not to waste time in homesickness but to channel his energies into discovering all that was useful in each temporary billet. He learned where the real authority in a household was to be found, where he might play his fiddle without fear of interruption, whom he could trust a little and whom not at all.

In Matthew Dawlish's house it was Nathaniel, the ostler's boy, who had become his chief ally. Although only a few years older than Luke he was a strapping great lad, and besides that he had his master's respect for being a natural-born preacher who testified on Sundays to the part the Lord God played in his life. At first Nathaniel had been troubled by the effect Luke's music produced on him. 'Are those not Satan's tunes?' But Luke, seeing his eagerness to be persuaded, had replied easily, 'The Lord would never have made the world so beautiful, nor given us the gift of melody, if He had not intended us to use it.' Where had he heard such certainty before? A picture floated into his mind of a sun-warmed cliff-top, soft turf and the scent of gorse and bracken in the air, Hedge's muffled voice barking down a rabbit hole, and he seemed to hear his mother's voice reassuring him . . . but he could not be certain of it. The important thing was that Nathaniel was convinced and from then on he would sit happily for hours in the loft above the stables, listening. And keeping watch for Luke.

Like most people in Plymouth, Nathaniel had heard stories in plenty about Richard Treveryan. While other men were risking and losing their lives in the fighting, he made no secret of his intention to follow no principle but profit. Obviously such a man's rapid rise to fortune had not been made by lawful trade alone . . . and the God of Justice had punished his sins with the affliction of a barren wife.

Luke listened and said nothing but, if he had wished, he could have added plenty of seasoning to their rumours. Every now and then he still awoke covered in the sweat of humiliation from a dream where the boys of Porthew were taunting him, slandering his mother with words he did not understand but whose scurrilous intent was clear enough. He had been in Plymouth sufficient time to know what a whore was (but his mother had a home of her own and a husband?) and from the older apprentices he had learned the meaning of 'adulteress' . . . When Treveryan had asked him if he wished to see his mother again his agreement had sprung from him before he had time to consider his reply, but now all certainty was fading. Why had she not tried to see him before? What connection was there now between her and Treveryan? Would he return only to be mocked as before, simply for being her son? Did Father know? Whichever way he turned there was only confusion.

Besides, there were weightier matters to consider. Nathaniel and he had talked deeply on many occasions. Parliament and the True Church of God were struggling to maintain a hold in the West Country and only Plymouth still held out for the faith. Nathaniel was planning to run away from the Dawlish household and join God's army in the fight against the armies of darkness. Supposing Luke went with him? Most likely he would be considered too young to fight, but the soldiers would surely be encouraged by the music.

An end to the confusion. A chance not only to be a soldier in the cause of right but also to be free, to be his own master at last, to walk with Nathaniel wherever they chose and to be at no man's beck and call. To play his fiddle by an open fire with never a fear that his music would be banned.

Anyone wishing to observe the change that, by the summer of 1643, had turned the Cornish troops from a shambling group of country boys to a battle-seasoned force needed to look no further than Nicolas Sutton. The features were the same, the abundant brown hair, the handsome face, the full, almost girlish lips. He was grown leaner, browner – but the alteration was much more than that. He now possessed a honed-down quality, as though he no longer had time for non-essentials. His manner was harsher, and yet at the same time there was a gentleness that Margaret sensed as soon as he came into the room and greeted her with unaccustomed courtesy. As she watched him now talking with Richard in the long gallery, Margaret tried to put her finger on the precise nature of the change that had been wrought in him by weeks of sharing hardship with his troops, suffering observed, the self-knowledge gained from the terror and exhilaration of battle, and she came to the conclusion that Nicolas Sutton had at last grown up.

He had been slightly wounded at Chagford and returned to Rossmere to recover during the truce that had been negotiated in Cornwall during March and April. But now the truce had been over for a fortnight and on the following day he was to return to his place among the 'Cornish malignants' as their opponents now called them.

'Alice suggests that I feign illness for a little longer, at least until her confinement in August, and Heaven help me I am almost tempted. I think I never saw Rossmere look so beautiful as it does now and the boys are becoming champion horsemen under my teaching.'

'Then you should attend to what she says and stay at home,' said Richard briskly.

Nicolas slid him a wary glance. 'How can you stand idly by, Richard, when every gentleman in Cornwall has made up his mind for one side or the other? My God, I truly believe I'd sooner you were my enemy than a mere spectator to this deadly business.'

'I'll not join the Parliament men, Nick, not even to please you. Besides, I'm not idle always. My ships are busily employed in harrying the Plymouth supplies.'

'Rumour has it your captains have orders to attack any ships that are vulnerable, whether Parliament's or the King's.'

Richard stared into the middle distance. 'Dame Rumour was always a malicious hag,' he commented lightly.

Nicolas turned away in disgust. 'And yet you do not deny it. How can you be so unscrupulous when men are dying every day to preserve our monarchy and our Church? I was with Godolphin on the night he was killed. A small group of us was returning through the town. We were keeping our spirits up with the pretence that we would spend the night at a well-appointed inn and imagining what meal we would order up that evening. Godolphin had just startled us all by claiming that nothing could beat a well-seasoned rabbit pie when there was a sudden noise – it didn't seem loud enough for a musket shot – and he exclaimed, "Oh God, I am hurt," and rolled from his horse. I thought it was all part of our earlier play-acting and was on the point of telling him it was in poor taste, when one of our companions cried out that he was dead. Whoever shot him cannot have taken aim, it was too dark. Some believe the musket went off by accident . . . he was a poet, damn it, a courtier and a poet, not a soldier, and he had as many friends on the Parliament side as on ours. We buried him at Okehampton . . .'

Nicolas fell silent. It was not the first time he had told them the story, but his pain did not seem to lessen with each telling. After some little while Richard said gently, 'Sidney Godolphin was a good man, though he did cheat me at skittles when we were boys, but if he and half the men of Cornwall are killed it will not make this battle mine.'

Nicolas sighed and began folding a sheet of paper into a dart which he then tossed into the empty fireplace. Richard said to him, 'Don't fret, Nick, within a week or two I shall quit this rusty island altogether and find battles of my own to fight across the sea. We might settle in the New World, or maybe a little closer so that you can visit us.'

But Nicolas shook his head. 'When I next return from this wretched war,' he said, 'no power on earth will ever make me leave Rossmere until they carry me out in a wooden box.'

He talked on for a little longer, describing his oldest boy's prowess on a horse, his eagerness to reach manhood so he could join his father in fighting for the King. Richard listened without comment, then excused himself, saying there was a brief matter that needed his attention. Nicolas and Margaret, left alone for the first time since the day of Ambrose's attack on Richard, sat for a while in uneasy silence.

At length Nicolas said, 'You have more influence with him than I do, Mistress Hollar. Won't you try and persuade him to join me when I ride east tomorrow?'

Margaret was so startled to hear Nicolas appealing to her for help that it was a moment or two before she could think of a reply. When she did, she said coldly, 'Richard makes his own decisions, and I'm sure he always will.'

'Yet he would listen to you.'

'I doubt –'

'You know he would.'

For the first time her eyes met his. She looked away quickly. 'And why should I attempt to make Richard choose what will only be injury for me?'

Nicolas hesitated, then said simply, 'Because I believe you are a woman of honour, Mistress Hollar, and that you would not wish the man you love to betray his own people.'

'Honour, Mr Sutton?' She laughed. 'Not many would accuse a woman in my position of that particular virtue.'

'Maybe not. And I myself have been guilty of . . . Mistress Hollar, I believe I owe you an apology. When I talked with you last September I was over-hasty and said things that I now regret. And for that I wish now to apologise.'

'Thank you, Mr Sutton. And I accept your apology. May I ask what has brought about your change of heart?'

'I suppose one learns to see things differently when all the world is turned topsy-turvy by war. And I cannot remain blind to the changes in Richard over these last few months. You have made him happy, and no one else has done that before. And because he has always been my closest friend, I am glad to see him so content, though I wish it did not keep him from the fighting. When we spoke before I told you that unhallowed unions never endure. Well, as a general rule, I believe that still. Only now I hope that you and Richard may prove to be the exception.'

'Thank you again, Mr Sutton. As you can imagine, I share that hope,' she smiled.

'Hmm. And now that I've beguiled you with my quite uncalled-for blessing, I hope you will use your influence on Richard to –'

She burst out laughing. 'And I thought you were sincere! I'm sorry, Mr Sutton, I have no intention of trying to persuade Richard to leave me. On the contrary, if he shows any signs of interest in the battles, I shall do my utmost to dissuade him.'

'Well, you are honest, at least. And you and Richard are well matched in stubbornness. By the way, I did not mention it to him just now, but your friend Treloar has been fighting with Sir Bevil's own pikemen since the winter.'

'Ambrose? Is he in danger?'

'Not of arrest, he's far too valuable to our own side. Sir Bevil knows his history, but the fellow is such a formidable fighter he'll probably return with a knighthood. It's not just his own strength, but his presence alone among a group of men seems to give them all the strength of Trojans. The story is that several Roundheads have died of fright just at the sight of him.'

'Does Lizzie know?'

'I told her so myself when I returned.'

Margaret was on the point of thanking Nicolas for the third time that morning when Richard strode into the room and said cheerfully, 'There, Nick, though I do not join you in this fight myself, I am sending you my best man to further the King's noble cause. Giles is an honest lad, as you know, brave and loyal and resourceful . . . but if I praise him any more I shall regret my generosity in parting with him. I would have given you Will Stevens as well but he is in Plymouth on private business. I have given Giles leave to make his farewells today and he will join you at Rossmere by dawn tomorrow.'

'Is he the lad with the large ears?'

'As an elephant's.'

'And he saved Richard's life,' added Margaret.

'A useful fellow,' said Nick, 'but I'd sooner you were joining us yourself.'

'Don't waste time appealing to my conscience, Nick. I have risked my life a score of times when I thought there might be profit in it, but this foolishness of the King's is nothing to do with me.'

Nicolas was frowning. Surely there must be words somewhere that would persuade Richard of the importance of the royal cause – but if there were, he lacked the skills to find them. As a conventional and good-natured youth he had followed Richard for years with a baffled fascination. Perhaps he had not changed so very much after all. He still could not understand how Richard, normally so belligerent, could remain aloof at precisely that moment when all his fellow countrymen were being roused to warlike passions. Richard's neutrality maddened him, and he would gladly have left on a quarrel – but the old friendship proved too strong.

They all three walked down the steps into the sunshine as Nicolas's roan mare was led round to the front of the house. Nicolas looked about him thoughtfully. A couple of men were clipping the low box hedging that had been planted in intricate patterns beyond the gravel walk.

'I'm surprised you're in such a hurry for foreign parts,' he mused, 'when you have such a fine home here. Not a patch on Rossmere, of course, but still, in its own way . . .' He grinned, then, turning to Margaret, he took her hand and raised it to his lips. 'I wish you every happiness, Mistress Hollar.'

She smiled. 'And for you, a speedy return to Rossmere.'

He turned to Richard, hesitated only a moment before embracing him warmly. 'Damn you, Richard,' he said roughly, 'I wish you were with us in this fight, but since you refuse . . . well then, God give you comfort in your choice.'

'And may He grant you the courage of a lion so your enemies are soon defeated.'

'Amen to that.' He placed his hands on the saddle to

mount up, then turned and confessed with a rueful smile, 'But the sad truth is that my brother Stephen has all the courage in our family. I have discovered these past few months that I am ill-suited for a soldier's life.'

'Don't be afraid, Nick.'

'But that's the whole trouble. As soon as I leave Rossmere, I become a coward through and through. I cannot abide the discomfort, nor the sight of the injured.' Then, fearing that he was grown too sombre he said cheerfully, 'But I daresay courage comes with practice.' He swung up into the saddle. 'Farewell, Richard, Mistress Hollar.'

'Farewell, Nick.'

Nicolas grinned down at the sight of the man and woman standing side by side. He seemed to be on the point of saying something, but then he thought better of it, halooed his servants to follow and set off at a canter down the driveway between banks of bluebells and the frothing white and green lace of cow parsley.

Margaret slipped her hand through Richard's arm. 'He cares no more for this fight than you do,' she said.

Richard shrugged. 'Then let him quit it,' he said briskly. 'Forget about him, Meg. Forget about the fighting. In a couple of days your son will be here, and then there will be nothing to prevent us from leaving.'

'Two days? So long? I thought perhaps –'

'At least two days,' said Richard firmly, 'you'll wear your eyes out with searching the road if you begin now and God knows, your sight is weak enough already. Come inside, Meg. Luke will be here soon enough.'

But that night, under cover of a moonless dark, Luke and Nathaniel slipped through the lines of the royalist soldiers besieging Plymouth and made their way to the homestead in Devon where Nathaniel's parents and brothers still farmed. From there they planned to travel east to join the Parliamentary army led by the Earl of Essex.

28

Nicolas was able to rejoin the West Country Royalists in time to take part in the battle at Stratton in the northeast of the county on the sixteenth of May. The Cornish troops acquitted themselves with their now customary efficiency and by evening the Parliamentary soldiers, who had begun the day with the advantage of high ground, were put to flight. Nearly two thousand prisoners were taken, as well as money and guns. If he felt fear at any time during that day, Nicolas never showed it. He was energetic and cheerful, as popular with the men as with his fellow officers.

Only Plymouth still held out for Parliament: a small contingent was therefore left to continue the siege while three thousand battle-proud Cornish soldiers marched across the Tamar and through Devon to swell the numbers of Prince Maurice's army in Somerset. And none was prouder than the tight-knit band of Porthew men, basking in the reflected glory of being neighbours and kin to the renowned Ambrose Treloar.

When the servant returned empty-handed from his mission to Plymouth, Margaret at first refused to accept his report that Luke had left Matthew Dawlish's house of his own free will. She was convinced that he had been abducted, or threatened and frightened . . . or that William had somehow gained word of her plan and had spirited the boy to another secret hiding place . . . he was surely hidden, hiding, the men must return to Plymouth and seek again. She herself would leave at once. But a couple of days later Will Stevens came back, having taken it on himself to follow the boys as far as Nathaniel's Devon home. There he had learned from Nathaniel's parents, whom he described as honest and godly folk, of Luke's enthusiasm to join the battle. Will had decided there was little point in pursuing him further, since it had never been his orders to bring the boy home against his will.

Forced by Will's report to accept that her son had indeed escaped of his own free will, Margaret sank into despair. For several days she hardly stirred from the tower rooms, barely ate or drank or spoke. Nor did she grieve. Richard grew anxious; alternately he tried to console her or grew angry, but whatever he said she only stared at him with leaden eyes and told him he might do as he wished, nothing mattered any more. Richard began to think he must be touched with madness himself to endure such a companion. Several times he was on the point of leaving, but each time, at the last moment, something persuaded him to change his mind.

A few days after Will's return, Richard was working in the library on some plans that Thomas had drawn up for the second phase of building. Although they talked as if its completion was a certainty, each man privately doubted if the work would even begin, at least while the country was feeding all its able-bodied men to far-off battles. Richard considered ruefully that if he was to be burdened with a cheerless mistress, he needed some future challenge to distract him.

It had been raining steadily since early morning and the room was filled with a greeny dark. Try as he might to concentrate on Thomas's talk of gables and cross-beams, Richard could not shake off a growing sense of oppression. The sound of the rain drumming against the ground outside was so loud that he did not hear the door open, and only looked up when there was a rustle of skirts at his side.

'Meg?' He eyed her warily. Her face was without expression but he noted that she had taken care to brush out her hair and put on fresh clothes.

'May I speak with you alone, Richard?'

'Yes.' He glanced quickly at Thomas, who did not bother to make any protest beyond a hard-done-by sigh as he gathered up his papers and said that he would be ready to continue their discussion when Richard wished.

As soon as they were alone she said, 'If you're still prepared to take me with you, I'll go.' The words were spoken in a flat voice, bleached of all emotion.

Richard frowned. 'Is that what you want?'

'Yes.'

'Why the change now?'

'Because –' her hands were twisting the bunched up fabric of her skirt – 'because he has gone. Of his own free will he has gone. And I believe that we can never be truly happy, you and I, while we remain here.'

'Are you sure?'

'Yes.'

He stood up. Until now she had resisted all his efforts to comfort her. Almost tentatively, he took her hands in his and said, 'Then I'm glad, Meg. And yes, of course I want you to leave with me as we planned. And once we are away from here –'

He did not finish. She was gripping his hands so tightly that her knuckles were taut white and she began to shake. 'Oh Richard!' she burst out on a sob. 'He ran away, when he knew I was coming he ran away. I have lost him and I do not think I can bear it!'

Richard held her in his arms while she wept and when the first passion of her grief was passed he told her that Luke was too young to come to harm in the wars, would be sure to come home again soon enough and then Will would take care of him until they could all be reunited. And he told her of the journey they would make together, the places they would visit. And then for the first time he told her of his hope that she would one day have his child, a child that would mean as much to each of them as Luke had meant to her.

Thomas waited outside until his stomach told him it was past dinner time, and when he came back from the kitchen the closed door, and the sound of low voices, indicated that his employer was still occupied. And when the door was at length flung open Richard merely told him to order wine and food from the kitchen and to send word to the stable that the horses should be ready at the usual time for their ride, now that Mistress Hollar was herself again.

The preparations for their departure took a considerable time but, by the middle of July, all was settled. Margaret threw herself into the activity with an energy that was partly to dull the pain of Luke's loss, partly because of her great eagerness, now that her decision had been made, to leave. They were delayed by a continuing lawsuit over a nearby tenancy, but once that was dealt with, the steward was empowered to manage all the western estates. Thomas was told that for the time being he was merely to supervise the final details of the work that had been undertaken already. The seemingly unending barrage of complaint and threat issuing from Kitty in Saltash was parried, money was organised for the journey and a ship sailed west from Fowey.

Towards late afternoon on a day when his ship, the *Herald*, stood offshore in readiness for their departure, Richard and Margaret walked down to the wrought-iron bench by the yew tree overlooking the bay. The spot where they had sat together on the August afternoon of her first visit to him at Trecarne, had long been a favourite. It had rained intermittently during the day but now the clouds were passing and the landscape glittered in cold sunlight. A blackbird, hidden in the green darkness behind them, poured out his bubbling song and a pair of ducks, long necks outstretched, flew homewards towards their roost among the willows. A couple of dogs which had followed Richard from the house flopped down in front of them and snoozed.

Richard asked with a smile, 'And how do you like my little ship?'

They had been rowed out to the *Herald* that morning and Richard had shown her the living space which, although cramped after the large rooms at Trecarne, was well appointed. They had both been drenched to the skin but Margaret had been delighted by the compact efficiency of the little ship.

'You know I loved it,' she told him, 'you just like to hear me flatter you again.'

'Of course I do. By the way, I thought I might have the tapestry taken down from the tower room and hung in our cabin. Just in case you feel homesick for Paris and his three beauties.'

'Is that wise?' All day boats had been ferrying books and possessions out to the ship and Margaret had watched each fresh load with growing anxiety. 'Aren't you afraid the *Herald* will be weighed too low in the water?'

He laughed. 'I have no intention of sinking into a watery grave for the sake of a bed-hanging, never fear. And that reminds me, I thought maybe we should rename her *La Reine Marguerite*.'

'What on earth for?' asked Margaret, who spoke no French.

'It sounds more poetical than the *Queen Meg* which was my first choice, and it means the same thing.'

Margaret burst out laughing and told him he could name the ship as he liked. They sat for a while in contented silence. Margaret found, to her surprise and annoyance, that she was almost afraid. For most of her life she had wanted nothing more than to leave these few square miles which were all she had ever known, yet now that the dream was about to become reality, doubts had come to nag her. After expecting so much and for so long, she might now be disappointed. Or disillusioned. (Or suffer seasickness.) Could those distant lands and cities Richard had described so many times ever match her fervent imaginings?

After a while she broke the silence. 'I wonder if I'll ever come back to this spot? Did I ever tell you how much I love your house, Richard?'

'No.'

'You must know that I do. And in spite of everything, I've been happier here than ever in my life before. Except, perhaps, in the little barn in Porthew.'

'I'll have it moved here stone by stone.'

'I hope we'll return. One day.'

'Of course we will. I plan to sit here with you, Meg, when we are both old and feeble. We'll smoke a pipe together and sink into remembrance of our travels.'

She laughed easily. 'You'll have a younger mistress then, for sure.'

'Probably,' he grinned, 'but there'll always be a special place for you in my heart.'

It was the old fiction they maintained, that their time together was a fleeting moment and sure to pass, but just at that moment, neither of them believed it.

Silence enfolded them once again, a silence broken only

by the far murmur of the sea and the blackbird singing above them. Margaret fell to wondering what sounds she would remember for Trecarne. In her mind the farm at Conwinnion was wreathed around with the cries of rooks while William's Porthew house was dominated by the constant calling of the gulls, but here . . . ? She was not sure. Once she was far away, then she would know.

Richard looked up, frowning. 'Who the devil comes to disturb us now?'

There was the scrunch of footsteps stumbling over the gravel path towards them and a rasping breath.

They both turned at once but it was a few moments before either of them recognised the filthy and exhausted figure who stood before them. But those huge ears could only belong to Giles.

'What's the matter, man? Are you wounded?'

He shook his head.

'Then why – ?' Richard's voice was harsh. 'I sent you to be a soldier, did you lose courage so soon?'

Giles was gulping deep breaths but he seemed incapable of speech. He was covered from head to toe in a pale layer of dried mud from his journey; only his eyes, huge and staring, were clear. Margaret stood up and took him by the arm.

'Heavens above, Richard, the poor fellow is so weary he can hardly stand. Come to the house, Giles, when you've had a bite to eat you can –'

'Wait! Let him tell us now.'

Giles swayed, then, sinking down on his knees in front of Richard he stammered, 'I . . . he . . .' before falling silent once again.

A strange smile began to spread across Richard's face. He said, 'Your orders were to stay with Mr Sutton. I trust you have not –'

The lad shook his head and said suddenly, 'You told me to stay with Mr Sutton until he . . . until – this day he lies at Rossmere,' and he sank back on his heels and buried his face in his hands while his whole body shook with noiseless grief.

Richard's face was a cold mask of fury. 'Nick?' he said. 'Dead?'

648

Giles nodded hopelessly.

No one spoke. The stillness of the evening was huge, a vast shroud of silence stretching as far as anyone could see. The sun was sinking behind the steep roofs of the house and in the shadows it was grown suddenly cold.

Margaret looked first at Richard, then at the groom. 'Sit down, Giles,' she said gently, 'and you can tell us everything.'

She helped him on to the bench and then stood in front of the two men. Giles wiped his eyes on his sleeve and, staring at a patch of ground just in front of his boots he began, 'I don't know if I did right, but when he fell . . . he told me to take him home again and his wound was not grave, or so it seemed to me then . . .' He swallowed, took a deep breath, carried on, 'He rode like a man possessed. I had a hard time keeping up with him, but I remembered what you had told me and I tried . . . the shoulder of his coat was a mess of blood, but he would not stop, not hardly to sleep at night. Then, as we were coming over Bodmin Moor he slowed up a bit and turned round to say something, but I could not catch his words. So I shouted out to him, "What was that, Mr Sutton?" and I kicked my horse on so that I could draw up alongside him . . . but he just stared at me. And then he slid down from his horse and when I went to fetch him up again, he was dead.' Giles's face was streaked with tears. 'Did I do right, Mr Treveryan? I keep thinking that maybe –'

Richard interrupted him coldly. 'His body is now at Rossmere?'

Giles nodded.

'Then tell me exactly what happened, and slowly, and I can judge if you have acted well or –'

'Very good, sir,' he paused, took a long breath to calm himself and began again, 'We'd gone a long way from Cornwall, somewhere between Cornwall and London, Mr Sutton told me, but I never knew exactly where. We all knew that everybody feared the Cornish. We'd had a fine victory at Stratton, I daresay you've already heard how the rebels ran from us like rabbits and hardly any of our side were injured. That was when Sir Bevil Grenvile told us we were the best troops in the King's army and that's the truth –'

'Get on with it, Giles. And after Stratton?'

'We marched. We were all so fired up after our victory that it didn't seem too bad and we marched for days, I've lost count of how many. Then we joined up with another army, even larger than ours. You've never seen so many men, Mr Treveryan, there must have been thousands of them, tens of thousands, it made me giddy just to look at them. When I saw how many were fighting with us I thought the war must be over soon, for sure. Everybody was in good spirits to see so many on the King's side, even though we were far from home. With such an army we thought it would be simple enough to march on towards London, join up with the King himself on the way and bring the rebels to heel. We were confident of being home again soon.'

'And so?'

'We never got to London. The rebels had taken a hill, near to a town they called Bath and I believe that's pretty near to London. It was a good choice, being a steep hill and easy enough to defend. They had placed musket men all around it, behind all the hedges and ditches and there were plenty who said it would be madness to try to shift them. But Sir Bevil said the Cornish could take the hill and he led the pikemen on and Mr Sutton rode with him. I truly believe we would have followed them into the mouth of Hell itself if they had told us so. The rebels had cannon and muskets and cavalry and they beat us back once and then again, but we kept on. Ambrose Treloar was there at the head of the pikemen and he was roaring and fighting like ten men, and Mr Sutton rode past and cheered him on. But there was such a cloud of smoke from the muskets it was worse than a sea fog and you could barely see your hand in front of your face.

'Twice we fought our way up that hill and twice we were beaten back, but the third time all the pikemen were packed so close together, and Sir Bevil and Mr Sutton riding with them and I was there too and they could not force us back. And when we had word that Sir Bevil was killed, there was such a rage against the rebels that no power on Heaven or earth would have shifted us from that spot and have him die for nothing. And someone lifted Sir Bevil's son on to

650

his horse and put his father's sword in his hand – the lad's only a child, not more than twelve – and the boy was so shocked you could see he hardly knew what he was doing, but he kicked his horse on all the same, and Mr Sutton and the others stayed close by to shield him from harm – and then we kept on until we knew for sure that we had won. No one could ever budge us from that hill. Lansdown Hill, they called it. And the officers all rode up then and said it was the best victory for King Charles since the fighting began. And it was the Cornish that did it, Mr Treveryan, those up-country cavalrymen were no more use than a three-legged pony –'

'And Mr Sutton?'

'He fought like a soldier born, no one could touch him for bravery. But the battle was so thick as we approached the summit of the hill that I lost sight of him towards the end. When I found him again it was nearly dark and he was sitting with a group of gentlemen and laughing with them. It was them who said what a great victory this had been. And then I said, "Mr Sutton, sir, look at your shoulder, it's all bloody," and he told me not to bother with it, he would get it dressed by and by. But the next morning when I spoke to him again, he just smiled and patted me on the shoulder and said, "We've done our bit for the King, I think, Giles. Now let's get ourselves back to Rossmere." And I wanted to do something for his shoulder, but he would not even take off his coat to let anyone see the wound – I think in his heart he knew already it was mortal. But all he said was, "Let's get moving, Giles, I've a mind to see my home once more." And so we saddled up and left. Did I do right, Mr Treveryan? I'm plagued with the thought that if I had but made him wait, if someone had only dressed his wound –'

Richard ignored the question. He was staring down the valley at the iron-grey sea and the white rim of foam in the bay and his face was without expression; he seemed hardly to have been listening. Then he muttered harshly, 'Nick, you've always been a fool for that damned home of yours.'

'Did I do right, Mr Treveryan, sir?'

Only then did Richard acknowledge the question, but all

he answered was, 'Right? What has right got to do with it? He's dead, isn't he?'

Margaret reached out her hand to comfort him, but he brushed her angrily aside and strode off towards the bay.

Giles buried his face in his hands. Margaret touched his shoulder and said gently, 'You could not have stopped him once his heart was set on coming home.'

'Do you really think so?'

'I'm quite sure of it,' she told him. 'Come to the house, Giles. I'll order up food and drink for you and then you can rest. You have done all that you could.'

But Margaret was haunted by the image of Sir Bevil Grenvile's twelve-year-old son in the thick of the battle and when Giles had downed a mug of ale she asked him, 'Did you hear anything of my Luke? They say he is marching with the rebels. He's too young to fight, but he plays the fiddle.'

Giles had no news. Margaret told herself that it was only gentlemen's sons who were useful in battle, a child like Luke was sure to be left behind with the baggage and the wounded.

In fact Giles had barely heard her question, so dazed was he by exhaustion and the events of the previous few days. He had grown to like Nicolas Sutton, who was cheerful and an easy-going master to serve, but his grief was more a reaction to the piled-up horrors he had witnessed at Lansdown, the frightening responsibility of bringing his injured master home and then, worst of all, the long long journey, hardly daring to pause for sleep, with the corpse draped over the second horse. Ghosts and imps had always frightened Giles more than any rebel army could have done, and by the time he deposited his tragic burden at Rossmere, he was almost out of his wits with fear. Margaret, perhaps sensing this, or perhaps because she needed to occupy herself somehow while Richard coped alone with the first impact of his loss, stayed with him and talked to him until he collapsed on the settle by the kitchen fire, and slept.

Richard was gone for a long while, not returning until grey dusk was filling the corners and passageways of the house with shadow. Margaret was in the lower tower room. She was busy with some sewing, a task she normally avoided, and repeating under her breath the names of the ports they were to call at on their voyage: anything to keep her mind occupied and away from thoughts of the twelve-year-old boy in the midst of the fighting, away from thoughts of Mistress Sutton at Rossmere and the handsome, wounded, tomb-cold body of her young husband. The work kept those unwelcome images at bay, just as she had learned not to brood herself into misery over the fate of her lost son.

She looked up. Richard was standing in the doorway watching her. There was something so dejected, so haggard in his stance that, for the first time since Giles had come with the news, Margaret felt her eyes fill with tears.

'Oh Richard,' she stood up, laying aside her sewing, 'I am so sorry. I know how much you cared for him.'

She began to go towards him but he raised an arm as though to ward her off and said in a harsh voice, 'Confound you, Meg. It is you have done this to me.'

'What? What have I done?' She stood quite still.

'You have made me –' He broke off.

Suddenly Margaret was afraid to move or speak. Her fear grew until it was a huge thing, banishing grief.

'It's no use, Meg –'

'No. Don't say anything. Not now, not yet. Wait –'

'I must. We cannot sail on the *Herald* after all.'

'Dear God, no, don't speak, please don't.'

He turned away from her agonised face, slumped down hopelessly in a chair and said, 'I cannot leave them now.'

'But why – ?'

'I hardly know the reason. I only know I cannot do it. Maybe later. When this slaughter is ended.'

Margaret drew in a sudden breath. 'You surely do not mean to fight?'

'So help me God, I do.'

'Why?'

He shrugged. 'I wish I knew. Not for the King, nor for principle, nor for the bishops or the old ways or . . . you see, Meg, I thought I could stay detached from this war, as I have always been detached from the concerns that most affected others but now –' he fell silent for a moment, musing – 'but now I find that is no longer possible.'

Margaret was staring at him without speaking, but then,

as though suddenly recollecting herself, she became brisk, moving up and down the room and speaking decisively, as though she had worked out a plan in her head. 'You have always told me, Richard, that anything is possible if one only decides to make it so. This news has been a shock and you are not yourself. As soon as we are on board the *Herald* and out of sight of land you will forget these quarrels. You have told me a hundred times that you care not which side wins, and in the morning, once you are rested and have had time to think this over calmly –'

But he caught her by the hand, interrupting. 'Hush, Meg. It's no use now. Everything has changed.'

'No! Don't say it! You must wait!'

'For what? My mind is already made up.'

'Oh!' She snatched her hand away angrily. She went to stand by the window and hugged her arms about her chest as though for comfort. She said in a low voice, 'And all because of Nicolas Sutton.'

'In part. Perhaps.' Richard's voice was gentle.

'How stupid,' she muttered, 'as though by fighting you can bring him back to life.'

'Only listen to me, try to understand. If I left the country now, how could I live with myself in the future? Sidney Godolphin, Sir Bevil, and now Nick. Meg, these are the men I have known all my life –'

'Yes, and many's the time you said how much you scorned them.'

'Did I? Ah, well,' he smiled awkwardly, 'and maybe I do, maybe I did. But now that they are casting their lives away in a senseless cause, my scorn seems a paltry thing. I cannot abandon them now.'

'In the name of all that's holy,' she turned to him in fury, 'why not? For pity's sake, Richard, they are *dead*! It's too late for them, too late to do anything to help them now. Think of the living, it's not too late for us. We can still leave tomorrow.'

'Impossible.'

'And what of me?' she flung at him. 'Am I now so unimportant that I must make way for corpses? I was prepared to leave behind my own child, my *living* child. I gave up my family and friends, all the ties I had, and willingly, and

654

now you tell me you cannot leave. Richard, do I mean nothing to you at all?'

Her question was a wail of pure despair. Gone was the pretence that she saw their liaison as a passing pleasure that would surely fade as the seasons fade. Seeing her naked pain, Richard longed to take her in his arms and tell her that together or apart, he could never love anyone but her.

Then he remembered Nicolas, and those others, neighbours, friends and enemies alike, and he knew that his present task was to accomplish this difficult parting as smoothly as possible and he said only, 'Yet surely you must understand the reason for my going.'

'How can I?'

In spite of himself he smiled. 'I rather think this is your doing, Meg, this change in me.'

'Oh, what nonsense! Do you mean to drive me mad?'

'You know you're not the kind of vapouring maid who crumbles into pieces when she is left alone for a few months. Listen to me, Meg, and let me try to explain,' and now he was serious again, and pleading with her, 'though Heaven knows I barely understand myself, yet I do believe that you have changed me. Perhaps if we had never had these months together, if I was still . . . then maybe I could turn my back and convince myself that Grenvile's death, Godolphin's death and . . . and now Nick's death too and a hundred others besides, that all these were no concern of mine, but now . . . well, now I find I cannot do it.' She was staring at him as he spoke and she saw that his gaze was very steady, very sure. 'And I do not believe, for all your protest, that you would have me decide any other way.'

For a little while she did not speak. She was remembering the last conversation she had had alone with Nicolas. He had appealed to her as a woman of honour to use her influence to persuade Richard to join the fight. She did not feel herself, just then, to be a woman of honour. She felt that Nicolas, by dying, had beaten her at last, and briefly, she hated him for it.

'But you're wrong, Richard. I do not want you to fight. I want nothing that threatens to come between us.'

'If you were in my position, you know you would do the same.'

'Would I? Richard, I turned my back on my own people when I left Porthew.'

'But never completely, Meg. At the time it was not always easy for me to understand you, but I tried. When you refused to leave because of Luke, I did not really understand your reasons, but I tried to, you know I did. And then again, when you stopped me from shooting at Treloar –'

'Oh, that's not fair!'

'Isn't it? I'm asking you now to believe that I *must* fight, even though it seems a nonsense to you.'

'Oh Richard, why?' She sank down on her knees in front of him and laid her cheek against his sleeve. 'I only know,' she said in a low voice, 'that if anything ever happens to you, then I shall die.'

'Never worry on my account,' he smiled, 'I'm not such a hero that I intend to throw my life away in their wretched cause.' And he began to stroke her hair gently. 'Besides, after their great victory at Lansdown I'm sure the fighting must be nearly over and I shall arrive just in time to get a knighthood for my valour and be back at harvest.'

'God make it so. But still I wish you would change your mind. You know I have never asked anything of you before, but now . . . now I am afraid. If we do not take this chance, I have a great fear there will never be another.'

'Don't be so faint-hearted. If you care for me half so much as you say, then you will be waiting for me here when I return.'

She twisted herself away with a sudden gesture of annoyance. 'If!' she exclaimed. '*If*. Why must you torment me always with that *if*?'

He did not answer.

She went on bitterly, 'What must I do to convince you of my feelings? I have given up everything for you, even my child, and you continue to insult me with your doubts.'

Richard remained silent. He was reminded suddenly, uncomfortably, of those times in the beginning when Kitty had wept and raged in her attempts to keep him at her side. He grew impatient. Already he was beginning to consider which men to take with him when he left, and he began to see that parting might be less painful if it was done with coolness.

He said, 'I was not aware that you regarded this as such a sacrifice.' He stood up and looked down at her coldly. 'You may rest assured that you will be well provided for during my absence. And now I must give orders for my departure.'

Margaret watched him leave the room and her face was taut with anger and despair. As though all her future was rushing from her grasp and there was nothing whatsoever that she could do to prevent the certain catastrophe.

That evening, when they sat down at the polished oak table, they were stiff and formal with each other, and their appetites were as impoverished as their conversation. The plates of food were sent back virtually untouched.

Towards the end of the meal Richard looked up and commented, casually enough, 'If at any time during my absence you decide to quit this place, I shall leave orders with the steward that you are to be given any money you require, or whatever else is necessary.'

Margaret raised her eyes to gaze at him across the table, then looked quickly away. She was wearing a dress of deep blue material that glowed with all the shifting colours of a summer sea. Richard thought with a stab of pain that he had never seen her look so beautiful, and he was on the point of retracting his harsh words, when she replied scornfully, 'I sometimes wonder, Richard, if you have ever known me at all.'

And later, when they drew the tapestry curtains around the bed and laid themselves down for sleep, they barely spoke, no words to break the sound of the gentle winds shifting through the oak woods. Margaret, lying wide-eyed in the darkness, tried not to think of the small pack that stood waiting by the coffer for Richard's early departure in the morning. Nor of her own quantity of belongings all packed and ready for a journey that had been postponed, perhaps for ever. Nor of the endless days of waiting that lay ahead. Nor of Richard lying beside her in the huge bed, so close, yet already, in spirit, so infinitely far away.

Separate and cold as stone effigies on a grey tomb they eventually slid into sleep. Yet when they awoke in the early

657

dawn light their bodies were entwined in their usual tangle of affection, arms around each other as if their quarrel had never been.

'Our flesh is wiser than we know,' murmured Richard, brushing his lips against her cheek.

Margaret did not trust herself to speak, only wound her arms around his back, felt the press of his body against hers, his warm night-time smell, the bones and skin and muscle and hair that she knew and loved better than her own, and she closed her eyes and willed this moment to stretch into eternity.

Soon, too soon, his tall bay was saddled and brought round to the front of the house and Richard, dressed in the buff coat and breast-plate of a soldier, a heavy sword hanging by his side and pistols in position across his saddle, was ready to depart. Now that he was girded about with the accoutrements of a soldier, he found himself eager to be a part of the conflict which he had ignored for so long. But when he took Margaret in his arms for the last time, he wanted only to remain here with her for ever.

Almost angrily he pushed her away, ignored the tears that were brimming in her eyes.

'Will you be standing here when I return?' he asked.

Her laugh was almost harsh. 'You know I must, Richard. After all, I have nowhere else to go.' And then, as he turned to walk away from her and down the steps to where his waiting horse whinnied and fretted to be off, she burst out, 'I have loved you from the day I saw you first, Richard. How could I stop loving you now?'

He came to an abrupt halt. Her question echoed through the noontime stillness. He hesitated, but did not turn to face her. She saw the flicker of a muscle on the edge of his cheek, his hand twitch as though he was about to reach out, reach back . . . but then, gathering up all his strength and coldness, he continued resolutely down the flight of steps and took the reins from Giles's hands and swung up into the saddle.

At the head of a small retinue of tenants and serving-men, each hastily cobbled together in a variety of costumes suitable to a soldier's life, Richard cantered off down the driveway that had once been a part of the Treloars' near meadow.

Margaret stood on the step for a long time, shielding her eyes with her hand, and watched the emptiness where the riders had been.

29

Richard had not travelled far along the Helston road when he took his men, without a word of explanation, down the side road that led to Rossmere. He had not told Margaret of his intention, not wishing to add to her distress, but he planned a last visit to Rossmere before the long journey to seek out and join the main body of the King's army in the west.

The day was overcast and a fine sprinkling of rain was beginning to fall as the troop of horsemen rode the last mile to the house, and Richard noticed, in an abstracted way, that Sir John's avenue of young limes was now grown to a commendable size. As they passed beneath the archway into the stable-yard a flock of pigeons and white doves rose into the air and curved in a wide arc to settle again on the stable roofs.

Richard dismounted and, as had always been his habit, entered through the back of the house. The kitchen was unnaturally quiet. Joan Treworgie sat plucking a brace of ducks near an open window and the feathers fell light as ash from an autumn bonfire around her feet. He was reminded suddenly of the occasion – how many years ago had it been? twelve? thirteen? – when he had raced through the goose-feather-snowy kitchen because he expected to find Alice Laniver waiting for him so that together they could tell the world they were to be married.

And now he was visiting her again, and she was another man's widow.

He paused, turned to say something to Joan Treworgie, but noticed that her face was blotched with tears and she had not even noticed him. Quietly, he went on through the kitchen, crossed the grassy courtyard to the hall.

The high-ceilinged hall where he had fought with Nicolas was empty, save for a wooden coffin supported by two stools before the hearth. Glad at least of solitude, Richard went and stood beside the coffin. His face betrayed no emotion as he stared down at its polished surface. The lid was not yet secured but he found he had no wish to lift it free. Better to remember the vigorous, living face of the friend who had always cared for him, and never understood . . . He remained for a long time without moving, until, with a rustle of petticoats, Alice herself came into the room.

'Richard.' She did not sound pleased to see him.

He turned to look at her and saw that she was very pale. 'I wanted to come here once again before I left. To say goodbye.'

'Ah yes,' she said coldly, 'you intend to travel abroad.'

'My plans have changed. I am on my way to join the King's forces.'

Richard noticed then that despite the pallor of her face and the shadows under her eyes which told of a sleepless night, she did not look as if she had been crying. He guessed that she was still protected by the merciful calm of shock.

'So why this sudden change of heart? Nick . . .' her voice faltered slightly, she frowned and went on, 'Nick told me many times that you refused absolutely to be a part of this fight and showed a perverse determination to remain aloof. He could not comprehend it.'

Richard's mouth twisted in a wry smile. 'Just as I have trouble understanding my present wish to be a soldier. Except that it is somehow connected with –' and he gestured towards the coffin – 'to do with this.'

She avoided looking at the coffin. 'Nick was always grieved by your decision.'

'I know. And I'm sorry. He should have known me better than to be surprised. And he has no reason now to grieve.'

'No!' Her voice was a little squeak of anger. 'Not now he's dead!' She turned abruptly and went to stand by the window. The slump of her shoulders was so dejected that he hesitated only for a moment before crossing the room to join her.

'Alice,' he said in a low voice, 'I am so sorry.'

'Yes,' she twisted round to face him, 'I know.'

'If I could only bring him back . . .' And he put his arms around her and held her tightly, and wondered at how small and plump she was, and though she did not cry he could feel waves of emotion shuddering through her body.

After a little while she detached herself carefully, patted her cheeks with a kerchief and smoothed her hair before saying gently, 'Will you do one last thing for me, Richard?'

'If I can.'

'Then stay at Rossmere tonight. I have been so frightened here since . . . since the news came. The house has changed, I don't know how to explain, but it feels as if it is full of ghosts, and not only because of –' Still she could not bring herself to look at the coffin. 'Sir John is all demented with the shock and Stephen and most of the men are away and I do not know what to say to the children to comfort them. Be company for me, Richard. Tomorrow I'll be strong again.'

He did not see how he could refuse.

'Very well. If arrangements can be made for my men to rest here also. But I must leave early.'

At some stage during that long afternoon and evening Richard came bitterly to regret his decision. It was not the sorrow in the household that troubled him: he talked with Sir John and with the older children and with those of the servants who had been most deeply affected by the loss, and there was a kind of grim satisfaction, almost a rightness, in their eagerness to share memories of the dead man. And Richard was glad to do it, as much for his own sake as for theirs.

It was Alice herself whose company so grated on him that by dusk he was wondering if there was an excuse he could conjure up to bring forward the hour of his departure without heaping fresh offence on her sorrow.

That evening they ate in the solar. Sir John was persuaded to join them but he was too distracted to eat and his man-servant helped him early to bed. Alice had ordered up a copious supply of good wine and by the time Sir John departed and they were left alone together her cheeks were flushed and her eyes glittered.

Richard could not help noticing how much she had grown to resemble her mother, that fluffy duckling of a woman who had so infuriated his own mother on the occasion of

Alice's betrothal to Nicolas. Her hands fluttered with the same ineffectual gestures, displaying jewelled rings, and her voice bumbled on like the drone of some blundering, pollen-heavy bee.

She hardly spoke of her husband. Perhaps she was trying to protect herself from the heartache that was to come. And yet, Richard could not help reflecting, she used strange stratagems. Several times she referred to her youthful courtship with him, and he lost track of the number of occasions she endeavoured, much to his annoyance, to steer their conversation round to the subject of Margaret Hollar. It was clear that the presence of the draper's wife in his house had rankled with her all these months. Richard found it was all he could do to stop himself from telling her to be silent about matters she had no hope of understanding.

He was just wondering how to divert her from the topic when she said, 'And then there was that tiresome business between my poor husband and the blacksmith's simpering wife. Her sister, I believe.' She picked a grape from the bunch in the centre of the table and popped it into her round mouth. 'But of course it was soon over. These liaisons never last,' and she glanced at him quickly, 'do they?'

Richard, who had never considered himself an arbiter of good taste, was dismayed that she should be remembering Nicolas's infidelities in quite such a dispassionate way, on this of all evenings.

'On the contrary,' he said coldly, surprising himself by his reply, 'I believe that where there is true affection —'

'Oh nonsense, Richard,' and she dimpled him a girlish smile, 'you are too much a man of the world to confuse true affection and carnal pleasures.'

Richard forced himself to remain silent.

But worse was to come. The candles were guttering low and Richard could no longer hide his yawns when Alice said suddenly, 'Before you leave in the morning, can you please try to talk some sense into Sir John?'

'Sense?'

'He has mentioned . . . I am fearful he might try to alter his affairs now, our sons still being so young, and leave the estate to . . . If ever I have to play second fiddle to some young wife of Stephen's I do not think I could endure it.'

And for the first time that evening, he saw her eyes fill with tears.

'I'll see what I can do, though I doubt –'

She looked at him cannily through her tears. 'Nicolas owed you money, I know. If you ever hope to have it repaid, you'd be well advised to help his heirs, for your own sake.'

Richard flinched, then, 'I may have the reputation of a self-seeking scoundrel, Alice, but I am quite capable of helping the family of my greatest friend for his sake and theirs, not my own.'

'Good.'

Richard did not know if he was glad or sorry that she had not even noticed his reproach. He rose abruptly and said that as he had a long ride ahead of him the following day he would retire early. And he was sure she must be tired also.

She raised the candle and came to stand beside him in the doorway.

'Do you remember,' she began, dipping her eyelids in a gesture that verged on coquettishness, 'how you pulled back this very door long ago and all Sir John's serving-men who had been pounding against it came tumbling in a heap? And his expression –! I shall never forget it.'

She continued as they climbed the wide stairs. 'I am glad you have decided to fight for the King. Nicolas said you refused to join him because you had been bewitched by that Hollar woman and . . . I did not like to think of you being bewitched by anyone.'

Except for me, her eyes said as she bade him good night.

A huge sadness was weighing Richard down as he closed the door of his chamber and prepared himself for bed. He had come here out of some vague desire to say farewell, to make a peace with Nicolas – and had spent the evening being subjected to his widow's flirtatious advances. He wished he was not quite so clear-sighted, that he had not been forced to see in quite such brutal detail the woman in whose company he had been obliged to pass these last few hours. It was not that the young girl with whom he had believed himself to be in love for so many years had been transformed into a shallow and self-centred woman; for he knew, with a certainty that weighed him down more heavily than mere physical fatigue, that Alice Sutton had barely changed at all. As he had seen her that evening, so had she always been. He had squandered years and emotions on an idle dream.

Cynic that he was, his foolishness should have been vastly entertaining, but all he could think of as he fell asleep that night, was a sense of waste.

In the nextdoor bedroom Alice, though light-headed with fatigue and wine and shock, took even longer to fall asleep. She had probably gained even less satisfaction from her flirting than Richard had. There had been no disloyalty to her husband in her actions. In her view of things Nicolas had been her life, the father of her children, partner and, so far as she was capable of it, her love. In the years of widowhood that lay ahead she would never seriously consider remarriage but would fight like a vixen to see Nicolas's children well provided for. And Richard would continue to hold a special position in her affections. She regarded him as her Lancelot; his role was to wear her colours on his armour. When he had fought for her love, her prosaic life had been briefly touched with romance and she had never forgotten it. To her it was unthinkable that her knight errant should debase himself with a tawdry affair with a mere merchant's wife.

She would never tell Richard of the letter she had burnt, but its words returned this night to haunt her. 'Oh my dear heart,' the shameless woman had written, 'how I do miss your laughter and your loving.'

And Alice, half-asleep now, imagined that Nicolas had donned his shift and was lying in the bed beside her. She reached out her arm and, finding only the emptiness of smooth sheets beneath her hands, began at last to comprehend the hugeness of her loss.

There was a bitter aftertaste in Richard's mouth as he rode from Rossmere in the early-morning sunshine, accompanied by his little troop of horsemen. Birdsong and the gossamer beauty of fields and hedgerows, seemed only to taunt him for his folly.

For as long as he could remember he had believed himself

to be moated about with cynicism, yet all the time that very cynicism had been a self-deception and he had been as blind in his dreaming as the most witless schoolboy. He had held fast to the image of what might have been, had turned his first love into an icon that no one else could ever match. He had believed in the illusion of what he had lost. And he had lost nothing. Alice's rejection of him in the letter his mother had brought that day at the mews had been, after all, neither more nor less than a merciful escape.

The horses slowed their pace to climb a long hill and, as they reached the summit, Richard saw, beyond a fold in the hills, a glimpse of blue sea. His spirits began to lift.

He had been a fool and he had wasted time but it was not yet too late to make amends. There was no real reason to lament the loss of his youthful dream, since that delusion had only blinded him to his present good fortune. There was a sense of well-being deep inside him that neither Nicolas's death nor Alice's fall from grace could take away; it was a fullness he had enjoyed for over a year without ever troubling to identify the cause.

Suddenly Richard found himself laughing. Startling his little group of horsemen further by letting out a whoop of joy, he reined his horse to a halt at the top of the hill.

'Giles,' he commanded, 'take them on at a steady pace and wait for me at the Bear in Grampound. I'll catch you up as soon as I can.'

'Why – ?'

'None of your business,' Richard grinned. He wheeled his horse around and set off at a gallop. When Giles saw that he was heading back towards Trecarne the young groom, who was of a soft-hearted disposition and had been troubled by something out of joint in the leave-taking he had witnessed on the steps the previous day, began to ride towards Grampound, well pleased.

Intoxicated by the heady morning air and the richness of all he wished to share with the woman who was waiting for him at Trecarne, Richard galloped between banks of fox-glove and campion. *If* you love me, he had taunted her time and again. *If* . . . as if he had not known the strength of passion that bound them and would bind them always. He did not know by what miracle this had come about, he only knew that he, who had always believed himself to be aloof from any ties, had been ringed about with love from the day Margaret left Porthew and rode with him to Trecarne. Ever since then he had dwelt within the charmed circle of loving that he had glimpsed when he turned to look back on Jennie Treloar and her crippled husband.

Meg . . . Meg . . . there was such a world of words he longed to share with her that came tumbling through his mind as he galloped through the woods towards Trecarne. Their parting had been shabby, a tawdry thing, and the fault was all his. Thank the Lord there was still time to set matters right between them.

Now that he could see matters plainly, their future was clear enough. They must marry. It would be a simple matter to have her marriage annulled: non-consummation would be easy to prove. His own divorce from Kitty would be a more difficult business, but with money and persistence all things were possible, and it was likely that in this topsy-turvy time of war legal niceties could be more easily done away with. He was brimming with impatience as he thought of Margaret's surprise at seeing him back so soon, her pleasure when he told her all that was in his heart.

Meg . . . he murmured, urging his horse on, my own Meg . . .

As was always his preference, he followed the route across the high ground, and the little patch of moor, and soon the steep roofs of Trecarne were below him, and the wide valley of alder and willow that stretched down towards the sea.

Margaret's brief despondency when she saw Richard ride away did not last long. Every parting is a little death, she knew that well enough, but she had believed him when he said he had no intention of throwing his life away in a doubtful cause and she persuaded herself that he would return again as soon as he had seen action enough to purge the memory of Nicolas's death. She had heard it said many times that his ships and his knowledge of the sea were the chief gifts he could offer the King's cause, and as soon as he was once more a master of his own ship, then no power on earth would keep her from his side.

And in the meantime she knew that the first day of

loneliness was always the hardest, so she set about filling the time as best she could. She paid a visit to one of the farm labourers who had injured his back in a fall from a hay wagon, and she arranged with the steward for him and his family to be provided for until he was able to work again. Although Richard had remained true to his vow that he would never allow her to choose those who worked for him, there was little he could do to stop her from ministering to those he did employ and she spent a good while tending a young lad who had injured himself by stepping on a scythe. As she walked back past the mews and the stables she was struck by the uncommon silence of the place: most of the men who worked near the house and almost all the horses had accompanied Richard when he left that morning. Only Will Stevens, too rheumaticky since the illness incurred following his vigils at Ia's Wood to survive a soldier's hardships, remained to tend the unbroken horses and the foals and the single brood mare.

Glancing up from his work he nodded his greeting: although Mistress Hollar's position in the household was irregular to say the least, she had, over the past eighteen months, won the grudging respect of the servants and, whenever she gave orders, she was obeyed at once. Only Hester continued to resent her presence and made no secret of her dislike – but then she had enjoyed the luxury of undisputed power in the days when there had been no mistress at Trecarne to hinder her, and Margaret understood that the old woman missed her former freedom.

In the long gallery she came upon Thomas, a pattern book in his hand. He was vexed with himself because he had forgotten to discuss with Richard the detail he required for the wooden overmantel. He rather thought a heraldic motif might be most suitable but the griffon illustrated looked too much like a lap dog for his taste. He appealed to Margaret.

She was not impressed by the griffon either, and after some thought she suggested that the wood carvers might be more comfortable with a simpler design enhanced by some suitable lettering.

'You have something in mind?'

He had seen the glint in her eye as she had the idea.

'Of course.'

She sat down with paper and ink and he read over her shoulder, *'Nulla domus . . .'* His knowledge of Latin was sufficient to make him smile as he recognised the text.

'Will Mr Treveryan approve?'

'I hope so,' she said, adding inconsequentially, 'it isn't granite, but still, I hope it will suffice. Besides,' she added, and this was what clinched it, 'if he does not, I shall take full responsibility for the decision.'

Thomas was delighted, but Margaret, it seemed, had not yet run out of ideas for surprises for Mr Treveryan.

'You are a painter, are you not, Thomas?'

'It is my first love, but, alas, not profitable.'

'Could you do a portrait of me?'

He looked at her. 'It would be a pleasure. Standing there just as you are by the window, perhaps with a book in your hand. And that dress. I could do it with a simplicity and a care for the light that would rival the Dutch.'

Margaret, who knew nothing of Dutch painting, suggested that they begin at once. And so it was that when Parson Weaver arrived a couple of hours later he found her in a pose of uncharacteristic idleness, standing by one of the windows in the long gallery, a book in her hand while Thomas sketched in the outline and told her about his childhood which had been nothing if not turbulent. His parents, it transpired, had been fervent Catholics and his mother had narrowly escaped execution for harbouring Jesuits.

'That is why I am so scrupulous in my church attendance,' he said with a wry smile; 'outward conformity is all important to someone from a family such as mine.'

'And inwardly?'

He frowned at the canvas. 'I rather think there is no "inwardly". The creation of objects of beauty, such as this fine house and, if we are fortunate, your portrait, seems to be the only act of worship of which I am capable.'

'But you are –' Just what she thought Thomas was, she never said, for at that moment Parson Weaver came into the room. In that instant Margaret realised that she had never seen him dishevelled before. She had seen him irritated, she had seen him bored, but now he looked as though one little thing more would blow him apart entirely. His hair was unkempt, his face flushed, and the look in his eyes . . .

'Parson, what is it? What's the matter?'

'I . . . they . . .' He stared about him wildly. Margaret hurried over to take his hands. He was trembling.

'Is it – ?' She found she was unable to finish her question. Thomas was standing quite motionless in front of the canvas.

'I wanted . . .' the parson stammered, 'both . . . they both . . .' He sank down on his knees and buried his face in her skirts and sobbed like a child.

At first she was so taken aback that she could do no more than murmur meaningless words of comfort while a dread of what he might be going to tell her spread like a film of ice through her heart.

Half-kneeling, she cradled him in her arms. 'Parson, for God's sake tell me, what has happened?'

'My boys –' he choked, 'both my boys – Andrew and Peter, both – both killed at Lansdown. Oh my poor boys –!'

'Oh no! The Lord have mercy on us all,' murmured Margaret, and hung her head in shame at the sweet relief that flooded through her with her sorrow, and she breathed a silent prayer of thanks: praise God it was not news of Luke that had brought the parson to this grief.

'Both my boys –' he kept repeating, 'both my boys –'

Margaret listened and wept with him and in time she sent Thomas to fetch wine. A little later, when the parson was calmer, they sat alone together by the open window and when he had drunk some of the wine, he was able to give her what details he knew. Both his sons had been slain in the savage and foolishly brave assault on the Parliament's hill-top position near Bath, the assault that had claimed Sir Bevil's life and Nicolas Sutton's and a thousand others and which, at huge cost, had earned for the Cornish an unparalleled reputation for heroism. Andrew had died from a musket shot to the head, Peter's leg had been blown away by a cannonball and he had died from loss of blood and shock by nightfall. The list of local men who had been killed or injured in the battle, though not yet complete, was already long.

'And Tom?' Margaret asked in a whisper.

'I have heard nothing, so, God willing, he is spared. And Ambrose too, I know. It is said he sent a dozen rebels to meet their Maker before he reached the top of that cursed hill.'

Margaret thought of the Puritans she had known and their fervent desire to be better acquainted with their Maker and she had a sudden, hysterical urge to laugh, as she imagined how they might thank Ambrose for his assistance.

Instead she said, 'And Nicolas Sutton is dead also.'

The parson leaned his head back against the window breast and closed his eyes. 'And there are many more will die before this slaughter is ended.'

'Richard left to join the King's forces this morning.' Margaret shuddered.

'I thought he was determined to have no part of this fight.'

'He was. But Nicolas's death changed that.'

'So you are alone here now. I did not know. Perhaps that makes it easier.'

'How so?'

He did not answer. Margaret hugged herself for comfort. She felt suddenly cold. 'Dear heavens, what kind of madness makes men fight and kill their own kin?'

'It is not madness, Margaret.' He sighed. 'I could not grieve at home; my poor wife has taken this news so hard, I do not think she will survive it.'

'You are always welcome here, Parson, you know that.'

'I know. But that was not the reason for this visit.'

Margaret said nothing. She was watching a butterfly that was trapped behind the windowpane and wondering whether to reach up and rescue it, but just at that moment, any kind of movement seemed impossible.

The parson continued in a low voice, 'All night I was on my knees in prayer. I was praying for God's guidance, to try to understand why these terrible things are sent to afflict us.'

Margaret noted with interest that the butterfly had now ascended to the top of the window frame and she would have to stand on the seat in order to reach it.

'"I the Lord thy God am a jealous God,"' he said, '"and visit the sins of the fathers upon the children even until the third and fourth generation."'

'This war is men's doing,' she asserted firmly.

'No, Margaret. Just as God sent the flood in the time of Noah, so He has sent this punishment –'

'But Andrew and Peter were fine young men. I do not believe Our Lord is so cruel.'

'Margaret, listen –' his eyes were still closed and a single tear was trickling down his cheek, 'I have not told you all.'

She stood up and shook out her skirts. 'Would you like more wine? You must be hungry. I shall go to the kitchen and arrange for some food to be sent –'

'No –' he waved his hand, motioning her to stay, 'listen to me, Margaret –'

'But it tires you so to speak, Parson. Rest awhile and –'

He opened his eyes, stared directly at her. 'Our Luke has been wounded.'

'Dear God, no.' She sank down beside him.

'Be calm, Margaret, he is not dead. At least I do not think –'

But she did not hear the rest. Although she had been half-expecting the words, in that instant it seemed to her that the floor and the walls, the ceiling and the window and the furniture and everything that had ever been familiar in her life was falling, rushing away on a roaring wind like the wind at the end of the world. Gradually she became aware of the parson's hand gripping hers very tightly, the gentle insistence of his voice.

He was telling her that Master Payne had been killed on the Parliament side. And that the manservant who had brought his body home had told the parson that he had seen Luke on the evening of the battle. He did not know how it had come about but the boy had received a wound to his arm. Being occupied with Master Payne the man had not troubled to find out the severity of his wound, but the lad had lost a good deal of blood and seemed likely to lose his arm as well.

At length Margaret drew her hands away from his and stood up very straight. 'I shall go to this Lansdown Hill,' she said, 'and find him again.'

'That is not the way, Margaret. You will never find him and your efforts would be useless.'

'Maybe not. But I cannot remain here and do nothing –'

'That is the reason for my visit. To tell you what you must do, what we both must do, to make sure he is returned to us, safe and well.'

'I don't understand.'

'Don't you? I have been a sinner all my life, Margaret, and I have comforted myself with the pretence that Our Lord is merciful. Peter and Andrew have been my punishment –'

'Parson, you are overwrought. You surely cannot blame yourself for their deaths?'

'Yes, don't you see? Luke's injury is God's warning to us, but he may yet be saved.'

She was staring at him. 'How?'

'Leave off your evil life. No, wait, hear me out. Why did Luke run away to join the Parliament men rather than come home to you? Was it not his shame at the life you are leading? Don't you know how he was tormented by the other children in the months before William had him taken away?'

'But he need never go back to Porthew. He will be safe with me here.'

'He'll never come back while you are here. Repentance is not enough, Margaret. I know in my heart that I must amend my ways, but if God is to send our son home again, then we both must change. Our God is not mocked.'

After a pause, Margaret said in a voice like stone, 'You waste your time, Parson. I have not seen my son in nearly two years and I cannot believe this is the way to bring him home again.'

'Or is the truth rather that you are not prepared to make the sacrifice? There was a time when you threatened starvation to make William bring him back, yet now, even a little thing is too much.'

'A little thing? Parson, this wicked life, as you call it, is all that I have left.'

'And how long will this last? It has pleased Treveryan to have your company here for nearly two years, but what of the future?'

Margaret said nothing.

'When he has abandoned you and you are alone in the world and have the rest of your life in which to reflect, how will you then look back on a decision that may cost our son his life?'

'Parson, stop! That is not fair!'

But Parson Weaver was not so easily put off. His arguments were relentless and his determination to save his favourite child knew no stopping. He told Margaret all that she had ever been taught of right and wrong and punishment and retribution – all that she had tried so hard to forget. He told her that William Hollar had left Porthew to help the Puritan cause in Plymouth, that Viney and Dorcas were left to manage house and shop between them somehow. He assured her that she would come to no harm on her return to her right home, that he would give her every protection and that besides, the whole world was turned upside-down by the fighting and old scandals were barely noticed any more. He did not tell her, for even in his state of new-found understanding he was still blind to the truth about himself, that he had always wanted her for his own, that he had seized the chance to marry her to a man whom he knew would never be a husband to her because he could not endure the thought that she might one day find happiness with anyone but him; that it had been a kind of torment, these past eighteen months, to witness her happiness while she was with Treveryan.

Nor did he know – no one but Margaret would ever know – how ready she was to believe his words. It seemed to her then as she listened to him, argued with him, pleaded with him, that all her life she had been in the wrong; ever since, when she was hardly more than a child, she had allowed herself to trust this man who had always been a part of her life. She should have given up the temptation of her lessons, should have pushed him away and never returned. She should never have drunk the green potion that her stepmother prepared for her, nor trudged in secret to Father Pym's shack on the moors. She had been glad when she thought William drowned in the storm, she had wanted his death, she who always thought herself so tender-hearted. Worse, worst of all, she had fallen in love with Richard Treveryan when all the instincts of family and friendship should have bound her to her husband, to Lizzie and Ambrose, to Jennie Treloar and her crippled husband. And

674

now she was being told that her son was paying the price for her transgressions.

At length she could stand it no longer. She shouted at him to leave her in peace. 'For God's sake, go!' she wailed. 'Let me decide this for myself.'

Suddenly Parson Weaver was drained of all energy. He had wanted so passionately to make amends for a lifetime's wrongdoing, to bring about the miracle that would restore Luke to the home where he was loved, but now all he could think of was that he was tired. Dog-tired, weary in his very marrow. And that his mouth and throat were parched with a great thirst. He finished the measure of wine that had been brought for him – hours ago, or so it seemed to him now.

'I shall leave you, then. But be warned, I shall not rest in this matter until Luke is safe again.'

He picked up his hat. Margaret was still standing by the window, just as she had been when he came into the room; she was gazing down towards the valley and the bay that he knew her eyes were too weak to see.

He said, 'Goodbye, Margaret.'

But she did not answer.

Hardly making a sound, Parson Weaver left the room.

Will Stevens was well accustomed to sleepless nights. On this July evening it was the brood mare who kept him from his bed. Her foal was coming and she was fretful, showing signs of discomfort.

All day he had missed the company of the stable-hands and others who had ridden away with Richard Treveryan but now, in the summer darkness, he was glad of solitude. Like everyone else in Cornwall at that time, he was absorbing the changed landscape of loss. He had worked many years at Rossmere before coming to Trecarne and he could remember Nicolas Sutton as a cheerful curly-haired boy whom he had placed on his first pony one spring morning in a meadow starred with buttercups, when he himself had been free of his present aches and pains. He had been acquainted with the parson's two sons and besides, his sister's new husband was among those reported dead.

Towards midnight he became aware that he was not the

only person at Trecarne to be kept from their sleep. There was a candle burning in the tower bedroom; he could see it clearly whenever he went out into the stable-yard to stretch his legs. From time to time he saw the candle flame move, as though someone was pacing the room. Restlessly pacing back and forth, unable to remain still. Once or twice he thought he saw a pale face at the window, but in the darkness he could not be sure. It filled him with a sense of unease, that solitary flame, crossing and recrossing in front of the window: like the beacons that men use, he thought, to lure unwary ships on to the rocks.

The foal was born some little while after dawn; a bright, sunshiny dawn after the sombre cloud of the previous day. It was a filly, still slippery black but strong already and quick to struggle to her feet and search out for milk.

Will had just settled himself down on a bench that caught the best of the early-morning sun to indulge himself with a pipe and a well-earned stoop of ale, when he saw a figure crossing the yard towards him. It was a moment or two before he recognised Mistress Hollar; she was wearing a dress of sober grey material and instead of her usual brisk pace she moved slowly, wearily, almost with the gait of an old woman. She carried a small bundle under one arm.

He stood up instinctively and said, 'Mistress Hollar . . .'

'I am leaving, Will.' It was an effort for her to speak. 'It is . . . inevitable, some time. I shall not come back.'

'Why?'

She was about to speak, then she shrugged hopelessly. 'It does not matter. I am leaving, that is all.'

He was silent for a few moments. He noticed that her hands were bare of rings. He asked, 'And the master?'

'I don't know how . . .' She tugged anxiously at the strap on her bundle.

'Your mind is made up?'

She nodded.

'Then shall I saddle you a horse, my lady?' It was the first time that he had addressed her that way, and he was not quite sure why he did so now. 'The best are all gone, but I can find a pony will serve –'

But she shook her head. 'I shall leave as I came,' she said, 'with nothing. Goodbye, Will.'

'God be with you, Mistress Hollar.' To his annoyance Will found that his eyes had filled with tears and he considered it most unfair that he should be confronted with yet more sorrows when he had spent the night in contemplation of so many. Yet although this was a small tragedy on the scale of the great griefs that were sweeping through Cornwall at that time, Will found himself regretting that the rheumatism in his joints caused by long hours waiting at Ia's Wood had been all in vain.

She had only taken a few steps when she hesitated, then turned back to him once again. 'Will, may I ask you something?'

'Of course.'

'If Mr Treveryan returns – *when* Mr Treveryan returns, you must tell him that . . .' She broke off, frowned, plucked anxiously at the cuff of her sleeve, began again, 'Tell him never to try to follow me. I never wish to see him again. Tell him that – tell him that I found I could not wait for him, after all.'

'Is that all?'

'Yes. I could not wait.'

'Very well then, I shall tell him.' Will tried not to imagine the likely response this news would provoke in his master.

'Thank you,' she said.

And with that she turned and walked quickly away. And although the morning was warm, with no breeze at all, she walked with the dogged steps, shoulders hunched and head bowed, of someone who must make their way against a tremendous wind.

She took the road back to Porthew along which she had walked on those spring mornings when a fardel of cloth was all the excuse she needed. And she was so absorbed in the painful necessity of her journey that she never heard the horseman galloping back towards Trecarne along the higher ground.

30

The Cornish infantry who had achieved such a heroic victory at Lansdown Hill went on, before July 1643 was over, to storm the Parliamentary citadel of Bristol. This city, second only to London in importance, was a crucial acquisition for the King's side. But a terrible price was paid for their achievement. Sir Bevil had died at Lansdown, Sir Nicolas Slanning and John Trevanion were both killed in the assault on Bristol, and by that time half the men who had left their homes with such high hopes to join the royal army had been slaughtered with them. Those who remained were weakened and demoralised. It was their local leaders they had followed. Now they found themselves far from home at harvest time, in the service of strangers and a distant king.

In the south-west, only the city of Plymouth was doggedly holding out for Parliament, and repeated attempts to capture it were unsuccessful. Richard Treveryan, as Margaret had anticipated, soon abandoned soldiering for, from a strategic point of view, the more profitable task of using his ships to harass the Parliament-controlled navy.

Yet within twelve months of the great victories at Lansdown and Bristol, the West Country, for so long the bedrock of royalist strength, was crumbling before a Roundhead army of eight thousand men led by the Earl of Essex. At the beginning of July 1644, almost exactly a year after Margaret had left Trecarne for the last time, the King's forces in the west were facing catastrophe. Sir Richard Grenvile, younger brother of Sir Bevil and a recent recruit to the Stuart cause, was forced to abandon the siege of Plymouth and retreat across the Tamar and into Cornwall. He took with him less than a thousand men and many of these, believing their cause already lost, were negotiating in secret with the Earl of Essex, hoping to salvage merciful terms for themselves when the inevitable defeat took place.

By the end of July Sir Richard Grenvile had been driven as far as the south-western coast and had come to a halt in Penryn. His situation appeared hopeless: his troops were outnumbered ten to one by the massive army which had already reached Bodmin, only twenty miles to the north, and which was now poised for the final assault. Among the many meetings that took place in Penryn during those frantic summer days were several with Richard Treveryan, who had two ships standing offshore to supply the beleaguered Royalists and protect them from harassment by the Earl of Warwick's navy.

His business with Grenvile having brought him once more to the west of the county, Richard decided to use this opportunity to pay a visit to Trecarne. He had not returned to the place in over a year, not since Will had given him the news which had put him into such a towering rage that he had ridden his horse to the point of death as he galloped away from his home. Prosecution of the war provided an excellent excuse for his long absence – and yet he knew that even if the country had been at peace he would have found some reason to stay away. It vexed him now to think that the memory of old ghosts might hamper his present actions. Besides, Kitty had been obliged to flee her now precarious house in Saltash and had made her way to Trecarne a week or so earlier. Grimly, he ordered one of his captains, of a ship called the *Falcon*, to sail the short distance from Penryn and drop anchor beyond the harbour mouth at Porthew. Four seamen rowed him and a manservant to shore.

Once landed, he was obliged to linger for a while near the entrance to the churchyard while a horse was fetched. Several people recognised him but, as he would have expected had he bothered to give the matter any thought, no one approached to speak with him.

The day was hot. Impatient of any delay, he was glad when a bay gelding was brought: a meaner mount than he was accustomed to but in these times all the decent horses had long ago been taken for the army. He left the town by the road that led past William Hollar's tall house, but he looked neither to the right nor left and soon he had passed the slaughterhouse and the smithy, and had left behind the stench of drains and fish that hung about the town in summer, and was riding between lush hedgerows and fields of silk pale corn.

At the first glimpse of Trecarne he reined his horse to a halt. Work on the central portion of the house had been pretty well completed when he saw it last, and though in his mind's eye, as he gazed down upon it, he sketched in the outlines of the four wings that were also a part of the grand design he and Thomas had planned together, he doubted now that they would ever be built. His manservant, who had picked up scraps of gossip here and there, watched his master carefully as they paused, but Richard's face remained impassive. Hugh Gribble, a Plymouth man who had only been in Richard's employ for six months or so, was hardly surprised: he had never seen his master express any emotion except, under extreme pressure, a cold and lasting rage.

They rode on slowly. Kitty, who had been watching out for her husband's arrival all morning, controlled the impulse, which was strong, to run out on the steps to greet him, and instead remained indoors. In the hallway she welcomed him with her usual combination of eagerness and anxiety. Having arrived at the house a week before, she had quickly put the servants to work altering the arrangements of the rooms. She more than half-expected Richard to react with anger and insist that all be restored to its former condition but, to her surprise (though only half-surprise, she thought, since if she was sure of anything in this life it was that her husband always surprised her) he told her she might do as she wished – and then he ruined her brief moment of satisfaction by adding that the arrangements of the rooms were of no interest to him whatsoever.

Only briefly deterred, Kitty accompanied him on a tour of the house, pointing out improvements both intended and already under way or completed. He paused only to warn her that in the present turmoil of war, her concern for the house was likely to be a waste of time. Kitty suggested they look at the long gallery.

She had been pleased to discover that since her last visit the long gallery, running the entire length of the first floor between the two towers, had been adorned with several excellent paintings that Richard had acquired in the course of his travels. Now she suggested several others that might be brought from Saltash, 'If,' she added petulantly, 'our poor home has not already been plundered by those barbarous rebels.' Richard was aware that much of Kitty's animosity towards the Parliamentarians in Plymouth was due to the fact that her father was prominent among them. His only comment was that she might choose whichever paintings she wanted. His attention had, however, been caught by some lettering carved on the overmantel. Scowling, he demanded of the steward by whose orders the words had been placed there. The steward anxiously replied that he understood Thomas to have commissioned the inscription before he left the previous autumn. To the steward's relief Richard merely shrugged and said it hardly mattered.

Kitty had paused briefly in her chatter. She went to stand beside a canvas, not yet framed, that leaned face against the wall. For a moment or two she stood there, anxiously chewing the inside of her cheek. Since her arrival she had had several long and extremely interesting conversations with Hester, who was now the wealthier by several items of warm clothing that Kitty no longer needed. So far today all had gone well, but even so, she never did know which trivial thing would trigger Richard's anger. Still . . . watching his expression closely she pulled the canvas out and turned it towards him. There was the beginnings of a sketch in oils; a woman, obviously, a woman standing, but the face was a blank. It could have been anyone. Kitty had even considered whether to have her own face placed there, the pose was so tall and stately. To her satisfaction Richard's expression only briefly changed – a passing hint of annoyance.

She enquired mildly, 'And this, my dear?'

His dark eyes met her gaze steadily for a few moments before he turned away and said, with a dismissive gesture, 'I suggest you have it burned.'

More confident than before, Kitty led the way towards the tower.

Here the lower room was so sunny and pleasantly proportioned that she had no hesitation in ordering it to be furnished as her own private retiring room. Richard made no comment, except to congratulate her – in that tone which could have been sincere, or could have been mocking, she had never learned to distinguish the two – on her excellent good taste. One of her first acts had been to move the tapestries depicting Paris choosing among his three goddesses from the four-poster bed in the room above to cover instead these bare walls. For a moment she was afraid that Richard had lost patience with her, since he appeared reluctant to follow her and admire the changes that she had made in the tower bedroom, changes of which she was particularly proud, but then he frowned suddenly and said that he fully intended to see everything, now that he was here again.

Kitty had replaced the tapestries, which she had always thought highly unsuitable, with bed hangings of deep red brocade which she now proudly showed to him. She did not know if she was disappointed or relieved when Richard displayed as little interest in these alterations as he had in all the others. After looking about him briefly he said that while she was, of course, free to sleep where she wished, he had always found this room, with its windows on two sides, to be both inconvenient and draughty. Moreover, he warned her, on winter nights the sound of the wind in the oak woods could be especially tiresome. He would sleep elsewhere.

Kitty pouted and had a hard job to stop herself from stamping her foot. With difficulty she managed a smile and a firm, 'Then I shall sleep where *you* choose.'

Richard looked bored. But just as he was about to tell her that he was to rejoin his ship that day and would remain at sea until the King had no further use for him, so she would be well advised to sleep in the room of her choice, there was the sound of commotion in the room below. And then, a few moments later, the commotion could be heard coming up the stairs.

The door flew open and women's raised voices, the staccato noise of struggle, burst in through the narrow doorway in the shape of three figures, all in varying stages of dishevelment.

Kitty was staring in astonishment at the trio and she

exclaimed to the only one she recognised, 'Hester! What on earth is the meaning of this?'

The housekeeper's face was taut with bitterness at having so obviously been the loser in the recent struggle. Beside her stood a mean-looking fellow with dark hair and a long, doleful face and behind him was panting a woman who was almost as broad as she was tall, and quite remarkably ugly. Though Kitty searched her memory she could not recall ever having seen them before – and she did not think either would be easy to forget.

Hester was just drawing breath to answer the question, when the man took half a pace forward and, looking mournfully at Richard, said, 'If I could beg a few words with you alone, m'lord.'

Richard, who had recognised him at once, answered coldly, 'Explain this outrage at once!'

'But in *private*, m'lord,' he begged.

'You may speak in front of my wife. We have no secrets.'

Kitty experienced a glow of pleasure. She had no idea who this rude-looking fellow might be, but she felt obscurely that Richard was snubbing him on her behalf and the feeling that gave her was as gratifying as it was rare. She did wonder if the bulging woman who had waddled into the room despite all Hester's efforts might be suffering from some form of shock: she was staring at Richard and trembling from head to foot and her eyes were very round. From time to time she opened her mouth but only odd little moans escaped her.

The man licked his lips nervously and ran his fingers round the inside of his collar. Kitty observed that he had a neck like a turkey's gizzard. At length he summoned up his courage and said, 'It was Dorcas here who made me come. She had the idea when she saw you ride past the house, nothing would stop her and I thought . . . well, I hoped . . . well, you see, I could not let her come alone.'

Kitty went to stand by Richard's side and slipped her hand through his arm. She wished to appear like a woman whose husband has no secrets from her, but she was unable to keep the anxiety from her voice. 'Richard, who are these people?'

As if explaining an obscure point of local custom, Richard

said to her, 'First, my dear, you have to understand that there exist, in these wild regions, a few people who have perfected the curious art of mismanaging their households. They select only cretins and vagrants to serve them.' And then, with sudden ferocity he turned to Viney. 'Damn you, man, take your hands away from your throat and tell me why you dare to interrupt us in this outrageous fashion!'

Viney let out a groan. 'Concerning the Mistress Hollar's child, sir –'

Kitty tightened her grip on her husband's arm. Suddenly she found that she was extremely interested in what this dismal-looking man had to say.

Her husband's face remained expressionless. 'Has the lad returned, then?'

'No, sir, there has been no word . . . that is to say . . . I have not heard . . .'

As his words died away the fat woman beside him began to babble, but in her obvious excitement the meaning of her words was somehow lost.

Richard turned to her. 'Dorcas, until you have gained sufficient mastery over the English language to make yourself understood, for God's sake hold your peace or –'

But Dorcas was silent at once. Eyes bulging in remembered terror.

Viney was mumbling in a manner that implied he half-hoped he would not be heard, '– had a daughter at Easter time, m'lord –'

But his words were so indistinct that Richard snapped, 'What did you say?' and Viney had to repeat himself more clearly.

'My mistress had a daughter born at Easter, m'lord.' Viney was not sure if it was correct to address Richard Treveryan as 'm'lord' but in present circumstances it seemed advisable to err on the side of flattery.

Richard flinched as though he had been struck. He did not seem to hear the second part of the man's sentence, that they had brought the child with them from Porthew and that she had been left, at Hester's insistence, in the room below.

It did not seem that Richard heard anything. Gently detaching Kitty's hand from his arm, he walked slowly to the window and stood looking through the rippling glass.

His head was bowed in thought. He might have been quite alone. Memories were flooding through him and he was powerless to prevent them. He remembered the echo of her laughter, her soft voice shaping his name. He remembered the gleam of the pendant lying between her breasts as she stood before him, quite naked in the sunlight. He was remembering how Margaret, when distracted, would put more logs on the fire and how more than once he had warned her that she would one day set the house blazing about their ears. He remembered . . . no more. He bunched his hand into a fist. How he wished now that this whole cursed house was burning, blazing, walls aflame and roof-beams crashing about their ears. However hard he tried to obliterate the image nothing could save him from seeing, with agonising clarity, his own Meg sitting in the large four-poster, curtained all about with Paris and his beauties. She was smiling up at him and, cradled in her arms, there lay a child, her child, their child – and he could almost walk across the room and reach out to touch . . . And this fugitive, hopeless vision was so unbearable that he spun around with a snarl of fury and told Viney to leave the house at once or he'd administer the thrashing himself.

But Kitty, having done some quick calculations concerning dates, had already taken advantage of his brief moment of inattention to assume command of the situation and had sent the seething Hester to fetch this mysterious child. Hester was more out of sorts than ever as she stumped up the stairs a few moments later carrying a tightly wrapped bundle which Dorcas promptly snatched from her arms. A few snuffles from the bundle, and then a feeble wailing.

Kitty had a face like stone. Her shoulders twitched. Nervously she peered towards the swaddled infant.

The next moment she had started back and snapped, 'This is outrageous!'

'Are you gone mad to think of bringing the infant here?' exclaimed Richard.

It appeared that Dorcas had gained some courage by possession of the child, for she glared at Richard and declared, 'But *you* must look after her now!'

'Indeed? Can the woman not even care for her own child?'

Viney began to reply, 'The mistress is –' but Richard's

question had upset Dorcas so much that she began to sob loudly. As the baby was still crying also, Viney had to raise his voice to be heard above the noise. 'Mistress Hollar has been stricken with the fever for nearly a month!' he shouted. 'Dame Watkins is sure she'll die.'

All the colour had drained from Richard's face. He picked up a small statuette that Kitty had placed on the mantelshelf that very morning, and examined it carefully before replacing it once again. At last he said, 'A likely story.'

'It's God's holy truth,' said Viney, and one glance at Dorcas, who was surely incapable of feigning her feelings, was proof enough.

Richard scowled. 'That woman's health is no concern of mine,' he said. 'Now, begone from here, and take these damned caterwaulers with you.'

Viney, sensing defeat, drooped more than ever, but he began to steer Dorcas towards the door. It was Kitty who stopped them. 'Wait a moment,' she said, her voice still stern, but a strange eagerness lighting up her eyes, 'the child appears frail. Has the mother not cared for it properly?'

'She would, she did. But now she cannot, ma'am.' Viney was fidgeting with embarrassment. 'Being so ill . . . and her milk all gone with the fever.'

'I see.' Drawing courage from such clear evidence of a rival's incompetence, Kitty took the still-weeping infant from Dorcas's arms and began to jig it up and down. The wailing developed into howls of anguish.

'For God's sake, Kitty, put the brat down,' said Richard. 'Whether the creature lives or dies, it is no concern of ours. Viney, you must take it back to the draper and if the mother –' he broke off, for some reason unable to finish that particular sentence – 'and if she can no longer care for it herself then he must make other arrangements.'

At the mention of William Hollar, Viney made a sudden, placatory gesture. 'But you see, m'lord, that's just the problem. Mr Hollar sent word from Plymouth that he'll not be foisted with a second –' here the man cleared his throat and glanced anxiously towards Kitty – 'a second bastard, m'lord. He sent word to say that when he returns, if it is not got rid of somehow first, he'll see the child settled where they know how to treat unwanted foundlings. I do think,' and here he lowered his voice to a more confidential tone, 'I do think it was hearing his message made the mistress worsen so fast. For two days now, she's been delirious.'

A chill smile was spreading across Richard's face as he listened, not so much a smile as something resembling the grin of a cornered animal. He said softly, 'Ever the gentleman, God's Fox.'

His words, though gentle, were heard throughout an abruptly silent room. Dorcas had left off her sobbing and was gazing at Kitty with awe. For Kitty, having got nowhere with bouncing the baby up and down, had suddenly taken it into her head to pop her little finger in its mouth. For a few moments there was no sound but a contented sucking, while a confused range of emotions spread across Kitty's pinched little face.

'Oh Richard, look, do look!' She glanced up at him in bewilderment. 'She's smiling at me!'

Richard did not look. 'Then I daresay the poor wretch has already learned to be mercenary,' was his only comment. Then, seeing her delight, he flung up his hands in mock despair and exclaimed, 'However, if you insist on being charitable, then we can give them some money. I'm sure it's all they want, and a good deal more than they deserve.'

But Kitty had not even heard him. Hurrying over to his side, she pulled back the shawl that was covering the baby's head. 'But only look at her, Richard. She is yours entirely. See, she has your eyes and nose. We cannot possibly send her away.'

Richard stared in astonishment at his wife. He had never known such a radiance lighting up her eyes. Not, at any rate, since a Christmas Eve he had long ago forgotten.

'What on earth do you mean by that?'

'Why, that I shall care for her, and keep her. She will be our daughter.'

It was seldom that anyone surprised him, and Kitty he had come to think of as entirely predictable, but he was quite unprepared for this response.

He said sternly, 'Are you joking with me, Kitty?'

She hugged the infant tightly against her embroidered bosom, causing it to whimper once again. 'I was never so serious in all my life.'

And suddenly he knew that she meant it. He glanced briefly at the child – who did indeed appear to have his features, so dark and wizened, poor thing, an unlikely result of the marriage of the fair-haired Mr Hollar and his worthy wife, and so much the worse for her – and turned away to show that he had no further interest in the matter.

'Take her then, by all means, if it amuses you. I'm sure you'll tire of the diversion soon enough.'

Kitty was still holding the child tightly in her arms; she did not look as if she could ever tire of such a gift. Richard smiled at her with sudden indulgence. 'I know how much you have longed for a child. But tell me, are you not troubled by the origins of this one?'

She looked first at the face of her husband, then at the infant, but for once in her life Kitty's emotions were too powerful to allow for speech. Still clutching the bundle tightly to her chest as though afraid someone might yet come and snatch it away from her, she shook her head in silent reply to his question and hurried from the room to search out Will's youngest daughter who had recently had a child herself and was, at present, the only suitable candidate for wet-nurse that she could think of.

Richard turned to Viney. 'A resounding success,' he commented drily, 'you must be very pleased with yourself. Now be off at once, before your luck changes.'

But Dorcas blurted out, 'We must stay with the baby.'

And Viney nodded his agreement. 'We cannot go back to Porthew.'

'What fresh madness is this?' exclaimed Richard in exasperation. 'My wife has shown great kindness towards the child, but you can hardly expect her to adopt you both as well. She is not as soft-hearted as –' he flushed, checking himself just in time.

'We cannot go back,' Viney repeated stubbornly.

'I'm sure your mistress has need of your services.'

'Her sister cares for her now. And Mr Hollar is sure to turn us out when he learns of our visit here today.'

There was no arguing with that statement. Richard asked, 'So why risk your livelihood and home for the sake of a bastard infant?'

'We did not do it for the child. Only for Mistress Hollar.

She gave us everything.' And to his fury, Richard saw that the man's eyes were brimming with hopeless tears.

Ignored by both the men, Dorcas suddenly took in a gulp of air and clasped her hands around her huge stomach and began to explain, patiently, as if to a child, 'Mistress said we must take care of her child and stay with her and see she comes to no harm and always take care of her. And you told me I must always obey Mistress Hollar and do what she said, and so I have and so I will. And so I must stay.'

Richard saw that it would be easier to argue with a pillar of salt than with Dorcas once she believed herself to be acting under orders. Besides, he would soon be aboard his ship again and this whole circus would be behind him. So he gave in. 'Then stay, both of you, and be damned. But in my household, unlike some others, all must work for their keep, and if I ever hear ill-report of either one of you, then you'll both be turned out of doors with a flogging. Hester, take them, and make sure they are useful.'

Hester, looking as though she would rather have administered the flogging, did as she was told. Dorcas was confused as they hustled her from the room since she did not know if it was food or a flogging that lay in store, but Viney was heartily relieved. He could not abide the prospect of returning to the draper's house in Porthew, not because of any promise made on behalf of the baby. But the sight of Margaret's long illness troubled him more than anything he could remember in his life, and he did not want to have to witness her death.

Left alone at last in the tower bedroom, Richard walked slowly towards the bed. He seemed lost in thought as his hand smoothed the rich brocade of the wine-red hangings. His first instinct, now that Margaret's child had been deposited in his care, was to quit the place at once. But he reminded himself that the purpose of this visit had been the vanquishing of old ghosts, and he did not propose to let a mere scrap of an infant send him so quickly into scurrying retreat.

Kitty would have been surprised if she could have seen the half-smile that twisted his mouth as he wondered what magic still lingered in this room that could have made him agree to let that pair remain, the idiot woman and her drunkard husband.

A powerful magic, surely. Some brooding presence that remained to infect the very air he breathed . . . His thoughts were wandering down a dangerous path and he checked them brutally. Darkness and oblivion. The thoughts, those half-remembered fragments of conversation, the echo of a laugh and the bloom of pale skin in the morning light – all these he had learned to strangle in their infancy. He had never allowed himself to grieve for Margaret's loss, and if she was dying now, then he would not grieve for that either. She had chosen her own destiny when she chose to desert him and now she was suffering the consequences. If he had ever thought of her at all during these past months of welcome warfare and bloodshed, it was to remind himself of her betrayal. She had not waited, not even for a day, had left no word of comfort or explanation to soften the blow of her going. Perhaps, he thought cruelly, the truth was that her affections were diluted by being so widely spread. Her sympathy was evoked by every misformed and woebegone creature she came across, and yet she did not have the courage, the tenacity, the loyalty . . . she had not waited. Her great sea of love had turned out to be a paltry thing after all.

He had found strength in hating her this past year. And that strength did not fail him now. He told himself grimly that he was glad of her present illness, her death would not trouble him in the least. The presence of their child in his household was an irritant, might prove to be an unwelcome reminder of what he was determined only to forget, but he did not doubt that Kitty would be weary of her new plaything soon enough.

His hand was no longer smoothing the shining folds of the brocade. It was clenched in a tight fist and the fabric was being crushed into ugly lines. He had decided what he must do. He would stay with Kitty tonight and delay his return to the *Falcon*. In this tower bedroom he would purge the memories once and for all and would give pleasure to his lawful wife who, after all, was nothing if not loyal. And when he rode from here tomorrow it would be as if that other woman had never existed. Once again he would savour the bitter strength of solitude.

Kitty spent a good deal of time trying to choose a name for the brown-haired baby, only to be told by Viney, when Richard had ridden off again next morning, that the girl had already been given a name. He did not say by whom, but then he did not need to. Kitty had for some time been fascinated by and more than a little afraid of this strange woman who had exerted such a powerful influence on her life. She wished she could remember what she looked like, but had only seen her once and had only the haziest memory of the occasion. But during the years since then Kitty had visited so many oracles and soothsayers, and had dabbled so much in those shadowy areas of belief where the teaching of the Church blends with darker secrets and the edge of witchcraft itself in her long search for a child, that she regarded the sudden appearance of this infant as nothing short of a miracle. She would not dream of doing anything that might jeopardise her almost supernatural good fortune. And so, although she might consider the natural mother's choice of name an odd one, she did not for a moment think of challenging it.

Besides, this other woman's influence, which had caused Kitty so many weeks and months of misery when she fretted powerless and neglected in Saltash, seemed now to have been transformed into a power that brought nothing but good. And the woman herself was dying (not before time, Kitty might have added). The evening after the infant's arrival, Richard had taken her to bed in the tower room and had made love to her with a tenderness and passion that brought the years of unhappiness and neglect falling from her body like a shabby coat.

And when she emerged from their night together, she was so mindful of the double miracle that had occurred, that she would have accepted any name, and joyfully.

On reflection she thought the name was not so bad. It had a certain oblique charm.

She learned that when Mistress Hollar's illness took a turn for the worse (and she had not been herself, Viney explained, since the child's birth at Easter time) and she began to consider how her daughter might have to survive alone in a hostile world, she named her Perdita.

By the time Kitty had learned the meaning of the name she had grown too used to it to think of changing.

Perdita, the lost one.

31

At the end of July 1644, while Paul Viney and Dorcas were adjusting to their new life, the royalist defenders of Cornwall, trapped on three sides by the sea and on the fourth by a Parliamentary army of eight thousand men, were on the point of surrender. But on the third of August occurred one of those sudden reversals of fortune which seemed proof to many of divine intervention: the King himself crossed the Tamar at the head of an army sixteen thousand strong and marched into Launceston. Now it was the Earl of Essex and his forces, outnumbered more than two to one and in enemy territory, who found themselves trapped and helpless in the Cornish noose.

Essex, to his lasting shame, slipped away from Fowey in the brief darkness of a summer's night and reached the safety of Plymouth in a fishing boat. His men were not so lucky. The terms of their surrender were generous enough, but the inhabitants of East Cornwall, who had lived in terror of these alien troops for months, were less inclined to be reasonable. The remnants of the Parliamentary army were beaten and robbed as they tried to escape and not many survived the journey.

The devout Puritans of Plymouth still held out for Parliament, but for the rest, the King's cause was secure again. Kitty was able to move her household back to Saltash and the panic that had sent them helter-skelter to Trecarne at the end of July came to have the unreality of a half-remembered nightmare. The Royalists were not yet defeated.

And Margaret Hollar did not die.

When Ambrose Treloar, who had been wounded in the fight at Pennycomequick, returned to the Forge in the late autumn of 1644, he found his sister-in-law still being nursed in his home. For his part, he was glad to leave soldiering behind him, and as his father had died during the summer, he was needed to run the smithy.

Margaret was stronger now, and talking of returning to Porthew. But Ambrose, who had not seen her in nearly two years, was shocked at the change in her. Sometimes he could hardly believe it was the same person who had so stirred and muddled him in his youth: her face seemed somehow washed out, as though the flame that had illuminated it for as long as he could remember, had been extinguished. But then, when he was working in the smithy, he sometimes caught the clear ring of her laughter as she and Lizzie shared some nonsense together over their work in the kitchen. And on a winter's evening, while the wind blew beyond the windows, he saw how her eyes lit up as she held his children spellbound with one of the stories of the heroes she had always loved. And he was reminded of Mattie Pearce again.

Her presence in his house was unsettling. She had been a traitor to everything he held dear, to everything he understood. She had flouted every rule, turned her back on family and friends; above all she had betrayed him by her liaison with his enemy. Yet here she was, eating at his table, playing with his children and chatting with her sister as if nothing whatsoever had changed. He thought he should turn her out, but found he could not even be angry.

Margaret was well aware of his discomfort – but she chose to ignore it. She was discovering that most of her former friends and neighbours could be persuaded to accept her on her own terms. In spite of everything, she had learned to walk about Porthew with her head high, insisting they treat her with respect. And so they did – to her face at least. And what people whispered behind her back, she did not care in the slightest.

The tall house on the outskirts of the town had stood empty for so long that it was cold and damp and dirty. On her return, just before Christmas 1644, she threw open all the windows and lit fires in every room and cleaned both house and shop from top to bottom. A serving-girl was engaged, not quite Dorcas's equal for incompetence, but one who had been deaf since a childhood accident and whose speech hardly anyone but Margaret could understand. Also, a lad was taken from the stocks where he had been placed for petty pilfering and set to be an apprentice in the shop. Hedge, who had reverted almost to a wild state while Margaret was at the Forge, greeted her return with delirious enthusiasm. On the surface at least, a kind of normality was restored.

Margaret worked long hours in the shop. Trade remained slow as long as the country was bled dry by war, but even so, she began to win back some of William's former customers. Even Alice Sutton made her way to buy fabric from Mistress Hollar, and she lingered more than was necessary, attempting to see what, in those pale, tired, almost expressionless features, had exerted such a baffling hold over Richard Treveryan. She went away with no answers to her question, only with the thought that the woman must be cold and heartless who could give up her only remaining child with never a show of regret.

Just how wrong she was, only Margaret knew. And even she sometimes wondered if some essential part of her being had been frozen into a kind of unyielding marble during her difficult pregnancy and the long illness which followed Perdita's birth. She, who had half-expected to die of the unhappiness of parting, had found herself on the contrary to be very much alive. The routines of life continued unchanged, though she herself might pass through the days like a sleepwalker. Eating and sleeping and haggling over prices and living with the rhythms of the church bells and the tides and the changing winds of the seasons. There was pleasure to be had from a warm fire and a glass of wine, pleasure in the first sunshiny days of spring, wildflowers in a jug on the table and the shifting colours of the sea.

And there was satisfaction in her work. She learned the qualities of each type of cloth, its strengths and suitability; she learned to understand her customers and their preferences and foibles. As her health returned she took care to allow herself no time for brooding. She was, however, much troubled by headaches and these were often so severe that for a day or two at a time she could barely move at all. Her search for a cure took her to the wise woman at Coverack who prescribed an infusion of herbs which was sometimes helpful. Margaret also consulted her about her missing son: was he still alive? would he ever return? The woman's answers were ambiguous, leaving Margaret more frustrated and uncertain than before. Of her daughter, growing up in another woman's household, she never spoke to anyone.

Sometimes her long impatience broke out in a kind of helpless rage against the parson. Almost as if she held him to blame for Luke's continuing absence. 'You *told* me he would come back!' she scolded him. 'I have done everything I could but you have done nothing, less than nothing.'

Parson Weaver was feeble in his own defence. Since the death of his sons and that of his wife and youngest child, he was foundering in a sea of confusion. He did not know if he had any regrets; he only knew that when sober he was almost always unhappy and afraid. The remedy was close at hand, and Margaret hardly ever saw him these days but he was drunk, and often incoherent. She turned from him in disgust. It seemed all part of the way her world had been turned upside-down, that this man who had throughout her childhood been the chief source of knowledge and authority, should appear now as a pathetic fool, not even worthy of her anger.

In 1646 the war ended in defeat for the King. The great victories in the West Country were offset by the even greater defeats in far-off Marston Moor and Naseby. Richard Treveryan's house at Trecarne, along with the rest of his property in the area, was given to one of Cromwell's men and no one locally regretted Treveryan's fall. There were various rumours concerning his subsequent fate: he had followed the young Prince of Wales into exile; he had drowned in a skirmish off the Scillies; he had changed his principles to save his skin and was marching with the Puritan army through Ireland; his wife had given birth to a second son . . . Margaret heard the rumours – she could hardly avoid them – but what she made of them, no one could ever tell.

With the lifting of the siege of Plymouth, William Hollar was free to come home. His faith in the God who had saved him from the storm to execute His will, had been daily reinforced by the heroism and fervour of the siege. His life had been in peril a hundred times, others had been slaughtered or maimed – and he had been spared. His belief was now unquenchable. But his body was all but destroyed. Near-starvation, fasting and sleepless nights spent in prayer, the constant din and danger of cannonfire had left him a prey to sudden fevers and bouts of weeping. Often he had hardly the strength to cross the room and an unexpected noise could put him into a state of shock and trembling that lasted all day.

He was furious at what he called Margaret's gross presumption in taking over the shop, but her days of compromise were over. A series of bitter arguments took place. But it became obvious, almost at once, that William no longer had the stamina to do much more than fret over his bookkeeping from time to time; the bolts of cloth were too heavy for him to lift and the customers irritated him. His few reserves of strength were needed for prayer and reading the Bible. So Margaret remained in command of the shop. The arguments died down and William discovered that the apprentice she had hired was quick to learn. He took pleasure in encouraging the boy's progress.

And then, one day towards midsummer, a tall gangling youth was seen approaching on the Helston road. He paused briefly at the Forge for a sup of ale and a bite to eat – long enough at any rate to set Lizzie sobbing into her apron for joy – before travelling the last half-mile to the draper's house. He was so thin you could count the ribs on his chest and there was a long scar that ran the length of his arm from shoulder to wrist, and a strange look in his eyes of a youth who, too soon in childhood, had seen the horrors that men do, but Margaret, glancing up from the bowl of rose petals she had gathered for drying and seeing the stranger who stooped to enter the kitchen doorway, recognised him at once, as she would have recognised him if she had had to wait until they were both old and wizened before they met again.

'Oh –' she was trembling from head to foot, 'Oh –'

'Mother,' he said, almost fearfully, 'it's me.'

'Oh my Luke!'

He laid his fiddle down on the table and took a step towards her and she put her arms about his bony shoulders. 'Oh Luke, I don't believe it.'

'It's me, Mother. I'm home. Please don't cry.'

But she could not help it. On the day Luke came home she cried as she had never cried when he left, nor when she had walked away from Trecarne, nor when Viney and Dorcas had removed her infant daughter for safe-keeping. And William, who had always loved him like a son, watched from the parlour doorway and wept with them.

Luke comforted her as best he could. Mother and son were shy with each other at first; so much love between strangers is hard to comprehend. That evening Parson Weaver came to the house to hear the wanderer's story, and he remained sober for three whole days afterwards.

Over the following weeks Luke told his mother much of his adventures (though not all: there was much that had happened which he never spoke of). How Nathaniel, the ostler with whom he had run away from Plymouth, had managed to get him back to his family's farm in Devon; the slow healing of his wounds; the suffering endured by the country people as first one army and then another stripped the land bare of crops and animals and every last crumb of food and the sea of war washed back and forth and seemed as though it would never end. Of how he had saved the money for his journey home only to be robbed at the first inn where he stopped for the night.

That was the summer when the changes that William had so long prayed for were finally set in motion throughout the Church in Cornwall. At first Parson Weaver, like most of the clergy, bowed to the inevitable and, unable to square his conscience, he drowned it in alcohol instead. But then he discovered a fixed point within himself beyond which he could not persuade himself to go and so he was 'outed'. His position was taken by a young vicar much given to talk of smiting and lamentation and who disapproved of the frivolity of Christmas and music and dancing. For a couple of years Parson Weaver eked out a scant existence on charity; Margaret was visiting him with cheese and ale on the morning that he died.

He had been waiting for her. He wanted to tell her that all his life he had been wrong; he had always seen Death as his enemy. In countless sickrooms he had fought with that spectral figure, had feared him and tried to outwit him. But now, as he prepared for the next stage of his journey, he saw that Death was not his enemy at all, but rather a friend, a welcome deliverer.

But when Margaret set down her basket beside his bed, he found that he only had the strength to tell her that whatever he had done, he had always had her interests at heart. Margaret did not answer straight away. She smoothed his rumpled sheets and thought for a while. She had been angry with him for so long but now she did not have the heart to contradict his lie.

Eventually she said, 'There is nothing in my life that I regret, Parson. If I had it all to live again I'm sure I'd make the same mistakes. Luke is home. And I've been lucky.'

Later, as she walked home, she wondered if her words had been only to comfort the parson, or to comfort herself, or if, perhaps, they had been the truth. It was a grey-cold March day and the primroses that lined the path seemed too early, too palely fragile to survive. In spite of everything, Margaret decided, she had indeed been lucky. She had known what it was to love and to be loved. And in spite of everything, one single prayer remained – that she would one day hold Richard Treveryan in her arms again, and tell him she would always love him.

On the morning of Parson Weaver's funeral (and no one, locally, could ever leave off the habit of calling him Parson, no matter how much the zealous new minister might fret) Margaret came into the kitchen to find Luke replacing one of the strings on his fiddle.

'Are you not going to the funeral?' she asked.

'I might.' He seemed intent on his task but then, in a voice so soft she barely caught the words, he asked, 'He was my father, wasn't he?'

Margaret stood very still. 'Yes,' she replied, 'do you want me to tell you?'

He shook his head. His glance slid sideways, avoiding her. Margaret waited, hardly daring to breathe. Luke smiled cruelly. 'You made a muddle of everything right from the start, didn't you?'

Margaret could have defended herself against anyone else, against all the world, but never against him. She said only, 'It made sense at the time.'

He raised his eyes to look at her, and his smile was no longer cruel. 'There's no one else like you.' He put his arms

699

around her shoulders and hugged her. 'You and your loving muddles.'

A few months later Luke told them he was leaving. Margaret noted with satisfaction that he was looking younger now than on the day when he had arrived; his tall frame was fleshed out, his cheeks had a good colour and his eyes had lost their restless, shifting expression and looked directly at the person to whom he spoke. She had known for some time that he no longer felt at ease in Porthew, and that he had not yet reached the age when a settled life has any appeal and so she had been expecting his decision. She heard him out with equanimity and then, just before he left, she gave him the ring she always wore, the one that had been the foreigner's. 'You and I have much in common,' she told him. 'This will always be our home, yet neither of us ever truly belongs here.' He told her that he would return within a year, two at the most.

So Margaret was once more alone with her husband in the draper's tall house. And to their neighbours it seemed that they had achieved a kind of contentment.

The Cornish had ceased to play any real part in the events taking place on the wider stage. Most of them had supported the King with all the strength and energy they had, thousands had died, thousands more were injured, and in the end it was not enough. In February 1649, a winter of raw cold and drizzle, came the news that was at first met with stunned disbelief: King Charles himself had been sentenced to death by Parliament and, in the palace yard at Westminster, beheaded. For several days a kind of shocked silence, a numbness, hung in the dank winter air and men and women went about their work quietly. This murder of a lawful king seemed an act beyond treason, a kind of blasphemy, and people waited for certain retribution on the culprits. They waited in vain. Incredible though it might be, the perpetrators of this foul act of regicide were not struck down; on the contrary, they prospered, order was restored to the country, trade flourished, and that year's harvest was better than most. Defeated and baffled, people turned their backs on events in London and Plymouth. They might fret about the dour morality that Parliament had seen fit to impose, but the spirit of rebellion had been extinguished.

Or merely driven underground. A king may be executed but there will always be a successor. Charles Stuart, son of the martyr, had survived to provide a focus of hope for all those who wanted the monarchy restored. And the Cornish were surprised when it was the Scots, those very men whose insurrection against Charles I had been the origin of all his troubles, who now crowned the son King Charles II in his place.

Richard Treveryan had always had a grudging respect, a liking even, for the young king. He had seen enough of the youth during his flight from Fairfax's army, first at his base on the Scillies and later in Jersey, to know that this was a man who not only inherited his father's unquestioned courage, but who had cunning and integrity as well.

And so Treveryan chose to march with the new king on his ill-fated 'conquest' of the North Country in 1651. He did not have much to lose, after all. Unless the King was restored, his own prospects were bleak: two of his ships had been seized by the Parliamentary navy; a third had gone down in a storm and the remaining two managed to survive occasional acts of piracy, but their legitimate trade was at a standstill. He himself had been too closely associated with the King's cause in the last years of the war to expect generous terms from the victors. Besides, he was too proud, too angry still, to sue for mercy. As his father-in-law had supported Parliament throughout, there was no need to fear for Kitty's future, though on the rare occasions when he had risked a secret visit to their Saltash home, he had found her chafing in what she considered a state of abject poverty.

Richard liked the young king and he liked a gamble, and so he stood beside Charles Stuart at Worcester. And at the end of that long day he fled with the King when the relentless might of Cromwell's army broke upon the city in a wave of steel and gunfire, and the narrow streets were packed with the bodies of the dead and wounded and the cobbles were slippery with blood.

He had been prepared to gamble with death – but with capture and imprisonment, no. That humiliation was one fate he knew he could never endure. At all costs he must find a way to the coast, and a friendly ship to take him to France.

In the weeks following the débâcle at Worcester, all through September and October of 1651, the highways and ports of England were crawling with soldiers and spies seeking out the remnants of royalist resistance. Two thousand men had died in a single day of fighting at Worcester, another nine thousand were taken prisoner over the next few days and weeks, and almost all the remainder were either killed or captured eventually. Richard Treveryan, riding south on a stolen horse, vowed to die before he was numbered among them.

He was soon obliged to abandon the horse. A man alone can hide in a thicket or a copse, but a horse, even a tired-looking jade like the one he had stolen, always attracts attention. For the first time in his life he had reason to be thankful for his ruffianly appearance. Once he had exchanged his lawn shirt and Spanish leather boots for the coarse clothes of a (somewhat bemused) shepherd boy, he was able to pass himself off as an itinerant labourer returning to his home in Plymouth, and the few people to whom he spoke appeared to accept his story.

He was lucky. Unknown to Richard, who was cut off from all news from the day he fled the fighting and was therefore ignorant of the King's fate, Parliament was offering a reward of a thousand pounds for the capture of Charles Stuart – and any stranger, especially a tall one with dark hair, was certain to excite some interest on his journey towards the sea.

Sensing danger, Richard travelled mostly by night and slept as best he could by day. Food was hard to come by and by the time he reached the outskirts of Tavistock weakness and fatigue were beginning to make him careless. His plan was to get word to Giles, now employed by Kitty and of impeccable loyalty, he was sure, to arrange a passage for him from one of the multitude of hidden creeks and waterways near Plymouth.

Towards noon, one day in the middle of September, he was set upon by two men as he slept on a patch of grass near a stream. Whether they had thought to rob him, or whether they hoped they had captured the King himself, or whether they simply objected to strangers sleeping on their land, Richard never discovered. He still had a knife concealed beneath his shirt and he killed one of the men instantly and wounded the second badly enough to send him howling off in the afternoon sunshine. But he himself had not escaped unharmed. His head and shoulders were bruised and bleeding and there was a knife wound just above his knee.

Cursing the dead man and his injured accomplice, Richard knew his only hope was to quit the area before the justices and God only knew who else came searching for him. They would expect him to flee towards Plymouth; on an instinct he turned north-west and crossed the Tamar into Cornwall by night just north of Horsebridge. He had bandaged his leg as best he could but he was losing blood and weakening by the hour. Though he was beginning to grow confused, he knew he could never reach the sea on foot in his present state. Just before dawn he stole a horse from a lonely farm and cantered westwards away from the rising sun, gaining the illusion of strength from the movement of the horse that carried him. He rode all day and as evening fell he tumbled from his horse and into sleep and dreamed that he was riding once more between the oak woods that led towards Trecarne. And by the yew tree that overlooked the bay, there was a woman standing, a tall straight woman with fair hair, and as he rode up to her she turned to him, and smiled her welcome.

When he awoke he found it hard to know what was dream and what reality. All he was certain of was the grinding ache of his wounds and a great weariness and the knowledge that his life's strength was seeping away with the blood that spread through the bandage around his leg. Slowly he rode on, always westwards.

Too late now to consider enlisting Giles's help. Thoughts of Giles reminded him of Nicolas and his fierce determination to see Rossmere again before he died, and he wondered if his fate was, after all, to be buried beside his friend. And the thought of them both entwined like lovers in a common grave was so ludicrous that he laughed out loud and awoke from his reverie just as the horse stepped in a rabbit hole and stumbled, throwing him to the ground.

He was stunned by the fall, but as soon as he had recovered consciousness he saw that the horse was injured beyond saving. He must once more continue on foot.

The pain had taken over his whole body and now he walked only because he knew that the moment he stopped would be the moment he began to die. He barely knew where he was, only that the lanes, the landscape, when he could make them out through his state of near-delirium, were growing always more familiar, and he walked on, encouraged by the smell of the salt breeze from the sea on his face.

But when he reached Trecarne there was no woman waiting to greet him by the yew tree. He still had sense enough to wait until it had been dark for some time, and the moon had risen. It was that time of night when all those lucky enough to have beds and a clear conscience are lost in sleep.

Richard crept round to the stables. A solitary lamp was burning and, peering through the half-open door, he could just make out the familiar features of Will Stevens who had risen to tend a sickly yearling.

'Will? Are you alone?'

At first Will almost thought his eyes must be playing tricks on him: that dark vagabond, more dead than alive, could never be his former master.

'Mr Treveryan?'

But Richard only murmured, 'Sweet Jesus, help me,' and slumped down against the half-open door.

Will had remained at Trecarne when it changed hands; he was a skilled man with the horses and the new owner was pleased to take possession of men like him along with the property. Treveryan's appearance put him now in an impossible quandary. Any fool could see the man needed food and rest before he made his escape, yet to be caught harbouring a traitor now would cost him his home and his livelihood, and maybe his freedom too. Will felt himself too old for acts of heroism; yet found he could not betray such a direct appeal.

He was determined to be rid of Treveryan as soon as possible. Having hidden him in the stable loft he went to fetch food and ale, but on his return he found Treveryan was unconscious and nothing would rouse him. Hardly daring to imagine how he would explain away a dead Royalist, he hurried to Porthew as soon as it was light to make discreet enquiries.

He returned in the early afternoon, well pleased with his luck. A Penzance boat had put into Porthew the previous evening and was due to leave the following day. The owner, Will knew, had been a firm supporter of the King in the late war and was too sensible to ask questions about a wounded gentleman who needed urgent passage to France and who would, Will assured him, hoping it was true, be well able to pay for the service. A boat would be sent ashore to receive him once it was dark.

By evening Richard had recovered sufficiently to have a few mouthfuls of food. Will, more accustomed to tending horses than men, had dealt with his wound as best he could. 'Are you able to walk, Mr Treveryan?' he asked. 'It will only attract notice if we take a horse.'

'Then I must walk,' his former master smiled.

Will had to admit a grudging admiration for the man's courage as they set off, a little later, towards Porthew. Several times he was obliged to catch him round the waist to prevent him falling, but Treveryan only mocked his own weakness.

'It's a good few years since you and I journeyed to Porthew of an evening, Will,' he said.

'Hush sir,' Will looked about him anxiously in the fading light, 'someone might recognise your voice.'

But Ambrose, hiding in the deeper twilight of the woods, had already heard and seen everything.

Ambrose had been working in the smithy with his oldest son Robert at his side, when he first heard the news of the injured man who had been seen falling from his horse somewhere on the moors. He knew at once that it was Treveryan. For the previous week he had dreamed of him every night and in each dream his revenge had taken a different form.

By noon Lizzie had heard the rumours too. She came into the forge and laid her hand on Ambrose's arm. 'You've heard, haven't you?' she asked.

He nodded.

'Ignore it, Ambrose. Let him go.'

He told her not to worry, he'd come to no harm. Only half-satisfied, Lizzie returned to her washing. And worried the whole afternoon.

Ambrose hardly knew what he meant to do. The longing for revenge had become so much a part of his life that he could not imagine how he could let this opportunity pass. But then again, he had had his fill of killing in the recent war, had lost count of the number of men he had slaughtered, and at some stage in his journey through the seemingly endless battles, he had lost the taste for fighting. On the other hand, he reasoned, if he had killed so many strangers, men with whom he had no real quarrel except that they wore different colours than his own, why should he now let his old enemy go free? Then he caught sight of his son Robert who was growing up to be a fine young man, not quite his equal in strength but clever – he must have got that from his mother's side, thought Ambrose, puzzling things out while he hammered the steel to thinness on the anvil, as he had done years before when he watched out for Margaret and Lizzie and their little brother to come running down the hillside towards the Forge. He took pleasure in his family now and was especially proud of his boy – why should he do anything that might upset the balance of his life? But then, just before he put the white-hot metal in the butt to cool it, he caught sight of his disfigured face and as the steam hissed up in a cloud he knew he must follow the man, and if opportunity arose . . .

When his day's work was done he sat in the shade at the front of the smithy as was his custom and enjoyed a tankard of cool ale. His youngest daughter, the one with red hair and freckles to match his own, had been making patterns in the dusty road with a stick, but when she saw that he was idle she ran over and scrambled up on to his knee and snuggled close and told him all the grievances of her day. Lizzie, when she came out to refill his tankard, smiled to see them together because now she was sure he meant to stay. But a little later the child came sulking into the kitchen and complained that Daddy had gone off to hunt rabbits, and had taken his knife.

Ambrose did not expect to use the knife. As he had proved time and again in the late war, his bare hands were all the weapons he needed. He cut through the woods and waited until he saw the two men begin their slow journey towards Porthew. But he had no quarrel with Will Stevens, whose mother had been a cousin on his uncle's side, and besides, a strange fatalism had crept over him: he was becoming sure that God had sent this opportunity for vengeance, and he reasoned that the exact moment would reveal itself soon enough.

Unnaturally quiet for a man of his height and size, Ambrose padded along in the darkness, keeping always at a safe distance behind them, the old man and the injured one, as they made their way painfully towards the town.

Just beyond Ia's Bridge he saw them stop. He heard them talking together in low voices and he crept closer to listen. Then he heard Treveryan laugh, that low laugh that he had always loathed, and say softly, 'I'll wait here until it is dark. Then I'll go on to the town. If you're not at the shambles, then I'll hide myself in the old place. Do you know where I mean?'

'I do, sir. Take care.'

Ambrose could hardly believe his good fortune when he saw Will hurry off towards the town, leaving the injured man hidden by the side of the road. He had seen Treveryan's weakness, could almost smell his utter helplessness. He was grinning. It occurred to him that the man who killed the hated traitor might well be rewarded for his courage by the new men now ruling in Cornwall. Stealthy as a cat he began to move forward, when he was checked by the sound of voices. Silently cursing he fell back into the shadows. A courting couple were dawdling up the road from Porthew, whispering and giggling and pausing every couple of steps to kiss each other.

By the time they had passed – and they seemed to Ambrose to take an age – it was almost dark, and a shadowy figure was already limping down the road ahead of him. Patience, Ambrose told himself, patience. The perfect moment is sure to come.

At the crossroads on the edge of town Treveryan stopped and turned around unexpectedly. It seemed to Ambrose that the fellow was staring straight at him, although his reason told him that the darkness made him invisible. He saw Treveryan finger something that gleamed like a knife at his belt, before turning and continuing slowly towards the harbour.

Just past the shambles he paused again: then, as Ambrose had somehow known he would, he followed the narrow lane that led down behind the houses. When he came to the garden behind Mistress Hollar's house, Ambrose heard the click of a latch being lifted and the creak of a gate.

From within the house, a dog began to bark.

William Hollar, reading the Scriptures by the light of a candle in the parlour, snapped at the dog to be quiet. Next door, in the kitchen, Margaret repeated the order more gently, but Hedge ignored them both.

Margaret sighed. She had been trying to teach the serving-girl to write her name but found it impossible to concentrate on the task. Already her thoughts had flown ahead of her. Tomorrow, at last, she was to leave Porthew on the boat that was waiting off shore and go to France to sell and purchase cloth. Her wish to travel had been with her so long that she could hardly believe it was about to come true. Just to stand on board the little ship, feel the movement of the sea, watch Porthew fade to an insignificant dot on the land.

She leaned back in her chair and smiled. Now that she was about to leave, she had allowed herself to think of Trecarne again, and an old puzzle had been solved. When she and Richard had been on the point of leaving for their travels she had wondered what sound she would remember for his home. Until now she had never known. But now that she was about to depart she knew what it was. Not the owl, nor the lonely curlew, nor the bright songs of blackbirds and thrushes. It was the unending whisper of the wind in the oak woods, that soft echo of all her greatest happiness.

William was standing in the parlour door. 'How can you sit there smiling while that dog is barking fit to wake the dead?' he demanded.

'Is he? I had not noticed.'

'You *know* how these things upset me.' It was true. He was almost weeping.

Margaret preferred to talk to the dog. 'What is it, Hedge?

Is it a fox after our chickens? We'd best go and see.'

She was wrapping a shawl around her shoulders and had lifted the lantern from its hook on the wall when William stopped her. 'Take care, Margaret. Take a knife. I've heard rumours of strangers the past day or so.'

She smiled at him scornfully. 'Don't tell me you are concerned for my safety, William.'

William frowned, plucked anxiously at the sleeve of his jacket, then muttered nervously, 'I have always cared about you, Margaret. I sometimes think that if I had been . . . if God had made me a true husband to you, we might have been . . . well suited.'

She stared at him incredulously for a few moments. Then shrugged. It must be thoughts of parting that were making him speak so strangely.

'Heavens above, William –' She stooped and picked up a log of wood and placed it on the fire.

'At least take a knife with you. Take some protection.'

'Why? You know full well I could never use a knife, not even on a fox.' She pushed open the door and Hedge leapt out barking joyously and raced down the path towards the barn.

'I'll make sure the chickens are safe,' she said. Briefly she paused, and looked back into the little kitchen. William, very pale, was still standing in the parlour doorway; Beth had nodded off to sleep over her slate, her name still unwritten, the old cat was drowsing by the fire.

She took a deep breath and thought how sweet the autumnal air was after the dusty days of summer. Pulling her shawl more tightly around her shoulders, she stepped outside into the mild September darkness.

The Falling Years

London, October 1660

On the morning of his audience with the King, Sir Richard Treveryan awoke late, and in a bad temper. He much preferred to rise while his wife was still asleep, so that the business of dressing and preparing for the day might be completed with Viney in undemanding silence. But the potion he had taken in the small hours of the night had caused him to sleep on and now the morning sunlight was slanting in through the lattice windows and Kitty, more animated at the prospect of an audience with His Most Royal Majesty than Richard had ever seen her, was chattering like a whole flock of starlings at once.

As usual, the topic which was causing the words to tumble from her mouth at such an unrelenting pace was Dress: her clothes, his clothes, the clothes of their children and those of the servants who were to accompany them to Whitehall. This had been the focus of her attention ever since she learned of the coming audience. In a lighter mood, some days before, Richard had told his wife she would surely spend the precious hours of Judgement Day, while others were reviewing the ledger of their souls, in trying to decide whether the Almighty would prefer to see her in amber damask or deep blue taffeta. But on this particular morning, the constant rattle of her voice was so intolerable that he told her he would appear before the King dressed in his old buff coat and breeches if she did not leave him in peace.

Appalled, disbelieving, she began, 'You wouldn't –' but then, seeing from his black expression that yes indeed he surely would, she stifled a sob and fled from the room to vent her frustrations on the servants. Through the thin walls of their lodgings, the sounds of a household in turmoil were unmistakable: Kitty scolding Belinda, the boys quarrelling between themselves and Perdita . . . for all Richard knew Perdita was cross and weeping as she had been since their conversation together the day before. He turned from the thought with distaste.

'This damned house is worse than a rabbit coop,' Richard complained to Viney, 'one more night in this town and I shall have my whole family committed to Bedlam. I am going out to see to the horses. Prepare my things for the journey west; I shall leave for Devon this evening.'

Viney merely grunted, his lugubrious face displaying no expression. It was his taciturnity that Richard valued.

Not so the rest of his family. As he descended the narrow stairs Richard could hear Kitty's voice behind the parlour door rising to a positive frenzy of vexation over the problems of mismatched Holland lace. His anger could banish her but he knew no magic that could subdue her tongue. Suddenly he found himself remembering Dorcas, and how the threat of goblin mischief was enough to make her clamp her mouth tight shut though her eyes might be popping with fear.

Dorcas had died in Saltash in the year following the execution of Charles I. Kitty had forgotten to lock the door of her still room and Dorcas, having stolen in when no one was looking, had begun to eat her way around the laden shelves. A few hours later she had died of a surfeit of bottled fruit and syrups and potions and preserves and goodness only knew what else besides. Obviously she had glimpsed Heaven before her death, though Kitty was concerned about the waste.

Richard, returning to Saltash the next day on one of those semi-secret visits that were still possible before the catastrophe at Worcester, had learned of her death, and that Viney had vanished. Furious at the man's backsliding, Richard had hunted for him through all the taverns of Saltash and Plymouth, during the course·of which he learned that Miriam Porter had died at about the same time. And the knowledge that the woman who had given him such a warm welcome to the city twenty years before had died alone and in bitter poverty, made him so angry that by the time he tracked Viney down in an ale-house near the Hoe, he had himself begun to drink and found his manservant a tolerable companion for his bitter mood. Viney, as happened to him very seldom, was grown tearful and garrulous.

Perhaps to justify his present condition, he began to praise Dorcas in such glowing terms that Richard found himself wondering if they were talking of the same person. By the time Viney began to talk of Margaret Hollar, Richard was himself too drunk to stop him. Viney, with many rambling detours, gave his opinion that Mistress Hollar's heart had broken when she left Trecarne. He said he had gathered, from scraps of conversation overheard and from fragments she had uttered in the delirium of her illness, that it had been the parson who forced her to leave. He had made her think (and maybe he had been right after all, Viney added judiciously, for he was not one to judge his fellow man) that her son's safe return from Lansdown, where he had been injured, depended entirely on her giving up her wicked life and returning to her husband. Richard could not help but hear what was said, but he drank until the pain of it was wiped away.

The next morning Richard had been aware of little more than a fearful hangover. Viney was briefly flogged for his waywardness but, by mutual agreement though hardly a word had been exchanged between them, the next time Richard left Saltash it was Viney, as silent and doleful-looking as ever, who accompanied him. And whatever Richard remembered of their drunken exchange in the ale-house was shut away behind the door deep inside him that had long ago been locked and soundly bolted.

Unwelcome thoughts and memories stuck like splinters in his brain as Richard walked down the stairs on this bright October morning. His body felt heavy, after-effects of late sleeping made worse by his uncomfortably new clothes (since he could never please Kitty with regard to fundamentals, he sometimes gave way to her on petty details, such as the wearing of a new suit of clothes). As he began to cross the hallway a door flew open and Perdita, shouting an angry something to the servant who had been attending her, burst into the narrow hall and ran smack into her father.

He pushed her away just as she stepped backwards. He looked down at her scornfully as a whole multitude of emotions – hope, anger, fear, love, despair and something that was very close to raw hatred – crossed her face. Her features were so pitiful, eyes dark-shadowed from lack of sleep, that he was prompted to cruelty.

He said, 'Your appearance does little credit to your family,' and saw her flinch in response, and then, 'and tell your mother – your mother my *wife*, that is – that I plan to leave for the West Country as soon as this business with His Majesty is completed,' which made her gasp with astonishment.

'But . . . but . . .'

'Yes?'

'You said Mr Nashe was to visit this evening. And I thought –' Her voice faltered and her face grew more pinched and miserable than ever.

Richard who, in his eagerness to be free of the city and of his family, had quite forgotten his obligations to Perdita's would-be suitor, the armourer from Coventry, swore vehemently and swung out of the house without another word.

As the cold bright air of the street stung him into wakefulness, Richard could hear his only daughter racing up the stairs to her mother and wailing that he was determined to abandon them and never to see her married at all.

By the time Richard had visited the horses he had purchased since arriving in London and had taken a stroll around St James's Fields, his bad humour had almost lifted and all that remained was a weary impatience to see the business of the day completed so that he could make his escape. He had suffered too long in close confinement with his family in this teeming ant-heap of a city. And yet, as he walked through the open spaces beyond the Palace of St James, he was forced to admit that autumn was a season of dignity, beauty even, in this eastern corner of the kingdom. Crisp clear mornings such as this one, tall trees still proudly decked in yellow and red, and frost-hard ground that crunched beneath his boots – a vivid contrast to the dark dank days of a Cornish autumn, trees stunted by the wind, roads and pathways foundering in a tide of mud.

Strange then, that it was always at this dying, falling season of the year that the pull of the West Country, that yearning that was almost like a sickness, proved hardest to resist.

It was typical of her husband, thought Kitty irritably, that having put everyone out of humour at the start of the day, he should now return in a better temper than she had seen him in all week. However, she was so relieved to hear no more about old buff coats or quitting the city without anything settled concerning Perdita's marriage, that she stifled her anger easily. Richard's coat of jackdaw-grey velvet with the slashed sleeves and the lining that gleamed jewel-bright when he moved, not to mention her own gown of shimmering yellow silk, gave her such intense pleasure that, for a brief moment, all her woes were forgotten.

Richard saw her brittle-eager upturned face, saw his two sons fidgeting and trying to smother their excitement at the coming meeting with the King and he felt a kind of affection for them. And then he looked at Perdita, and saw from her sullen expression that she was trying to persuade herself she cared nothing for her father's opinion, good or bad. But the despairing droop of her mouth was proof enough that she did care, very much indeed. And for his daughter, that cuckoo child who had brought his wife such happiness, for Perdita he could find no affection at all.

Sensing their nervousness, he tossed them random compliments, which Kitty seized on eagerly ('Do you *truly* like this style? You do not consider, perhaps, that the waist should have been a little lower? Or the colour – ?') and which Perdita, in her slough of misery, scorned, with bitter accuracy, as meaningless.

Kitty and the children were to travel by coach. Richard hurled his wife into a fresh flurry of anxiety by insisting that he would walk. But there was nothing she could do to alter his decision, as she said a hundred times and in a hundred different ways while they journeyed the short distance to the royal palace at Whitehall.

Once arrived, they were reunited in the palace yard and Kitty was able to reassure herself that Richard was still as scrupulously elegant as he had been when she saw him some ten minutes before. Kitty's desperate fear of being late meant that they had a good deal of time in which to wait and to her dismay they found themselves joining a curious throng of people, all of whom seemed to be hoping, with

717

varying degrees of optimism, to meet with the King.

Such a crowd presented Kitty with fresh cause for panic and she herded her three children into a space near the inner door where they were in less danger from muddy shoes and other hazards. Richard, as always, took up a position a little apart from them. Through a tall window he could make out the smudge of a high-flying bird against the blue expanse of sky. A buzzard perhaps? It was a few moments before he became aware of a man tugging at his sleeve and repeating in a low, urgent voice, 'Sir Richard, Sir Richard Treveryan! Do you remember Porthew?'

Richard shook him off angrily. 'Damn it, man, what do you mean by this?'

'Sir Richard, I've waited a long time to see you again. They told me you were to be presented to His Majesty today and the moment I set eyes on you, I knew that you were the man –'

'What in God's name are you blabbering about?'

'I knew you would wish to repay me for what I –'

'I'll repay you with a broken head if you don't leave me in peace.'

'– to repay me for saving your life.'

Richard stared down at the man in disgust. He did not relish the idea of owing such an intimate debt to any man, least of all to one of this quality. He was small and hungry-looking, dirty and almost certainly verminous. He had the toothless grin and the bright eyes of a born liar and trickster. Richard was in half a mind to call the guards and have him thrown out at once (how in the world had he wormed his way in here in the first place?) but the man had mentioned Porthew . . .

He said, 'What are you talking about?'

'The month after Worcester, Sir Richard. I was employed on the ship that carried you to France. And at Porthew I was the one that saved your life.'

Richard was sceptical, and on the brink of dismissing the fellow. But something made him hold back. He could remember nothing of his escape from Porthew. He had some vague and fevered memories of visiting Will in the stables at Trecarne, of that endless painful walk through the dusk

718

to Porthew, and of his growing certainty, that instinctive knowledge that men have sometimes when they are bound to one another in hatred, that Ambrose Treloar had smelled him out, had divined his weakness and his fever and the deep and festering wound to his leg, realised that he was outcast, and alone. He knew that Ambrose meant to kill him, and he had known too that he was powerless any longer to defend himself, too befuddled by the fever and exhaustion to put up any kind of fight, certainly nothing of any use against the hatred of the disfigured smith.

And Richard had been afraid, as never before or since in his life. Terror had been a raw taste rising to fill his mouth. He had wanted to cover his head with his arms and crawl into a safe hiding place like a sick animal. It was not death he feared; if he could fall asleep and find rest from his weariness and pain he would ask nothing more. But he cringed from the prospect of being delivered into the hands of the man he had maimed, a man with reason to be cruel in his murder.

That was the fear which drove him to seek shelter in the Hollars' barn, though he knew Ambrose would find him there. Even now the memory of his abject terror was shameful, though from the moment he had stumbled into the hay-sweet barn he could remember nothing, and he had never known what occurred between then and his arrival in France. And now this wretched specimen was claiming to have saved his life.

He was a liar, Richard was sure of it. Since the King's triumphant return from exile, London had been humming with those who claimed to have rendered services to both him and his supporters which had yet to be repaid. The numbers now claiming to have helped Charles Stuart in his flight after Worcester were legion, most of them imposters. As this man almost certainly was too.

'Your name?'

'Jem Bridges, Sir Richard.'

His accent had already shown that he was not a West Country man.

'Where are you from, Jem Bridges?'

'Kent, sir. I was born in Folkestone. But I've been a sailor all my life and I was working on Master Chiswick's boat, the *George*, when it put into Porthew. It was the *George* that took you to –'

'I'm well aware of the name of the boat,' Richard interrupted him, 'and so are a thousand others. You have made this up because you hope to profit –'

'No, no, Sir Richard,' Jem Bridges caught hold of his sleeve once again, 'I'd never lie on so grave a matter. I was there, I swear it. I was one of the party sent into town to find you when the old fellow said you were too weak to walk.'

'The old fellow?'

'He had white hair and a stiff way of walking. And such Cornishness in his speech I could barely understand him.'

Will Stevens. That stiff rheumaticky walk. Richard was only half-convinced. It could be the man had heard this story from someone else and hoped to profit by it himself. Yet even so, this man knew more than he did, for he had never heard the story of his escape from anyone.

'Tell me your story, then, Jem Bridges. But if you dare to lie to me then I'll ram your words back down your throat and choke you on them.'

'Very good, Sir Richard.' Bridges cleared his throat uneasily before proceeding. 'We had seen the old fellow, the one with the white hair, talking with the captain earlier in the day. And as it grew towards dusk three of us were detailed to row ashore to meet with that same fellow, for he said there was a passenger to be brought on board in secret. Captain said that same passenger might be ill and need carrying –'

'Then why did he choose you?' Richard surveyed the man's scrawny frame. 'Surely he had stronger men on board.'

The birdlike eyes darted nervously. 'I was strong as any man on the ship in those days. But the past few years I've been often ill,' and here Bridges coughed loudly, establishing his credentials as an invalid.

Richard indicated with a nod that he should continue.

'We rowed to shore just as it was getting dark and after we had waited for a while below the harbour wall, the old fellow came down to find us. He told us the man who was to be taken on board was too ill to go the last distance unaided so two of us, a sailor by the name of Brady and myself, went with him into the town and the third man stayed behind with the boat.'

In spite of his mistrust, Richard was listening intently now. So far it all sounded plausible enough. He was no longer aware of the crowded room in which he stood, nor the chatter of voices all around. In his mind he could hear the gentle slap of the sea against the Porthew harbour wall on a still September night, could smell the salt wind and woodsmoke and rotting fish that seemed to permeate the very stones of the little town. In his mind he followed the three men as they walked, quietly, but not wasting any time, up the alley that led behind the houses.

'We did not go along the main street. The old man led us up a narrow lane and then we came to a stone building, some kind of shed. That was where you'd gone to ground, Sir Richard. We could see right away you could not walk any further.'

'And so you helped me to the ship, and now you want payment. Well then, here's sixpence for your charity.'

'No, no, Sir Richard, there was more. I'm coming to it now. You'd hidden yourself so deep among the straw that we had trouble raising you up, but just as we were about to quit the place, a huge man, a giant I thought he was at first, came in and blocked the doorway.'

'Did you notice anything about him, other than his great size?'

Seeing that he held his listener's attention at last, Bridges's eyes glittered with excitement. 'Oh yes indeed, Sir Richard, even in that poor light it was plain to see that the man had something monstrous wrong with his face. One side of it was all bunched up as if he had suffered a terrible injury. It was a fearsome face.'

Richard nodded. 'Ambrose Treloar,' he murmured under his breath. His face was very pale. 'Go on.'

Jem Bridges continued with growing confidence. 'The big man was in a towering anger. Brady was standing in front of you and when he would not make way, the giant picked him up and broke his neck as easily as if he'd been no more than a chicken ready for plucking. And then he would have killed you too, but that I pulled out my knife and stepped forward and finished him off myself.'

Here Bridges stopped abruptly and looked up at Richard with an expression eager for praise, gratitude, some suitable reward. But Richard, who had followed his story carefully so far, found that final scene impossible to imagine.

His eyes narrowed. 'Ambrose Treloar would have dealt with you as swiftly as he did with your companion. You'd not stand a chance against him, you'd not even try. You're lying, Jem Bridges, and I warned you –'

'I'm not, Sir Richard! I swear it's only God's sweet truth. Maybe he might have killed me too, but there was a woman came to the door of the barn and she was carrying a lantern; and there was a dog with her that was barking and in the moment of his distraction I – I killed him!'

'Liar!' In a murderous rush of fury Richard took Bridges by the throat and rammed him against the wall. 'Tell me the truth or by Jesus I'll kill you here and now!'

'Please, Sir Richard, I did not mean –'

'I know what you meant to do, you lying rogue; you thought to twist the truth to your own advantage, but you've a coward's face, Jem Bridges, and you'd no more tackle Ambrose Treloar in a fight than jump from the rigging and fly. But you were there, that night, I believe that much. And you'll tell me the truth of it if I have to –'

'Yes, yes, I'll tell you. Only let me go!'

With obvious reluctance, Richard relaxed his grip. All the chattering in the room had ceased abruptly and people were gathering round, forming a natural circle, the better to witness this strange encounter between the hero of Worcester and the scrawny sparrow of a man who had so unceremoniously accosted him. Neither of the combatants was aware that all eyes were now fixed on them.

'Very well then, continue.' Richard's hand had moved unconsciously to rest on the hilt of his sword. 'You say the big man killed your companion. Is that the truth?'

He nodded. 'I swear it, Sir Richard –'

'Then my guess is you tried to hide, or run away.'

'I could not run, Sir Richard, the door being blocked –'

'So?'

'I hid behind some sacks.'

'Now I begin to believe you, Jem Bridges. And Will Stevens, the old man?'

'The big fellow pushed him away. Told him not to meddle in what was none of his concern. That his only quarrel was with you.'

'And then?'

'The old man did not fight him. He warned the big man not to be a fool, but then he turned away. There was nothing he could do.'

'Quite so. Go on.'

'When the big man caught hold of you, you seemed to revive a little. Until then you were dead to the world; truth to tell, Sir Richard, I thought you'd had it, anyway. But just then you roused yourself somehow and pulled a knife from under your coat. But it was no use. The big man knocked it out of your hand as easily as if it was a toy. And the strangest part of all was that he was laughing.'

Richard said nothing, only flexed the muscles of his hand. That blow when Ambrose knocked away his knife would explain why he had a broken hand in addition to his other injuries on his arrival in France.

'He was hitting you, but it was like it was a game. Like watching a cat baiting a mouse.'

'You could see much from your hiding place behind the sacks.'

'Everything, Sir Richard. I swear it was as clear as day because the woman was carrying a lantern.'

'What woman?'

'I never knew who she was.'

'Can you remember her face?'

'She was tall. Her hair was a light sort of colour, maybe grey.'

'Was she beautiful?'

Bridges searched his memory, hoping, among the truth, to salvage some detail that would win Treveryan's favour, but, 'Nothing special,' he answered, 'she was not young.'

Richard was staring at him blankly. 'Go on.'

Something in his opponent's face made Bridges increasingly uneasy, although he had no option but to carry on. All thoughts of a reward had long gone; his only concern now was how to conclude this meeting without further injury.

He said, 'She ordered the big man to let you alone. She seemed to know him well. He said he would not, that he had waited a long time for this chance, and he knew there'd never be another. By then he had his hands about your neck. He could have killed you straight out but he seemed to want to do it slowly, because he was enjoying it. The woman began to shout at him that he *must* stop; I think maybe she struck him once or twice about the shoulders but her blows could make no impression on such a man. He paid her no heed at all and she was growing more frantic all the time. You'd gone limp by then, Sir Richard, I swear I thought you were dead and the woman she was shouting and crying and the dog was jumping around and barking. But nothing would stop the big man.'

Unaware of what he was doing, Richard had moved his hands to his throat, as if to protect himself, while he listened.

'Then suddenly the woman stopped shouting. She bent down and picked up the knife you had let fall in the straw. She ordered him to stop, she warned him, but he only laughed at her and told her she was too soft-hearted. He was laughing still when she raised the knife above her head. I saw the metal blade flash in the light from the lantern and she brought it down and plunged it into the big man's throat. The blood spurted out all over her face and hair. He let go of you at once and you fell down in a heap in the straw. The big man was looking at her and he looked puzzled and angry all at once, but he caught her such a blow across her neck that I think it must have broken at once. I think she died right away then but him, he was a longer time in dying . . .'

'My God . . .' Richard had gone white as death.

Jem Bridges continued, though now his voice was barely above a whisper. 'The lantern that she had set down was knocked over and the straw began to burn. I wanted to run away but my legs would not move. The old fellow, the one you called Will, he came over to me and shook me by the shoulder and it was like waking up. The dog was howling and licking the woman's face. We had to push her body aside to lift you up and God knows how we managed to carry you out of that place. As we went down the hill, we could hear the sound of commotion – people were running to put out the fire and pull the bodies clear. Luckily they were all too busy to look out for us and we were able to get you safe on board, though it was at least three days before we knew for certain you would live.'

Richard did not speak. He seemed to be staring at some place that no one else could see. His mind could not absorb that image of Margaret, his own Meg who could not bear to see a wounded bird or a baited animal, could not imagine those work-worn gentle hands raising a blade to kill . . . He murmured, 'I cannot believe –'

'There was one thing further,' Jem Bridges, aware now that his tale, though no longer much to his credit, was causing a momentous impact on its hearer, added eagerly, 'she said something that got fixed in my mind, somehow. Because there was no sense to it, or none that I could make out. I think she said it when she raised the knife, or maybe it was later, when she caught hold of you just before the big man killed her.'

'She said?'

Bridges shifted uncomfortably. 'She said – I know it sounds wrong but I heard it so plain – she said, "No less or more," and then again, in a sort of whisper, "No less or more." And I shall remember her face all my life, she looked so happy.'

Richard let out a low groan. Oblivious to all around him he turned and stepped towards the high window and leaned his forehead against the cool glass. He closed his eyes. No less or more, the man had heard. And Richard alone knew what the woman had said as she died. *Nullus amor* . . . letters printed on the pages of an old book, letters scratched on a snow-covered lawn, letters carved to surprise him over the fireplace in the long gallery at Trecarne. Those words had been the talisman of her hopes and dreams, the watchword of their love. *Nullus amor* – 'No love ever joined lovers in such a bond.' The words flooded through him on a huge tide of grief and passion and he knew, as perhaps he had always known, but never admitted, that she had never wavered for an instant in her love. That it had only been his hurt pride, his habit of anger and doubt which had caused him to question her sincerity. She had always loved him; every look and word and gesture had told him so a hundred times each day.

As he had always loved her, perhaps even from the day when she stood before the crowds at Porthew and delivered her oration and he had believed her warm smile to be a gift for him alone. Or perhaps from that evening when they had danced together at her wedding and he had sensed a wildness in her movements. Certainly from the sleepless night that followed when they had sat beside the kitchen fire and she had shown him her precious book of Latin verses. *Nullus amor* – it was to his own Meg that he owed his life, that dubious gift that he would gladly throw away tomorrow if in return he could spend one hour in her company again. He owed her his life, as he had owed her so much more besides.

A glow of yellow at his side, a rustle of silk skirts and a claw-like hand was tugging nervously at his arm. 'Richard,' said Kitty, 'word has come through that the King awaits us. He is ready now.'

Kitty feared that she would never be able to rouse him from his dreamlike state but then, as her husband opened his eyes and turned slowly to look at her, there was surprise on his face, almost as if he had been expecting to see someone else standing beside him. She stepped backwards with a little cry of astonishment. 'Why Richard, whatever is the matter? I do believe you're weeping!'

He was a long time staring at her and his face was haggard, like that of an old man. Then he smiled, a slow strange smile. 'I have good reason to weep,' was all he said.

'But the King, Richard! You must not keep him waiting. Here, let me –'

But he stopped her busy hands. 'All in good time, Kitty. The King is only a man, after all, and sometimes even kings must wait.'

'Oh Richard –!'

He looked about him, as if searching for something, or someone, and after a few moments his gaze settled on the anxious face of his daughter, who stood watching from a little distance away. 'Yes, that's it,' he murmured, 'it may be too late for some things, but perhaps I can still make amends. Kitty, go and fetch Perdita –'

'Later, surely –'

'Go and fetch Perdita and tell her that when this royal business is done with, she and I will talk alone. Tell her that there are many things she should know and that I have kept them from her far too long. For that I am sorry. She will not lack a father now.'

'But the King, Richard!'

He took her jewel-encrusted hand and raised it to his lips. 'Go,' he said, 'go tell my daughter, so she may enjoy her brush with royalty.'

Despairing, but too baffled to argue, Kitty hurried off to gather Perdita and the boys and convey their father's curious message.

Richard stood alone, swathed in silence, realising slowly that regret would be with him all his days, as well as remembered love. If he had only trusted her, if he had followed her to Porthew the day she left and told her all that was in his heart. If . . . but his love had been vulnerable and selfish and hers had been unable to withstand what she believed to be her obligation to her son. And yet their love had been a fine, true thing, the best part of their lives. It had not been enough, though it had seemed everything once.

Only gradually did he become aware of the scurvy-looking man who had crept once more to his side. He was not yet so altered that he regarded the fellow with anything but contempt, but his words sounded gentle enough. 'Wait here, Jem Bridges. You are a liar and a rogue, but long ago I knew someone who had a care for scoundrels such as you. When my meeting with His Majesty is done, I shall see you are duly recompensed.'

The man began to babble his thanks but was silenced by a brusque gesture. Richard glanced once more through the high window, at the pale blue vault of the sky where the smudge of the bird was no longer visible.

He murmured something under his breath, a woman's name perhaps, but in a voice so quiet that no one could ever hear him. He turned and walked towards the inner door where Kitty was waiting with the children. The two boys, smiling and proud. Perdita . . .

He looked at her carefully, a thing he had always been studious to avoid before, and he was dismayed to see how she flinched from his scrutiny. Two bright spots of colour on her cheeks told him that Kitty had conveyed some version of his message and that Perdita was as yet too suspicious and confused to believe it.

'Perdita –' he said gently. Her head jerked backwards in nervous defiance. And then for the first time he saw that the line of her jaw, the graceful curve of her cheek, was like another that he had thought long since forgotten.

'Now we'll begin,' he said, his hand hovering over her dark hair, 'pray God we're not too late.' Those around him assumed he was talking of the coming meeting with the King, only Perdita wondered if perhaps it had another meaning, one she hardly dared to hope of. Then he smiled. 'Come,' he said.

They gathered around him, his tiny wife, his two sons and his dark-haired daughter. The wide doors were thrown open and, his face still wet with tears, Sir Richard Treveryan stepped forward to greet his King.

DINAH LAMPITT

THE KING'S WOMEN

France in the Middle Ages; torn by internecine strife, menaced by the might of England's King Henry V. At the country's head; a frightened youth, the Dauphin Charles.

Yet fate has decreed that it is he who will become the most victorious king of all, who will drive the English from French soil. And it is through the love of women that this prophecy will come true.

The magnificent Yolande, more a mother to him than the depraved Queen Isabeau; Marie, his plain but intelligent wife; Agnes, his exquisite mistress. All will play a part. Yet above all will be Jehanne, the un-blemished girl who will ride at the head of his army whilst swearing allegiance to the mysterious Knights Templar. The girl who will become known to legend as Joan of Arc.

'A meaty dish of lust and medieval intrigue'
Maureen Owen, *Daily Mail*

'Ingenious, long and highly readable'
Philippa Toomey, *The Times*

'Best writer of her kind'

Kent Messenger

HODDER AND STOUGHTON PAPERBACKS

ELIZABETH GOUDGE

THE BIRD IN THE TREE TRILOGY

The Bird in the Tree is the first of Elizabeth Goudge's famous trilogy of novels about the Eliots of Damerosehay. The tranquil, happy existence of this closely-knit family seems suddenly threatened when David and Nadine fall in love with one another. Lucilla, who has spent a lifetime making Damerosehay a special haven for her family, feels that their happiness would be shattered by a marriage between her favourite grandson and her beautiful daughter-in-law and is determined to prevent it.

'Genuine discernment and poignancy'
The Sunday Times

'Triumphantly accomplishes its aim of leaving the reader with a warm glow in the emotions . . . only Miss Goudge could have written it'
The Times Literary Supplement

Don't miss the other two books in this trilogy: *The Herb of Grace* and *The Heart of the Family*.

HODDER AND STOUGHTON PAPERBACKS

YVONNE ADAMSON

BRIDEY'S MOUNTAIN

Telluride, Colorado. The most beautiful place on earth, about to strike it rich with the discovery of gold in the 1890s.

Telluride in the 1990s is still the loveliest place in the world but is hanging on to its wilderness by a thread as the jet set moves in.

And two remarkable women are linked to it and each other across the generations: Morna Gregory, a mysterious Irish beauty who fled there at the turn of the century to escape her dangerous past; and Ariana MacAllister, a young woman determined to preserve her inheritance, her great-grandmother's mountain . . .

HODDER AND STOUGHTON PAPERBACKS

JOANNA HINES

DORA'S ROOM

The brilliant and mesmerising first novel from a dazzling new talent.

When timid unworldly Fern unexpectedly inherits the entire estate of her rich and forbidding grandfather she has to force herself to claim the family house inhabited by relatives who have never acknowledged her.

Orphaned years before by violent death and insanity, Fern has been brought up to bury the things that hurt. But Chatton Heights evokes memories of a long-forgotten childhood happiness. Searching for the source within her parents' shattered past she uncovers a tragic love story of innocence betrayed.

This is now her terrible legacy. As she struggles to reverse the past and find the elusive 'Dora', someone is trying to silence her for ever.

HODDER AND STOUGHTON PAPERBACKS

BARBARA WHITNELL

CHARMED CIRCLE

The Rossiters lived just over the garden fence – and inhabited a completely different world.

Rachel was lonely, missing her parents, forced to live with her disapproving, strait-laced grandmother.

The family next door was noisy, colourful, careless of convention: bubbly Alannah, sensitive Barney, Diana, so casually beautiful and clever. And Gavin, who she could only adore from afar.

Invited into their charmed circle, yet never quite part of it, the Rossiters became the emotional centre of her life.

But as the shadow of terrible events begins to loom over their seemingly secure pre-war life, Rachel finds her relationships with the Rossiters becoming more complex, more adult – and more disturbing.

'Here is a strong story, well told, with an abundance of real feeling and a winning spice of humour. Above all, characters that live, and live on in the mind (and dare I say the heart) long after you finish reading. Warmly recommended'

Sarah Harrison

'A compelling read'

Dee Remington, *Family Circle*

HODDER AND STOUGHTON PAPERBACKS